Praise for the Soul Screamers series
by *New York Times* bestselling author
RACHEL VINCENT

"Twilight fans will love it."
—*Kirkus Reviews*

"The story ~~~~~ (for ~~~~~ and adults, I might add)."

"Fans o   p

"A must for any reading wish list."
—*Tez Says*

"A book like this is one of the reasons that I add authors
to my auto-buy list. This is definitely a keeper."
—*TeensReadToo.com*

SOUL SCREAMERS

≪ VOLUME TWO ≫

RACHEL VINCENT

HARLEQUIN®
entertain, enrich, inspire™

Recycling programs
for this product may
not exist in your area.

ISBN-13: 978-0-373-21079-4

SOUL SCREAMERS VOLUME TWO
Copyright © 2012 by Harlequin Books S.A.

The publisher acknowledges the copyright holder of the individual works as follows:

MY SOUL TO KEEP
Copyright © 2010 by Rachel Vincent

MY SOUL TO STEAL
Copyright © 2011 by Rachel Vincent

REAPER
Copyright © 2010 by Rachel Vincent

CONTENTS

• MY SOUL TO KEEP •

To Amy, Michelle, and Josh.

My memories of you from high school make the non-fantasy elements of Kaylee's life feel so real to me...

THE WHOLE THING STARTED with a wasted jock and a totaled car. Or so I thought. But as usual, the truth was a bit more complicated....

"SO, HOW DOES IT FEEL to be free again?" Nash leaned against my car, flashing that smile I couldn't resist. The one that made his dimples stand out and his eyes shine, and made me melt like chocolate in the sun, in spite of the mid-December chill.

I sucked in a deep, cold breath. "Like I'm seeing the sun for the first time in a month." I pushed my car door closed and twisted the key in the lock. I didn't like parking on the street; it didn't seem like a very safe place to leave my most valuable possession. Not that my car was expensive, or anything. It was more than a decade old, and hardly anything to *oooh* over. But it was mine, and it was paid for, and unlike some of my more financially fortunate classmates, I'd never be able to afford another one, should some idiot veer too close to the curb.

But Scott Carter's driveway was full long before we'd arrived, and the street was lined with cars, most much nicer than mine. Of course, they all probably had more than liability coverage....

Fortunately, the party was in a very good section of our little Dallas suburb, where the lawn manicures cost more than my father made in six months.

"Relax, Kaylee." Nash pulled me close as we walked. "You look like you'd rather gouge your own eyes out than hang for a couple of hours with some friends."

"They're your friends, not mine," I insisted as we passed the third convertible on our way to the well-lit house at the end of the cul-de-sac, already thumping with some bass-heavy song I couldn't yet identify.

"They'd be yours if you'd get to know them."

I couldn't help rolling my eyes. "Yeah, I'm sure the glitter-and-gloss throng is waiting for *me* to give *them* a chance."

Nash shrugged. "They know all they need to know about you—you're smart, pretty, and crazy in love with me," he teased, squeezing me tighter.

I laughed. "Who started *that* vicious rumor?" I'd never said it, because as addictive as Nash was—as special as he made me feel—I wasn't going to toss off words like *love* and *forever* until I was sure. Until I was sure *he* was sure. Forever can be a very long time for *bean sidhes,* and so far his track record looked more like the fifty-yard dash than the Boston marathon. I'd been burned before by guys without much staying power.

When I looked up, I found Nash watching me, his hazel eyes swirling with streaks of green and brown in the orange glow from the streetlights. I almost felt sorry for all the humans who wouldn't be able to see that—to read emotion in another's eyes.

That was a *bean sidhe* thing, and easily my favorite part of my recently discovered heritage.

"All I'm saying is it would be nice to get to hang out with my friends and my girlfriend at the same time."

I rolled my eyes again. "Oh, fine. I'll play nice with the pretty people." At least Emma would be there to keep me company—she'd started going out with one of Nash's teammates while I was grounded. And the truth was that most of Nash's friends weren't that bad. Their girlfriends were another story.

Speaking of bloodthirsty hyenas...

A car door slammed in the driveway ahead and my cousin, Sophie, stood next to Scott Carter's metallic-blue convertible, her huge green eyes shadowed dramatically by the streetlight overhead. "Nash!" She smiled at him, ignoring me in spite of the fact that we'd shared a home for the past thirteen of her fifteen years, until my dad had moved back from Ireland in late September.

Or maybe *because* of that.

"Can you give me a hand?" As we stepped onto the driveway, she rounded the end of her boyfriend's car in a slinky, sleeveless pink top and designer jeans, a case of beer clutched awkwardly to her chest. Two more cases sat at her feet, and I glanced around to see if any of the neighbors were watching my fifteen-year-old cousin show off an armload of alcoholic beverages. But the neighbors were probably all out, spending their Saturday evening at the theater, or the ballet, or in some restaurant I couldn't even afford to park near.

And most of their kids were at Scott's house, waiting for us to come in with the beer.

Nash let go of me to take the case from Sophie, then grabbed another one from the ground. Sophie beamed at him, then shot a haughty sneer at my plain jacket before turning on one wedge-heeled foot to strut after him.

I sighed and picked up the remaining box, then followed them both inside. The front door opened before Nash could pound on it, and a tall, thick senior in a green-and-white-letter jacket slapped Nash's shoulder and took one of the cases from him. Nash twisted with his empty arm extended, clearly ready to wrap it around me, but found Sophie instead. He side-stepped her—ignoring her plump-lipped pout—and took the case from me, then stood back to let me go in first.

"Hudson!" Scott Carter greeted Nash, shouting to be heard over the music. He took one of the cases and led us toward a large kitchen crowded with bodies, scantily clad and shiny with sweat. In spite of the winter chill outside, it was hot and humid indoors, the hormone level rising with each new song that played.

I took off my jacket, revealing my snug red blouse, and almost immediately wished I could cover myself back up. I didn't have much to show off, but it was all now on display, thanks to the top Emma had picked out for me that afternoon, which suddenly seemed much more daring than it had in the privacy of my own room.

Nash set the remaining case of beer on the counter as Scott slid the first one into the refrigerator. "Kaylee Cavanaugh," Scott said when he stood, having apparently noticed me for the first time. He eyed me up and down while I resisted the urge to cross my arms over my chest. "Lookin' good." He glanced from me to Sophie, then back, while my cousin tried to fry me alive with the heat of her glare. "I'm starting to see the family resemblance."

"All I see is you," Nash said, pulling me close when he realized Sophie and I weren't happy with the comparison.

I smiled and kissed him impulsively, convinced by the slow churn of colors in his irises that he meant what he said.

Scott shoved the last case of beer into the fridge, then slapped a cold can into Nash's hand as I finally pulled away from him, my face flaming. "See? Family resemblance." Then he headed off into the crowd with Sophie, popping the top on a can of his own. Three steps later they were grinding to the music, one of Scott's hands around his drink, the other splayed across my cousin's lower back.

"Wow, that was…unexpected," Nash said, drawing my gaze from the familiar faces talking, dancing, drinking, and… otherwise engaged. And it took me a moment to realize he meant the kiss.

"Good unexpected, or bad unexpected?"

"Very, very good." He set his can on the counter at my back, then pulled me closer for a repeat performance, one hand sliding up my side. That time I didn't pull away until someone poked my shoulder. I twisted in Nash's arms to find Emma Marshall, my best friend, watching us with an amused half smile.

"Hey." Her grin grew as she glanced from me to Nash, then back. "You're blocking the fridge."

"There's a cooler in the other room." Nash nodded toward the main part of the house.

Emma shrugged. "Yeah, but no one's making out in front of it." She pulled open the fridge, grabbed a beer, then popped the can open as she pushed the door shut with a toss of one shapely hip. It wasn't fair. Emma and her sisters inherited crazy curves—a genetic jackpot—and all I got from my relatives was a really gnarled family tree.

There were times when I would gladly have traded all my *bean sidhe* "gifts"—did a glass-shattering screech and the ability to travel between the human world and the Netherworld even count as gifts?—for a little more of what she had. But this was not one of those times. Not while Nash's hands were on my waist, his taste still on my lips, and the greens and browns in his eyes swirling languorously with blatant desire. For *me*.

Em drank from her can, and I grabbed the car keys dangling from her hand, then showed them to her before stuffing them into my hip pocket, along with my own. She could stay the night with me, and I'd bring her back for her car in the morning. Emma smiled and nodded, already moving to the music when someone called her name from the living-room doorway.

"Hey, Em!" a voice called over the music, and I turned to see Doug Fuller leaning with one bulging arm on the door frame. "Come dance with me."

Emma smiled, drained her can, then danced into the living room with Doug's hands on her already swaying hips. Nash and I joined them, and he returned greeting after greeting from the glitter crowd writhing around us. But then he was mine. We moved with the music as if the room was empty but for the stereo and the heat we shared.

I had stolen Nash from a room full of his adoring devotees with nothing but the secret connection we shared. A connection no other girl could possibly compete with.

We'd combined our *bean sidhe* abilities to bring my best friend back from the dead and to reclaim a damned soul from the hellion who'd bought it. We'd literally saved lives, fought evil, and almost died together. No mere pretty face could compete with that, no matter how much gloss and mascara she applied.

An hour later, Em tapped my shoulder and pointed toward the kitchen. I shook my head—after a month without him, I could have danced with Nash all night—but after Emma left,

Nash kept glancing at the kitchen door like it was going to suddenly slam closed and lock us out.

"Need a break?" I asked, and he smiled in relief.

"Just for a minute." He tugged me through the crowd while my heart still raced to the beat, both of us damp with sweat.

In the kitchen, Emma drank from a fresh can of beer while Doug argued with Brant Williams about a bad call during some basketball game I hadn't seen.

"Here." Nash handed me a cold soda. "I'll be right back." Then he pushed his way through the crowd without a backward glance.

I looked at Emma with both brows raised, but she only shrugged.

I popped open my Coke and noticed that Doug and Brant's argument had become a whispered conversation I couldn't follow, and Emma hadn't even noticed. For several minutes, she prattled about her sister refusing to lend her a blouse that made Cara look lumpy, anyway.

Before I could decide how to respond, someone called my name, and I looked up to find Brant watching me. "Yeah?" Obviously I'd missed a question.

"I said, 'Where's your boyfriend?'"

"Um…bathroom," I said, unwilling to admit that I wasn't sure.

Brant shook his head slowly. "Hudson's falling down on the job. You wanna dance till he gets back? I won't bite." He held out one large brown hand for mine, and I took it.

Brant Williams was tall, and dark, and always smiling. He was the football team's kicker, a senior, and the friendliest jock I'd ever met, not counting Nash. He was also the only other person in the house I would dance with, other than Emma.

I danced with Brant for two songs, glancing around for

Nash the whole time. I was just starting to wonder if he'd gotten sick when I spotted him across the room, standing with Sophie in an arched doorway leading to a dark hall. He brushed a strand of hair from her forehead, then leaned closer to be heard over the music.

My chest ached like I couldn't breathe.

When he saw me looking, he stepped away from Sophie and scowled at my partner, then waved me over. I thanked Brant for the dance, then made my way across the room, dread building inside me like heartburn. Nash had ditched me at a party, then showed up with Sophie. Deep down, I'd known this day would come. I'd figured he'd eventually look elsewhere for what he hadn't had in the two and a half months we'd been going out. But with Sophie? A flash of anger burned in my cheeks. He may as well have just spit in my face!

Please, please be imagining things, Kaylee....

I stopped five feet away, my heart bruising my chest with each labored beat. Yes, Sophie had a boyfriend, but that didn't mean she wouldn't try to take mine.

Nash took one look at my face, at my eyes, which were surely swirling with pain and anger I couldn't hide, then followed my gaze to Sophie. His eyes widened with comprehension. Then he smiled and grabbed my hand.

"Sophie was just looking for Scott. Right?" But then he tugged me down the dark hall before she could answer, leaving my cousin all alone in the crowd. "We can talk in here," Nash whispered, pressing me into a closed door.

The full body contact was promising, but I couldn't banish doubt. "Were you talking to her the whole time?" I asked around the hitch in my breath as his cheek brushed mine.

"I just went outside to cool off, and when I came back in, she cornered me. That's it." He fumbled for the handle near my hip, and the door swung open, revealing Scott's dad's posh office.

"Swear?"

"Do I really need to?" Nash stepped back so I could see his eyes in the dim light of the desk lamp, and I saw the truth swirling in them. He didn't want Sophie, no matter what she might do that I hadn't.

I felt myself flush. "Sorry. I just thought—"

Nash closed the door and cut my apology off with a kiss. He tasted good. Like mint. We wound up on Mr. Carter's burgundy leather couch, and I had just enough time to think that psychiatrists made *waaaay* too much money before Nash's mouth found mine again, and thinking became impossible.

"You know I'm not interested in Sophie," he whispered. "I wouldn't do that to you or Scott." He leaned down and kissed me again. "There's only you, Kaylee."

My entire body tingled in wave after wave of warm, exhilarating shivers, and I let my lips trail over the rough stubble on his chin, delighting in the coarse texture.

"Oh, blah, blah, *blah,*" a jaded voice said, drenching our privacy with a cold dose of sarcasm. "You love him, he loves you, and we're all one big, happy, sloppy, dorky family."

"*Damn* it, Tod!" Nash stiffened. I closed my eyes and sighed. The couch creaked beneath us as we sat up to see Nash's undead brother—fully corporeal for once—sitting backward in Mr. Carter's desk chair, arms crossed over the top as he watched us in boredom barely softened by the slight upturn of his cherubic lips. "If you don't quit it with the Peeping Tom routine, I'm going to tell your boss you get off watching other people make out."

"He knows," Tod and I said in unison. I straightened my

shirt, scowling at the intruder, though my irritation was already fading.

Unlike Nash, I had trouble staying mad at Tod lately because I considered his recent reappearance a good sign. We hadn't seen him for nearly a month after his ex-girlfriend died in October—without her soul. And when I say we'd *not seen* him, I mean that literally. As a grim reaper, Tod could choose when and where he wanted to be seen, and by whom.

But now he was back, and up to his old tricks. Which seemed to consist entirely of preventing me and Nash from having any quality alone time. He was almost as bad as my dad.

"Shouldn't you be at work?" I ran one hand through my long brown hair to smooth it.

Tod shrugged. "I'm on my lunch break."

I lifted both brows. "You don't eat."

He only shrugged again, and smiled.

"Get out," Nash growled, tossing his head toward the door. Like Tod would actually have to use it. One of the other perks of being dead, technically speaking, was the ability to walk through things. Or simply disappear, then reappear somewhere else. That's right. I got swirling eyes and the capacity to shatter windows with my bare voice. Tod got teleportation and invisibility.

The supernatural world is *so* far from fair.

Tod stood and kicked the chair aside, running one hand through short blond curls that not even the afterlife could tame. "I'm not here to watch you two, anyway."

Great. I scowled at the reaper, my eyes narrowed in true irritation now. "I told you to stay away from her." Emma had met him once, briefly, and we'd made the mistake of telling her what he really was. He'd been watching her covertly before, but after Addison's death and his obvious heartbreak, I'd assumed that had stopped.

Tod mirrored his brother with his arms crossed over his chest. "So you won't let me go near her, but you'll let her get in the car with some drunk jock? That doesn't even kinda make sense."

"Damn it." Nash was off the couch in an instant and I followed, whispering a thank-you to Tod as I passed him. But he'd already blinked out of the office.

I trailed Nash down the hall and through the packed living room, accidentally bumping a beer from a cheerleader's hand on the way. We ran out the front door and I wished I'd stopped to find my jacket when the frigid air raised goose bumps all over my skin.

We paused at the end of the walkway, and I spotted Emma near the mouth of the cul-de-sac, a brief glimpse of long blond hair. "There." I pointed and we took off again. We got there just as Doug pulled his passenger's side door open. He had Em pressed against the side of the car, his tongue in her mouth, his free hand up her shirt.

Emma was totally into it, and though I didn't think she'd have gone so far in public if not for the beer, that was her business. But getting in the car with a drunk crossed the line from stupid into dangerous.

"Em," I said as Nash slapped one hand on Doug's shoulder and pulled him backward.

"What the hell, man!" Doug slurred as his hand pulled free from Emma's bra hard enough that the elastic slapped her skin.

"Kaylee!" Emma smiled and fell against me, and I glared at Doug. She didn't know what she was doing, and *he* was being a complete asshole.

"Em, you know how it goes." I wrapped one arm around

her waist when she stumbled. "Come together, stay to-gether…"

"…leave together," she finished with a wide-eyed, pseudo-serious expression. "But we didn't come together, Kay…"

"I know, but the last part still applies."

"Fuller, she's drunk." Nash angled him so that Doug fell into his own passenger's seat. "And so are you."

"Noooo…" Emma giggled, blowing beer breath at me. "He's not drinking, so he gets to drive."

"Em, he's wasted," Nash insisted, then glanced at me and tossed his head toward the house. "Take her back in."

I started walking Emma up the sidewalk, trying to keep her quiet as she told me how nice Doug was. She wasn't just drunk, she was *gone.* I should have watched her more closely.

A minute later, Nash caught up to us as I was lowering Emma onto the porch. "Did you get his keys?" I asked, and Nash frowned. Then, as he turned to head back toward Doug's car, an engine growled to life and a sick feeling settled into the pit of my stomach. Nash took off running and I leaned Emma against the top step. "Tod?" I called, glancing around the dark yard, grateful there was no one around to see me talking to myself.

"What?" the reaper said at my back, and I whirled around, wondering why he always appeared behind me.

"Can you sit with her for a minute?"

He scowled and glanced at Emma, who stared up at us, blinking her big brown eyes in intoxicated innocence. "You told me to stay away from her."

"Hey, I remember you," Emma slurred, loud enough to make me wince. "You're dead."

We both ignored Em. "I know. Just watch her for a min-ute, and don't let her get into any cars. Please." Then I raced after Nash past the entrance to the cul-de-sac, confident Tod would watch Emma. That he'd probably been doing it all night, though he'd catch hell for missing work.

Ahead, streetlights shone on the glossy surface of Doug's car, gliding past like a slice of the night itself. Then, as I caught up to Nash, Doug leaned suddenly to one side, and his car lurched forward and to the right.

There was a loud pop, followed by the crunch of metal. Then the crash of something more substantial.

"Shit!" Nash took off running again and I followed as that sick feeling in my stomach enveloped the rest of me. "Oh, no, Kaylee…"

I knew before I even saw it. The street was lined with expensive, highly insured cars belonging to people who could easily afford to replace them. But the drunk jock had hit mine. When I got closer, I saw that he'd not only hit it, he'd rammed it up onto the sidewalk and *through* a neighbor's brick mailbox.

My car was *crunched*. The driver's side door was buckled. Bricks and chunks of mortar lay everywhere.

Behind us, Scott's front door squealed opened and voices erupted into the dark behind me. I glanced back to find Tod— now fully corporeal—ushering Emma away from the crowd pouring into the yard. When I was sure she was okay, I turned to my poor, dead car.

Until I noticed that Doug Fuller had yet to emerge from his. *Crap.*

"Help me with him," Nash called, and I rounded the car as he pulled open the completely unscathed driver's side door of the Mustang. Doug's head lolled on his shoulders, and he was mumbling drunk nonsense under his breath. "…with me. Somebody else in my *car,* dude…"

Nash leaned inside to unlatch the seat belt—what kind of

drunk remembers to buckle up?—but he couldn't fit between his friend and the steering wheel, which had been shoved way too close to Doug's chest. "Kay, could you get the belt?"

I sighed and crawled across his lap, wedging my torso between the wheel and his chest as I felt around for the button. "Scared the *shit* out of me…" he mumbled into the hair that had fallen over my ear. "He was just *there,* outta nowhere!"

"Shut up, Doug," I snapped, seriously considering leaving him in the car until the cops arrived. "You're drunk." When I had the belt unlatched, I backed out of the linebacker's lap and he exhaled right into my face.

I froze, one hand braced against his thigh, and that sick feeling in my stomach became a full-body cramp. Ice-cold fingers of horror clenched my heart and shot through my veins. Emma was right. Doug hadn't been drinking.

Somehow, Eastlake High School's completely human first-string linebacker had gotten his big, dumb hands on the most dangerous controlled substance in the Netherworld.

Doug Fuller absolutely *reeked* of Demon's Breath.

"Are you sure?" Nash whispered, brows drawn low as, behind him, a big man in a grease-stained coat hooked the front of my smashed car up to the huge chain dangling from the back of his tow truck.

"Yes. I'm sure." He'd already asked me four times. I'd only had two brief whiffs of Demon's Breath a month earlier, but that bittersweet, biting tang—more like an aftertaste than a true scent—was emblazoned on my brain, along with other memorial gems like the feel of nylon straps lashing me to a narrow hospital bed.

"Where would he even get it?" I murmured, zipping the jacket Nash had gotten for me as a motor rumbled to life on the street and the big chain was wound tighter, raising the front of my poor car off the ground.

"I don't know." Nash wrapped his arms around me from behind, cocooning me in a familiar warmth.

"Humans can't cross into the Netherworld and hellions can't cross into ours," I murmured, thinking out loud while no one else was close enough to hear me. "So there has to be some way to get Demon's Breath into the human world without bringing the hellion who provided it." Because the name was a very literal description: Demon's Breath was the toxic exhalation of a hellion, a very powerful drug in the Netherworld. And evidently a hell of a high in our world, too.

But Demon's Breath could rot the soul of a reaper who held it in his lungs for too long. Did the same hold true for humans? Had Doug breathed enough of it to damage his soul? How had he gotten it in the first place?

"I'm gonna take a look around," I whispered, and Nash shook his head.

"No!" He stepped closer to me, so everyone else would think he was comforting me over the loss of my car. "You can't cross over. Hellions don't like to lose, and Avari's going to be out for your soul for the rest of your life, Kaylee."

Because I'd escaped with mine when we'd crossed over to reclaim the Page sisters' souls.

"I'm just going to peek." Like looking through a window into the Netherworld, instead of actually walking through the door. "And anyway, Avari won't be there." I frowned. "Here." Or whatever. "At Scott Carter's party."

The Netherworld was like a warped mirror image of our own world. The two were connected at certain points, wherever the bleed-through of human energy was strong enough to anchor the Netherworld to ours, like a toothpick through layers of a sandwich.

"Kaylee, I don't think—"

I cut him off with a glance. I didn't have time to argue. "Just stand in front of me so no one can see me. It'll only take a second."

When he hesitated, I stepped behind him and closed my eyes. And I remembered death.

I thought back to the first time it had happened—at least, the first time I remembered—forcing myself to relive the horror. The certainty that the poor kid in the wheelchair was going to die. That dark knowledge that only I had. The shadows that churned around him. Through him.

The memory of death was enough, fortunately, and the scream began to build deep in my throat. A female *bean sidhe*'s wail heralds death and can suspend the deceased's soul long enough for a male *bean sidhe* to redirect it. But my wail would also let me—and any other *bean sidhe* near enough to hear me—see into the Netherworld. To cross into it, if we wanted to.

But I had no desire to go to the Netherworld. Ever again.

I held the scream back, trapping it in my throat and in my heart so that Nash heard only a thin ribbon of sound, and no one else would hear a thing.

Nash took my hand, but I could barely feel the warmth of his fingers around mine. I opened my eyes and gasped. Scott Carter's street had been enveloped by a thin gray film, like a storm cloud had settled to the ground. My world was still there—police, tow trucks, an ambulance, and a small crowd of onlookers.

But beneath that—deeper than that—was the Netherworld.

A field of olive-colored razor wheat swayed in a breeze I knew would be cold, if I could have felt it, the brittle stalks tinkling like wind chimes as they brushed together. The sky was dark purple streaked with greens and blues like bruises on the face of the world.

It was both beautiful and terrifying. And blessedly empty. No hellions. No fiends. No creatures waiting to eat us or to breathe toxic breath on Doug Fuller, even if we'd found some kind of hole in the barrier between worlds.

"Okay, it's clear. Let it go," Nash whispered, and I swallowed my scream.

The gray began to clear and the *wrong* colors faded, leaving only the upper-class suburban neighborhood, somehow less intimidating to me now that I'd seen what lay beneath. The Netherworld version of Scott's neighborhood looked just like mine.

I wrapped my arms around Nash, discomforted by the glimpse of a world that had once tried to swallow us both whole. "However he got it, it didn't come straight from the source," I said, then I let go of Nash to face the real world.

Only a few brave—and sober—partyers had stayed once word got out that the police were on their way, and the stragglers were gathered around Scott on his front lawn, watching the cleanup from a safe distance. The cops knew there'd been a party, and they obviously knew Scott had been drinking. But so long as he stayed in his own yard and didn't try to get behind the wheel, they were clearly willing to look the other way, thanks to his elite address and his father's considerable influence in the community.

Emma wouldn't be so lucky. She and Sophie had taken refuge four doors down, in Laura Bell's living room. Laura—Sophie's best friend and fellow dancer—had only let Emma in because Nash used the male *bean sidhe's* vocal Influence to convince her.

But just in case, we'd sent Tod to watch out for Emma. Invisibly, of course.

Nash's arms tightened around me as a uniformed policeman clomped across the street toward us. "Miss—" he glanced at the notebook in his hands "—Cavanaugh, are you sure you don't need a ride?"

"I have one, thanks." I let him think Nash was my ride so I wouldn't have to mention Emma or her car.

The cop glanced at Nash, and my heart fell into my stomach. He'd finished his one drink hours earlier, but suddenly I was afraid the cop would make him walk the line or breathe into something. But when Nash didn't flinch beneath the appraisal, the cop's gaze found me again.

"You want me to call your parents?"

I hesitated, trying to look like I was seriously considering that option. Then I shook my head decisively. "Um, no thanks." I waved my cell for him to see. "I'll call my dad."

He shrugged. "They're hauling your car to the body shop on Third, and the guys there should have an estimate for you in a couple of days. But personally, I think an angry word from your lawyer could get this Fuller kid's parents to buy you a new one. He looks like he can afford it—" the cop shot a contemptuous glance over one shoulder "—and I'm willing to bet a year's pay that kid's baked hotter than an apple pie. They're taking him to Arlington Memorial, so make sure your lawyer gets a look at his blood-test results."

I nodded, numb, and the cop glanced at Nash over my head. "Get her home safely."

Nash's chin brushed the back of my head as he nodded, and when the cop was out of hearing range, I twisted to find Nash's irises swirling languidly with none of the urgent fear skittering through me.

"Do you think the blood test will show anything?"

"No way." Nash shook his head firmly. "There's not a human lab built that can detect a Netherworld substance, and that cop lacks the necessary equipment to do it himself." He tapped my nose and smiled reassuringly, and for a moment, I felt like a supernatural bloodhound. "You ready to go?"

"I guess." I stared as the tow truck pulled away with my car, and a second one backed slowly toward Doug's Mustang.

Doug sat on the floor of the ambulance, legs dangling over the edge, and as I watched, another officer held out a small electronic device with a mouthpiece on one end. Doug blew into the breathalyzer, and the cop glanced at the reading, then smacked the device on the palm of his hand. Like it wasn't working.

It probably showed at least one beer, but nowhere near enough to account for his current state. Nash was right; neither humans nor technology could detect Demon's Breath. I wasn't sure whether to be happy about that, or scared out of my mind.

We knocked on Laura Bell's door as the ambulance pulled away, followed closely by the second wrecker pulling Doug's car. Laura led us through a large, tiled foyer and into a sunken living room full of dark colors and expensive woods.

Emma sat in a stiff wingback chair, looking lost and half-asleep. When I reached to help her up, Tod popped into view a foot away and I nearly jumped out of my skin. Would I never get used to that?

"She's fine," Tod said as I knelt to look into Emma's heavy-lidded eyes, and I knew by the lack of a reaction from anyone else—including Nash—that no one else could see him. "She just needs to sleep it off. And to get away from these squawking harpies you call friends."

In fact, I did *not* call Sophie and Laura friends, but I couldn't explain that without looking crazy to everyone who didn't see the invisible dead boy. So I scowled at the reaper as I helped Emma up, and Nash wrapped her other arm around his neck.

"Hey, Sophie, do you want a ride?" I asked as we passed

my cousin, standing with her hand propped on one denim-clad hip.

She sneered at me with shiny pink lips. "Didn't Doug just wrap your rolling scrap pile around a mailbox?"

"In Emma's car," I said through gritted teeth.

Sophie sank onto the couch and crossed one skinny leg over the other. "I'm staying with Laura."

"Fine." They deserved each other. "Thanks for watching her," I said to Tod.

"Someone had to." But before I could answer, the reaper popped out of existence again, presumably gone back to the hospital, where he was no doubt overdue.

"Just get her out of here before my parents get home," Laura said, assuming I was talking to her. "They don't like me hanging out with drunk sluts." I bit back a dozen replies about the irony of her friendship with Sophie and settled for slamming the door on our way out.

I called my dad on the drive home, but he was working overtime again, and I got his voice mail. I hung up without leaving a message, because somehow "my car got rammed by a linebacker high on Demon's Breath" just seemed like the kind of thing he'd want to hear in person.

It was almost midnight—my official curfew—when I pulled into my driveway, and Emma had fallen asleep in her own backseat. Nash carried her inside and put her on my bed. I took off her shoes, then curled up next to Nash on the couch with a bowl of popcorn and a sci-fi channel broadcast of the original *Night of the Living Dead*—a holiday classic if I'd ever seen one.

My front door opened just as the first zombie ripped its way into the farmhouse on-screen, and I jumped, dumping popcorn everywhere.

My father trudged through the door in faded jeans and a flannel shirt, an entirely different kind of zombie thanks to shift after shift on an assembly line, trying to keep us both clothed and fed. Then he stopped and backed onto the porch again, and I knew exactly what he was looking for.

"Where's your car?" Dread warred with the exhaustion in his voice as he tossed his jacket over the back of a living room chair.

I stood while Nash began dropping stray kernels into the bowl. "Um, there was a little accident, and—"

"Are you okay?" My dad frowned, eyeing me from head to toe for injuries.

"Yeah, I wasn't even in the car." I stuffed my hands into my back pockets because I didn't know what else to do with them.

"What? Where were you?"

"At a party. When Doug Fuller left, he accidentally…hit my car."

My dad's dark brows furrowed until they almost met. "Were you drinking?"

"No." *Thank goodness.* I wouldn't put it past him to whip out a plastic cup and demand a urine sample. I swear, he would have been a great parole officer.

My father studied me, and I could see the exact moment he decided he believed me. And with that settled, his gaze fixed behind me, where Nash now stood with the bowl of spilled popcorn. "Nash, go home." The most common words in his verbal arsenal.

Nash handed me the bowl. "You want me to take Emma home?"

"Emma…?" My dad sighed and ran one hand through his thick brown hair. "Where is she?"

"In my bed."

"Drunk?"

I thought about lying. I had no idea how he would react, even if I wasn't the one drinking. But Em smelled like beer; my lie would never float.

"Yeah. What was I supposed to do, toss her the keys and wish her luck?"

My dad sighed. Then to my complete shock, he shook his head. "No, you did the right thing."

"So she can stay?" I couldn't believe it. He didn't even sound mad.

"This time. But next time, I'm calling her mother. Nash, I'm sure we'll see you tomorrow."

"Yes, sir." Nash squeezed my hand, then headed for the door. He would walk to his house, two streets away, like he'd done every time he'd come over since I'd been grounded. Including several times when my father'd had no idea he was there.

"What happened?" My dad locked the door behind Nash, then sank into his favorite armchair as I settled onto the couch, trying to decide whether or not to tell him the whole truth. About the Demon's Breath. He was being pretty cool so far, but the Netherworld element was guaranteed to push him over the edge.

"I told you. Doug Fuller hit my car."

"How bad is it?"

I sighed, mentally steeling myself for an explosion. "He wrapped it around a neighbor's brick mailbox."

Air whistled as he inhaled sharply, and I flinched.

"He was drinking, wasn't he?" my father demanded, and I almost smiled in relief. Part of me had been sure he'd know about the Demon's Breath from my posture, or my expression, or some kind of weird *bean sidhe* parenting telepathy I didn't know about. But he thought it was just regular teenage drama, and if I wasn't mistaken, he looked a little relieved, too.

I was not going to burst his bubble. "I don't know. Maybe. But he *is* about as smart as a tractor."

"Where'd they take the car?"

"To the body shop on Third."

My dad stood and actually smiled at me, and I could almost taste his relief. He was thrilled to finally be faced with a normal parent's problem. "I'll go look at it in the morning. I assume this Fuller kid is insured?"

"Yeah. The cops gave me this." I held out the form with Doug's contact information and his insurance company's number. "And he said his dad would pay for it."

"Yes, he *will*." My father took the form into the kitchen, where the light was better. "Go get some sleep. You and Em are working in the morning, aren't you?"

"Yeah." From noon to four, we'd be selling tickets and serving popcorn at the Cinemark in the never-ending quest for gas money. Which we spent going to and from work. It was a vicious cycle.

Dismissed, and feeling like I'd just been pardoned from death row, I changed into my pj's, brushed my teeth, and lay down next to Emma in the bed. And as I listened to her breathe, I couldn't help thinking about how badly everything might have turned out if she'd actually gotten into that car.

I'd already lost Emma once and had no intention of losing her again anytime soon. Which meant I'd have to find out how her boyfriend got his human hands on Demon's Breath— then make sure that never happened again.

3

"KAYLEE, COME ON IN!" Harmony Hudson brushed blond curls back from her face and held the door for me as I stepped into her small, neat living room, stuffing my freezing hands into my jacket pockets. "Do we have a lesson this morning?"

"No, I just came to see Nash."

"Oh!" She smiled and closed the door, cutting off the frigid draft. "Then you must have served out your sentence."

"As of yesterday."

Nash had been grounded, too, but he only got two weeks, to my four. I think he would have gotten more if he'd still been underage, but it's hard to ground an eighteen-year-old. And punishing Tod wasn't even an option, considering he was fully grown and technically dead, and had unlimited access to the Netherworld. She couldn't even keep him in one room—not to mention corporeal—long enough to yell at him.

"He's still asleep. What did you guys do last night, anyway?"

I dropped my duffel on the faded couch, going for non-chalance, though I hated withholding information from her even worse than from my father. "Party at Scott's house. Doug Fuller rammed my parked car with an '08 Mustang."

"Oh, no!" Harmony stopped in the kitchen doorway, holding the swinging door open with one palm. "You're insured, right?"

"Liability only." That's all I could afford, working twelve hours a week at the Cinemark. "But Doug's parents are loaded, and there's no way they can say I'm at fault. I wasn't even in the car."

"Well, that's good at least, right?" I nodded, and she waved one hand toward the short hallway branching off from the opposite side of the living room. "Go wake up van Winkle and see if you can get him to eat something. I'm making apple-cinnamon muffins."

Harmony was always baking something, and always from scratch. She was really more like a grandmother than a mom, in that respect, though she looked more like Nash's older sister. She was eighty-two years old, with the face and body of a thirty-year-old.

So far, slow postpuberty aging was the only real advantage I'd discovered to being a *bean sidhe*. My father was one hundred thirty-two and didn't look a day over forty.

Nash didn't answer when I knocked, so I slipped into his room, then closed the door and leaned against it, watching him sleep. He looked so vulnerable in his boxers, one side of his face buried in the pillow, one leg tangled near the bottom of his sheet.

I knelt by the bed and brushed thick brown hair from his forehead. The room was warm, but his skin was cool, so I started to cover him up, but before I could, his face twisted into a grimace, his eyes still squeezed shut.

He was breathing too fast. Almost panting. His teeth ground

together, then he made a helpless mewling sound. His arms tensed. He clenched handfuls of the fitted sheet.

I watched Nash's nightmare from the outside, trying to decide if I should wake him up or let the dream play out. But then his eyes flew open and he gasped, his gaze still unfocused. He scuttled over the mattress, bare chest heaving, and stood against the far wall, staring across the bed at me. His irises churned in terror for several seconds before recognition settled into place and by then my own heart was racing in response to his fear.

"Kaylee?" He whispered my name, like he wasn't sure he could trust his own eyes.

"Yeah, it's me." I stood as his breathing slowed and he started to calm down. "Nightmare?"

He rubbed both hands over his face, and when he met my gaze again he was calm, back in control of his expression. And of his eyes. "Yeah, I guess."

"What was it about?"

"I don't remember." He frowned and sank onto the mattress. "I just know it was bad. But the waking up part is good so far..."

Nash pulled me onto his lap. "So, what's with the personal wake-up?" He swept my hair over one shoulder and suddenly I was acutely aware that he was half-naked and now very close. "Phone calls just aren't as satisfying anymore?" he whispered, trailing feather-soft kisses down my neck.

He leaned us both back, and before I even realized what had happened, I was lying on his bed, his weight pressing me into the mattress. His lips trailed down my neck again and his hand roamed over my shirt, and all I could think was that I didn't want to stop him. He'd waited long enough. I wanted to just let it happen...

My next exhale was ragged, and I couldn't control my racing pulse.

"I, uh…" What was I saying? What did he ask? Suddenly it didn't seem to matter….

His hand slid beneath my shirt, but his fingers were freezing on my skin, and the shock woke me up. Irritated, I pulled Nash away and sat up to frown at him. "Are you Influencing me?"

He shrugged, a heated grin turned up one side of his mouth. "Just helping you relax."

"Don't Influence me, Nash!" I stood, struggling to sustain my anger with his voice still slithering through my mind. "Don't ever do that to me when I'm not singing for someone's soul." Sometimes his voice helped me quiet my *bean sidhe* wail, but that's not what this was. Not even close. "I hate losing control. It's like falling off a cliff in slow motion." Or being sedated. "And that's not what I came in here for," I insisted, waving one hand at the bed.

Nash scowled, and that tremendous, irresistible false calm deserted me, leaving only the chill of its sudden absence and his obvious irritation. "How am I supposed to know that? I wake up and you're in my bedroom with the door closed. What was I supposed to think? That you want to play Scrabble?"

"I…" I frowned, unsure how to finish that thought. Had I sent him some kind of signal? Was I wearing my "I'm done with my virginity, please get rid of it for me" T-shirt? "Your mom's in the other room!"

"Whatever." He sighed and pulled me closer by one hand. "Forgive me?"

"Only if you promise to play nice."

"I swear. So, what's up?" He leaned back on a pillow

propped against his headboard, hands linked behind his skull, putting himself on display in case I changed my mind.

"You said you'd give me a ride."

His eyes swirled with mischief, and my cheeks blazed when I realized what I'd said. "Um…you're the one who said no."

"A ride to *work*." I'd just discovered the cause of spontaneous combustion. Surely I'd burst into flames any moment.

"I guess I could do that, too."

"I'm serious!" But not too serious to let my gaze wander. After all, I was being invited to look… "I need a lift to work, and I was hoping we could make a stop first."

"Where?"

I closed my eyes and took a deep breath. "Doug Fuller's."

"Kaylee…" he began, and I could already hear the protest forming. He sat up and I let one leg hang off the bed. "Whatever Fuller's into is none of our business."

"He's taking *Demon's Breath,*" I whispered with a nervous glance at the closed door, hoping his mother was still in the kitchen. "How is that none of our business?"

"It has nothing to do with us." He stood and snatched a shirt from the back of his desk chair.

"Don't you want to know where he got it? He could have killed someone last night. And if he takes any more of it, he'll probably kill himself."

Nash sank into his desk chair. "You're overreacting, Kaylee."

"No, you're *under*reacting." I scooted to the edge of his bed. "What happened to looking out for your friends?"

"What am I supposed to do?" He shrugged, frustration clear in the tense line of his shoulders. "Go up to Fuller and say, 'Hey, man, I'm not sure where you're getting secondhand air from a demon you don't even know exists, but you need to lay

off it before you kill yourself'? *That's* not gonna sound weird."
He kicked a shoe across the room to punctuate his sarcasm.

I crossed my arms over my chest, struggling to keep my
voice low. "You're worried about sounding weird in front of
a guy who's getting high off someone else's breath?"

"Why do you care, anyway?" Nash demanded. "You don't
even like Fuller."

"That doesn't mean I want to watch him die." Especially
considering that his impending death would send me into an
uncontrollable, screaming *bean sidhe* fit, forcing us to decide
whether or not to try to save him. "And I won't let him take
Emma with him."

Nash's scowl wilted, giving way to confusion. "What are
you talking about?"

"They were all over each other last night, Nash. While he
was high on Demon's Breath. And it probably wasn't the first
time. She could be accidentally inhaling what he exhales."

Horror flitted across Nash's face, greens and browns twisting in his irises, then he closed his eyes and reset his expression
before I was even sure of what I'd seen, effectively locking me
out of his thought process.

I leaned against his headboard and fiddled with his pil-
lowcase. "Tod says it's highly addictive and ultimately *deadly*
to humans. What if she gets hooked on it, too? What if she
already is?"

Nash sighed and sank onto the bed, facing me. "Look, we
don't even know that Fuller's actually addicted, okay? We just
know he took some last night. And to even be exposed, Emma
would have had to suck air straight from his lungs, right after
he inhaled. And the chances of that are almost nil. Right?"

"How do you know? He was still exhaling enough for me
to smell it on him, and they've been all over each other for the

past two weeks. Are you sure she couldn't have gotten even a tiny bit by kissing him?"

"I seriously doubt it, Kaylee." But before he regained control of his eyes, I saw the truth in the nervous swirl of color. Nash wasn't sure. And he was scared.

He exhaled heavily, then met my gaze again. "Okay, we'll find out if he knows what he was taking and where he got it. But if he doesn't know, don't tell him what it is, okay? No more full disclosures to friends. Emma was plenty."

"Fine." I wasn't exactly eager to tell anyone else I wasn't human, anyway.

"You have to be at work at noon?" I nodded, and he pulled off the shirt he'd just put on, then tossed it at his open hamper like a basketball. "We'll leave as soon as I get out of the shower."

"After breakfast," I corrected on my way to the door, smiling over my victory. "Your mom's making muffins."

In the kitchen, I waited for Nash in a rickety chair at the scratched, round table, watching Harmony wash dishes.

"So are you enjoying your freedom?" She glanced at me over her shoulder as she set a metal bowl in the dish drainer.

I shrugged. "I haven't experienced much of it yet."

She dried a clean, plastic-coated whisk, dropped it into an open drawer, then leaned against the counter and eyed me in blatant curiosity. "Was it worth it?"

"Was it worth being grounded?" I asked, and she nodded. "Yes. And no. Getting Regan's soul back was totally worth it." Four weeks of house arrest were nothing compared to the eternity she would have suffered without her soul. "But there was nothing we could do for Addy." And every time I thought about that, my stomach pitched like I was in freefall, a mixture of guilt and horror over my failure.

"Do you still hear from Regan?" Harmony asked when I didn't elaborate.

"Not very often. I think it's easier for her to try to forget about what happened with Addy." About the fact that her sister had been damned to eternal torment because she died without her soul. With nothing to release upon her death but a lungful of Demon's Breath.

And suddenly I had an idea... "Do you think Regan will be okay? Because of the Demon's Breath, I mean. Tod said it's really dangerous."

Harmony nodded absently, opening the oven door to check the muffins. "It certainly can be. Demon's Breath decays your soul. It rots the parts of you that make you you."

Okay, that's not terrifying....

"But on the surface, it acts a bit like a very strong hallucinogenic drug. It'll make you see and hear things that aren't there."

Which would explain why Doug thought someone had been in the car with him...

Harmony continued, sounding every bit like the nurse she was. "It's also highly addictive, and even if it doesn't kill you quickly, long-term use can lead to brain damage and psychosis."

I swallowed the huge lump that had formed in my throat and hoped my voice sounded normal. "Psychosis, like, insanity?"

"Simply put, yes. A complete loss of contact with reality." She used a pot holder to pull the muffin pan from the oven, then kicked the oven door closed. "And withdrawal is even worse. It sends the entire system into shock and can easily be fatal, even to someone who survived the substance itself."

"Great…" I whispered. So cutting off Doug's supply might kill him even faster than the Demon's Breath would.

"Oh, no, hon!" I looked up to find her watching the horror surely growing on my face. "Don't worry about Regan. She wasn't huffing Demon's Breath for a high—she was sustained by it in the absence of her soul. That's a totally different ball game. Still very dangerous, for obvious reasons," she conceded with a shrug. "That whole sell-your-soul thing. But very little risk to her, physically."

"Because she didn't have a soul…" My mind was racing. "But if she inhaled Demon's Breath now that her soul's back in place…"

Harmony frowned. "She'd be in very serious trouble."

AN HOUR LATER Nash turned his mother's car onto a brick driveway in front of a huge house with a coordinating brick-and-stone facade. And I'd thought Scott's place was crazy. Whatever Doug Fuller's parents did, they made some serious cash.

"You think he's home?" I asked, and Nash pointed at the spotless, late-model sports car in the driveway, with a rental sticker on the rear windshield.

He turned off the engine and stuffed the keys into his pocket. "Let's get this over with."

Doug answered the door on the third ring in nothing but the sweatpants he'd obviously slept in, then backed into a bright, open entryway to let us in. We followed him to a sunken den dominated by a wall-size television, where a video game character I couldn't identify stood frozen with a pistol aimed at the entire room.

"Sorry about your car." Doug plopped onto a black leather home theater chair without even glancing at me.

"Um…" But before I could finish the nonthought, he waved off my reply and picked up a video controller from the arm of his chair.

"My dad'll pay for the damages. The rental place is supposed to deliver your loaner this afternoon. I got you a V6."

Just like that? Was he serious? I got weird death visions and a supersonic shriek, and Doug Fuller got unreasonable wealth. That was a serious imbalance of karma.

"Trust me—it's a step up."

My fists clenched in my coat pockets. How could Emma stand him?

"Um, thanks," I said, for lack of anything even resembling an intelligent reply. I looked at Nash with both brows raised, silently asking what he was waiting for. He dropped onto a black leather couch and I sat next to him.

"So was your dad pissed about the drug test? You must have been high as a satellite to hit a parked car." Nash slouched into the couch, sounding almost jealous, and that must have been the right approach because Doug grinned and paused his game.

"Dude, I was in *orbit*." He set the remote on the arm of his chair and grabbed a can of Coke from the drink holder. "But the test came out clean, other than a little alcohol. The E.R. doc told my dad I was probably euphoric from shock."

"What the hell were you taking?" Nash leaned forward and took two Cokes from the minifridge doubling as an end table.

"Somethin' called frost. It's like huffing duster inside a deep freeze, but then you're high for hours…."

Chill bumps popped up all over my skin and I shuddered at the memory of dozens of creepy little fiends crawling all over one another in the Netherworld, desperate for a single hit of Demon's Breath—preferably straight from the source.

Nash handed me a can and raised one brow to ask if I was

okay. He'd noticed the shudder. I nodded and popped the top on my Coke.

"Where'd you get it?" Nash leaned back on the couch and opened his own soda.

"From some guy named Everett. I think that's his last name. I got a physical next Tuesday, and he swore this frost shit wouldn't show up in a blood test." Doug's focus shifted to me. "Hey, Kaylee, do you know if Em's working tonight?"

"Yeah. I think she's closing." Actually, we'd both be off by four in the afternoon, but I didn't want her hanging out with Doug until I was sure he wasn't going to freeze-dry her lungs with every kiss.

Nash set his can on the minifridge. "You have any more of this frost?"

"Nah. I had an extra balloon, but I sold it yesterday." One corner of his mouth twitched twice, and my stomach flipped. The fiend we'd met in the Netherworld had twitched just like that, from withdrawal. "And I huffed the last of mine last night."

"It comes in a balloon?" Nash frowned and his irises suddenly went still, like he'd flipped the off switch on his emotional gauge.

"Yeah. Black party balloons, like the kind we used to pop in the back of the class to watch Ms. Eddin's substitute jump. Remember, back in eighth grade?"

Nash nodded absently.

"What friend?" I demanded, my hands both clenched around my Coke. "Who did you sell the other balloon to?" But I knew the answer before Doug even opened his mouth. Because that's just the kind of luck I had.

Doug picked up his game controller, his hand twitching around the plastic. "Scott Carter."

My heart dropped into my stomach. I was right. He'd sold his other balloon to my cousin's boyfriend. And Sophie was cold enough on her own, without exposure to secondhand frost.

4

"THAT'S JUST GREAT!" I buckled my seat belt as Nash shifted into Reverse. "Doug exposes Emma, then sells half his supply to Scott, who's just going to turn around and drag Sophie into the whole mess. It's an epidemic. How are we supposed to stop an epidemic?"

"It's not an epidemic." Nash twisted in his seat to check behind us while he backed down the driveway. "It's two guys who have no idea what they're into." The car rocked as the tires dropped from the brick driveway onto the smoother surface of the road, then Nash settled into his seat facing forward. "And I really don't think they could expose Emma or Sophie to secondhand Demon's Breath. Or would that actually be thirdhand?" He tried on a halfhearted grin to go with his joke, but couldn't pull it off.

"But you don't actually know that, right? You can't know for sure that they haven't been exposed."

"No, but I don't think—"

"Why are you trying to brush this off? This isn't like having a drink at a party or lighting up behind the shop building. We're talking about humans inhaling the toxic life force sucked out of a demon from another *world*." Quite possibly the weirdest sentence I'd ever said aloud… "And according to your mom, if they survive addiction—and that's a big if—their scrambled brains'll make Ozzy Osbourne look rational and coherent."

And as far as I was concerned, insanity—including the risk of being locked up in some mental ward—was worse than death, which would simply put an end to the terminal drama and angst of human existence. Unless you were stupid enough to sell your immortal soul like Addy had…

Nash's silence drew my gaze, and I found him staring at me, rather than at the road. "You asked my *mother* about Demon's Breath?" His voice held a hard quality I'd rarely heard from him before, like his words formed the bricks in a wall I was destined to crash into.

"In reference to Regan." I rubbed my palms over the denim covering my legs. "I didn't mention Doug or Emma." At least, not in the same sentence as Demon's Breath. "I'm not stupid, Nash."

"Neither is she!" His palm slammed into the steering wheel and I jumped, then a sharp jolt of anger skittered up my spine. "She knows. You ran your mouth off, and now she knows everything. Great, Kaylee. Thanks."

"She doesn't know. What is *wrong* with you?" I demanded, fighting to keep from shouting.

"Even if she doesn't know yet, if this gets as bad as you seem to think it will, she's going to figure out why you were asking, and then we're both going to be in serious trouble, Kaylee!"

I rolled my eyes. "If this gets as bad as I *know* it will, having your mother mad at us will be the least of our problems." I paused, waiting until my point had a chance to sink in, and when his grip on the wheel eased, I continued, trying to ignore his clenched jaw and tense posture. "We need to know if Scott's tried it yet." Thus, whether Sophie was in any potential danger. "And we have to get that balloon away from him, then figure out where this Everett guy is getting his supply."

Nash exhaled heavily and answered without looking at me. "Yeah. You're right." But he didn't seem very happy about it.

The rest of the ride was quiet and uncomfortable. I was mad at him for getting mad at me, and I didn't know how to deal with any of that. We'd never had a real fight before.

So we rode in silence and I got lost in my own head, trying to figure out how Demon's Breath had gotten into the human world in the first place, and how best to wrestle it from the privileged, demanding hands of the Eastlake football team without turning both of us into social rejects.

I didn't even realize I'd fallen asleep until I woke up in the Cinemark parking lot with my face against the cold passenger's side window. Confused, I blinked and sat up to find Nash watching me, frowning, his hands clenched around the wheel again.

"You okay?" He looked upset, but made no move to reach for me across the center console.

"Yeah." I stomped on the floorboard, trying to ease the tingling in my left foot, which hadn't woken up along with the rest of my body. "Just worried about this whole frost mess." I glanced at the dashboard clock, surprised to see that my shift started in ten minutes. "And tired, I guess."

Nash nodded, but his worried look held. "Hey, I'm sorry I got mad. I'll find out if Scott's tried it yet."

"Thanks." I smiled, determined to take him at his word. I didn't understand his change of heart, but I'd take it.

"You need a ride home?" he asked as I opened the car door and hauled my duffel into my lap from the rear floorboard.

"Em said she'd take me. I'll call you when I get home."

His grin that time looked more natural. "Is your dad still working overtime?"

"Yeah."

"I'll bring pizza if you pick up a movie."

"Deal."

He leaned in for a kiss, and I kissed him back, trying to believe everything would be okay. "Don't worry about Scott's balloon," he said as I got out of the car. "I'll take care of it."

I CHANGED INTO my ugly red-and-blue polyester uniform in the bathroom, then pulled my hair into a ponytail and met Emma in the box office, where she was already counting the cash in her drawer. Somehow she'd scored us matching shifts selling tickets, which almost never happened. Usually one or the other of us got stuck scooping popcorn or emptying trash cans.

I counted my own drawer in silence, trying to decide whether or not to tell her to stay away from Doug. And what to cite as the reason.

I wasn't sure if she knew what he was taking, and even if she did, I couldn't tell her what frost really was. Not without scaring the crap out of her, anyway. And my policy on Emma and Netherworld stuff was to keep the two as far apart as possible, for as long as possible. How was I supposed to know Netherworld trouble would find her all on its own?

Finally, after two hours, a steady stream of customers, and a snack break during which I'd done little more than nod along with her chatter, she went suddenly silent on the stool next to mine, sitting straighter as she aimed a bright smile through the window in front of us. I looked up to find a familiar face halfway down the line across from Emma's register.

Doug Fuller.

I had to nudge Emma into giving change to an elderly lady taking a small child to see a PG-13 comedy. Emma slid the change and receipt under the window, then glanced at me as her next customer ordered two tickets for a Japanese horror flick. "Doug's here," she whispered.

I ran a debit card through the scanner, then dropped it into the dip in the counter beneath the pane of glass. "I see him." And I didn't like what I saw.

Oh, I understood the attraction. He was tall, and dark, and undeniably hot, and was just edgy enough—he didn't care what *anyone* thought of him, including his own friends— to intrigue Emma. But Doug wasn't just "she's so drunk she doesn't know what she's doing" dangerous. He was "spend the rest of your life in a padded cell" dangerous. And that was the best-case scenario.

"I knew I should have waited to take my break." Emma slid three tickets and a receipt beneath the glass to her next customer, glancing at Doug every chance she got.

"Em, what do you see in him? I mean, other than the obvious." Because for a short-term, nontoxic, casual good time, the obvious would have been plenty.

She shrugged and slid two more tickets under the glass. "I don't know. He's hot and he's fun. Why does it have to be deeper than that? We're not all looking for a lifetime commitment at sixteen, Kay."

"I'm not…" I started to argue, then gave up. I wasn't sure what I was looking for from Nash, but it definitely wasn't short-term fun. "Em, I don't think you should—"

"Shhhh!" she hissed as Doug stepped up to the counter,

his lopsided grin showing off just one dimple, and I knew I'd lost her. She smiled and leaned forward on the counter, and somehow her uniform clung to her curves, where mine only hung from my angles. "Hey."

"Hey. So, you wanna come over after you close?" he said, and the people in line behind him started grumbling.

I slid a debit card beneath the glass on my side of the counter and tried not to groan out loud.

Reason number eighteen that Kaylee should not lie: she never gets away with it.

Em frowned. "I'm not closing—it's a school night. I get off in two hours."

"But Kaylee said…" Doug glanced at me, and I stared at the counter, relieved when the customer behind him moved into my line, giving me something to do.

"She was wrong." Em was mad. Of *course* she was mad. "Meet me at five?"

"Uh, I gotta do something first." His hand jerked on the counter, and my stomach pitched. "I'll pick you up at seven."

"Okay." Emma smiled for him, but didn't even look at me until he'd stepped out of line, already heading down the steps toward the parking lot. She served her next customer in silence while I handed back change, then both lines were empty for the moment.

Emma turned on me while Doug veered toward the rental I'd seen in his driveway, now double-parked in two handicapped spots on the front row. "What the hell, Kaylee?"

I twisted on my stool, brainstorming damage control that would not come. "I'm sorry. I just… I don't think he's good for you."

"Because he hit your car? That was an accident, and I'm sure he'll pay for it."

"Yeah. He already got me a loaner."

"Then what's the problem?"

I sighed, grasping for some way to explain without...well...
explaining. My urge to protect her from all things Netherworld
was overwhelming, and my gut was all I had to go on at the
moment. "He's not safe, Emma."

She rolled her eyes. "I don't want safe. I want fun, and
Doug is fun."

"Yeah, he's so fun he tried to haul you off while you were
drunk. What do you think would have happened next, Em?"

"Nothing I didn't want to do." She crossed her arms beneath her breasts. "What? You think Nash is perfect?"

My pulse spiked and I thought about him Influencing his
way up my shirt that morning. But Em didn't know about
that. "What's that supposed to mean?"

"Nothing." Emma sighed and leaned with both elbows on
the counter, watching through the glass as Doug unlocked his
car. "I'm just saying guys only come in a couple of models, and
Nash didn't exactly break the mold. So lay off my boyfriend
until you're ready to take a closer look at yours."

I had no idea what to say to that. So Nash was getting a
little pushy. That was nothing compared to Doug breathing
toxic fumes all over her.

In the lot, Doug's arm twitched as he pulled open his
car door. Emma didn't even notice, but I knew what those
twitches meant, and I was pretty sure I knew what he had to
do before he picked her up. I had to tell her something—had
to at least warn her, if I couldn't keep her away from him.

I took a deep breath and twisted on my stool to face her as
Doug pulled out of the lot. "Emma, Doug's into something
new. Something really bad. It's called frost."

She frowned, ignoring the customer who stepped up to her window. "What are you talking about?"

"Just listen. Please. It comes in a black balloon, and it *will* kill him. And if you inhale any of it, it could kill you, too. Or drive you insane. For real."

Emma's frown deepened. "You're serious?"

"*So* serious." I looked straight into her brown eyes, wishing she could see the sincerity surely swirling in mine. "Nash and I saved your life once and I'm trying to do it again. If you see Doug with a black balloon or even if he just starts acting weird, go home. Okay? Whatever you're doing, just stop and go home."

The man in front of the glass knocked on the window, but we both ignored him.

Emma's eyes widened and she clutched the counter. "Kaylee, you're kind of creeping me out."

"I know." I took both of her hands when she started to turn toward the window. "But you have to promise you'll go home if he starts acting weird. Swear."

"Fine, I swear," she said as the man knocked harder and a second customer appeared in front of my window. "But I gotta tell ya, you're the one acting weird right now, Kay."

I knew that, too. But at least my brand of weird probably wasn't going to get anybody killed. No one other than me, anyway.

"You want the good news, or the bad?" Nash asked as soon as I opened the front door. I took the pizza from him and he pulled the door shut as he stepped inside.

"Bad first." Because I was a "get it out of the way" kind of gal. I set the pizza box on the coffee table and headed into the kitchen for a couple of sodas. He tossed his jacket over one of the chairs around the table in our eat-in kitchen.

"Okay, Carter has tried the balloon, and I think he was still flying pretty high when I got there this afternoon. He was talking fast and leaping from one subject to the next. I could hardly keep up with him."

"But Doug didn't act anything like that. He was slurring and reacting kind of sluggish. And seeing things."

"I know." Nash flipped open the pizza box and sank onto the couch. "It seems to be affecting them both differently. But the good news is that Sophie's at the Winter Carnival committee fundraiser, so the chances of her inhaling anything from him tonight are pretty slim. If that's even possible. She's probably safe until tomorrow."

"This good news isn't sounding so good." I set a Coke can on the end table nearest him.

"Okay, then how 'bout this…" He pulled me onto his lap, and my unopened soda fell from my hand to roll under the coffee table. "I talked him into bringing the balloon to school tomorrow, so I can 'try' it."

My smile reflected his own. "And we're gonna get rid of it before he has a chance to share, right?"

Nash's grin widened, and he kissed me before lowering me to the couch next to him. "That's the plan."

"Okay, I like that part. So, how are we going to get the balloon? Ask Tod to pop in and snatch it for us?"

"Even better." He leaned to one side and dug in his hip pocket, then pulled out a single key with an electronic lock on a plain silver ring.

I frowned. "You stole Scott's car key?" Yes, it was convenient, and meant we wouldn't have to actually break into the car, which was equally illegal. Still…

Nash shook his head. "I just borrowed it from the kitchen junk drawer. He won't notice it's gone until he locks himself out of his car again, and with any luck, I'll have it back way before then. How else are we supposed to get into his car?"

"Tod can do it without stealing a key."

He raised a brow in challenge, pulling one slice of pizza free from the others. "Does that make it morally acceptable?"

"No, that makes it easier and safer. Tod won't get caught, and we won't be connected to a B and E on school grounds."

"Tod got in trouble for missing too much work," Nash said around a mouthful of pepperoni. "So he's working for the next forty-eight hours straight, with no breaks. Evidently some poor old lady lingered on the wrong side of a second heart attack when the first should have done the job."

Great…

"So unless you know how to pop a car lock, this is our best bet." Nash held up the key, and his nonchalance made me distinctly uncomfortable. Unfortunately, he was right.

Was unlawful entry really any worse than theft, anyway? And did confiscating a toxic Netherworld substance even count as theft?

I nodded reluctantly, and Nash slid the key into his pocket. "You don't trust me."

"It's not about trust. I don't want to get caught breaking into Scott's car."

"We're not gonna get caught. And if we do, he won't get mad. No one ever gets mad at me, Kaylee. I have a way with words…." He leaned closer, teasing me with a short kiss, his mouth open just enough to invite me in. Just enough so that I missed his lips the moment they were gone.

"I got mad at you this morning," I whispered as he angled

us back on the couch, reaching down to lift my right leg onto the cushion.

He pulled my left leg up on his other side, bent at the knee, then leaned over me, propped up on his elbows. "Yeah, but you got over it." Nash kissed me, and I got lost in him. I *wanted* to be lost in Nash, to forget about fear, and danger, and death, and everything that wasn't him, and me, and us. Just for a few minutes, to forget about everything else. Nash made that possible. He made that inevitable.

He made me feel so good. Beautiful, and wanted, and needed, in a way I'd never been needed before. Like if he didn't have me, he wouldn't have *anything*.

And I wanted him to have me. I wanted to have him. But I couldn't. Because what if Emma was right? What if he was like all the others, and once I'd been had, he'd need someone else?

His tongue trailed down my neck and my head fell back on the throw pillow, my mouth open. My eyes closed. His hand slid beneath my shirt and I gripped the cushion under me. I could feel him through our clothes. Ready. Needing.

But Nash was right before—I didn't trust him. I couldn't, because if he wasn't perfect, I didn't want to know about it. Not yet. I wanted to sleep with Nash, but that's not what I needed.

I needed him to break the mold.

"Wait."

"Hmm?" But then he kissed me before I could repeat myself. His hand slid farther, his cold fingers crawling over my ribs. His mouth sucked at mine, and I couldn't talk. I could hardly breathe.

When his other hand found the waist of my jeans, I turned my head and shoved him with both hands. "I said stop."

He frowned. "What's the problem? I'm not using any Influence."

"I know. Just…slow down."

He sat up and frowned while I tugged my shirt back into place. "If we go any slower, we'll be moving back in time. You've been teasing me for months, Kaylee. Anyone else would already have walked away."

My face burned like he'd slapped me. "I'm not a tease, but you're starting to sound like a real jackass. If you wanna walk, I'm sure you won't have any trouble finding someone a little more cooperative."

Nash sighed, scrubbing his face with both hands. "I don't want someone else. I want you."

Yeah. More of me than I was ready to give. But I wanted him, too. "Let's just watch the movie, okay?"

"Fine."

The ache in my heart eclipsed the other aches I was trying to ignore, but before I could figure out what to say to make it better without giving in, he stood and crossed the room to start the DVD.

I ran my hands through my hair, searching for a change of subject to act as a reset button on the entire evening.

"Doug showed up at the Cinemark this afternoon," I said, grabbing my Coke from the floor. I tapped the top to settle the bubbles. "He's picking Emma up tonight, so I made her promise to go home if he starts acting weird." Hopefully she wouldn't think twice about taking his rental, since she wouldn't have her car.

Nash turned to look at me, his eyes narrowed. "You didn't tell her…"

"What frost really is?" I shook my head. "I just told her that he'd gotten ahold of something bad." I searched his eyes for disapproval, but found only leftover frustration. "I had to tell her something."

"I know." Nash grabbed the remote from the top of the TV and changed the input. "How did Fuller look?"

"Twitchy." I turned and dropped my feet onto his lap when he sank onto the opposite end of the couch, universal remote in hand. "I think he's picking up another balloon tonight." I made a mental note to call and check on Emma before bed, to make sure she sounded like herself and that Doug hadn't gone all psych ward on her.

I sipped from my soda as thoughts—dark possibilities, really—sloshed in my mind like murky swamp water. "Did Scott say anything about Everett? Does he know him?"

"Nope." Nash grabbed the slice of pizza he'd already started on and handed another one to me. "He's never met the guy. He thinks Fuller's holding out on him." He tore a bite from his pizza and spoke around it. "So what do you think a party balloon goes for on the street these days?" Nash grinned, trying to lighten the mood, but the idea of some creepy Pennywise peddling balloons full of Demon's Breath on the corner scared the crap out of me, and I struggled to purge the visual.

What if we'd discovered the problem too late? What if Doug's dealer had already been peddling his product all over central Texas, or worse, all over the state? Or the entire south? After all, what were the chances that we *happened* to go to school with the only human in the area who huffed Demon's Breath?

No, my inner logic insisted. If people were dropping dead or being admitted to mental hospitals in record numbers, we'd have heard about it. This was just starting, which meant it was still fixable. It had to be.

I took a deep breath, then another drink from my can.

"I think the real question is, what is Everett? If he's human, where's he getting his supply? And if he's not, what is he doing here?"

Nash shrugged. "Evil, would be my guess. That's kind of a Netherworld specialty."

"Okay, but as far as diabolical Netherworld schemes go, getting a bunch of human teenagers high, hooked, then dead is kind of lame." I looked at my pizza, but couldn't bring myself to actually eat it. "I mean, how good can the repeat business be if the customers are all gonna die?"

Nash chewed some more, apparently giving the idea some serious thought. "Nobody's dead yet."

But we both knew that was only a matter of time.

Or was it?

I dropped my uneaten slice into the box and grabbed the remote, poking the pause button until the image on the screen froze. "Maybe no one's going to die from this. You can't die if it's not your time, right? If you're not on the list?" The reaper's list, which contained the names of everyone whose soul was scheduled to be collected on a given day. Tod talked about the list like it was scribbled by the hand of Fate herself, thus could not be changed.

Of course, being driven insane wasn't much better than death. But at least I wouldn't have to scream for those hauled away in straitjackets.

But Nash didn't look very relieved.

"Kay, it doesn't work like that. Demon's Breath is a Netherworld element. It trumps the list, just like actually crossing into the Netherworld."

My heart hurt like it was being twisted within my chest, and my throat felt almost too thick to breathe through. "So, even if we got in touch with Tod and he got his hands on the master list, he couldn't tell us who's most at risk from this. Or how far it's going to spread."

Nash shook his head slowly. "There's no way to track this, and no way to know who's going to die from it. Not until…"

He didn't have to say it. I knew.

"Not until I start screaming."

5

"WHAT'S WRONG WITH YOU two today?" Emma speared a
cherry tomato in her salad. Which was really just a mountain of iceberg lettuce dotted with croutons and smothered
in cheese, ham, and ranch dressing. Emma didn't do health
food, and I'd always respected that about her. "You look like
you're waiting for a bomb to go off."

Not a bomb. A football player. We'd seen Scott Carter in
the hall before first period, and his eyes had a familiar fevered
look, yet his breath was too-sweet and *cold,* like he'd been
chewing ice. He was high. On frost. At school.

Maybe having him bring it with him wasn't such a good
idea, after all....

Before I could come up with an answer, Emma's gaze
strayed over Nash's shoulder and her eyes flashed with something like desire or anticipation, only stronger. More fervent.
I twisted on the bench to see Doug pushing his way through
a huddle of freshmen in front of the pizza line.

Emma smiled at him, and I wanted to break my own skull
open on the white brick wall behind her.

Around us, the cafeteria buzzed with conversation, individual words and voices muted by the steady swell of sound. Our school was a closed campus for the entire first semester, thanks to a fender bender in the parking lot the second week of school, so nearly a third of the student body was crammed into four rows of indoor picnic-style tables. For most of the year, Em and I ate outside in the quad, but in December, even Texas was too cold for all but the truly hardy—and those in desperate need of a secret smoke—to brave the winter chill.

"So, I take it last night went well?" I dipped a corn chip into my cheese sauce, but couldn't bring myself to eat it as I watched her closely for some sign that her attraction to Doug went beyond the usual hormonal tidal wave. But I saw nothing but the hair tosses and challenging eye contact she usually saved for guys old enough to drink. Or at least date her college-age sisters.

"Does she really *like* this ass-wipe?" Tod said, appearing suddenly on the bench beside me.

The corn chip in my hand shattered, but for once I managed not to jump and look like an idiot in front of Nash and Em, who clearly couldn't see the reaper this time. Wasn't he supposed to be a virtual prisoner at Arlington Memorial for another day or so?

But I couldn't ask without looking crazy in front of half the varsity football team sitting at the other end of the table.

"*So* well." Emma's voice went deep and throaty, and I glanced briefly at Tod with one raised brow, silently asking if that answered his question.

He scowled, then blinked out, and I wiped cheese sauce from my fingers with a paper napkin. I knew what I had against Doug, but why did Tod care who Emma liked? I'd assumed he'd let go of his crush on her when Addison had stepped back into—then quickly out of—his life a month ago.

Evidently, I was wrong, and the implications of that settled into my gut like a brick in a bucket of water. How would a grim reaper—someone no longer bound by the limitations of mortal existence—deal with the potential competition Doug Fuller represented?

Oh, *crap!*

Someone was selling Demon's Breath in the human world, and Tod had on-demand access to the Netherworld. Doug had sworn someone had appeared in his passenger's seat on Saturday night when he'd hit my car, and Tod had the infuriating habit of popping in anywhere he wanted, whenever he wanted, to whomever he wanted....

Was it possible?

No. I almost shook my head before I realized no one else knew what I was thinking. Tod wouldn't do that. Not that he'd hesitate to sabotage the competition if he ever decided he was serious about Emma. But he wouldn't do anything to jeopardize his job—because an unemployed reaper was a dead reaper—or Emma, one of the few humans he actually cared about.

Still... I made a mental note to mention the possibility—however slim—to Nash the next time we were alone.

"Hey." Doug dropped onto the bench next to Emma, straddling the seat with his left thigh against her backside. He reached across the table to slap Nash's hand in greeting, then turned to me. "How's the loaner working out?"

"Fine." I dunked another chip and tried to hate Doug quietly, so Emma wouldn't notice. It would be hard to protect her if she wasn't speaking to me.

Doug ran one hand slowly up and down Emma's back. "What are you doing after school?"

"Working. But then I'll be home. Alone."

"Want some company?"

"Maybe…" She bit into a cube of ham speared on her plastic fork, and Doug's hand moved slowly beneath the table, probably working its way up her thigh. Then something behind me caught his eye, and he tossed his head at someone over my shoulder.

I turned to find Scott Carter making his way across the cafeteria toward us, a tray in one hand, his other arm around Sophie's thin shoulders. Scott set his tray down and sank onto the bench next to Doug. Sophie took a bruised red apple from Scott's tray and bit into it, chewing in angry silence while she tried to avoid my eyes.

Or maybe she was trying to avoid being seen with me.

"We still on for this afternoon?" Scott asked Nash, twisting the lid on a bottle of Coke, then tightening it before it could fizz over. "I'm parked on the west side, near the gym." His eyes looked a little clearer, and I could no longer smell the Demon's Breath on him. He was coming down from his initial high, and I couldn't help but wonder how long it would be before he'd need another fix. And what that need would look like on him.

Would Sophie notice something was wrong? Would his teachers? His parents were still out of town….

"Yeah." Nash shoved the last bite of his cafeteria hamburger into his mouth and picked up his own soda. "I'll be there right after the last bell."

But Scott's stash would *not*.

"You still have what I gave you?" Doug glanced anxiously between Nash and Scott, having caught on to the subject.

"What you *sold* me," Scott corrected.

"Whatever." Doug finally removed his hand from Emma's thigh and leaned closer to Scott. I chewed, pretending not to listen while Sophie and Emma exchanged rare twin looks of confusion. "I need to buy it back, but I can replace it this weekend."

Scott squirted a mustard packet on his hamburger. "I thought you were gonna have more today?"

Doug shook his head. "Didn't pan out. Sell me yours. I'll pay extra."

"No way." Scott shook his head and picked up his burger. Sophie and Emma weren't even pretending to eat anymore. "But you can have a hit after school with Hudson—" he nodded in Nash's direction "—if you give me your guy's name and number."

Doug's jaw tightened and his eyes narrowed. "I already gave you his name, and there *is* no number. But I'm gonna see him this weekend for sure. I can get you another one then, if you pay up front."

Nash stiffened next to me, and I knew he was thinking what I was thinking. Everett. This weekend. That was our best chance.

"Same as last time?" Scott asked, and my stomach twisted in on itself as Emma glanced at me, brows arched in question.

"Yeah," Doug said, and Sophie rolled her eyes, glossy pink fingernails digging into the skin of her apple.

"I'm bored," she whined. "You guys are like walking sedatives."

"You got something more interesting to talk about?" Scott snapped, dipping a limp French fry in ketchup. "And don't say the Winter Carnival."

Sophie pouted, gesturing with her apple. "It's on Saturday,

and you guys *promised* you'd help with the booths this afternoon." They all had their afternoons free, since football season had ended with a loss to the new Texas state AA champions.

"I'm not feelin' it, Soph." Scott raised one brow and his frown grew into a lecherous grin. "But maybe you could convince me…" He pushed his tray across the table and leaned back, watching her expectantly.

Sophie went from shrew to succubus in less than a second, straddling Scott so boldly that I glanced around, sure there would be a teacher stomping toward us from somewhere, intent on peeling her off.

But no teacher came. The two on duty were busy trying to confiscate a cell phone from some senior rumored to be showing off naked pictures of his girlfriend.

Sophie performed like a trained seal, and I was humiliated for her—because she didn't have the sense to be—but I couldn't look away from my cousin's spectacle. Until Scott's hand inched down from her waist toward the back of her overpriced jeans.

"Sophie, that's enough. Sit down before you get suspended."

The look she shot me could have frozen Satan's crotch, but she slithered off her boyfriend's lap, licking her lips like she could still taste him, while Doug, Scott, and the rest of the team watched her like she'd just danced around a pole. I shot Nash a "why the hell do you hang out with these jackholes" look, but he was unavailable to receive my withering glance. Because he was watching my cousin. But Emma was watching me, *I told you so* written clearly in her expression.

I frowned and elbowed Nash while Sophie reapplied her lipstick with a compact mirror. "So…" She snapped the compact closed and dropped it into her purse. "Any volunteers?"

"I'm in," Scott said, and I understood that Sophie's show

was actually a preview of things to come. Was that how she got everything she wanted? "You guys got a couple of hours to spare this afternoon?" Scott glanced around the table for more volunteers.

Nash nodded, but Emma leaned around Doug to answer for us both. "Kaylee and I have to work."

"Oh, well." Sophie shrugged, and the bitch was back. "We'll miss you…" her mouth said, but as usual, her eyes said something entirely different.

When the bell rang, everyone got up to dump their trays, but Nash and I headed into the quad against the flow of smoke-scented traffic into the building, his cold fingers intertwined with mine. When the late bell rang eight minutes later, we sneaked around the outside of the school—the gym side, where there were no windows—and into the parking lot, ducking to run between the cars until we spotted Scott's. Fortunately, he'd parked out of view from the building exit.

The top was up on Scott's shiny, metallic-blue convertible, and through the rear window I saw nothing but a spotless interior; the car was so clean he probably made Sophie take off her shoes before getting in. On the back passenger's side floorboard sat a large green duffel bag. "It's either in there, or in the trunk," I whispered, though there was no one else around to hear us.

Nash dug in his left pocket and pulled out Scott's key. "Then let's get this over with."

He slid the key into the lock—presumably to avoid the telltale thump of the automatic lock disengaging—and glanced toward the building to make sure we were alone.

With the driver's door open, he reached through to unlock the back door, then pulled it open and gestured toward the rear seat. "Be my guest."

Rolling my eyes, I crawled into the backseat and tugged the bag into my lap. My heart thumped as I unzipped it, and I was suddenly sure Scott had put the balloon in his trunk. But there it was, a solid black balloon, next to a football and on top of a pair of green gym shorts, which weren't exactly fresh. I pulled the balloon out with both hands and gasped at the chill that sank immediately through my fingers. The balloon was so cold ice should have glazed its surface, flaking off to melt on my skin.

Yet, other than the temperature and the weighted black plastic clasp holding it closed, the balloon felt just like any other latex party balloon. It was only half inflated and I wondered how full it had been, and how much of the contents Scott had already inhaled. When I squeezed it gently, my fingers dimpled the surface and the rubber seemed to grow even colder.

"It's cold," I whispered, without taking my eyes off the balloon. *"Freezing…"*

Nash nodded. "There's a reason they call it frost. Don't you remember what Avari did to that office when he got pissed?"

I did remember. When the hellion had gotten mad, a lacy sheet of ice had spread across the desk beneath him and onto the floor, inching toward our feet, surging faster every time his anger peaked.

"Okay, zip the bag up and let's g—"

"Hudson?" A booming voice called from across the parking lot, and my blood ran as cold as the balloon.

Coach Rundell, the head football coach.

Nash waved his hand downward, inches from my head, and I dropped onto the backseat, bent in half over the balloon. On the way down, I glimpsed the coach between Scott's leather headrests. The middle-aged former jock stomped toward us from the double gym doors, his soft bulk confined by a slick green-and-white workout suit, bulging at the zipper.

"You're not allowed in the parking lot during the school day, Hudson," the coach barked. "You know that." That ridiculous rule was supposed to stop kids from sneaking cigarettes or making out in backseats, and to prevent the occasional car break-in. Which we were committing, at that very moment.

Panicked now, as the cold from the balloon leached through my shirt and into my stomach, I craned my neck to see Nash digging frantically in his hip pocket. "Sorry, coach. I left my book in here this morning, and I need it for class."

"Isn't that Carter's car?"

Nash shrugged. "He gave me a ride."

Actually, Nash had ridden with me, in my new loaner. But Coach Rundell wasn't going to question his first-string running back. Even if he didn't believe Nash.

"Well, get what you came for and get back to class. You need a pass?"

"Yeah, thanks," Nash said, and I rolled my eyes as he bent into the backseat behind the headrest, where the coach couldn't see him clearly.

That figures. The football player steals a friend's key and breaks into his car, and he winds up with a free hall pass for his trouble. I'd probably be expelled.

Nash pressed Scott's car key into my hand. "Wait until we go in, then lock the balloon in your trunk. Got it?"

I shook my head, pocketing the key reluctantly. "I'm just going to pop it. That way no one else can get ahold of it."

Sudden panic whirled in Nash's irises. "You can't *pop* it, Kaylee. What if you accidentally breathe some of it in?"

My pulse raced at the thought, fear chilling me almost as

badly as the balloon I was trying not to crush. "Is it…as dangerous to *bean sidhes* as it is to humans?" I whispered.

Nash sighed. "No, but…" He stopped and shook his head sharply, as if to clear it. "I don't know. It's a controlled substance for a reason. It has to be disposed of carefully. I'm going to give it to Tod to take to the disposal facility in the Netherworld. Okay?"

I nodded grudgingly. "Fine."

Nash kissed me quickly on the cheek, then leaned past me to grab the chemistry book I'd brought to lunch. "I'll give it back to you after school." Hopefully the coach wouldn't know Nash was taking physics this year.…

He backed out of the car, held the book up for the coach's benefit, then closed the door, leaving me alone in the quarterback's car, with his stolen key and his stash of a rare, expensive inhalant.

No pressure, Kay.

I peeked between the headrests until Nash and the coach disappeared around the corner of the gym, then I sat up and shoved the frigid black balloon off my lap and onto the floor. I zipped Scott's duffel and put it back exactly where I'd found it, then glanced around the lot again before easing the door open. When I was sure I was alone, I grabbed the balloon, lurched out of the car, and shoved the door closed, then clicked a button on the key to lock it. Then I raced across the lot holding the balloon by its clip, to keep the unnaturally cold latex from touching my skin.

On my way across the asphalt, I slid Scott's key into my back pocket, then dug my own from my hip pocket, holding it ready as I skidded to a stop behind the rental. I jabbed the key into the trunk lock and twisted, relieved when the trunk popped open an inch on the first try. I'd never opened it and,

according to Murphy's Law—which they might as well rename after me—it would malfunction when I needed it most.

I dropped the balloon into the carpeted compartment, glad
when it sank with the weighted clip. Then I slammed the
trunk closed and made myself walk toward the building, concentrating on regulating my breathing and heartbeat with
each step.

The last thing I needed was to arrive for class flushed and
out of breath.

Although now that I thought of it, that would give me an
interesting alibi. Everyone would assume Nash and I had been
occupied, and had missed the bell.

I smiled at that thought, and the smile stayed in place until I
opened the door to my fifth-period English class, where every
head in the room swiveled to look at me. And that's when I
realized I'd forgotten to stop by my locker for my book.

"Miss Cavanaugh," Mr. Tuttle said, perched on the edge
of his desk with one sockless loafer dangling a foot from the
floor. "How nice of you to join us. I don't suppose you have
a late pass? Or a textbook?"

I shook my head mutely and felt myself flush. So much for
avoiding rumors…

"Well, now you *do* have detention."

Naturally. Because detention seems like an appropriate reward for someone trying to save her school from a deadly
Netherworld toxin, right?

<< 6 >>

"DETENTION FOR YOUR FIRST tardy?" Nash looked skeptical as he slammed his locker and tossed his backpack over one shoulder. All around us, other lockers squealed open and clanged closed. The hall was a steady din of white noise—the constant overlap of voices. The final bell had rung three minutes earlier and the entire student body had split into two streams: most of the underclassmen flowing toward the front doors and a line of long yellow buses, and most of the upperclassmen toward the parking lot.

"It was my third," I admitted, turning with Nash as he wrapped his free arm around my waist. "I was late twice last month, since *some*body thought it would be fun to take a private tour of the gym equipment closet while Coach Rundell was out for lunch."

Nash looked pleased with himself, rather than penitent. "Yeah, sorry about that."

"I bet *you* weren't counted tardy for either of those, were you?"

He shrugged. "No one cares if you're late to study hall."

I rolled my eyes. "Not so long as you're wearing a green-and-white jacket."

"You want to borrow it?" He grinned and made a show of pulling one arm from his sleeve. He seemed much more relaxed now that we'd relieved Scott of his Netherworldly burden.

"No, thanks. I have too much self-respect."

"For school spirit?" He frowned, but his eyes still sparkled with mischief.

"For being the unmerited exception to the rules the rest of us plebeians have to follow."

"What rules?" Doug Fuller walked toward us with one arm around Emma, his hand splayed over the band of bare hip visible between the hem of her tee and the low waist of her jeans.

I scowled. "My point exactly."

"Hudson, your girlfriend's too serious." Doug dropped his duffel and ran one hand through a wavy mop of thick dark hair, pulling Emma closer.

"She can't help it," a familiar, cold-edged voice said from behind me, and I turned to find Sophie and Laura Bell leaning against the lockers, malice glinting in their eyes like sunlight off the point of a sharp knife. "The staff in the psycho ward *shocked* the fun right out of her."

Simultaneous waves of anger and humiliation surged through me, and for just a minute, I considered letting her take a hit from her boyfriend's balloon. Why was I trying so hard to save someone who would rather see me dead than return the favor?

"Don't look now, Sophie, but your insecurity's showing like the roots on a bad bleach job." Emma smiled sweetly, then glanced pointedly at Sophie's hairline. Then she turned on one wedge-heeled foot and headed down the hall toward the parking lot exit. Laughing, Doug jogged to catch up with her.

Nash and I trailed them while Sophie stood speechless. "You know, she loves it when you let her piss you off."

"Gee, thanks, Dad," I snapped, bending beneath the weight of my own sarcasm. "You think if I just ignore her, she'll go away?"

"No." Nash's hand tightened around mine and I glanced up to find him eyeing me steadily. "I think she's going to be a bitch no matter what you do. But you don't have to make it so easy for her. Make her work for it."

"Yeah." But that was a lot easier for him to suggest than for me to do. "It *kills* me that she has no idea that we saved her life. Or that she'd be just like me, if not for winning the genetic lottery." Sophie's father—my dad's younger brother—was a *bean sidhe,* and because her mother was human, Sophie could have been born like either of her parents. Fate, or luck, or whatever unfair advantage ruled her privileged life, had given her the normal, human genetic sequence, and a snottier-than-thou disposition that seemed to grow more toxic by the day.

"There's nothing you can do about that, Kaylee." Nash pushed open the door into the parking lot and a cold gust of wind blew my hair back as I stepped outside. "And anyway, considering that her mother died and her boyfriend's spending a small fortune to get high off someone else's bad breath, I'd say Sophie's next in line for therapy. At least you know who and what you are," he pointed out with an infuriating rationality. "Sophie knows there's something we're not telling her. Something about her family, and how her own mom died. And she may never find out the truth."

Because Uncle Brendon didn't want her to know that her

mother had stolen five innocent lives and souls—including Sophie's, by accident—in exchange for eternal youth.

Nash shrugged. "For me, knowing that I actually feel sorry for her makes it a little easier to put up with the shit she's shoveling."

A warm satisfaction filtered through me at the realization that it *did* help to think of her as an object of pity: a prospect that would horrify my pampered cousin to no end.

"And Kaylee, I'm sorry about last night. I can wait. You know that, right?"

"I know." He was calmer and happier now. Less intense than he'd been the night before. He'd obviously gotten plenty of sleep and backed off the caffeine.

"Thank you." I stood on my toes for a mint-flavored kiss— a better kiss than what he usually got on school grounds—and only pulled back when shouting from the other end of the parking lot caught our attention.

Scott had just discovered his frost was missing.

"Come on…" Nash took off and I held my backpack strap in place while I raced after him. My boots clomped on the concrete as we tore past my loaner, Doug's loaner, and dozens of other cars still parked in the lot. We had to be there to look surprised by Scott's loss.

Doug and Emma were huddled together in the empty space to the left of Scott's car, hands stuffed into their jacket pockets against the cold. Doug scowled, almost as angry as Scott over the loss. Next to him stood Brant Williams, who'd obviously been promised a sample, too. Other students watched all over the lot, curious but uninvolved.

And suddenly I was really glad we'd taken the balloon, in

spite of the risk. This crowd was too big. How were we supposed to protect the entire school?

"Are you sure you brought it?" Doug tugged his duffel higher on his shoulder and his hand twitched around the strap.

"Hell, *yes,* I'm sure." Scott punched the back of his front seat, which he'd folded forward for more room in the backseat. "I took a hit this morning before I got out of the car, then stuffed it in my gym bag. And now it's gone."

"What happened?" Nash asked as I wandered to the edge of the small crowd to stand with Emma. She tucked a long blond strand of hair behind one pierced ear, then shrugged to say she had no idea what was going on.

"Somebody broke into my car and stole my *shit,*" Scott snapped, and I wasn't the only one surprised by the sharp edge of fury in his voice. Not just anger, or frustration, or disbelief. Scott's words dripped with *rage,* laced with some dark, desperate need no one else seemed to understand. Not even Doug. But as his hand convulsed around the edge of the open car door, *I* understood.

Scott was going into withdrawal. For real. He wasn't just itching for another hit—he was physically, psychologically, maybe even soulfully, addicted. He couldn't function without frost now.

But that couldn't be right. He'd only had one balloon, and it was still half-full. How could this happen so fast?

With that thought, a new fear twisted in my stomach. Had we made everything worse by taking the balloon? Harmony had said withdrawal could be just as deadly as Demon's Breath itself....

But what were we supposed to do, give the balloon back, with our blessings? Let him sink into insanity and brain damage, and possibly drag Sophie along for the ride?

"Dude, calm down," Doug said, sniffling in the frigid wind, and I was relieved by the composed—if stuffy—quality of his voice. Somehow, though he'd been on frost longer than Scott and had taken more of it, he was obviously much less dependent on it. "Unless you want to explain to Coach what you're yelling about."

Scott only scowled and ducked into the backseat again, digging in the green-and-white duffel. But the volume of his anger and denial dropped low enough to avoid notice by the teachers monitoring the parking lot from near the west school entrance.

Nash dropped his bag at my feet, and I was impressed by how steady his cold-reddened hands were as he knelt to examine Scott's driver's side door, concentrating on the seal at the base of the window. "It doesn't look like it was forced, but all that would take is a coat hanger or a slim jim…" He stood and wiped his hands on his jeans, then opened the door wider and fiddled with the automatic lock to demonstrate that it still worked. "There doesn't seem to be any damage…."

But Scott wasn't listening. He was still digging in his bag, anger exaggerating his jerky movements, like he might somehow have overlooked a half-filled black latex balloon among the sweaty sports equipment.

I glanced around the lot for Sophie and found her watching with a couple of her dancer friends, all bundled up as they unloaded several gallons of paint and new brushes from Laura's trunk. Presumably to be used on the booths for the Winter Carnival.

"What's wrong with him?" Emma whispered, still staring at Scott's breakdown. "He's really freaking out."

I shrugged and shoved my frozen hands into my pockets. "I guess frost is pretty hard to come by."

Em huffed, and a white puff of her breath hung on the air. "What is it, anyway? Some kind of inhalant?"

"I don't know." I felt bad about lying to Emma, even if it was for her own good, so I compensated with a little bit of the truth. "But it's not good, Em. Look what it's doing to Scott."

Scott's anger simmered just shy of the boiling point. Fortunately, the small crowd had dispersed—all but the central players—and there weren't many people left to watch as Doug and Nash tried to talk him down. Less than a minute later, their efforts failed.

"Screw this!" Scott threw his bag into the car, where it smacked the passenger's side window, then tumbled to the floorboard. "I can't be here right now." He dropped into the driver's seat and shoved his key into the ignition. Then he slammed the door and gunned his engine before taking off straight across the parking lot. Bright winter sunlight glinted on his rear fender as he raced between two parked cars, sending students scrambling out of his way.

Across the lot, the teachers on duty scowled and crossed their arms over their chests, but there was nothing they could do, except be grateful no one was hit. And possibly recommend that the principal suspend his parking pass.

With Scott gone, and Nash and Doug conferring softly in the space he'd just vacated, my gaze settled on Sophie, who now stood alone in front of her friend's car, a bucket of paint hanging from each clenched fist. Her mouth hung open, her nose red from the cold, and I got a rare glimpse of pain and disappointment before she donned her usual arrogant scowl and marched across the lot in a pair of trendy flats, as if she couldn't care less that her boyfriend had just bailed on his promise to her without a word.

And everyone knew it.

"YOU SURE SCOTT'S OKAY to drive?" I asked as Nash placed his palms flat against my temporary car, on either side of me. I was trapped, but willingly, *deliciously* so, and when he leaned in for a kiss, I stood on my toes to meet him.

"Yeah, he's fine." Nash's mouth pressed briefly against mine, then he murmured his next sentence against my cheek, near my ear, which lent his words a tantalizing intimacy, in spite of the subject matter. "He's pissed, not high." Another kiss, this one a little longer and a lot deeper. "And I'll check on him when we get done here." He and Doug were going to stay and help the carnival committee, to honor their friend's promise in his time of…withdrawal. "Call me when you get off work?"

I ran my hand up the cold leather sleeve of his jacket. "Yeah. My dad's working late, and I think I might need help with my anatomy."

Nash's brows shot up. "You're not taking anatomy."

I grinned. "I know."

The next kiss was longer, and ended only when Sophie made a rude noise in the back of her throat, wordlessly calling on Nash to help carry the five-gallon buckets of white paint. He waved her off without turning away from me. "Leave them here, and I'll bring them in a minute."

Sophie stomped off, obviously irritated, but silent for once.

"Here, let me get the balloon before you go." Nash glanced around the lot to make sure no one was within hearing range as he unzipped his nearly empty backpack.

"Why don't you just come over and get it tonight?" I said, reaching to open the driver's door.

Nash frowned. "Has your dad checked out the loaner yet?"

"No. He passed out right after dinner last night."

"So what if he gets off early today and decides to take a look? You want him to find that in your car?"

"He's not gonna search the trunk, Nash."

His gaze hardened. "Just give me the balloon, Kaylee," he snapped.

I stepped back, surprised. "What's wrong with you? You're being a dick." And whatever was wrong with him was about more than a couple of strung out friends. It had to be.

Nash sighed and closed his eyes. "I'm sorry. I just don't want you driving around with that in your car. Please let me take care of it, so I won't have to worry about you."

"Fine." It was *not* fine, but I didn't want to argue. Again. "Give me your bag." I rounded the car and opened the trunk, standing ready in case the weighted balloon somehow rose and escaped. It did not. Instead of handing me his bag, Nash leaned into the trunk with it and shoved the balloon inside, then zipped it before anyone could see what he was doing. "Don't get caught with that," I warned. None of the teachers would know what it was, but anyone who'd seen Scott's melt-down might. "And don't forget to put his key back."

He grinned, good mood intact once again. "I'm a big boy."

"I know." But on the drive to work with Emma, all I could think about was Nash walking around with a balloon full of Demon's Breath in his backpack, where anyone might find it.

So after a later-than-expected shift at the Cinemark, I called him as I was getting ready for bed—I wouldn't be able to sleep until I knew he'd safely disposed of the balloon. He assured me he had given it to Tod, and we talked for about half an hour, until my dad knocked on my door and told me to hang up and go to sleep.

Rolling my eyes, I said good-night to Nash and turned off my lamp. But even once I'd curled up with one leg tossed over my extra pillow, I couldn't stop the slideshow playing behind my eyes.

Doug's car smashing into mine.

Scott's fit in the parking lot.

Nash holding the stolen balloon.

We were in deep with the Demon's Breath, and as I lay in my dark room, trying to sleep, something told me that taking Scott's stash was about as helpful as plugging a hole in the Hoover Dam with a chewed-up piece of gum....

"Noooo!" My own shout echoed in my head like gunfire in a closed room, shocking me into semiawareness in spite of the thick gray haze swirling languidly around my ankles. The haze was like smoke—heavier than air and impossible to see through—except that it carried no heat and no stench of burned debris.

Hesitant to move when I couldn't see my surroundings, I turned in place, then turned again, searching the gray haze desperately for some familiar landmark. Or even an *unfamiliar* landmark. For anything that could tell me where I was. But I saw nothing but more grayness, as if I'd gone blind, and what lay behind my eyelids now was not the sparking, staticky darkness of closed eyes, but a vast, featureless expanse of gray.

A thing of nightmares.

Okay, Kaylee, think! I demanded silently. *Why were you screaming?*

For one long, terrifying moment, the answer wouldn't come. I didn't *know* why I'd been screaming. Then I sucked in a deep, fog-bitter breath and held it, focusing on how thick and oily the grayness tasted in my mouth. I wanted to spit it out, but I couldn't stop breathing it, because there was no fresh air to be found.

Then the answer came to me, slithering softly into my head like a snake into the solace of a dark pond. Hoping to escape notice.

I'd had a premonition. I'd been screaming because someone was going to die.

Crap! I was in the Netherworld. I had to be, because no place in my world had fog like the thick haze oozing over my jeans to curl around my hands, brushing my fingers like swabs of damp cotton.

Wait, that wasn't right, either. I'd never actually *seen* fog in the Netherworld. I'd only seen it layered over my own reality when I peeked into the Netherworld. So, was I peeking? And if so, why could I now feel the fog, which had always been a simple visual element before?

Something was wrong. I wasn't in the real Netherworld. I was in some stylized version of it as if I were…

Dreaming.

That's it! I was asleep, dreaming about someone's death. Which put me in some dream version of the Netherworld, the best approximation my subconscious mind could come up with. And even as that truth sank in, the scream welled up in my throat again, greeting the dark, fuzzy form coming toward me out of the fog.

The walking dead.

It was human. Or at least humanlike, with head and shoulders in the proper proportions, and presumably matching pairs of arms and legs. I couldn't tell the figure's gender, though it was only feet from me now, because it was thoroughly obscured by the grayness, which seemed to thicken even as I thought of it.

I clamped my jaws shut against the scream scraping my throat raw and clenched my fists hard enough to draw blood with my nails, hoping to wake myself up. To leave this sleep-version Netherworld before I saw whose demise I was dreaming. Whose death my subconscious was predicting with every bit of stubborn certainty my waking body put into each screech that left my mouth.

But nothing happened. I felt no pain in my palms, saw no blood, and certainly did not wake up. And the figure kept coming.

Five feet away now, and its steps made no sound on the ground. Four feet away, yet there was no brush of fabric or click of heels.

Three feet, and the features started to come into focus through the Nether-smog. A nose. Two shadowy eyes, like the hollows of an unlit jack-o'-lantern. And a mouth like a great, dark void...

My throat hurt so bad I thought it would swell shut. It felt like I'd swallowed rose stems, thorns and all, and someone was trying to pull them back up.

Yet the sound kept coming.

In front of me, as I stood frozen in disharmonic agony, the figure stumbled and went down on one knee. A ghostly hand reached out for me, fingers penetrating the haze for one tortured moment before the hand fell, too, disappearing completely into the fog, along with the body.

But before the haze melted away, before the features came in clearly enough for me to identify, the real scream burst from my throat, slicing through the night—or day?—like a foghorn through the stormy sea.

And still I screamed.

I tried to bring one hand up to cover my mouth, to stop the sound rattling my teeth. But my hand was pinned to my side, though nothing held it there. My limbs were frozen, and with that realization, my panic doubled, dumping a fresh dose of adrenaline on top of the premonition-panic already fueling my wail.

And finally, with nothing left to try, I closed my eyes tight—relieved that they, at least, still seemed to follow my commands—and prepared to ride out the scream.

When the last hoarse note slipped through my mouth like the exhale of a dying man, I licked my lips, then swallowed gingerly. My throat hurt like I'd been gargling shards of glass.

A frigid breeze blew against my bare legs, raising chill bumps the length of my body, and a soft, eerie tinkling sound tickled my ears, a thousand wind chimes all jingling at once.

Wait, *bare legs?* Where did my jeans go?

My eyes flew open and devastating, terrifying comprehension sank through me, anchoring me to the ground where I stood as if I were mired in concrete. But I wasn't. I was mired in razor wheat, and the tinkling hadn't come from wind chimes. It had come from hundreds of tall, olive-colored stalks of grass brushing against one another, as sharp and brittle as blown glass.

I wasn't sure when the dream ended and the real horror began, but I'd woken up at some point, still wailing, and accidentally crossed into the Netherworld. In my tank top and pj shorts. Barefoot and freezing.

Oh, shit!

Gone were my warm bed, fluffy pillows, and worn-thin carpet. Instead, I stood on bare dirt—oddly gray in color—with my big toe pressed against the base of one cold, fragile stalk of razor wheat. Another stalk brushed my elbow as the cold wind blew it toward me, and I froze to keep from shattering it and being pricked by thousands of glasslike slivers.

Harmony had said it wasn't possible. That we couldn't accidentally cross over, because moving from one world into the next required intent, in addition to the *bean sidhe* wail. So what did this mean? That I secretly wanted to cross over?

If so, I'd certainly been keeping that secret well. Even from myself.

But there would be time to figure that out later—hopefully. My immediate concern was getting my defenseless *bean sidhe* butt out of the Netherworld before something predatory came along to eat me. And in the Netherworld, that could be anything. Including the plant life.

I had plenty of intent to cross over when I called forth my wail this time, but nothing came out but a soft, hoarse croak. I'd lost my voice screaming my way *into* the Netherworld, and now had no way out. Nor could I move from the spot where I stood without slicing my bare feet open on every stalk of wheat I shattered.

Then, with panic looming, my hands actually shaking from both the cold and my slim chance of escape, a sudden crashing, furiously chiming sound made me jump. My elbow hit the stalk to my left, and it shattered into tiny needle-sharp shards. Several points scraped my leg as they fell, three or four actually lodging in my skin, but I couldn't bend to examine the damage without breaking more of the wheat. So I stood as still as possible, my mind racing in search of a way out, and I flinched each time the racket from my left grew louder.

The sound was like the tinkling of shattering razor wheat, only it echoed, and each burst followed a heavy metallic crash.

Desperate now, I held Emma's death in my mind—remembering how she'd looked as she'd collapsed to the gym floor, her eyes empty, her hands uncurling at her sides—as I tried to work up enough saliva to swallow and ease the pain in my throat. Which would hopefully make it possible for me to wail, at least long enough to cross over.

My pulse raced. My palms began to sweat in spite of the cold eating at my skin, echoing the sting of the wheat shards in my flesh. The crashing continued, headed toward me, and I flinched with each new burst of sound.

I swallowed convulsively, wishing I dared to move enough to rub my throat, and wishing even harder that I had something to drink. Something warm and sweet, like the hot tea Harmony always made after I wailed.

Another crash, alarmingly close, and my stomach leaped into my throat. The next was closer still—just yards away now. On my left, stalks of grass swayed to either side in a nearly straight line, like the part between a little girl's pigtails. But the seed clumps at the top of the stalks were eye height on me, so I couldn't see much more than the movement itself.

Drowning in fresh panic, I opened my mouth and forced a sound out, devastated when the croak warbled, then faded.

I swallowed again and clenched my fists at my sides. Then I pictured Emma's pale, dead face in my mind and let loose my wail with everything I had left in me.

A new scream tore free from my throat, just as painful as the last one, but nowhere near as loud. The sound fractured, and I scrambled to pull it back together, closing my eyes in concentration. And when the notes finally steadied, I opened my eyes again to see that the grass around me had gone still. I no longer heard the crashing, but then, I could rarely hear anything over my own wailing. Yet I knew instinctively that the creature in the wheat with me had stopped moving, either scared or surprised by my wail.

The stalks bent in my direction again. I screamed harder. Razor wheat shattered. My pulse raced. My throat ached. My stomach was leading a revolt of my entire body. Then, finally, a familiar gray fog swept in to overlay my vision, heralding my return to my own world.

Just in time.

And as my bedroom began to reform around me—pale walls and furniture oddly overlaid across the still-real olive-tinted field—the crashing creature penetrated the wall of wheat at my side, bursting into view.

I almost laughed out loud.

It wasn't some weird, Netherworld monster, eager to eat me. It was an ordinary trash-can lid. An old-fashioned metal disk, wielded by the handle on the topside. The suburban knight had used his shield to break the stalks ahead of him, to avoid being sliced to bits by the literal blades of grass.

It was brilliant, really. I wished I'd thought of it.

The improvised shield began to lower, and with the last breath I took in the Netherworld, my gaze landed on a pair of bright brown eyes set into a dark face not much older than my own, crowned by a nest of tight curls and the slightest shadow of a beard.

Then I was back in my room, those eyes fading slowly from the image burned into the backs of my eyelids.

"Well, then, get dressed! Harmony, you have to come *right now!*" my father yelled. Terror echoed in his voice like a shout from a lost cave.

My feet shifted on something soft and springy, and my eyes popped open. I stood in the middle of my bed. My bare toes curled around a fold in my comforter, still smudged with gray

Netherworld dirt and dotted with tiny spots of blood from splinters of razor wheat. My father stood at the foot of my bed with his back to me, the home phone pressed to his ear.

"She's crossed over, and I can't get into the Netherworld without you!" he yelled.

"Dad?"

He whirled toward me, eyes going wide even as the line of his jaw softened with relief.

"Never mind, she's back," he whispered into the phone. Then he hung it up and dropped the receiver on the blankets at my feet. "Kaylee, are you okay?"

"Fine." I whispered, then followed his gaze to the thin shards of razor wheat still protruding from my bloodstained left thigh. "Just scratches," I said, reaching down to pluck the needle-sharp splinters from my skin. I collected them loosely in my other palm, and breathed a sigh of relief that razor wheat—while painful—wasn't poisonous.

"Where the *hell* did you go?" He stomped around the foot-board and lifted me from the mattress like a naughty toddler caught jumping on the bed. "I heard you wailing, but by the time I got here you'd crossed over. What were you doing?"

"It was an accident," I muttered, my mouth pressed into his shoulder as he hugged me so tight I couldn't catch my breath. The scruff on his chin scratched my neck, and I felt his heart racing through my nightshirt. "I dreamed someone died, and woke up in the Netherworld."

"What?" He shook his head slowly. "That's not possible." My dad held me at arm's length, searching my eyes for any sign of a lie, but he must have found none, because he didn't get mad. Instead, he got scared. Obviously and truly frightened— a terrifying expression to find on a man who should represent all things strong and safe. "You crossed over in your sleep?"

"Yeah." I set the shards on my nightstand, then sank onto the edge of my bed, holding my dirty feet away from the mattress. "Please tell me that's never going to happen again. Only say it better than Harmony did, because she said we couldn't cross over accidentally, and she was *wrong*."

He sank wearily into my desk chair, the golds and browns in his eyes churning fiercely in fear. "I wish I could, Kay, but I've never heard of anything like this. How did this happen? Who were you dreaming about?"

I shrugged, reaching for the clear plastic bottle on my nightstand, wincing as the movement tugged at the fresh cuts on my leg. "I don't know. I'm not sure I even knew in the dream." I gulped lukewarm water, watching my father as he watched me. "What if it happens again?" My voice came out soft with fear, and hoarse because of my raw throat.

"We'll just have to make sure it doesn't." My father's sigh was carried on a breath of determination. "How 'bout some hot chocolate?"

I glanced at my alarm clock, frustrated to see that it was only a quarter to four on Wednesday morning. "Make it coffee, and I'm in." Because I wouldn't be sleeping any more that night. Or any other night until I figured out how to keep from waking up in the Netherworld.

"You drink coffee?" My father frowned as he picked up the phone and followed me into the hall.

"Not if I can help it."

The phone rang in his hand, and he glanced at the display, then handed it to me as we turned into the small galley-style kitchen. "It's Harmony. Tell her you're okay before she and Nash show up with the cavalry."

I answered the phone and assured Harmony—and Nash, by extension—that I was fine, in spite of having crossed over in my sleep. She sounded almost as horrified as I felt, and she promised to see what she could find out about preventing a repeat performance. Then she put Nash on the phone so we could say good-night—or rather, good-morning—and by the time we hung up, the smell of fresh coffee—always better than the taste, in my opinion—was wafting into the kitchen.

Over heavily creamed and sweetened coffee, I told my dad about the field of razor wheat in the Netherworld version of our property and about the trash-can-lid-wielding boy stomping through it. And when we'd exhausted our theories about both the mystery boy and my unscheduled trip, he refilled both of our mugs and started a second pot.

For the next three hours, I sat at the rickety kitchen table with my father, talking about the only thing—other than our species—that we had in common: my mother. He'd always been reluctant to talk about her before; this time he told me everything he could remember about her, probably because, for a few minutes, he'd thought he'd lost me, too. He even answered my questions as I interrupted with them. The only thing we didn't touch on was my death—followed by hers, to save me.

That discussion would have to wait, in spite of the questions I had ready. We were both too tired and distraught from the latest shock to my not-so-human system to handle memories so painful.

But by the time my alarm clock went off, I felt like I truly knew my mother for the first time since my third birthday.

And like I knew my father a little better, too.

NASH'S ARMS WRAPPED around me from behind as I swung my locker door shut, and his voice relaxed me like little else could. "Hey, beautiful," he whispered, dropping a kiss on my neck, just below my ear. "Rough night?"

"Seriously rough. I can't even explain how messed up last night was." I sighed and settled into him, letting the warmth of his chest against my back ease some of the tension left over from my interdimensional field trip. But he couldn't help me fight exhaustion. Fortunately, for that I had two twenty-ounce sodas in my backpack, their condensation probably making a soggy mess out of the chemistry homework I'd forgotten to finish.

"You really crossed over in your sleep?"

I twisted in his arms to face him, laying my cheek against the thick chenille weave of the white letter *E* on his jacket. "Yeah, it was weird. Scary. I was asleep, dreaming that someone died, and in the dream, I was standing in a bunch of that gray fog you see when you peek into…"

I lifted my head to make sure no one else was close enough

to hear. Across the hall, a small cluster of students was gathered around a girl showing off the answers from her algebra homework, but they hadn't even glanced our way. The mohawked junior with the locker next to mine was rifling through his stuff, but his headphones were playing loud enough for me to recognize the bass line of Korn's "Evolution," so there was no way he could hear me.

"…into the *Netherworld*," I continued, whispering just in case. "I couldn't see who was dying, and I couldn't move. Couldn't do anything but scream."

Nash's arms tightened around me and the greens and browns in his eyes swirled rapidly as he listened.

"And when I woke up, I was screaming for real, and I'd already crossed over. I was standing in a field of razor wheat, barefoot. In my pajamas."

Before Nash could reply, Mohawk man slammed his locker and took off down the hall in the growing stream of early-morning students.

"Damn, Kaylee." Nash sank onto the cold tile floor in front of the lockers and drew me down with him, brushing aside a crumpled piece of notebook paper. "How could that happen?"

I shook my head slowly, almost washed away by the wave of fear that crashed over me at the reminder that I still had none of the answers I needed. "My dad thinks that because I subconsciously repressed so much of my *bean sidhe* heritage for so long—" because no one had told me I wasn't human "—that now it's basically demanding to be recognized." I hesitated, reluctant to mention my father's other theory. "That, or I've somehow developed too strong a connection with the Netherworld." Or with someone—or some*thing*—in it.

Nash paled, which almost sent me into a tailspin of panic. I'd hoped for something more optimistic from him than I'd gotten from my father, as grateful as I was for my dad's honesty. But Nash had no comfort to give. "That's the scariest thing I've ever heard."

I rolled my eyes and pulled my backpack onto my lap. "Thanks, Nash," I snapped. "You're a huge help." I'd just about reached the limit of how much fright and frustration I could take. At least, on so little sleep.

"Sorry." He turned so that I could see him. "You're sure you can't remember who died in your dream?"

I nodded. "I'm not sure I knew even *during* the dream. All I saw was an outline in the fog. I couldn't even tell if it was male or female."

"Do you think it was just a normal dream, or could it have been part premonition, too? Maybe the way your brain deals with them when you're asleep?"

I shrugged and leaned with my left shoulder against Mohawk man's locker. "I don't see how it could have been a premonition. I've only had them about people I'm physically close to at the time, and there was no one else in the house but my..."

Oh, no... Terror lit my nerve endings, which blazed until it felt like my entire body was on fire. I sat up, and when I looked at Nash, I knew from his expression that my irises were swirling madly.

"What if it's my dad?" I demanded in a horrified whisper. I'd already lost my mother and had just gotten my father back. I couldn't lose him again so quickly. I *couldn't.*

"No." Nash shook his head calmly, running one hand up my arm, over my sleeve. "It can't be. When you have a premonition, someone dies quickly, right?"

I nodded, not yet willing to grasp the branch of hope he held out to me. "Usually within the hour."

"See? And you had that dream in the middle of the night, right?"

I glanced at my watch and counted backward silently. "Almost five hours ago."

"And your dad's still alive, right?" Nash grinned like he'd just discovered the meaning of life, or the root of all evil, or something equally unlikely, but I was already digging in my pocket for my phone. "What are you doing? Didn't you see him right before you left?"

"Yeah. But I have to be sure." I autodialed my father, hoping the school's no-cell-calls policy didn't apply before the first bell.

"Hello?" my dad said into my ear, over the rush of highway traffic, and I let my head fall against the lockers in relief. "Kaylee? What's wrong?"

"Nothing." I could practically hear the smile in my own voice. "I just wanted to make sure you're not asleep at the wheel or anything, since I got you up so early."

"I'm fine." He paused, and I heard his blinker ding faintly. "Thanks for checking, though."

"No problem. I gotta go." I hung up and slid my phone back into my pocket.

"Feel better?" Nash asked, brows raised.

"Marginally." The front doors opened at the end of the hall, admitting a frigid draft, as well as several dozen freshmen and sophomores. The buses had arrived, and class would start in less than ten minutes. "I gotta go finish my chemistry homework," I said, using the lock on the locker below mine to haul myself to my feet.

Nash stood with me. "I'll walk with you."

I wrapped my arms around Nash's chest, content for the moment just to lean against him and breathe him in—until his next words drenched my warm, cozy feeling like a cold wave crashing over a sleeping sunbather.

"Have you seen Carter this morning?"

"No." In fact, I hadn't seen him since he'd torn out of the student lot on Monday afternoon. He'd skipped school on Tuesday—his parents were still out of town, but rumor had it he'd convinced the maid to call him in sick—presumably too ill from withdrawal to deal with the usual school crap. And I hadn't given him a second thought so far today, thanks to my nearly sleepless Tuesday night.

"His car's in the lot," Nash continued, voice low to keep anyone else from overhearing us as the hall filled with students. "But we don't have any classes together till after lunch, and I'm afraid he's—"

"There he is," I interrupted the moment I saw Scott Carter turn the corner from the gym hallway, strutting as confidently as he ever had.

Nash followed my gaze. "He looks happy." Which—assuming he hadn't found a miracle cure for addiction or withdrawal—could only mean one thing. He'd found Doug's supplier and made another purchase.

"Maybe he's just a quick healer," I suggested, determined to be optimistic because the alternative made me want to rip out my own hair.

"We'll know in a minute." Nash held one hand up and called down the hall, "Hey, Carter, where were you yesterday?"

Scott threaded a path through the crowd toward us, greeting guys he knew on the way, and shared a hand slap with Nash, whose face froze the moment they touched. And if I'd had any doubts before, they were obliterated a second later when Scott's hand brushed mine on its way to his side.

His skin was freezing, and his breath smelled like he'd inhaled a hellion *whole*.

"Sick," Scott said, smiling broadly for no reason I could see. "I could barely get out of bed. Had to get Carlita to call me in sick. Good thing she's picking up some English, right?"

Nash shrugged. "You got a lot of makeup work?"

But Scott wasn't listening. He frowned, eyes narrowed and jaw tense as he stared over my shoulder. I turned to see what he was looking at and found only our own shadows stretched over the lockers, cast by bright light from the office window. But I couldn't help wondering what *he* was seeing....

"Carter?" Nash repeated, turning to follow my gaze while Scott shook his head, as if to clear it.

"Nah," he said finally, like he'd heard the question on some kind of time delay. "I don't think they'll make me do any of it but that quiz in civics." He stepped back and made a sweeping gesture to encompass his entire body. "I'm Scott Carter, man. Nobody's willing to piss off my dad until the football team gets those new pads and tackling dummies for next season."

"Jeez, you say your name like it should be written in all caps," I mumbled, slapping a smile on at the last minute, hoping they'd think I was joking.

Scott did. Sophie did not.

"It should be," she purred, stopping at Scott's side to run one hand over his shoulder and down his back. "But I guess you usually see *yours* handwritten by some nut job with a half-eaten crayon. Isn't that how they label stuff in the psych ward?"

"Only when *you're* in residence," I snapped. I was too tired to put up with Sophie's crap that morning, and for a moment, awe at my own nerve energized me better than three cups of early-morning coffee had.

Scott laughed while Sophie fumed, cheeks hot enough to

spontaneously combust. He slapped Nash on the back, still grinning. "Sounds like your little puss grew some claws! Does she purr when you stroke her? 'Cause this one sure does." He pulled Sophie closer, his hand inching toward the denim pocket curved around her rear.

She smiled and squirmed for his benefit, but when her gaze landed on me, it was cold enough to build a layer of ice in hell.

I rolled my eyes and stepped around my cousin, tugging my backpack higher on my shoulder as I walked briskly toward my first class. Behind me, Scott asked Sophie if she felt like skipping fourth period with him.

I didn't hear her answer—though I was pretty sure it was a yes—because Nash's footsteps pounded rapidly on the tile after me. "Wow. That was…unexpected," he said, slowing to walk beside me.

"Me, or Scott?"

"You." I heard the grin in Nash's voice, but glanced up at him to be sure. "I liked it."

"She had it coming. But Scott…"

"He's just messing around," Nash insisted as we passed his class without slowing. Mine was on the other end of the main hallway.

"I don't care about that." Scott's flirting didn't bother me because it drove Sophie half out of her mind. "But, Nash. He was staring at the lockers behind us like he expected monsters to jump out and drag him off." Which really only happens in the Netherworld. "He's wasted."

"I know."

"We have to do something." I lowered my voice for the next part, leaning closer to him to be heard. "Obviously stealing his stash was a short-term solution."

"I *know*," Nash whispered as we slowed to a stop several

feet from my advanced-math classroom. "He's hallucinating, but I don't think he's hearing things yet, and he's still making sense." Nash shrugged. "As much sense as he ever did, anyway. So I don't think it's too late for him yet."

"What does that mean?" Suddenly I had chill bumps beneath my jacket sleeves. "Why would it be too late?"

Nash's face fell in a mixture of sympathy and surprise, and he tugged me toward the lockers, out of the stream of traffic. "Kaylee, the effects of Demon's Breath on a human are irreversible. If he takes enough to actually sever his tie to reality, cutting off his source may save his life, but it won't fix him. He'll wind up locked in a padded room." He hesitated, searching my face for the truth. "My mom didn't tell you that?"

"No…" I closed my eyes in horror until I had my expression under control. "She didn't know anyone was actually taking it." I pulled my backpack higher on my shoulder, almost fascinated by the irony—the Netherworld had proved to me that I wasn't crazy, but its effect on Doug and Scott would be the opposite.

"How do you know all this?" I glanced at the wall clock over his shoulder to see that we had less than two minutes until the bell. *So much for doing my chemistry homework.…*

Nash ran one cool finger down my jaw to the point of my chin. "Most *bean sidhes* don't grow up thinking they're human, Kay." He glanced around at the rapidly emptying hall, then back at me. "Anyway, we have to cut off Carter's access and figure out how to treat him for withdrawal, or…"

"…eventually frost will literally drive him crazy. Or kill him," I finished, leaning against a row of green lockers.

"Yeah, if by 'eventually,' you mean very, very soon," Nash said, a flash of true fear stirring in his eyes. "He's obviously really sensitive to it."

"What do you mean?"

"Scott probably doesn't have any non-human blood in his gene pool. Sophie, for instance, is human, but she'd probably be much less sensitive to the side effects of Demon's Breath—though she could become just as physically addicted to it—because of her dad's non-human blood."

"And by 'non-human'—" my voice dropped even lower and I leaned closer to him "—you mean *bean sidhes?*"

"Yes, us, and anyone else originally native to the Netherworld. There are a few other species that live here in the human world with us. Like harpies, and sirens, and—"

"Whoa…" I felt my eyes widen, and could only hope I didn't look like a complete drooling idiot to the rest of the student body. "You're serious?"

His irises swam in sympathy. "I keep forgetting you grew up in virtual darkness."

"Well, that makes one of us," I mumbled, frustrated all over again by how much I still had to learn about the Netherworld and its non- or part-human elements. Like *me.*

"Anyway, the less human you are, the less susceptible to the effects of Demon's Breath. Though fiends are the obvious exception."

Because those little buggers only existed in one of two states: stoned, and trying to be stoned.

"So, since Doug's addiction isn't progressing as quickly, he probably has some non-human blood in his family somewhere, right?"

"It's possible." Nash glanced over his shoulder to where my math teacher was eyeing us both and tapping her watch. He headed toward the classroom with me. "But it could be way, way back in his family tree, and he probably knows nothing about it."

"Are you joining us today, Ms. Cavanaugh?" my math teacher asked.

I nodded, and Nash squeezed my hand, then he trotted backward down the hall. "See you at lunch...."

I ducked into my classroom, sliding into my seat just as the tardy bell rang, but while my classmates pulled out homework assignments and frantically filled in the blanks they'd forgotten, I couldn't stop thinking about Doug Fuller, and the only thing we had in common, other than Emma.

What I hadn't known about my family nearly got me killed. But what he didn't know about his might just save his life.

9

"DID SCOTT SAY WHERE he got it?" I asked, bending to dip my paintbrush in white latex paint.

Nash had roped me into helping with the carnival booths after school to keep him company, so I'd pulled the same thing on Emma. Which was how she, Nash, Doug, and I wound up in the school gym at four o'clock on a Wednesday afternoon, slopping white paint and fake snowflakes on booths made of plywood and construction staples. Along with twenty other bright-'n'-shiny cheerleaders, basketball players, and student-council members I'd rarely ever spoken to.

"He said he got it from Fuller again."

I sank to my knees on the canvas drop cloth protecting the gym floor from my subpar artistic efforts and glanced across the basketball court to where Emma and Doug were working on the ice-carving registration booth. And by "working," I mean making out, half-hidden by their booth, with dried-stiff brushes dangling from paint-speckled hands.

"I assume he got it from that same guy? Everett?"

Nash shrugged and used his brush to smooth out a drip on my side of the hot-chocolate stand. "I guess."

"We have to find this guy. Can you get Doug to introduce you? Maybe pretend you want to buy some from him?"

He frowned, critically eyeing the giant marshmallows he was painting on top of a cutout of a mug full of brown liquid. "But then wouldn't I have to sample the product?"

Crap. "Probably. Can't you just fake it?" I sighed, already rethinking my request. Did I want to put Nash in that kind of danger? What if he couldn't fake it and had to take a hit? What if he accidentally inhaled Demon's Breath? Either way, his exposure would be my fault. And I couldn't live with that.

"You know what? Never mind. I'll do it." I stood, trailing my damp brush along the corner of the booth, where I'd evidently left streaks on my first pass. "I'll meet him, and pretend to sample the product, and find out where he gets it. And whether he knows what it really is—"

"No," Nash said. I turned around, and he was so close onlookers would think he was either challenging me to a dance battle, or staring down my shirt.

"Why? Because I'm a girl?"

His irises churned with…panic? But as I watched, he made them go still—obviously an effort—and there was nothing left to read on his face but the angry line of his jaw. "Because you don't seem to understand that the world isn't yours to save. This isn't a game, Kaylee. You're not an undercover cop. You're just a little girl who's in way over her head, and I'm not going to let you get yourself killed over some stupid hero complex."

I stepped back and my cheeks flamed like I'd been slapped. "I'm not a little girl." And he'd never spoken to me like that. Not ever. "I don't know what your problem is, but unless you pay the rent on my house or wear the black suspenders at the Cinemark, you don't get to tell me what to do."

"Or what? You'll slop paint all over my jacket?" Nash's lighthearted grin irritated me.

"Stop smiling. I'm serious," I insisted.

"Yeah. I can see you're fully prepared to deface my letter jacket. Which is exactly why you should let me do this. A Netherworld drug dealer isn't going to be scared of your drippy paintbrush." He tried to take it from me, and when I refused to relinquish the handle, Nash wrapped his hand around both my fingers and the paintbrush and slowly pushed my arm down to my side. "Just let me do this. I don't want you anywhere near Everett." He let me see truth in his eyes, but that did little to placate me. You don't have to be a jock to know when you're being sidelined.

"What if I don't want you near him, either?"

He shrugged. "I'm bigger than you, and I've been taking hits from guys bigger than me for the past six years."

"Well, that experience should come in handy, so long as you're both wearing football helmets and pads. Assuming Everett's even human."

"So long as he's not a hellion, I can take him if I need to." And hellions couldn't cross over, so the chances of that were good. "And Fuller will be there, too."

Though I had serious doubts that Doug would choose Nash over his dealer if he ever wanted to see another hit of frost.

"Fine," I relented. Nash kissed my nose, then let go of my hand, and I glanced up to find Emma dipping her brush into her paint can, grinning at Doug like he'd invented kissing. My stomach churned at the very real possibility that *he* wasn't what made her feel so good. "Look, they came up for air. This is your shot."

Nash laid his brush carefully across the top of his open paint can. "Be right back." He walked across the gym, exchanging greetings with friends and teammates, and I dipped my brush into the can, wishing I could read lips. I was about to put the finishing touches on the top of our booth when sharp words from the hallway caught my attention through the open doorway several feet to my left.

"Get your ass back in there. Now." It was Sophie, her voice low and unusually soft with anger. I'd never heard her so mad, and she got mad at me a lot. "You are *not* going to bail on us again."

"I'll be right back," Scott snapped, and I knew from the rough edge to his voice that he'd come down from his high. And was getting desperate to regain it. "I have to get something from my football."

"What?" Sophie snapped, and I edged closer to the door, backing along the canvas until I could see Scott, though my cousin remained out of sight.

"I mean my *car*." Scott rubbed his forehead in frustration. "I can't think with all that noise!" He glared toward the gym, and I ducked out of sight, glancing around the gym at the other volunteers. Yes, everyone was chatting while they worked, but the gym was huge, and it was nowhere near capacity. Nor were we very loud.

Scott was hearing things. Auditory hallucinations? *Not good…*

"I need to get something…" he mumbled, and I risked scooting forward again to see him staring at the wall to his left, as if something were about to burst through it.

"Yeah, and then you won't come back," Sophie spat. "You promised you'd help, and every time you walk out, I look like an idiot in front of my friends."

"Then you need better friends. Or maybe you're not the only one clawing to be crowned Ice Bitch this year."

"It's Snow Queen. And what good would it do me to win if no one's there to escort me?"

Nash had reached Doug and Emma by then, and had drawn Doug closer to the bleachers for their private chat, and it felt weird to be watching them while I eavesdropped on my cousin and her boyfriend.

"I said I'd be there." Scott spoke through gritted teeth that time, and my pulse jumped at the intensity of the anger in his voice.

"You also said you'd help us all week, and this is the first time you've shown up. And now you're ready to bail."

His sneakers squeaked on the tile as he turned and stomped away from her, and her flats clacked after him. "Damn it, Sophie, get *off!*" Then I heard a thud, and a stunned *oof* from Sophie. I whirled back toward the hall to see her sitting on the floor, propped up by both hands, legs splayed in front of her.

"You *ass!*" she hissed, cloth rustling as she picked herself up.

He exhaled slowly, looking both sorry and impatient. "You just…you never know when to quit."

"That sounds like *your* problem," she snapped, and I almost applauded, surprised to find that for once she and I agreed. And I was just as surprised that she'd picked up on his problem. But I shouldn't have been. She was mean, not stupid. "You're acting like more of a freak than Kaylee."

And…there she'd lost me again.

"Whatever." Scott stomped off, his left arm twitching violently, and just before he passed out of my line of sight, he glanced over his shoulder one last time, not at Sophie, but at the row of lockers to his right. As if he saw something that no one else could see.

Sophie straightened her blouse and I hurried back to the hot-chocolate stand as Nash started across the basketball court toward me. An instant later, Sophie clacked into the gym—and stopped short when her gaze met mine.

Her face paled when she realized I'd heard their argument. Then, in true Sophie style, her critical eye took me in from head to toe and a sneer formed on her perfectly made-up mouth. "You're dripping on your shoe," she said, then stomped off to join a group of dancers gathered around the temporary Snow Queen stage with handfuls of fake snow.

"What's wrong with her?" Nash bent to pick up his paint-brush.

"I heard her fighting with Scott. Who just left for another huff from his balloon. I swear, he and Doug are like babies with pacifiers. And Scott's sounding less coherent by the min-ute."

"Great." Nash's jaw tightened, but then his gaze caught on the white paint splattered all over my right foot, and he smiled. "You look like you're bleeding milk."

"So I hear." Disgusted, I dropped my brush into my half-empty bucket and knelt to work on my shoe. "What did Doug say?"

Nash sat on the canvas to touch up the bottom of the booth. "He's having a party Friday night, and Everett's going to be there. He said I can buy my own then, but he's not selling any more of his."

I dabbed at the paint on my shoe with a damp rag, but only smeared it. "So, we're going to the party?"

"Looks like." He sighed and glanced around to make sure we weren't being overheard. "But I don't see how that will help. Even if we meet Everett, what are we supposed to do? Haul him out the back door and demand he stop selling in the human world? If he's selling Demon's Breath, he must have a supplier, and there nothing we can do against another hellion." He grabbed the rag I'd dropped to wipe another drip before I could sit in it.

"I know." Or rather, I didn't know. I had no solution. No way of stopping Everett—or the hellion backing him—and no way of knowing that cutting off the supply and sending them into withdrawal would actually help Scott and Doug, rather than hurt them. But we couldn't stand by and watch a couple of incidents turn into the epidemic I'd originally feared. "We're gonna have to bring in someone else."

"Like who?"

"I don't know. My dad? Your mom? Uncle Brendon?" I held my breath in anticipation of Nash's argument.

"Kaylee…"

"Wait, I know how that sounds." I set my brush across the top of the can, like I'd seen him do, and edged closer to him on the canvas so I could lower my voice. "But we wouldn't really be ratting anyone out. No cops, no arrests. Nash, if we don't do something, Scott's going to go insane. Like, talking-to-himself, showing-up-half-dressed, cowering-in-the-shadows *insane*. And that's just the beginning. The same thing will happen to Doug, and everyone he passes a balloon to. And possibly to Emma and Sophie, and anyone else who breathes too deeply near someone who's just inhaled. We have to get rid of Everett and his supply, and we can't do that on our own."

"Okaaay…" Nash frowned. "So what's your dad going to say when he finds out you've known about this for nearly a week and didn't tell him? When he finds out your car was totaled by a guy wasted on Demon's Breath? He'll never let you out of the house again. You want to be grounded for the rest of your life?"

"Of course not. But so what if he does ground me? At least Scott and Doug will still be alive." And hopefully sane. And frankly, being grounded again seemed like a small price to pay in exchange for someone else's life. "Not to mention Emma, and even Sophie. What happens if we don't say anything, and Sophie gets drawn into this? How can I ever look my uncle in the eye, knowing I let his daughter die? Again?"

Nash closed his eyes and breathed deeply, and he didn't look at me until his knuckles were no longer white around the paintbrush he clutched like a lifeline. "Fine. It's not like I can argue with that logic." But he certainly looked like he wanted to. "But let's try it ourselves first, okay? Let's go to the party and meet Everett. Let me see what kind of system he has going before we go tattle. I'm only asking you for two more days. All right?"

I hesitated. I understood Nash's reluctance to rat out his friends, but I did *not* understand his reluctance to keep them alive. "Fine. But if we can't do anything about him, I'm telling my dad. That night. I'm not kidding, Nash. This has already gone too far."

Nash nodded and dropped his paintbrush on the white-splattered canvas. "I agree with you there," he whispered, eyes swirling slowly with frustration and a little fear. "This whole thing has gone way too far."

10

WEDNESDAY NIGHT WAS hell on earth.

After painting carnival booths until dinnertime, Nash and I grabbed fast-food burgers and ate while I rushed through only the homework that *had* to be done, for the teachers who actually checked. Then I fell asleep on my couch with my head on his lap while he watched old action movies until my dad got home.

When the front door slammed, I woke up and rolled over to find my father staring down at me, looking pissed beyond words. Apparently napping with my nose pressed into my boyfriend's denim-clad crotch was not on the list of approved sleeping arrangements.

Who knew?

But when I broke into tears explaining that I was afraid to sleep alone, in case I woke up in the Netherworld again, my dad's scowl softened into a sympathetic frown, and he suggested we camp out in the living room that night, to put both of our fears to rest. That way, if I started screaming, he could wake me up before I crossed over.

A living-room slumber party with my dad sounded a little juvenile, but I was willing to try anything that might keep me anchored to my own reality.

Unfortunately, his plan worked out better in theory than in practice.

Around midnight, my dad fell asleep in his recliner, head rolled to one side, bottom lip jiggling each time a snore rumbled from his mouth. But I was still awake two hours later, when the *Judge Judy* marathon gave way to an infomercial advertising men's hair-loss products. I couldn't relax. I was *terrified* of waking up in a field of razor wheat, barefoot and hoarse, and unable to move without getting shredded like secret government documents.

So after twenty minutes of watching old men have their hair spray-painted on, I exchanged my pj bottoms and Betty Boop slippers for jeans, a thick pair of socks, and my heaviest pair of boots from the bottom of my closet. After slipping on the black quilted jacket Aunt Val had given me for Christmas the year before, I snuck back into the living room and collapsed on the couch, finally feeling armed for sleep.

That way, if I crossed over, at least I'd be warm, and dressed in defense of razor-sharp, literal blades of grass.

I even considered running outside for the lid to the old trash can we raked leaves into, but in the end decided that would only bring up more questions from my father when the crash of metal woke him up.

Finally prepared for the worst, I managed four hours of light dozing, during which several extra loud commercials broke through my delicate slumber. But by six in the morning, I was awake for good, reading the directions on the back of the coffee grounds, hoping I wouldn't mess up my first pot too badly.

By the time I'd showered and dressed, my father was padding wearily around the kitchen in his bare feet, and the coffee was done. "Not bad." He held up a nearly full mug. "Your first batch?"

Sighing, I sank onto a chair to pull mismatched socks from my feet. "Yeah." I forced an exhausted smile, wondering how I would ever make it through my history review session if I couldn't even find a proper pair of socks from the pile of clean laundry in the basket in my room.

I had to hand it to Aunt Val: she may have been a vain, soul-stealing, interdimensional criminal, but she'd always kept the laundry neatly folded...

"Harmony and Brendon are coming over tonight to discuss your problem. To see if we can't figure out how and why it's happening." My father paused, pouring coffee into another mug for me—this one oversize. "I didn't hear you sing." Which was how male *bean sidhes* heard the female *bean sidhe's* wail. "Does that mean you didn't have any death dreams?"

I shook my head, rubbing my temples. "I had another one. Same as last time, from what I remember. But this time the Geico gecko woke me up before the screaming started."

My dad frowned and crossed the room to set a heavily doctored mug of coffee on the table in front of me. "I could call you in sick, if you want to stay home and rest."

"Thanks, but I better go." I cradled my mug in both hands and blew on the surface before taking the first long, bitter sip. "We're reviewing for midterms today." And as awesome as staying home sounded, I needed to be there to watch Scott and Doug for further signs that their sanity was slipping. And Emma and Sophie, for any signs that they'd gotten a contact buzz from breathing near their own boyfriends. "Besides, I could dream about death as easily in the daytime as I can at night, right?"

"I guess so." My father put one hand on the back of my chair, watching me in concern as he brought his own mug to his mouth. "Just be careful, okay? I can't follow you into the Netherworld, and by the time I find someone to take me—" Harmony, presumably "—there's no telling where you'll be."

I nodded and bit my tongue to keep from reminding him that—barring catastrophe, like injured vocal cords—I could get myself out the same way I got myself in. I'd done it several times already.

But something told me that reminder would reassure him no more than it reassured me.

I WANDERED AROUND SCHOOL in a daze on Thursday, feeling almost as out of it as Scott looked. I fell asleep during individual study time and slept through the bell, so I was almost late to my next class.

In the hall before lunch, Nash told me Scott had showed up twenty minutes late for economics with his shirt inside out, carrying the wrong textbook. Then he laughed out loud during Mr. Pierson's lecture on the influence of the American stock market on the global financial community.

When Pierson asked what he found so funny, Scott said the teacher's shadow had flipped him off.

Half the class laughed along with Scott, assuming he was either high—on something human in origin, presumably—or making fun of Pierson in some way they didn't understand. The other half looked at him like he'd lost his mind, which was much closer to the truth. We'd waited too long, and Scott had gotten in too deep. He was living in his own world now, and I became more certain with each painful beat of my heart that Nash was right: we wouldn't be able to fix him.

At lunch, Scott refused to sit with us—or with anyone else

in the room. He stood in front of our table, glancing nervously back and forth between it and the narrow, floor-to-ceiling windows along the outside of the room, which cast student-shaped shadows on the opposite wall. He looked from one of us to the next, then at the silhouettes lined up along the wall behind us, muttering under his breath. He said something about being followed, then covered his ears, spun one hundred and eighty degrees, and ran straight down the center aisle and out the double doors, leaving Sophie and her friends—and everyone else in the cafeteria—to stare after him.

Sophie's friends burst into laughter, watching their toppled football idol with the same derisive dismissal they usually reserved for stoners and loners. Sophie looked like she'd either scream or vomit as she marched to their usual table.

I almost felt sorry for her. Almost.

Nash and I followed Scott into the main hall, ignoring curious looks from the other students, but he was already gone. We glanced into each empty classroom we passed, Nash's irises roiling with fear, regret, and guilt. I knew exactly how he felt. If we'd told someone sooner—if I'd insisted on telling our parents the night Doug hit my car—Scott might never have gotten his hands on Demon's Breath in the first place.

At the end of the main hall, a flash of movement caught my eye from the parking lot beyond the glass door. "He's going for his car," I said, and Nash nodded, then glanced at me with both brows raised, waiting for my opinion before he charged ahead. Most exterior doors locked automatically. If we followed Scott into the parking lot, we'd have to walk around the building to reenter through either the office or the cafeteria, where I'd come in after we'd taken that first balloon.

I shrugged and shoved the door open, flinching as a cold draft chilled me instantly. But a little discomfort and a hike around the school meant nothing compared to the friend we'd failed to save.

Nash followed me outside and across the lot, both of us crossing our arms over our chests for warmth. We headed toward Scott's usual parking spot and found his car three rows back, just to the left of the gym entrance. As we got closer, we could see Scott behind the wheel, alternately shaking his head, and vehemently gesturing as he yelled at no one.

He'd progressed from hallucinating to carrying on conversations with his own delusions.

Had I looked that crazy, strapped to a bed in the hospital, when I couldn't stop singing for some stranger's soul?

"Come on." Nash grabbed my hand and we raced across the lot toward Scott. But the moment he saw us coming, he twisted his key in the ignition and slammed his gearshift into Reverse, peeling out of his space way too fast. His rear bumper plowed into the front of another car, then he tore down the aisle and out of the lot, newly dented bumper winking at us in the sunlight as he pulled onto the road.

Nash and I changed directions, and I dug my keys from my pocket as we ran. Our school day was over. We couldn't let him drive all over town in his current state of…crazy. I popped the lock from several feet away and Nash made it into his seat before I did. I backed out carefully—still unfamiliar with the length of my borrowed car—then raced after Scott.

"I think he's heading home." Nash shoved his seat belt into the clasp and braced one hand on the dashboard as I took a sharp turn just after the light turned red. Fortunately, no one else was coming.

But Scott zoomed through the next yellow light, and I got stuck behind a pizza delivery car. By the time we got to Scott's house, his car was slanted across the driveway, the driver's side door still open, and he was nowhere in sight. I turned off the engine, shoved the keys into my pocket, and raced up the driveway after Nash, fully expecting the front door to be locked.

It was open. Nash led the way into the house, which had recovered nicely from the previous weekend's party. Thanks, no doubt, to the unseen and likely unthanked Carlita.

"Scott?" Nash clomped through the foyer onto the spotless white carpet in the formal living room. There was no answer. We peeked into the den, kitchen, dining room, laundry room, and two guest bedrooms before coming to Mr. Carter's office at the end of the hall—a space I remembered fondly.

The room was dark, and it took a minute for my eyes to adjust to what little light fell from the cracks in the wooden blinds drawn shut over both windows.

"Close the door!" Scott shouted, and I jumped as he lifted one hand to block the light from the hallway. Nash nudged me farther into the room and pushed the door closed softly, cutting off so much light that I had to wait for my eyes to adjust again.

Scott cowered on the far end of the brown leather couch, and as Nash approached him, Scott began to mumble-chant under his breath.

"No light, no shadow. No light, no shadow..."

Chill bumps popped up all over my arms, in spite of the warm air flowing from the vent overhead.

"What's wrong, Carter?" Nash squatted on the floor in front of his friend, one hand on the arm of the couch for balance. "Does the light hurt your eyes? Does your head hurt?"

Scott didn't answer. He just kept mumbling, eyes squeezed shut.

"I think he's afraid of the shadows," I whispered, remembering Scott's horror when he'd eyed our silhouettes in the cafeteria and his own shadow in the hall the afternoon before.

"Is that right?" Nash asked without looking at me, his profile tense with fear and concern. "Is something wrong with your shadow?"

"Not mine anymore," Scott whispered, his voice high and reedy, like a scared child's. He punched the sides of his head with both fists at once, as if he could beat down whatever he was seeing and hearing. "Not my shadow."

"Whose shadow is it?" I whispered, fascinated in spite of the cold fingers of terror inching up my back, leaving chills in their wake.

"His. He stole it."

My chest seemed to contract around my heart as a jolt of fear shot through it.

Nash shifted, trying to get comfortable in his squat. "Who stole it?"

"Like Peter Pan. Make Wendy sew my shadow back on…"

I glanced at Nash, and Scott froze with his eyes closed and his head cocked to one side, like a dog listening for a whistle humans can't hear. Then he opened his eyes and looked straight at Nash, from less than a foot away. "Can you get me a soda, Hudson? I don't think I ate lunch." The sudden normalcy of his voice scared me almost as badly as the childlike quality had, and I glanced at Nash in surprise. But he only nodded and stood.

"Just watch him," he whispered, squeezing my hand on his way out the door, which he left ajar a couple of inches.

Uncomfortable staring at Scott in his current state, I glanced around the room, admiring the built-in shelves behind a massive antique desk with scrolled feet and a tall, commanding chair.

"You can go look," Scott said, and I jumped, in spite of my best effort to remain calm.

"What?"

"You like to read, right?" He cocked his head to one side, as if he heard a reply I hadn't made. "Some of them are really old. Several first editions."

I hesitated, but he looked so hopeful, so encouraging, that I rounded the corner of the desk farthest from him, drawn by the spine of an old copy of *Tess of the d'Urbervilles*. It was on the second shelf from the top, and I had to stand on my toes to reach it. To brush my fingers over the gold print on the spine.

The soft click of a door closing shot through the room, as loud as a peal of thunder in my head. I dropped to my heels and whirled to see Scott standing in front of the now-closed door, mumbling something like soft, inarticulate chanting.

My heart thudded in my chest, my own pulse roaring in my ears. "Scott? What's wrong?"

His head snapped up, his fevered gaze focusing on me briefly. Then his mumbling rose in volume, and he seemed to be arguing now, but I couldn't make out the words. He shook his head fiercely, like he had in his car. "Can you hear him?"

I stepped slowly toward the desk between us. "Hear who, Scott? What do you hear?"

"He says you can't hear him," Scott continued, his gaze momentarily holding mine again. Then, "No, no, no, no…"

I tried to sound calm as I inched toward him. "Who do you hear?"

"Him. Can't see him in the dark, but I hear him. *In. My. Head!*" He punctuated each word with a blow to his own temple. "Stole my shadow. But I still hear him…"

Shivers traveled the length of my arms and legs, and my hands shook at my sides. Was Scott actually seeing someone the rest of us couldn't? Hearing something meant only for his ears? Thanks to Tod, I knew better than most how very possible that was....

But this didn't feel like the work of a reaper. Reapers couldn't steal someone's shadow. Could they?

Scott rolled his eyes from side to side, as if to catch movement on the edge of his vision. My stomach tried to heave itself through my chest and out my throat. I knew that motion. I did the same thing when I peeked into the Netherworld. When I tried to get a clear view of the heard-but-unseen creatures skittering and sliding through the impenetrable gray fog.

Could he see the fog? Could he see the *things?* Was something from the Netherworld talking to him?

No. It's not possible. But my chill bumps were as big as mosquito bites.

"What is he saying?" I was past the desk, four feet from him now, and closing. When Nash came back, I would peek into the Netherworld to rule out that impossibility. To verify that Scott wasn't seeing and hearing something from that other reality. From a world he didn't even know existed.

Because creatures that couldn't cross over couldn't shout across the barrier, either. Right?

Scott looked up and smiled, but it was the kind of smile a cancer patient wears when he's realized chemo isn't worth the pain and nausea. When he's finally decided to give up and let Death claim him. "Take me to him. He'll fix me if you take me to him."

Dread burned like ice in my veins, and I edged back when Scott stepped toward me. "Take you where?"

"There." He rubbed his brow, as if to soothe a bad headache. "Where he is. He says you know how to cross."

Cross. *No.* My eyes closed briefly, and I sucked in a long, devastated breath.

Scott's shadow man wanted me to take him to the Nether-world.

11

"Who is he, Scott?" I shuffled back another step and trailed my fingers over the top of his father's desk, hoping the smooth, cool surface would ground me, in spite of my rapidly thumping heart. I needed to peek into the Netherworld, to see for myself who was talking to him, but I was afraid to take any of my attention from Scott.

"Take me…" he whispered fiercely, matching each of my steps with a larger one of his own. "We have to cross!"

Not gonna happen. I might not have Harmony's experience, or my dad's wisdom and pathological caution, but I was nowhere near naive enough to believe that whoever was tormenting Scott would simply "fix" him if I took him to the Netherworld.

The Netherworld didn't do charity. This shadow man would claim us both, body and soul, and we'd never see the human world again.

Over Scott's shoulder, the doorknob turned, and relief washed over me as Nash's voice called out. "Kaylee?"

But the door didn't open—it was locked—and I never should have taken my eyes off Scott.

"Nash, he's not having delus—"

Scott grabbed my arm and jerked me forward. He pinned me to his chest and I gasped, more surprised than afraid. Something sharp bit into my throat, just below my jaw, and the shout I'd been about to unleash died on my tongue.

"Take me…" he demanded, and a cold, nauseatingly sweet puff of Demon's Breath wafted over my face.

My breath hitched as I tried not to inhale, and my pulse pounded in my head. I wasn't sure exactly where my jugular ran through my neck, but I was pretty sure accuracy wasn't as important as enthusiasm in the art of throat slashing.

"If you don't take me, I'm gonna die. And you're gonna die with me," Scott whispered, his voice shaky with terror.

His skin was cold, even through both layers of our clothing, and the blade—something small…a paring knife, maybe?—felt warm by comparison. "Scott, you don't want to go there." I had to force the words out, afraid that any movement of my throat would force the metal through my skin. "Trust me."

"Carter, what are you doing?" Nash asked through the door, and I was worried by how composed he sounded—his best friend was about to cut my head off! Not that Nash knew about the knife…

"She won't take me!" Scott hissed, his grip bruising my arm.

"He has a *knife*," I said as loudly as I dared with the blade still pressed against my skin.

"Take you where?" Nash asked, ignoring my contribution to the exchange. And that's when I realized he was Influencing Scott—trying to talk him down with a little *bean sidhe* push. "Let me in, and we'll talk about this."

"He's not delusional, Nash," I said, struggling to stay calm.

"Something wants me to cross over with him. Could you please help me explain why that's not a good idea?"

I needed Nash to do the talking, if there was any chance of his Influence actually working. And I was fighting complete panic at the feel of the blade against my throat.

In theory, if my time was up—if my name was on the list—I would die, and no amount of talking or fighting would stop that.

And if it wasn't my time, so long as I stayed in the human world and avoided Netherworld elements, I wouldn't die, no matter what. That not-death could come about in any number of ways. Scott might turn out to have colossally bad aim with a knife, or Nash might do everything right to stop the bleeding. Or Tod might blink in, then blink me instantly to the hospital. Or we might actually talk Scott out of violence.

Or…Scott could maim me beyond recognition and normal physical function without actually killing me.

But no matter what might happen next, crossing over would be worse. Our expiration dates meant nothing in the Netherworld, which officially made it the scariest place in existence, and the place I was least likely to take Scott.

"You're confused," Nash said to Scott from the other side of the door, and his voice slid over me like a warm breeze. "I can help you. Let me in, and I'll help you."

"No!" Scott shouted, his hand tightening around my arm. "He knows about you. Your voice makes people do things. Shut up or I'll kill her."

My pulse spiked again, and there was only silence from the hallway. Tears filled my eyes, blurring the closed door until I blinked them away and mentally closed the well. Crying would not help me, nor would it help Scott. But there had to be a way out of this.

The light beneath the door flickered, like Nash had stepped closer. "How?" he asked softly, and his normal voice now sounded flat compared to the rich tones that accompanied his Influence.

"How what?" Scott asked, and his grip on my arm loosened slightly.

"How will you cross over if you kill her?" Nash clarified, and I almost smiled, in spite of my predicament. Scott knew about his vocal influence—sort of—so Nash was working without it. He was being smart. If I wanted to live, I'd have to get smart, too.

I closed my eyes, ignoring the hum from the heating vent overhead and the eerie coolness of the body pressed against my back. "Nash can't take you," I whispered, just loud enough for Scott to hear me.

Scott stiffened. "You're lying."

I started to shake my head, then remembered the knife and opened my eyes again. "Nash can't take you, and neither can *he*. If he could, he wouldn't need me, would he?" Scott didn't answer, but he pulled me back a step across the thick, soft carpet. "Ask him. Not Nash. Ask *him*."

Scott remained silent and rigid against me, and I wondered if whoever he was listening to could hear me, or if Scott had to ask him directly. Silently or otherwise.

Finally Scott seemed to sag against me, though the blade never left my throat. "Take me there. Please take me. Please make it stop," he begged. He was close to his breaking point, which meant that whoever wanted him must be getting desperate.

Scott went quiet again, listening to something we couldn't hear, and I was almost surprised to realize daylight still slipped through the cracks in the closed blinds. It felt like we'd been in that room forever, but it couldn't have been more than a few minutes. Then Scott leaned into me, dragging my thoughts back to the crisis at hand. His mouth brushed my right ear, through my hair. "He says this is all your fault."

What? A wash of confusion diluted my fear. What did any of this have to do with me?

"Scott, if I take you there, he'll kill us both. Or worse."

He stiffened again, and his knife hand twitched. I gasped as the point of the blade pierced my skin with a sharp slice of pain. A warm bead of blood trailed slowly down my neck, and I froze.

"He says I'll die here. You say I'll die there. But if I can't get him out of my head, none of that matters!" He sobbed, then stood straighter, drawing me up with him as the blade pressed more firmly against my broken skin. "Take me there now, or I'll cut your throat wide open."

"Okay…" I said, my heart pounding so hard I could barely hear my own words, much less my thoughts. "I'll take you. Just…put the knife down."

"Kaylee?" Nash demanded from the other side of the door, and something thumped to the floor. He'd dropped the soda.

"No way." Scott shook his head, jostling us both, ignoring Nash completely. "He says you'll run."

I closed my eyes and breathed deeply, trying to slow my racing thoughts. And my racing pulse. Then I opened my eyes to find the doorknob twisting again as Nash tried to force his way into the room.

"If this shadow man is so smart—" my voice wavered with nerves "—he'll know it takes a lot of concentration to cross over. And I can't concentrate with a knife at my throat."

Nash pounded the door. "Kaylee, no…!" he shouted, but he was too upset now to manage much Influence on either of us.

Scott went still behind me, listening to his shadow man again. Then, "Fine. But if you run, he says I should gut you like a goat on an altar."

My heart beat so hard my head hurt, and adrenaline was turning my fight-or-flight instinct into a demand. I knew what I had to do, but had no idea if I could actually pull it off. He was a lot bigger than I was, and a lot stronger and faster. And Nash would be no help from the other side of the door.

Slowly, Scott removed the knife from my neck, and more blood trickled down my throat. A moment later, the blade poked at my back through my jacket and my thin tee. "Yes, that's much more relaxing," I snapped, unable to censor my sarcasm, even with my life in mortal peril.

I stared at the closed door and tried to communicate my intentions to Nash silently, desperately wishing *bean sidhes* were psychic. But that was just another on a long list of really cool abilities I didn't get.

"Okay, this is gonna feel kind of funny," I warned Scott, closing my eyes as I silently wished myself luck. "Your skin will tingle, and it'll feel like you're falling." Which wasn't true in the least. Nash stopped pounding on the door for a moment, as if to listen. He knew I was lying, and had hopefully gathered from that fact that I had no intention of taking Scott to the Netherworld.

But then what I was really planning sank in, and he kicked the door so hard it shook in its frame.

"So, don't freak out if you lose your balance, okay?" I continued for Scott's benefit, doing my best to ignore Nash. "You ready?"

"Yeah." But Scott's voice had gone squeaky, and his grip on my arm was cutting off my circulation. He was terrified.

Good. So was I.

I took another deep breath. Then I spun away from the knife and twisted my arm from Scott's grip. He shouted. The knife arced toward me. I threw my arm up to shield my face. Pain sliced across the fleshy part of my forearm. I screamed and kicked him. My boot hit his hip, and Scott stumbled toward the desk. He tripped over his own foot and went down like a felled tree.

I whirled around before he landed and fumbled with the lock, twisting the knob twice before it would turn. I pulled the door open and Nash shoved me behind him even as he charged into the room, armed with nothing but his own outrage.

Scott lay motionless on the floor, the knife clutched loosely in his fist.

For a moment, I thought he was dead. That his shadow man had been right—he'd died because he hadn't crossed over. Then I saw his chest rise and fall, and realized he was unconscious. He'd hit his head on the desk when he fell.

Nash dug his phone from his pocket and was dialing before I'd even processed what happened. Distantly, I heard him answer the 9-1-1 operator's questions, telling her that his best friend, Scott Carter, had gone crazy. That he'd attacked me with a knife, then fell and hit his head on a desk and knocked himself out.

The operator said help would be there soon. She was right.

Nash was still wrapping my bleeding arm with a kitchen towel when the sirens screamed down the street. "Just go along with whatever I say," he insisted as flashing red lights drew to stop in front of the house, easily visible through the glass front door. He pushed me gently onto a couch in the living room. "Everyone at school will back us up. They all saw him acting crazy."

My eyes watered and the room blurred. "You're going to get him committed..." I whispered, unsure whether or not I meant it as a question.

"There's no other choice," Nash insisted, walking backward toward the front door to let the EMTs in. "There's nothing we can do for him now, and the only way to keep him from hurting anyone else is to lock him up."

"This is our fault, Nash," I sobbed, wiping scalding tears from my cheek with the back of my good arm. "We should have done something sooner."

"I know." His eyes swirled with grief, and guilt, and regret. Then he turned his back on me and opened the front door.

"TELL ME AGAIN WHY you left school?" the police officer said, scooting his chair closer to the E.R. gurney I sat on, my legs crossed beneath me like a kindergartner. Only he wasn't just an officer. He was a detective. Because attempted murder—or manslaughter, or whatever they would wind up calling it—was a felony, and even though Scott was strapped to a bed in the same mental health ward I'd once spent a week in, he couldn't officially plead his mental defect until his parents called in their fancy, overpriced attorney to replace the court-appointed rookie currently shaking in his loafers upstairs.

And if anyone deserved to get off on temporary insanity, it was Scott Carter. He hadn't really meant to kill me. Well, maybe he had, but he would never have done it if he weren't in withdrawal from Demon's Breath and under the manipulation of an as-yet-unidentified Netherworld monster. Both circumstances I was convinced Nash and I could have prevented, if we'd acted sooner. Called in reinforcements.

"Kaitlyn? Kaitlyn, are you okay?" the cop asked, and Nash squeezed my good hand until I glanced up, surprised to find everyone staring at me.

"It's Kaylee…" I mumbled, staring at the neat row of stitches on the arm I held stiffly in front of me, awaiting a sterile bandage. "My name is Kaylee." I was grateful for the local anesthetic, and a bit surprised that it seemed to have numbed my mind, as well as my arm.

Or maybe that was shock.

"I'm sorry. Kaylee," the detective corrected himself, shifting uncomfortably in his chair. I'd insisted he sit, because I didn't like him towering over me. He made me nervous, probably because I felt guilty, though he didn't seem to suspect me of anything. "Kaylee, please tell me again why you followed Mr. Carter from the school parking lot."

Behind him, the thin blue curtain slid back on its metal track and an elderly nurse appeared, nearly swallowed by her purple scrubs. She carried several small, sealed packages, and I eyed them suspiciously.

"Because he was acting…crazy." *There. Maybe I could help with Scott's defense….* "He wasn't making any sense, and we didn't think he should be driving. So we followed to make sure he was okay."

"And he went straight home?"

I glanced at Nash, who nodded. "Yeah. The front door was open, so we went in. He was in his dad's office."

The nurse ripped open a package of sterile bandages and I flinched, startled.

"And he just attacked you with a knife?" The detective was still scribbling in his notebook, not even watching me as I nodded. "Did he say anything?"

"Um… He wanted me to take him somewhere."

Finally the cop looked up, surprised. "Where?"

"He didn't say." Which was true, technically. "He just said he'd kill me if I didn't take him. I told him I'd take him wherever he wanted to go if he'd put the knife down. So he moved it from my throat to my back, and when I tried to get away, he slashed me." I held up my injured arm for emphasis, foiling the nurse's attempt to bandage it.

"Okay, thank you, Kaylee." The detective stood and flipped his notebook closed, then slid it into the right pocket of his long coat. "Your dad's on his way—" I hadn't been able to stop them from calling him and scaring him to death "—and it looks like you're in good hands until he gets here." The cop smiled first at Nash, who didn't even seem to notice him, then at the nurse, whose cold hands shook as they pressed the bandage gently on the long line of stitches curving over the bony part of my forearm onto the fleshier underside. "We'll be following up with you soon, when we know more about what happened. Okay?"

I nodded as he headed toward the exit. He already had one hand on the doorknob when I looked up. "What's going to happen to Scott?"

Nash glanced at me in surprise almost equal to the cop's, but the nurse didn't even pause in her work.

"Well, that all depends on his attorney. But Mr. Carter—Scott's father—has testified in several cases around here and, for a psychiatrist, he knows a fair bit about the law. I wouldn't worry about Scott. He'll get the best legal and mental care available."

I nodded, but only because I didn't know how else to respond. No amount of money or treatment could fix Scott now, and for all I knew, he'd hear that voice in his head—see that shape in the shadows—for the rest of his life. Even if he never again saw the outside of a padded room.

12

"JUST COME STRAIGHT HOME," Harmony said into her cell phone as I sank onto my couch with my bandaged arm in my lap. She pushed the front door closed, cutting off the chill from outside, then marched into the kitchen, already digging through my fridge for something that hadn't started to mold.

On the other end of the line, my father tried to argue, but she interrupted him with the confidence of a woman accustomed to giving orders. "I already picked her up."

My dad worked at a factory in Fort Worth, while Harmony worked in the very hospital they'd taken us to. So even coming from home—she'd worked the third shift—she'd gotten there nearly half an hour earlier than my dad could have made it.

"Because I was closer to the hospital than you were." And because Nash's Influence had convinced the doc to release me to someone other than my legal guardian.

Harmony held the phone away from her ear while my father blustered, complained, and questioned. "She's fine, physically. We'll talk about it when you get here." With that, she flipped her phone closed and shoved it into her front pocket with a finality that suggested she would *not* answer if he called back.

Wow. I'd never seen anyone handle my dad like that, and I was so impressed I forgot to argue that I was fine mentally, too. I thought I was handling the whole thing pretty well, considering I'd nearly been killed. Again.

"Kaylee, do you believe in déjà vu?" Harmony smiled amiably and pulled a carton of milk from the fridge. "Because the sight of you lying injured on that couch is starting to look awfully familiar."

"I don't go looking for trouble," I insisted, a little miffed.

Nash set the keys to the rental on the half wall between the entry and the living room, then dropped onto the couch next to me with his head thrown back like it weighed a ton. We'd stopped by the Carters' house on the way home so Nash could follow us in the loaner. Scott's parents had been called back from Cancún early, but they wouldn't get in until the next day, so his house was completely dark and looked oddly deserted, even in the middle of a sunny winter day.

It was creepy, to say the least.

Harmony set a tub of margarine on the counter, then pulled half-full bags of flour and sugar from the depths of a cabinet I'd rarely peeked into. "Yet trouble manages to find you, whether you're looking for it or not."

"In this case, I think 'trouble' is a bit of an understatement," I mumbled, twisting carefully to lean on Nash as he wrapped one arm around me. "Don't you want to know what happened?" I asked, watching her through the wide kitchen doorway.

"Not yet." Her voice echoed from inside another cabinet. "You'll have to explain it all over again when your father gets here, so I'll just wait for that."

"Well, *I* won't," Tod snapped, and I glanced up to find him leaning against the kitchen door frame. He'd shown up in my room in the E.R. right after the detective left, demanding answers we couldn't give him while the nurse was still there. Then he'd blinked out to find his mother, only to discover her already on the way to the hospital. One of her fellow nurses had called her when she recognized Nash.

"Yes, you will." Harmony finally stood and faced her older, mostly dead son, a box of baking soda in one hand. "Making her repeat herself won't make her feel any better."

"Not that there's any chance of that, anyway..." My dad was going to go *apocalyptic* when he heard about the Demon's Breath. And I wasn't entirely convinced Harmony wouldn't join him, once she knew the whole story.

Tod grumbled and dropped into my father's recliner, apparently willing to physically wait with the rest of us for once.

I sat up and shrugged out from under Nash's arm so I could see his face, but he wouldn't look at me. His eyes were closed, one wave of brown hair fallen over his eyebrow. I might have thought he was asleep, if not for the tense lines of his shoulders and jaw. Nash was just as upset as I was, and probably suffering an even heavier burden of guilt, because Scott was his friend.

Metal clanged against the faded Formica as Harmony set our good mixing bowl on the counter.

A labored engine roared down the street out front, then rumbled to a stop in the driveway. My father was home, and considering how quickly he'd arrived, I was surprised not to hear police sirens following him.

Moments later, the front door flew open and smashed against the half wall. My dad's keys dangled from his hand and his chest heaved as if he'd just run all the way from work.

His breathing didn't slow until his gaze found mine. "Are you okay?"

I scooted forward on the couch as Nash sat up straight next to me. "Yeah. I'm good." Thanks to twenty-eight stitches and a strong local anesthetic. But I wasn't looking forward to the next hour of my life. The nurse who'd bandaged my arm had given me two Tylenol tablets. Because once the local anesthetic wore off, she'd said, I'd feel like someone sliced my arm open.

I think that was her idea of a joke.

"What the hell happened?" my dad demanded, still standing in the open doorway as a cold draft swirled across the room, fluttering the opened bills on one end table and raising chill bumps on my legs. "Don't they have teachers at that school? Why wasn't anyone there to stop this?"

Well, crap. I guess there's no way to avoid the whole truancy aspect....

"We weren't actually *at* school." I squeezed my eyes shut, hoping I looked pathetic enough to thwart the bulk of his temper.

The front door slammed and I opened my eyes to see anger and concern warring behind my father's pained expression. "I don't even know where to start, Kaylee. I've only been back for three months, and you've nearly been killed twice. What do I have to do to keep you safe? Are you out *looking* for trouble?"

In spite of the growing pain in my arm and my general state of guilt and grief, I managed a wry grin, trying to lighten the mood. "You missed that part of the discussion." When his worried scowl deepened, the smile died on my face.

My father sighed and pulled his coat off as he clomped across the living room, bringing with him the scents of sweat and metal from the factory where he worked. He'd had to leave early—giving up part of his paycheck—thanks to me. "How's your arm?"

"Fine." I held out my hand when he reached for it, and he studied my arm, as if he could actually see through the long, thick bandage. "The doctor said there's no permanent damage. It's just a few stitches, Dad."

Tod huffed and propped his feet on the footrest of my father's recliner. "Try twenty-eight," he said, and my dad actually jerked in surprise. I was almost amused to realize that, though he could clearly hear the reaper, my father couldn't see him.

"Damn it, Tod!" He glared in the reaper's general direction. "Do not sneak up on me in my own house—I don't care *how* dead you are! Show yourself or get out."

Harmony and I shared a small smile, but my father didn't notice.

The reaper shrugged and grinned at me, then blinked out of the chair and onto the carpet at my father's back, now fully corporeal. "Fine," he said, inches from my dad's ear, and my father nearly jumped out of his shirt. "Your house, your rules."

My dad spun around, his flush deepening until I thought his face would explode. "I changed my mind. Get out!"

Tod shrugged again and a single blond curl fell over his forehead. "I'll get the scoop from Kaylee later. My break's over, anyway." Then he winked silently out of existence, leaving my father still fuming, his fists clenched at his sides in anger that had no outlet.

I looked up at the clock in the kitchen. It was 2:05 p.m. Tod's shift had only started at noon. If he didn't watch it, he was going to get fired.

"Is he really gone?" My dad glanced first at me, then at

Harmony, who shrugged, clearly trying to hide a grin as she shoved several fallen ringlets back from her face.

"As far as I can tell."

Tod didn't torment his mother or me much because he couldn't get such a rise out of us. My father and Nash were his favorite targets, because they took themselves so seriously.

My dad closed his eyes and sucked in a long, hopefully calming breath, then refocused his attention on me. "Where were we?"

"I was telling you I'm fine. No permanent damage." No need to mention the twenty-eight stitches again...

"But you could have been killed," he insisted, and I couldn't argue with that, so I kept my mouth shut. "Come in here where I can get a better look at you." He stomped into the kitchen and gestured for me to take a seat at the table, beneath the brightest light in the house.

I sat, and he sank into the chair next to mine, studying my face as if it now held foreign planes and angles. "Who did this?" He took my chin in one hand and carefully turned my head for a better look at the short, shallow cut on my neck, which the nurse had cleaned and left unbandaged. It hadn't even required stitches.

I sighed and pulled away from his gentle grip, already dreading the explanation I was about to launch. "Scott Carter."

"The same kid who trashed your car?"

"No, that was Doug Fuller."

My father twisted in his seat to glare at Nash, who was now hunched over on the couch, his head cradled in both hands, his broad shoulders slumped. "And they're both friends of yours? Teammates?"

Harmony crossed her arms over her chest. "Aiden, Nash had nothing to do with this."

"Oh, really?" My father turned on her, and I hoped she understood that the sharpness in his voice reflected more worry than anger. "So it's just a coincidence that one of his teammates rammed her car through a brick mailbox, and less than a week later another one tries to hack her head off."

Well, at least I know where I get my penchant for exaggeration....

"Scott's kind of been borrowing trouble from Doug," I said, picking at the edge of my bandage. "But Nash has nothing to do with any of it."

I glanced at Nash for confirmation, but he still had his head buried in his hands. He was really taking Scott's breakdown hard, and I couldn't blame him. I'd be devastated if anything happened to Emma. Especially something I could have prevented. Which was why the whole thing had to end now, even if that meant turning the whole mess over to my dad.

"Exactly what kind of trouble are these boys in?" my father demanded softly. "And what does it have to do with you?"

Nash finally looked up, his eyes shiny and rimmed in red. His hands shook, clenched in his lap, and I wanted to sink onto the couch next to him and tell him it would be okay. That none of it was really his fault. He hadn't given his friends the Demon's Breath, and we didn't know for sure that acting earlier would actually have saved Scott. For all we knew, sending him into withdrawal earlier might only have escalated his breakdown.

But I stayed at the table because Nash looked like he wanted to wallow in private misery. I wanted to respect that. To give him some time. But if he so much as looked at me, I'd be across the room in an instant.

I shrugged, meeting my dad's gaze reluctantly. "I don't think it has anything to do with me." Though Scott's shadow man's insistence that the whole thing was my fault was certainly nagging at the back of my mind. I sucked in a deep breath and spat out the rest of it before I could chicken out.

"Scott and Doug are taking Demon's Breath, and it's making them crazy. Literally."

"What?" my father demanded, at the exact moment Harmony dropped an egg on the kitchen floor. She just stood there, her open hand palm up and empty, slimy egg white oozing over the linoleum toward the toe of one worn sneaker.

Then understanding sank in—I saw its progression across her face—and she stepped absently over the busted egg. "That's why you were asking—"

My father turned on her. "You knew about this?"

"No!" Harmony glanced at me, and the hurt in her slowly swirling eyes withered my self-respect. "I thought she was talking about Regan Page! I had no idea there was Demon's Breath in their school!" Then her gaze narrowed on me again. "You didn't take any of it, did you?"

"Of course not!" It killed me that she even had to ask. But then, I had lied to her—if indirectly—in my search for facts. "Don't you think I've spent enough time strapped to a bed?"

My dad flinched and I almost felt guilty for throwing such a low blow. But he wasn't the one who'd had me hospitalized. My aunt and uncle had done that, in a very ill-thought-out attempt to help me "deal" with abilities I neither knew about nor understood. My father's only crime was leaving me with them in the first place.

"Nash and I were just trying to cut off their supply." I shrugged, hating how unsure of myself I sounded. And how juvenile our attempts at intervention must look to a couple of *bean sidhes* with a combined age of more than two centuries. "Dad, these guys have no idea what they're taking, or what it's doing to them. We took Scott's first balloon and gave it to Tod to dispose of, but he got another one, and—"

"You did *what?*" My father's voice was as hard as ice, and about as warm. "Tod knows about this?"

I shrugged and glanced at Nash, who looked like he wanted to disappear as he avoided his mother's look of disbelief and confusion. "We were assuming you wouldn't want us to take the balloon to the Netherworld ourselves…."

"You assumed right." Yet somehow my father didn't look very happy about my display of uncommon sense. "How did two human boys get their hands on Demon's Breath in the first place?"

"They…" I started, but then a sharp shake of Nash's head caught my attention, and I looked up to find him staring at me intently. And suddenly I wasn't sure what to do. We'd agreed to tell our parents about the Demon's Breath, and technically we'd done that. But Nash clearly didn't want them to know about Everett. Or maybe about the party.

My father watched me expectantly, waiting for me to finish my aborted thought. "They bought it from some guy who sells it in party balloons. He calls it frost." Which was true… "We could ask Doug—"

"No!" My father's palm slapped the table and it shook beneath my arm. "Stay away from him, Kaylee. Harmony, Brendon, and I will take care of this. I don't want you anywhere near that kid. Ever."

I nodded slowly, unsure what else to do. My dad was starting to sound paranoid. I had to go to school, and unless he'd miraculously graduated in the past few hours, so did Doug.

Harmony knelt on the kitchen floor in front of the cracked egg with a dish rag in one hand, but her attention was focused on me. "How bad off are they? Scott and Doug."

"They're both seeing things, but it's obviously affecting Scott a lot worse than Doug," I said, thinking about Nash's conjecture that Doug had a little Netherworld blood somewhere in his genealogy.

"Scott totally lost it today at school," Nash added, and I glanced at him in surprise; he'd hardly spoken since we'd left the hospital. "He was seeing things, and hearing things, and he was literally scared of his own shadow."

"Assuming it really is his shadow…" I said. Nash and I hadn't discussed my theory that Scott wasn't really hallucinating, but I figured if anyone would know for sure about the side effects of Demon's Breath, it would be Harmony.

"What do you mean?" she asked.

But Nash answered before I could. "Kaylee got creeped out by Scott's shadow fixation. He was talking to them, and listening to them, and the whole thing was pretty convincing. Plus, there was the knife." He shrugged and shot me a concerned, almost condescending look of sympathy. "It's no wonder she started to believe him. She was terrified. I was scared, too."

I bristled, glaring at him. "You think I'm imagining this? I was *not* creeped out!" Though I wasn't going to deny being afraid of the knife.

"Kay…" Nash stood and made his way into the kitchen, his voice flowing over me like warm silk. "He was delusional, and you were scared, and bleeding, and in shock. Anyone would have been freaked out, but try not to read too much into anything Scott said or did. He's not playing with a full deck anymore."

I shook my head so hard my brain felt like it was bouncing in my skull, but I couldn't shake the seductive feel of his voice in my mind. The overwhelming urge to nod my head, close my mouth, and let the whole thing play out without me.

I fought it, but struggling was like trying to swim in a huge vat of warm honey, when it would have been so much easier simply to sink into the sweetness. "Stop Influencing me," I whispered, when what I really wanted to do was shout.

"Nash!" Harmony snapped, and his warm mental presence dissipated like fog in bright sunlight.

Furious now, I pushed my chair away from the table, twisting my injured arm in the process. I gasped over the fresh throb and clutched my arm to my chest, but the pain helped clear my head and I rounded on him, fighting angry tears and the sharp sting of betrayal. "I'm not some hysterical kid, and *I am not crazy!*" Even the implication that my logic had been compromised triggered my very worst fears.

And Nash damn well knew that.

"Kay, no one's saying you're crazy." My father stood, too, and when he reached out for me, I let him pull me close. "You've had a traumatic day, and he was just trying to calm you down, though admittedly he's going about it the wrong way." He shot a pointed scowl at Nash, who had the decency to look horrified by what he'd done. So why the hell had he done it?

"I'm sorry, Kaylee." Nash let me see the swirl of regret in his eyes. But I couldn't forgive him. Not for this. Not yet.

"Stay out of my head, Nash." I stepped back when he reached for me, and he looked like I'd punched him in the gut. Some small part of me felt bad about that, but the rest of me was pissed. I had more to say about this, but not in front of our parents.

So I sat at the table again and ground my teeth when he sat in the chair next to mine.

"I assume people noticed Scott acting strange?" my dad

asked as he crossed the kitchen, obviously eager to pull the discussion back on track.

"Um, yeah." Nash fought to catch my gaze, and when I refused to look at him, he fingered a crack in the weathered kitchen table. "But they all think he was high on something… normal." He glanced at his mother, who'd just finished cleaning up the egg slime. "Is there anything we can do for him?"

Harmony shook her head slowly. "The damage to his brain is permanent. And withdrawal will be very hard on him in a human hospital, because all they can do is restrain him to keep him from hurting himself. The only medications I know of that can make him feel better come from the Netherworld."

"Can you get him any of those?" I asked. "Assuming they keep him at Arlington Memorial?"

She leaned with one hip on the counter, drying her hands on a damp dishrag. "I don't work in mental health, but I can probably get in to see him once or twice. And if I can't, Tod can."

"What about Doug?" I asked. "He's not as bad off as Scott is, but the night he hit my car, he said he saw someone in his passenger's seat."

"That's easy enough," Nash shrugged, looking optimistic for the first time since we'd left school. "Next time we hang out, I'll just slip whatever weird medication he needs into his drink." He glanced at Harmony again, eyes shining in either hope or desperation. "You can get whatever he needs, right?"

"I think so. But it won't do any good until the Demon's Breath is completely out of his system…"

"And we still don't know how to cut off the supply," I finished.

"You let us worry about that," my father said with a note of finality he'd probably perfected kicking drunks out of his parents' pub in Ireland. "Let's get you something to eat, then I want you to take a nap while I'm here to make sure you wake up in your own bed."

I didn't even try to argue. I was exhausted, and I wouldn't be any help to Emma or Doug until I could think straight.

My dad and Harmony messed around in the kitchen, trying to put together a decent meal and discuss the situation without saying anything that would upset me. Because apparently exhaustion and blood loss had combined to make me look about as sturdy as a blown-glass vase.

After several minutes spent listening to them whisper, I plodded to my room without even a glance in Nash's direction.

He followed me.

I collapsed stomach-down on my bed while he stood in the doorway. "Go away."

He took that as an invitation to sit at my desk.

"I'm sorry."

"You should be." I turned to face the window, fluffing my pillow under one cheek, and my desk chair creaked as he stood. A moment later, he knelt on the opposite side of the bed, inches from my face. "What the hell is wrong with you lately?" I was worried about the frost invasion too, but it hadn't turned me into a controlling bitch.

"Kaylee, please..."

"That was messed up, Nash. That was...slimy." I sat up and scooted back on the bed to put distance between us. "You make me think I want things I don't really want to do, and it's like losing control of myself. It's worse than being strapped to a hospital bed because it's not some stranger who has to let me up when I stop fighting. It's you, and I shouldn't have to fight you." I blinked back tears, almost as mad at myself for crying as I was at him for invading my mind. "I don't want your voice in my head anymore. Not even to help me."

Nash nodded slowly, his eyes churning with too many emotions for me to interpret. "I'm so sorry, Kaylee. I swear it'll never happen again." He swallowed and glanced at his hands, where they gripped the edge of my mattress. "It's just that everything is so messed up, and it's all my fault. Scott could have killed you, and I...I'm just not thinking straight right now."

"I know." I wasn't, either. I was running on caffeine and adrenaline, both of which were fading fast.

But before he could say anything else, my phone dinged, and I leaned to one side to dig it from my front pocket.

There was a text from Emma. R U OK? LB said you narced on Scott.

Crap. I'd forgotten that Laura Bell—LB—had been home sick all day. She'd obviously seen them load me and Scott into ambulances—his under police escort—and had reported her version of the event.

It was probably all over school. And since I couldn't tell anyone the truth, Laura's version—which evidently blamed me for getting the quarterback arrested on drug charges—would stand on the record.

Great.

I tried to text her back, but I couldn't type very well without my right hand, so after two failed attempts, Nash held out his hand for my phone, watching my face closely. Letting him help would mean I'd forgiven him.

I sighed and gave him my phone. "Tell her I'm fine, and I'll explain later," I said, and he nodded, typing almost as fast with two thumbs as I could. "And that I did *not* rat on Scott."

The part about Scott trying to kill me could wait for another day.

13

EMMA EYED ME in concern when I collapsed into my chair beside her in chemistry on Friday morning. She'd been pre-occupied with Doug for most of yesterday and hadn't noticed my exhaustion, but evidently my zombie impersonation was now too obvious to be overlooked.

"Wow, Kaylee, you look like crap," she whispered as the girl in front of me passed a stapled test packet over her shoulder.

"Thanks." I shot Emma a good-humored smile. At least, I hoped it looked good-humored. "I haven't been getting much sleep."

After Nash and Harmony left the night before, I'd collapsed on the couch—again in my homemade protective gear—but got very little rest, because this time my father refused to sleep and I could feel him watching me. I had two death dreams in a four-hour span, and my dad woke me up from both of them the moment the first note of a soul song erupted from my mouth.

Each time, he sat on the coffee table with a spiral-bound notebook, pen ready to go, but I had no new details to offer.

Same dark figure. Same falling through the Nether-smog. Same panic welling inside my dream throat. Same featureless face I couldn't identify.

Between the dream-screaming, the butchered forearm, and my near-death experience, peaceful sleep was a fond and somewhat distant memory. Yet, thanks to Scott's absence and Laura Bell's sensational but inaccurate gossip, the last school day of the semester was even worse than the sleepless night it followed.

I could feel them staring at me as I flipped open my test booklet. They'd been watching me all morning. Ogling the bandage my right sleeve wouldn't cover, which made it obvious that something big had gone down the day before, but left the details tantalizingly vague.

I pretended not to hear the whispers in the hall, rumors linking my name with Scott's. Wondering if he and I had been cheating on Nash and Sophie, which was easily the most ridiculous speculation I'd ever heard.

Until I heard someone claim that Nash had cut me—and was the source of whatever mysterious damage Scott had suffered—when he caught the two of us together.

There were other, quieter rumors from people who'd seen Scott's breakdown in class or in the cafeteria. They knew something had been wrong with him before we'd ever left school, but their tales were less exciting and never really caught on. Which left me and Nash to bear the brunt of the rumors and the stares.

And Sophie, of course. Her conspicuous absence only fanned the flames of the rumor bonfire consuming the school, and for the first time, she found herself tied to a stake at the center of the blaze, condemned to burn alongside me.

I couldn't really blame her for skipping school. Especially

considering she had no idea what had really happened between me, Scott, and Nash. For all I knew, she'd actually bought the load of crap Laura was shoveling.

"Just ignore them." Emma glared across the room at a couple of juniors whispering and staring at me while they waited for test booklets. "Their own lives aren't interesting enough to warrant gossip," she said, loud enough for the whole class to hear.

Mrs. Knott frowned and cleared her throat, and Emma avoided her eyes as she flipped open her test. But as soon as the teacher turned away, Em kicked my chair softly to regain my attention. "I'm really worried about Doug," she whispered. "He didn't show up for his English midterm this morning." Ever since Scott's freakout at school, she'd been watching Doug closely for signs that he was headed down the same path. "He's hardly eating anything. And this is going to sound stupid, but his hands are always cold."

I tried to smile and calm her down. She couldn't help him, so worrying would do her no good. "I'm sure that doesn't mean anything, Em. Nash's hands are usually freezing, and he's…"

No. I closed my eyes and swallowed thickly. It was a coincidence. Nash wasn't using. He was helping me get rid of frost for good. He knew how dangerous it was, and he was just as repulsed by the thought of sucking hellion breath as I was.

But Doug *was* using, and it *would* kill him.

I hadn't told Emma the truth about the Demon's Breath, even after what happened with Scott, because Dad and Harmony agreed that the less she knew, the safer she'd be from Everett and his Netherworld supplier. But watching her now, forehead wrinkled in concern for the first high school guy she'd shown any interest in, I couldn't help thinking that Dad and Harmony were wrong this time.

I knew better than most that ignorance was neither blissful nor safe, and it didn't seem fair to put Emma through what I'd suffered. Especially considering that Scott had turned out to be dangerous on Demon's Breath.

What if Doug did, too?

"Em, I need to tell you something." Her brows rose, and she nodded, but then Mrs. Knott walked down the aisle between us and I'd lost my chance to speak. The test had begun. "After class," I mouthed, then turned my attention to my midterm.

Unfortunately, Doug was waiting for Emma after class, and she waved to me apologetically as she wrapped one arm around his waist, promising she'd catch me at lunch.

At first, I was surprised that Doug hadn't asked me what happened to Scott. Until I noticed the half-eaten candy bar in his fist as they walked off. He held it without the wrapper, and despite his tight grip, the chocolate wasn't melting against his skin. He was frosted, and probably not thinking about anything but staying that way.

Tod's hospital shift started at noon, so I'd fully expected him to pop into class during one of my early midterms, demanding to know what he'd missed when I couldn't possibly answer him. But I didn't see him all morning, and I couldn't help wondering why he was never around during his off hours, but would skip out on work to come bug me and Nash.

By eleven-thirty, my morning overdose of caffeine had worn off and I wobbled on my feet, flinching when I caught myself against the wall with my bad arm. I'd survived my first three midterms—though I couldn't swear I'd aced them—and had three still to go. But after only twelve hours of sleep over the past three days, I could barely spell my name right, and passing the remaining tests seemed like a long shot, at best.

So during lunch, Nash and I snuck out of the cafeteria and into the parking lot, where I slept in the reclined seat of my rental car while he devoured a cafeteria cheeseburger and crammed for his physics test, ready to wake me if I so much as hummed in my sleep.

I jolted awake thirty-eight minutes into our forty-five-minute lunch period, sitting straight up in the driver's seat with Nash staring at me like I'd just recited the U.S. presidents in my sleep. An ability which probably would have come in handy during my history test.

"What happened?" I blinked, confused, until I remembered I was still at school, in a car I hadn't completely gotten used to yet. Was that why I felt so…disoriented? But exhaustion couldn't explain why I'd evidently sat up in my sleep.

Nash's eyes churned steadily with fear and with some emotion I couldn't quite identify, and as I watched, his irises began to settle as he got a handle on the scare I'd obviously given him. "You were making weird noises. So I woke you up."

I was? I didn't remember having any dreams at all, much less the horrifying, recurring death dream. But something had obviously happened, and it had clearly scared the crap out of Nash.

In spite of my rude—and odd—awakening, the short nap helped more than I'd thought possible. Or maybe that was the Mountain Dew Nash handed me as we walked back into the building, just in time for fifth period. "Drink fast and work hard," he said, giving me the sweetest, peppermint-scented kiss on the nose. "I'll see you in the gym after school."

He was trying really hard to make up for our fight the day before, and the caffeine fix was good for several bonus points.

But by the time the final bell rang, the Mountain Dew was wearing off and my arm was really starting to throb. I couldn't stand the thought of spending my Friday afternoon painting booths for my cousin's pet project—left-handed, thanks to my injury—while her friends stared and whispered. If Sophie was skipping, we could, too. So I drove Nash home and crashed on his bed while he played Xbox.

Nash shook me awake a couple of hours later, with hands so cold I could feel them through my shirt. I was relieved to discover that I had neither dreamed nor struck any odd positions in my sleep. "You have to get up if we're going to make it to the party," he whispered, soft, warm lips brushing my cheek.

The setting sun cast slanted shadow bars across Nash's room through his half-closed blinds, and I blinked in the crimson glare, trying to fully wake up. The alarm clock on his bedside table said it was almost five-thirty. "Mmmm…" He smelled so good I wanted to bury my face in his shirt and breathe him in. Then go back to sleep.

Who needs food and water? Nash and slumber would be enough to sustain me. Right?

"What party?" I mumbled, pushing myself up on my good arm, in spite of the heavy hand of sleep threatening to pull me back under.

"Fuller's. Remember? We were going to find Everett?"

And that's when reality came crashing in on me, washing away the serenity that waking up next to Nash had lent me.

Doug's party. Everett's balloons. Scott's knife. My sliced-up arm. Suddenly my head hurt and my stomach was churning in dread.

"I can't believe he's still throwing a party, with one of his best friends in the hospital." And charged with a felony.

Nash shrugged. "The crowd will be bigger than ever tonight, everyone hoping to hear what really happened to Carter."

Well, they wouldn't hear it from me. "My dad'll kill me if we go to Doug's." Not that my father's caution had ever stopped me from helping a friend in need before.

Nash rolled his eyes and pressed the power button on his Xbox, then shoved it against the scratched chest of drawers his television sat on. "If we don't go, who's going to watch out for Emma?"

"Tod…?" I started, but the flaw in that plan was immediately obvious. "Well, I assume he has to actually show up for work at some point."

"Let's hope." Nash hesitated as I ran my fingers through long, sleep-tangled hair. "Maybe you can talk her out of going…" he finally suggested. "You two could do something girlie tonight and let me handle Everett."

I shook my head as I stepped into my first sneaker. "I already tried that. After what happened with Scott, she's determined to keep an eye on Doug." I had to sit on the bed to tug the second shoe on, then I met Nash's frustrated gaze with one of my own.

Nash sighed and sat on the edge of his desk, and I sat straighter as a new thought occurred to me. "Maybe we're making this too hard. Why don't we just get him alone at the party, cross over with him, and leave him in the Netherworld?" Which was a virtual death sentence—or worse—for anyone native to the human world. Yet I felt only a fleeting pang of guilt over that thought, after what Everett's little enterprise had done to Scott, and would do to anyone else who sampled his stash. "I mean, he can't *sell* in our world if he can't *get* to our world. Right?"

His brows rose. "You think he can't cross on his own?

If that's true, how is he getting Demon's Breath in the first place?"

Crap. My disappointment crested in a wave of embarrassment.

Either Everett could cross over on his own—which meant he couldn't be trapped in the Netherworld—or he was working with someone who could. In which case getting rid of Everett wouldn't stop the distribution of frost into our world.

I grabbed my backpack from the floor and tossed it over one shoulder, squinting against the reddish light peeking through the blinds. "Nash, we have to tell my dad about Everett."

Nash rolled his eyes. "What's your dad going to do that we can't? Other than make sure we're never welcome at another party…"

"I don't know. But what are we supposed to do? Threaten to scream until Everett's ears bleed?"

Nash sighed and grabbed my keys from the desktop, where I'd dropped them when we came in. "Look, if your dad busts up the party, Fuller will wind up hanging out alone with Emma all night. Either high off his new stash, or crazy from withdrawal."

My heart dropped into my stomach. I swear I heard it splash into the Mountain Dew I drank instead of eating lunch.

He was right. My dad could break up the party and possibly even stop Everett from selling to everyone there. At least for one night. But he couldn't save Emma from Doug once they were alone.

That was up to me.

We went to my house first, so I could change and pack an overnight bag. On the way out, I left a note for my dad on the fridge, telling him I was going out with Nash and that I'd be spending the night with Emma—so she wouldn't have a chance to be alone with Doug—and that he was welcome to call and check up on me. It's not like I'd be sleeping. Ever again, evidently.

Then, because I knew he couldn't answer his cell at work, I called and left a voice mail saying the same thing. He was working late again, to make up for the pay he'd lost the day before thanks to my trip to the hospital, and with any luck he wouldn't get either message until his double shift was over. Around midnight. By which time I hoped to be stretched out on Emma's bedroom floor, halfway through a pint of Death by Chocolate and a B-grade '80s horror flick, safe from the perils of the real world.

Make that *both* worlds.

EMMA'S AFTERNOON SHIFT at the Cinemark didn't end until seven, so she couldn't make it to the party until eight. Nash and I stopped for cheap tacos and still got there by seven-thirty.

Mr. Fuller had taken Doug's twenty-eight-year-old step-mother with him to some professional conference in New York, leaving Doug alone in a house big enough to sleep the whole football team.

Or host the entire senior class.

We parked at the end of the street again, and I felt marginally more confident in the safety of my car this time, because it wasn't really mine and because Doug wouldn't be driving. He was already home.

The party was in full swing long before we got there—music blasting, drinks flowing, people dancing, and couples ducking out the back door or up the stairs. In the den, a dozen upperclassmen had gathered around two guys with video game controllers, engrossed in some virtual tournament. One room over, two half-dressed couples had found an alternate use for

Mr. Fuller's pool table, and in the kitchen, one of the football team's managers was manning a keg someone's big brother had bought.

I waved to Brant Williams across the living room and he smiled back, dark, friendly eyes shining at me over the heads of most of our classmates. As Nash pulled me through the crowd, I spared a moment to hope Brant miraculously decided he needed to be somewhere else before Everett showed up.

People everywhere shouted greetings to Nash, and more than a few of them looked surprised to find me with him. Evidently seeing us together discredited the worst of the rumors about me and Scott. Several guys asked Nash how Scott was doing, and he told them all he hadn't heard anything since yesterday.

He'd called the hospital that afternoon, but they would only release information to family members. We were hoping Tod could give us an update, but neither of us had seen him since he'd disappeared from my living room the afternoon before.

Sophie was a no-show at the party. While I was glad she was staying out of trouble—and out of my way—I was starting to wonder if she'd even show up for the carnival she'd helped organize. I considered calling her, but she wouldn't answer her phone if it showed my number, so I decided to check in with her dad in the morning. Uncle Brendon knew what was going on—much more than Sophie knew, anyway—and had no doubt taken the Netherworld element into consideration when he let her skip school.

I almost felt sorry for her.

We found Doug near the back of the living room, pouring something stronger than beer into a clear plastic cup of soda. "Hey, man, is Em with you?" He handed Nash a can of Coke from a cooler sitting on a thick rug thrown over the hardwood floor.

"She'll be here around eight," I said as Doug rooted through the cooler again. He came up with a Diet Coke and a regular, holding them both up for me to choose from. I pointed to the regular, and he grinned as he dropped the diet back into the cooler.

"Atta girl. Want somethin' extra?" He held up the small bottle of Absolut he'd poured into his own cup.

"No thanks." There was no way I'd handicap my logic or coordination with Everett the Netherworld crack dealer scheduled to make an appearance.

"She has control issues," Nash said, and I could have kicked him into the next time zone.

Doug raised one brow at me, then shot Nash a sympathetic look. "Lucky you."

"I'm driving," I insisted, but the damage was already done.

"Whatever," Doug said, then something behind me caught his attention and he grinned.

"Hey, guys!" Emma threw her arm around my waist. She smelled like vanilla and looked like sex poured into a skirt. Her sister's skirt, if I had to guess.

"I thought you had to work," I said as she let Doug pull her close.

"I got off early." She stood on her toes to kiss Doug as his hand wandered down from her waist, and I had a moment to hope he hadn't yet unsealed a fresh balloon before she grinned at me like she'd been huffing goofy gas. But this high was natural. I could tell because, as I watched, Doug's hand twitched around her hip.

He hadn't had his fix yet. Which meant we hadn't missed our chance.

"I didn't think you'd come after yesterday," Emma said, her smile fading with the memory of what little I'd told her about Scott and his knife.

Nash popped open his Coke. "She needed a little fun."

Emma grinned. "Me, too."

"Well, then, start with this." Doug handed Emma the cup he'd spiked for himself, and she drained half of it in one gulp.

"Hey, Em, can I crash with you tonight?" I asked, popping the top on my own can.

"Sure. Your dad being a pain?"

I shrugged, letting her draw her own conclusions.

"Hey, Fuller, is your friend here yet?" Nash asked, his hand tightening almost imperceptibly around mine.

But Doug shook his head. "I wish he'd hurry up."

"What friend?" Emma asked, but instead of answering, Doug pushed her cup toward her mouth until she emptied it, then pulled her into the crowd of writhing bodies, already moving to the heavy beat.

With nothing else to do until Everett showed up, Nash and I joined them on the dance floor and I was just starting to relax when a dark smudge on the edge of my vision seemed to freeze my blood in my veins.

I went still while all around me bodies moved in time to the song, oblivious to the danger now walking among them. I couldn't see the door through the crowd, but I couldn't miss the dark shape hovering near the ceiling—a huge black balloon bouquet, like the centerpiece of an over-the-hill birthday party.

Everett had arrived. And he'd brought enough frost to bake the entire senior class.

14

"Look!" I shouted into Nash's ear, to be heard over the thumping, blaring music. I clutched his arm, unable to tear my horrified gaze from the balloons floating a couple of feet below Fuller's twelve-foot ceiling. Before Nash had a chance to focus on the problem, I tugged him toward the edge of the crowd, hoping the noise would abate so we could hear each other.

And maybe see more than three feet into the crowd.

Near the edge of the room I let Nash go and nodded toward the foyer, where the bouquet still hovered over the room like a poisonous cloud. What kind of dealer walks right in the front door? But then, I guess it's hard to be discreet carrying that many balloons.

"That's Everett, right?" We couldn't see him, but who else would bring three dozen black balloons to a high school party?

Nash looked up. Blood drained from his face so quickly I wasn't sure how he remained conscious. He nodded slowly and began making his way through the crowd, still clutching my hand. I tried not to step on too many feet or bump into anyone with my bandaged arm as my heart raced fast enough to leave me light-headed. Everett was here. And we still had no plan.

Nash stopped when we got to the front window and had a clear view into the entryway, and his hand clenched tighter around mine. I followed his swirling gaze to see that the guy holding the balloons wasn't much older than the crowd—twenty, at the outside—and that he was flanked by two of the most beautiful, eerily flawless girls I'd ever seen.

Between them, Everett, who looked human, was tall and too thin, his slight build only exaggerated by an oversize T-shirt and jeans that barely hung from the points of his hips. I couldn't help wondering if he would let go of the balloons to pull his pants up if they fell off, which was a definite possibility. Based on the hazy look in his eyes and his death grip on the collection of strings, I would have bet my life the answer was no.

Everett wasn't just selling; he was using. Though I couldn't imagine how he stayed sane enough to run his business.

"It's about time!" Doug called across the room, and I looked up to see him shoving his way through the crowd, dragging Emma behind him. "I have a room set up for you in the back." Doug's gaze jumped from the balloons to Everett's face, his hand twitching at his side. He was hurting—bad—and surely we weren't the only ones who could see that.

Emma raised both perfectly arched brows as she wandered toward me. "Who's that?"

"Everett," I said, desperately wishing I'd been able to keep her away from the party. "Doug's supplier."

"Yeah, I puzzled that out on my own. Who are *they?*" She nodded toward the foyer again and I realized she meant the girls. So I took a closer look and finally realized what was bothering me about them. It wasn't their surreal beauty—

though, for the record, nothing so perfect should ever really exist.

Nor was it the fact that they were identical—not like twins, but like two copies of the same person. The *exact* same person. Same long, straight, white-blond hair parted on the left, with exactly the same crook halfway down the part. The same black eyes shining like they were lit from within. They had the same brilliant white teeth and exactly the same pale skin with the barest brush of pink on unfreckled cheekbones. And they stood at exactly the same height, with their right legs bent at the knee.

The whole carbon-copy aspect was definitely creepy, but it wasn't what nagged at the back of my mind, like a skeletal finger tapping my shoulder. What bothered me was their stance. The girls flanked Everett not like arm candy, but like bodyguards.

But I had to be imagining that. Right? What could two slim, unarmed girls in identical white-lace minidresses do in defense of a man six inches taller, with feet the size of small boats?

The crowd parted for Doug and his strange entourage, and they passed through the living room and out of sight in seconds.

"I need another drink," I said for Emma's benefit, already moving back into the crowd. Em had figured out who Everett was, but not what he was really selling, and I didn't want her involved in…whatever was about to go down.

"Let's go!" I whispered, tugging on Nash's arm when he made no move to follow me.

Emma shrugged and held up her empty cup. "I could use a refill, too."

I groaned inwardly, trying to catch Nash's eye. He finally

met my gaze and nodded. He had a plan. But instead of clueing me in, he walked off toward the kitchen, apparently expecting us to follow.

Irritated, I smiled at Emma and wound my way through the crowd after Nash. Several feet from the kitchen, he turned to walk backward, facing us with a glance at Emma's empty cup. "What are you drink—?"

Nash tripped over his own foot and grabbed the arm of the girl next to him for balance. She squealed and overcompensated, dumping her beer all over Emma's shirt.

Em screeched and pulled the cold, wet material away from her skin.

"I'm so sorry, Emma!" Nash ducked into the kitchen and grabbed a towel from the counter, then tossed it to her as his eyes met mine, swirling with mischief.

"What if that hadn't worked?" I whispered, reaching around him to pull a strip of paper towels from a wooden rack.

"Then the keg would have had a malfunction." He turned back to Emma, faking a concerned expression that made me want to laugh. Until I heard his next words. "Kaylee, your overnight bag's in the car, right? You have a shirt she can borrow?"

I glared at Nash in a cold wash of comprehension. He wasn't just trying to get Emma out of the way, he was getting rid of me, too! But I wasn't going to be pushed out of danger because of some prehistoric sense of chivalry. Nash couldn't even cross over on his own! He needed me.

My jaw clenched, and I had to force my mouth open to answer the question, as Emma stared at me beseechingly, still holding the front of her drenched top. "Of course." I dug my keys from my pocket, intending to hand them to her when Nash shot me a warning look and stepped close enough to whisper in my ear, though it probably looked like he was going for a much more intimate contact. "Go with her and keep her out there for a few minutes. I don't want her to come back looking for us and walk in on something she shouldn't see or hear. Do you?" he continued, before I could protest.

And I could hardly say no. Keeping Emma out of danger was my idea. I just hadn't planned on overseeing that part of the plan personally....

I nodded grimly and clenched my keys in my fist, glaring straight at Nash so he could see the anger surely churning in my eyes.

But he only shrugged apologetically, then watched me lead her out the door and into the frigid night, headed toward my car and away from the action—and the answers I was desperate for.

"This f-f-figures," Emma said, chattering violently as we clacked down the brick driveway. "I actually remembered to bring a change of clothes to work and I got off early. I should have known something would go wrong." She crossed her arms over her chest in spite of the cold beer probably freezing to her bra at that very moment. "Maybe we should stay at your house tonight, so I can wash the beer out of this shirt before my mom smells it. Or Traci. Traci's going to kill me."

"It's your sister's shirt?" I rubbed my arms, trying to get rid of the chill bumps prickling my skin.

"You think my mom would let me buy something like this?" She held her arms out to show off the plunging neckline of the clingy, sparkly top.

When I had the car unlocked, Emma crawled into the backseat and pulled her shirt off while I dug in my bag for the one I'd planned to wear in the morning. It was just a T-shirt, but because I was smaller than Emma up top, it would look much better on her. Unfortunately, for that same reason, she'd either have to go braless or stay cold, wet, and smelly. My spare bra wouldn't fit her unless she could time-travel back to age twelve.

"Does this look obscene?" Em asked, and I turned to see her pulling my snug, crimson T-shirt into place over her bra-less chest.

"Yes."

"Good." She grinned and glanced at the rearview mirror. "Do you have a brush in there?" Em nodded at the bag I still held in my lap.

"I forgot it." I'd packed in a hurry. "But I think Nash keeps a comb in his duffel." I pointed to the right rear floorboard, where Nash had tossed his gym bag after school.

Emma lifted the bag onto the seat with one hand and laughed. "Not planning to do much reading over the holiday, is he?"

"Not if I can help it." I grinned, thinking about two straight weeks with nothing to keep us apart but a few shifts at the Cinemark and what little sleep we couldn't do without. Assuming we ever solved my current sleeping issues.

Emma unzipped the bag. "What's this? It's *cold*." Something red and shapeless took up half of the duffel. Emma pulled it out with one hand, and her brows rose in confusion.

My next words died in my throat. I could barely breathe around them.

She held a bright red balloon, closed by a weighted black plastic clip.

No. My hand clenched around the back of the front passenger's seat as I twisted for a better look.

"I thought Nash wasn't into this." The surprise in Emma's voice was a weak echo of the denial I wanted to shout.

"He's not," I insisted, in spite of the traitorous voice of doubt in my head and the painful pounding of my heart. "Everett's balloons are black." But that didn't mean anything. Regardless of color, why else would Nash have a clipped, weighted party balloon in his gym bag? A very *cold* clipped, weighted party balloon…

It's not his. Maybe he'd confiscated it from another teammate Doug had sold to. After all, I'd never seen Nash talking to his own shadow or twitching from withdrawal. Nor had I ever smelled Demon's Breath on him. In fact, I'd only smelled…

Peppermint. When did Nash start chewing gum?

No. He'd helped me get rid of Scott's first balloon, and…

I sank into the driver's seat, devastated, as the pieces started to fall into place. I hadn't actually seen Nash give the balloon to Tod. I'd just assumed he had because he'd said he would.

The mood swings. Aggression. Cold hands. He'd stopped me from telling my dad about Everett. Then he'd sent me outside with Emma instead of letting me confront the dealer.

Nash was using. Tears burned in my eyes. I'd wondered briefly before, then dismissed my suspicion as paranoia. I hadn't wanted to believe it. But I couldn't deny it now. *How could I be so stupid?*

"Kaylee?" Emma said, one hand on the back of my seat.

"We have to go. Now." I started to shove my key into the ignition, then stopped when I remembered the balloon. I would *not* have that thing in the car with us.

My vision swimming in tears, I twisted and grabbed the balloon from her. "Stay here," I said, then got out and slammed my door, leaving Emma to stare after me in surprise.

I'd only made it ten steps from the car, my nose already freezing and dripping, when Nash stepped out of Doug's house and pulled the front door closed. He jogged down the steps and onto the sidewalk, shoving cold-reddened hands into his pockets, then stopped when he saw me.

I wanted to believe his eyes were swirling with something painful—regret, guilt, shame. But the truth was that it was too dark for me to tell.

"Tell me this isn't yours." Holding the balloon like a bomb, I stopped about eight feet from him—close enough to read his expression, but not to see his irises—and my stomach flip-flopped painfully. I took a deep breath, so cold it burned my lungs. "Tell me the truth, Nash."

He flinched and dropped his gaze. So I tried again. "Tell me this isn't yours."

Nash sucked in a deep breath and met my gaze. His shoulders slumped and his throat worked furiously, like it was trying to stop whatever he intended to say.

"I can't, Kaylee. It's mine."

15

Nash's admission shattered my fragile composure, splintering my thoughts like jagged shards of ice. For a moment, I could only stare at him, in shock so complete my whole body went numb—and not from the cold. Then the truth of his statement sank in. I spun around and stomped toward my car, anger and confusion raging inside me like two storm fronts about to collide.

"Kaylee, wait!" His words weren't what stopped me. It was the anguish in his voice, the crack on the last syllable, that made my feet pause and my hands clench dangerously around the unnaturally cold balloon.

Forcing my grip to relax, I turned slowly, struggling to unclench my jaw so I could speak. "This is what nearly got me killed yesterday, Nash." My voice was low and hoarse from both the winter air and the raw, holding-back-tears ache in my throat. "What can you possibly say to make me feel better about that? To make it okay that you've been taking the same *shit* Doug and Scott are taking, and lying to me about it?"

The bitter wind stung my face, almost as painfully cold as

the balloon stiffening my fingers, and when he didn't answer, I turned and headed for my car again. But this time his feet pounded on the sidewalk after me. "Kaylee, stop!"

Instead, I broke into a jog. Emma started to open her door, but I shook my head, telling her I was fine. And to stay in the car.

"It was an accident, Kay! Give me a chance to explain."

I whirled on him so fast he skidded to a halt, surprised by my sudden, furious stand. "You accidentally took a lethal inhalant native to another reality? How is that even possible, Nash? You just happen to breathe in at the wrong time?"

"Yeah." He shrugged, as if it were that simple, and I could only blink, unsure whether or not to take him seriously. Or if it even mattered. Even if he *had* inhaled unintentionally, what was he doing close enough to a hellion to breathe in its used air? Beyond that, what was he doing in the Netherworld in the first place?

"Can we go somewhere and talk?" Nash's voice was steady now, though his hands trembled visibly, even when he crossed his arms over his chest.

"I'm not leaving Emma alone, with Doug inside replenishing his stock. Are you going to help me get rid of the dealer, or don't you care if the rest of your friends wind up sharing a padded room with Scott?"

Nash flinched, and I almost felt guilty when I recognized the devastating regret etched in every line on his face. "Everett's gone, Kaylee," he said, remorse riding each word. "I told him to get out, or I'd call in a personal favor from a reaper." Nash forced a halfhearted grin, trying to evoke one from me, but I clung to my stony expression. "Let's go in and talk. Please."

I shook my head. "I'm not taking Emma back in there." I'd already seen what withdrawal from frost could do.

"Fine. Let's talk here." Nash shrugged out of his jacket and handed it to me, but I stepped back. I didn't want his coat *or* his borrowed warmth. Not knowing he'd been lying, and that he could be one missed fix away from hearing Scott's shadow man.

"You're shivering. Take the jacket." He shoved it at me again, and this time I gave in. I didn't want to hear his excuses, but I needed to hear everything he knew about Demon's Breath, and I was nearly frozen solid.

Nash reached for the balloon so I could put his jacket on, but I twisted harshly, angling it away from him. "Like I'm going to give this to *you*."

His eyes widened, irises swirling in pain and disappointment. But he had no right to look hurt; I was the one with a grievance.

I jogged back to my car, where Emma still watched us from the back window, and pulled open the front passenger's door.

"Are you gonna dump him?" she asked as I set the balloon on the leather seat.

"I don't know, but I have to talk to him. I need you to stay here until I get back. And don't mess with the balloon, okay? Don't even touch it."

Emma shrugged. "It creeps me out, anyway." She crossed both arms over the thin tee she'd borrowed. "But I need to go back in and check on Doug. He could be in there singing like the Chipmunks by now."

I shook my head and gave her a half smile. "Nash got rid of Everett before he could sell anything."

"Good. I'm going back in." Emma reached for the door handle, but I shook my head again.

"Em, I need you to trust me. The party's not safe anymore."

She hesitated. "Is this *bean sidhe* business?" We'd used that phrase to refer to anything involving the Netherworld that I couldn't fully explain to her. Considering that Nash and I had brought her back from the dead, she was usually pretty willing to let it go at that. For which I was unspeakably grateful.

I nodded and she frowned, but settled back into her seat. I dug in my pocket, then held out the key to the rental. "Here. Start the engine and turn on the heat. I'll be back in ten minutes, then we'll get some ice cream and a DVD."

"Fine. But I get to pick the movie. And the ice cream."

I forced a grin. "Deal."

She leaned over the seat and started the engine as I headed back to Nash, tossing my head toward the small winter garden to the left of Doug's house. I'd seen several thickly bundled couples on lawn chairs around the covered pool out back, but the enclosed side yard was deserted. And thanks to the music still thumping from the house, the chances of us being overheard were minimal.

Nash followed me through the gate and latched it behind us. "You want to sit?" He gestured toward one of the ornate stone benches in front of a line of tall evergreen shrubs.

I sat, and the cold seeped instantly through my jeans and into my skin. "The gum?" I eyed him frankly and was pleased to see him flinch.

"Covers the scent," he admitted, squinting in the harsh glow from a ground level floodlight.

My heart ached in disappointment, though I'd guessed as much, and I shifted on the cold, hard bench. "The chilly hands?" He nodded again, swallowing thickly, and I sucked in a painfully frigid breath before continuing. "And you didn't want to tell our parents…"

"I messed up—"

"You kept Scott's balloon, didn't you?" I demanded, vaguely frightened by the flat, hopeless quality of my own voice. "You weren't trying to help him. You were getting your fix for free."

Nash looked miserable. "Kaylee—"

"*Weren't* you?" I stood, anger pulsing through my veins, scorching my soul with each excruciating beat.

"Yes. But it was a weaker concentration than what I'm—" he shook his head and corrected his phrasing "—what I *was* getting. Mine comes in red balloons, and the black one wasn't really enough to…"

"Enough to do the job?" I could hear disgust in my voice. "How long?" I asked, but he only frowned, confused. "How long have you been lying to me?"

His eyes closed, and the stark shadow cast behind him slumped as his shoulders fell. "A month." He opened his eyes and stepped out of the light to watch me closely, like he was looking for something specific in my expression. "It happened when we crossed over, Kaylee. In a way, you started it."

"What?" We'd actually crossed into the Netherworld several times, but I had no memory of exposing either of us to Demon's Breath. "You're blaming me for this?"

"No." He sighed. "I'm just frustrated by the irony. The balloons were originally your idea. Remember?"

I did remember. I sank onto the bench again and barely felt the cold this time as shock roared through me like a roll of thunder.

I remembered thinking the balloon idea was a stroke of genius—a simple, innocent storage solution for a toxic, hard-to-transport substance. I remembered feeling like an enabler when we'd brought three balloons full of the Demon's Breath stored in Addy's lungs as payment for information from a desperate fiend. We'd taunted him with them, denying his need until he gave us what we wanted. I'd never felt so slimy in my life.

And then one of the balloons had popped, and...

Oh, *no*. One of the balloons had popped in Nash's face. He'd coughed and choked—because he'd accidentally inhaled.

And I hadn't even noticed.

"Why didn't you tell me?" I heard the sob in my voice, and it seemed to warble in time with the unsteady rhythm of my heart.

Nash sank onto the bench next to me and stared at his hands in his lap. "I didn't realize what had happened at first, and by the time I started feeling it, you were dying from Crimson Creeper venom. What was my stupid contact buzz compared to your life and Addy's soul?" He shrugged again, as if choosing my problem over his was no big deal. "But I couldn't fight it, and by the time you got better, I was hooked. It just snowballed from there."

Stunned, I let my head fall into my hands, my mind now as numb from shock as my nose was from the cold. How could I not have known? How could I have seen him nearly every day, and not noticed what was going on?

But that was just it. I'd barely seen Nash in the month after he was exposed, other than a few minutes between classes and half an hour at lunch. I'd been grounded on a massive scale, unavailable to him when he'd needed me most. When it was my fault he was exposed in the first place. I'd dragged him to the Netherworld, and I'd made Addy blow up those balloons.

Focus, Kaylee. There would be time to feel guilty later.

"You should have told me," I groaned, staring up at him again. "I could have helped you."

He shrugged, shoving chapped, clenched fists into his jeans

pockets. "I thought I could quit on my own, and you'd never have to know."

"I had a right to know!" I swiped the back of one frozen hand across my dripping nose. "I told you every secret I have—even the ones I wish I could forget—because I thought I could trust you." My hands clenched around nothing, as if I could wring the composure I needed from the air. "But you were lying the whole time. Why, Nash?"

"Because I didn't want you to know!" He stood and stomped across the concrete tiles, staring into the hedges before turning to face me, gesturing helplessly with one cold-reddened hand. "I can't fight it, Kaylee. I don't even *want* to fight it." He blinked, and his irises churned with fervor—with desperation for something I couldn't offer—and an ache settled deep into my chest like a bad cold.

"It feels like the whole world is buzzing, and when you come down from it, everything feels flat and colorless, and all you want to do is get that feeling back. Even before the withdrawal sets in, you'll do *anything* to get that feeling back, because as long as it lasts, nothing's wrong. It doesn't matter if you forget something, or lose something. Or if you fail someone. Nothing's wrong and everything feels good, and you never want it to end. Okay? I didn't want you to know that I don't ever want it to end...."

He sank onto the bench across from mine as his last tortured sentence trailed into silence, but for the thumping bass from the house behind me.

I could only stare at him, trying desperately to calm the storm of fear, disappointment, and anger lashing around inside me. "Nothing's wrong when you're on Demon's Breath because nothing's *important*." And I wanted to be important.

I wanted so badly to matter to him. To mean more than his next fix.

"Nash, it should matter to you that you let it go this far. That your habit got Scott locked up and nearly got me killed."

"No." Nash shook his head vehemently, his damp lashes glittering in the glare from the floodlight. "That had nothing to do with me. The guys have never even seen me with a balloon."

I believed him. He was meeting my eyes too boldly to be lying, his irises swirling calmly with sincerity. But the coincidence was too…coincidental. He had to be connected, even if he didn't know it.

I slid my frozen hands into my borrowed jacket pockets, and the right one curled around something cold and hard. I pulled out a weighted, black plastic balloon clip. "So, I'm assuming Everett is your supplier, too?"

Nash sighed. "Yeah. But I swear I had no idea he was selling to humans until Fuller actually said his name."

Again, I believed him. But again, it didn't matter. "He got to them through you. He must have. None of this makes sense otherwise."

"No." Nash shook his head, and I wasn't sure which one of us he was trying to convince. "Everett doesn't know my name, and I never gave him anyone else's."

I shrugged, a thin thread of panic tightening around the base of my spine, sending cold fingers across my flesh from the inside. "So, he followed you. He saw you at school and realized there's an entire untapped market out there. A whole world full of spoiled, careless kids with more money than sense."

"I don't know. Maybe…" Nash finally conceded.

"What's Everett's last name?" I sank onto the bench again

and hunched into Nash's jacket, suddenly overwhelmed by the exhaustion I'd been holding back by sheer will and caffeine.

"I don't know," Nash said, and I raised both brows at him. "I swear!" He shrugged defensively.

"Is he human?"

"Half. His mother's a harpy."

I bet that was a weird childhood. And his mixed blood certainly explained how he'd survived addiction long enough to turn a profit…. "What about those girls?"

Nash shrugged again, and dropped wearily onto the bench beside me. "I don't know. I've never seen them before. Junkies, maybe?"

They didn't look like junkies to me. But then, neither did Nash or Doug.

"How did you get hooked up with Everett?" My teeth had begun to chatter, and I had to concentrate to make myself understood. "How does one even find a Netherworld drug dealer?"

Nash exhaled, then stared at the white puff of breath, obviously avoiding my gaze. "I was referred to him."

That sick feeling returned, churning the contents of my stomach mercilessly. "Referred?"

"You have to understand, Kaylee," he began, turning suddenly toward me with a fevered look in his slowly swirling eyes. "You were still sick from the Creeper venom. We hadn't even buried Addy yet, and I started feeling weak, like I had low blood sugar or something. I couldn't concentrate on anything, but I didn't know what was wrong until I started shaking and twitching, like that fiend, when he was desperate for a hit. I didn't know what else to do. So I got Tod to cross over with me."

"*Tod* took you to the Netherworld?" Normally nothing Tod

did surprised me. He didn't see things from the normal human perspective—or even the normal *bean sidhe* perspective—and his moral compass always seemed to point just to the left of north. But Tod would never intentionally hurt Nash. Or let him hurt himself.

"He didn't know why," Nash insisted. "He owed me another favor—don't ask," he added when I opened my mouth to do just that. "And I called it in, no questions asked. He crossed me over, then came back for me half an hour later."

"So you, what? Tripped over Everett in the Netherworld?" I wiped my dripping nose on a tissue from Nash's left jacket pocket. "Can half harpies cross over?"

"Not on their own. I don't think Everett's ever been there." Nash glanced down at his lap, where his hands had nearly gone purple from the cold.

It took me a minute to understand. If he hadn't crossed over to find a dealer...

I felt the blood drain from my face and I backed away from him on the bench. "Please tell me you didn't go there looking for a hellion." Sucking Demon's Breath from a balloon was bad enough, but from the *source?*

Nash frowned, conflict written in every line of his face. "I didn't know what else to do. I was desperate."

"What hellion?" I demanded, so softly I could barely hear my own words. I only knew of two in the area—or the Netherworld version of our area—and was horrified by the thought of Nash going near either of them.

"I had to, Kaylee." His voice pleaded with me to understand. "I thought I was dying. You don't know what it's like."

"Nash, who was it?"

"Avari," he whispered.

My heart dropped into my stomach. A face flashed from

my memory, along with a chill that had nothing to do with the seasonal temperature.

Avari was the demon of greed who'd made a bid for my soul when I was dying in the Netherworld. His icy voice haunted my nightmares, promising that he would one day feast from my suffering, even if he had to destroy everyone I loved to get to me.

Evidently he'd started with Nash.

16

Terror and anger twisted through me like vines dripping poison into my veins. I shot off the bench, and Nash grabbed my arm to stop me from leaving. "Kaylee, please…" he begged, his warm fingers leaching some of the chill from my own. If his skin had been colder than mine—if I'd had any reason to suspect he still had frost in his system—I'd have run all the way to my car without looking back.

But because he was warm, I turned and made myself look at him. "So, how did it work?" I demanded, my voice as cold as the fingers he still gripped. "He blew up a balloon for you? Just like that?"

"Um, no." And I swear I saw Nash flush, in spite of the little available light. "The initial transfer was more…personal."

Eewww! "You kissed Avari?" My own lips went cold at the thought, and I couldn't help being creeped out that a Netherworld hellion and I had indirectly shared intimate contact through my boyfriend.

"It was more like artificial respiration," he insisted, but his rationalization couldn't make the facts sound any better.

The thought of kissing a hellion sent me into realms of terror and disgust I hadn't even known existed. "And after that first time, he set things up with Everett, so I wouldn't have to cross over again."

"Well, wasn't that nice of him!" I snapped, jerking my fingers from his grip.

Nash ignored my sarcasm. "I thought so at the time, and I couldn't figure out why he'd go to that much trouble. But the payoff's obvious now." He gestured toward the house, and the party full of teenagers who'd nearly become the client base of an alternate-realm drug dealer.

But the payoff wasn't obvious to me. "What's Avari getting out of this?"

"My guess is that he'll feed from their suffering until they die. Hell, Carter's just become a twenty-four-hour buffet...."

And suddenly my stomach wanted to send those tacos back up. "Do you think he's given up on them?" I waved my hand at the party still in progress.

"Not a chance. But it'll give us some time to think."

Mentally and physically exhausted, I sank back onto the bench, far from encouraged by the temporary reprieve. "So, you know how to get in touch with Everett, right? You call him when you need...more?" The very thought gave me chills, but if Nash knew how to find him, at least we'd have some valuable information to give my dad. Or whoever was most qualified to deal with a half-harpy Netherworld drug dealer.

Did we even have people like that? A supernatural equivalent of the police? Or was this a neighborhood-watch kind of operation?

I honestly wasn't sure which possibility frightened me more....

"Not exactly," Nash said, avoiding my eyes again. "I don't know how it works with his human…clients, but in my case, Everett is just the mule. Avari collects the payment personally."

I closed my eyes, trying to sort the facts out in my head. It was physically impossible for hellions to cross into our world, and Nash said he wasn't crossing over, either…. "I don't get it," I said as a new foreboding twisted my guts even tighter. "How does he take payment if neither of you crosses over?"

"It's kind of a long-distance operation." Nash sighed and finally met my gaze before I could show off another confused frown. "There are a few ways for a hellion to interact with the human world, and they all suck."

He shuddered with some horrible memory, and a sudden wave of intuition rolled over me, dropping another piece of the puzzle into place in my head. "Your nightmare… Avari talks to you in your sleep?"

His eyes closed, like he was scrambling for composure—or for control of the telltale swirling in his irises—and when he met my gaze again, his own seemed somehow closed off. Like he'd slammed shut the windows to his soul. "I wouldn't call it talking, but yeah. In my dreams, or through an… intermediary."

"An intermediary?"

Nash sighed. "He can sometimes talk to me through someone in this world—anyone he has a connection with."

"You mean, like, possession?" *That's not creepy or anything…*

"For lack of a better term, yes. And I'm pretty sure he's Carter's shadow man, too. I think you were right about his hallucinations."

Though I hadn't realized who Scott was actually hearing.

"You knew that, didn't you?" I demanded, my voice actually shaking with anger. I scooted back to put distance between us. "You knew Scott was really hearing Avari, but you made me sound like an idiot in front of my dad. Why?"

"I'm sorry." His gaze dropped like an anchor. "I was afraid that if they knew he was hearing a hellion, they'd want to know who that hellion was, and would eventually connect him to me."

"So, you made me look *crazy* to cover your own tracks? How very chivalrous of you," I spat. The Nash I'd met three months earlier had given me strength and confidence. He'd sacrificed his own safety to help protect me. But now he was lying to me, and Influencing me, and covering up information that could have helped save his best friend. Was it all because of the Demon's Breath? Could breathing from Avari actually change him? Was it already rotting his soul?

"I'm so sorry, Kaylee..." Nash started, but I cut him off with a harsh wave of one hand. I was already tired of pointless apologies.

"Is Avari giving me nightmares, too? Are these death dreams because of him?"

Nash shrugged miserably. "I don't think hellions can make you have premonitions if no one's dying, but I honestly don't know."

I didn't realize I'd been grinding my teeth until my jaw began to ache. How could he answer so many questions with so little information? "So, does this mean you don't have Everett's number, or email, or anything?"

Nash shook his head again. "Avari just tells me where and when to meet him. That's why I had to come to the party. Because I can't get in touch with Everett on my own." I started to interrupt, but Nash rushed on. "Neither can Fuller. I already asked him. Everett calls him and sets up a meeting, and his number shows up as *Unidentified*."

Nash scowled and rubbed his hands together for warmth. I was freezing, too, in spite of his jacket, and part of me wanted to slide closer to him for heat. But I wasn't ready to be that close to him yet.

"So, Avari feeds from the suffering he causes and Everett gets the money," I said, scooting farther away from him for good measure. "But you're not suffering like Doug and Scott are." Presumably because he wasn't human. "And you don't have any money. So how does Avari plan to turn a profit on you?"

Nash's gaze fell to where his hands now clenched the edge of the stone bench on either side of his thighs. And suddenly a devastating new understanding crashed over me, threatening to crush me.

"He already is, isn't he?" My pulse roared in my ears, and I wasn't sure I really wanted the answer. But I had to ask. "How do you pay, Nash?"

He shook his head. "Kaylee, you don't want to—"

"Service?" I interrupted, twisting on the bench to pin him with my eyes. "You're not selling for him, are you?" I whispered, because that was all the volume I could muster.

"No!" Nash insisted, rubbing my back through his jacket. "It's not like that."

"Then what is it like?" I shrugged out from under his hand, silently begging him—*daring* him—to tell me the truth. "What are you paying him, Nash?"

He sighed, and his entire body seemed to deflate as his jaw tensed. "Emotions, in the past tense."

"What?" I felt my forehead crinkle. "What does that mean? You're giving him your emotions? So, you can't feel anything?" The horror rising through me had no equivalent. The only thing that even came close was the black scream that built inside me when I felt Death coming.

"No, not my current emotions," Nash insisted, trying to reassure me, but the gloom in his eyes didn't match his tone, so the look was more frightening than comforting. "The emotions in some of my memories."

"He's eating your *memories?*" I couldn't imagine a more personal violation. Nash was giving away the experiences that made him the person he was.

The person I loved.

I ran my hand over the smooth, cold bench, desperate for something real and sturdy to cement me in reality. In a world where food was food, and memories were invulnerable. Untouchable.

"No." He shook his head vehemently and put one warm hand over mine on the bench. Yet somehow, he seemed to steal my waning warmth, rather than fortify it. "Just the feelings from them. When I think about things from my past, I don't feel how I felt when they actually happened. *Past* emotions." He tried to smile reassuringly, but failed. Miserably. "I don't need those, anyway, right?"

My vision went dark and my hearing began to fade as shock and horror sank through me, cutting my ties to the world. Then my senses came roaring back, stronger than ever, the floodlight glaring in my eyes, the cold numbing my skin. "You don't need those? You don't need to revisit feelings from your past?" I snatched my hand from his and jumped from the bench again, and this time he was too slow to catch me.

"In most cases, it's a mercy, Kaylee," he insisted as I backed slowly away from him, wondering if I'd be making things better or worse if I simply walked away. Would I be giving us time to think, and to miss each other? Or time to realize we shouldn't have been together in the first place. After all, I'd dragged him into the Netherworld where he'd been exposed to Demon's Breath. And he'd lied to me and left me alone with Scott, who'd tried to slit my throat.

Maybe we *didn't* belong together....

"It's like mental anesthesia," he continued, pleading with me silently to understand. "The things that used to hurt..." He shrugged. "Now they're just...numb."

"Numbness is a mercy?" What kind of screwed-up perspective was that? "Do you have any idea what I'd give for more memories of my mother, Nash? What I'd give to remember how she lived, and what it felt like when she died? And you're just throwing your past away!"

"It's not like that." He closed his eyes and inhaled deeply, in spite of the cold, sharp air. "I'm not losing the memories. They're still there."

"What does that matter, if you can't feel them?" I'd never felt so frustrated or disappointed in my entire life. How could he let Avari have such an important part of himself?

Nash sighed again, and the small slip of air through his lips conveyed a devastating weight of hopelessness. Of despair. "It was the only acceptable price, Kaylee. It's all I was willing to part with. And you'd understand if you knew what he really wanted from me."

His soul? His blood? His service? That time I didn't ask. Those were all unacceptable prices for me, but I'd never been in his position. What might I have given to save myself from the Creeper toxin, if we hadn't made it back to the human world in time? Certainly not my soul. But would I have given my memory-emotions in exchange for my life?

Depends on the memories in question...

"What memories, Nash?" I demanded, suddenly afraid that

he'd set no limits on what Avari could take. "Potty training? Pulling your first tooth? Your first independent bike ride? What did you lose?"

He shook his head slowly. "The most intense," he admitted finally. "Only the ones with real value to me have value to him."

I took a deep, cold breath and it caught in my throat, stuck behind a sob. *"Us?"* I closed my eyes, blinking back tears when I remembered all the times in the past few days when his irises had abruptly gone still instead of swirling with emotion. Had he been remembering something all those times? Trying to feel what used to be there?

"Do you still feel what you felt when we met? At Taboo?" I stepped closer for a better look at his eyes, testing the most painful theory I'd ever explored. "When you calmed me so I wouldn't scream? When you figured out what I was? That I was like you?"

His eyes swam in tears, but his irises held painfully steady. Not so much as a twitch of color shifting in the browns and greens I'd always loved.

I swallowed thickly. "Kissing me for the first time?"

Nash closed his eyes to keep me from seeing the truth, and a whip of anger coiled tightly around my spine. *No!* How could he give that away? Did my most precious memories mean less to him than his next high?

What else had he sold?

"Your dad dying? Tod dying? Do you feel what you felt when *I* was dying?" I demanded at last, and when he shook his head, tears slipping from closed eyes, I'd had all I could take.

"It's all gone, Kaylee."

And so was I.

I shrugged out of his jacket and dropped it on the brick

patio, gasping out loud when the cold hit me full force. The roar of my pulse in my ears drowned out the noise from the party as I ran across the stone path toward the quaint wooden gate.

"Kaylee, please…" Nash's whisper hit my back with a last, desperate surge of Influence, but I stiffened my spine and kept going. I was too devastated by my own loss—the boyfriend who remembered *why* he loved me—to worry about his.

I swiped scalding tears from my frozen cheeks when I stopped to shove the gate open and was jogging again by the time I rounded the front corner of the house, headed for my car. And for my human best friend, who would soothe me with junk food, though she could never understand the source of my pain.

But bleak panic hit the moment I spotted my car, two blocks down the street. The instant I saw the form leaning against my front passenger's side door, that familiar dark terror wound its way around my spine, sending thick, hot fingers toward the base of my throat.

The beam from a streetlight shone on the bright red balloon clasped between two pale hands, but darkness slanted across their owner's broad torso, leaving the face obscured. Why had Emma left the balloon unattended?

"Kaylee, are you okay?" Emma asked, and I whirled to see her close Doug's front door, already jogging down the steps toward me, wearing her jacket now. "Where's Nash?"

I shook my head and clenched my jaw shut, unable to answer her without screaming as the death wail took me over. It wrapped around my throat like a thorn-spiked glove, and I tasted blood on the back of my tongue. This premonition was strong; he would die very, very soon.

I glanced pointedly from Emma to my car, trying to guide

her gaze. To speak to her with only my eyes. But she wasn't Nash. She didn't understand.

"What's wrong, Kaylee?"

Frustrated, I turned my back on her and ran for my car, racing toward death for the first time ever, because this time my effort wasn't pointless. Nash had said deaths caused by Netherworld elements were unscripted, so whoever he was, if Demon's Breath was the problem, I could save him—if I got there in time.

I'd just passed the dark, silent house next door when the old wooden gate squealed open again and winter-dead grass crunched under someone's feet. "What's wrong?" Nash called out behind me.

"I don't know!" Emma shouted as his steps pounded after us. "She won't tell me!"

And that was enough for Nash.

"Kaylee, stop!" he yelled, even as he raced after me. "Wait!" But I couldn't stop. I'd let Nash down. I'd let Scott down. But I could save this one.

Thirty feet. My nose dripped, and my throat burned.

"Stay here," Nash ordered Emma, but his footsteps never slowed. "Kaylee, stop!"

Twenty feet. The form against my car came into focus, his features coalescing in the swirling shadows to form a face I recognized. He raised the balloon. The weighted clip hit the ground.

Ten feet. My jaws ached from being clenched. My throat felt like I'd swallowed razors from holding back his soul song. My hands clenched into fists at my sides, pumping as I ran. And now I could hear him.

"Hudson, you've been holdin' out on me!" His smile was joyous. Relieved. Uncomprehending. "I'll pay you back…."

"No!" Nash shouted behind me, but I didn't turn. There was no time. "It's too strong!"

But Doug put the balloon to his mouth, anyway, and drew in a long, deep breath.

He smiled, even as he began to convulse....

⟨ 17 ⟩

"No!" NASH YELLED AGAIN, and in the next instant, time seemed to shift into fast-forward. My world hurtled through space and time so quickly my head spun and the neighborhood around me swam in and out of focus.

Doug shook violently and fell against the car. Strands of shaggy brown hair flopped into his wide, empty eyes. His hands seized around the balloon. Demon's Breath burst from it in a frosty white vapor. I skidded to a stop two feet from him, one hand over my mouth to hold the scream back. But I was out of breath and couldn't help sucking in air through my nose to satisfy my abused lungs.

Strong hands grabbed my arms from behind, lifting me. The world spun around me as I inhaled. The air I pulled in was clear and cold. And clean. The hands shoved me forward and I stumbled onto the neighbor's yard, my feet barely brushing the ground.

I fell facedown on cold, dead grass, recently sprayed green with fertilizer. My graceless landing jarred my mouth open, and the scream ripped free from my throat, calling out to Doug's soul as it prepared to leave his body.

Doug fell forward, draped across the sidewalk, still convulsing. His shoes slammed into the road. His knuckles scraped the sidewalk. His skull bounced on the grass. Dark, translucent shadows swirled all around him.

The Nether-fog rolled in from nowhere, swallowing my world whole.

Nash grabbed the balloon he'd dropped and tied the opening into a quick knot, trapping what little vapor hadn't escaped into the air. Then he dropped to his knees at Doug's side, two fingers at his throat, feeling for a pulse, uninhibited by the fog he couldn't see.

I saw both layers of reality, and was desperate to separate them. To push the fog back. Yet still I screamed.

"No!" Emma's mouth formed soundless words of denial. She sank into the fog next to me, hands covering her ears, hunched over her knees in shock. Dark things scuttled around her, and revulsion skittered up my spine. Tears filled my eyes, then ran over. "No!" she shouted again, though I couldn't hear her over my own screaming.

Nash looked up.

His eyes reflected pain, and regret, and guilt, and horror, swirling as madly now as they'd sat calm moments earlier. He left his friend still seizing in the fog and churning shadows and dropped to his knees beside me. Nash turned me so that I couldn't see Doug. His lips brushed my ear, but I couldn't hear him. He wasn't using his Influence. Because I'd told him not to.

He leaned back and shouted at me, as Emma sobbed, but I couldn't hear either of them. Yet I knew what Nash was saying. *Pull it back. You can do it, Kaylee. You have to let him go....*

It was hard. It was so hard without Nash's help. But I couldn't let him back in my head.

I closed my eyes and slapped both hands over my mouth, but that wasn't enough. I could practically feel the gray haze lapping at my skin. I forced my jaw closed, but the screaming still leaked from my sealed lips, scraping my insides raw. So I swallowed it, fists clenched against the pain, locking the wail inside myself, where it bounced around my throat like a swarm of angry wasps.

When I opened my eyes, the fog was gone. Nash was still watching me. Doug was still convulsing. Em was still crying. Nash glanced from one of us to the other, and finally his anxious gaze settled on me. "Can you drive?" he asked, and I nodded, relieved to be able to hear him. I wasn't sure I really could drive, with Doug's death song consuming me from the inside, but Emma had been drinking.

It was either me or a cab.

"Okay." He left Doug—still convulsing—and hauled Emma up by both arms, as gently as he had time for. "Em, you have to calm down. He's still alive, and I'm going to do what I can for him." We both knew Doug was as good as dead, but maybe Emma didn't know I'd never yet had a false premonition. "But I need you and Kaylee to get out of here before she starts screaming again." He walked with her as he spoke and carefully settled her into the passenger's seat, then closed the door.

"Go straight to her house," he said, circling the car to open my door for me as I held one hand firmly over my mouth. "Drive slowly, just in case. I'll call you later."

I nodded. I would answer his call, even though we'd just had the biggest fight in the history of fights, because things weren't as simple as "break up and make up" between me and Nash.

What we had was life or death. Literally.

He closed the door and I twisted the key in the engine with my free hand. Then I grabbed the wheel and hit the gas. The last thing I saw in the mirror before I turned the corner was Nash kneeling on the ground next to one of his best friends, already pulling his phone from his pocket. No one had come out yet—the whole thing couldn't have taken two minutes, and the music from the party had helped cover my screaming—but it wouldn't be long before someone wandered outside, and the second party in a week would end in disaster.

When I turned the corner—swerving too sharply in haste—the panic began to ebb, and my throat started to relax. The pincushion feeling faded slowly, and two blocks later, I opened my mouth and sucked in a deep breath, grateful when the only sound that escaped was the rasp of air through my throat.

And that's when I realized Emma was still crying.

She sat huddled in one corner of the passenger's seat, knees to her chest, seat belt unbuckled, right temple pressed against the cold window. Her shoulders shook with each soft sob, and as I watched, she raised one arm to wipe her face with her jacket sleeve.

"Are you okay?" I flicked on my blinker for the next turn, then slowed to a stop at the red light.

"No. Is he dead?"

"I don't know." I wished I wasn't driving so I could really look at her. So I'd know how she was handling this. "But if he isn't yet, he will be soon."

Emma twisted toward me, her brown eyes wide. Imploring. "Can't you save him? Like you saved me?" Her voice cracked on the last word, and she reached up to wipe more tears.

I shook my head slowly, sadly, then glanced at her as passing streetlights lit the car, one after another. Would this explanation ever get any easier? "Em, if we'd saved him, someone else would have to die in his place." Because even though we hadn't seen him or her, there was a reaper somewhere nearby waiting to claim Doug's soul, and if we snatched it back, the reaper would simply take another.

At least, that's how it usually worked. I wasn't sure about unscripted cases, but I wasn't gonna risk it. "You, Nash, and I were the only ones there to choose from, and I'm not willing to sacrifice any of us to save someone else." *Not even your boyfriend.* Though I couldn't say that aloud.

"What if it's not really his time to die? It wasn't my time when I died."

Okay, she had a good point. And a very hard question.

I closed my eyes and exhaled softly, then forced my gaze back to the road. I'd wondered the same thing. But ultimately... "It wouldn't really matter." I slowed for the next turn and flicked my blinker on. "You, and those other girls, and Sophie—none of you were supposed to die. But saving you still meant killing someone else. I can't risk that again."

"Wait...*Sophie?*" Emma said, and for a moment, surprise eclipsed the hurt and confusion she wore like a funeral veil. "Sophie died, too?"

Crap. "Yeah. But she doesn't know, so please don't tell her."

"Like I'm gonna go looking for a reason to talk to Sophie." Emma paused, and curiosity shined through her tears. "What happened?"

I stepped on the gas to make it through a yellow light, then dropped back to the speed limit. Getting pulled over while Emma still had beer on her breath would *not* be a good way to end the most horrible week in the history of...weeks.

"Aunt Val took her place." Making the very same sacrifice for her daughter that my mother had made for me. Except that it was Aunt Val's fault Sophie died in the first place. Which kind of mitigated her sacrifice, in my eyes.

"That's how your aunt died?" Em wiped tear-damp mascara onto her sleeve.

I shrugged. "Sophie thinks she passed out from shock, and when she woke up, her mother was dead. She has no idea why or how it happened, but she knows I was involved and she's decided I'm somehow responsible." Which couldn't have been further from the truth, but no one—including me—wanted to tell my cousin that her mother had tried to trade five innocent souls for her own everlasting youth and beauty.

"No wonder she hates you…"

"Yeah." But the truth was that Sophie had never exactly been warm and fuzzy.

For several minutes, Emma stared out the window, though I had a feeling she wasn't really seeing the dark houses we passed. Then she turned to look at me, and the weight behind her gaze was devastating. "Kaylee, what was in the balloon?"

I blinked at the road and exhaled slowly. "Nothing you want to know much about."

"I saw how Nash pulled you away." Leather creaked as she shifted in her seat. "He didn't even want you to get a whiff of it, so whatever it is, it must be pretty damn scary."

"It is." Yet he hadn't hesitated to kiss me and breathe all over me while he was taking it. How much could I possibly mean to him if he'd risk exposing me?

"I should have done something." Emma groaned. "I knew he was taking too much, and I just let him!" She stomped the floorboard hard enough to rock the whole car, and my heart broke for her.

"Em, you couldn't have stopped him." I was sure of that, yet I was equally sure that Nash and I could have. I'd failed Scott and Doug, but it wasn't too late to help Nash. No matter what he'd done, I couldn't live with myself if I let him turn out like his friends.

"I should be there." Emma sat straighter, oblivious to the turn my thoughts had taken. "Can you take me to the hospital? He might not be gone yet, and I should be there. I know that sounds stupid—it's not like we were in love or anything—but I feel awful for just leaving him."

I shook my head slowly and made the turn onto her street. "It doesn't sound stupid. But Em, they're not going to let you in. You're not family." And Doug's family—just the father and stepmother, as far as I knew—were still in New York on a working vacation. Did that mean Doug would die alone? Surely Nash could Influence his way into the room…. "Besides, Emma, the last place you need to be is in a hospital swarming with cops."

Emma sighed and sank into her seat as I pulled to a stop on the street in front of her mailbox. Her house was dark.

"Where is everybody?" The hum of the engine faded as I pulled the keys from the ignition.

"Traci's working, and Cara's at her sorority's Christmas party," Emma said as I pushed my car door opened. I hadn't really expected either of her sisters to be home on a Friday night, but I was worried about her mom catching Emma before we'd washed her shirt and brushed her teeth. "And Mom has a date, if you can believe that." She shoved her own door open and stepped onto the grass, surprisingly steady.

Evidently death is sobering. No real shock there.

I grabbed my overnight bag—now minus one T-shirt—then swung the door shut and locked the car. Emma was already halfway up the cute stone path, digging in her pocket for her keys before she remembered that I'd taken them. I gave them to her, but her hand shook too badly to slide the key into the lock, so I took it back and opened the door myself.

"I feel so helpless!" Emma dropped onto the overstuffed couch as I bolted the door behind us. "Worthless. So frustrated and…impotent!" She sat up straight then and punched the arm of her couch so hard I wasn't surprised when her knuckles came away skinned and oozing blood from the rough weave.

I handed her a tissue from a box on the end table. "That's not a phrase you hear very often from girls." I forced a smile, but my joke landed like a brick dropped from a skyscraper.

I knew exactly how she felt.

"I'm serious." She dabbed at her fist, then dropped the tissue on the coffee table. "What's the point of knowing someone's going to die if you can't do anything about it? How can you stand this?" she demanded. "All this death? How can you stand knowing about it before anyone else does?"

I took my shoes off and lined them up with the others in the front closet, then sank onto the couch beside her, leaning my head on her shoulder. "Have you ever known anyone who died?" Her parents had divorced when Em was only four, but I was pretty sure her dad was still alive. Somewhere.

"Just Roger."

"Who's Roger?"

"The hamster we had when I was seven. Does he count?"

"I don't think so." I almost smiled, but held it back when I realized she might be offended. For all I knew, she and Roger had been very close.

"Then, no." She folded one leg beneath the other and twisted to face me. "And I've certainly never had to *look* at someone, knowing he'd be dead soon. How can you stand this?" she asked again. And in that moment, I came very close to telling her the truth: that I couldn't. Not without Nash.

"It's not easy." I stood and pulled Emma up by both hands. "In fact, it sucks. Do you have ice cream?"

"Yeah." She wiped fresh tears from her face and gestured vaguely toward the kitchen. "Traci's boyfriend dumped her yesterday. Fourth one this year." Which made no sense to me. The Marshall girls were gorgeous beyond all reason. "There's a pint of Phish Food in the freezer."

"Great. Pick out a movie while I get the ice cream."

Emma nodded hesitantly, then crossed the living room toward the rack of DVDs to the left of a slim, simple entertainment center. "Bring two spoons!" she shouted over her shoulder as she knelt to scan the titles.

For the first half hour of the movie—a lighthearted, predictable romantic comedy—Emma shoveled ice cream into her mouth and glanced regularly at my cell lying on her nightstand, obviously willing it to ring with an update from Nash.

But my phone never rang.

By the time the credits rolled, Emma had fallen asleep, her spoon still dangling from one hand, several drops of chocolate ice cream dotting the front of the shirt she'd borrowed from me. When I got up to turn off the movie, her spoon thumped to the floor, so I rolled carefully off the bed and took both spoons and the empty ice cream container into the kitchen, yawning so hard my jaw ached.

The clock on the microwave read a quarter to one, and I wondered idly how late Ms. Marshall would be out. I had no frame of reference for adult dating.

I grabbed a Coke from the fridge, then padded back to Emma's room, intending to call Nash. But when I reached for my phone from the nightstand on Emma's side of the bed, her eyes popped wide-open, as if some unseen clasp holding them closed had just been released.

Startled, I squealed and jumped back. "Em, you okay?" But even when she finally blinked, her face still pressed into the pillow, her eyes didn't lose that sleep haze, nor did they focus on me. Or on anything else. "Em?"

She snapped upright in a single, eerily stiff motion and blinked at me, then glanced around her room like she'd never seen it before—easily one of the weirdest things I'd seen in my entire life.

In either world.

"Emma?" I backed slowly away from the bed, my phone clenched in my left hand, as a strange, heavy, fluttery feeling settled into my stomach. Like I'd swallowed a swarm of iron butterflies.

"Not exactly…" A low, scratchy, *unfamiliar* voice said as my best friend's mouth moved.

My heart rate exploded and my pulse roared in my ears. "Who, then, exactly?"

"I am Alec. As presented through Emma Dawn Marshall."

As presented…?

Whoa…

"Who are you, and what the hell are you doing *in* my best friend?" I backed farther from the bed, my empty hand stretched behind me to warn me before I bumped into anything. Part of me—most of me, in fact—wanted to make a break for the door. But I couldn't leave Emma alone with… whatever was talking through her. Possessing her. Because that's obviously what this was.

"I apologize for contacting you through an intermediary, but my options are pretty limited at the moment," Emma said with Alec's voice, and the effect was disjointed, like a bad voice-over in a foreign film. Except the actor and the voice were both speaking the same language. "I promise your friend won't remember any of this. She might wake up sleepy and disoriented, but none the worse for wear." He extended his borrowed arms, like he was testing the fit of a new shirt.

My stomach roiled at the casual gesture and the gruesome image that accompanied it, and my mind raced, trying to make sense of what I was seeing and hearing. Without much luck. Emma was speaking to me in *someone else's voice*. She was being used as a human microphone—this "Alec's" intermediary.

And suddenly a horrifying understanding clicked into place in my nearly scrambled brain. The blood seemed to drain from my face, leaving me cold.

Nash had said Avari contacted him through an intermediary— by possessing someone in our world. And several times in the past few weeks I'd fallen asleep with Nash, only to wake up disoriented and unsure where I was, even during his few covert visits while I was grounded. In the past week alone, it had happened on the way to work, then in the school parking lot during my lunchtime nap....

Nooo!

My hands clenched into fists at my sides, and I had to force my grip on my phone to loosen. Anger and fear rolled through me like thunder across the sky, dark, and low, and threatening. And accompanied by a vicious, white-hot bolt of betrayal that singed every nerve in my body.

I'd played intermediary between Nash and Avari. The hellion had used me as his own personal walkie-talkie.

And Nash had let it happen.

18

"GET OUT!" I GLANCED around Emma's room for a weapon—until I realized I couldn't hurt the hellion without hurting Emma, too. "Get out of her! She has nothing to do with any of this!" Whatever "this" was. "Emma's human, and she knows nothing about hellions, or the Netherworld, or Demon's Breath, or anything else to do with your warped, twisted, toxic hellhole of an alternate dimension."

Keeping Emma in the dark about everything that went bump in the night was supposed to protect her from those bumps. So why was she now speaking to me with a hellion's voice? What kind of "connection" could she possibly have to this Netherworld possessor? For that matter, what connection did I have to Avari?

My best friend's carefully arched brows rose in surprise. "*My* warped, twisted...?" Then comprehension washed over her face. Alec grinned with Emma's mouth, and I was floored by how unlike Emma that look was, considering that she smiled at me all the time with those same features. He swung both of her denim-clad legs over the edge of the bed. "You think

I'm a hellion." It wasn't a question, and Alec sounded every bit as surprised as Emma looked.

He shook her head slowly, and their shared smile faded into a bittersweet melancholy. "I'm human. Only I have the misfortune to be stuck in the Netherworld."

Surprised, I gripped the edge of Emma's desk to anchor myself to the only thing that made sense while I tried to puzzle through Alec's maze of misinformation.

He started to stand in Emma's body, but I threw one hand out, fingers splayed. "Stay there!"

She shrugged and sank back onto the mattress. "If that makes you more comfortable…"

Like comfort was even a possibility.

"You're lying." I forced my other hand to relax around my phone, to keep from bringing it to his attention. "You're not human." He couldn't be, because humans can't survive in the Netherworld with both soul and body intact.

Which meant that Alec was either lying or soulless. Or that there were big things going on in the Netherworld. Things I didn't understand well enough to fully grasp.

Knowing my luck, it was all three.

"Not solely human, no," Alec admitted, tilting Emma's head so that a strand of straight blond hair fell over her shoulder. "But I swear to you that I mean neither of you any harm." I huffed in disbelief and he continued, furrowing the delicate lines of Emma's forehead. "If I wanted to hurt her, I could have already fed her a bottle of pills or made her cut her own throat." Alec drew one of Emma's own long fingernails slowly across her slim neck, and terror crawled over me like an army of spiders marching up my spine. "But that's not why I'm here."

Somehow, I wasn't very comforted.

"What else are you? Other than human?" I wanted both my hands empty, in case I had to defend myself. Or Emma. But I was reluctant to put down the phone—my security blanket and only connection to the rest of the world. The human world, anyway.

Alec crossed Emma's arms beneath her breasts, looking physically comfortable for the first time since he'd claimed her body. Yet her expression spoke of long-term anger and resentment. Of a grudge that had been allowed to fester. "I am a proxy to a hellion in the Netherworld."

"A proxy?"

Alec's frown deepened as his obvious self-loathing swelled. "I'm used as a servant and energy storage unit. Like an assistant you can eat."

"Eat?" I didn't bother to hide my horror, and Alec nodded, pushing back a strand of Emma's hair when it fell into her eyes.

"Not literally, of course. Well, not like we eat, anyway." Emma's shoulders shrugged within the borrowed shirt. "Many hellions do consume flesh. Fortunately, the one I serve does not. He uses me like a sports bottle," Alec continued. "An emergency drink when there isn't enough human energy bleeding over from your world."

Eewww! No wonder Alec's grudge was festering.

"Sorry about the whole human Gatorade thing," I said, glancing at the alarm clock on the nightstand—1:08 a.m. What were the chances that Ms. Marshall would stay out long enough for me to get rid of Emma's visitor? "But what does that have to do with Emma?"

"Nothing. It has to do with you." He smiled, like I should have been flattered. "Emma was the closest available intermediary."

"She wasn't available!" I snapped, indignation on her behalf bolstering my courage. "She was asleep." But then something new occurred to me, when I remembered passing out as Nash drove me to work on Sunday. "Did you make her fall asleep?"

Alec shook Emma's head somberly. "That's beyond my ability. The most we can do is give someone who's already tired a little *push* toward slumber. During sleep, the mind is more susceptible to sharing space in the body."

"So you pushed Emma out of her body?"

"No." He chuckled. The talking "boost" actually laughed! "She's still in here. I just pushed her over a bit." He shrugged, looking almost as unconcerned by his violation of her free will as Tod was by his regular violation of closed doors. "She was almost asleep, anyway."

My next breath was an exasperated huff. I'd had it with people—and non-people—taking liberties with moral norms! Personal boundaries—whether body, mind, or home—were not up for negotiation!

"Get out of Emma, and don't ever 'push her over' again!" I propped both hands on my hips, hoping to look threatening, though surely he knew I wouldn't hurt my best friend, even to hurt him. "Pick another intermediary. Or better yet, stay out of my friends and away from me!"

Alec's sigh slipped through Emma's lips. "I would gladly use another body—preferably one without breasts…" My best friend glanced down at her own chest as if she didn't know what to do with such generous curves. "Unfortunately, you don't surround yourself with many potential intermediaries." A hint of desperation leaked through onto Emma's features. "But I swear to you, on both my life and my soul, that if you help me—if you let us help each other—my need for an intermediary will soon be a thing of the past."

I blinked at Emma/Alec in disbelief. "You're asking me for a favor?"

Emma's head nodded steadily. "And offering one, as well."

Curiosity overwhelmed me, in spite of my desperation to put Emma back in control of her body. "What could you possibly do for me?"

His smile widened on her face, and Emma's straight white teeth seemed to taunt me. "Return your damaged lover."

My what?

Confusion must have shown clearly on my face, because Emma/Alec raised both brows in a rather masculine look of amusement. "Your boyfriend. Nash. I assume you remember him. Or does the heart forget so soon?"

Terror shot through me in a jolt of white-hot adrenaline, then settled into my gut like lead. My free hand gripped the back of Emma's desk chair and I sank into it, stunned. "What are you talking about?"

Emma's smile faded and her forehead furrowed as he stepped closer, moving stiffly in the unfamiliar body. "My boss has your boyfriend in the Netherworld. I can help you get him back—in exchange for passage into your world."

Vertigo crashed over me and I wobbled on the chair as Alec's claim truly sank in. *"No."* I shook my head so hard Emma's bedroom swam wildly. Nash couldn't be in the Netherworld. I'd left him at the party less than two hours ago.

"No, you won't cross me over, or no, you don't believe me?"

"No, Nash can't be in the Netherworld." Confused and horrified, I stood and spun away from him, my gaze skipping around the room in search of answers Emma's clothes and furniture could never provide. "He can't cross over."

How did Alec know *I* could cross over?

"Oh, he had help," Alec said, ducking Emma's head to catch my gaze.

Help? Not Tod. He would never intentionally do anything that could hurt Nash.

Except take him to the Netherworld to repay a favor, no questions asked...

Tod, if you're involved in this, I'll kill you! Except you can't kill someone who's already dead. But I could get him fired....

Assuming Alec was telling the truth, which was a big assumption. He could be lying about the whole thing.

Then where was Nash? Why hadn't he called or answered the two text messages I'd sent?

"You actually saw Nash there? Tonight?"

Emma's head nodded, and Alec said, "Not ten minutes ago, my time." Because in the Netherworld, time was not a constant. It sped up at odd intervals, depending on how closely a specific place was tied to its equivalent location in our world.

"What was he wearing?"

Emma's eyes rolled, and she sank onto the bed again. "Jeans and a T-shirt, with a green-and-white jacket. And I have to tell you, jeans have changed since I last bought a pair."

My eyes widened before I could regain control of my expression. *He'd bought jeans?* Unless the Netherworld had recently become active in the retail market, Alec must have been topside at some point. I couldn't help wondering how long ago that had been, considering his odd mix of hellion-formal and human-colloquial language.

But then, on the tail of that momentary surprise, came a more devastating near-certainty. Alec *had* seen Nash that night. Not necessarily in the Netherworld—he could easily have seen Nash in our world, through another hijacked body—but I wasn't willing to take that chance.

If Nash had crossed over, I had to get him back.

"So, all I have to do is cross over and bring you both back? Just like that?" It sounded too easy.

"Well…" Emma hedged with Alec's voice. "It may not be quite that simple."

Aaaand here comes the catch… "Why not?"

"Because Nash is with my boss right now. But once he's alone, I can get to him."

I closed my eyes, trying not to let frustration and the incredibly small chance I had of ever seeing Nash alive again get me down. "Your boss, the hellion? Nash is with *that* boss?"

"That's the one."

"Why?" I demanded, standing so quickly Em's chair thumped against the desk behind me. "Why is he in the Netherworld? What does your boss want with him?"

Alec shrugged, pulling my T-shirt tight across Emma's chest. "I don't know. Another proxy, maybe?"

Nash, as a demon's proxy? "Why does your hellion need two?"

Emma's bright brown eyes rolled, and Alec leaned her back on the mattress, propping her up on one elbow like a life-size doll. "You're asking the wrong man. I don't think he needs any proxies, but he's had as many as eight at a time." She shrugged again. "What can I say? He's a hellion of greed."

Greed? *No…*

I drew in a deep, slow breath, wishing I didn't have to ask. "Your boss? Is his name Avari?"

Emma's eyes widened to anime proportions. "You know him?"

I sighed and dropped onto the chair again. "We've met, but I doubt he'd consider me a friend."

Emma snorted, and I couldn't resist a small smile. That was

the first sound Alec had made that truly sounded like my best friend. "Friendship isn't a popular concept here."

No surprise there. Everything in the Netherworld was food for something else, and no one was safe except those at the top of the food chain: hellions. And in the three short months I'd known about my species and the existence of the Netherworld, I'd managed to piss off two of them.

But they'd pissed me off, too. "How soon can you get Nash alone?"

Alec stared at the comforter he—they—lay on. "That's the hard part. He's Avari's new toy, and the boss won't want to let go for a while." If I'd had any doubt that Emma was not in control of her body, that doubt died when his gaze met mine. My best friend was not the one staring at me with those big brown eyes. "But there's this thing tomorrow night. A sort of party. I can get to him then with no problem."

"Tomorrow night!" I had to suck in deep, calming breaths through my nose. "You want me to leave him there for an entire day?"

Emma's body sat up and her gaze went hard. "You don't have any choice. You can't get to him without me, and I can't get him alone until then. Beyond that, if we miss our chance tomorrow, we may never get another one."

The entire room tilted as I reeled from shock. I had to close my eyes and grip the sides of the chair to regain my balance.

"Do you understand, Kaylee? It's tomorrow, or never."

"I get it." I swallowed thickly. "So, we wait until tomorrow night, and when you say the word, I cross over and haul you both out. Right? That's it?"

"With any luck, yes."

Luck? We were depending on luck?

Nash is so screwed….

"Is there anything else I need to know?" I leaned forward with both elbows propped on my knees. "Anything you're not telling me? Are we expecting an ambush? Or a giant boot to descend from the sky and squish us all?"

Or a trap waiting to be sprung?

As scared as I was for Nash, I couldn't quite buy the coincidence. Two days earlier, Scott's shadow man—who turned out to be Avari—had tried to get me into the Netherworld, and now Alec the proxy was trying the same thing, on behalf of the same hellion. Albeit, this time the bait was much better, but I was far from prepared to trust him.

And frankly, I was proud of myself for remembering to expect the unexpected—a good rule of thumb when traveling to the Netherworld.

Well, that, and "expect to be eaten by *everything…*"

Alec only shrugged. "The only other thing I can tell you is this…" He leaned forward, peering at me earnestly through Emma's eyes, her pouty lips pressed into a firm, pink line. "You're going to cross over into a big celebration. The biggest event I've seen in my time here. The place will be crawling with Netherworlders."

"And your point is…" Though, by then, I was pretty sure I already knew.

"I know you're going to be tempted to bring backup. Someone older and wiser, maybe?"

My father, of course. I hadn't actually decided to bring him in yet, but I'll admit I was considering it. He knew much more about the Netherworld than I did, and Nash's life was on the line.

When I refused to answer, Alec continued. "Kaylee, you may be able to cross back into your world with nothing more than a thought…"

Yeah, like it's that easy!

"...but if you bring anyone who can't cross over on his own, he's as good as dead. You know that, right?"

My stomach flipped and twisted at the thought of getting separated from my father in the Netherworld. If that happened, he'd never make it out.

"And trying to get more than two of us out at a time will slow you down enough to get us all killed. Do you understand? It's not just your life on the line here. Not just mine or Nash's, either. If you bring help, you're as good as slitting his throat. Though I can promise you his actual death will be neither that quick nor painless."

I swallowed the sudden need to vomit and nodded. He was right. But I didn't like it.

The growl of an engine outside broke through the excruciating silence Alec's last words had woven. Ms. Marshall was home.

But Emma was not.

I spun in the chair, as if I could see through all the walls between me and the driveway. My heart raced, and I turned back to Alec. "You have to go. Now."

He shook her head and stood, foreign panic playing behind Emma's eyes. "We have to make plans. We're only going to get one chance, and we can't afford to mess it up."

"I know. But not now." I glanced toward the hall again as a key turned in the front door. "I need some time to get rid of her mother." *And talk to Tod.*

As badly as I wanted to save Nash, I was not just going to jump into the Netherworld with someone I'd never met— someone whose humanity I couldn't even confirm—without proof that Nash was actually missing.

And I *definitely* wasn't going to do it without backup. Tod could get himself out, and he could take someone with him, if necessary. And if this whole thing turned out to be a trap—an attempt by Avari to regain the soul that got away—I wanted someone I mostly trusted in my corner.

"How long?" Alec asked as the front door swung open across the house.

"Shhhh…" I hissed, my pulse racing. Then, "Two hours. Can you do that, with the time difference?"

Emma nodded. "I think so."

As loath as I was to subject Emma to another possession, I saw no other choice. "Fine. Now go!"

Alec frowned. Then Emma's eyes closed, and she fell over backward on the bed.

"Em, are you home?" Ms. Marshall called, her heels clacking down the hall toward us.

"Mmm?" Emma's eyes fluttered and she rolled over, one hand rising automatically to run through her hair.

"We're back here!" I crossed the room and sank onto the bed next to Emma. "We fell asleep watching a movie."

Ms. Marshall appeared in the doorway, leaning against the frame with one high-heeled foot crossed over the other, the empty ice cream carton in one hand. She lifted the carton and glanced at the DVD case on Emma's dresser. "Wild night?"

You have no idea….

19

"Tod!" I whispered as I slammed the car door shut, glancing frantically around the dark concrete maze at mostly empty parking spaces. The chances of the reaper being in the parking garage were slim to none, but honestly, Tod was hardly ever where I expected to find him.

When he didn't answer, I clicked the automatic lock on my rented key bauble and headed for the entrance, wishing I'd thought to change clothes before I left Emma's. But since I hadn't, my walk across the dank parking garage was accented by the clunking of my wedge heels against the concrete and the flash of my shiny blouse in the dim industrial lights overhead.

When the glass door closed behind me with a soft air-sucking sound, I glanced around the empty, sterile hallway, desperate for a glimpse of the reaper Nash and I usually couldn't get rid of. "Tod! Get your invisible butt down here!" Or up here, or over here, or whichever way he'd have to travel to get to me.

Regrettably, superhearing was not among a reaper's many awesome abilities, so I'd have to be within normal hearing range to catch his attention. And since I couldn't see him—he considered corporeality at work to be unprofessional, though evidently shouting at the patients to *hurry up and die!* didn't offend his delicate moral fiber—putting myself within that hearing range could prove quite a challenge.

When he didn't show up in the back hallway, I race-walked down the corridor and around the corner, then through the swinging double doors into the emergency room, where Tod spent most of his working hours. If I didn't find him there, I was screwed, because there was no way a teenage girl would go unnoticed wandering around the intensive-care unit by herself in the middle of the night.

Unfortunately, even at two in the morning, the emergency room was half-full and most of the patients looked awake enough to notice me calling out to someone who wasn't there.

"Tod!" I whispered, stepping into the vending machine alcove. Stubbornly resisting a bag of Doritos taunting me from behind the glass, I checked both restrooms opposite the water fountain with no luck.

Back in the waiting area, I jogged past the triage nurse's station and had one palm on the door leading into the bowels of the E.R. when a familiar voice spoke up from behind me. "Is Emma with you?"

Startled, my heart thumping, I whirled around to find Tod standing with his hands shoved deep into the pockets of a faded, baggy pair of jeans. His sleeves were short and his jacket missing, as usual. Evidently the mostly dead don't feel the cold like the rest of us do. Or maybe that was part of his big bad reaper routine.

"No. Why?" I asked, and the triage nurse glanced at me in surprise, clearly unable to see or hear the reaper. I was going to have to start wearing a Bluetooth headset, or talking to Tod was going to get me locked up again.

"Her boyfriend came in by ambulance a few hours ago, and it's getting pretty tense back there," he said, unbothered by the nurse's presence as I smiled at her and subtly led him away from the double doors, hoping none of the staff recognized me from my visit the night before.

In the waiting area again, I raised my brows to tell him to go on, and Tod shrugged. "His dad's some big-shot lawyer. The governor's personal attorney, or some crap like that. He showed up about fifteen minutes ago, straight from the airport, and has been raising hell ever since. He's threatening to sue the hospital for negligence, and the attending physician for malpractice, and the damned *janitor* who mopped the floor he slipped on, even though there was one of those orange 'slippery' signs right next to him when he went down."

"So Doug's still…alive?" I whispered as he followed me into the rear corridor.

"Nah. He was brain-dead but breathing when he got here, and I put him out of his misery about an hour later. The weird thing is that he isn't on the list. Levi sent a runner with this about twenty minutes after Richie Rich came in." Tod pulled an uneven square of yellow paper from his right pocket and handed it to me.

My hands shook as I unfolded it. It was the bottom half torn from a sheet of legal paper. Neat, loopy handwriting slanted across the lines: *Douglas Aaron Fuller 23:47:33.*

"What is this?" I couldn't refold the paper fast enough. I shoved it at Tod, and he slid it back into his pocket.

"It's an addendum. An unscheduled reaping. The job should have gone to whoever works the sector where Em's boyfriend dropped, but our office didn't get word in time. So they sent it to me here."

Exhaustion and shock had taken their toll, and my eyes didn't want to focus. The hallway blurred until I blinked to clear my vision. "So this didn't have to happen..."

Tod shrugged. "It probably *shouldn't* have happened. This is only the second addendum I've seen in two years, and it just happens to be Emma's new boy toy. And she didn't come in with him. What's going on, Kaylee?"

And suddenly Doug's death hit me—not as a *bean sidhe,* but as a person—grief suffocating me beneath the weight of my own guilt. I tripped over one wedge heel and caught myself against the wall, barely flinching at the pain in my bandaged arm because it was nothing compared to the ache in my heart.

"You okay?" Tod asked, and he sounded like he actually cared.

"No." I pushed myself away from the wall and tugged him down the hall with me, grateful when my fingers didn't sink right through his arm. "Do they know what Doug died of?"

Tod shrugged. "He had some cuts and bruises, but the doc thinks he got them during a seizure. Blood tests show alcohol, but not enough to kill him. Nothing else has come back yet, but Richie, Sr., insists his kid is clean, and if the tests show otherwise, he'll sue the lab. Man, I hope I'm working when *his* name comes up on the list."

I took the next left to put us farther from the E.R., and from Mr. Fuller. "Someday, someplace, karma is waiting to kick your teeth in, Tod."

"I'm dead." He made a sweeping gesture to encompass his entire body—which death had not damaged in the least. "My teeth have already been kicked in."

Well, he had a point there....

"So, where're Nash and Emma? And aren't you a little over-dressed for two-thirty in the morning?"

"Is it that late?" I glanced at my watch and groaned. Talking Emma back to sleep had taken half an hour, and hunting for Tod had taken longer than I'd expected. I now had less than forty-five minutes to be back in Emma's room, waiting for another call on the human telephone.

"It's a long story." Flustered, I ran one hand through my tangled hair, then crossed my arms over my blouse. "And Nash is the reason I'm here. Did he come in with Doug?"

The reaper frowned. "No. Why would he?"

"Because he's the reason Doug died."

Tod's confusion twisted into dark distress, and I could have sworn I saw blood drain from his face. Though I wasn't sure that was even possible for a dead guy. "What the hell are you talking about?"

But before I could answer, the door at the end of the hall opened, admitting a gust of wind and a couple in their mid-forties, whose stress and fatigue showed in every line on their faces.

"I need to sit," I suggested, irritated when the hand I wrapped around his arm went right through his flesh this time. "Cafeteria?" I whispered, shoving my hands into my pockets.

Tod huffed, already heading down the hall. "The coffee tastes like swamp water tonight, but sure." He led me down the long hallway and around two corners, then through the double doors into an outdated but functional cafeteria dotted with old square tables and cheap '70s-style, vinyl-covered chairs. "You know, you're lucky you caught me here. My shift ended at midnight, and if I weren't filling in for a friend, you'd be out of luck."

Yeah, right. I passed by the stack of trays and pulled a bottle of Coke from a refrigerated shelf. After his shift, Tod would have had nothing to do but hang around and spy on either me or Nash. He was almost always around, whether we needed—or wanted—him or not. At least, he had been until Addison died.

But all I said, as I dug a five from my pocket to pay for my soda, was, "You have a friend?"

Tod scowled. "Well, I wouldn't call him a friend according to the traditional definition, but in the sense that he imposes on me constantly and isn't afraid to point out my flaws, I'd say he qualifies."

"Sounds more like a cousin." I picked the table farthest from the food line and sank into a chair against the wall. Tod sat on my left, where he could see the rest of the room.

"Okay, spit it out." His chair squealed against the floor as he scooted toward the table, and I realized that he was now fully corporeal and visible to everyone in the room—and probably had been since we'd come through the doors. "What's Nash caught up in?" His brows were low and his voice was deep, but he didn't sound surprised. He'd known something was wrong. Maybe he'd known longer than I had.

"Demon's Breath," I whispered, to keep from being overheard. "He's been hooked for about a month, but last week a couple of his teammates got mixed up in it without knowing what they were taking. Doug found Nash's red balloon and now he's dead, and Scott's strapped to a bed in the mental health unit. Did you already know about that? And now Nash is stuck in the Netherworld, and it may be a setup, but even if it is, *we have to get him out!*"

"Whoa, take a breath!" Tod reached for my hand across the table, physically unclenching my fingers so he could squeeze them, and I was surprised by his warmth. Weren't dead guys supposed to be cold to the touch? Or was that only in the movies? "Nash is taking Demon's Breath?"

"Yeah, but it gets a lot worse than that."

"So I gathered." His gaze strayed to the bandage forming a lump beneath my sleeve. "But none of the rest of that made any sense."

"I know." I wiped unshed tears from my eyes with the back of my free hand, and lowered my voice when I noticed the custodian staring at me. "It's all messed up, and Alec says we only have one chance to get Nash back, but I'm *not* going to cross over until I know for sure that Nash is there."

Tod's eyes widened, thick blond boy-lashes nearly touching his eyebrows. "Okay, I need you to slow down and start over." He leaned back in his chair and brushed a stray, pale ringlet from his forehead. I nodded, and he forced a smile. "First of all, what does Nash have to do with the Fuller kid's unscheduled reaping?"

I took a deep breath and forced my throat to relax, though it felt hot and sore from holding back tears. "Demon's Breath— the dealer calls it frost—is sold in black party balloons. Except for Nash's. His are red." I clenched my hands together on the cracked, faded tabletop and looked into Tod's bright blue eyes, somehow undulled by death. "Doug found Nash's balloon and took a hit, but Nash's concentration is too strong for humans. Or something like that. Then Doug started convulsing, and I started screaming, so Nash put me and Emma in my car—though, actually, it's a rental—and told us to go. He was supposed to call us with an update, but he never did. Then this guy named Alec *possessed* Emma and said his boss has Nash in the Netherworld, and that if I want him back, I have to help him cross back into our world."

"Wait…" Tod held both hands out to slow me down. "You have to help who cross over? Nash or Alec?"

"Alec. Well, both of them, really. But Alec won't help me find Nash unless I promise to bring him back with us."

"Who's Alec?"

"I have no idea." I shrugged helplessly. "He just…showed up tonight, talking through Emma's mouth. He says he's human, but he lives in the Netherworld. But humans don't live in the Netherworld. They can't, right? It doesn't make any sense."

Tod sighed. "It might, if you weren't saying it so fast."

"Sorry. But I have to be back in half an hour." My mouth was so dry I could barely talk, so I opened my soda and drained half of it. I'd definitely need the caffeine, since I obviously wasn't going to get any sleep for the third night in a row. "Alec says he's a proxy for Avari, who's holding Nash in the Netherworld. Have you ever heard of a proxy?"

Tod nodded slowly. Bleakly. "They're like assistants you can snack on. If you're a hellion. But they're rare, because humans don't hold up very well in the Netherworld, and eventually they'll wear out. It sounds like this hellion is looking to upgrade. With Nash."

I shook my head. "I don't think so. Alec didn't sound very worn-out."

"Okay, let's start with Nash." Tod leaned both elbows on the table, which put his eyes almost exactly level with mine. "He's been taking Demon's Breath for how long?"

"About a month."

The reaper's blue eyes went dark like the ocean at night, and his fist thumped on the table. "Why the hell didn't you tell me!"

"Because you weren't around, and I didn't know!" I hissed, glancing around the cafeteria to make sure no one was listening. "And it's your fault he was exposed in the first place! He accidentally inhaled some when we crossed over trying to save your girlfriend! Then *you* took him back to make his first purchase!"

"I never…" But his denial faded into shocked silence when the pieces fell together in his head. "I didn't know what he was doing, and he wouldn't tell me. He just said he was calling in his favor, and that's all I needed to know. And honestly, I didn't even push him for information. I was so messed up then, I wasn't even thinking."

Because Addison had just died without her soul. His absence and absentmindedness had worried me. But I should have been worried about Nash.

"I should have followed him. I could have stopped this before it even started!" Tod ran one hand through his hair, and several curls fell over his forehead. And when he finally looked up, I couldn't decide whether I was more surprised by his admission or by the guilt and anger churning slowly in his eyes.

I almost never saw Tod's eyes swirl.…

"Me, too." I stared at my hands, still clenched tightly on the tabletop. "I should have noticed something was wrong. A pack of gum, and four weeks of school and back, shouldn't have been enough to make me miss something this big."

Tod sighed. "How did he get into the Netherworld this time?"

"You didn't take him?"

"Hell, no, I didn't take him!" Tod said, loud enough to draw several looks our way.

I leaned across the table and lowered my voice. "Then I have no idea. He was supposed to be here with Doug, but you said he wasn't…?"

Tod shook his head in confirmation. "Not that I saw, and I

was here when they brought him in. How did he get Nash's...
balloon?"

I sighed and took another sip from my bottle. "Emma found
it in Nash's bag during the party. I left Em in the car with the
balloon. But she had to go to the bathroom." As she'd explained while we watched the movie. "We think Doug went
looking for her and found the balloon instead." I sighed and
stared at the table. "I wish we'd never gone to Doug's house
tonight. But we couldn't let Em go alone." I glanced up at
Tod, searching for agreement in his expression. For some sign
that this whole catastrophe wasn't solely the result of my poor
judgment. "Not with Everett bringing enough balloons to
make a house float."

"Everett?" Tod's hand fell from his hair to land on the tabletop with a thud. "The dealer's name is Everett? Are you sure?"

"Yeah. He's tall and kind of angular. Nash says he's half
harpy, which is why we can't figure out how he's getting his
supply here from the Netherworld."

"Everett. That damned pointy-looking, son-of-a-*shrew*,"
Tod snapped. Then he met my gaze again. "I know how he's
getting it." He clenched the cheap plastic saltshaker like it held
untold secrets of the universe. "I swear I had no idea what I
was carrying, but...*I* brought it over."

≪ 20 ≫

"What?" Questions tumbled in my head like shoes in the
dryer, clanking painfully as they slammed into one another.
Tod was ferrying Demon's Breath from the Netherworld for
Avari? "Have you and Nash both lost your minds? This is really a very simple concept—one that you taught me! Hellion
equals evil. Period!"

Tod's exhale was long, and low, and heavy. "Avari had
something I needed, and he doesn't take cash or checks. Not
that I have either one, but I could have come up with some
money." The reaper shrugged. "But he already knew what
he wanted from me. And Kaylee, I swear I had no idea what
I was carrying."

The numbness in my brain and body faded, replaced by a
scalding anger. "Is that supposed to make it okay? That you
didn't care enough to ask what you were hauling? What did
you *think* he was sending up? Fuzzy kittens and care packages for the children's ward?" People were staring at us now,
but I was *so* far beyond caring. "Isn't working for a hellion a
conflict of interest?" I demanded through gritted teeth, my

open-arm gesture taking in the entire hospital, and the job Tod carried out there.

"It would be, if I were selling him poached souls, or something like that. But my business with him has nothing to do with my job, or with my abilities as a reaper."

"Are you serious?" I shoved my chair back and my pitch rose so high on the last word that dogs all over the neighborhood were probably howling in sympathy. Or maybe in pain. "Your reaper skills are what get you to and from the Netherworld. Without them, you wouldn't have interested Avari except as a snack. Another soul to suck. You're *totally* abusing your abilities. And because of what you've done, one kid is dead, one's gone clinically insane, and your own brother is wandering around in the Netherworld like a protein bar with legs!"

People were starting to openly stare, so I looked at the table and counted to ten to get my temper back under control. When I looked up, Tod was wiping both hands over his face, the muscles in his arms bunched with tension.

"I hope it's worth it, whatever he's giving you," I spat as softly as I could. "I hope it's worth the three lives you've ruined." Four, if you counted Emma's, and five if you counted mine, because there was no guarantee I'd walk away from the Netherworld alive this time. Or at all.

Tod flinched, but didn't break eye contact. "It's Addison," he said, his voice so low and heavy I wasn't sure I'd heard it at all. "I traded my service as a courier for an hour a day with Addy."

Huh?

"Tod, Addison's dead."

He nodded slowly. "Her body is. But her soul is alive and not so well in the Netherworld, and the only way I can help

her is to give her an hour a day free from torture and humiliation. To keep her sane. It seemed like the least I could do,
considering I failed to get her soul back before she died." Tod's
jaw tightened, and he held my gaze, steadily. Unashamed. Yet
I saw the flicker of pain and determination in his eyes.

I felt my heart splinter and thought for a moment that I
could actually hear the cracks. How was I supposed to stay
mad at him now? Tod had been ruining lives with his own
postmodern, interdimensional version of chivalry.

Will all the real men please stand up?

"I swear I didn't know what I was carrying...."

I wanted to ask if that would have mattered. If he'd known
what he was really agreeing to, would he have considered
five ruined lives—and potentially countless more—worth an
hour of comfort a day for Addison? But I didn't ask, because
I already knew that where Addy was concerned, Tod had no
limits. He'd been willing to let me die in the Netherworld
to save her soul. There was nothing he wouldn't do for her.
To be with her.

Even beyond the grave.

I sighed and rubbed both hands over my face. "Okay, so
how does this work? You blink into the Netherworld and he
lets you see Addison for an hour, then hands you a balloon
bouquet on your way out?"

Tod's brows rose in bitter amusement. "Do I look like
a party clown? It's just a canvas duffel bag with a padlock
through the zipper. I could have broken it, or cut the bag open,
but honestly, considering what Addy and I have to lose, it
didn't seem smart to stick my nose into Netherworld business."

"I hate to tell you this, Tod, but you're already up to your
eyebrows in it. And thanks to you and Nash, so are Doug,
and Scott, and Emma, and me." Not to mention whoever else

Doug might have introduced to frost. I couldn't help marveling at the irony of both Hudson brothers playing separate, secret parts in whatever Avari was up to.

He leaned back in his chair and exhaled heavily. "Avari's going to be pissed when he finds out I'm out of the drug-trafficking business, and he'll probably take it out on Addison. But the more immediate problem is Nash. If we don't get him out before I refuse the next shipment, we'll probably never have another shot."

"Alec says our best chance is tomorrow night. They're having some kind of big party…" And I couldn't help wondering what there was to celebrate in the Netherworld.

The reaper nodded, pale curls bobbing. "Yeah, I've seen them setting up for it. Creepy."

"…and he thinks he can get to Nash during the commotion. He's gonna call me back in about half an hour—" I glanced at my watch "—make that twenty minutes, to make plans." I stood, and Tod stood with me, and we headed for the hall by unspoken agreement.

"There are no cell phone towers in the Netherworld," he whispered. "How's Alec going to call you?"

I swallowed the horror and disgust my answer brought with it as I pushed open the double doors. "Through Emma."

Confusion narrowed Tod's eyes, then sudden comprehension flowed in, chased by a wave of obvious repulsion. "He's using her as an intermediary? That's what you meant by possession?" he hissed, without bothering to check the cold, sterile hall for humans.

I nodded. "It's awful. She still looks like herself, but she sounds like someone else, and she doesn't move, or sit, or laugh like Emma. She's being *worn*. It's creepy."

"Yeah." Tod's scowl deepened as he walked, and I rushed to

keep up with him. "I've only seen the show once, but it was one of the ugliest things I've ever seen." Which surely meant something coming from a reaper. "And it's hard on the host, because he subconsciously fights the invasion. It can leave you exhausted for days afterward."

"Tell me about it." No wonder I was so tired all the time. In addition to giving up sleep to avoid waking up in the Nether-world, I'd had my body invaded by an uninvited visitor twice in the past week.

Tod stopped abruptly and his gaze narrowed on me. "What does that mean?"

I sighed and cradled my bandaged arm. "Avari's been using me to communicate with Nash. I didn't realize it until I saw it happen to Emma, but I'm sure that's what's been happening." I shuddered at the sudden clear understanding that I'd been used, both physically and emotionally. That Avari had been in my body, without my knowledge or permission. Could there be a more horrifying, revolting violation?

I'd never seen a stronger look of disgust—or protective *rage*—than the one on Tod's face. His eyes practically blazed with twisting blue flames. "How could Nash let that happen?"

I shrugged, dropping my empty soda bottle in the trash against the wall. "I don't think he had any choice. I sure didn't when Alec took over Emma."

Tod shoved the parking garage door open with both hands, though he could have walked through it. "You didn't know what was going on, and you had to play nice to get your boy-friend back. Nash had a choice. If he'd wanted to get rid of Avari, he would have found a way. But he just let it happen—let that bastard use you—and he didn't even tell you." His mouth snapped shut against the rest of what he wanted to say, but I heard it, anyway.

If I were as important to Nash as his next fix, he would never have let it happen.

"What the hell is wrong with him?"

"He's not the same, Tod," I said, race-walking to keep up with him, though he had no idea where I'd parked. "He's been Influencing me, and he's lying all the time. He said he gave Scott's first balloon to you to get rid of, but I'm guessing you never saw it."

Tod scowled, adjusting his course when I veered toward my rental. "When was that?"

I clicked the button to unlock the car. "Monday, when you were working double shifts with no breaks." Except that Tod had popped into the cafeteria at lunch that day to ask me if Emma was serious about Doug... "You were never in trouble with Levi, were you? No double shifts?"

Tod shook his head, teeth grinding furiously. "To my never-ending dismay and boredom, we only get a few deaths a day in a hospital this size. I wander off during the lulls all the time, and Levi doesn't care, so long as I don't miss an appointment. And Nash damn well knows it."

"I'm such an idiot!" I kicked the front tire, but that only scuffed my shoe. "Why couldn't I see what he was doing?"

"I didn't see it, either." Tod's footsteps went silent as he circled the car toward the passenger's side, and I knew that no one else could see him. Still, I was grateful that he hadn't simply blinked into Emma's bedroom, leaving me to drive back alone.

"So, you're not going to get in trouble for leaving now?" I asked as I settled into the driver's seat.

He shrugged, unconcerned. "It's a slow night. No one's scheduled to tumble into the abyss for another hour and a half, and if I'm not back by then, I'll get someone else to cover for me."

"What if you get another...addendum?"

His brows rose, but the corners of his cherubic mouth turned down as he sank onto the leather seat. "Then we have bigger worries than my absence."

I buckled up and started the engine, then twisted to watch out the rear windshield as I backed out of the parking space. "We need help, but my dad can't do it. Bringing someone who can't cross over would just be creating more work for ourselves," I said, then rushed on before he could interrupt. "I think we should bring your mom in on this."

"No," Tod said, and I glanced at him as I shifted into Drive, surprised to find his expression completely unreadable. "Absolutely not."

"But she's five times my age, and she can cross over on her own." I turned left out of the garage and onto the street, trying not to let frustration leak into my voice. "She's the only option that makes sense."

"We are not dragging my mother into the Netherworld. And we can't tell her about Nash, or she'll go on her own and get killed." His hand landed on mine on the gearshift, and again I was surprised by its warmth. "I'm serious, Kaylee. If you want to bring your dad or your uncle, that's your call. But leave my mother out of this. I've already lost my dad and Addison, and now possibly Nash. I will *not* add my mom to the list."

I could only nod, impressed by his fervor and surprised by the brief glimpse into his heart. *Maybe he doesn't think so differently from the living, after all....*

"Fine." I nodded once more, decisively. "No parents."

EMMA WAS STILL ASLEEP when I snuck back into her room at ten minutes after three. Fortunately, her mother was snoring from behind her bedroom door, and both of her sisters were still out. Obviously the best part about college was the lack of a curfew.

In the bedroom, I knelt to check on Emma, half convinced she would show some delayed ill effect from the abuse of her body, but she seemed to be sleeping peacefully. And deeply. Probably because, as I'd discovered, possession is exhausting.

"She looks okay," Tod said, echoing my own thoughts. "Hopefully one more round won't hurt her. But let's keep this Alec on a short leash, just in case."

I nodded, yawning as I pushed myself to my feet with one hand on the mattress. Considering I'd never actually met Alec, his leash would be no longer than my pinkie finger.

"How much time do we have?" Tod leaned over Emma and ran one finger gently over her lower lip.

I glanced at the clock on Emma's DVD player. "About five minutes. Don't touch her! You'll wake her up."

He huffed softly. "I doubt that. She looks like she could sleep through the end of the world."

"No thanks to you." I shooed him away from the bed, then had to force my eyes open wide when they threatened to close. "I need a Coke." What I *really* needed was a shot of adrenaline straight to the heart, but caffeine would have to do. "I think you should fade out," I said, backing toward the hall. "Alec doesn't want me to bring backup…." Which was one of the main reasons I found him hard to trust. Well, that and the fact that he'd contacted me through the unconscious body of my best friend. "So we should probably keep you a secret."

"No problem." Tod grinned, and though I could see no difference in him, I had no doubt that he no longer existed physically in the room. If he ever had.

I tiptoed into the kitchen in my socks and grabbed another

can of Coke from the fridge. I had drained half of it by the time I made it back to Emma's room. "Do you—" I began, intending to ask the reaper if he wanted a soda. Though I couldn't remember ever seeing him consume anything before.

"Shhhh!" Tod hissed the moment I stepped in from the hall. "He's here."

My voice faded into a tense silence as I glanced from the reaper to the girl lying curled up on one side on the bed. Emma hadn't moved since I left the room, but if Tod thought Alec had arrived—a full four minutes early—I wasn't taking any chances.

Sipping from my can as casually as possible, I strolled across the room toward Emma, and this time when her eyes popped open, I was ready. I didn't spill a single drop.

"Do I what?" Alec asked through Emma's mouth as he stared up at me through her deep brown eyes.

"I was going to ask if you wanted a soda."

Emma frowned, then pushed herself upright on the mattress. "How did you know I was here?"

"You went tense when I walked into the room." I shrugged, totally ad-libbing. "So, you want a drink or not?" I asked before he had a chance to think about my answer.

Emma's brows shot up. "Can I do that? Have a drink while I'm in here?" He spread her arms to indicate her entire form.

I shrugged again. "How would I know? I've never been in someone else's body."

The grin was all Alec. "Me, neither—before tonight."

"Are you serious?" I shot him a legitimate scowl. "You're new at this? Here, they don't let new drivers behind the wheel alone, but I bet there's no one in there with you to slam on the brakes if this thing goes downhill."

His grin faded. "Trust me, Kaylee, there's no one else here you'd trust in your friend's body."

"No one here, either…" Tod quipped, and it was all I could do not to acknowledge his joke—or his presence.

"So, how 'bout that drink?" Alec swung Emma's bare feet onto the floor. "Do you have anything stronger than Coke?"

Yeah. Drano. But even if I knew for a fact that he was drawing me into a trap, I couldn't poison Emma. "She's had quite enough to drink tonight, thank you."

"Well, that explains why she was so easy to push toward sleep." When I showed no sign of relenting, he sighed and shrugged Emma's shoulders. "A Coke would be great, thanks. I haven't had one in years."

Tod followed me to the kitchen, as I'd hoped he would, and I whirled on him the minute we were out of sight from the hallway. "Just shut up and listen in there, or I swear I'll tell your boss you're moonlighting as a Netherworld mule," I hissed. Then I grabbed another can from the fridge and marched back down the hall before he could reply.

In Emma's room, Alec stood with Em's arms crossed beneath her chest, eyeing the collection of pictures on her dresser. "Here. Drink fast and talk faster. This little powwow's over if anyone wakes up or comes home. Got it?"

Alec nodded, then broke one of Emma's nails popping open the tab on his can. She was definitely going to notice that. "Mmm," he said, swallowing his first mouthful of soda. "I'd forgotten how it fizzes on your tongue. It almost hurts. Do you have any idea how long it's been since I had a soda? I can't believe I can feel it through her. Maybe I should just stay here…"

"No, you shouldn't. Don't you want to feel things in your own body?"

Emma shrugged. "Well, one without breasts would be nice. These things get in the way every time I move my arms."

I rolled my eyes and sank into the desk chair. "I wouldn't know. But she should get her period in a couple of days. Unless you want to stick around for that—" and I could tell from the comically horrified look on her face, and from Tod's less-than-subtle snort, that my dart had hit the bull's-eye "—I suggest you start talking. What's the plan?"

"Okay, here goes…" Alec took his can and settled Emma onto the edge of the bed, leaning forward with one elbow on her knee, her legs spread wide. Like a guy would sit. "Tomorrow is the winter solstice, in both worlds, and for the first time in something like sixty years, Avari has the resources to hold a true Liminal Celebration. I've truly never seen anything like the effort they're putting into this."

"What's a Liminal Celebration?" I asked, sipping from my own can, wishing that the caffeine would kick in almost as badly as I wished Alec would get to the part that included the actual plan.

"It's a festival in honor of the liminal times and places. Do you understand liminality?" I shook my head and, to my irritation, he made Emma nod, as if she'd expected as much. "Liminalities are the spaces and moments between."

"Between what?" I asked, exhaustion having used up all my patience.

"Between anything. Dusk and dawn, for example, are the liminal times between daylight and dark. Doorways are the liminal spaces between in and out. Make sense?" he asked, and I nodded slowly, though I was far from sure I actually understood.

"So, noon would be a liminal time between morning and afternoon, right?" I said, sinking into the desk chair.

Emma's head nodded, and her borrowed eyes lit with satisfaction. "Liminalities are very important, because they thin the boundaries between the two worlds and make human energy easier for those in the Netherworld to access. And the summer and winter solstices are the biggest, most important liminalities of all. They represent the points of balance in the year between the shortening of days and the lengthening of days. The winter solstice is like their New Year."

I drained my can and reached back to set it on the desk behind me. "So, you guys are basically throwing a big New Year's Eve party, and you want me to crash it?"

"Sort of." Emma's eyes narrowed in thought. "I think I can take advantage of the distraction to get your boyfriend alone. Then you should be able to cross over and take us both back with you."

Sounded reasonable enough to me—assuming he was telling the truth.

"Where is this big festival?"

Alec sighed through Emma's mouth. "As near as I can figure, not having been on your side of the gray fog in quite a while, it's across the street from the city park. That's where they're setting everything up. And whatever they've built where the old county courthouse stood must be heavily populated, because the building bleeds through almost entirely. Long hallways and room after empty room."

My heart dropped into my stomach. He was talking about the high school. *My* high school. It had been built five years earlier, after the courthouse burned down and the county seat was moved.

"What time does this party start?" I whispered as chill bumps popped up beneath my sleeves.

"Dusk. The last minutes between sunset and full darkness,

when you can still make out things around you, but you can also see stars and planets in the sky. It's the perfect liminal moment."

Crap. Of course it started at dusk. Our Winter Carnival opened at 5:30—which was about when the sun went down in mid-winter—the exact time and place as their Liminal Celebration.

There's no way on earth that was a coincidence. Something bad was going on. Something even worse than the frost invasion and Nash being stuck in the Netherworld, though that hardly seemed possible. And according to the clock on Emma's DVD player, I only had about fourteen hours before dusk brought my one chance to bring Nash back to our world.

"So, I'll meet you at five-thirty by the front steps of the—" *high school* "—new building, and we'll go from—"

But Alec interrupted before I could finish that thought.

"Shhhh, he's coming," he hissed. Then, "Yes. Five-thirty, by the steps, no matter what else happens. I have to—" And just like that, Alec was gone.

Only instead of slumping back into sleep, as she'd done the last time Alec vacated her body, Emma stood suddenly stiff and straight as a bedpost. Her head swiveled slowly on her shoulders, steadily taking in the room and its furnishings before her eyes met mine. Then her mouth curled into a slow, taunting smile.

"Well, isn't this interesting...."

Though I hadn't seen him in a month, I'd know that voice anywhere.

Avari.

"Ms. Cavanaugh, how delightful to find you here." The hellion paused, glancing around the room again through Emma's eyes. "Wherever *here* is."

I shuddered beneath a bolt of near-paralyzing terror, then exhaled silently in relief. If he didn't know where he was, he probably didn't know who he was *in*. Which surely meant it would be hard for him to ever take Emma over again.

But then Em's eyes narrowed as Avari stared through them at a framed photo on the dresser: a shot of me and Emma standing in front of my new-to-me car, on the day I'd gotten it. "Well, isn't my proxy clever?" Avari crossed the room in Emma's bare feet, hips swinging in the exaggerated motion of a man who isn't used to wielding them. His gaze flicked to the mirror behind the picture and his eyes widened in lecherous appreciation. "And doesn't he have the most exquisite taste?"

Seeing Avari in her was a thousand times worse than watching Alec interact through Emma's body. I couldn't stand it. How was I ever going to look her in the face again?

"Get out!" I whispered through clenched teeth, my hands

curling into powerless fists at my sides. Avari ignored me and reached for the picture with one of Emma's delicate, graceful hands. "Don't touch that!"

His gaze flicked my way in surprise and I choked on my next breath, shocked and disturbed by how unlike Emma her own eyes could look. "What would you rather I touch?" Avari asked, his smooth, sinister words violating her throat just as brutally as his presence desecrated her existence. "This?" The thin hand changed directions and Emma's fingers splayed across her flat stomach, thumb brushing her sternum, pinkie tucking beneath the elastic waistband of her pj pants.

"Or this?" Avari's voice deepened suggestively, and the hand slid up Emma's torso to lift her left breast through the thin cotton of her nightshirt.

My pulse pounded so fast and hard my vision started to go dark. "Get *out* of her, *now!*" When Avari turned back to the mirror, unbothered by my powerless protest, I glanced at Tod for help, but he could only shrug and press one finger against his lips in a "shhhh" gesture, reminding me not to give away his presence. He couldn't control Avari any more than I could, but if the hellion found out the reaper was helping me, he would take his anger out on Nash, and on Addison's soul.

"Oh, nooo…" Avari ran Emma's hand down her side and over the generous curve of her hip, cocking it to one side for a better view in the mirror. "I like this one. Truly lovely. She is definitely worth the effort of exploration."

My jaws ached from being clenched, but I forced my feet to remain still. There was nothing I could do to hurt Avari without hurting Emma, and I wasn't sure what abilities, if any, Avari brought with him to the body he possessed. Knowing my luck, if I tried to throw a punch—not that I even knew how—he'd freeze me where I stood, or do something worse than groping with Emma's borrowed hands.

"How could I not have noticed her before? She feels familiar…." Both of Emma's hands slid around her hips to cup her backside as Avari's gaze traveled down in the mirror. "But not obviously so. How did Alec ever find her…?" Avari blinked, then turned from the mirror to meet my furious gaze through narrowed eyes. "I do *love* a resourceful proxy." But the hard, angry line of Emma's jaw said that wasn't entirely true. Alec had been up to something without Avari's knowledge, and the hellion was pissed. "And Alec has always been exactly that."

"How long have you…had him?" I asked, stalling for time as my brain whirred almost audibly, grinding in search of some way to get rid of the hellion.

Avari tilted Emma's head to one side, as if surprised by my interest. And suspicious of it. "Oh, two or three decades," he finally said. "And he has proven most useful." Yet that little twitch of irritation was back. "Even when he doesn't intend to." Emma's body stepped closer to me, one hip cocked, one side of her mouth curved up in a lewd grin. "For instance, you are a hard child to get in touch with. Though I must say you aren't particularly difficult to get *inside* of…"

Rage and horror battled within me as Emma's borrowed gaze swept the length of my form before finally returning to my eyes. I had the sudden urge to cover what little flesh my clothes didn't hide, and couldn't help wondering what the hellion had done with my body when he'd occupied it. And how often that had been.

If I actually got Nash back alive, he was going to tell me every single thing that happened while I was literally out of my own mind—or I'd kill him myself. And based on Tod's angry, narrowed eyes, he was thinking something very similar.

Emma stepped forward again, and I answered with another step back, my pulse racing, my jaws clenched so hard I was half-afraid my teeth would crack. "How many times?" I whispered, trying to showcase my anger while hiding my terror.

He took another slinky step toward me, wearing my best friend's body like a slut wears spandex. And this time when I backed away, my thighs hit the edge of the desk. I had nowhere left to go, unless I was willing to let him follow me through the rest of Emma's house. Which I was not.

"How many times have I been in you?" Avari asked, leering at me with Emma's wide, brown eyes, and I flinched over his phrasing. My skin crawled just thinking about him being on the inside of my flesh, breaching the most sacred of my boundaries: that which defined my soul.

"Several," the hellion answered at last, and his next step put him—put them—less than a foot away. "And I must say it's a genuine pleasure." Emma's body leaned forward and her cheek skimmed mine, my pulse roaring in my ears.

"Each…" Her lips brushed my jaw, and I swallowed thickly.

"…and every…" Her hot, damp breath puffed against my earlobe, and I closed my eyes, trying not to breathe.

"…time." Avari's last word stirred the sensitive hairs on my neck, just below my ear, and I swallowed the whimper caught in my throat.

I opened my eyes, and over Emma's shoulder I saw Tod standing with his fists clenched, his face flushed in fury, jaw bulging as he silently ground his teeth.

Then the hellion stepped back, smiling through Emma's pouty mouth, and her eyes took on a lecherous glint so disturbing and disorienting that my whole body shuddered. "But as much fun as I've had playing teenage *bean sidhe*—once when your boyfriend didn't even realize you'd stepped out of your body…"

Rage raced through my veins so fast and hot I thought I would combust. What the *hell* had he done! What had he made *me* do? And did Nash really think it was me doing…whatever Avari had done with my body?

"…I have yet to find a good way to communicate with you. Though we came so close with your classmate the other day." Confusion must have shown through my mounting fury, because as Avari turned, running one of Emma's slim fingers over the desktop, he lifted one of her artfully arched brows and continued. "How is your arm, by the way?" Her loaded gaze traveled to the bandaged bulge beneath my right sleeve.

Understanding slammed into me like a hammer to my skull. It all came back to Avari. All of it.

Nash was right. Avari was Scott's shadow man. He was the hallucination Doug had seen in his passenger's seat. He was the hellion selling its breath to Nash. Avari had possession of Addison's soul. He'd bribed Tod and Everett into delivering and disseminating his toxic byproduct. He was holding Nash captive in the Netherworld. And Avari was organizing the Liminal Celebration, which would conveniently coincide with our Winter Carnival.

How could I not have seen it earlier? All roads led back to Avari. And for some reason, he'd been trying to get in touch with me.

"What do you want?" I demanded, suddenly sure I'd finally asked the right question.

Avari wrapped one of Emma's arms around the shoulder-high post at the foot of her bed and swung her around to face me, exposing a smooth strip of skin at her waist. "You." The hellion's voice went deep and dark, and sounded surreal coming from Emma's still-pink mouth. "I want you. And if you cross over right now, you have my word that I will send your boyfriend back to your world."

From my left, near Emma's closet, Tod shook his head frantically, and it was all I could do not to look directly at him and clue Avari in to his presence. But I didn't need to see Tod to know what he was thinking. Avari might send Nash back, but there was no telling when, where, or in what condition he would arrive.

Or in how many pieces.

"Why me?" I asked, ice-cold dread surging through my veins in place of blood. "Don't you have enough proxies, or servants, or snacks running around?"

"There are never enough proxies." *Of course.* I almost forgot I was talking to a hellion of avarice. "But that is not my interest in you." Emma grinned, easily the most genuine expression Avari had twisted her features into yet. "If you want to know more, you'll have to cross over so we can have this conversation in person."

I shook my head firmly and crossed my arms over my chest. "Not going to happen."

"Even to save your boyfriend?"

I swallowed thickly. Crossing over into Avari's hands was not my only chance to get Nash back, but that didn't make it any easier to say what came next. In fact, the words stuck so firmly in my throat that I had to clear it just to speak. "I don't want a boyfriend who cares more about his next fix than about me." The tears in my eyes were authentic, but with any luck, he'd attribute them to the emotional loss of my boyfriend, rather than to the crippling pain born from my knowledge that I was betraying Nash, and maybe damning his soul. "And

I certainly don't want one who lets you step into my body without even telling me I'm being worn like a used condom."

Surprise and amusement glittered in Emma's eyes, and Avari almost looked…satisfied. As if he were pleased to discover something he actually respected in me.

Which sent an even stronger chill through me.

"Is that a no?"

I nodded slowly, as if the decision were difficult for me. As if I weren't planning to come later, on my own terms. With backup. "A very firm no."

I had an instant to hope I hadn't just made a very big mistake, then Avari smiled cruelly with Emma's lips. "In that case, I hope you said a very firm goodbye to your boyfriend."

Emma's eyes closed and her legs folded beneath her. She collapsed to the carpet with a single soft, feminine exhale, and I dropped to my knees beside her as her eyes fluttered open once. Then twice. Then they flew open again and stayed open, focusing on me sluggishly.

"Kaylee?" she asked in her own voice, and relief flavored my next breath, as if the very air tasted better now that Avari had left the building. "What happened?"

"I don't know." I shrugged and glanced at Tod, who now knelt on her other side, though she clearly could neither see nor hear him. "I went to the bathroom, and when I got back you were on the floor. Did you roll off the bed?"

And now I'm lying to my best friend…

Emma frowned and propped herself up on both palms. "I don't think so." Then her gaze narrowed on my blouse before trailing to my jeans, and I knew I'd messed up. Em was smart and she knew I had secrets. "You were sleeping in your clothes?"

I sighed and shot her a crooked smile, scrambling to think on my feet. "I was hoping Nash would call and we'd make up."

"You were going to go over there in the middle of the night?" Her own smile snuck up on me, and I was surprised to realize that our fight had bothered her, too.

"Yeah. But he didn't call." And my next trip to see Nash would involve much more than a mile-and-a-half drive through suburban Texas.

"He will." Emma pushed herself to her feet. Her eyes were already trying to close, and her next words were stretched through a lion-size yawn. "And everything will be okay. Because Nash loves you, and that's all that matters. Right?"

I nodded as Em sank back onto the bed, and I couldn't help wishing that, for once, things really were that simple.

"Hey, Dad," I said into my phone, then covered the mouthpiece to thank the waitress pouring ice water into my glass.

"You're up awfully early after a sleepover," my father said, relief obvious in his voice. This time I couldn't blame him for worrying, even though I'd left voice messages several times throughout the night to tell him I was okay. And still in the human world.

"It doesn't count as a sleepover if you don't sleep," I said, stifling a yawn. "But Emma was nice enough to help me stay awake all night." Which was technically true. After seeing her body taken over by two different Netherworld entities, I couldn't have slept if I'd wanted to. "We watched movies and ate ice cream."

Across the table, Tod rolled his eyes, apparently feeling cheated by the lack of slumber party clichés. After all, what were a couple of teenage possessions compared to the half-naked pillow fight he'd hoped for in reward for staying the rest of the night with us—invisibly—just in case I fell asleep. Or Avari reappeared.

Not that my dad needed to know about either the reaper or the hellion. I saw no reason to worry him, since even the noblest of intentions on his part would only get him trapped in the Netherworld. Or worse.

Tod nodded in thanks when the waitress set a glass of orange juice in front of him. I'd refused to talk to him if he didn't go completely corporeal at the restaurant.

Over the line I heard the clink of glass-on-plastic as the coffeepot bumped the rim of my father's travel mug. "I'm about to leave for work." Which he had no choice but to do, even in the middle of a *bean sidhe* crisis, if we wanted to be able to make next month's rent. And honestly, the only thing I could think of worse than being wanted by a hellion was being *homeless* and wanted by a hellion. "I don't want you alone today. You need rest, and it's not safe for you to sleep alone right now."

A very odd statement coming from my father... But I knew what he meant.

"I'm fine, Dad. I'm being careful." Whatever that meant... I was too tired at the moment for much coherence.

"You're not fine, Kaylee." His mug clunked against the countertop. "You can't function on so little sleep, and you're only going to make yourself sick by trying."

"So what do you suggest?" I asked as the waitress set a plate of chocolate chip pancakes on the table in front of me. Sugar would keep me awake, right? I thanked her, then pushed the melting scoop of butter around with my knife.

My dad sighed. "I don't know. We're still working on it. Can you stay with Nash or Harmony? As little as I trust that boy in some respects, I do trust him to wake you up if you start screaming."

Unfortunately, hanging out with Nash wasn't an option, unless I was willing to cross into the Netherworld and hand over my soul for the privilege. And I couldn't stay with Harmony without having to explain her son's absence. So maybe Emma, once Tod went to work…?

"Yeah," I said around a sweet, chocolaty mouthful. "Don't worry, I won't be alone."

"Okay, I have to go." He paused, and I heard doubt and concern in the short silence. "I'll call to check up on you, so answer your phone when it rings. And I'll see you tonight."

"Count on it," I said, desperately hoping I wasn't jinxing myself with that one.

I hung up my phone and slid it into my front pocket, then looked up to find Tod eyeing my pancakes. "Do you want something? Do reapers even need food?" To my surprise, he was already halfway through his juice, but I couldn't remember ever seeing him actually eat.

"We don't need it, just like we don't need sleep, but all the same pleasure sensors are still there and functioning. Including taste buds," he clarified when I grinned with one raised brow. "Unfortunately, the reaper gig doesn't pay in human currency, so I'm perpetually low on funds."

Oh. Now *that* I understood.

"Here. This is more than I need, anyway." I pushed my plate to the center of the table, and handed him a napkin-wrapped bundle of silverware. "I can't eat with you drooling like a starving child."

"Thanks." He dug in, and I watched, amused by the thought that Death had a sweet tooth.

"So, I assume I'm not the only one who isn't buying this Winter Carnival/Liminal Celebration coincidence, right?"

We hadn't been able to talk it through before, with Emma around—or even dozing.

Tod swallowed his first bite, nodding. "There's no way they're unrelated. My guess is that Avari's planning a big Netherworld feast to take advantage of such a large concentration of human energy when the boundary between the worlds is so thin. They'll be able to soak it all up with minimal effort in the hour surrounding dusk."

I nodded, chewing my own syrup-soaked bite. "But surely that's not all there is to it. I mean, really? A big picnic? That's Avari's master plan? That makes him sound about as dangerous as Yogi Bear."

Tod shrugged. "Yeah. If Yogi were a soul-sucking, body-stealing, boyfriend-snatching, damned-soul-torturing evil demon from another world. Besides, what else could he be planning?"

"I don't know. But the winter solstice happens every year, and Alec said this was their first festival in decades. Why? What's different about this year?" I took another bite, chewing while I waited for an answer neither of us had. "Whatever it is, we need to know before we get there. Are you supposed to see Addison today?"

Tod nodded and dropped his fork on the plate. "Yeah. But if I refuse to take the shipment afterward, Avari's going to know something's up."

I shrugged and cut another bite. "So take it. Just don't deliver it to Everett. We'll figure out how to get rid of it after we've gotten Nash out of there."

Tod frowned, a bite hovering halfway to his mouth. "Kaylee, we don't even know if Alec is going to show up, now that Avari caught E.T. phoning home. For all we know, he'll have his proxy locked up even tighter than Addison, and we'll cross over into this massive chaos swarming with freaks ready to chew our eyeballs and slurp up our intestines."

I felt my brows arch halfway up my forehead. "Eyeballs and intestines? You've been crossing over every day for a month. Has anyone even looked twice at your soft tissues?"

"No, but I was there working for Avari." He leaned closer to whisper over the table. "Or maybe it's because I'm dead, and even most Netherworlders won't eat dead meat. But you're not dead and you don't have permission to be there. So it's *your* soft tissues we should be worrying about." He shrugged when I swallowed thickly, and leaned back in his chair, crossing his arms over the tee stretched across his well-toned chest. "I just thought you should know what you're getting into."

A chill shot down my spine in spite of the hot coffee warming my belly. "Which is why I need you to keep your eyes and ears open while you're with Addison," I said. "We need to know what happened to Alec, and where they're keeping Nash, and what kind of shape he's in, in case Alec isn't there to help us. We also need everything you can find out about this Liminal Celebration And even if you can manage all that, I have a feeling we'll be walking into a very unpleasant surprise tonight."

"Agreed." Tod mopped up a puddle of syrup with the last bite of pancake. "But I'm not making any promises on this spy mission. It's not like I have free rein of the Netherworld."

I hadn't assumed he did, but… "Don't you do half of your job there? I mean, isn't that where you take the souls to be recycled?"

Tod's brows shot up, and I couldn't tell if he was amused or horrified by that thought. "To the Netherworld? No. If I took souls there, they'd be eaten, instead of recycled. Reapers have access to the Netherworld by virtue of being dead, Kaylee. Not as an employee benefit."

Ohhhh… I felt my face flush at my own stupidity. "So, where do you take them?"

"I can't tell you that." And that time, his grin looked genuine. "Company policy. And as for my business in the Netherworld, I pop into Avari's office—the one we were in when Addy died—and he brings her in. We get an hour, most of which I spend talking to her, to keep her mind from slipping under the strain of constant torture and abuse."

"She has a mind?" I couldn't wrap my own mind around that one, though I couldn't imagine why he would visit her if she didn't. "But she's dead."

"So am I." Tod set his fork on my empty, syrup-smeared plate. "You have to stop thinking of death as the end of everything. Yes, in most cases the soul is recycled, but if that doesn't happen, there are a bunch of ways to be dead, with or without a body, a memory, and a soul. Addy has everything but her body, and I'm not even missing that, as you may have noticed." He spread his very corporeal arms for emphasis and almost smacked some poor waitress carrying a huge tray of food.

"I know. But how does Addy have her soul if she sold it to Avari?"

"She and her soul have been reunited in the Netherworld, but he actually owns it. Thus the constant torture."

"Oh." I made a mental note to keep my mouth shut about things I didn't understand. And to let Tod go invisible whenever he wanted—though I would never have believed it, he actually caused less trouble that way. "Just keep your ears open while you're there, okay?"

Tod nodded reluctantly, and I understood his frustration.

The only special skills a reaper could use in the Netherworld were his actual soul-harvesting ability and the ability to cross back over, which made sense, now that I knew he didn't work there. He couldn't go invisible, or walk through walls, or project his voice to only select occupants in a room.

He'd be practically human, and he didn't look very pleased by the thought.

"What about you? What are you going to do?" He glanced to the left, at a clock hanging over the door into the commercial kitchen. "We still have nine hours to kill. Eight, if you want to get there early."

Which I did, for obvious reasons.

"I'm going to see if I can crash at Emma's. It's okay to tell her about my sleeping issues, right, since they have nothing to do with the Demon's Breath epidemic or Nash being missing?"

But Tod shook his head slowly. "Kay, I think you should stay away from Emma for a while."

I frowned, my nearly empty mug of heavily doctored coffee hovering in front of my mouth. "Why?" We could keep an eye on each other. Her, for the demons in my dreams, and me for the demons in her body. "I need to know if Avari possesses her again."

Tod leaned forward with his arms crossed on the table, eyeing me intently. "I know, but the truth is that if you're with her, that's much more likely to happen. Emma is a very convenient direct line of communication to you. But if you're not with her, no one can talk to you through her."

So the best way to protect Emma was to stay away from her.

Well, crap. Looks like I'm on my own today.

Tod glanced at the table for a moment before meeting my eyes. "I'll have a little time between visiting Addy and going to work." And he would *have* to work at least a half shift, because an unemployed reaper was a dead reaper, and a dead reaper was no good to anyone. "So I'll pop in then and you can take a nap."

I couldn't stifle the yawn that came at the very thought of sleep. "Thanks." A nap sounded *sooo* good. Assuming I could keep myself in my own world long enough to enjoy it.

<< 22 >>

OVER THE NEXT HOUR and a half, I drank an entire pot of coffee in front of the TV and fielded phone calls from Emma and my dad, while avoiding one call each from Harmony and Sophie. Emma called in tears, and it took me nearly twenty minutes to calm her down. Thanks to his father's position in the community and his threat to sue the hospital, Doug's death was getting a lot of coverage on the local stations. I felt horrible about not being able to comfort her in person, but Tod's warning kept me firmly on my own couch, telling my-self over and over again that I was staying away from Emma for her own good.

My dad was just calling to check up on me, and as bad as I felt about having to lie to him, if I'd told him I was alone, he would have left work—and possibly lost his job—to come sit with me while I napped.

Sophie left me a furious voice mail demanding to know why my presence at a party—or anywhere else, for that matter—seemed to usher in disaster. She'd seen the news and one of her friends had told her Nash and I were at the party. Fortunately, Sophie seemed to have no clue that Nash was missing, which meant I wouldn't have to call her back to find out if she'd seen him before he disappeared.

Harmony called the home phone looking for Nash, who wasn't answering his cell. But since she'd just gotten home from work, she didn't know how long he'd been gone, and she didn't sound too worried yet. Though that would no doubt change as the day wore on with no contact from him. Especially once she heard about Doug's death on the news.

At the end of the message, she said she might have found a way to keep me anchored to our world when I slept. As grateful as I was for that little tidbit of hope, I sat on my hands to keep from answering the phone for details, because then I'd have to lie to her, too, and for some reason, lying to Nash's mom made me feel even worse than lying to my own father.

An hour after her phone call, I was sitting on the couch sipping from the last can of Jolt, watching the loudest action movie I could find on one of the cable networks, shivering in a short-sleeved T-shirt and a pair of jeans. I'd turned off the heat and opened all the windows, hoping cold air would help keep me awake. Yet in spite of the caffeine, the temperature, and the noise, my eyes were just starting to close when the home phone startled me upright with its sharp, electronic bleating.

The caller ID read *Unknown,* so I dropped the phone back onto the cradle without answering. But my gaze stayed glued to the phone dock as the answering machine kicked in.

My father's voice filled the room, asking the caller to please leave a message after the tone, then an obnoxious electronic beep skewered my exhausted, overworked brain. For a moment, the machine produced only soft static, and I started to relax, assuming it was a wrong number.

Then a familiar voice called my name, and I whirled around so fast I nearly fell off the couch.

"Kaaayleeeee," Avari said, and the discordance of a hellion's voice on my regular, human-manufactured answering machine was enough to make me dizzy. "I know you're there. Where else would you be without your boyfriend to keep you warm, or your father to keep you safe?"

What?

I scrambled over the couch so fast my knee slammed into the armrest and my bad arm brushed the rough upholstery, but I barely felt the pain in my rush to get to the phone. "What do you know about my dad?" I demanded, before the phone even made it to my ear.

"I know that he's sitting four feet from me, unconscious but breathing. For the moment."

"You're lying!" I shouted, panic thudding in my head with each beat of my heart. "He can't cross over."

Avari laughed, and the sound was like shards of ice shattering on concrete. "Neither can Mr. Hudson, yet here they sit, waiting for you to come save them."

Noooo… He was lying. He had to be. "Prove it."

The hellion laughed again, and the callous racket was sharp enough to scrape the flesh from my bones. "Your father is a large man, but about as frightening as a stuffed bear. And when he cries in his sleep, as he's doing at this moment, he calls you 'Kay-Bear.' He also asks for a woman named Darcy, whom I can only assume was your ill-fated mother."

Anguish crashed over me, and I sank onto the couch. For a moment, I heard nothing but the beating of my own heart and felt nothing but a hopeless, almost pleasant numbness crawling over my entire body.

"What do you want?" I asked when I was capable of speech

again, and my voice sounded like it was being whispered from the other end of a long tube.

"I have already answered that question," Avari said. "And my answer hasn't changed. Cross over now, and I will let them go."

Or...he'd keep all three of us, and I would officially qualify as the dumbest girl on the face of the planet. But if I refused to come, would he kill them? Could I bluff him, or stall him somehow?

The room around me swam with my tears. My hand clenched around the phone. My chill bumps now had nothing to do with the cold room.

"Kaylee? What's wrong?" Tod asked, and I looked up to find him standing on the other side of the coffee table, watching me in concern. For once I was too upset to be startled by his sudden appearance. "And why is it colder than *polar bear piss* in here?"

"Shhhh..." I whispered, covering the mouthpiece with one hand while I wiped hot tears from my face with the other.

He waved my warning off. "No one else can hear me. Who is that?"

"He has my dad..." But before I could say any more, the hellion spoke again.

"Time waits for no *bean sidhe,* Ms. Cavanaugh. Are you coming or not?"

"Avari? On the phone?" Tod's jaws bulged with fury, and he spun around like he'd punch something, but there was nothing within reach. "How the hell did he...?" The reaper swung back around to face me, eyes narrowed on me. "Who is he *in?*"

Oh, crap. I hadn't even thought of that.

I covered the mouthpiece again, and the words fell from my lips so quickly even I could hardly understand them, but

Tod seemed to have no trouble. "Emma. It has to be. Can you help her?"

He scowled, his fists clenching around air at his sides. "I don't know. I'll be right back." Then Tod was gone, and I was alone in my freezing living room with the very voice of evil.

"How did you get to him?" I demanded, uncovering the receiver. Yes, I was stalling, but I also needed to know how he'd crossed my father over, so I could stop him from doing it again. Otherwise, bargaining for my dad's freedom, or even his life, would be like holding ice in my palm in July; it would only melt away again.

"My resources are vast, Ms. Cavanaugh, and unlike you, I have no moral qualms preventing me from using them to my advantage."

I stood, pacing the length of my living room as I spoke. "Is that your way of saying you have people?"

He chuckled again, sounding genuinely amused that time. "I suppose so. I have many, many people. One more, in fact, than I had an hour ago."

My anger raged again at his implication, but I did my best to contain it. Avari was trying to make me mad. Trying to rush me into a snap decision that would likely get all three of us killed.

Out of the corner of my eye, something moved, and I glanced up to see that Tod had returned. "It's not Emma," he said, breathing hard, as if he'd actually had to exert himself for that piece of information. Or as if he was too furious to breathe properly. "She's having brunch with her mom and one of her sisters. It's not my mom, either. I already checked."

Crap! Who else could it be?

"So what about your people, Ms. Cavanaugh?" Avari asked,

blessedly oblivious to the other conversation I was holding. "What are you willing to do to save them?"

I covered the mouthpiece again and sank onto the edge of the coffee table, my head spinning with anger, frustration, and exhaustion. "It could be anyone…" I moaned to Tod, staring up at him in desperation. "What are there now, six billion people on the planet?"

Tod shook his head. "He can't just possess some random sleeping stranger, Kaylee. The host has to be someone with a connection to the Netherworld. Someone who's left a psychic imprint there, either by crossing over or by tasting death in one form or another. Which is how he got Emma. She was technically dead for a couple of minutes back in September, right?"

I nodded, my thoughts as scattered as dandelion fuzz on the breeze. Em had died, and I'd crossed over. Those were our connections. Were we both now fair game for demon possession?

"It probably also has to be someone with a connection to you. Otherwise, how would he get your phone number? It's unlisted, right?"

"Kaylee?" Avari's impatience reclaimed my attention, as Tod's new information began to process in the back of my mind.

"It's not about what I'm willing to risk!" I snapped into the phone, having hit the limit of my own tolerance. "It's about what I stand to gain from that risk. Which is nothing, because we both know you'll never let them go if I cross over." After all, he was a hellion of greed.

"I might not," the hellion agreed, and in my mind, I saw a featureless, borrowed head nodding sagely. "But you'll have to take that chance if you ever want to see your father and boyfriend again."

I covered the mouthpiece and met Tod's eyes. "Someone who's tasted death and has a connection to me. Like Emma…" Oh, no. *No, no, no…* "It's Sophie." My eyes closed in horror, but I knew I was right. "Avari's in Sophie."

Tod frowned, then he was gone again.

"Well?" Avari said into my ear. "Which do you value more—their lives, or your freedom?"

But I had no answer to that because it wasn't a fair question—if I crossed over, I'd be giving up both options. "Give me a gesture of goodwill," I demanded. "A sign that you intend to keep your word."

Avari laughed so hard they probably heard him in the next dimension. "What did you have in mind?" he asked, amusement still ringing loud and clear in his voice. "A pinkie swear?"

I rolled my eyes. Where did he get his cultural references, Hannah Montana? "Send one of them back now," I clarified. "And I'll cross over, then you can release the other." Of course, I had no intention of crossing over, because I didn't believe for a second that he'd actually give back either my father or Nash. So his next question stunned me into speechlessness.

"Which one?"

"What?" I asked when his words finally sank in.

"Which one will you trade yourself for? Which one will you save?"

"Oh, right," I snapped, digging deep to find the courage for a few more words—and desperately hoping my bravado didn't get anyone killed. "Like you're actually going to let one of them go."

Avari chuckled softly, and the sound skittered up my spine like spiders crawling on long-dead bones. "I'm just intrigued enough by your proposition to actually send one of them back.

But only because your agony over the decision promises to be a rare and extravagant treat."

As if I would ever let him snack on my pain...

Still, it was a chance to get one of them out alive, immediately, which meant Tod and I would only have to escape the Netherworld with two passengers, instead of three.

"So, which one will it be? The father or the lover? Which do you love more?"

I don't know. My father, who loved me, but abandoned me to his brother. Or my boyfriend, who loved me, but lied to me, Influenced me, and let a hellion wear my body.

There were no guarantees that I'd make it out of the Netherworld alive with whichever one I left in Avari's...care. So the only one whose safety was guaranteed—assuming the hellion's *people* couldn't get to him again—was whichever one he sent over immediately.

And I couldn't choose.

"This offer expires in two minutes, Kaylee..." Avari's intimate whisper made me feel dirty, and promised much worse things to come when we met in his territory. Things that may have already happened to my father and Nash. And I couldn't decide which of them to rescue....

Fortunately, before I could squeak out a desperate, impulsive answer, I heard a dull thud over the line, then the smack of something hitting the floor.

An instant later, Tod's voice spoke to me over the line. "You were right. It was Sophie."

"What did you do?" I demanded. My momentary relief was eclipsed by concern for my cousin, who hadn't exactly volunteered her body for hostile occupation. Even if her own occupation of it was usually hostile.

Tod chuckled. "You can't possess someone who doesn't

have control over his or her own body. That's like stealing a horse without grabbing the reins—how are you supposed to control the animal?"

Had he just compared my pampered cousin to a beast of burden? *I shouldn't like the comparison, but I do....*

Still... "So what did you do?" I repeated.

"I hit Sophie on the back of the head with a universal remote. This thing is huge. It's like a cell phone from the '90s."

"You were supposed to get rid of Avari without hurting the host!"

"Yeah, I didn't get that memo. Maybe next time you should be a little more specific when you boss me around while I'm saving your ass. Though, frankly, this whiny little shrew is lucky she only has one bump, 'cause she's had this coming for a while."

Well, I couldn't argue with him there. "Is she still breathing?"

"It was a remote, not a sledgehammer. Anyway, it's not her time. She'll be fine."

"She better be." I sighed and sank onto the couch again, desperately hoping I hadn't just signed my father's death warrant. Or Nash's. "But the real question is how can we keep it from happening again? What's to stop Avari from taking over everyone I know?"

"Other than the qualifications for an intermediary? I mean, how many people do you know who have a connection to the Netherworld?"

Not many, fortunately. Not that I knew of, anyway. But there were a few—Emma, Sophie, Uncle Brendon, and Harmony—none of whom I wanted to see hurt. Especially because of me.

"Besides," Tod continued, suddenly appearing in the middle

of my living room floor, still holding Sophie's home phone. "I think the key to keeping Avari out of your friends and family is right in front of us."

"It is?" I dropped my phone back into its cradle as Tod nodded solemnly, ignoring the static bleeding from the receiver in his grip.

"Alec."

"The proxy?" Finally wide-awake, I made my way toward the open kitchen window.

"Yeah." The reaper's gaze followed me, but in true Tod fashion, he made no move to help as I used most of my weight to force the first heavy pane of glass closed. "Possession takes an enormous amount of energy, and most hellions can only do it every now and then, and only for short periods of time. A few minutes, at the most. But Avari's been possessing you regularly for a month now, right?"

I latched the kitchen window, then moved on to the two in the living room. "As near as I can tell." I felt sick just thinking about it. How could Nash let Avari possess me? Had he even *tried* to evict the body snatcher? Even once I forgave Nash for lying about the Demon's Breath—after all, he'd been exposed while helping me—I wasn't sure I could forgive him for letting Avari inside me. And even if I could forgive, I could never forget....

"And he's been able to do it twice in two days, since he got his hands on Nash and your dad," Tod continued, dragging my thoughts back on topic. "Which suggests that he's using them as additional energy supplements—logical for a hellion of greed, don't you think?" The reaper raised one brow for emphasis.

"Yeah." And that also supported my theory that Avari had

no intention of returning them, no matter what I did. Especially now that I'd blown the "one now" deal.

"But without proxies to boost his energy level, Avari won't have the power to possess his own wardrobe, much less the entire cast of the Kaylee Cavanaugh show."

"Okay, that makes sense…" I nodded slowly as I reached into the fridge for another Coke. "But won't he just get more proxies?"

The sides of Tod's mouth lifted in the first true smile I'd seen from him in a very long time. "He'll try. But we're banking on the fact that proxies like he has now are few and far between."

"Wait, Dad and Nash are *bean sidhes*—I get that. But Avari was possessing me way before he had either of them, back when Alec was his only walking snack. And Alec is human, right? He called himself a human proxy."

The reaper shook his head slowly. "I don't know exactly what this Alec is, but I'd bet my afterlife that he isn't only human. If he were, there's no way he could have possessed Emma for so long. Or twice in one night."

So Tod was right. The key to disabling Avari's human-telephone mode was to get Alec away from him. Not to mention my father and Nash. But since he'd just been physically expelled from my cousin's body by an unknown third party, the hellion would probably guess that not only would I be coming for my men, but I'd have backup.

Something told me that getting us all out of the Netherworld would *not* be as easy as Alec seemed to think.…

23

Tod had to report to work at noon, but before he popped out of my living room at three minutes 'til, he swore he'd be back by five o'clock. That he would find someone to cover his shift, even though he'd already burned most of those bridges with his previous absences. Then he disappeared from my reality, leaving me alone with thoughts of my missing father and boyfriend.

Well, with those, and with Sophie's phone.

Great.

With a frustrated sigh, I grabbed her phone and my keys, then shrugged into my coat on the way out the door. All the way to Sophie's house, I tried out different explanations for how I'd gotten her phone, and why she'd woken up on her living-room floor with a big bump on the back of her head. But my efforts turned out to be unnecessary—she was still unconscious when I got there.

My old house key still worked, and when I pushed the front door open, I found Sophie lying facedown on the living-room floor, her cheek against the carpet, her eyes closed.

She looked so fragile without her figurative fangs bared at me, or her eyes flashing in bitter triumph over the advantages her life had over mine. Unconscious, she looked frail and tragically human, and it was easier than usual to remind myself that she hadn't chosen her own path in life any more than I had chosen mine. And she certainly hadn't chosen to have her body hijacked by a nefarious Netherworld entity she didn't even know existed.

Even if she had deserved the whack on the head. *Speaking of which…*

I knelt on the spotless white carpet next to the huge remote control and gently prodded the lump on the back of my cousin's skull. Sophie didn't even flinch. How hard had Tod hit her?

Resigned, I sat on the coffee table and slid my cell from my front pocket, dialing my uncle's cell number from my contacts list. He answered on the second ring.

"Kaylee? What's wrong?"

Jeez, what isn't wrong? I honestly had no idea where to start, without completely freaking him out. "Okay, Uncle Brendon, I have to tell you something, but first I need you to promise you won't tell Harmony. I swore to Tod that we'd keep his mother out of this, no matter what."

Something clicked, and background music died, leaving only highway noise and the sound of his engine. He was in the car. Hopefully on the way home. "Did something happen to Nash?"

I sighed. "Just promise, or I can't tell you until it's over."

"Kaylee, you're scaring me…"

"Then promise."

He exhaled heavily. "I promise."

"Thank you." I sucked in a deep breath, then spit the whole

story out, as coherently as I could, considering my current state of exhaustion, stress, and fear. "Avari the hellion of greed is holding Nash and my dad in the Netherworld, and after he took them, he possessed Sophie so he could call me and try to talk me into trading myself for them. But I know he's not really going to send them back. So Tod hit Sophie on the back of the head with your universal remote to kick Avari out of her body. It worked, but now Sophie's unconscious on the living-room floor with a big bump on her head. Could you come home and take a look at her? And maybe let me nap on your couch for a couple of hours?"

For a moment, there was only silence on the other end of the line. Then my uncle released the breath he'd been holding. "I'll be right there." The phone went dead in my hand, and I smiled, more relieved than I could express that he and my father were two completely different people.

Twenty-five minutes later, my uncle walked through his own front door, and he seemed almost as relieved to find me still there as he was upset to find Sophie still unconscious. "I think part of it is exhaustion from being possessed," I said as he knelt beside me. "Emma slept for a long time afterward, too."

"Emma Marshall?" he asked, gently turning his daughter over. "This hellion possessed her, too?"

I nodded solemnly. "Tod said that so long as they're sleeping, he can get anyone with a connection to the Netherworld. Which Em and Sophie both have, since they've both been technically dead."

"Yes, but that takes an enormous amount of energy from a hellion. He shouldn't be able to do it very frequently or for very long." He brushed Sophie's hair back from her face and pulled back her eyelids to check her dilation. "Otherwise, you'd hear about people committing crimes in their 'sleep' all the time."

I shrugged and perched on the end of the coffee table. "Well, he has a proxy, and Tod thinks he's feeding off my dad and Nash, now that he has them."

Uncle Brendon's expression went as hard as I've ever seen it. "I'll kill him." Presumably Avari, not Tod. Tod was already dead. But was Avari actually living?

"That'd be great, except we don't think you can kill a hellion, and you can't cross over on your own."

"Take me." He stood in one fluid motion, lifting his daughter like a sleeping toddler.

"No way." I shook my head. "You have to stay here and watch Sophie, to make sure Avari doesn't take her over again." *And because you can neither defend yourself in nor escape from the Netherworld...* "Don't leave her vulnerable just because you want revenge, Uncle Brendon."

"I don't just want revenge." My uncle stomped down the hall and into Sophie's room so quickly I had to jog to keep up. "I want my brother back. And Harmony's lost enough already. We can't let her lose Nash."

"I want them back, too." I crossed my arms over my chest and sat on the edge of my cousin's desk. "And we're going to get them tonight. But you have to stay here, and you already promised not to tell Harmony. If you do, she'll run out after Nash and get herself killed. Or worse. And it'll be your fault."

Uncle Brendon frowned at me like I'd lost my mind. Again. "The same could happen to you, Kaylee. What am I supposed to tell your father then?"

I raised both brows at him as he lowered his daughter gently onto her bed. "If I don't make it back, there won't be any father to tell."

My uncle sighed so deeply I thought his entire body would deflate. "One hour." He stood straight and scowled at me, and I knew that was the best we'd get, and only because we'd given him no other choice. "You and Tod have one hour in the Netherworld, then Harmony and I are coming after you. Do you understand?"

I nodded. "But we can't cross over till five. Can I sleep here until then?"

He pulled the desk chair closer to the bed and sank into it, folding his daughter's limp hand into his own. "You know you're always welcome here, Kaylee."

Yeah. So long as Sophie was unconscious. "Great. It'll be like old times." Except that now there was a Netherworld demon out for my soul and my cousin's body.

Something hard poked my elbow, and I struggled to rise from the mire of sleep that had swallowed me like a sinkhole. A warm, soft, peaceful sinkhole…

The poke came again, hard enough to jar my injured arm that time. "Why are you passed out on our couch? This is not a park bench."

Sophie.

I opened my eyes to find her glaring at me in full beauty-pageant makeup, both hands propped on her bony hips. But my relief at seeing her alive and well was dampened a bit by the contempt shining in her eyes.

"Did your dad finally kick you out?" Sophie sneered, then her expression tightened into a mask of dread and irritation. "You're not moving back in, are you?"

I pushed myself upright with my good arm, rolling my head on my neck to alleviate the stiffness that had set in. I wasn't dumb enough to expect a thank-you for helping save her from demon possession, or for calling her dad when she was hurt, but a little courtesy would have been nice. Or even just a little quiet while I slept.

Of course, I wasn't sure what Uncle Brendon had told her, but I doubted it referenced much of the truth, or my part in it. As usual.

"I was just taking a nap," I said, leaning forward to fish my shoes from under the end table.

"Well, nap somewhere else. I have to get ready for the carnival, and I don't need you hanging around, sucking all the normal out of the room."

The Winter Carnival. *Crap.*

Sophie started toward her room and the pageant dress hanging over her door, pausing halfway to glance back at me over one shoulder. "Laura thinks we should cancel the whole thing, because of what happened to Doug, but I don't think Doug would want his tragic death to take food out of the mouths of impoverished children, right? And anyway, we're gonna open with a moment of silence, and there's that whole memorial service next week."

I shot her a blank stare. Untimely and tragic as his death may be considered in certain social circles, I seriously doubted Doug Fuller had ever given much thought to mouths that didn't belong to hot, willing teenage girls. But if Sophie wanted to rationalize a way to preserve her party—despite the death of a friend and the mental breakdown of her own boyfriend—nothing I said would change her mind. And without the Winter Carnival, there would be no reason for Netherworlders to gather, and no way for us to get a fair shot at stealing back Nash and my dad.

I hopped into the kitchen on one foot while wedging my

shoe onto the other. The clock over the stove read four fifty-five. I was running late.

"Where's Uncle Brendon?" I shoved one arm into my coat sleeve on my way to the front door.

"Testing Christmas lights in the garage." Sophie smoothed a wrinkle from the skirt of her hanging gown without even glancing my way. "I have a massive headache, and the blinking was making it worse."

I raised one brow and tried not to smirk as I dug my keys from my jacket pocket, then hesitated with my hand on the doorknob, twisting to eye my cousin critically. "How do you feel?"

The sudden flush in her cheeks was hard to miss. "Dad told you I fell?" Her mouth stretched into a long, hard line. "I swear, Kaylee, if you tell anyone I was sleepwalking, I'll make sure—"

"Sleepwalking?" I laughed. I couldn't help it. Of all the ridiculous explanations Uncle Brendon had fed her to cover past *bean sidhe* activity, he was really pushing the credibility envelope with that one. "You sleepwalk?"

Sophie's gaze hardened. "I never have before. But it figures that you'd show up the first time it happens." Her frown deepened. "Somehow, you're always there whenever anything really weird goes down. You're like a walking bad luck charm."

"Have fun at your carnival, Sophie," I said, pulling open the front door. "I'm sure you're a shoo-in for the Ice Bitch crown." I slammed the door before she could reply.

I was halfway down the driveway when Tod materialized in front of me, wearing his usual loose jeans and dark tee. "You okay?"

"I overslept. Sophie's fine, too, by the way."

The reaper shrugged. "Like I'm going to pass up an opportunity to smack your cousin."

I grinned, half hoping that next time she was ~~possessed, I'd~~ be there to do the honors. "You ready?"

"As ready as I'm gonna be." He strode past me toward the car, sneakers squeaking on the concrete.

"You think Alec will make it?"

"Addy said she'd do her best. They won't let her near Nash or your dad, but she thinks she can get to Alec. She'll pay for it later, though." Tod's jaw bulged and he stuffed tightly clenched fists into his pockets. "We shouldn't have involved her."

"That's her call, Tod. If she wants to help, she has every right. And we're kind of screwed if she can't get to Alec."

"I know." Conflict was clear on his face as he stepped through the passenger's-side door and settled onto the seat with that weird, selective corporeality reapers typically flaunted. It must have been hell having to choose between the girl he loved and his own brother. Maybe as hard as it was for me to choose between Nash and my dad. Only Tod hadn't gotten out of making his decision.

The school parking lot was already half-full when we got there, the pink-and-purple sunset reflecting broad streaks of color on row after row of windshields. Once the carnival actually began, cars would line the street in both directions. Fortunately, the park across the street was still mostly empty, and thanks to the frigid temperature, no one sat in front of the fountain. In our reality, anyway.

I parked as close as I could, then hunched into the fading warmth my coat held as Tod and I made our way toward the fountain. It was a simple scalloped circle of brick with a smooth concrete ledge, surrounding a single broad jet of water, still spraying in spite of the near-freezing temperature. We were hoping that since we were half an hour early, the crowd in the Netherworld would be as sparse as the one in our world.

"You want me to check first?" Tod asked, after one look at the terror which must have been churning in my eyes.

"That'd be great." What I really wanted was for him to find out where Nash and my dad were being held, so we could cross over right next to them, then escape before anyone noticed we'd arrived. Unfortunately, they were probably being held in the Netherworld version of some building I didn't have access to in our world.

Which was why we needed Alec.

"I'll be right back," Tod said. "And if for some reason I'm not, do *not* cross over alone. Okay?"

I nodded, but we both knew I was lying. If he didn't come back, there would be no one left to go with me, and I wasn't going to leave Nash and my father to die in the Netherworld. Or worse.

Tod shot me his lopsided, cherubic grin, then blinked out of existence.

I sat on the edge of the fountain, just out of reach of the frigid spray, prepared to wait as long as it took. Which turned out to be about fifteen seconds.

"This isn't gonna work," Tod said, and I heard the first word almost before he materialized in front of me. "They're everywhere. It's like that big Halloween party they have downtown, only the costumes are real. And everybody looks hungry."

Great. My pulse swooshed rapidly in my ears, and my heart began to ache from beating so hard. "Did anyone see you?"

He shrugged. "I don't know, but I don't think it matters. Reapers aren't very appetizing. You're the one we have to worry about. "

"Okay, so what do you suggest? A costume?" I asked, thinking about the furry werewolf mask in a box at the top of my closet.

Tod frowned. "No costume you could possibly own would make you look like an actual monster. Some of them don't look all that different from us, anyway…" His voice trailed off, and I saw the idea the moment it sparkled in his eyes. "But everyone is all dressed up for the festival, so if you had a fancy dress or something, you might pass for one of the harpies, or a visiting siren. I could pop into a store and try to find you something." He stepped back and eyed me critically. "What size do you wear?"

"No need…" I said as movement from the school lot caught my eye. If I hadn't known her all my life, I might never have recognized my cousin from such a distance, but there was no mistaking that slim build, or easy, rhythmic sway of nonexistent hips as she walked down the sidewalk with a skinny friend who could only be Laura Bell. And if Sophie had arrived, so had her pageant gown. "Come on. I think I know where we can get one."

Assuming I could squeeze my normal-size body into her skeleton-size dress.

We found Laura's car in the third row, and when we were sure we were alone in the lot, Tod stepped through the door and sat in the driver's seat with one leg hanging out as he popped the trunk from the inside. I pulled up the trunk lid when it bounced open, then lifted the long, white dress box from inside, hoping the gown would be long enough to cover my sneakers. Because even if I managed to squeeze myself into Sophie's dress, I could never wear her size-five heels, and running around the Netherworld barefoot was not an option. Not after I'd nearly died when a Crimson Creeper vine had lashed itself around my ankle.

I changed into the dress from the semiprivacy of my own backseat, but had to emerge and suck in a deep breath so Tod could force the zipper past my hips. And finally I understood why pageant contestants had such good posture: they had no choice. I couldn't breathe in the stupid dress, much less slouch.

"Wow." Tod stepped back for a better look, and I had to glance down to see why he was staring. Sophie's dress was too small for me, which meant that my meager assets were heaped above the strapless, gold-embroidered bodice, and my waist cinched by the torturous ribbing. The skirt flared with several gathered layers of material, and only barely brushed the ground around my shoes. It would have been longer on Sophie, but I wasn't going to complain about the length of a stolen dress.

"You really think I'm going to blend in wearing this thing?" I eyed him skeptically, suddenly certain the reaper was playing a horrible, ill-timed joke.

He grinned. "Actually, now I'm pretty sure you're gonna stand out, but in a good way."

"But I still look human." Especially with chill bumps popping up all over my exposed arms and shoulders.

"So do sirens. And anyway, they'll probably assume there's a tail or a third leg under your skirt."

"How very comforting..." I mumbled, slamming the front door. Then I took a step forward and realized I'd closed Sophie's skirt in the car. Frustrated, I opened the door and pulled the material free, wincing at the grease stain obvious on the white beaded satin, even in the rapidly fading daylight. Sophie was going to *kill* me. "Let's get this over with."

With any luck, I could reclaim my men and return Sophie's dress before she discovered it missing. And under the circumstances, I'd be happy to let her wonder about the unexplained stain for the rest of her life.

"Okay, now try to walk around like you belong there, but don't make eye contact with anyone," Tod said, taking my hand as he half led, half tugged me across the street. "And if it looks like it's going to go bad at any time, I want you to cross back over. You won't do anyone any good if you get caught."

"The same goes for you," I pointed out, then clenched my jaw to stop my teeth from chattering as we came to a stop in front of the still-spraying fountain.

"Acknowledged." Tod grinned again, but this time his smile felt forced. "You ready?"

"Not even a little bit." But I bid a silent farewell to the human world, anyway, and closed my eyes as his hand tightened around mine. Tod was going to cross me over, so I could save my voice for the return trip.

Since they didn't have to conjure up a death song, reapers crossed almost instantly, and I found the process disorienting, compared to my own routine.

While my eyes were still closed, the air around me took on a different quality as it brushed my bare arms and shoulders. It was every bit as cold as the December chill in the human world, but felt somehow sharper. More dangerous.

The sounds from my reality faded rapidly. Gone were the growl of a distant engine and the Christmas music tinkling faintly from inside the school gym. The park lights no longer buzzed overhead, nor did the wind rattle the skeletal branches of the trees all around us.

Instead, a constant hum of strange conversation filtered into my ears, and even the familiar words were spoken with an unfamiliar lilt, or pitch, or syllabic stress. Even the light pitter sound of the fountain had changed, as if something thicker than water now splashed onto the brick ledge to my left.

I opened my eyes and gasped. I now stood beside the stone

park fountain in Sophie's white Snow Queen dress, both of which had bled through from one reality to the other without so much as an atom out of place. Except that now the fountain shot a thin stream of blood high into the air, to splatter into the gruesome crimson pool at its base.

I really should have seen that coming.

But the fountain was just the beginning. Unlike the park in our world, on this side of the gray fog, Tod and I were no longer alone.

Not by a long shot.

24

"You okay?" Tod whispered, leaning so close I could feel his breath on my ear, warm in contrast to the bone-deep chill of the Netherworld.

"Mmm-hmm," I mumbled, afraid to speak for fear of somehow giving away my species. His hand squeezed mine, reassuring me with the physical presence he couldn't avoid in the Netherworld.

All around us bodies milled, clustered in restless groups or walking aimlessly around the grassless park. Some whispered words as thin and wispy as the wind, while others thundered in deep, round tones. Everywhere I turned, sparkling, flowing gowns were decked with large multilobed feathers from birds I couldn't identify. Long swaths of crystalline material draped forms whose gender I couldn't determine.

Several people wore masks, and as I watched, a man with three legs and a tail lowered a visage painted with four glittering lilac eyes to reveal a smooth, featureless expanse of chalk-white flesh where his face should have been. I gasped, and Tod squeezed my hand, then pulled me swiftly through the crowd.

He stopped at a tree with a massive, twisting trunk in varying shades of a deep, earthy gold and tugged me beneath branches bowed with thick, spiky, rust-colored foliage. "If you want to blend in—" he whispered "—it might help *not* to flinch and gasp every time you see a Netherworlder. I hear they're pretty common around here."

"I know. I'm sorry." But the featureless face was new to me. As were the short, thick creatures with wickedly curved claws instead of fingers, and long, sharp beaks where their noses should have been. "Do you see Alec?"

"I don't know. What does he look like?"

"You've never seen him?" Frustrated, I reached up to brush a spiky, orange-ish plant pod from my hair, then stopped myself just in time. For all I knew, the tree we stood under was just as poisonous as the Crimson Creeper that had nearly killed me a month earlier.

"When would I have seen Avari's proxy? You think he parades his staff in front of me every time I visit Addison?"

Lovely. "Well, we know he's human." I shrugged. "Or at least he thinks he's human." But then again, so had I.

Tod stared out at the crowd. "Okay, so we're looking for someone who probably stands out almost as badly as we do. How hard can that be?"

It turned out to be pretty damn hard. People were everywhere—"people" defined as beings able to move under their own power—and while the vast majority of them looked terrifying to my humanoid-accustomed eyes, sprinkled throughout the array of extra limbs, missing extremities, backward joints, wings, horns, claws, and the odd tentacle were the occasional normal-looking beings with the proper proportions and standard number of appendages.

Some of these creatures, upon closer examination, were

very definitely *not* human. One normal-looking woman turned out to have perfectly round, anime eyes with bright teal irises, surrounded by rich, deep rings of lavender. Another man's flesh, when I saw it up close, was covered in shallow but pervasive wrinkles, like a Sphinx kitten, and for several seconds, I battled a horrifying impulse to tug on a flap of the skin drooping from his arm to see how far it would stretch.

Yet others could easily have been kids in my third-period class, or the parents who picked them up after school. The variety of shapes, sizes, and colors was truly astounding and almost too disorienting for me to process, with shock and fear still racing through my veins. So when my gaze finally settled on a familiar profile in the crowd, it was all I could do not to shout her name across the multitude, which would surely have gotten us all killed.

Instead, I grabbed Tod's arm, trying to guide his gaze with my own. "Addison…" I whispered, standing on my toes to get as close as I could to his ear.

As if she heard me, Addy suddenly turned, and my breath caught in my throat, trapped by horror so profound it had no expression. Addison's profile was just as I remembered it, bright blue eye, heavily lashed lid, and a flawless cheek and nose. But the other side of her face was a ruined mass of oozing red wounds and black crusted flesh, stretching from her scalp—where most of her beautiful blond hair had been burned off—to below her collarbone, where her skin disappeared beneath her shirt.

My hand tightened around Tod's arm, but he only pried my fingers loose and squeezed them, then let me go.

I forced my gaze away from Addy to glance at Tod, who betrayed neither horror nor shock. He exhaled in relief, then headed for Addison with quick, determined strides.

Gathering Sophie's stupid long skirt in both hands, I rushed after him and caught up as he sidestepped a tall, skeletal woman with dark eyes and cheeks hollow enough to cradle a pool ball. "What happened to her?" I whispered as we walked, my horror on Addison's behalf almost eclipsing my terror of the creatures all around us.

"It looks like he lit her on fire today."

"Today?"

Tod nodded grimly as Addy's gaze found him, and her half-scarred mouth struggled into a gruesome smile. "What part of 'eternal torture' don't you understand? Yesterday he peeled her flesh off while she screamed, and you could see her teeth through her cheek. He always leaves one side perfect, though, so she can mourn her own beauty. Her room is walled-in mirrors, and the damage goes all the way down her body."

I couldn't voice my horror; I had neither the words nor the nerve. Questions were all I could manage, and my voice croaked as I forced it into the bone-cold air. "How does she even have a body? We buried her. I saw her in the coffin."

"Avari gave it back to her."

I dodged a man with a suspicious lump roiling beneath his broad white shirt, lowering my gaze at the last second to avoid his. "But is it real?"

Tod's jaw tightened. "Real enough to feel every second of agony."

By then we'd reached Addison, and I forced my mouth closed, unwilling to embarrass either of us with my ignorance. Tod slid one arm around her waist and, though Addy winced, she didn't shrug out of his grip. Without a word, he led us back toward that same weird tree, and only once we were hidden by the heavy branches did he exhale, and even Addison seemed to relax.

"Kaylee, you look beautiful!" She reached out with one mutilated hand—fingers fixed into a clawlike position by her fresh, puckered scars—to touch Sophie's pristine white satin dress.

"Thanks." I wished I could say the same to her, but the most I could manage was a small smile to cover my horror. "It's my cousin's."

It's not your fault, I thought for at least the twelfth time as I stared at my skirt to avoid looking at her wounds. I hadn't done this to Addison; she'd done it to herself when she sold her soul. All I'd done was fail to save her....

"Did you find him?" Tod said, rescuing me from my own guilt and denial.

Addy nodded eagerly, then winced when the skin on the right half of her face stretched. "I let him out. He's supposed to meet us here when he finds your brother. And your dad," she added, glancing at me in sympathy. "Hey, there he is!"

I twisted to peer between two low-hanging branches, and my eyes nearly fell out of my skull. Walking briskly toward us from the edge of the crowd was the trash-can-lid-wielding boy I'd seen in the field of razor wheat when I'd woken up in the Netherworld.

"You!" I said as he ducked beneath the limbs into our private powwow.

"You, too," the boy said, in a voice I'd last heard from Emma's mouth.

"You know each other?" Tod's eyes narrowed as he glanced back and forth between us. But I couldn't tear my gaze from Avari's proxy.

"You're Alec?"

"Since the day I was born." He shrugged, dark eyes watching me closely. "Though the name's about all I have left from that existence."

"I saw you in the razor wheat on Wednesday."

Alec nodded. "I was looking for you, and your house seemed like a good place to start."

Great. A *sarcastic* demon proxy.

"But I have to say you look better in formal wear than pajamas," he continued, eyeing Sophie's dress—and me in it—appreciatively. Suddenly I wanted a coat, to cope with more than just the cold.

"Wait, why were you looking for her on Wednesday?" Tod asked. "Nash didn't go missing until yesterday."

"Yes, but I wanted out of here two and a half decades ago, and she seemed like my best shot in years."

I propped both hands on my hips. As badly as I wanted to know who he was and how he'd known I could get him out, I had more important things to worry about at the moment. "I'm not taking you anywhere until you take me to Nash and my father."

"Are they at Prime Life?" Tod asked. The Netherworld version of Prime Life, one of the largest life insurance companies in the country, was Avari's home base when he was in town.

Addison shook her head in stiff, obviously painful motions. "Not that I could find. And I looked everywhere I had access."

"They're in there." Alec pointed off into the throng and I followed his finger toward the building rising over the heads of the crowd gathered in front of it. Eastlake High.

Or the Netherworld version of it, anyway.

"Why are they in the school?" I asked, dread clenching around my stomach with an iron grip.

"Avari's planning something big, and I think he wants them

both nearby to boost his energy," the proxy said, and Addison nodded.

"He wants them near?" I repeated, glancing again at the second floor of the school, which was all I could see over the crowd. "Does that mean they're not actually with him?"

"They don't have to be in the same room, no," Alec said. "They just have to be close enough to draw power from."

I shrugged, a thin pulse of hope threading through me. "So, we can just go get them, right?"

"In theory..." Addison started, and that was enough for me.

"Let's go." Human-looking people were rare enough in the Netherworld that four of us together might be noticed, so Addy and Alec each started off on their own, one veering to the left and one to the right. Tod and I stayed together for strength in numbers, since neither of us belonged there or had any defensive abilities. We headed down the middle, hoping to avoid notice at the edge of the throng, where the crowd was least dense.

The multitude swallowed us whole, and I let it, breathing deeply through my mouth as we walked, trying to calm my racing pulse in case any of the predators could hear it. Sophie's skirt swished around my ankles, brushing other pieces of clothing made of rich, iridescent materials I didn't recognize, several of which seemed to move independently of their wearers.

A tail brushed my hand and I shivered. A soft, warm breeze caressed my face and exposed cleavage, and as it passed, I both heard and felt the words it whispered into my ears, though I couldn't understand a bit of what was said.

I clung to Tod's hand as we crossed the crowded street, grateful for how very *there* he felt in the Netherworld, though no doubt his physical vulnerability made him feel exposed and defenseless. And finally, when we stepped past the edge of the crowd onto the sidewalk in front of the school, I exhaled. We were still alive, and we were almost there.

"Ready?" Addison appeared at Tod's side and took his hand, just as Alec emerged on my right.

We both nodded. Then the double front doors of the school opened, and my gaze was drawn toward the literally dazzling figure that emerged.

"Who's that?" I stared at the girl, who looked completely human except that she glowed with a beautiful, intense inner light. As if she were lit from within, like a human candle, shining so brightly it hurt my eyes to look at her.

Her eyes were dark pinpoints in a face so brilliant I couldn't make out her actual features, and though her short, fitted dress was a pristine white, it was dull in comparison to flesh that gleamed and glittered like sunlight on the ocean. In one glowing hand, she carried a slim, dark cylinder I couldn't identify from that distance.

"That's Lana. She's one of the lampades," Alec whispered as the girl sank onto the top step, like a school kid waiting for a ride. "She's one of Avari's favorite pets in decades. This whole celebration is for the lampades. *About* them. And Avari has two of them for the first time in living memory. Lana, and her sister, Luci. They just got here yesterday."

"What are they?" I asked, unable to drag my focus from the girl glowing like a living jack-o'-lantern, even though the light hurt my eyes.

"Lampades are the only creatures I know of that exist in both worlds at once, in the exact same time and place." Alec headed slowly away from the crowd and we followed him, the cold Netherworld wind seeming to push us along. "If you were to cross over, you'd see her sitting there in your world just like she is here. Lampades are walking liminalities. You see how Lana's glowing like someone shoved a lightbulb up her butt?" Alec asked, and I nodded, amused by the visual in spite of the circumstances. "That's liminal light, and it runs through her like blood runs through us. A concentration of that light can temporarily merge corresponding sections of the Netherworld and your world if she shines it at a liminal space, like a window, or a threshold."

Sudden brutal understanding uncoiled like a whip inside me, snapping tight around my brain. "Can someone go through that…merged space? Like a doorway?" I whispered, dreading the answer even as I asked the question.

"Maybe…" Alec began, and I recognized comprehension as it swept over Tod, and the reaper met my gaze. "But he'd have to move fast. Shining her light is like bleeding for a lampade, and she'll bleed to death if she's not careful."

"But you said there are two of them, right?" I asked, and the proxy nodded, dark curls almost blending with the shadow of the building. "So if they worked together…"

"…they'd only have to bleed half as much," Alec finished, and the deep furrows in his forehead said he was starting to understand.

"That's how he got them," Tod said, and I nodded. "These lampades took Nash and your dad."

My eyes closed in sudden cruel certainty. "And I could have stopped them."

"How?" Addison asked, stepping from the sidewalk onto the umber-colored grass on one side of the school's front lawn.

I gestured toward the steps, where Lana now sat with her hands clasped over her knees. "I think I met both of them last night. They came to Doug Fuller's party with Everett. Nash ran them off, but they must have come back after Em and I left. After Doug died."

"What?" Tod's eyes flashed in anger, and I knew exactly how he felt.

"These lampades? I'd bet my life they were the arm candy hovering over Everett last night at the party. Only they didn't glow then."

Alec rubbed one hand over his forehead, like he was fending off a headache. "They only glow here. In your world, they'd look like normal people."

I rolled my eyes. "Yeah, except they're identical, and flawlessly gorgeous." More than enough to give a regular girl an inferiority complex, without adding evil to the mix. "I'm going to cross over and make sure I'm right."

"Want me to come with you?" Tod asked, but I shook my head.

"Stay here with them." I knew he didn't want to leave Addy, and I needed him to keep an eye on Alec, whom I had no intention of bringing with me until we found Nash and my father. "I'll be right back."

I rounded the corner of the building quickly to cross over without being seen in either world, and my silent scream came fairly easily that time, which scared me almost as much as the necessity of using it. I faded into my own world near the back corner of the parking lot, then hugged the wall of the building all the way to the front of the school, to keep from being seen. Sophie's satin gown whispered against the rough bricks, and twice I had to tug the material free when it snagged. My cousin was going to *kill* me.

Assuming I survived long enough to be murdered.

At the edge of the building, I peeked around the corner to see Lana—definitely one of the girls I'd seen with Everett—sitting on the front step, exactly where she'd been in the Neth-

MY SOUL TO KEEP •

erworld. Only now she held an ornately decorated metal flashlight. It was unlit—for the moment.

I crossed back over and rejoined the group without bothering to lift the hem of Sophie's skirt when I walked. "It's her," I said, shivering from the cold. "The lampades are the girls from the party."

"What are they doing here?" Addison asked as the front door of the school opened and Luci joined her sister on the top step, holding an identical unlit flashlight. "Waiting to be celebrated?"

"They're obviously waiting for something," I said, and no sooner had the last word fallen from my lips than the girls twisted in unison to glance at the sky to the east of the school, where the sun was just starting to sink below the horizon, a mirror image to the sunset in the human world, but for the bruised green-and-purple of the Netherworld sky.

"Uh-oh…" A heavy new dread anchored my sneakered feet to the sidewalk.

"What?" Tod asked, but my gaze found Alec—the man with the answers.

"What effect would other liminalities have on this doorway a lampade can create? Big liminalities. Like, once-a-year events." Such as the winter solstice.

Alec's eyes closed in alarm as the reaper tensed visibly. "They would amplify the power of the liminal light."

"And would that make this doorway any bigger? Or hold it open any longer?"

The proxy nodded, because words were no longer necessary. We finally understood the purpose of Avari's Liminal Celebration. "He's using the solstice to bridge the gap, when the veil between the two worlds is thinnest," I whispered, terror rendering my voice a hoarse echo of itself.

Even as I spoke, the lampade sisters stood and took up positions on either side of the double front doors, facing each other. And that's when the last piece of the puzzle fell into place. "Crap!" I whispered fiercely, grabbing Addison's scarred hand without thinking. "They're about to start."

"Start what?" she asked, pulling her blistered hand firmly out of my grip.

"Don't you get it? Avari's planned the whole thing out! The school, a carnival full of high schoolers, the solstice... Dusk is a liminal time, the lampades are liminal creatures, the front door is a liminal place, and teenagers are at a liminal age in life. Lana and Luci will shine their light across the threshold at dusk. And when the carnival opens, instead of heading into the front hall, a couple of hundred teenagers will cross directly into the Netherworld, like lambs to the slaughter."

25

MY HEAD THROBBED in time with the stitched gash on my right arm, and my heart ached like never before. Of all the trouble I'd walked into since finding out I was a *bean sidhe,* nothing compared to this. To the abduction of a couple hundred teenagers right through the front door of our own school. Disappearances the human authorities would never be able to understand, much less solve.

And we were the only ones who could stop it.

"If he's planning some kind of forced migration, why bother bringing Nash and your dad over?" Addison asked as Tod guided us subtly toward the right edge of the crowd. Suddenly, standing directly in front of the lampades didn't seem like such a good idea.

"For more power." Alec rubbed his arms, fighting chills from the bitterly cold breeze. "I thought he was just being greedy, which makes sense, and is probably half-true. But he needs every bit of power he can get—as well as what he'd hoped to get from Kaylee. He'll have to pour energy into

Lana and Luci to keep them alive while they hold the doorway open."

"Would Nash and my dad survive that?" I asked, rubbing my own chill bump-covered arms.

"No. And neither will they." Alec nodded toward the lampades. "Though I doubt they know that."

"So, how do we stop it?" I asked. "Take away their flashlights?"

Alec shook his head. "The flashlights are just focal points—decoys to fool the humans. The lampades shed their own light, and you can't extinguish it without killing them."

Which I wasn't ready to do yet, no matter how much of a threat to humanity they represented. Because despite everything they'd done, Lana and Luci were being used by Avari just like Nash and my father were, and death seemed like an unfair penalty for that. Especially considering they'd probably die, anyway, if Avari got what he wanted.

"What if we take the girls?" I asked, still looking for an alternative to murder.

"Take them where?" Tod ground his teeth in frustration, his fingers linked through those on Addy's good hand. "It's not like you can just cross over with them. They're in both places at once."

"Can't we just...chase them away from the doorway? And maybe separate them?" I propped both hands on the waist of Sophie's gown, wishing I weren't dressed like a china doll during what might turn out to be the last moments of my life. "If they're not together—and at the threshold—they won't be able to open this door, right?"

"Well, not the big door Avari's counting on," Alec agreed. "So that might work, at least long enough to get Nash and your dad out of here. Which will rob Avari of the power he needs to make this work."

"If we're gonna do it, we better do it now," Tod whispered as the buzz of the crowd around us faded into an eerie quiet. Almost as one, the audience turned toward the school doors, clearly readying themselves for the main attraction—a building full of food, ready to be harvested. "Because we're about to lose our chance."

We turned, too, to avoid standing out, as badly as it nauseated me to be standing among the wolves, waiting for the sheep to be slaughtered. Or eaten. Or slurped up. Or whatever.

"We should do this from our world," I said, so softly I could barely hear myself. "To keep Avari from interfering."

"I'm on it." Tod squeezed Addy's good hand again, then met my gaze, speaking softly through one corner of his mouth. "I'm gonna grab one of the walking Lite-Brites, then I'll be back to help with Nash and your dad. Will you be okay here?"

I nodded, careful not to let my uncertainty show. "Yeah. I'm good. But work fast."

An instant later, Tod was gone.

A moment after that, one of the lampades let out a piercing scream, and Lana was suddenly pulled off her feet by... nothing we could see. The effect was bizarre, and reminded me of a scene in an old slasher movie, where a teenager stuck in a nightmare is hauled up her bedroom wall by an invisible evil force.

Lana fell backward, smashing the front door open, then disappeared from sight.

The crowd around us roared in surprise and outrage, shouts varying from high-pitched squeals to rumbles low enough to reverberate deep within my bones. There were even several protests I seemed to hear in my head, rather than through my ears.

A minute later, as several dozen representatives from the mob raced toward the stunned and abandoned Luci, Tod reappeared at my side, wearing the biggest Cheshire cat grin I'd ever seen outside of *Alice in Wonderland*.

And what a bizarre wonderland we'd fallen into…

"Where is she?" I stood on my toes to yell into his ear as the shouts around us reached a brain-numbing crescendo.

"In the utility closet by the art room. I had to knock her out, but that should hold her for a while. Let's find Nash and your dad, then get the hell out of here before Avari puts Humpty Dumpty back together again." Then his gaze met Addison's and regret took over his face. He took her hand as if to apologize for leaving her, but she only smiled and shook her head.

"Go find your brother. We knew this would end sooner or later, and I'm grateful for the time we had. The time you gave me."

Tod nodded, then squeezed her hand and turned to follow me and Alec as we raced toward the other side of the school, hidden in plain sight among the outraged crowd. Alec was fast, and as the proxy's head disappeared into the crowd ahead of me, my foot came down on something thick and lumpy. I lost my balance when whatever I'd stepped on was jerked out from under me, and a horrific, bleating roar trumpeted over my head. My right foot snagged in the hem of Sophie's dress and one hand went automatically to my ear to protect my hearing, while the other flew out in front of me to keep my face from hitting the asphalt.

But before my palm could hit the ground, someone hauled me to my feet, tearing the dress with a dull thread-popping sound. Tod pulled me back, pressing me into his own chest as the creature on our right drew himself up to a terrifying height. Gray, leathery wings beat at his back, stirring the heavy skirt of Sophie's dress as his tail—which I'd obviously stepped on—whipped around his legs to lash my ankles.

"I'm so sorry!" I cried as Tod backed us swiftly away from the beast whose grayish cheekbones were literally sharp enough to slice the flesh from his face. The creature roared again and knelt like a bull about to charge. But then his massive right wing clipped the shoulder of the hairy fellow at his back, and both Netherworlders exploded into sudden violence like two giant cats with claws bared.

Tod and I raced away, thrilled to realize we didn't represent a big enough threat to keep the beast's attention.

Ahead, Alec's brown curls bobbed through the crowd, and we followed him, Tod occasionally pulling me out of the path of another stampeding monster. We didn't stop to catch our breath until we rounded the corner of the building. The empty span of gray grass—representing the quad in my version of the school—was still unoccupied and relatively peaceful, at least until the Netherworld residents discovered that the building had more than one entrance.

I led Tod and Alec to the cafeteria door, and we frantically searched every classroom, peering in through the windows of the locked doors and ducking around corners whenever footsteps headed our way, be they heavy, lumbering thuds or sharp, quick scuttles.

The first floor was deserted, except for the closet where Tod had stashed the unconscious lampade, so we ran up the wide staircase and repeated the search again, racing from room to room. And finally, through the rectangular window in the last door on the right, I spotted my father, slumped over a warped and dented metal teacher's desk, still in the flannel shirt he'd worn to work.

My heart leaped into my throat and I struggled to breathe around it as I twisted the knob desperately. But it wouldn't turn, nor would the door budge. "Dad!" I shouted, begging him frantically to wake up and let us in. To help us help him. But he didn't move, and only once I'd forced myself to go still and concentrate could I see that he was still breathing.

"Here, let me try." Tod pushed me aside with one outstretched arm, and I remembered that he couldn't walk through walls in the Netherworld. Alec and I stepped back, and the reaper exploded into motion. His foot flew, connecting with the door just beneath the knob with an echoing crack of wood. But the door didn't open, so Tod backed up and tried again, this time letting loose a heartfelt grunt as his leg shot out.

That time more wood splintered and the door swung open with the metallic groan of little-used hinges. I rushed past Tod and dropped onto my knees on the floor next to my father. "Dad?" I ran one hand down his ruddy, stubbly cheek. His eyes didn't open, but he moaned, and his head fell to one side. "I think he's okay." I glanced up at Tod and laid one hand on my father's shoulder. "I'm going to cross over with him, but I'll be right back."

"Take me, too." Alec's voice trembled, and for the first time I saw true fear shining in his greenish eyes. "Please. You don't need me anymore."

"You're not going anywhere until we find Nash," I insisted, folding my hand around my father's. I almost felt guilty, knowing that if we left Alec, he'd probably be punished like Addy had, or worse, for his part in my father's escape. But as callous as it sounded, even after everything he'd done, Nash meant more to me than any stranger. Even a stranger who'd helped me find my father. "I'll be right back."

Before either the proxy or the reaper could protest, I closed my eyes and called forth my wail with practiced speed, trying not to think about the fact that the more often I crossed over, the harder it would be to stop myself from doing that very thing by accident. As my recent dream-shrieking had shown me.

The odd cacophony from outside faded into a more familiar, benign, excited buzz. I opened my eyes to find myself standing in one of the Spanish classrooms, surrounded by empty desks and travel posters from Spain, Mexico, and South America. My father sat beside me, and as soon as I was sure he was still breathing, I stood and dug my cell phone from my pocket, only mildly relieved to be in the relative safety of my native reality.

I dialed by memory, and the familiar electronic tone rang in my ear. "Kaylee?" Uncle Brendon said, his voice thick with tension. "Are you okay? Did you get them back?"

"I got my dad, and I need you to come get him out of here. He's in the last classroom on the right, on the second floor. The door's open."

"You're at the school?"

I rushed across the room and twisted the lock to open the door. "Yeah, and I have to go back for Nash and Alec, or Avari's going to use the lampades to open a big doorway into the Netherworld, and everyone here's going to walk right through it."

"No, that's impossible. Kaylee, Sophie's there."

"I know. I'm wearing her dress."

"What?" Over the line, I heard a door slam, then an engine

purred to life. My uncle was already on his way. "Kaylee, you have to get her out of there."

"I can't, Uncle Brendon. I have to go back for Nash and Alec. Call Sophie and tell her to go home. And tell her I'm sorry about her dress."

"Wait, Kaylee, who's Alec—?"

But I hung up without answering, then kissed my unconscious father on the cheek and summoned my wail to cross over one more time.

In the Netherworld classroom, Alec had his hands curled around clumps of dark curls on either side of his skull, as if he were about to rip them out. Tod stood in the doorway, staring down the hall in case anyone else showed up. "Okay, let's go find Nash," I said, and both heads whipped in my direction.

"You came back…" Alec said, relief and disbelief warring for control of his wavering voice.

"Of course I came back. You think I'd leave Nash here?" The proxy frowned, and I couldn't help but smile. "Or you? Let's go!"

But we'd only made it halfway down the hall when a sudden unanimous roar of triumph from outside made my blood run cold in my veins. I grabbed two thick handfuls of white satin skirt and ran into the nearest classroom and over to the row of windows set into the outside wall, which—thanks to the H-shaped footprint of the school—looked out over the broad front lawn.

I yanked on the dusty pull-cord dangling in front of my face and the aluminum blinds ratcheted up, shining the dying, anemic light from outside into the dark classroom. The crowd gathered in front of the school had nearly doubled since we'd come inside. And every single bizarre, misshapen face was turned toward the broad front porch, where three familiar figures now stood.

In the center was a tall, darkly elegant male form who could only have been Avari, the host of the night's twisted jamboree. And on either side of him stood a glowing, white-clad female figure.

Avari had found the missing lampade, and the night's festivities were back on schedule.

As if to punctuate that fact, Alec suddenly doubled over, arms wrapped around his middle like his guts were being twisted from within. "He's drawing power from me. It's too much, too fast, without a supplement from your dad." The proxy gasped, and struggled to stand in spite of obvious pain. "He's feeding them, and it's going to kill me. And your boyfriend."

"Tod, do something!" I insisted, panicked, unable to tear my gaze from the spectacle outside. "Whatever it takes to stop them from opening that doorway."

The reaper glanced from my desperate, earnest expression to the spectacle outside, to the now-pallid proxy, then back to me. "I'm not leaving you here, Kaylee."

"I'll be fine. I have Alec, right?" I insisted, and the proxy nodded halfheartedly, his face now waxy with pain. "We'll cross over as soon as I find Nash. Now go, or none of us will get that chance!"

After another moment's hesitation, Tod nodded, then disappeared from the Netherworld just as a sudden swell of bright light from the ground drew an eerie "Ahh…" from the crowd below, and a low groan from Alec. And while all eyes were focused on the light shining from the front of the school, a sudden, darker movement in the opposite direction caught my gaze.

Something was moving in the crowd. Something headed steadily away from the lampades, while everyone else was easing gradually toward them.

I squinted against the painful glare of living light and finally made out Addison's long, half-head-full of straight blond hair, the other half of which had been singed from her scarred, pink skull. And just behind her, being pulled along by her good hand, was a form I would have recognized anywhere, in any reality, even hunched over in obvious pain.

Nash.

"There he is!" I cried, my voice approaching dog-whistle pitch. I pointed with one finger pressed to the cold window glass, and Alec's pained gaze followed mine as he clutched the windowsill for balance. "See? Heading for the tree at the back of the crowd?" The one we'd huddled beneath only a quarter of an hour earlier.

Alec nodded and stifled a moan. "I see him."

Unfortunately, while Addison was pulling him away from the Netherworld crowd and Avari's new pets, she was also pulling him away from us, and I wasn't sure we could get to them in time. Not without being noticed.

But we had to try.

"Come on!" I hiked up Sophie's dirt-smudged skirt and pulled Alec out of the room and down the hall, fervently hoping he wouldn't trip, or collapse entirely. At the top of the staircase, I paused and glanced back at him with one finger pressed to my lips in the international—and hopefully cross-reality—symbol for "shhhh." Then I took the stairs as softly as I could in sneakers, my hand tight around his.

From the bottom step, I could see Avari and the brightly glowing lampades clearly through the glass front doors, and my pulse raced as I paused to stare for a moment, desperately hoping they couldn't hear my heart pounding in my chest louder than a jackhammer through concrete.

"What are you doing?" Alec whispered pulling me weakly away from the front entrance. "Is there another way out of here?"

I blinked as tears filled my eyes to defend them from the bright light still forming red circles behind my eyelids. "Yeah. The gym." One arm around his waist now, I led the way down the hall and through the double doors into the gym. I half carried him across the deserted wooden floor—absent of any basketball court makings—and paused at the closest exit while I crossed my mental fingers.

Then I pushed the door open slowly, just enough to peer outside.

The excited mass mumblings from the crowd swelled immediately, but there wasn't a single creature in sight on this side of the building. Glancing back, I nodded at Alec, then pushed the door open far enough for us to slip through—snagging the hem of Sophie's dress on something sharp once again. I tugged the material free and held the door open for Alec, then let it close gently.

Now came the hard part; we had to sneak across the school yard, around and behind the crowd, just like Addison had, without getting caught. And it might have worked—except that all hell broke loose at that very moment.

Suddenly the powerful shine from the front door dimmed into a dull glow, and the crowd's excited mumblings shifted into fresh cries of outrage. Tod had done his job. Unfortunately, he was now hauling Luci away from the school and around the human-world version of the crowd toward us, drawing all eyes our way.

"Come on!" I shouted, and took off toward the tree, pulling Alec behind me. Fortunately, with the hellion no longer feeding his pets, the proxy grew steadily stronger until he was running on his own.

We were ten feet from the tree when Avari stepped out from under the branches, one hand wrapped cruelly around Addison's scorched arm, the other around Nash's. My heart nearly burst through my chest in terror and surprise.

Stupid hellion powers!

To my horror, Nash didn't seem to know who held him. Or even where he was. I'd never seen him like that before. His eyes were focused on nothing, and as I watched, they actually rolled back into his head. He was as high as the international space station. Nash would be no help in his own rescue.

"I knew you'd show up eventually," Avari said, and a soft crackling drew my gaze to the ground at his feet, where a thin, delicate layer of ice was now spreading toward us over the gray grass.

"It's too late," I said, drawing my gaze back up to his. "You're missing a lampade, and you can't open a doorway of any size without both of them."

"Not yet." The hellion nodded formally in concession, and the layer of ice thickened, obscuring the gray ground it covered. "But the summer equinox is only six short months away, and I'm sure we can find some way to amuse ourselves until then. Since we'll all be here together..."

Alec squeezed my hand and tugged me backward, his cold fingers trembling in mine. "Cross over!" he hissed, without taking his eyes from the hellion.

Avari shook his head slowly, confidently, wrinkling the collar of his starched white shirt. "She won't go without this one." He jerked ruthlessly on Nash's arm, hauling him upright hard enough to make me flinch. "Loyalty is her weakness. It renders her predictable and tells me just where to aim. If only the rest of your world were so feeble… Ahh, but then where would be the fun?"

"Kaylee, *cross!*" Alec begged, tugging on my arm, but I shook my head again.

"I won't leave him here!"

"You won't have to," Addison said. And before I could register her intent, she jerked her arm free from the hellion and spun around behind him, screaming in pain when the sudden movement split her crusted skin. Blood streamed down her torn flesh, and when Avari reached for her, his fingers slipped in the crimson streaks. Addison's screams hit all new notes as more raw skin tore when she tried to run.

As the hellion's hand closed around the charred remains of her hair, she shoved Nash with an agonized grunt. He stumbled forward. Alec and I raced toward him. Nash fell to his knees, and we knelt beside him.

"Take him!" Addy screeched. I expected to find her trying to pull Avari away from us. But instead, she clung to him, her fingers barely clasped around his torso, and as I watched, as his fury grew, a thin, bluish film of ice traveled over her, freezing the blood that flowed from her new wounds. "Now!" she screamed.

Avari gave a mighty snarl and threw his arms away from his body, literally breaking her hold. Her scarred forearm shattered and fell to the ground in several gruesome, frozen chunks.

Addison screamed again, holding her severed arm up as her broken body thudded to the ground. I'd seen all I could stand.

My heart pounding, I grabbed both Nash and Alec, then closed my eyes. My wail that time was for Addison, whose pain had only begun at her death, and who would endure it for eternity, or until Avari died. Neither of which seemed imminent.

As my throat began to sting and burn, the imprisoned cry scraping my flesh raw, Avari's roar of fury faded from my ears, and the unnatural cold of the Netherworld became a benign December wind, stinging my bare arms and shoulders above the ruined pageant gown.

On my left, Alec dropped onto the frozen grass and burst into tears of relief. He knelt on his hands and knees, sucking in breath after frigid breath as if he'd never tasted anything sweeter than normal, everyday air.

Nash sagged on his feet, his stare as heartbreakingly vacant in the human world as it had been in the Netherworld. He didn't seem to know we'd crossed over at all.

Harmony would know what to do for him. Surely she'd know how to bring back the Nash who'd first asked me to dance three months earlier, even if he never again remembered how that moment felt.

Exhausted, I sank onto the freezing ground next to him and lay on my back in Sophie's dress. I barely felt the cold on my bare shoulders, or the grass that tangled in my hair. All I could think was that I was alive. We all were. Except for Addison, and though it bruised my soul to admit it, there was nothing else I could do for her.

The tree branches overhead were skeletal in the human world, devoid of weird spiky pods, and beyond, I saw a vast, clear sky full of blessedly familiar constellations. We were alone on our side of the gray fog, because the human crowd had gathered on the front lawn of the school, kids and adults alike waiting in a long line to enter the building.

I propped myself up on one elbow to see that the front doors had opened. And not one of the carnival-goers was disappearing into a painfully bright void. Tod had done his job. Sort of.

A sudden commotion from our left drew my attention, and I glanced up to find the reaper running toward us, fully corporeal, dragging Luci the lampade—in her human guise—across the frozen ground. Two school security guards ran several feet behind them, overweight and panting, their cheeks flushed by the cold. Tod stopped beneath the tree branches and abruptly dropped Luci's arm, his eyes swirling with both relief and pain at having left Addy. Then he shot one worried look at Nash and blinked out of existence, hopefully having returned to the hospital to finish his aborted shift.

Assuming he had a job to return to.

"Where'd he go?" The security guard stumbled to a stop in front of me. He was bent in half, wheezing with both hands propped on his knees.

I stood, brushing my hands on the ruined skirt of Sophie's dress. "Where'd who go?" I asked, my eyes wide in innocence as the astonished lampade gaped at me.

The guard scowled, thick forehead furrowed. "The…boy. Who was pulling her…"

"There's no one here but us," Alec said, wiping tears of joy on his sleeve. He looked like he'd almost laughed himself to death.

"Are you okay?" the other guard asked Luci, and she could only nod, no doubt stunned by events on both sides of the gray fog, which she could see simultaneously.

"I'm f-fine," she stuttered, her voice high and clear. "Thank you."

"Let us know if he shows up again," the first guard said, then the pair waddled off toward the carnival again, shaking their heads in confusion. When they were gone, the motley members of our odd gathering could only eye one another warily, *bean sidhe,* former proxy, and lampade each equally stunned by our near capture.

"He'll send us after them again," Luci said finally, glancing briefly at Nash as if he held no interest to her at all. As if she didn't care one way or another which world he occupied.

"Yeah, but if you take Nash and my father back to Avari— if you give him anyone else strong enough to power his little human generator—you may as well put a gun in your mouth. And your sister's, too."

Luci frowned, and I realized I had truly captured her attention for the first time. "What does that mean?"

"He would have killed you both," I said as I pulled Nash closer with one arm. He came willingly, but made no move on his own. "Avari was going to bleed you both until you died powering his pedestrian bridge to nowhere. And he still will, if you give him a chance." I held Nash tight as he began to chatter, his freezing skin leaching the warmth from my own.

Luci only blinked at me, her stunned expression edged by distrust. "You're lying."

I shrugged. "Fine. Believe what you want. But we both know Tod could have killed you if he'd wanted to. Twice. And I'm sure he was tempted, considering you kidnapped his brother. But he didn't so much as bruise your arm dragging you away from certain death. What does that tell you about who means you harm and who doesn't?"

Luci's frown deepened, and true fear flitted across her face. But she hadn't so much as glanced at Nash in regret, and had yet to ask about my father.

"Look, I don't care where you go or what you do, so long as you stay away from us. And if you want to live, you should get your sister and stay away from Avari, too."

And finally, Luci nodded. She was still nodding when Alec and I walked off with Nash wobbling between us.

"Kaylee Cavanaugh, you bitch!" A shrill voice called as I pulled open the front door of my rental car minutes later. "That's a *six-hundred-dollar* gown, and you ruined it! What the hell are you doing in my dress?" Sophie demanded, flanked by two other Snow Queen contestants in long formal gowns, while she still wore jeans and an angora sweater beneath a pink quilted down jacket.

"Saving the day," I said, closing Nash's door as Alec settled himself into the backseat. I crossed in front of the car and sank into my own seat, tucking the voluminous, ruined skirt in around my legs. "You're welcome."

Then I slammed my door and drove off, leaving Sophie and her friends to stare after us in astonishment.

26

MY HAND SHOOK as I turned off the car and pulled the key from the ignition. Nash's front porch light shone through the windshield, highlighting his face, but all I could think about was how he'd kept me in the dark, fighting an evil he'd already embraced. He leaned against the passenger's-side window, staring at his unlit house. His mother was out, and hopefully blissfully ignorant of what we'd gone through. That wouldn't last long; we'd have to tell her everything soon, because if we didn't, my father would.

But for the moment, this private, temporary reprieve from chaos was too valuable to waste.

For lack of any place else to take him, I'd left Alec at my house with my dad and my uncle when I'd gone in to change clothes. My dad was worried about me, furious with Nash, and understandably scared by the whole thing, though he covered it with almost believable bravado.

Uncle Brendon was relieved that everyone had survived and that Sophie hadn't been sucked into the Netherworld. And he didn't give a damn about the ruined pageant gown.

He'd promised to work on calming down my dad while I took Nash home.

But taking him home was as far ahead as I'd planned.

When I dropped the keys in my lap, Nash twisted in his seat to face me. "What now?" His skin was pale and damp with sweat, in spite of the temperature, but his eyes were clear. He was coherent, and withdrawal hadn't set in yet. If we were going to talk, this was the time.

"I don't know." I fiddled with the key bauble, trying to bring my scattered thoughts into focus. But they didn't want to focus. They wanted to remain mercifully blurry, so I wouldn't have to come to terms with what I'd almost lost. What I might still have to give up.

"Kaylee…"

"Inside." I shoved open my car door without looking at him. "I don't want to do this here." In the driveway. Within sight of any neighbors who happened to peek out the window.

I locked the car while he unlocked the house. He held his front door open, then closed it behind me after I brushed past him into the living room. I followed him down the hall and into his room—we both knew the way, even in the dark—then closed the door at my back. I didn't think Harmony would mind this time, even if she'd been home. My plans for the evening included neither Nash's hands, nor his bed.

Nash kicked his shoes into the corner, then pulled his shirt over his head and dropped it on the floor. He collapsed onto the bed, leaning against his headboard, but for once I wasn't tempted by the display. Nash looked like hell.

Avari had nearly drained him.

I pulled out his desk chair and sat, swiveling to face him. Without taking off my coat. "Nash, I don't know where to st—"

"I'm sorry. Kaylee, I'm so sorry." He looked like he wanted to touch me, but knew better than to try. "I don't even know how to tell you how sorry I am." He watched me, studying my reaction, but I could only stare at my hands in my lap, blinking away unshed tears. "But that's not enough, is it?"

Two months earlier, it would have been. Nash had been the sun lighting up the horizon of my life, outshining everything else in my world. I'd thought once that he was too good to be true.

Turns out I was right.

"Kaylee?" he asked, and his voice was like thin, brittle glass. One heavy word from me, and he would shatter.

"I don't know." I made myself look at him, though the pain and regret swirling in his eyes bruised me, deep inside. I didn't want to be the cause of so much suffering. But I didn't want to feel it, either, and he wasn't the only one hurting. "You lied to me."

"I know. I lied to everyone." His voice echoed with shame, but it wasn't enough. Regret couldn't fix what he'd broken. Apologies couldn't bring back what he'd lost. What *we'd* lost.

"But you lied to *me,* Nash." I swallowed more tears and cleared my throat. "You said you loved me. Then you lied to me, you Influenced me, you tried to make me sound crazy in front of my dad, and you let Avari possess me and do—I can't even imagine what—with my body."

"Kaylee, I'm…"

I sat straighter, anger overwhelming everything else for the moment. "Don't say you're sorry. That won't fix this." I wasn't sure *anything* could fix this—now.

But if I'd been paying more attention… If I'd thought more about Nash and less about being grounded, I'd have seen what was happening before it got so bad. If I'd watched him as closely as I'd watched his loser friends, who'd started using of their own free will... If I'd told my dad earlier... If I'd never taken those stupid balloons to the Netherworld in the first place...

There were a million what-ifs that could have stopped the whole thing. A million things I wished I'd done differently. But in the end, I was left with what actually happened. With my mistakes and his.

And with the question of which mistakes I could live with.

"How many times?" I demanded, so soft I barely heard my own words. I picked at my cuticles because I couldn't stand to watch him struggle for an answer. "How many times did you let him...use me?"

Nash sighed, and the bed creaked as he moved closer, but I didn't look up. "I don't know. I wasn't counting. I was trying to forget."

You should have been trying to stop him. "Make a guess." I rolled away from the bed until the chair back hit the desktop.

"I didn't see you very often when you were grounded. So... maybe once a week. Until the last week of school."

"Twice that week?" I asked, and Nash nodded miserably. "So, six times?"

He shrugged. "I guess so."

"What did I do?" I demanded, far from sure I really wanted the answer.

"Kaylee, you don't want to—"

"No, *you* don't want to," I snapped. Because the guilt was killing him. I could see that. But I needed to know. "Tell me."

"Most of the time, he just talked through you. Told me where and when to meet Everett. Made me remember things, so he could take his payment." A concept which horrified me to no end.

"But it was more than that once, right?" Unless Avari was lying. Please, please let him be lying...

Nash closed his eyes and let his skull thump into the headboard. "The first time." He opened his eyes and met my gaze so I could see the earnest colors swirling in his irises. The brutal honesty. "I didn't know what was going on, Kaylee. I swear, I had no idea. I didn't even know it was possible."

"What happened?"

"Your dad was at work, and I came over with a movie. You fell asleep on the couch, and I was gonna let you sleep. But then you woke up, and we started...kissing."

"That's it?" I could tell that wasn't it. The thought of Avari kissing him with my mouth was revolting, but it wasn't bad enough to account for the crimson flush of shame in his cheeks.

"No. You... *He* let me...touch you. He took your shirt off. I should have known it wasn't you, but I—"

"Yeah, you should have!" My head was a maelstrom of rage and humiliation, spinning fast and hard enough to make me dizzy. I pulled my jacket closed over my shirt, as if that could somehow block what he'd already seen. What he'd touched. But I couldn't undo it. It was done when I couldn't stop it, and he *didn't* stop it.

I stood, breathing too fast. Terrified by the thought that I could have been so out of control of my own body. *I can't do this.* It was too much.

I whirled on him, anger burning deep inside me. "You can't remember what our real firsts felt like, and I wasn't even *there* for this one. How am I supposed to deal with that?" I scrubbed both hands over my face. "I'm lost, Nash. What happened while I wasn't here—what you thought you were doing with me—may have been no big deal to you, but it would have been special to me. Something *I* was supposed to give to you, but someone else gave it to you instead, and now it's ruined. And I want it back, but you can't give it back to me…" I blinked away more tears, struggling to cling to anger instead.

Nash stood, too, but gave me space. "Kaylee, I swear I had no idea what was going on."

"You didn't want to know! You saw what you wanted and took it, and it didn't occur to you that something wasn't right until…" I stopped, my focus narrowing on him as my stomach pitched with a sudden horrifying certainty. "When did you know? Did you stop on your own? Did you figure it out, or did he tell you?"

Nash dropped his gaze. His hands curled into fists, and he shoved them into his jeans pockets. "We were… He said something, and it wasn't your voice."

The churning in my stomach grew into full-fledged nausea. "So he stopped you, probably only because cluing you in would be more fun. How far would you have gone if he hadn't? Would you have stopped at all?"

Had Nash Hudson ever waited three months for anyone to give it up before? Could he even be expected to have that kind of willpower, when I wasn't saying no?

Nash read the fear on my face. "Kaylee, no. I would have figured it out." He stepped forward, and I backed up until my spine hit the wall, and I had nowhere else to go. He stopped, begging me silently to listen. To try to understand. "I know your limits. I know *you*. I would have figured it out. I would have stopped."

"Why should I believe you?" I felt used. I felt cheated and dirty, and though I knew that wasn't entirely Nash's fault, I couldn't help hating him a little bit, for letting it happen. "You called me a tease. You said anyone else would have walked away already. But would you have, if I seemed willing? You've already tried to Influence me out of my clothes."

"Kaylee, that's not fair. I wasn't thinking. I was…"

"High?" I raised both brows, and he nodded miserably. "Yeah. You were. And you're right—it wasn't fair. So why should I believe you now?"

"Because he never fooled me again." Nash made eye contact and held it, letting me see the truth. "I know you. I love you, Kaylee. I know you probably can't forgive me—hell, I don't think I can forgive myself—but I swear on my life that it'll never happen again. Any of it. No more frost. No more lies. No more Influence. Please, just give me a chance to prove it. Will you give me one more chance?"

"I…"

But before I could come up with an answer, Tod appeared in the desk chair, where I'd sat minutes earlier. "Hey. Am I interrupting something?"

"Yes," Nash said. "Get out."

But Tod was watching me, and I could tell from the angry line of his jaw that he'd been listening long before he showed himself. He'd heard what Avari had done to me. What Nash had let him do.

"You want me to go?" Tod asked me, his back to his brother.

Nash implored me silently to say yes. Tod waited patiently.

"No," I said, looking right at Nash. He scowled, and his shoulders sagged.

"Good." Tod stood and kicked the rolling chair out of his way. "I just checked on your friend in the straitjacket. But first…" The reaper swung before either of us realized what he intended to do.

Tod's very solid fist slammed into Nash's jaw. Nash's head

snapped back. He stumbled into the wall. Tod shook his hand like it hurt. "That's for what you let him do to Kaylee."

Nash shoved himself away from the wall, swinging at his brother. But his fist went right through the reaper's incorporeal head, and Tod only frowned, turning back to me while his brother seethed.

I gaped at them both, surprised beyond speech.

Tod pushed the rolling chair toward me, and I sat. Nash sank onto his bed, glaring at his brother and rubbing his jaw. "How's Scott?" I asked, still trying to absorb the abbreviated fistfight and avoid answering Nash's last question. "Still hearing voices?"

"Just that one voice,"

Tod said. "According to the chatter at the nurses' station he's been much worse tonight. I figure Avari's been throwing fits ever since we crossed over."

And if Avari was taking his rage out on Scott, I didn't want to know what he was doing to Addy.

"How does he look?" Nash asked, staring at the floor rather than look at his brother.

"Crazy." Tod shrugged. "He stares at the walls like they're going to swallow him, and they're keeping the room lit from all four sides to eliminate shadows. Even at night. Otherwise, he screams until they have to sedate him." The very thought of which triggered memories of my own time strapped to a bed. "They seem to think his fear of shadows is part of his neurosis."

But we knew the truth: the shadows really *were* out to get Scott Carter.

Because Avari was in the shadows.

"Mom says they're connected now. Because Scott inhaled so much of his breath, Avari has a permanent, hardwired connection to his brain. The bastard's playing with the shadows, and probably planting thoughts directly in his head."

I swallowed true horror.

"That won't happen to me," Nash insisted, obviously having read the fear on my face. Or in my eyes. "If Avari could have spoken to me directly, he would have." But he couldn't. Avari's serial possession of me was proof of that.

I nodded. Nash seemed to be immune to the connected-consciousness thing by virtue of being a *bean sidhe.*

"So…you talked to Mom?" Nash frowned at his brother.

"Yeah. I didn't tell her everything, but I had to tell her you crossed over. She's on her way here." Tod raised one brow at his brother. "Consider this your heads-up."

"Thanks for the warning." Nash stood to show Tod that his presence was no longer required. He was still pissed over being punched, but obviously realized that fighting the reaper would do no more good than trying to argue with him.

Tod glanced at me in question.

I sighed and nodded. I couldn't avoid Nash's question forever. "Thanks, Tod," I said. Then, acting on impulse, I stood and gave him a hug before he could blink out. I wasn't sure whether I was thanking him for helping save Nash and my dad, or for watching over Scott, or for giving a damn what happened to me. Maybe it was all three.

But more than any of that, I was thankful for the possibility he'd shown me: that a man really could love a woman enough that he'd do anything to protect her. That's how much Tod loved Addy.

That's how much I wanted Nash to love me.

When I let him go, Tod held my gaze for a long moment, searching my eyes. Then he blinked out of sight without a word.

I turned to face Nash slowly, my pulse racing. I stared at the floor as I weighed my options, the possibilities, and my own heart.

"Kaylee?" Nash whispered, and I looked up to find him watching me. Still waiting for my answer, as if Tod had never interrupted. "I know it doesn't do any good for me to make promises, because you don't trust me right now. But I swear, I'll spend every day earning your trust back. Let me prove it. Give us one more shot, Kaylee." He stood, and his eyes were shiny with tears. "Please. I need you."

I didn't know what to say. Needing me wasn't enough. Not after what he'd done. Love should have meant more than getting high. *I* should have meant more…

Nash did love me. I could see the truth of that in his eyes and I desperately wanted it to be enough. But Avari would never die, and even though he was clean now, Nash would always be addicted to him. And what if he started using again?

I'd already lost classmates, and free will, and trust, and I'd almost lost both my father and Nash. How much more could I afford to lose if he fell off the wagon?

"I can't, Nash. Not yet. I'm sorry." My eyes watered, but I blinked away the tears and opened the door.

"Kaylee, wait." He pulled my hand from the doorknob and held it, and I saw that his eyes were damp, too. "What do you want? Tell me, and I'll do it. Please."

My next breath was painful, but I held it for several seconds, swallowing tears I refused to let fall. Then I looked into his eyes, trying not to see the honest pain and regret in them.

"I want to take it all back. I want to save Doug, and heal Scott, and protect Emma. I want to fix your memories, so you can remember what this felt like the first time." I stood on my toes and kissed him, long and slow, and hot tears rolled down my cheeks, because I knew that—at least for now—I was kissing him goodbye. Then I leaned against his chest, listening to his heartbeat. Already missing it.

"Nash, I want you to get better, so I can have you back."

I tugged my hand from his grip and stepped into the hall, pulling the door closed behind me. Then I ran for my car.

And cried all the way home.

★ ★ ★ ★ ★

ACKNOWLEDGMENTS

THANKS MOST OF ALL TO #1, who takes over so many real life duties so I can live and work in my own little world.

Thanks to Rinda Elliott, for one honest opinion after another, to the Deadline Dames, for camaraderie, and to Jocelynn Drake and Kim Haynes, for friendships I grow more grateful for every year.

Thanks, as always, to my agent, Miriam Kriss, for making things happen.

And thank you to my editor Mary-Theresa Hussey and to Elizabeth Mazer and everyone else behind the scenes. Without your patience and enthusiasm, this book would never have made it onto the shelf.

• MY SOUL TO STEAL •

To all the real-life couples, exes,
and unrequited romantic interests, tangled up in love
and nightmares. Sometimes that frayed knot is the best lifeline
in the world. Other times, it works more like a straitjacket....

By the time the second semester of my junior year began, I'd already faced down rogue grim reapers, an evil entertainment mogul, and hellions determined to possess my soul. But I never would have guessed that the most infuriating beast of all, I had yet to meet. My boyfriend's ex-girlfriend was a thing of nightmares. Literally.

"I won't bite." Nash looked up at me with a green bean speared on his fork, and I realized I was staring. I'd stopped on the bottom step, surprised to see him at school, and even more surprised to see him sitting alone at lunch, outside in the January cold, where I'd come to get away from the gossip and stares in the cafeteria.

Obviously he'd had the same idea.

I glanced over my shoulder through the window in the cafeteria door, looking for Emma, but she hadn't shown up yet.

Nash frowned when he noticed my hesitation. But I wasn't worried about him. I was worried about me. I was afraid that if I got within touching distance of him—within reach of the arms that had once been my biggest comfort and those gorgeous hazel eyes that could read me at a glance—that I would give in. That I would forgive, even if I couldn't forget, and that would be bad.

I mean, it would *feel* good, but that would be bad.

The past two weeks had been the most difficult of my life. In the past few months alone, I'd survived horrors most sixteen-year-old girls didn't even know existed. But a couple of weeks without Nash—our entire winter vacation—had nearly been enough to break me.

Whoever said it is better to have loved and lost than never to have loved was full of crap. If I'd never loved Nash in the first place, I wouldn't know what I was missing now.

"Kaylee?" Nash dropped his fork onto his tray, green bean untouched. "I get it. You're not ready to talk."

I shook my head and set my tray on the table across from his, then sank onto the opposite bench. "No, I just… I didn't think you'd be here." I hadn't gone to see him, because that would have been unfair to us both—being together, when we couldn't really be together. But I knew he'd been very sick from withdrawal, because my father, of all people, had called regularly to check on him.

And based on his brief reports, withdrawal from Demon's Breath—known as frost, in human circles—was hell on earth.

"Are you…okay?" I asked, poking at runny spaghetti sauce with my own fork.

"Better." He shrugged. "Still working toward okay."

"But you're well enough for school?"

Another shrug. "My mom was giving me a sedative made from some weird Netherworld plant for a while, to help with the shakes, but it just made me sleep all the time. Without dreams," he added, when he saw my horrified expression. The hellion whose breath he'd been huffing had communicated with Nash through his dreams sometimes. And through me, the rest of the time. By hijacking my body while I slept.

I'd been willing to work through the addiction with Nash—after all, it was my fault he'd been exposed to Demon's Breath in the first place. But his failure to stop the serial possession of my body—or even tell me it was happening—was the last straw for me. I couldn't be with him until I was sure nothing like that would ever happen again.

Unfortunately, what my head wanted and what my heart wanted were two completely different things.

"I still don't have much appetite, but what I do eat is staying down now." Nash stared at his full tray. He'd lost weight. His face looked…sharper. The flesh under his eyes was dark and puffy, and he hadn't bothered to artfully muss his hair that morning. The bright, charismatic Nash I'd first met had been replaced with this dimmer, somber version I barely recognized. A version I was afraid I didn't know on the inside, either. Not like I'd known *my* Nash, anyway.

"Maybe you should have stayed home a little longer," I suggested, slowly twirling noodles around my plastic fork.

"I wanted to see you."

The fissure in my heart cracked open a little wider, and I looked up to find regret and longing slowly twisting the greens and browns in his irises. Humans wouldn't see that, even if we'd had company. But because Nash and I were both *bean sidhes*—banshees, to the uninformed—we could see the colors swirling in each other's eyes, and with a little practice, I'd learned to interpret what I saw in his. To read his emotions through the windows of his soul—when he let me see them.

"Nash…"

"No pressure," he interrupted, before I could spit out the protest I'd practiced, but hoped not to have to use. "I just wanted to see your face. Hear your voice."

Translation: *You didn't visit me. Or even call.*

I closed my eyes, trying to work through an awkwardness I'd never felt with Nash before. "I wanted to." More than I could possibly express. "But it's just too hard to…"

"To see, but not touch?" he finished for me, and I met his rueful gaze. "Trust me, I know." He sighed and stirred a glob of mass-produced peach cobbler. "So, what now? We're friends?"

Yeah. If friends could be in love, but not together. In sync, but out of touch. Willing to die for each other, but unable to trust.

"I don't think there are words for what we are, Nash." Yet I could think of at least one: *broken.*

Nash and I were like the wreckage of two cars that had hit head-on. We were tangled up in each other so thoroughly that I could no longer tell which parts of us were him and which were me. We could probably never be truly untangled—not after what we'd been through together—but I had serious doubts we could ever really recapture what we'd had.

"I just… I need some time."

He nodded, and his eyes shone with the first flash of hope I'd seen from him in ages. "Yeah. We have time."

In fact, we had lots and lots of time. *Bean sidhes* age very slowly from puberty on, so while I'd likely be carded until I was forty, if Nash and I actually managed to work things out, we'd have nearly four hundred years together, barring catastrophe.

Although actually barring catastrophe seemed highly un-likely, considering that since the school year began, my life had been defined by a series of disasters, barely held together by the beautifully strong thread of Nash's presence in my life. At least, until recently. But now I was clinging to the wreck-age of my existence, holding the pieces together on my own, trying to decide if I would be helping us both or hurting us by letting him back in.

"So, how's Em?" Nash asked, his voice lowered as he glanced at something over my shoulder.

I twisted to see Emma Marshall, my best friend, heading toward us across the nearly deserted quad. Everyone with half a brain—or nothing to hide—was eating inside, where it was warm. Em carried a tray holding a slice of pizza and a Diet Coke, content to eat with us outside, not because she couldn't face the crowd ready to judge her, but because she didn't care what they thought.

"Em's strong. She's dealing." And though she didn't know it, in many ways, Emma was my hero, based on her resilience alone.

Doug Fuller, Em's boyfriend of almost a month, had died from an overdose of frost two weeks earlier, and though they'd been connected at the crotch, rather than at the heart, she'd been understandably upset by his death. Especially considering that she couldn't comprehend the Netherworld origin of the drug that had killed him.

Nash lowered his voice even further as she walked toward us. "Did you go to the funeral?"

"Yeah." Doug had been one of Eastlake High's starting linebackers. Practically the whole school had shown up at his funeral—except for Nash. He'd been too sick from withdrawal to get out of bed. And Scott, their third musketeer. Scott had survived addiction to frost—but at a devastating price. He'd suffered brain damage and now had a permanent, hardwired mental connection to the hellion whose breath had killed Doug and mortally wounded my relationship with Nash.

"Hey." Emma came to a stop on my right and glanced from me to Nash, then back before taking a seat next to me. "Someone bring me up to speed. Are we making up or breaking up?

'Cause this limbo is kind of driving me nuts." She grinned, and I could have thanked the universe in that moment for the ray of sunshine that was Emma.

"How low can you go?" I asked, then crunched into a French fry.

"Lower than you know…" Nash replied, with a hint of an awkward grin.

Em rolled her eyes. "So…more limbo?"

Nash looked just as ready for my answer as she did. I exhaled heavily. "For now."

He sighed and Emma frowned. Like I was being unreasonable. But she didn't know the details of our breakup. I couldn't tell her that he'd let a hellion take over my body and play doctor with him—to Nash's credit, he hadn't known it wasn't me that first time—without even telling me I was being worn like a human costume.

I couldn't tell her because the same thing had happened to her, and for her own safety and sense of security, I didn't want her to know that her body had been hijacked by the hellion responsible for her boyfriend's death. Her friendship with me had already put her in more than enough danger.

"Oh, fine. Drag out the melodrama for as long as you want. At least it'll give everyone around here something else to talk about." Something other than Doug and Scott.

If they hadn't already had two weeks to deal with grief and let off steam, the whole school probably would have been reeling from the double loss. The looks and whispers when we passed in the hall were hard enough to deal with as it was.

"So, did you see the new girl?" Emma asked, making a valiant attempt to change the subject as she tore the crust from her triangle of pizza.

"What new girl?" I didn't really care, but the switch in topic gave me a chance to think—or at least talk—about something other than me and Nash, and the fact that there was currently no me and Nash.

"Don't remember her name." Emma dipped her crust into a paper condiment cup full of French dressing. "But she's a senior. Can you imagine? Switching schools the last semester of your senior year?"

"Yeah, that would suck," I agreed, staring at my tray, pretending I didn't notice Nash staring at me. Was it going to be like this from now on? Us sitting across from each other, watching—or pointedly not watching—each other? Sitting in silence or talking about nothing anyone really cared about? *Maybe I should have stayed in the cafeteria. This isn't gonna work....*

"She's in my English class. She looked pretty lonely, so I invited her to sit with us." Emma bit into her crust and chewed while I glanced up at her in surprise.

First of all, Em didn't have other girlfriends. Most girls didn't like Emma for the same reason guys couldn't stay away from her. It had been just the two of us since the seventh grade, when her mouth and her brand-new C-cups intimidated the entire female half of the student body.

Second of all...

"Why is there a senior in your junior English class?" Nash said it before I could.

Emma shrugged while she chewed, then swallowed and dipped her crust again. "She got behind somehow, and they're letting her take two English classes at once, so she can graduate on time. I mean, would you want to be here for a whole 'nother year, just to take one class?"

"No." Nash stabbed another green bean he probably wasn't going to eat. "But I wouldn't want to read *Macbeth* and *To Kill a Mockingbird* at the same time, either."

"Better her than me." Em bit into her crust again, then

twisted on the bench as footsteps crunched on the grass behind us. "Hey, here she comes," she said around a full mouth.

I started to turn, but stopped when I noticed Nash staring. And not at me. His wide-eyed gaze was trained over my
head, and if his jaw got any looser, he'd have to pick it up off
his tray. "Sabine?" he said, his voice soft and stunned.

Emma slapped the table. "*That's* her name!" She twisted
and called over her shoulder. "Sabine, over here!" Then she
glanced back at Nash. "Wait, you've already met her?"

Nash didn't answer. Instead, he stood, nearly tripping over
his own bench seat, and when he rounded the table toward
the new girl, I finally turned to look at her. And instantly understood why she wasn't intimidated by Emma.

Sabine was an entirely different kind of gorgeous.

She was a contrast of pale skin and dark hair, where Em was
golden. Slim and lithe, where Em was curvy. She swaggered,
where Emma glided. And she'd stopped cold, her lunch tray
obviously forgotten, and was staring not at me or her new
friend Emma, but at *my* boyfriend.

My kind-of boyfriend. Or whatever.

"Sabine?" Nash whispered this time, and his familiar,
stunned tone set off alarm bells in my head.

"Nash Hudson. Holy shit, it *is* you!" the new girl said, tossing long dark hair over one shoulder to reveal a mismatched
set of hoops in her double-pierced right ear.

Nash rounded the table and walked past me without a
glance in my direction. Sabine set her tray on the nearest
table and ran at him. He opened his arms, and she flew into
them so hard they spun in a tight circle. Together.

My chest burned like I'd swallowed an entire jar of hot salsa.

"What are you doing here?" Nash asked, setting her down,
as she said, "I can't believe it!"

But I was pretty sure she could believe it. She looked more

thrilled than surprised. "I heard your name this morning, but I didn't think it would really be you!"

"It's me. So…what? You go to school here now?"

"Yeah. New foster home. Moved in last week." She smiled, and her dark eyes lit up. "I can't believe this!"

"Me, neither." Em stood and pulled me up. "What is it we're not believing?"

And finally Nash turned, one arm still wrapped casually around Sabine's waist, as if he'd forgotten it was still there. "Sabine went to my school in Fort Worth, before I moved here."

"Yeah, before you ran off and left me!" She twisted out of his grip to punch him in the shoulder, but she didn't look mad.

"Hey, you left first, remember?" Nash grinned.

"Not by choice!" Her scowl was almost as dark as her grin was blinding.

What the hell were they talking about?

I'd already opened my mouth to say…something, when Tod winked into existence on my left. Fortunately, I was still too confused by the arrival of Nash's old friend—*please, please* just be a friend!—to be surprised by the sudden appearance of his mostly dead grim reaper brother.

"Hey, Kaylee, you…" Tod began, running one hand through pale blond curls, then stopped when he saw Sabine and Nash, still chatting like long-lost relatives, while the rest of us watched. "Uh-oh. I'm too late."

"Too late for what?" Emma asked, but I could tell from the lack of a reaction from either Nash or Sabine that Em and I were currently the only ones who could see Tod. Selective corporeality was one of several really cool reaper abilities, and now that Emma knew about him, Tod rarely appeared to me alone. For which I was more than grateful—Em was one less person who thought I went around talking to myself when I was really talking to the reaper.

"To warn you," Tod continued. "About Sabine."

"She comes with a warning label?" Em whispered.

I crossed my arms over the front of my jacket. "Well, it can't be sewn into her clothes, or we'd see the outline." Sabine's black sleeveless top was so tight I could practically count her abs.

Emma raised one brow at me. "Catty, much?"

"Well, look at her!" I whispered, both relieved and very, very irritated that neither Nash nor Sabine had given us a second look. A strip of bare skin showed between the low waist of her army-green carpenter pants and the hem of her shirt—an obvious violation of the school dress code—and she wore enough dark eye shadow to scare small children. And—most grating of all—the look worked for her. And it obviously worked for Nash. He couldn't look away.

"I don't think it's her you have a problem with," Emma whispered. "It's *them*."

I ignored her and turned to Tod. "I take it they were involved in Fort Worth?"

Tod nodded. "Yeah. If you're into really dramatic understatements."

Great.

"Hey, you two, care to introduce those of us on the periphery?" Emma called, betraying no hint of Tod's presence. She was a fast learner.

Nash looked up in surprise. "Sorry." He guided Sabine closer. "I'm guessing you've already met Emma?" he said, and the new girl—his *old* girl—nodded. "And this is my…" Confusion flashed in Nash's swirling eyes, and he dropped his hand from Sabine's waist. "This is Kaylee Cavanaugh."

Sabine truly looked at me for the first time, and I caught my breath at the intensity of her scrutiny. Her eyes were pools of ink that seemed to see right through me, and in that moment, the certainty—the terror—that Nash would want nothing to do with me now that she'd arrived was enough to constrict my throat and make my stomach pitch.

"Kaylee…" Sabine said my name like she was tasting it, trying to decide whether to swallow me whole or spit me back out, and in the end, I wasn't sure which she'd chosen. "Kaylee Cavanaugh. You must be the new ex."

Resisting the overwhelming urge to take a step back from Sabine, I shot Nash a questioning look, but he only shrugged. He hadn't told her. He hadn't even known she was there until she walked into the quad.

"I…" But I didn't know how to finish that thought.

Sabine laughed and fresh chill bumps popped up on my arms, beneath my jacket. "Don't worry 'bout it. Happens to the best of us." Then she turned—pointedly dismissing me—and grabbed her forgotten tray in one hand and Nash's arm in the other. "Let's eat. I'm starving!"

He glanced back at me then, and a flicker of uncertainty flashed in the swirling greens and browns of Nash's irises before he turned with her and headed for our table.

As they sat, I turned to find Tod watching them warily. "How long ago did they break up?" I asked, without bothering to whisper. Nash and Sabine no longer knew we existed.

"Well…" Tod hesitated, and I frowned at him. Like Emma, he was usually blunt bordering on rude.

"What?" I demanded.

Tod exhaled heavily. "Technically speaking, they never did."

"So, HOW SERIOUS were they?" I handed change and a receipt to a balding man in his forties. He shoved them both into his front pocket, then took off toward the north wing of the theater with a greasy jumbo popcorn.

"You sure you want to hear this?" Tod sat on the snack counter in his usual jeans and snug white tee, invisible and inaudible to everyone but me and Em. Not that it mattered. Monday afternoons were dead at the Cinemark. But then, so was Tod.

Emma leaned over the counter next to him. "I'm sure *I* want to hear it." She was on a break from her shift in the ticket booth, but Tod and I were obviously much more entertaining than anything going on in the break room.

"I didn't come to rub your face in it," the reaper insisted, watching me as he snatched a kernel from Emma's small bag of popcorn.

"No, you came because you're bored, and my problems obviously amuse you."

Tod had just switched to the midnight-to-noon shift reaping souls at the local hospital, and since reapers didn't need sleep, he was now free every afternoon to bug his still-living friends. Which consisted of me, Em, and Nash.

Tod shrugged. "Yeah, that, and for the free food."

"Why are you eating, anyway?" Emma pulled her paper bag out of his reach. "Can you even metabolize this?"

Tod raised one pale brow at her. "I may be dead, but I'm still perfectly functional. More functional than ever, in fact. Watch me function." He reached around her and grabbed another handful of popcorn while she laughed. "And that's not all I can do..."

"Can we save the live demo for later, please? *Bean sidhe* in angst, here." But the truth was that it felt good to laugh, after what we'd all been through in the past few months. "Seriously, tell me about Sabine."

Emma grinned. "Does she have a last name, or is she a superstahh? Like Beyoncé, or the pope?"

I threw a jelly bean at her, from the open box I kept under the counter. "You know that's not his name, right?"

Em threw the jelly bean back.

"Anyway..." Tod began. "Vital stats—here we go... Her name is Sabine Campbell, and she's probably seventeen by now. She likes long walks down dark alleys, conspicuous piercings, and, if memory serves, chocolate milk—shaken, not stirred." Tod paused dramatically, and the good humor shining in his eyes dulled a bit. "And she and Nash were the real thing."

My grape jelly bean went sour on my tongue, and I had to force myself to chew. But he'd said *were*. They *were* the real thing. As in, past tense. Because I was Nash's present tense. Right? We were taking a break so he could get clean, and I could come to terms with what had happened, but that didn't mean he was free for the taking!

"Wait, the real thing, like hearts and candy and flowers?" Em asked, wrinkling her nose over the cupid cliché.

Tod started to laugh, but choked off the sound with one look at my face. "More like obsession and codependence and… sex," the reaper finished reluctantly.

I rolled my eyes and poked through my box of jelly beans for another grape. "I know he's not a virgin."

"Well, he was when he met Sabine."

"Ohh," Emma breathed, and I dropped my jelly beans into the trash.

"Okay, so what?" I opened the door to the storage closet and grabbed the broom. "So she was his first. That doesn't mean anything." I swept up crushed popcorn kernels and smooshed Milk Duds in short, vicious strokes. "She didn't save lives with him. She didn't risk her soul to rescue him from the Netherworld. Whatever they had can't compete with that, right?"

"Right." Emma watched me, her eyes wide in sympathy. "Besides, we don't even know that she's still interested in him. They were probably just surprised to see each other."

I stilled the broom and raised both brows at her.

Emma shrugged. "Okay, she's totally still into him. Sorry, Kay."

"It doesn't matter. So long as *he's* not into *her*." I resumed sweeping, and accidentally smacked the popcorn machine with the broom handle.

Tod hopped down from the counter and held one blessedly corporeal hand out. "Hand over the broom, and no one will get hurt." But I found that hard to believe. Sabine was making me doubt everything I'd thought I knew. And I'd spent less than fifteen minutes with her.

I gave Tod the broom and he put it back in the closet. "He hasn't seen her in more than two years. Give him a chance to get used to her being here, and everything will go back to normal."

Normal. I could hardly even remember what that word meant anymore. "You really think so?"

Tod shrugged. "I give it a fifty-fifty chance."

"Doesn't that mean I have a better chance of being struck by lightning at least once before I die?"

Em laughed. "Knowing your luck? Yeah."

I pulled a plastic-wrapped stack of large cups from under the counter and began restocking the cup dispensers. "So, what's the deal? How did they hook up?"

"I was limited by real-world physics at the time, so I don't know the whole story," Tod said, leaning back with his elbows propped on the counter.

"Just tell me what you do know."

The reaper shrugged. "Nash was only fifteen when they met, and still coming into his full *bean sidhe* abilities— Influence doesn't come on full-strength until puberty."

"Really?" Emma said, a kernel of popcorn halfway to her mouth. "I didn't know that."

I hadn't, either. But I was tired of sounding ignorant about my own species, so I kept my mouth shut.

"Yeah. Otherwise, the terrible twos would turn any little *bean sidhe* boy into a tyrant. Can you imagine Nash ordering our mom around from the time he could talk?"

Actually, I could, having had a taste of what out-of-control Influence looked and felt like.

"So, anyway, Nash was coming into his own, but he didn't have our dad around to teach him stuff, like I did, so he was kind of mixed up. Sabine was abandoned as a kid, and she'd been through a bunch of foster parents. When they met, she had it pretty rough at home, and she'd gotten into some trouble. She had a temper, but nothing too serious. She and Nash just kind of fell into each other. I think he thought he could help her."

Yeah, that sounded like Nash and his hero complex. We'd gotten together the same way.

I stared at the gritty floor, trying not to feel sorry for Sabine. Something told me she wouldn't welcome my sympathy any more than she'd welcome my currently undefined presence in Nash's life.

"Did Harmony like her?" I asked, unable to deny the queasy feeling my question brought on. I didn't want Nash's mother to like any of his exes better than she liked me, but the new fear went beyond that. Harmony and I shared *bean sidhe* abilities. We'd bonded beyond our mutual interest in Nash, and I wanted her for myself, just like I wanted Nash.

Tod shrugged. "Mom likes everyone. The two of them together scared the shit out of her, though, the same way you and Nash being together probably gives your dad nightmares."

"So what happened?" Em asked, while I was still trying to process the fact that Nash and Sabine's bond had been strong enough to worry Harmony.

When Tod didn't answer, I looked up and he shrugged again. "I died."

Emma blinked. "You…died?" She knew he was dead, of course, but that didn't make his proclamation sound any more…normal.

"Yeah. I died, and Mom and Nash didn't know I'd be coming back in my current incarnation." He spread his arms to indicate his existence as a reaper—and his completely unharmed-by-death physique. "So they moved for a fresh start, just like we did after my dad died. We'd lived around here when Nash and I were kids, so this probably felt a little like coming home for my mom. It made everything harder for Nash, though. Because of leaving Sabine."

"And he and Sabine never broke up?" I moved on to the jumbo plastic cups, fascinated in spite of myself by Tod's story.

"He couldn't get in touch with her. She was kind of…in state custody at the time. No email. No phone calls, except from family. Which she doesn't have."

Emma stood straight, brown eyes wide. "She got arrested?"

"I told you she got into some trouble."

"Yeah, but you didn't mention that she was a criminal." I shoved the cups down harder than was probably necessary. Nash's ex-girlfriend—his former "real thing"—was a convict? *That's* not scary or anything.

Obviously at some point his tastes had changed. Dramatically.

"What'd she do?" Emma said, asking the question I most wanted answered, but refused to ask myself.

Tod shrugged. "Nash never told me. But she got probation and a halfway house instead of prison, so it couldn't have been too bad."

"I'm guessing that's a matter of opinion." I twisted the end of the cellophane around the remaining cups and shoved them under the counter. "Maybe I should call him after work."

"What are you gonna say?" Emma asked. "'I'm not sure I want you back, but I'm sure I don't want your ex-con ex-girlfriend to have you, either'? Yeah. That'll start this little triangle off on the right foot."

"This is not a triangle. This is—" *a disaster* "—nothing. Exes turn into friends all the time, right?" Emma and Tod exchanged a glance. "Right?" I demanded, when neither of them answered.

"I don't know, Kay." Emma crumpled her empty popcorn bag and tossed it into the trash can from across the counter. "But on the bright side, according to Mrs. Garner, the triangle is the most stable geometric shape. That has to count for something, right?"

"This is not a triangle," I repeated, turning my back on them both to check the number of nacho cheese containers lined up beneath the heat lamp. I couldn't afford to let my decision about me and Nash be influenced by Sabine's arrival. Or her criminal record. Or her prior claim on my boyfriend.

When I turned back around, Em was still watching me. "Maybe you shouldn't start grilling Nash about his ex until he's back on his feet for sure."

"Yeah." Except by then she could have swept him off of them. Or knocked them out from under him. Either way, Nash off his feet would be bad.

"Marshall, your break's over!" the new assistant manager called from across the lobby, fleshy hands propped on his considerable gut. "Back in the ticket booth!" His name was Becker, but when she made fun of him after work, Em replaced the capital *B* with a *P.* She'd called him Pecker to his face once, by accident, and he'd been yelling at her ever since.

Emma rolled her eyes, pushed the remainder of her soda toward Tod, and headed backward across the lobby. "See you after work." We'd ridden together, as we usually did when we had the same shift. But now, more often than not, we had a third carpooler.

As if he'd read my mind—not a reaper ability, as far as I knew—Tod glanced around the snack bar as a group of junior high kids came through the front door, wearing matching aftercare shirts. "Where's Alec?"

Tod, Nash, and Harmony were the only ones—other than my dad—who knew the truth about Alec, that he'd spent a quarter of a century enslaved by a hellion in the Netherworld. Until we'd rescued him in exchange for his help saving my dad and Nash from that same hellion.

I glanced at the clock. "He's on his break, but he should be back any minute." I'd given him my keys so he could eat a bag of Doritos in the car, by himself. Alec had grown comfortable with me and my dad, but the same could not be said for the rest of the general populace.

For the most part, Alec had adjusted well to being back in the human world. He was fascinated with the internet, DVDs, and laptops, none of which had been around in the eighties, when he'd become Avari's Netherworld proxy—a weird combination of a personal assistant and snack food. I hadn't even seen my iPod in days.

But he was still sometimes overwhelmed by crowds, not because of the numbers—he'd regularly faced large groups of terrifying monsters in the Netherworld—but because of the culture shock. He was getting to know the twenty-first century at his own speed through TV, newspapers—evidently people still read them in his day—and all the movies he saw for free at the Cinemark. But he got nervous when he had to actually interact with groups of people who didn't understand his cultural handicap. So far, "Medium or large?" and "Would you like butter on your popcorn?" were the most we'd gotten out of him at work.

"Want me to find him?" Tod asked, as the gaggle of kids descended on Emma in the ticket booth. But before I could answer, Alec rounded a corner into the lobby, tucking his uniform shirt into his pants.

"Sorry. Fell asleep," he said, then ducked into a small hall leading to the break room and service entrance. When he stepped into the snack bar a second later, scruffing one brown hand over short-cropped, tight curls, I couldn't help noticing that he still looked only half-awake.

"Just in time. We're about to get hit hard." I pointed to the swarm of tweens, and his dark eyes widened. "Don't worry, kids usually get Slurpees, candy, and some popcorn. Nothing complicated."

Alec just stared at me as I dumped a bag of popcorn seeds into the popper, careful not to burn myself. "Hey, you missed the inside scoop on Sabine." Em and I had told him about her on the ride to work, but his confused frown said he obviously hadn't been paying attention. Not that I could blame him. After twenty-six years spent serving a hellion in the Netherworld, high school drama probably felt trite and irrelevant.

But Sabine was anything but irrelevant to me.

"It turns out she's an ex-con. Or something like that. Tod doesn't know what she did, but…" I turned around to look for the reaper and wasn't surprised to realize he'd disappeared. I think the temptation to put a couple of the prepubescent punks out of their misery was a little too strong.

"Anyway, she definitely wants Nash back, and…" But before I could finish that thought, the kids descended on the snack bar, and my pity party was swallowed whole by the universal clamor for sugar and caffeine.

I pointed to the other register. "You take that one, and I'll cover this one."

Alec nodded, but when the first of the tween mob started shouting orders at him, he stared at his register screen like he'd never seen it before.

Great. Awesome time to succumb to culture shock. He'd been fine taking orders twenty minutes earlier, when there was no crowd. "Here. I'll take orders, you fill them." I stepped firmly between him and the register and shoved an empty popcorn bucket into his hands.

Alec scowled like he'd snap at me, then just nodded and turned toward the popcorn machine without a word.

I took several orders and filled the cups, but when I turned to grab popcorn from Alec, I found him staring at the machine, holding an empty bucket, like he'd rather wear it on his head than fill it.

"Alec…" I took the bucket from him and half filled it. "This is really not a good time for a breakdown." I squirted butter over the popcorn, then filled it the rest of the way and squirted more butter. "You okay?"

He frowned again, then nodded stiffly and grabbed another bucket.

I handed popcorn across the counter to the first customer and glanced up to find Emma jogging across the lobby toward me. "Hey, Pecker sent me to bail you out," she said, and several sixth graders giggled as she hopped up on the counter and swung her legs around to the business side. She thumped to the floor, and I started to thank her—until my gaze fell on four more extra large buckets of popcorn now lined up on the counter.

What the hell?

I turned the register over to Emma and picked up a medium paper bag, stepping close to Alec so the customers wouldn't hear me. "They're not all ordering extra large, Alec. You have to look at the ticket." I handed him a ticket for a medium popcorn and a large Coke, then scooped kernels into the bag. "Didn't they have tickets in the eighties? Or popcorn?"

Alec frowned. "This job is petty and pointless." He dropped into a squat to examine the rows of folded bags and stacked buckets.

"Um, yeah." I filled another bag in a single scoop. "That's why they give it to students." And forty-five-year-old cultural infants.

Alec had been nineteen when he crossed into the Netherworld—the circumstances of which he still wasn't ready to talk about—but hadn't aged a day while he was there.

"What's his problem?" Emma asked, as I handed her the medium bag.

"He's just tired." Em didn't know who he really was, because I didn't want her to find out that he'd once possessed her body in a desperate attempt to orchestrate his own rescue from the Netherworld. She thought he was a friend of the family, crashing on our couch while he saved up enough money for a place of his own and some online college classes.

When I turned back to Alec, I found him leaning with his palms on the counter, staring at the ground between his feet.

"Alec? You okay?" I put one hand on his shoulder, and he jumped, then stared at me like I'd appeared out of nowhere. He shook his head like he was shaking off sleep, then blinked and looked around the lobby in obvious confusion.

"Yeah. Sorry. I didn't get much sleep last night. What were you saying?"

"I said you have to look at the ticket. You can't just serve everyone an extra large."

Alec frowned and picked up the ticket on the counter in front of him. "I know. I've been doing this a week now, Kay. I got this."

I grinned at his colloquialism. He only used them on his good days, when he felt like he was fitting into the human world again. And honestly, in spite of his fleeting moments of confusion, some days, Alec seemed to fit into my world much better than I did.

THE HALLWAY IS COLD and sterile, and that should be my first clue. School is always cluttered and too warm, but today, cold and sterile makes sense.

I walk down the hall with Emma, but I stop when I see them. She doesn't stop. She doesn't notice anything wrong, but when I see them, I can't breathe. My chest feels too heavy. My lungs pull in just enough air to keep me conscious, but not enough to truly satisfy my need for oxygen. Like satisfaction is even a possibility with them standing there like that. In front of my locker, so I can't possibly miss the act.

I can't see her face, because it's sucking on his, but I know it's her. It's her hair, and her stupid guy-pants that look hot on her the same way his T-shirts probably look hot on her when that's all she's wearing. And I know she's worn his shirts. Hell, she's worn *him*, and if they weren't in the middle of the school, she'd probably be wearing him now. She practically is, anyway.

I stop in front of them so they can't ignore me, and she peels herself away and licks her lips, like she can't get enough *of the taste of him, and I know that's true. My teeth grind to-gether, and when I glance around, I realize there's a crowd.*

Of course there's a crowd. Crowds gather for a show, and this is one hell of a show.

I say his name. I don't want to say it. I don't want to ac-knowledge him and what he's doing, but I can't stop myself. It won't be real unless he says it, and part of me believes he won't say it. He'll say the right words instead. He'll say he's sorry, and he'll look like he's sorry, and he'll be sorry for a very long time, but then everything will be okay again.

Instead, he shrugs and glances around at the crowd, grin-ning at the faces. The faces leer and blur together. I can't tell them apart, but it doesn't matter, because the crowd only has one face. Crowds only ever have one face. Et tu, Brute? It's the mob mentality, and I am Caesar, about to be stabbed.

Or maybe I've already been stabbed, and I'm too stupid to know I'm bleeding all over the floor. But I know I'm dying inside. He's killing me.

"Sorry, Kay," he says at last, and I hate him for using my nickname. It sounds intimate and friendly, but he just had his tongue in her mouth, and now I want to cut it out of his head. "Sorry," he repeats, while my face flames, and my world blurs with tears. "She knows what I like. And she delivers…"

They're laughing now, and even though the crowd only has one face, it has many jeering voices. And they're all laughing at me. Even Emma.

"I told you," she says, shaking her head as she tries to hold back a giggle, and I love her for trying, even if, in the end, the laughter can't be denied. It's not her fault. She's just play-ing her part, and the lines must be spoken, even if each word burns like an open wound.

"I told you it wasn't worth saving. You can't win the game if you won't even play. You have to deliver…."

< 4 >

I SAT UP IN BED, sweating and cold, my heart beating so hard it practically bruised my sternum. I took a deep breath, threw the covers back, and stepped into my Betty Boop slippers, then padded silently down the hall and into the living room, where Alec lay on the couch with the blanket pulled over his head. His exposed feet were propped on the armrest at the opposite end, brown on top, and pale on the bottom. When I walked past him, his toes twitched, and I nearly jumped out of my skin.

In the kitchen, I got a glass of water, and I was on my way back across the living room when Alec folded the blanket back from his head and blinked up at me.

"Okay, that's starting to get creepy," I said, as he sat up. "What?"

"You. Lying there awake but covered." I sank into my dad's recliner and tucked my feet beneath me. "It's like watching a corpse sit up in the morgue."

"Sorry." He ran one hand absently over his smooth, dark chest. Twenty-six years in the Netherworld may have scarred him on the inside, but his outside still looked good as new. "I can't sleep. Can't get used to the silence."

"What, did Avari sing you to sleep in the Netherworld?"

"Funny." Alec leaned forward with his elbows on his knees, his head sagging on his shoulders. "Once you get used to all the screaming at night, it's hard to go to sleep without it. Not that I actually slept every night."

"Are you serious?" The fresh crop of chill bumps on my arms had nothing to do with my bad dream, and everything to do with his living nightmare.

Alec shrugged and sat up to meet my gaze. "Hellions don't sleep, so I passed out whenever I got a chance. Whenever Avari was busy with someone else."

I started to explain that I was horrified by the screaming, not by his irregular sleep patterns, then decided I didn't want to know any more about either. So I kept my mouth shut.

"What about you?" he asked, as I sipped my water.

"Bad dream." I set the glass over the existing water ring on the end table.

"What about?"

My exhale sounded heavy, even to me. "I dreamed Nash dumped me for his ex-girlfriend, in front of the whole school, after eating her face in front of my locker."

"Literally?" Alec frowned, and I realized that where he'd spent the past quarter century, literal face eating might have been a real concern.

"No. That might actually have been better."

He leaned back on the couch, arms crossed over his bare chest. "I thought you dumped him."

"I did. Kind of." Nash and I were too complicated for simple explanations, and something told me that would only get worse, with his ex suddenly in the picture.

"But now you want him back? Even after what he did?"

Alec knew exactly what Avari had done with my body when he'd possessed me, because he'd been there in the Netherworld with the hellion when it happened. I couldn't blame Nash for what Avari had done, but I couldn't help blaming him for not telling me. And for not even trying to stop it from happening again. And again. And for lying to me about taking Demon's Breath. And for using his Influence against me.

Alec knew all of it—even the parts Emma and my dad didn't know—because I'd needed to talk to someone who knew about things that go bump in the Netherworld, but who wouldn't hate Nash on my behalf before I'd decided how I felt about him myself. Alec had been my only option for a confidant. Fortunately, he'd turned out to be a good one.

"Well, yeah. I never stopped wanting him." Trust was our new stumbling block, and as much as Nash meant to me, I couldn't truly forgive him until I knew I could trust him again. I sighed and ran one finger through the condensation on the outside of my glass. "And I guess I kind of assumed that when we were both ready, we'd get back together. But now, with Sabine back in the picture..." I swallowed a bitter pang of jealousy. "It hurt to see them together."

They shared a history I hadn't even known existed. A connection that predated my presence in Nash's life and made me feel...irrelevant. And it wasn't just sex. She'd known him before Tod died. That was practically a lifetime ago. Was Nash very different then? Would I have liked him?

Would he have let a demon possess Sabine, when they were together? Would he now?

"And the dream..." But I couldn't finish. Being publicly humiliated and rejected like that by someone who claimed to love me—that was a whole new kind of terror, and even the memory of the dream left me cold.

"Tod says they were, like, *obsessed* with each other, and now she's back, and it turns out they never really broke up. She's not just gonna bow out gracefully, is she?"

Alec shrugged. "Honestly, I don't have a lot of experience with human girls—you're the first one I've really talked to in twenty-six years. But I do know a bit about obsession—you might recall Avari's ongoing quest to possess your soul?"

"That does ring a bell..." My hand clenched around my glass, and I gulped from it, trying to drown the pit of lingering terror that had opened up in my stomach.

"Well, whether she's obsessed with him or actually in love with him—or both—she's probably not gonna just walk away," Alec said, when I finally set my glass down. "But really, that's a good thing, in a way."

I gaped at him. "In what universe does Nash's ex wanting him back qualify as a good thing?"

Alec leaned back against the cushions. "Think of it as a second opinion on his value. If he wasn't worth the fight, wouldn't she just let him go? Wouldn't you?"

Hmm... Would I? *Should* I?

"How did you get so wise? You're like a giant Yoda, minus the pointy ears and green skin." I hesitated, eyeing him in curiosity. "They had *Star Wars* in the eighties, right?"

Alec laughed, and his deep brown eyes lit up. "Only the original trilogy. You sure know how to make a guy feel old." Then he frowned. "But I guess that makes sense. It's weird." He met my gaze again. "Physically, I'm still nineteen. But I'm old enough to be your dad."

I shook my head and grinned. "No way. My dad's a hundred and thirty." Though he didn't look a day over forty. "Why? Do you feel forty-five on the inside?"

Alec shook his head, holding my gaze with a serious, heavy sadness. "I feel way older, most of the time. Every day in the Netherworld was like a year, and I was there for something like twenty-six years. Doesn't even seem possible. Then, suddenly I'm out, and I'm here, and everything's different and fast and hard and shiny. I'm old and wise, according to some—" his eyes flashed in brief good humor on my behalf "—and in some ways, I feel ten thousand years old, because after everything I've seen, and everything I had to do to survive, shiny new Blu-ray disks and stereos that fit in your pocket seem so…irrelevant."

Alec shrugged again, looking lost. "But then sometimes I feel like a little kid, because these shiny bits of irrelevance are everyday parts of my life now, and half the time, I don't have a clue what they do."

"Wow." I grinned, trying to lighten the mood. "That was deep."

He returned my grin and raised a challenging eyebrow. "Isn't it past your bedtime?"

"You're sayin' I should listen to my elders?"

His smile died, and he glanced at the hands clasped in his lap, then back up at me. "I'm saying I wish I wasn't your elder." Another sigh. "I wish I hadn't lost twenty-six years of my life, and I wish to hell that it wasn't so hard to take advantage of what I have left."

Unfortunately, everyone he'd known before he left the human world was a quarter century older now, so he couldn't just show up on old friends' doorsteps—assuming he knew where to find them—with a smile and a suitcase. My dad and I were all Alec had at the moment, and we had no intention of cutting him loose.

But deep down, we all three knew that we couldn't replace his real family any more than my aunt and uncle had been able to replace my parents.

"I just wish I could turn back the clock and undo everything that went wrong."

I knew exactly how he felt.

TUESDAY MORNING, THE second day of the spring semester, I was waiting in front of Nash's locker when he arrived, walking down the hall alone for the first time since I could remember. His two best friends were gone, and we'd broken up. He was alone and probably miserable. And I couldn't help wondering how he'd gotten to school, considering he didn't have a car and no longer had anyone to bum a ride from.

Surely he hadn't taken the bus with the freshmen.

"Hey." His voice was casual, and completely Influence free, but his eyes swirled slowly in genuine pleasure. He was happy to see me.

My pulse spiked a little at that knowledge, and I resisted a relieved smile, trying to think of a way to ask him about Sabine without admitting that I wanted to nail her into a crate and ship her to the South Pole. Even though I'd just met her. "Hey. Can we talk?"

"Yeah." Nash opened his locker, then unzipped his backpack. "Actually, I need to tell you something. I wanted to say this yesterday, but then we got interrupted, and…" He set his bag down without taking anything out of it and looked right into my eyes, so I could see the sincerity swirling in his. "Kaylee, I just want you to know that I'm clean. It sucks, and it's hard, especially when I'm home by myself with nothing else to think about. But I'm totally clean. And I'm going to stay that way."

My heart ached. Part of me wanted to hug him and forgive him and take him back right then, because I was afraid that if I didn't, I'd lose my chance. Sabine would move in, and the time-out that was supposed to give Nash a chance to get better and me a chance to deal with what happened would only end up giving her a way into his life.

But I couldn't just forget about everything he'd done. If I took him back before I was sure we were both ready, we could fall apart for real. Forever. Rushing in could ruin everything for both of us.

Of course, so could Sabine.

"I'm glad. That's really good, Nash," I said, hating how lame I sounded. Did Hallmark make a card for former addict ex-boyfriends who were trying to stay clean?

"So…what did you want to talk about?" he asked, as I clung to the strap of my backpack like a life preserver. Why was I so nervous?

"I just…" I closed my eyes and took a deep breath, then made myself look at him. "How worried should I be about Sabine?"

At the mention of her name, Nash's irises exploded into motion, swirling so fast I couldn't interpret what he was feeling. And with sudden, frightening insight, I realized that was because he didn't *know* what he was feeling. Probably several conflicting emotions. But whatever they were, they were strong.

"Worried about her?" His irises went suddenly still, as he slammed the lid shut on his emotions, blocking me out. I couldn't blame him. Who wants to walk around looking like a giant mood ring? But I was desperate for a hint of what he really felt about her. And about me. I needed to know where I stood. "Why would you…"

But before he could finish, she was suddenly there, down the hall, shouting his name like she didn't care who heard. Or who turned to stare.

Sabine was fearless.

"Nash!" She jogged down the hall toward us, bag bouncing on her back, low-cut khakis barely hanging on to her hips. As she came to a stop, she reached into her hip pocket and pulled out a cell phone. Nash's cell phone. "You left this in my car. You know, you should really set it to autolock. Otherwise, all your information's just there for the taking…" Instead of handing him the phone, she stepped close and slid it slowly into his front left pocket, letting her fingers linger until he actually had to pull her hand from his pocket. Right there in the hall.

My face flamed. I could feel my cheeks burning and could see a scarlet half-moon at the bottom edge of my vision.

"Um…thanks," Nash said.

"Anytime," she purred, then finally seemed to notice me standing there. "Hey, Katie, what's up?" Her black eyes stared into mine, and I flashed back to my dream from the night before. Chill bumps popped up beneath my sleeves, and if I didn't know any better, I'd swear the fluorescent light overhead flickered just to cast deep shadows beneath her eyes.

It was everything I could do not to shudder. Something was wrong with her. How could Nash not see it? Looking into Sabine's eyes was like taking a breath with my head stuck inside the freezer.

"It's Kaylee," I said through gritted teeth, forcing the words out when what I really wanted was to excuse myself and walk away. Fast. "And we were talking."

"Oh, good!" She turned back to Nash, grinning like she'd just made a clever joke and I was the punch line, and I was ashamed of how relieved I was to no longer be the focus of her attention. "What are we talking about?"

"It's private," I said, my hand clenching around my backpack strap.

"Oh. Speaking of *private,* I actually slept pretty well last night, for once. I think I just needed to be *really* worn out to make it happen, you know?" She raised one brow at me, and I fought another chill as she turned to Nash. "Good thing your mom works nights now."

I reeled like I'd been punched in the gut. My breath deserted me, and my lungs refused to draw in more air.

"Kaylee…" Nash tried to reach for me, but I pushed him

away and stumbled backward into the lockers. When I could finally breathe, I looked right into his eyes, silently demanding that he let me see the truth.

"You were with her last night?"

"More like early this morning," Sabine said casually, like she couldn't tell I was upset. But she knew exactly what she was doing. I could tell from the way she watched for my reaction, rather than his. She was studying me. Sizing up the competition. And deep inside, I knew I should have been happy about that—that she considered me serious competition.

But closer to the surface, I was thoroughly pissed. Warm flames of rage battled the chill that resurged every time I glanced at her, until I felt half frozen, half roasted, and thoroughly confused.

"We had a lot to catch up on," she added, while Nash's jaw clenched. "That's not a problem, is it? I mean, you guys broke up, right? That's what Nash said…"

"Sabine," he said at last. "I'll see you at lunch. I need to talk to Kaylee before the bell."

She shrugged and smiled like she hadn't just ruined my whole day. Or like she'd meant to. "I gotta head to class, anyway. I'm trying out this punctuality thing. The guidance counselor says it's all the rage." She winked at him—actually winked!—then turned to squint at my cheek, like I'd suddenly grown a wart. "Hold still, Kay…" My pulse spiked at her unwelcome use of my nickname. "You've got an eyelash…."

Sabine reached out and brushed one finger slowly, deliberately across my cheek, but her gaze never left mine. In fact, it strengthened, as if she was trying to see through my eyes into the back of my skull.

I wanted to pull away, but I couldn't. I could only stare back as that instant stretched into eternity, and I stood frozen.

And for a second—just a single moment—her eyes suddenly looked darker, and that horrified, humiliated pain from my dream flashed through my head and throbbed miserably in my heart.

"Sabine..." Nash whispered, in the warning tone he usually saved for Tod.

She blinked, then smiled. "There. Got it." She held her finger up, then let her hand drop too fast for me to see the alleged eyelash. "Later, Kay..." she said, and I stood in shock as she sauntered down the hall without a glance back.

For a moment, Nash and I just looked at each other. I couldn't think past the surreal second that his ex-girlfriend's finger had lingered on my cheek. "What the hell was that?"

Nash sighed. "She's... Kaylee, Sabine's had it pretty rough. She doesn't remember her real parents, and she's been in more than a dozen foster homes, and she's never had many friends, so—"

"Maybe that's because she's a creepy bitch!" I spat, and Nash's eyes widened. He was almost as surprised by my snap judgment as I was. It usually took much longer than that for me to decide I didn't like someone, but Sabine had definitely found a shortcut.

"She's rough around the edges, I know, but that's not her fault."

"Tod told me her sob story," I snapped. "He also said she's a convicted criminal."

He frowned and his eyes narrowed slightly. He was looking for more. "He say anything else?"

"Yeah," I said, and Nash's eyes swirled in panic. "He said she was your first, and you two practically shared the same skin for, like, a year."

"Oh." Nash sagged against his locker, but he looked oddly relieved. "That was years ago, Kaylee. I haven't seen her since the summer before my sophomore year."

"You were with her last night," I reminded him, hating the warble in my voice.

"We were just talking," he insisted. "I swear."

"All night?"

He shrugged. "We had a lot to catch up on."

"Like, her latest felony and your latest conquest? Did you two laugh about me?" My heart throbbed, and suddenly I was sure that's exactly what they'd done. They'd laughed at me all night long. "Am I your little inside joke? 'Poor, frigid Kaylee has to be *possessed* before she'll let anyone touch her.'"

I started to walk away, tears forming in my eyes in spite of my best effort to stop them. But Nash grabbed my arm. "Kaylee, wait." He pulled me back, and I let him because I wanted him to deny it. Desperately.

What the hell was wrong with me? I wanted to be wrong, but I was terrified I was right. So scared of the truth that I could hardly breathe.

Nash looked down into my eyes, like he was looking for something specific in the shades of blue that were probably twisting out of control at the moment. "Damn it, Sabine..." he mumbled. Then, to me, "I'll talk to her. She doesn't mean anything by it. It's just habit."

"What's habit?" I was obviously missing something.

He closed his eyes and exhaled. "Nothing. Never mind." When he looked at me again, his eyes were infuriatingly still. "Look, Sabine and I haven't seen each other in a long time, and we were just getting caught up. Nothing happened, and nothing's going to happen. I know I messed up with you, but I'm trying to make it right, and I'm not going to let anything get in the way of that. Not even Sabine. Okay?"

"I..." I wanted to believe him. But I was so scared that he was lying. And if he was, I'd never know it. "Yeah. I just... I have to get to algebra."

"I'll see you at lunch?" he asked, as I walked away.

"Yeah." But he'd see her, too.

I dropped into my chair in Algebra II and stared at the wall, trying to ignore the whispers around me. No one knew the truth about what had happened to Doug and Scott, but they all knew that Nash and I had been involved. And that we'd broken up. And half of them had probably seen him getting out of Sabine's car.

Emma thought our classmates' theories were hilarious, and probably much worse than what had actually happened. But she was wrong. They couldn't begin to imagine anything as awful as how Doug had died. How Scott was now living.

After wallowing in unpleasant thoughts for a while, I looked at the clock. Class should have started eight minutes ago, but Mr. Wesner hadn't shown up. And neither had Emma. But just as I glanced toward the door, Emma came in from the hall, eyes wide, cheeks flushed.

She dropped into the chair next to mine, and I started talking, eager to share my misery with someone I knew I could trust. "You're not going to believe what just happened," I said, leaning in so no one else would hear.

"You're not going to believe this, either," she interrupted. "Mr. Wesner's dead. The custodian found him this morning, slumped over his desk." She turned and pointed toward the front of the class. "*That* desk."

AT FIRST, I just sat there. Stunned. Staring at Mr. Wesner's desk. And before I could ask for details, a crowd had formed around us, everyone looking at Emma.

"Wesner's dead?"

"He died here?"

"No way," one of the girls from the pom squad—Leah something or other—insisted. "I was here early to sell raffle tickets, and I didn't see anything. No police. No ambulance. No body. It's just a stupid rumor."

Em shook her head and gestured for silence. "It's true. I heard Principal Goody telling Mr. Wells in the office when I went in for a late slip. One of the custodians came in at six this morning to let a repairman into the cafeteria before breakfast, and he found Mr. Wesner. Right there." She pointed at the desk again, and every head pivoted, all voices silenced now, except for Emma's.

"Goody said the custodian called her, and the ambulance was already here by the time she got here at, like, dawn. They took him before any of us got here, but they're still in the office scrambling for a sub."

"Damn," someone said from behind me, and while I watched, the same stunned, vaguely frightened expression seemed to spread from face to face.

"How'd he die?" Brant Williams asked, clutching the back of my chair.

Emma shrugged and glanced at the desk again, and again, all eyes tracked her gaze. "I don't know. A stroke or something, I'm guessing. He was probably here all night."

"Ugh. That is *so* morbid," Chelsea Simms said, yet never paused in the notes she was taking for the school paper. But I couldn't help wondering if they'd actually let her run the story.

"This whole *year* has been morbid," Leah added, eyes round and a little scared, and everyone else nodded.

You have no idea....

Ironically, Mr. Wesner's stroke, or heart attack, or whatever, was the only normal death our school had experienced so far. Yet it was the one that most creeped people out.

Before anyone could ask any more questions, Mr. Wells, the vice principal, came in and officially announced Mr. Wesner's unfortunate, unexpected demise, then said that he'd be watching the class until a substitute could be found.

Wells seemed disinclined to dig through Mr. Wesner's desk for his lesson plan, though, so he gave us a free period. Which meant we were free to spend the period imagining Mr. Wesner slumped over the desk our vice principal obviously didn't want to sit behind.

"Can you believe this?" Em whispered, scooting her desk closer to mine. "Yesterday he was fine, and today he's dead. Right here in his own classroom."

"Weird, huh?" And I couldn't help wondering why Tod hadn't told me someone was scheduled to die at my school, just as a courtesy. If I'd been there when it actually happened, I'd have been compelled to sing—or scream—for his soul.

"And sad. Makes me feel bad about not bothering with homework for most of last semester. Do you think he was grading midterms when he died?"

I frowned when I realized she was serious. "Emma, your test did *not* give him a stroke."

"I think you underestimate my incomprehension of sign, cosign, and tangent," she said, obviously trying to lighten the mood. And failing miserably. Her eyes narrowed as she watched me. "Everyone else is completely weirded out by this. Why isn't this freaking you out, Kaylee?"

I could only shrug. "It is. It's just that…" I lowered my voice and leaned closer to her. "I've seen a lot of death in the past few months, and every bit of it has been weird and *wrong*. After all that, it's actually kind of good to know that Mr. Wesner died at his own time and that his soul isn't being tortured for all of eternity. For once, death worked the way it was supposed to, and honestly, that's kind of a relief." Even if it did happen at school.

"I guess I can understand that," Emma said at last. But I had my doubts. "Okay, enough of this. I'm depressing myself." Emma shook her head, then forced her gaze to meet mine. "So…what were you going to say earlier?"

My news didn't seem quite as catastrophic as it had before I'd found out my algebra teacher died, but the very thought of Nash and Sabine alone at his house still made my blood boil. "Nash spent most of the night with Sabine."

"With her? Like, *with* her, with her?"

I shrugged. "He says they were just talking, but she's on the prowl, I swear. She actually reminded me that Nash and I broke up. Like that gives her some prior claim or something."

"Well, yeah, technically. You're both his exes now, so…"

Em hesitated, obviously wanting to say something I wouldn't want to hear. "Does he seem interested in her again?"

"His mouth says no, but his eyes… His irises churn like the ocean every time I say her name. There's definitely something still there, but I can't tell exactly what it is. It's strong, though. And she was spewing innuendo like some kind of gossip geyser, saying how great it is that Nash's mom works nights. She's making up for more than just lost time. Plus…" I felt like an idiot, saying it out loud, but it was the truth. "She's creepy."

"What do you mean, creepy?"

I scratched at a name carved into the corner of my desk. "I don't know. She gives me chills. I think there's something wrong with her. And Nash knows about it, whatever it is. He told me he'd talk to her. Like, he'd *take care* of her. I think she's seriously unstable."

Em raised both brows at me, and I rolled my eyes. "I know, that sounds hypocritical coming from me." Usually I was hypersensitive to references to mental instability, because I'd spent a week locked up in the mental health ward a year and a half ago. "I don't mean she's crazy. I mean she's…unbalanced. Dangerous. She's a criminal, Em."

Emma shrugged. "Tod says she did her time."

"Yeah. A few months in a halfway house. I'd hardly call that paying for her crimes."

"You don't even know what her crimes are."

"I'm guessing theft. She probably stole someone's boyfriend."

Emma laughed, and I gave in to a grin of my own. "I don't think you have anything to worry about, Kaylee. Whatever they had can't compare to what you and Nash have been through together. I mean, she's human, right? How well can she possibly know him?"

I sat a little straighter. Emma was right. Sabine was a non-issue. I'd faced down two hellions in the past four months, not to mention assorted Netherworld monsters. Compared to all that, what was one stupid ex-girlfriend?

Right?

BY LUNCHTIME, NEWS of Mr. Wesner's death had already been chewed up and regurgitated by the masses so many times that it bore little resemblance to the story Emma originally reported. In any other school, during any other year, a teacher's death would have been a headline all on its own. But we'd already lost four students, and the yearbook's In Memoriam page was getting regular updates. So while some of the snippets of conversation I overheard were flavored with either disbelief or morbid curiosity, most people sounded kind of relieved that life now made a little more sense than it had the day before.

After all, Mr. Wesner was pretty old and overweight enough that he'd wheezed with practically every breath. In a weird way, his death seemed to be giving people a sense of security, as if the world had somehow been shoved back into alignment with the natural order of things, wherein old, unhealthy people died, and young people talked about it over nachos and cafeteria hamburgers.

I paid for my food, then grabbed a Coke from the vending machine and made my way outside, where I found Nash sitting at a table on the far side of the quad. Alone. Again.

I felt bad for him. With the rest of the football team still reeling from their double loss, no one seemed to know what to say to the last surviving musketeer. But Nash's solitude was a definite advantage to me. I headed his way, hoping Emma would be late again and that Sabine would walk off the edge of the earth so he and I could talk.

His eyes lit up when I sat on the bench across from him,

and some of my tension eased. "Hey, did you hear about Mr. Wesner?" he asked. "Don't you have him this year?"

"First period." I twisted the cap off my bottle. "Em's the one who broke the story."

After that, he seemed at a loss for what else to say.

I knew exactly what *I* wanted to say—what I wanted to know—but I questioned the wisdom of actually asking. What's that they say about beating a dead horse?

But after a few sips of my soda and a lot of awkward silence from Nash, my curiosity overwhelmed my common sense. "So…what'd she do?"

"What'd who do?" Nash asked, around a mouthful of burger.

"Sabine. What'd she get arrested for?"

Nash groaned and swallowed his bite. "Kaylee, I don't want to talk about Sabine. Not again. Not now."

"Well, you sure had plenty to say *to* her." And in that moment, I hated Sabine for turning me into a paranoid, desperate shrew. Even more than I already half hated her for coming between me and Nash. But that wouldn't stop me from asking what I needed to know. "How late was she at your house?" I'd never been there past midnight when his mom wasn't home. If she was there after one, I was going to lose it. You don't stay at your ex's house alone with him past one in the morning to *talk*.

Nash exhaled, long and low. "Burglary and vandalism."

It did not escape my notice that he'd answered my first question, rather than the latest one. Not a good sign.

"What'd she steal?" I took the top bun off my hamburger and squirted ketchup onto the naked patty, just to have something to do with my hands.

"Nothing, really." Nash hesitated, poking his limp fries

with a fork. "She took a baseball bat, but she didn't actually leave with it."

"What does that even mean?" I dropped the bun back onto my burger and tried to pin him with my glare. "She took something, but she didn't really take it. What happened? She hit someone with it?" The poor, defenseless girlfriend of some guy she had a crush on, maybe?

"Not a person. A car. Thus, the vandalism charge."

"She beat up someone's car? Why?"

Nash dropped his fork onto his tray, exasperated. "Kaylee, that's really her business. If you want to know any more, you'll have to ask her." He hesitated again, then met my gaze across the table. "Only don't, okay? That's all in her past, and she's seriously trying to make a fresh start here. You wouldn't want some stranger asking questions about your week in mental health, would you?"

Damn.

"Okay, fair enough. So long as she didn't assault some*one*. I mean, if your ex hates me and is dangerous, you'd tell me that, right?"

Nash flinched, and my stomach pitched.

"What? I thought she just beat up a car?"

He set the remaining half of his burger down. "The assault charge came later, when she got picked up for violating probation."

"She hit a cop?" My horror knew no bounds. Why on earth would he have ever gone out with a creepy, violent thief and vandal, much less slept with her?

"No!" He leaned forward and lowered his pitch when the cafeteria door opened behind me and new voices came into the quad. "Kaylee, you're making this into a much bigger deal than it really is. Some asshole from our school in Fort Worth tried to make her do something she didn't want to do. If she'd told me about it, I'd have taken care of him."

The flash of pure fury in Nash's eyes told me how badly he wished he'd had that chance.

"But she's stubborn—like someone *else* I know—and she wanted to handle it herself. So she pounded on his car with his own bat. She got probation for that, but a few months later she missed curfew and was picked up for violating her parole. While she was in the detention center, waiting to see the judge, some idiot picked a fight with her in the cafeteria. Sabine broke her jaw with a lunch tray."

Words utterly deserted me. Concepts were even a bit iffy for a minute there. Then, suddenly, I couldn't speak fast enough.

"She broke someone's jaw with a lunch tray." I leaned forward, whispering fiercely. "She hates me, Nash—I can see it when she looks at me—and in case you haven't noticed, we all share a lunch period. Where there happens to be an abundance of lunch trays."

"She's not..." Nash stopped, closed his eyes, then started over. "She doesn't hate you, Kaylee. She's jealous of you. But she's not gonna hit you. Even if she wanted to, she wouldn't, because she knows that'd piss me off."

"Exactly what part of that is supposed to make me feel better?" Though, honestly, hearing that she was jealous of me did make me feel a *teeny, tiny* bit better.

He shrugged, but still looked pale and miserable. "I'm just answering your questions. What more do you want?"

What did I want? I wanted Nash. The old Nash, who'd loved me and wanted to protect me, and had risked both his life and his soul to help me. But I didn't know—couldn't *believe*—he'd had time to truly get himself back together. I wanted Sabine to transfer back to wherever she'd come from. I wanted to turn back time and make things right again.

"This isn't about what I want," I said at last. *When in doubt, change the subject.* "This is about what *she* wants. She wants you, Nash. You know that, right? Or is there some kind of testosterone-powered mind shield that prevents you from seeing her for what she is?"

Nash frowned and let a moment pass in tense silence before he answered. "I know what she wants, Kaylee. But that doesn't mean she's going to get it."

I should have been relieved. I should have been dancing on the table in joy. But something in his eyes said my celebration would have been premature. "She will if you keep letting her hang out in your room till two in the morning." *Please, please correct me. Say she wasn't there that late.*

But no correction came.

"You're not going to stop hanging out with her, are you?" My voice held a numbing combination of anger and disbelief.

For a moment, he watched me, studying my expression. "Are you asking me to?"

Damn it, why is this conversation so hard? I didn't have any right to tell him who not to hang out with! How pissed would I be if he told me to stop hanging out with Emma or Alec?

The answers were there, and they were clear, but I didn't like them.

"Nash, I just… I can't see any way for this to play out without one of the three of us—or maybe all three of us—getting hurt." And possibly actually injured.

Nash exhaled heavily and stared at the table for several seconds before finally dragging his gaze up to meet mine. "Kaylee, I still love you, and I still want you back. I miss you like you wouldn't believe, and I swear that not seeing you for the past couple of weeks—not even hearing your voice—hurt worse than the nausea and headaches combined. It kills me to sit here knowing I no longer have the right to lean over this table and kiss you. I want to be the first person you call the next time something goes wrong. I want to know that you're eventually going to be able to forgive me. And I'm not gonna do anything to jeopardize that possibility." He took a deep breath and held my gaze. "But Sabine needs me…"

"No…" I shook my head, but he spoke over me, refusing to be interrupted.

"Yes, she does. You may not like it or understand it, but that doesn't mean it's not true. And right now, I need her, too."

"You *need* her?" My nightmare came roaring back like a train about to run me over, and suddenly I wondered if it was more premonition than dream. I summoned anger to disguise the deep ache in my chest. "In what way do you *need* her exactly, and do *not* tell me she scratches the right itch, or I swear I will walk away right now, and this time I won't look back, Nash."

He exhaled again and his features suddenly looked heavy, like he couldn't have formed a smile if he'd wanted to. "I'm not sleeping with her, Kaylee. I swear on my soul."

I would have been relieved by his admission—and the confirmation I saw in his slowly swirling eyes—but I was too confused to process much of anything in that moment. "Then why would you possibly need her?"

Nash closed his eyes and inhaled deeply. Then he met my gaze over our forgotten lunches. "I'm two weeks clean, and every single day feels like starting all over. It never gets any easier, but yesterday truly sucked for me. Seeing you and not being able to touch you—hardly getting to talk to you… That made everything harder. Including willpower. Last night, I was one breath away from paying someone to cross me into the Netherworld."

I opened my mouth to ask who he could possibly have hired as a Netherworld ferry, but he continued before I could.

"Don't ask. There are places you can go. People—kind of—who will do it for the right price."

Fresh chill bumps crawled over my skin, followed by a bitter wash of revulsion. I hated it that he even knew things like that.

"But my point," Nash continued, "is that I was trying to talk myself out of it when she showed up on my porch. And we just talked. I swear that's all that happened, but it was enough. She gave me something to think about, other than how badly I wanted a hit, or an hour alone with you."

"So she's a substitute for me?" Suddenly my throat felt thick and hot. Bruised by the words I made myself swallow. How was I supposed to trust the two of them alone together, knowing that? "That's not fair, Nash. I can't…"

"I know. You're not ready to be alone with me, and I understand that. I deserve it. But I need *someone,* Kaylee. I need a friend. And in case you haven't noticed, no one else is exactly beating down the door to talk to me right now." His wide-armed gesture took in the entire table, still empty except for us.

"They just don't know what to say," I insisted. "People never know what to say when someone close to you dies, and it's even worse this time, thanks to the rumors about Scott." Half the student body thought he and I were cheating on Nash and my cousin, Sophie, and that we'd been caught the day of Scott's infamous breakdown.

"I know, but that doesn't change anything. I've been alone and sick from withdrawal for two weeks, and when I get back to school, people just stare at me and whisper."

"I get it." How could I not? But I had Emma and Alec to help distract me from Nash's absence. And even Tod had been coming around more lately… "What about Tod?" I asked, as the thought occurred to me. "Why can't you just hang out with your brother?"

"Because he won't talk to me. I haven't even seen him since that night. After the Winter Carnival." When he'd punched Nash for letting Avari possess me over and over. "Since he can't do anything else for Addy, he's decided that he's your white knight, and I don't think he's going to forgive me until you do."

Wow. "I had no idea."

Nash leaned forward and crossed his arms over the table, staring directly into my eyes. "I'm not making a play for your sympathy. I know I got myself into this. But I need some-one to talk to—someone to just hang out with—and I know you're not ready to play that role for me yet. But Sabine is. And she needs me for the same reason. She's new here, and she doesn't know anyone else, and she's trying to pull herself together. Just like I am."

I held his gaze, my next question stalled on my tongue, where I wanted it to wither and die. But I had to know. "Did you love her, Nash?"

His pause was barely noticeable. But I noticed. "Yeah. We were only fifteen, but yeah, I loved her." He blinked, then met my gaze again, letting me see the truth swirling in his. "But that was years ago. She's just a friend now, Kaylee."

My leg bounced under the table, uncontrollably. "Have you told her that?"

"Yeah. And eventually, it'll actually sink in. Look, I know she makes you uncomfortable, and I'm sorry about that. And if it's going to mean losing my second chance with you, I'll tell her to go away. But I'm asking you not to make me do that."

I bristled. "I can't make you do anything, Nash." Though the same could not be said for him and his Influence.

He frowned. "You know what I mean."

"You want my blessing to strike up a friendship with your

ex-girlfriend. The first girl you ever slept with, who's still in love with you and doesn't even deny it. Does that sum it up?"

Another long exhale. "Yeah. I think that covers it."

If I said yes, I'd be giving him permission to spend time with his hot, willing ex. If I said no, I'd be denying him what he needs to work through his addiction.

How did I even get into this mess?

He'd left me no real choice, unless I was ready to let him go. Or willing to pretend that the past six weeks of my life had never happened. And I couldn't do that, even if I wanted to. Not yet.

"Fine. Hang out with Sabine. But if this thing goes beyond friendship and support—"

I'll what? Leave him to find solace in her arms? Or her bed? That's exactly what she wanted, and in spite of Nash's good intentions, it wouldn't take him long to get over me, considering the kind of comfort she'd offer. I had no doubt of that.

"It won't," Nash insisted, saving me from grasping for a viable threat, and I hated the sudden surge of relief in his eyes. How could he not see what she was really like?

"Whatever. But don't expect me to spend time with the two of you." Though maybe Tod would, if I asked him. He couldn't watch them every second, but surely he'd see enough to report back on the true nature of their relationship....

Great, now I'm spying on Nash. I should have been ashamed. Instead, I was just...scared. Scared of losing him—even though I'd pushed him away—because now she was there to catch him.

"Just...be careful, okay? You may be looking for some kind of Netherworldly AA sponsor, but she's looking for trouble. I saw it in her eyes."

Nash's brows shot up, and a smile tugged at one side of his mouth. "That's not what you saw in her eyes. There's something else we need to talk about, but I don't want to do it here."

However, before he could elaborate, footsteps sounded at my back. A second later, Sabine appeared on my right, then settled onto the bench next to Nash. Her silverware clattered as she dropped her tray on the table.

"I don't know how you guys can eat this shit. It's an open campus, right? Let's go get some real burgers."

"It *is* an open campus," Nash said, both brows raised. "I almost forgot." The prohibition against off-campus lunch—the result of a wreck in the parking lot the second week of school—had expired with the fall semester.

"There's only twenty minutes left in lunch." It was all I could do to speak to her civilly. Every time I looked at her, I saw her making out with Nash in front of my locker, and that bitter, acrid fear from my dream sloshed around in my stomach, rotting the remains of my breakfast.

"Yeah, but you have study hall next, right?" Sabine said, ignoring me in favor of Nash. "And a decent burger would totally be worth a tardy in Spanish."

Nash glanced at me for an opinion, but I only shook my head. I couldn't afford another tardy in English. "Maybe tomorrow," he said at last, and Sabine scowled.

"Fine. But I'm not going to eat this crap." She shoved her tray across the table, and one corner of it knocked my open soda over. Coke poured from the bottle and splash-fizzed all over the front of my shirt. I jumped up to avoid getting drenched, and Sabine stood, too.

"Here, take my napkin." She plucked a single, thin cafeteria napkin from her tray and dropped it onto the table, where it was instantly soaked.

I glared at Nash and would have been appeased a bit by

how miserable he looked—if I weren't busy blotting my shirt, while Coke pooled where I'd sat a second earlier.

"I'll get more napkins," he muttered, then jogged toward the cafeteria, leaving me alone with Sabine.

"Sorry about the mess." Sabine stepped calmly around the table and added Nash's napkin to the puddle on my bench seat, apparently oblivious to everyone else in the quad now staring at us. "I just needed a chance to talk to you, girl-to-girl," she said, stepping too close to me so no one else would hear. "I figure it's best to get this out in the open."

"What?" I couldn't think beyond the cold, sticky spots on my shirt.

"It's cute, how he still thinks he loves you. Very chivalrous. Very Nash. But if you're not gonna make your move, don't blame me for making mine." She shrugged, and I saw that dark flash of…something in her eyes again. "Love, war, and all that. Right?"

Was she serious? Was this an open declaration of her intent to take my boyfriend? My kind-of boyfriend? Just like that?

My mouth opened and closed. *Say something!* I couldn't let her have the last word—that first little victory.

"So…which is this?" I asked, frustrated to realize that I sounded shell-shocked. "Love, or war?"

Sabine's smooth forehead wrinkled in surprise. "Both!" She smiled, a glaring ray of sunshine beneath storm-cloud eyes. "When it's good, it's always both. And Nash is so very, very *good*." Her eyes widened in mock regret, like she'd just let some vital secret out of the bag. "Oh, but you wouldn't know, would you?"

My face flushed. "He told you…?" Hadn't he already humiliated me enough?

Sabine shook her head slowly, exaggerating a show of sympathy. "He didn't have to. You may as well have a shiny white *V* stamped on your forehead."

Suddenly I hated her. Truly hated her, in spite of my generally forgiving temperament and everything Nash swore she'd been through.

Unfortunately, my abject hatred saw fit to express itself in utter speechlessness.

"Anyway, I don't have many girlfriends, so when this is all over, if you wanna hang out, I'm totally willing to let bygones be...well, bygones." She watched me expectantly—completely seriously—and I could only stare until Sabine blinked and shrugged again. "Or not. Either way, good luck!"

She reached out with her right hand and shook mine before I recovered the presence of mind to jerk away from her grip. When my skin touched hers, Sabine blinked, and her eyes stayed closed just an instant too long. When they opened and focused on me, her smile swelled, her irises darkened, and my chill bumps returned with a vengeance.

I pulled away from her and almost backed into Emma. "What happened?" Em asked, holding out a handful of napkins.

"I knocked her Coke over," Sabine said, as Nash jogged across the grass toward us. They soaked up the mess while I carried the soggy remains of my lunch to the trash can against the wall, desperate to put some distance between me and my new least favorite person in the whole world. In either world.

At least Avari'd never invaded my school.

"What the hell was that?" I whispered under my breath, as I dumped my empty bottle and my ruined hamburger into the can.

"*That* was Sabine," Tod said from my left, and I jumped, nearly dropping my sticky tray.

"Something's wrong with her," I whispered, when I'd recovered from the surprise. "If she wasn't human, I'd swear that…"

"Human?" Tod's brows rose. "She's not human, Kay. Not even close. Nash didn't tell you?"

Crap. He'd tried to tell me something about Sabine. Tried twice, but she'd suddenly shown up to prevent him both times. "What is she?" I said, turning to watch the cleanup effort under way at our table as my heart tried to sink into my stomach.

"She's your worst Nightmare, Kaylee," Tod said, his frown widening. "Literally."

I STOMPED THROUGH the empty hall, each step putting the cafeteria farther behind me. But I couldn't outrun anger and humiliation.

Sabine wasn't human. The one advantage I'd thought I had over her was that Nash and I had bonded through a mutual lack of humanity, which set us apart from everyone else at school. I knew what he really was and what he could do. I knew things about him that he could never tell anyone else.

But evidently, so did she. And Nash hadn't bothered to tell me.

Oh, he'd started to a couple of times, but I couldn't help thinking that if he'd really wanted me to know, he wouldn't have let Sabine's timely interruptions stop him.

Tod had started to tell me everything, but I'd cut him off. I wanted to hear it from Nash, when we had enough time and privacy for me to demand real answers. I needed to yell at him, but I didn't want to do it in front of Sabine. I couldn't let her know that her declaration was getting to me, nor was

I willing to let her see me mad at Nash. She would only take that wedge and drive it deeper.

I turned the corner and stomped past two open classroom doors, ignoring the chair squeaks and whispers from inside as my thoughts raced, my cheeks flaming with anger. The door to the parking lot called to me from the end of the hall. There were only five minutes left in lunch, and then I could escape into my English class, where no one could challenge me, lie to me, or threaten to take my boyfriend.

I had both hands on the door's press bar when Nash shout-whispered my name from behind. "Kaylee, wait!" I froze, then turned slowly. So much for escape.

He jogged to catch up with me and I crossed both arms over my chest, displaying my anger, in case he hadn't picked up on it yet.

"She's not human?" I demanded softly, when he came to a stop inches away. "Is that what you were going to tell me?"

"Along with some specifics, yeah." He shrugged apologetically. "I tried to tell you earlier, but…"

"Sabine got in the way, right? I have a feeling that's about to become routine."

Nash exhaled slowly. "Can we go somewhere and talk? Please? I want to explain everything, but I need to be able to speak to you alone for more than a few minutes at a time." And from the frustrated twist of color in his eyes, I knew he wanted to talk about more than just Sabine's species. We hadn't really spoken—not like we used to—in more than two weeks.

I missed talking to him.

"Please," he repeated. "Skipping one English class won't hurt anything."

Talking to him without Sabine around was *exactly* what I needed. I opened my mouth to say yes—then snapped my jaw closed before I could form a single word, terrified by the sudden, familiar thread of pain and primeval need winding its way up my throat.

No!

"Kaylee?" Nash whispered, while I glanced around the hall frantically. It was empty, but the dark panic inside me continued to swell. Someone nearby was going to die. Soon, based on the strength of the scream clawing its way up my throat.

I clamped one hand over my mouth and aimed a wide-eyed, desperate look at Nash. He knew the signs. His brow furrowed and his irises began to swirl with brown and green eddies of distress. "Who is it? Can you tell?"

I rolled my eyes and gestured with one hand at the empty hall at his back, trying to swallow the raw pain scraping its way toward my mouth as the scream demanded its exit.

Nash whirled around, and when he reached for my free hand, I let him have it. We raced past first one closed classroom door, then another, stopping to peek through the windows, but found nothing unusual. Until we got to the third door. I peered through the glass over Nash's shoulder to see Mrs. Bennigan slumped over at her desk, where she'd obviously fallen asleep during her lunch break. Her back rose and fell with each breath.

"Is it her?" Nash whispered, but I couldn't tell with the closed door separating us. So he pushed it open softly.

Shadows enveloped the sleeping teacher like a cocoon of darkness, where there'd been nothing a second before. Panic crashed over me, cold and unyielding. The scream reverberated in my head with blinding pain. A thin ribbon of sound began to leak from between my sealed lips, then spilled between the fingers covering them.

My hand clenched Nash's. Mrs. Bennigan was going to die. Any minute. And there was nothing we could do without condemning someone else to her fate instead. Because while Nash and I—a male and a female *bean sidhe*—could work together to restore a person's soul, we couldn't save one life without taking another.

"Come on." Nash took off down the hall, and I let him tug me all the way into the parking lot, one hand still clamped over my mouth. The urge to scream faded a little with each step, but even when the school door closed behind us—locking us out—the demand was still there, the unvoiced scream still scratching the back of my throat and reverberating in my teeth.

"Are you okay?" he asked, and I shook my head, clenching my teeth so hard my jaw ached. Of course I wasn't okay. Someone was dying—another teacher—and there was nothing I could do but wait for her soul to be claimed by whichever reaper had come for her, so the screaming fit would pass.

"Can I...? Will you let me help?" He stepped in front of me, blocking my view of the hall through the glass door, but I shook my head again. He couldn't help without using his Influence, and I couldn't let him do that to me again. Even with the best of intentions.

And anyway, I didn't need any help. I'd been handling it on my own just fine.

But when he pulled me close and silently wrapped his arms around me, I let him hold me. He felt so good. So warm and strong, as I battled the dark need trying to fight its way free from my body. So long as he didn't talk, holding me was fine. Holding me was *good*. It reminded me of the way things used to be between us, and that gave me something to think about, other than the fact that Mrs. Bennigan sat alone in her empty classroom, dying. And no one else had any idea.

The bell rang while Nash still held me, and for a moment, the shrill sound of it battled the ruthless screech still ringing inside my head. He pulled me to one side, out of sight from the hall, and I twisted in his grip to peek through the door.

The hall filled quickly, but I saw no faces. I couldn't tear my focus from that open doorway, waiting for someone to go inside and find her. And finally, as the excruciating pain began to fade in my throat and my jaw began to loosen, someone did. A freshman girl I knew only by sight stepped into the classroom.

I opened my mouth and inhaled. Nash's grip on me tightened from behind, offering wordless comfort. And maybe taking a little for himself.

And only seconds after she'd entered the room, the girl raced back into the hall. Her shout was muted by the glass between us and was only a fraction of the shrill sound I could have produced, but the crowd in the hallway froze. The dull static of gossip went silent. Everyone turned to look.

Nash pulled me away from the door as the first teacher came running, and I slid down the brick wall, my jacket catching on the rough edges. For the first time, I noticed the cold, and that my nose was running. "Are you okay?" he asked again, dropping to the ground in front of me, and that time I could answer.

"No. And neither is Mrs. Bennigan."

"What are the chances that this is a coincidence?" he asked, and I sucked in a deep breath, as if I'd actually emptied my lungs on the unvoiced scream.

"I don't believe in coincidence." Not anymore. "And even if I did, this is too much. Two teachers in one day? Something's wrong." I looked up to find a steady, tense swirl of green snaking through his irises. "Any idea what?"

He shook his head. "And I'm not sure I want to know. We've had enough to deal with this year, and I'm not..." His voiced faded into pained silence and he blinked, then started over. "Besides, this has nothing to do with us. Something's obviously going on, but it could be bad bean dip in the teachers' lounge, for all we know. Or some weird virus Wesner passed to Bennigan. Don't they sing in the same church choir, or something?"

I nodded slowly, trying to convince myself. Just because we'd lost four classmates to Netherworld interference didn't mean Mr. Wesner's and Mrs. Bennigan's deaths involved any extrahuman elements, right? Surely I was just letting my own fears and past experiences color my perception.

Please, please let me be overreacting....

But what if I wasn't?

"We better go in," Nash said, shoving himself to his feet.

"Yeah." Still half-stunned, we started around the building toward the cafeteria doors, which were kept unlocked during all lunch periods. And it wasn't until nearly an hour later, as I sat in my English class, that I remembered what Nash and I had been discussing when my *bean sidhe* heritage got in the way.

Sabine's species.

We'd been interrupted again.

AFTER SCHOOL, I STOOD in the parking lot next to my car with my keys in my hand, dialing up my courage as I waited for Nash to come out of the building. Most of my afternoon teachers had been reeling from the death of two colleagues in one day, and they'd made no attempt to actually involve students in their lesson plans. Which gave me plenty of time to avoid thinking about Mrs. Bennigan by planning my first move in Sabine's sadistic little game of love and war.

She'd laid down the challenge, and I could either rise to it or slink home alone and call Nash later for the scoop on his ex's inhuman specifics. And after the day I'd had, I just didn't feel like slinking anywhere.

I knew I'd made the right decision when they came through the double glass doors together. Sabine was laughing and Nash was watching her, and even from across the lot, I recognized the light in his expression.

That was the way he used to look at me.

I got into my car—newly made over by the local body shop, after Doug Fuller had totaled it a week before his death—and dropped my books onto the rear floorboard. Then I cranked the engine and took off across the lot as fast as I dared, one eye on potential pedestrian casualties, the other on Nash and Sabine, as he said something I couldn't hear. Something that made her laugh harder and made him watch her even more closely.

My car squealed to a stop in front of them as they hit the end of the sidewalk, two feet away. Nash looked surprised, but Sabine actually jumped back, and a tiny granule of bitter satisfaction formed in the pit of my stomach, like a grain of sand in an oyster. If I nourished it properly, would it grow into a pearl?

I didn't have automatic windows, so I had to shift into Park and lean across the passenger seat to shove the door open. The awkward movement dulled the sharp edge of my dramatic gesture, but I made up for that when Nash leaned down to see me beneath the roof of the car.

"Get in," I said, and he raised one brow.

"He came with me," Sabine said, before he could make up his mind.

"And I'm taking him home. Get in the car, Nash. We need to talk."

Sabine looked impressed in spite of herself, until he glanced from her to me, back to her. "What did I miss?"

"This is about what *I* missed," I said, shifting into Drive while the engine idled. "Get in the car."

Nash turned back to Sabine. "What did you do?" His voice held a single blended note of caution and curiosity, which made the hair stand up on the back of my neck. He wasn't even surprised to know she'd done something.

She grinned, one hand propped on a half-exposed hip that evidently felt no cold. "You don't really want the answer to that. Not yet."

"What do I really want?" Nash asked, humoring her, whereas I wanted to roll my car over her foot.

"You want to know why Kaylee's suddenly grown a pair."

He frowned. "Enlighten me."

She twisted one mismatched earring and shrugged. "I laid the cards out on the table. It's only fair that she knows the stakes, right?"

Except she'd left one of those cards out of her disclosure. They both had.

"Damn it, Bina."

"What?" She rolled her eyes, like *I* was the one being unreasonable. "I told her the truth. You can't get mad over the truth."

Oh, yes, we could. The truths between me and Nash hurt as badly as the lies.

Nash dropped his bag on my passenger's side floorboard and turned back to Sabine. "I'll see you later."

Sabine—Bina? Really?—scowled, then leaned in with one hand on the roof of my car, wearing an ironic, almost respectful smile. "Well played, Kaylee."

Nash got in and closed the door, and I drove off, leaving her standing there alone.

"I'm not playing her game, no matter what it looks like," I said, as I turned left out of the parking lot.

"Good. The only way to win is by refusing to play. Trust me." But he was smiling as he said it, like she was a toddler whose antics were still cute and harmless.

I did not find Sabine cute. Or harmless.

"Advice from your days in Fort Worth?"

Nash ran one hand through his thick brown hair, leaving it tussled in all the right places. "Based on observation, not experience. She doesn't play games with me. She doesn't need to."

"She's been back in your life for one day, and you sound like she was never gone." I braked at a red light, and unease crawled up my spine. How deep must their connection have been, if they could pick up right where they'd left off more than two years before?

He exhaled heavily. "How am I supposed to answer that?"

"It wasn't a question."

Nash twisted in his seat to face me, and his expression made my stomach churn. "We got caught up last night. And I'm sure once she gets used to the fact that I want you in my life, she'll—"

"No, she won't." I'd just met her, and I understood that much. My hand tightened on the wheel and I took a right at the next light. "She threw down the gauntlet, Nash. Like I'm gonna fight her for you."

"I know. I'm sorry, Kay. But it's not a physical fight she wants."

"What do *you* want?" I demanded, taking the next curve a little too fast. "You want us to fight over you? You get off on this—two girls, no waiting?"

He sighed and stared out his window. "Days like this I wish I had a car."

I rolled my eyes, though he wasn't watching. "Days like this I wish you'd tell me the whole truth for once, instead of leaving little bits of it lying around for me to follow like a trail of bread crumbs."

A moment passed in silence, except for the growl of my engine. Then he exhaled slowly and turned to look at me. "I'm guessing Tod told you?"

"He shouldn't have had to."

"I know. I tried to tell you, but Sabine…"

My pulse spiked in irritation. "You're going to be saying that a lot now, are you? 'But Sabine…'?"

"Do you want to talk, or are you just going to throw barbs at me?"

I exhaled deeply as I turned the car into his driveway. "I haven't decided. How's my aim?"

"Dead-on." He pushed his door open and hauled his backpack out of the car, and I slammed my own door, then followed him into the house. I hadn't been there in two weeks, but nothing had changed, except that someone had taken down the holiday decorations.

"You want something to eat? Mom made blondies." Nash dropped his backpack on the worn couch, then pushed through the swinging door into the kitchen.

"Just a Coke." I followed him into the kitchen, where Harmony Hudson glanced up from the breakfast table in surprise.

"Kaylee!" She crossed the small kitchen and wrapped her arms around me in a warm hug, her soft blond curls brushing my face. "I'm so glad you're back." Then she pulled away from me, frowning with her hands still on my shoulders. "You are back, aren't you?"

Nash groaned with his head stuck inside the fridge, then emerged with two cans. "*Laissez faire* parenting, Mom. We talked about this." He handed me a soda, and Harmony let me go to scowl at her son.

"That was before I spent two weeks nursing you through withdrawal from a substance more dangerous and addictive than anything the human world has ever even seen. I think that's earned me a little latitude, even if you are old enough to vote."

"Fine." Nash's jaw clenched in irritation, but he'd never

disrespect his mother. That much had not changed. "Kaylee's just here to talk. Let's try not to scare her away."

Harmony gave me a hopeful smile, then handed me a paper plate piled high with blondies and shooed us out of the kitchen.

I followed Nash to his bedroom, where he sat on the bed and leaned back on the headboard, leaving the desk chair for me.

"Was Sabine in here?" I set the plate on his nightstand, glancing around his room as if I'd never seen it.

Nash popped open his can, his posture tense and expectant. He watched me like I was a bomb about to explode. "Does it really matter?"

"Yeah." I set my can on his desk and faced him, fighting through suspicion and fear so I could focus on my anger. "Your ex-girlfriend just told me she has no problem going through me to get to you. So yes, Nash. It matters where you were when you talked to her until after two in the morning." Because that's as far as I'd narrowed it down so far. She was here until after two. When I was sound asleep, and probably already dreaming about them making out in front of my locker.

Nash closed his eyes, then opened them and took a long drink from his soda. Then he met my gaze. "Yeah. We were in here."

My chest ached. I don't know why finding out where they'd been made it worse—I knew they'd only talked. But knowing they'd been in his room made it more personal. Made it sting more.

"On the bed?" I asked, when I'd recovered my voice, hating how paranoid I sounded.

"Damn it, Kaylee, nothing happened!"

"Right. I heard. But did this 'nothing' happen on the bed?" I couldn't breathe, waiting for his answer. "Was she on your bed, Nash?"

"For the last time, she's just a friend," he said, his voice low, the wet can slipping lower in his grip. "She's the only friend I have right now who knows more about me than my football stats from last season."

I knew more about him than that. I knew a lot more. But I hadn't come to see him even once while he was working his way through withdrawal, because I couldn't deal with it. The wounds were still too fresh. Too raw. When I thought about Nash, I thought about Avari, and the things they'd each let the other do to me, when I wasn't in control of my own body.

In the painful silence, I popped open my Coke, just to have something to do with my hands. "So…what is she?"

Nash looked up, obviously confused. "I thought Tod told you…"

"He just said she's my worst nightmare. Whatever that means." But frankly, any girl openly trying to steal Nash from me would qualify as my nightmare. "So…what is she?" I repeated, hoping I wouldn't have to say it again. "Siren? Harpy?" I raised both brows at him in sudden comprehension. "She's a harpy, isn't she? She acts like a harpy." Not that I'd ever met one.

Nash laughed out loud. "She'd probably get a kick out of that." But I had my doubts. "She's a Nightmare, like Tod said. Only that's kind of an antiquated term. Now, they're called *maras*."

"There's a politically correct term for Nightmares? Would that make me a death portent?" I joked to cover my own confusion and ignorance, and Nash laughed again to oblige me.

"Sure. We could start a movement. 'Rename the *bean sidhe*.' You make picket signs, I'll call the governor. It's gonna be huge."

"Funny." Only it wasn't. "So what exactly is a *mara?*"

Nash leaned forward and met my gaze with a somber one

of his own. "Okay, I'll tell you everything, but you have to promise not to freak out. Remember, it was weird finding out you were a *bean sidhe* at first, too, right?"

Weird didn't begin to describe it. "Nash, I just found out she was on your bed at two o'clock this morning. With you. How much worse could this be?"

He gave me an apprehensive look, but didn't deny that they'd been on his bed together, and another little part of my heart shriveled up and died.

"*Maras* are a rare kind of parasite, and unique in that they aren't native to the Netherworld. At least, according to my mom."

"Did she and your mom get along?"

"Yeah." Nash shrugged. "Sabine didn't know what she was when I met her, and I'd figured out she wasn't human, but that's as far as I'd gotten. But my mom narrowed it down pretty fast. She wanted to help her."

Of course she had. Harmony's heart was too big for her own good. She wanted to help me, too, and I was definitely starting to see a pattern. Nash and his mother shared their hero complex—I should have seen that coming, considering that she was a nurse—and so far, only Tod seemed immune to the family calling to help people.

He killed them instead.

"So she's a parasite? That sounds…gross. If I get in her way, is she going to attach herself to my back and suck me dry like a tick? Or a vampire?"

Nash rolled his eyes. "There are no vampires. And no. *Maras* don't feed physically. They feed psychically. Off of human energy."

Alarms went off in my head. "She eats human energy? Like Avari?"

"No." Nash frowned, like he was mentally organizing his

thoughts, and it was a struggle. "Well, kind of. But she's not a hellion. Hellions thrive on pain and chaos, and they're strong enough to take it from the bleed-through of human energy between worlds. Parasites are nowhere near that strong. They have to feed through a direct connection, of one sort or another. And *maras,* specifically, feed from fear."

I blinked. Then blinked again, grasping for a nugget of comprehension from the words he seemed to be throwing at me at random. "She's a fear eater?" I said at last. "So…as long as I don't show her any fear, she can't feed from me?"

Nash took another long drink from his can, then set it on his nightstand. "Not exactly. There's a reason they used to be called Nightmares."

But before he could continue, movement from across the room caught my eye and I looked up to find Tod scowling at me. "You really think this is smart, after what he did?"

Nash obviously could neither see nor hear his brother, but he'd seen me stare off into space often enough to interpret the silence. "Damn it, Tod."

I sighed, glancing from one brother to the other. "I needed answers."

"I would have given them to you." Tod crossed his arms over his chest and glared at Nash, who stared at nothing, two feet from the space Tod actually occupied.

"He *owes* them to me."

"Show yourself or get out," Nash said, finally tired of being ignored. "Better yet, just get out."

Tod's eyes narrowed and he stepped forward, clearly stepping into sight, just to spite his brother. "Did you tell her about the dreams?"

Nash's frown deepened. "I was about to."

Dreams. Nightmares. Parasite. Sabine kissing Nash in front of my locker. No! But the pieces of the puzzle fit, so far as I could tell, and there was no denying the picture they formed. "She feeds during nightmares? She fed from *me,* during my sleep last night?"

"Probably," Tod said, while Nash asked, "What did you dream?"

I wasn't going to answer, but they were both looking at me, obviously waiting for a response. "I dreamed you and Sabine were making out in front of my locker. And you dumped me for her, because she 'delivers.'"

Nash flinched, while the reaper only shrugged. "Yeah, that sounds like Sabine."

"I'm sorry, Kay." Nash looked miserable. "I'll make sure she stops."

"Yeah. You will." I didn't even have words for how repulsed and scared I was by the fact that she'd been there while I slept, sucking energy from me through my dream. A very personal, horrifying dream.

"Kay, she didn't just feed from your nightmare," Tod explained, lowering his voice, as if that might soften whatever blow was coming. "She *gave* you that nightmare."

Huh? "What does that mean? How do you give someone a nightmare?" Other than scaring the living crap out of them. Which, come to think of it, fit Sabine to a T.

Nash tapped his empty can on the nightstand. "Sabine creates nightmares from a person's existing fear. It's a part of what she is, just like singing for people's souls is a part of who you are."

I felt my eyes go wide, as indignation burned deep inside me. "Yeah, but when I sing, I'm not sucking people dry! I'm trying to save their lives! That's the opposite of parasitic. Sabine and I are polar opposites!"

"Trust me, I know," Nash said. And if that was true, how could he possibly claim to love me, when he'd once loved her?

"Did you tell her how they feed?" Tod crossed the room to sit on the edge of the desk, taking his place at my side like an ally. And I'd never felt more like I needed one.

"Get out, Tod," Nash snapped. "I can handle this myself."

Tod scowled. "I'm not here to help *you*."

"How do they feed?" I demanded, when they both seemed more interested in measuring testosterone levels.

"Are you familiar with astral projection?" Nash asked, and I nodded.

"That's when someone's consciousness leaves the body and can go somewhere else, fully awake. Right?"

"Basically. What Sabine does is similar to that, except when her consciousness goes walking—she calls it Sleepwalking— she crafts people's fears into nightmares while they sleep. She says it's like weaving, only without physical thread." He shrugged. "Then she feeds from the fear laced into the dreams she's woven."

"By sitting on her victim's chest," Tod added, looking simultaneously satisfied and disgusted with his contribution to the explanation.

"Sitting on their…?" On *my* chest. My stomach churned. My horror knew no bounds. "You cannot be serious. While I was sleeping—minding my own business—she came into my room and sat on my chest, weaving some kind of metaphysical quilt out of fears she took right out of my own head?" That sentence sounded so crazy I was half-afraid men in white coats would burst through the door to drag me back to mental health.

"Not all of her. Just the part that was Sleepwalking," Nash insisted miserably.

"Is that supposed to make this any better? How could you not tell me this the minute she showed up at school?" I demanded, and when he had no answer for me, I turned around and stomped out of his room, through the house, and out the front door.

"Kaylee, wait!" he shouted, but I didn't wait. I got in my car and drove straight home, so angry my vision was tinged in red.

Sabine wants a nightmare?

That's exactly what she's gonna get...

7

NASH IS ON THE *floor watching me. He's not in the bed, and I
don't understand why, because he looks sick. His face is pale,
and beads of sweat dot his forehead and his bare chest. He
should be resting.*

*Instead, he's staring at me, and his eyes hold accusation
and pain and shame. His irises swirl with it all, so fast I can't
separate one emotion from the others. They blend together,
writhing violently, until the definitions no longer matter, because they're all aimed at me. Whatever's wrong with him,
it's my fault.*

*My stomach clenches around nothing and suddenly I'm
cold. I cross his bedroom and sink onto my knees in front of
him, in the corner. His eyes are unfocused. Half-closed. I take
his hand, and it's freezing.*

No! This can't be happening. Not again. He quit!

*Then I see it. In the corner, the opening pinched between
his fingers. A single red balloon, half-deflated. I hate that balloon. In that horrible, irrational moment, I hate all balloons.*

"Kaylee…?" he whispers, reaching for my face. His other

hand stays around the balloon, but that's not safe. Not with him like this. If he lets go, he'll pollute the whole room and probably kill us both.

I take the balloon from him, careful not to let the deadly vapor leak out. I twist the end into a knot, gritting my teeth as the unnatural chill seeps into my hands. My knuckles ache with the cold and my fingers are stiff. But the knot holds.

"I'm so sorry...."

Nash is gone. His body is here and his mouth keeps moving, keeps apologizing, but Elvis has left the building. Abandoned it to the toxin I hate. The poison that is rotting his soul, and corrupting him, and killing us.

"I tried," he whispers, and I need to move closer to hear him better. But I can't. I won't. I don't want to breathe what he's exhaling, and I can smell it from here. "I tried," he repeats. "But it was too hard on my own. You didn't come...."

Tears form in my eyes. He's right. I didn't come see him while he was getting clean. I didn't help. I could hardly look at him without remembering, and now he hasn't just fallen off the wagon, he's been run over by it.

And it's all my fault.

I want to get mad. I want to yell at him and scream, demanding to know why he can't just stand and shake it off. He's so strong in every other way. Why can't he do this one thing?

But I can't yell. I can't cling to my anger—not when everything I know is falling apart along with Nash. Anger is great. It's powerful, when you need something to hold you up. Something to steel your spine. But in the dark, when you're alone with the truth, anger can't survive. The only thing that can live in the dark with you is fear.

And I'm swimming in fear. I'm afraid of Nash when he's like this. Afraid of what he'll do or say. Afraid that he won't listen. That he won't stop. And I'm terrified of Demon's Breath. Of the vapor he loves more than he loves me.

Because that's the crux of it. The dark truth. I'm not enough for him. I can't keep him safe from Avari. Safe from himself. He doesn't care enough about me to let me try.

"It's okay," *I whisper back.* "It's gonna be fine." *But I can't say it with any strength, because it's a lie.*

"They're empty," *Nash says, as I sink onto the floor next to him, trying to warm his hand in both of mine. But that's a useless battle. His chill comes from within, and I can't fight it.*

"What's empty?" *I ask, and he's shaking now. Not shivering. More like tremors. His bare feet bump into each other over and over, and his empty hand flops on the floor.*

Convulsions. He took too much. I want to get rid of the balloon, but I can't pop it without polluting the entire room.

"Memories…" *His head rolls against the wall to face me.* "They're empty. Numb."

My heart beats too hard. It's going to rupture. Nash has sold the emotions in his memories to pay for this high, and even if he survives, he can never get those feelings back.

"Which memories?" *I don't really want to know. But I have to ask.*

"You." *His hand tightens around one of mine, but only a little. That's all the strength he has left.* "He only wants memories of you."

My throat closes and I can't breathe. It's all gone. He can never again look back on our history together and feel what he felt about me then. If there's no memory of love, can there still be love?

Finally, I suck in a deep breath, but it tastes bitter. Is this what I'm worth? A single latex balloon full of poison? If someone who loves me could sell me for so little, what value could I possibly have to anyone else?

My next breath comes before I can spit the last one out, and the next comes even faster. I'm hyperventilating. I know it, but I can't stop it.

I drop Nash's hand, and he stares at it blankly. Then he blinks and turns away from me, reaching for the balloon while I gasp and the room starts to go gray.

"It's a relief, really," he says, and I can hear him better now. Somehow he's stronger now, without me. "You're so needy, and clingy, and sealed up tighter than a nun. Too much work for too little payoff."

My tears run over, blurring him and the room and my whole pathetic life. His words burn like acid dripped onto my exposed heart. But he's sitting straighter now, like he draws strength from this. The truth is supposed to set you free, but it's killing me. And it is the truth. I can see that in his eyes, and his eyes don't lie. They can't.

I truly have no worth. And I don't think I can live with that.

"Go ahead and cry." Nash picks at the knot I tied, trying to loosen it. "Your tears are worth more than my memories, anyway. Wonder what I could get for the rest of you? Kaylee Cavanaugh, body and soul. Probably be enough to keep me high for life. Guess you're worth something, after all...."

8

I SAT UP IN BED, sticky with sweat. My pillow was damp from tears, and lingering fear pulsed through me, throbbing with each beat of my heart. I wasn't worth loving, or even remembering. I tried too hard, but gave too little. Nash had wasted his time on me, and selling me to Avari was the only way to recoup his loss.

My worst fears, ripped from my own soul and left bleeding like an open wound.

Then the room came into focus through my tears, and I shook off sleep. With awareness came logic. And anger.

Fury, like I'd never felt.

"Sabine, get the hell out of my room!" I snapped through clenched teeth, remembering not to yell at the last minute, to keep from waking my dad. "Stay out of my head and out of my dreams, and stay away from Nash, or I swear your last semester of high school will make you homesick for prison!"

Unfortunately, I wasn't even sure she was still there. But I had no doubt she *had* been. She'd given me the new nightmare, playing on my own fears. And that was the worst part.

Sabine was a horrible, cruel, emotional parasite, but she couldn't have played architect in my dreams if I hadn't given her the building material. The fears were real. Deep down, I was terrified that Nash wouldn't stay clean. That he didn't love me enough to even try. Because I wasn't worth loving. Why else would my father have left me with his brother and let me be hospitalized?

My resolve wavered again, and I clutched at it like a life preserver, refusing to give in. Refusing to wallow in my own fear, which was no doubt what Sabine wanted.

I threw back the covers and grabbed my cell from the nightstand, pacing back and forth on my rug while the phone rang. My alarm clock read 2:09.

"Kaylee?" Nash sounded groggy. "What's wrong?"

"Is she there?" I demanded, stomping all the way to my closet, then turning to stomp the length of my bed.

"Is who here?" As if he didn't know!

"Sabine. Is she there with you? Tell me the truth."

His bedsprings creaked. "You woke me up in the middle of the night to ask if Sabine's with me?"

"It's not like that's a stretch, considering how late she was there last night."

Nash groaned and I heard him roll over. "I sent her home hours ago. Before midnight," he added. "Why?"

"Because she just gave me another nightmare, Nash. She was feeding from me in my sleep, like a great big flea!" Which made me feel a bit like a dog and gave me a huge case of the creeps. "I don't want her in my head, or in my dreams, or in my room." Or in my life, or in his. "If you don't do something about her, I will."

I had no idea what I would do, but I'd come up with something. Fortunately, Nash didn't press for details.

"I will. I'll take care of it, Kaylee. I swear."

"What on earth did you guys talk about? 'Cause it obviously wasn't the fact that *she is not allowed to stalk my dreams!*"

"Kay, I'm sorry. It won't happen again."

"It better not." Sabine had invaded my most private thoughts. "It's almost as bad as having you in my head."

Nash's sigh sounded like it had completely deflated him. "I don't…" He stopped and started over. "I said I was sorry about that. *So* sorry. I wasn't thinking straight." Because he'd been high when he'd tried to Influence me into his bed. "It'll never happen again. Can we please just move on from that? Please?"

"*You* can, obviously. Forgive me if I'm having a little more trouble with that. Especially with your new girlfriend playing dreamweaver in my sleep!"

"She's not my girlfriend, Kaylee."

I sank onto my bed, clenching one fist around a handful of my comforter. "Well, she's not much of a friend to you, either, if this is how she treats your…people you care about."

He sighed again. "You have her at a disadvantage. She thinks she has to use her entire arsenal just to even the odds."

"I have *her* at a disadvantage? Tod says the two of you were attached at the hip. Or was it the crotch?" Yes, I was being petty and unreasonable. That may have had something to do with the fact that I wasn't getting any sleep, and I'd just had my psychic energy drained by my ex-boyfriend's leech of an ex-girlfriend.

Nash's bedsprings creaked again, and the soft click told me he'd just turned on his bedside lamp. "Are you mad at me because I slept with someone else two and a half years ago? Before I even met you?"

"Yes!" I stood again and rubbed my forehead, well aware that my lack of logic wasn't helping my case. But I couldn't help how I felt, and he wasn't doing much to alleviate my worries. "And don't say that's not fair, because 'fair' isn't even in the equation anymore. What you let happen to me wasn't fair, either. And I'm sure Scott would agree."

For a moment, I heard only silence over the line. I'd gone too far. I knew it, but I couldn't help it. I'd never been so mad in my life, and now that the dam had ruptured, I couldn't repair the damage. The overflow of anger wasn't just about Sabine and this nightmare. It was about everything beyond my control that had happened in the past couple of months. Everything I'd never vented about before, but suddenly *had* to address, or I'd explode.

"Are you trying to hurt me? It's okay if you are. I know I deserve it. I just want to be clear on the point of this whole conversation, so I'll know when we've accomplished whatever it is you need."

I had to think about that for a second. "No. I'm not trying to hurt you. I'm trying to heal me."

"Is it working?" He sounded so logical. So frustratingly reasonable, when I wanted to scream and shout and throw things until I felt better, logic be damned.

"I don't know," I had to admit at last, sinking into my desk chair.

More silence. Then, "What was the nightmare about?"

"It doesn't matter," I said, too quickly. I didn't want him to know how scared I was that he'd fall off the wagon. That he'd go back to selling his memories of me and trying to Influence me into things I wasn't ready for. That he might let Avari take over my body again, if that's what it took to get his next high.

Listing my fear—the facts—like that, the logical part of me couldn't even believe I was thinking about forgiving him. The smart thing would be to let Sabine have him. Let the ex-con and the former addict have each other, and wash my hands of the whole mess.

But I couldn't, because of the one truth it didn't hurt for me to think about: the guy who'd done those things to me wasn't the real Nash. *My* Nash was the guy who'd defied my family to save my sanity, and fought hellions alongside me, and put himself in danger just to help protect me.

This other boy—this boy whose addiction was literally the thing of my nightmares—he wasn't even real. It wasn't him doing those things, it was the frost. The Demon's Breath, which had suppressed—maybe even corroded—his soul. Changed who he was with each poisonous breath.

If he'd been human, the damage would have been irreversible. Part of it might be, anyway. But if it wasn't, then Nash was still the first and only guy outside of my family who'd ever loved me. And I couldn't turn my back on him if there was even a possibility of getting that Nash back.

I still wanted that Nash. I still needed to feel his hand in mine. I wanted to see him smile like he had before and know that I was the only thing he craved. I wanted to feel him behind me and know he had my back, whether we faced bitchy cousins or evil, soul-stealing hellions.

"Kay, can I come over?" Nash asked. "Can I please come see you?"

My heart thumped painfully, in spite of my best effort to calm it, and I sat up straight in my chair. "Now?"

"Yeah. I need to see you. We can just sit on the couch and talk. I just… I want to see you without the rest of the student body staring at us."

The ache in my chest spread into my throat, which tried to close around the only answer that made sense. "It's the middle of the night, Nash. My dad would kill you. Then he'd kill me." Just because he'd called to check up on Nash while he was sick didn't mean my dad wanted us back together. If he knew I was even thinking about taking Nash back, he'd make me get my head examined.

"Besides," I continued, standing to pace again before he could protest. "Alec's on the couch, so we wouldn't exactly have privacy."

"What?" Nash's voice went dark and angry with just that one syllable, and I realized I hadn't told him Alec was staying with us. I'd hardly spoken to him at all since the Winter Carnival. "He's there with you, while your dad's asleep? When your dad's not even there? And you didn't tell me?"

I rolled my eyes, though he couldn't see them. "Don't start. Sabine was in your room a couple of hours ago, actively trying to get into your pants while your mom was at work. And don't even get me started on the list of things you didn't tell me."

Another moment of silence. Then, "Fair enough. But I can handle Sabine. I know her. You don't know anything about Alec, except that he spent a quarter of a century working for a hellion. Not exactly a stellar recommendation. Has he tried anything?"

"Gross, Nash, he's forty-five years old."

"That won't matter when you're legal and he still looks nineteen."

I sank onto my bed and let my head thump against the headboard. "You're totally overreacting. He thinks I'm a kid."

"That's not going to stop him from looking."

"You don't even know him."

Nash laughed harshly, like I'd just told him rainbow-colored unicorns had flown through my bedroom window. "I know because he's there, and you're there, and he hasn't seen a girl without tentacles or claws in twenty-six years."

"Wow. You make me sound like such a catch."

"I can't win this argument, can I?"

"Nope. I'm going back to sleep now."

"Lock your bedroom door."

I laughed. I couldn't help it. "Good night, Nash. I'll see you tomorrow." I hung up before he could argue and turned off my lamp.

Unfortunately, I couldn't make myself go back to sleep for fear that Sabine would be waiting to attack me again from my own subconscious. Every time I closed my eyes, I saw Nash, huddled in a corner, telling me I wasn't worth staying clean for. So I got up and padded into the kitchen, where I found Alec wide-awake, fully dressed, and halfway through a box of snack cakes.

"You, too?" I asked, trudging past him to take a glass from the cabinet.

"Kaylee?" Alec coughed, nearly choking on his snack in surprise.

"Yeah. I live here, remember?" I ran tap water until it turned cold, then filled my glass.

"Of course. I didn't expect you to be awake. At this hour."

I raised one brow at him over my water glass. "You okay? You sound…tired." And less than perfectly coherent. "And Dad's going to kill you for eating all his cupcakes."

An annoyed expression passed over Alec's strong, dark features, but was gone almost before I'd seen it.

"You wanna hear something interesting?" I asked. "And by interesting, I mean terrifying beyond all reason…"

One dark brow rose as Alec closed the end of the snack box. "You have my attention."

I had his attention? "If you're trying to sound your real age, I think you're finally getting it right."

He frowned, like I'd spoken Greek and he was trying to translate.

"Anyway, remember my nightmare last night? I just had another one, but it turns out that they aren't real dreams. Well, not natural dreams, anyway." I leaned against the counter with the sink at my back. "Nash's ex is giving them to me. On purpose. She's a *mara,* if you can believe it. The living personification of a nightmare. How messed up is that?"

"Nash's former lover is a *mara?*" Alec wasn't even looking at me now. He was staring into space as if that little nugget of information took some time to sink in. I knew exactly how he felt.

"Yeah. She wants him back and has decided I'm in her way. But I have news for that little sleep-terrorist—it's going to take more than a couple of bad dreams to scare me off, so I hope she has something bigger up her sleeve."

But as soon as I'd said it, I wanted to take it back. Challenging Sabine felt a little bit like staring a lion in the mouth, daring it to pounce.

"You okay?" my dad asked, pouring coffee into his travel mug as I walked into the kitchen. He wore his usual jeans and steel-toed work boots, his chin scruffy with dark stubble above the collar of a flannel shirt.

"Just tired." I couldn't go back to sleep after my middle-of-the-night chat with Alec, so I'd stretched out on my bed, silently rehashing my argument with Nash, analyzing every word he'd said ad nauseam. "Can I have some of that?"

My father frowned at the pot of coffee, hesitating. Then he gave up and poured a second mug for me. "If you need coffee at sixteen, I hate to think what mornings will be like when you're my age."

Considering how many times I'd nearly died since the beginning of my junior year, I'd settle for just surviving to his age. But I knew better than to say that out loud.

"Hey, Dad?" I said, pulling a box of cereal from the cabinet overhead.

"Hmm?" He opened his carton of cupcakes—the breakfast of champions—and frowned into it. "Did you eat my snacks?"

"No. Dad, what do you think the chances are of two teachers dying on the same day?"

He looked up from his box, still frowning, but now at me. "I guess that depends on the circumstances. Why?"

"'Cause Mr. Wesner and Mrs. Bennigan both died yesterday. At their desks, at least six hours apart. You didn't see it on the news last night?" The story had been a short, somber community interest piece—a small Dallas suburb mourning the loss of two teachers at once. "There were no signs of foul play, so they're calling it a really weird, tragic coincidence."

"And you don't believe that?" His irises held steady—it took a lot to rattle my father—but unease was clear in the firm line of his jaw.

"I don't know what to think. It probably *is* just a coincidence, but with everything else that's gone down this year…" I couldn't help but wonder. And I could tell my dad was thinking the same thing.

"Well, let's not borrow trouble until we come up short. I can ask around." Meaning he'd talk to Harmony Hudson and my uncle Brendon. "But I want you to stay out of it. Just in case. Got it?"

I nodded and poured milk into my bowl. That's what I was hoping he'd say. And now that I'd been expressly forbidden from investigating the massively coincidental teacher deaths, I should have felt free from the compulsion to do just that. Right? So why was it so hard to get Mrs. Bennigan out of my head? Why did the soft rise and fall of her back haunt my memory?

Alec trudged into the kitchen and I shook off my morbid thoughts and sank into a chair at the table with my cold cereal. He headed straight for the coffeepot.

"You, too?" my dad asked, with one look at the bags under his eyes.

Alec shrugged and scrubbed one hand over his close-cropped curls. "I didn't get much sleep."

My dad's brows furrowed as he glanced from Alec to me, obviously leaping to a very weird conclusion. "Is there something I should know?" he half growled, glaring at Alec as he spooned sugar into his mug, completely oblivious to my father's suspicion and sudden tension.

I could only roll my eyes. "*He's* still adjusting to a human sleep cycle, and *I* had a...bad dream. Two completely separate, unconnected neuroses," I insisted, but my dad looked unconvinced.

He stepped too close to Alec, who looked up in surprise. "I haven't forgotten that you helped get me out of the Netherworld. But if you think that gives you some kind of claim on Kaylee, you're gravely mistaken. You lay one inappropriate finger on my daughter, and you'll learn that Avari isn't the scariest thing you've ever faced."

Alec stumbled backward, away from my father, and winced when his back hit the corner of the counter. "I don't know what you're talking about, Mr. Cavanaugh."

"Dad!" I stood, pushing my chair out of the way with the backs of my legs. "Back off! Why are men so suspicious? Is it hardwired into your brain? Jeez, he's forty-five years old!"

Alec actually frowned at that, and I felt bad about throwing his lost youth in his face.

"Not that you're not hot..." I backtracked. Totally tall, dark, and crush-worthy, if we'd been anywhere near the same age. Especially with the bonus haunted-past mystique.

Alec dared a faint grin, and my father scowled. "I'm not kidding, Kaylee. I know you and Nash just broke up, but that doesn't mean you need to..."

I dropped my spoon into my half-full bowl and grabbed my mug, already stomping out of the kitchen in humiliation. "I am not having this conversation with you." My dad didn't know exactly what had happened between me and Nash, but he knew Nash had been taking frost and he knew—and loved— that I'd taken a step back, at least while Nash recovered.

My father groaned, then called me back before I'd made it to the hall. "Wait, Kaylee. Please." The magic word. I stopped and turned to face him. "You're right. I'm overreacting. There are so many things I can't protect you from that I tend to go overboard in cases where I can actually make a difference. Come finish your breakfast. I'm sorry."

"You're trying to protect her from *me?*" Alec frowned into his cup of coffee.

Instead of answering, my father changed the subject, already on his way to the front door when he glanced back at Alec. "Don't forget the interview at one. Don't be late." My dad was trying to get Alec a job at the factory where he worked. With better pay and more hours than he got at the theater, Alec could afford his own apartment and really start to get his life back together. "And you owe me four chocolate cupcakes."

"Cupcakes? Is that the fee for getting me an interview?" Alec pulled off a very convincing confused look, and I couldn't quite hide my smile. But there was no way my dad would fall for that.

As soon as the front door closed behind my father, Alec turned to me, coffee mug halfway to his mouth. "You faced down a hellion to rescue three people from the Netherworld. Why the hell is he trying to protect you from me?"

I could only shrug. "He's my dad. That's what he does." And lately, that seemed to be the only normal aspect of my entire life.

I PULLED INTO the parking lot fifteen minutes before the first bell, hoping I'd beaten Nash to school. Hoping he'd find some way to school that didn't include Sabine, after what she'd done the night before. But four minutes after I arrived, her car pulled into a space two rows in front of mine, with a very familiar silhouette showing through the passenger's side window.

Maybe he was telling her to stay away from me. Maybe he was threatening her. Normally, I'm not big on physical threats. But normally, I don't have my dreams invaded by psychotic nightmare demons. Or whatever. I was willing to compromise a little on the former to get rid of the latter.

I followed them toward the building, hanging back so they wouldn't see me. When Sabine turned to brush hair from Nash's forehead, laughing at something he'd said, I dropped into a crouch next to a beat-up old Neon with faded blue paint. It certainly didn't *look* like he was telling her to back off, or else.

I wanted to see more tears. Less laughter and fewer you-light-up-my-life smiles. Nash had dumped countless other girls in his two and a half years at Eastlake, so why was he having trouble getting rid of this one? Had he forgotten how?

When Sabine's laughter was swallowed by the clang of the glass doors swinging shut, I stood, fuming, and kicked the front tire of the car I'd been hiding behind. Inside, I stomped straight to Nash's locker, intending to tell them both off before I lost my nerve. But to my unparalleled relief, Nash was alone, stuffing books from his bag into his locker. I leaned against the locker next to his and crossed my arms over my chest, frowning up at him.

"You really told her off, huh? I could tell by how hard she was laughing."

Nash glanced at me, then turned back to his locker. "I made her promise not to feed off you anymore."

"Just me?" I dropped my bag on the ground at my feet. "What about the rest of the school?" Or the rest of Texas, for that matter. "She can't just go around slurping up fear from the general population while they sleep."

Nash closed his locker door, then drew me into the alcove by the first-floor restrooms and water fountain, where we were less likely to be overheard. "Actually, she kind of has to. If she doesn't feed, she'll starve to death."

Stunned, I blinked at him. "You're serious?"

He frowned. "Why else would she do it?"

"I thought—" *hoped*… "—maybe it was recreational. Something she could quit, if she wanted to."

His frown deepened as my point sank in—a little too close to home. "Kaylee, she's not getting high. She's surviving. It's not her fault that food and water aren't enough to keep her alive."

"You seriously expect me to believe she doesn't enjoy it?"

Nash started to answer, then his mouth snapped shut as two freshmen came out of the girls' restroom, talking about some song one of them had just downloaded. When they were gone, he turned to me again, leaning against the painted cinder-block wall.

"I'm not saying she hates it. I'm just saying she has to do it, whether she likes it or not. Besides, what's wrong with liking what you eat? Don't tell me you hate pizza and chips and ice cream…"

He did *not* just compare me to junk food. My temper flared. "I'm not draining someone's life force every time I have a slice of pepperoni."

"She's a predator, Kaylee. She can't help that, and you can't change it. She has to eat something."

"You mean some*one*," I snapped, and Nash nodded, unfazed by my blunt phrasing. "But it doesn't have to be classmates, right? Why can't she eat bad guys? You know, feed from criminals. She could power up and serve society at the same time."

Nash laughed, and I gritted my teeth in irritation. He'd taken me seriously before she'd shown up, hadn't he? "Great idea, Kay. How would you suggest she identify these bad guys?"

"I'm thinking jail would be a good place to start." She'd probably feel right at home there. "Or Fort Worth gang territories. It can't be too hard to find someone worth scaring the crap out of, either way."

Nash's expression went hard. "I'm not going to tell her to drive downtown by herself in the middle of the night, to look for someone who deserves to be eaten in his sleep! She could get killed."

"But what about that whole astral projection thing? If she doesn't have a physical presence, she can't be hurt, right?"

"What do you want her to do, walk her astral self twenty miles and back? She can't *fly,* even when she's Sleepwalking.

Plus, there's a limit to how far her astral form can wander from her actual body, so she'd still be in physical danger."

"Nash, she's a walking Nightmare. She's probably the scariest thing out there, even in the middle of the night."

"That doesn't make her bulletproof!" He ran one hand through his hair and leaned back against the wall, obviously frustrated. "Look, I don't expect you two to braid each other's hair and share lip gloss, but you sound like you're trying to get her killed!"

I crossed my arms over my chest and leaned against the wall next to the water fountain. "I don't want her dead, I swear." *Though I might not object to a light maiming…*

But if she poked one more metaphysical finger into my dreams, I'd probably be singing a different tune.

"Good. Because no matter how tough she talks, she's really not that different from anyone else here." His wide-armed gesture took in the whole school.

"Yeah. Except for that whole creep-into-your-dreams-and-ruin-your-life angle."

Nash studied me, like he was weighing some options I didn't understand. "You know how you got creeped out just from looking at her a couple of times?"

"Like I'm gonna forget."

"She did that on purpose, because she's threatened by you. But she used to have no control over it. Until she learned to quit dripping creepy vibes like a leaky faucet, everyone she ever met had the same reaction to her. Her parents left her on the front steps of some big church in Dallas when she was a toddler. She'd creeped out twelve sets of foster parents before she was fourteen. And she's literally never had a friend, other than me. All because she was born a *mara*."

I blinked, confused. "Wait, why would her parents give her up? Weren't they *maras,* too?"

Nash shook his head, but didn't explain until a throng of girls in matching green—and—white letter jackets crossed between us and into the bathroom.

"It's different for *maras* than it is for us. They are always born to human families. Every seventh daughter of a seventh daughter is a Nightmare, and so is her life, until she figures out what she is and how to feed herself without driving off the rest of humanity. What do you think *your* life would have been like without your family? Or Emma?"

I didn't even want to imagine it. "Fine. I get it. She's had it rough. But that's all in the past. She can control herself now, so if she chooses not to, the consequences are all hers." And those consequences would include whatever happened when she eventually pushed me past my limit.

"I agree," Nash conceded, pulling his bag higher on his shoulder. "But I'm not going to send her to jail or to inner-city Fort Worth to feed. She doesn't deserve to get hurt just because you don't like what she eats." After another moment's hesitation, he exhaled and shrugged, like our argument wasn't worth fighting anymore. "It's not like she's hurting anyone. She'd never take too much."

My inner alarm flared to life inside my head, like a warbling siren. "Too much? What happens if she takes too much?"

"Kaylee, she's not going to…"

"What happens, Nash?" I demanded, stepping closer as the girls jostled their way out of the bathroom and into the hall.

"Not that Sabine's ever done this, but taking too much during a nightmare can leave the sleeper sick, unconscious, or…" He didn't finish. He didn't have to.

"Dead?" Chill bumps popped up on my arms at the memory of the dreams she'd woven for me.

Nash nodded. "But Sabine wouldn't…"

"So you keep saying. But if you're so sure she's not dangerous, how come I don't see you offering up *your* dreams to keep her sated?"

Nash's irises exploded into motion, and his brows rose. "I could do that..." he began. "But I didn't think you'd want Sabine—even her astral form—straddling me in my sleep, literally riding my dreams."

Damn it. My cheeks flamed. But I couldn't help being a little relieved by the fact that he hadn't let that happen.

"Fine. Then let's find her something more appropriate to eat. Okay?"

He shrugged. "At least that'll give us something to do, other than think about what we can't have."

I was confused for a moment, until his meaning sank in. "By 'us,' you mean you and Sabine, not you and me, don't you?" Of course he did. I'd just given them another reason to be together. Maybe I should have just let her snack on my cousin's dance team.

"Kaylee, no matter what she thinks she wants from me, what she *needs* is a friend." Traffic had picked up in the hallway, a sure sign the warning bell would soon ring. "You'll just have to believe me when I say her problems are bigger than a bitchy cousin, an absentee dad, and a species identity crisis."

I blinked and felt my face flame.

"I'm sorry..." Nash said, before I could recover from shock enough to even think about responding. "But the truth is that you've got it pretty good right now. Good grades, good friends, a decent place to live, and a dad who loves you so much he hardly wants to let you out of his sight. Sabine doesn't have any of that, and I don't have..." He swallowed, then met my gaze and continued. "I don't have you, and without you, it feels like what I *do* have doesn't matter."

The sudden sentimentality and the yearning clear in his eyes threw me off and dampened my anger. I didn't know how to respond. "I miss you, too," I said finally, and the swirling in his irises became frantic at my admission.

And suddenly we were talking about us.

"Then what's wrong?" Nash asked, trying to read the answer in my eyes.

"I just... I can't help thinking about how much she must mean to you, for you to go through so much trouble for her."

Nash let his bag slide to the floor and stepped close to me. I could feel the delicious heat from his body and had to look up to see the urgent swirling in his eyes.

"I love you, Kaylee. Nothing's going to change that, including Sabine. But she does mean a lot to me—as a friend I thought I'd lost. Sabine and I have a history we can't just erase, and I'm not going to drop her, like everyone else in her life has done. I don't *want* to drop her, because when she looks at me, she doesn't see an addict or a football player, or any of the other labels people keep trying to stick me with. She sees me. She sees what I was before, and she knows I'm trying, and that's enough for her. I really need someone who's okay with me the way I am right now, Kay, and I know that can't be you. So why can't you let it be her?"

I didn't want to answer. I wanted to be able to give him what he wanted—what he needed—to get through this and get back to the person he'd been when we'd met. But it wasn't that simple.

"Because you'll never see her coming, Nash. You think you know her, but you don't know how far she'll go to get what she wants, because back when you knew her, she didn't have to chase you. She already had you. But now she has to work for what she wants, and she's *really good*." That was obvious, based on the fact that she'd seamlessly sewn herself back into his life and he'd accepted her like she'd never been gone.

"You'll just be sitting there one day, alone with her, talking about someplace you went back in the day, and the next thing you know it, you'll be looking into each other's eyes, and it'll feel just like it used to. She'll kiss you—or maybe you'll kiss her—and it'll feel so good and familiar you won't even remember that you should stop it. So you won't. And then she'll have you, and I'll have lost you, all because I did the right thing, and she was willing to play dirty."

Nash shook his head slowly. "That's not going to happen, Kaylee. I wish you'd let me show you." He leaned into me, watching me so closely he seemed to see right through my eyes and into my soul.

He bent toward me, and my lips parted, my heart and body ready to take him back right then, even while my mind screamed in protest of abandoned logic.

My pulse raced, and his lips touched mine, just the slightest warm contact. Then a familiar voice at my back drenched our rediscovered heat with an auditory bucket of ice water.

"Well, this looks promising!"

I jerked away from Nash and turned to find Emma watching us both, her Cheshire cat grin firmly in place.

"It *was*," Nash mumbled, retrieving his bag from the floor.

"Yeah, well, timing is everything, and Coach Tucker is standing right over there, waiting to bust you for the public display. I just saved you both from detention."

I glanced over her shoulder to see that she was right. The girls' softball coach stood in the doorway across the hall, pink detention pad ready and waiting.

"And..." Em continued, thrusting a thick, worn textbook at me. "I brought you this."

I took my Algebra II book from her, frowning. "Why...?"

She shrugged, looking smug. "I noticed your heart-to-heart, so I stopped by your locker on the way to mine. I had a feeling you wouldn't be done in time to get your books."

Emma and I had known each other's locker combinations since our freshmen year. Just for occasions like this. "And I was right," she added, when the warning bell shrieked from the end of the hall.

In the event of a power outage, her smile could have powered the entire school for a week.

"Thanks, Em."

"You can thank me later by translating our French homework."

"No problem," I said, my heart still beating too hard over the almost-kiss, and the possibility it hinted at. "I better go. See you at lunch?"

Emma and Nash both nodded, and I took off toward first period algebra, while they headed in the opposite direction. Emma got to skip class that morning to meet with the guidance counselor, who wanted to make sure she was still okay, following Doug's death. Thanks to a call from her mom.

But I'd only gone a few feet when Sabine fell into step beside me in a snug polo, ratty jeans, and scuffed-up Converses. On the surface, she was even less Nash's type than I was—at least, Nash as he was known at Eastlake; I didn't know what he'd been like in Fort Worth—but he didn't seem to care. It probably didn't hurt that she was hot no matter what she wore. Sabine's look was overtly gearhead/gamer/troublemaker, but because she owned it, it worked for her.

Despite being new in the middle of her senior year and having no friends to speak of, Sabine had confidence and self-assurance I could only dream about. And that was just one more entry on my ever-growing list of reasons to dislike the *mara*.

"What do you want?" I walked faster, after a quick glance to make sure she wasn't armed. Her dark eyes creeped me out, even more so than before, now that I knew what she really was.

"You've got balls," she said, instead of answering my question, then launched into a high-pitched impersonation of me. "'Sabine, get the hell out of my room! Stay away from Nash, or I'll make you homesick for prison!'" she taunted, while I ground my teeth and stomped even faster through the hall. "That's some funny shit! Especially while you're still sitting in sweat-soaked sheets, heart racing from one hell of a nightmare. Though for the record, I was never in prison. The state detention center, halfway houses, and foster homes, sure. But never prison. What do you think I am, a hardened criminal?"

"Go away."

Sabine laughed. "I don't think you're truly getting into the spirit of this rivalry."

"This is not a rivalry. It's your own sad little delusion," I snapped, turning the corner so sharply my foot almost slipped out from under me.

When I paused to regain my balance, Sabine spun around to stand in front of me, one hand on the wall, effectively blocking my path. She smiled, but her eyes were even darker than usual, the fear they reflected as black as a starless night.

My hand clenched around the strap of my backpack, the other clutching my math book while Sabine leaned in so close her nose almost brushed my cheek. I held my breath, not sure what she was doing. Not sure what *I* should do.

"I'm not into girls, Kaylee," she whispered, her breath warm on my cheek. "But if I were, I think you'd be my type."

My breath froze in my throat, and she laughed, stepping back where I could see her whole face. "I'm starting to see why Nash wanted you. You got a backbone buried in there somewhere." She stepped back again and eyed me from head to toe, like a boxer assessing his opponent. "But if you don't loosen up, you're never gonna uncover enough of it in time."

"He doesn't love you," I said through gritted teeth, determined to maintain eye contact, even though that was about as comfortable as holding a jagged chunk of ice in the palm of my hand.

"I know." Sabine shrugged and crossed her arms over her chest. "But he *wants* me, and that's the first step, and there's nothing you can do about that. Know why?"

I didn't respond, so she answered her own question. "Because you're scared. You're one big ball of fear, wrapped inside a skinny, uptight little body you're not willing to share. But I won't hold back. I'll give him everything, Kaylee." Her gaze burned into mine. "Everything you're afraid to let him have."

My fingers twitched around my book. "Sounds like you already have," I spat, and she grinned, like making me talk was some kind of victory.

"I'm not talking about sex, though that offer's definitely on the table." Her eyes flashed with anticipation, and I hated her just a little more. "I'm talking about my heart, Kaylee. As cheesy as it sounds, I'm willing to give him my heart—everything I am and everything I have—and you're not. You're too scared to trust him, and you can't really love someone you don't trust. So if you care about him at all, you'll let him go, before you screw him up for good."

I forced myself to breathe slowly and evenly, to keep her from seeing how her words affected me. How scared I was—deep down—that she was right.

"You can't scare me away from him." I could see my algebra classroom over her shoulder, the door open, the new sub standing next to it, eyeing the stragglers in the hallway.

Sabine laughed and long dark hair fell over her shoulder. "Yeah, I can. But I don't think I'll have to. I think your conscience is gonna do most of the work for me, because you do care about Nash, and when you're brave enough to be honest with yourself, I think you'll understand that you're not what he needs."

I ground my teeth together, then unclenched my jaw. I didn't want to ask—didn't want to be drawn into her little mind game—but I had to know. "What is it you think he needs?"

Another shrug. "Someone who wants him as he is. Flaws and all. And that's never gonna be you. You're not ready to take him back, but you can't let him go. You're afraid to be with him, and you're afraid to be without him. You're paralyzed with fear, and it's eating you up on the inside and killing whatever you had with Nash."

"You got all that from my dream?"

"I got that from your *eyes*. Well, that, and a little peek into your darkest fears. But it's not like you keep those hidden."

"You don't even know me...."

Sabine laughed again, and I was starting to truly hate the sound. "I know you better than you know yourself. I can see the things you keep buried. The secrets you hide even from your conscious mind. And even if I couldn't, I know your type."

I glared at her, eyes narrowed until I could see nothing else. "I am not a type." Why was I still talking to her? I should have just walked away, but I couldn't help myself. Nash saw something in her. Something he liked. Something he'd once loved—and I wanted to know what that was.

"Oh, you're definitely a type. Self-righteous, like you've never done anything wrong and that gives you the right to point out everyone else's mistakes. You do what it takes to fit in, but not enough to get noticed, because you're afraid of scrutiny and because you think you're above the high school social scene. And frankly, you and I have that last bit in common."

I glanced around, hoping no one was close enough to hear her, and was relieved to find the hall nearly empty.

"You're *obviously* a virgin," Sabine continued, as I stood there, mortified, but unwilling to walk away because some part of me needed to hear this. Needed to hear what she thought of me. What she'd probably been saying about me to Nash. "And you think that makes you pure, but what it really makes you is uptight and scared. You won't admit it, but you think about sex. A lot. But you're not gonna do it, because then you wouldn't be special. You think your virginity is some kind of satin-wrapped, halo-topped gift that, someday, some perfect prince will be honored to receive. But you don't get it, and no one's had the heart to explain it to you yet. Fortunately for you, I'm *full* of heart today. So here's the truth: sex isn't a gift you give Mr. Right in exchange for 'forever' and a white dress. You're selling yourself short and making us all look bad with that kind of naiveté. Sex isn't something you do for *him*. It's something you do for yourself."

I blinked. Then I blinked again, stunned and humiliated. My face was on fire.

How on earth had Sabine's effort to scare me away from Nash become a lecture on sex, and why not to have it? But what was even more disturbing than the surprising turn her lecture had taken was the sincerity obvious on her face.

"Why are you telling me this? I mean, if this little explanation of yours is such valuable information, why waste it on someone you obviously hate?"

Sabine frowned. "I don't hate you. In fact, I kind of like you. I'm just not gonna let you stand between me and Nash."

I felt my brows furrow. "And you seriously think you can just…take him back?"

"Yeah." She nodded, betraying no hint of doubt. "I got this far, didn't I?" When I frowned, confused, she elaborated. "I didn't just *happen* to wind up in your school, Kaylee. Weren't you even a little suspicious of the coincidence?"

Maybe, for just a second... But the truth was that so much weird stuff had happened to me in the past few months that the appearance of an ex-girlfriend had hardly even seemed notable—at first.

"I came here for Nash. It took me a while to find him, and even longer to get myself placed in a foster home in the right district. But I'm here now, and I'm not going anywhere."

I blinked, surprised beyond words. Then impressed, in spite of myself. "You—"

But before I could finish that thought, the front doors of the school burst open behind me, and I whirled around to see two EMTs wheel a stretcher into the hall.

The tardy bell rang, but I barely noticed.

The office door opened and the attendance secretary motioned frantically to the EMTs. "He's in here," she said, her voice so breathy with shock that I could hardly hear her. "We found him a few minutes ago, but I don't think there's anything you can do for him. I think he's been gone for quite a while now."

⟨ 10 ⟩

"Yeah, it's some guy named John Wells," Tod said, sinking onto the bleachers next to me in the gym. No one else could see or hear him, and I was far enough from the other scattered groups of students that no one would be able to hear me, either. And with my earbuds in my ears, hopefully anyone who noticed me would think I was singing along with my iPod or learning to speak German, or something.

"Thanks." I leaned back, and the next bleacher poked into my spine. Tod had just confirmed one aspect of the rumors spreading like brushfire throughout the school.

"Who is he?"

"The vice principal." Found dead in his closed, locked office that morning, according to the rumors. Chelsea Simms had been running copies in the office before first period—the school newspaper's copier was out of toner—when Principal Goody unlocked her V.P.'s door to borrow a file, grumbling about Wells being late for possibly the first time ever. Until she found him, slumped over his desk like he'd fallen asleep, still wearing yesterday's clothes. Only they couldn't wake him up, and he was already cold.

But that's all Chelsea knew, because they'd kicked her out of the office while the secretary dialed 9-1-1.

"You think you can get a look at the list?" I asked, meaning the death list, which told reapers exactly when and to whom reapings were scheduled to occur in any given zone.

"Don't have to." Tod grinned. "I know the guy who works this sector and I already asked. Nothing's scheduled for East-lake High this week."

Nothing? He'd just blown Nash's coincidence theory out of the water. We'd had three deaths in two days, and not one of them was scheduled....

Sometimes I really hate being right.

"Wait, how do you just happen to know the guy who reaps at the high school?" I asked, trying not to be incredibly creeped out that such a position even existed.

"I don't *happen* to know him. I made it my *business* to know him, after what happened with Marg back in September."

Marg was the rogue reaper who'd killed four innocent girls and stolen their souls, which was part of my not-so-gentle introduction to the Netherworld and to the supernatural elements of my own world.

"I don't suppose you have any details about Wells?" I asked, as Tod leaned back next to me, staring across the gym at a bunch of freshmen grumbling their way through calisthenics. Thank goodness I'd already had my required year of P.E.

Tod shrugged. "They took him straight to the morgue, but I got a look at him before they put him on ice."

"Ew." Suddenly I had an image of Mr. Wells, wedged into a giant drink cooler alongside assorted cans of beer and soda, waiting to be consumed at some stupid party.

There hadn't been any parties since Doug Fuller died and

Scott Carter got run down by the crazy train. Most of the student body was still in social shock, struggling to deal with conflicting impulses to truly mourn two of our own, and to replace them. Because without someone at the top of the high school social ladder, the rest of the rungs might collapse, and life as we knew it would fall into chaos.

But waiting for the cream to float to the top of the social milk bucket—a rather organic process—took patience, and while a couple of front-runners had emerged—and some splinter faction might yet turn to Nash, once they'd figured out how to approach the last standing member of the former social power trifecta—no clear victor had been declared.

"It's really more like a big refrigerator with a bunch of meat drawers," Tod said, oblivious to the turn my thoughts had taken.

"Thanks. That's a much better visual."

Tod laughed, and I had to remind myself that death didn't affect him the way it affected…anyone else. Anyone living, anyway. He killed people for a living—as ironic as that sounded—and had outgrown the most common reactions to death: fear, sadness, and respect.

"So…notice anything weird about…the body?"

Tod shook his head, blond curls bouncing. "I got a pretty good look at him while they were filling out paperwork, and I didn't see anything noteworthy. No obvious injuries, no blood or bruises. And his eyes were already closed. He looked like he was sleeping."

Yeah. That's what I was afraid of.

I pulled one leg onto the bleacher with me, bent at the knee, and twisted to face Tod, hoping no one was watching me, because now I'd look like I was talking to myself. "I have to ask you something and I don't want you to freak out. Or say anything to Nash."

Tod's pale brows shot up, showcasing his curiosity while his blue eyes flashed in eagerness. "I'm not exactly known for either of those impulses."

Which was exactly what I was counting on. "What happens when a *mara* takes too much? Like, really gluts herself on someone's dream. Worst-case scenario." I'd already asked Nash, but his answer was biased by an intense need to protect Sabine, and was thus potentially unreliable.

Tod just stared at me for a minute, then slowly shook his head. "I know what you're getting at, but she didn't do this."

"That's not what I asked. Worst-case scenario. Could she kill someone?"

The reaper looked like he didn't want to answer, so I just waited, silently demanding a response. "Yeah, but…"

"And would it look like he'd died in his sleep?"

"Kaylee, I'm telling you, Sabine didn't do this. She and I may not have been best friends, but she's not a murderer."

"She's a thief and a vandal. And an assaulter. Or whatever." Based on her skills with a lunch tray. "It's just a hop, skip, and a jump from there to criminal overindulgence."

"That's not a hop, skip, *or* a jump," Tod insisted. "It's more like a vault over the Grand Canyon."

"Tod, three teachers died in two days. All at their desks, all possibly asleep. The week Sabine moved to town. You seriously think that's a coincidence?"

He shook his head slowly. "There are no coincidences." We'd learned that, if nothing else, during the first half of my insane junior year. "But that doesn't mean she had anything to do with it."

I swallowed a grunt of frustration. Was I the only one who recognized the *mara* as a potential psychopath? Case in point: her obsession with Nash! "Sabine comes here and teachers start dying. It doesn't take a genius to see the pattern."

"What pattern?" Emma dropped onto the bench below mine, staring just to the left of the reaper's head. I hadn't even noticed her climbing the steps. "I assume Tod's around here somewhere. Or else you've progressed to actually arguing with yourself."

"Hey, Em," Tod said, and Emma jumped a little, obviously startled to find him so close when he let her see him. "She thinks Sabine's—"

"Trying to get Nash back," I interrupted, and Tod glanced at me in surprise, then nodded when he understood. Emma didn't know Sabine wasn't human, and I wanted to keep it that way. At least until we knew whether or not she was a murderer.

"Well, yeah. That's been well-established." Em glanced from Tod to me. "Why? What did I miss?"

She was getting harder and harder to hide things from.

Tod crossed his arms over his snug white T-shirt, silently giving me the floor. Fortunately, I was prepared. "She ambushed me in the hall this morning and gave me a lecture on sex."

Tod's brows rose halfway to his hairline. "I hope you took notes...."

I elbowed his surprisingly solid ribs. "She told me that if I really cared about Nash, I'd let him go. Like he's just gonna fall into her arms if I give him up for good."

Tod and Emma both watched me, like they were waiting for me to clue in to the punch line of some horribly inappropriate joke.

"You think he would?" My heart throbbed with each beat, as if it were suddenly too big for my chest.

"He might fall into her, but he's more likely to land on her lap than in her arms," Tod said, pulling no punches, as usual.

"They have a history, and they're still really close, Kay,"

Emma said, watching for my reaction before continuing. "You're probably the only thing keeping them apart, and if you tell him he's never gonna get you back, and he should try to get over you, why *wouldn't* he turn to her?"

I had no answer that wouldn't be a lie, and the truth hurt too much to say out loud. "Doesn't matter, I guess," I said finally, studying the wood grain of the tread beneath my hand. "I'm not giving him up."

"Hey, shouldn't you guys be in class?" Tod asked, obviously trying to change the subject.

"I have a free period." And the only thing stopping me from going off campus for a long lunch was the fact that all of my friends had actual third period classes. Speaking of which…

"Are you supposed to be in art?" I asked Em.

She shrugged and held up the giant novelty paintbrush Mr. Bergman used as a bathroom pass. "I *might* be having a really bad menstrual cycle. Bergman's too squeamish to question it."

"That'll get you out of a whole class?" Tod frowned. "No fair using physiology against the entire male gender."

Em grinned. "Says the only person in the building who could put on a one-man version of *The Haunting*. Right, Casper?"

Tod scowled. "I'm a reaper, not a ghost."

"Whatever. Anyway, girl problems are good for fifteen minutes, max. Five, with a female teacher," she said, standing with the giant paintbrush. "So I gotta get back. See you at lunch?"

I nodded.

"Let's go get Chick-fil-A. I'd kill for some waffle fries," Tod said, as Em took the first two steps.

"You'd kill for a lot less than that," she shot over her shoulder.

"You got cash?" I asked, already warming to the idea of lunch off campus. Without Sabine.

Tod scowled. "No, but I can pay you back." He never had any money, because the reaper gig didn't pay in human currency.

"I'll buy you both lunch, if you bring me something." Emma was on her way up the steps again, already digging into her pocket. But coming back would mean dealing with Sabine at lunch.

Emma handed me a twenty, and I took it hesitantly. Disappoint my best friend with no explanation, or suffer through Sabine's infuriating presence...?

Finally I pocketed the twenty and stood. "What do you want?"

"Nuggets and fries. And a Coke. Thanks, Kay!" With that, she bounded down the steps and out the gym door as Tod and I made our way down the bleachers.

"You know, you could probably make a killing—no pun intended—working at Pizza Hut during your downtime." He worked twelve hours a day at the hospital and had the other twelve free, and he spent most of that time bored, since he didn't need to either eat or sleep. "I mean, you could just blink out of the parking lot and show up wherever the pizza's supposed to go, just like that." I snapped my fingers, then lowered my voice when I realized we were nearing a group of students. "You'd be the fastest delivery guy in history."

Tod huffed. "Like I want to spend my afterlife delivering pizza."

I shrugged. "At least that gig would pay in cash. And probably in pizza."

The reaper looked intrigued for a moment, then shook his head firmly. "Then who'd be around to pop in and drive you nuts when you start getting too serious? I perform an important role in your life, you know."

"Yeah, well, Sabine's starting to give you a run for your money," I whispered, as we headed out of the gym and into the hall.

We passed the closed art and music room doors on the way to the parking lot, but as we approached the library, a sudden shrieking shredded the midday quiet. Tod and I ran into the library to find Chris Metzer, president of the robotics club, standing between a table and the chair he'd obviously been sitting in moments earlier, face scarlet, eyes wide as everyone else in the room stared at him.

"Chris?" The librarian rounded her desk in a series of short, even steps, constricted by her long pencil skirt. "What happened? Are you okay?"

"Fine. Sorry." Chris scooped his books up from the table and I noticed the repeating-line imprint of a spiral-bound notebook on his left cheek. "It was just a stupid dream." Then he hurried past us and into the hall, cheeks still flaming.

I elbowed Tod, and he frowned. "I know, I know."

"Sabine," I whispered, as he followed me into the empty hall. "But when she Sleepwalks, her physical body looks like it's sleeping, right? Where could she go to sleep uninterrupted here at school?" Not the library. Not anymore, anyway…

Tod shrugged. "Storage closet? Locker room?"

I shook my head. During lunch or after school, sure. But those were both actively used during class periods. "Her car," I said, in a sudden stroke of inspiration.

I raced down the main hall and past several open classroom doors, crossing my fingers against any teachers vigilant enough to notice me. Tod followed, his silent footsteps signaling that no one else could see or hear him.

I shoved open the side exit door just in time to see Sabine

get out of her car in the third row. When she noticed me, she smiled and waved, then started around the side of the building toward the quad and the cafeteria. We had to jog to catch up with her, and when we finally did, we were almost to the quad.

"What the hell did you think you were doing?" I demanded, winded, but pleased to realize Tod hadn't deserted me for his waffle fries. Of course, I still had Emma's money.

Sabine shrugged without slowing. "Walking. The most common form of locomotion among American high school students." She glanced at my feet. "Looks like you've mastered the skill."

"I'm talking about Chris Metzer. You can't just Sleepwalk into people's dreams in the middle of the school day."

"I can if they fall asleep at school. Did you know Metzer's afraid of clowns? Like, *seriously* afraid of them. When he was four, he went to his cousin's birthday party and the clown cornered him behind the pool house and—"

"Sabine," Tod said, blessedly interrupting a sentence I desperately didn't want her to complete.

The *mara* blinked in surprise. But she recovered quickly. "Tod! Nash said you were back with us. So…how's the afterlife?"

Tod shrugged, amiable, now that she'd stopped publicly spewing someone else's darkest fears. "Dull, mostly. But there's no commute, and I don't have to exercise to maintain perfection." He spread his arms, inviting us both to inspect the form he was frozen in.

Sabine arched one eyebrow. "Sounds like a win."

Another shrug. "Death has its advantages."

I glared at them both, but neither noticed. How had I gotten stuck between a grim reaper and a walking nightmare?

"So, you get to see people as they die, right?" Sabine peered around me at Tod. "Do they get scared? Do you ever just sit back and think, 'Damn, I love my job!'"

"Yeah, there's usually some fear. I work at the hospital, so most of the ones I take know they're dying, so they have a little time to get worked up about it."

"Tod!" I snapped, more than fed up with their morbid social hour. "She was just *feeding* from someone in the middle of the school day. Can you at least *pretend* that's not okay?"

The reaper gave me a funny little smile—like he was more amused by my reaction than upset over what she'd done—then turned to the *mara,* plastering a frown over the grin I could still see leaking through.

"She's right, Sabine. You're getting careless. Is this about Nash?"

Sabine sat on the edge of the first picnic table in the quad and shrugged, glancing from one of us to the other. "I don't know *what* this is about. I was just minding my own business, having a little snack, when you two decided to team up on me. And not in the good way."

I rolled my eyes. "This is about you trying to kill Chris Metzer in the middle of third period, just hours after you drained Mr. Wells at his own desk. You're not just a murderer, you're a pig. Good thing you can't actually gain weight on psychic energy, or we'd have to roll you out of here like a giant marshmallow."

Sabine watched me calmly for a moment, and I became acutely aware that my cheeks were flaming in anger. Then she turned to Tod, completely unruffled by my accusation. "Is she supposed to be on medication, or something? What the hell is she talking about?"

"I'm talking about Wells." I stepped between her and the reaper, so she couldn't ignore me. "The vice principal? And Mr. Wesner. And Mrs. Bennigan. And now Chris Metzer.

You can't just walk around killing people every time your stomach growls!"

"I'm not sure where you're getting these delusions, but you need to step *away* from the crack pipe, Cavanaugh. I didn't hurt Metzer. He's never gonna miss what little energy I took, and if I'd wanted him dead, he'd be staring at the inside of a body bag right now. And as for those teachers, I've never even read their fears, much less played around in their dreams. Feeding from old-people fears is like eating tofu when you could have sirloin. I mean, why bother with the geriatric crowd, when guys my own age taste so much better?"

"You're lying," I said through gritted teeth, and Sabine only laughed.

"I've done a lot of things I'm not proud of—okay, I'm not really ashamed of them, either—but lying isn't one of them. Why would I give someone else credit for my hard work? For example, when I have my legs wrapped around your boyfriend, I'm not going to give you credit for losing him. I'm gonna give *me* credit for *taking* him."

My vision bled to red and my hand flew. But I didn't truly realize I'd slapped her until her hand swung up to cover her cheek and my palm started tingling like I'd just grabbed a live wire.

Tod gaped at me, obviously more surprised by how I'd reacted than by what she'd said.

Sabine stared at me, and I relished the shock clear in her eyes, even as a deep thrill of primal satisfaction burned hot in my gut.

But then she smiled and her hand fell to her side, revealing the angry red patch on her left cheek. "Atta girl! *Now* we're playin' the game! I wasn't gonna make this physical, but if you insist…" She pulled her fist back, and I flinched. But then Tod was suddenly between us, holding her back.

"Outta my way, reaper," Sabine growled, and even as my heart throbbed in my throat, I noticed that she looked much less creepy when she wasn't smiling. Anger suited her better, like the grin she usually wore was a weird, ironic mask. "She started it."

"You baited her." Tod shoved her back by both shoulders, and I realized he'd had to become completely corporeal to do it.

"If she wants to fight for him, I say let her. I'll play fair— no fear-reading, I swear."

Oh, crap. My pulse raced so fast my vision was starting to go gray. Why the hell had I hit her? Sabine had been to *jail,* and I'd never even thrown a punch.

Yet to my surprise, I realized I didn't regret it. Even though I'd probably get my jaw broken in front of the whole school. Sabine was a slutty, boyfriend-stealing, murdering Nightmare, and someone had to call her on it.

Evidently that someone was me.

"No, Sabine." Tod stepped to the left when she tried to dodge him, and I stood there like an idiot when she raised both brows at me over his shoulder.

"You gonna let living dead boy protect you, or are you gonna put on your big-girl pants and fight for your boyfriend?"

"This isn't about Nash," I insisted, secure from behind the reaper, at least for the moment. Anger, confusion, and fear swirled inside me like a thick, dark storm. "Okay, that last bit was about Nash. But the rest of it is about you leaving a series of dead bodies in your wake, like slime from a slug's trail."

Sabine stopped struggling with Tod and glanced up at him. "She's crazy. You do realize she's completely, mind-bogglingly insane, right?" And from the way she watched me for my reaction, I knew that she knew.

That righteous, burning feeling in my stomach turned ice cold. "Nash told you?"

"He didn't have to. I know what you're afraid of and why," she said, eyes glittering in satisfaction. "But I don't hold it against you." She shrugged. "We've both spent time in state institutions."

I stood there, shaking with rage, but Sabine wasn't done.

"I don't think you understand, Cavanaugh," she said around Tod's shoulder. Then she glanced up at him and gave him a shove. "Move, reaper, I'm not gonna hurt her." Tod stepped reluctantly out of her way, but stuck close to my side, just in case. For which I was profoundly grateful.

Sabine's attention turned back to me, and her eyes were endless black pits of despair. "Nash and I aren't a thing of the past. We're a thing of *forever*. You're a fleeting fascination for him. The only female *bean sidhe* he's ever met, other than his mom. Of course he's going to be curious, but curiosity's all it is. He'll get over that, and he'll get over *you,* and I'll be there waiting."

"It's not just curiosity," I insisted through clenched teeth, my throat thick with the denial. *It couldn't be.*

"You're right—it's part guilt." She crossed her arms over her chest and stood with her feet spread, guy-tough, yet somehow still hotter than I'd ever be. "You've managed to make him feel guilty for what he is, and for an addiction that's all your fault, even though he's killing himself trying to overcome them both. But he shouldn't have to. If you really cared about him, you'd be the one there with him at night, when he's shaking from needing a hit. When he's sick to his stomach, and sweating, and trying to look like he isn't dying inside."

I swallowed, guilt bubbling up inside me, but she wasn't done.

"If you really cared about him, you wouldn't have told him

to stay out of your head. His Influence is part of who and what he is, and you made it clear that he can't be that person when he's with you."

"You don't know what he did…" I started, blinking away tears I refused to let fall. "He didn't tell you that. I *know* he didn't."

"You're so naive it would be cute, if it weren't so pathetic." Sabine shook her head, but her focus never left me. "Nash and I don't have any secrets. He told me. It was this whole big confession for him, and the entire time he's telling me how he lied to you, and pushed you, and let that demon use you, he's looking at me like his fate's in my hands. Like he'll be damned forever if he sees judgment in my eyes. But he won't. He never will, because here's the thing—Nash can tell me anything. He can tell me how guilty he feels for using Influence to try to get into your pants. That's one of his very worst fears, and maybe it should be. He shouldn't have done that to you, because you can't take it. You're too fragile. One push too many, and you'll shatter into a million shards of Kaylee, all sharp and broken, and he'll be left to pick up the pieces.

"But I won't break," she continued. "And guess what else." Her voice dropped into an exaggerated whisper, and she leaned closer as Tod tensed beside me. "This may make me a dirty girl, but I *like* it. Nash's Influence? It's a game of control—a challenge to see who has it, which is a high all on its own for someone like me. Someone who has to be in control of herself for every minute of every single day, to keep from creeping out everyone she ever looks at. After that, letting someone else have control for a few minutes… It's something between a relief and a rush, and it's *fun*. Nash can't hurt me, and I can't hurt him. We can be ourselves around each other, and that's something you and he will never, ever have. Not ever. Because you don't trust him. And you never will. And in his heart, he knows it."

AT 4:23, SOMEONE KNOCKED on my front door. I'd just pulled a bag of popcorn out of the microwave and was about to do some research online, trying to dig up dirt on Sabine. Looking for anything that would make Nash and Tod take my suspicions seriously.

At first, I hesitated to answer the door. What if it was my own personal Nightmare, come to kick my teeth in when Tod wasn't there to stop her? But I shrugged that off. The last thing I needed was something else to be afraid of, and the truth was that in spite of her record, in-your-face violence didn't seem to be Sabine's style. She was much more likely to sneak in at night and make me dream she beat the crap out of me. Then had victory sex with Nash. Or something equally violent and crude.

Still, I peeked through the front window, just in case, and sucked in a surprised breath. *Nash*. I should have guessed from the fact that I hadn't heard a car pull up.

My heart beat a little harder when I opened the door, but I didn't invite him in.

He didn't smile. "Did you really hit Sabine?"

"Yeah." I went back to my homework on the couch and he followed me in, pushing the door shut at his back.

"Why?"

I lifted both brows at him and pulled open the popcorn bag from its corners. Fragrant steam puffed up onto my face. "The more logical question might be why I waited so long."

Nash sighed and sank into my father's chair while I dumped popcorn into a bowl on the coffee table. "She wouldn't tell me why."

I faked shock.. "I thought you two told each other everything? How could she keep a secret from her soul mate?"

Nash frowned, but looked more frustrated than angry. "If you don't tell me, I'll just ask Tod."

"What makes you think he'll talk?"

"He'll tell me if he thinks it'll help you, or piss her off."

"They sounded pretty chummy this afternoon. All dark and morbid together."

Nash shrugged. "He likes you better." He pulled off his jacket and laid it over the arm of the chair. "Please tell me, Kaylee. What the hell happened in third period?"

Tod and I had left for Chick-fil-A before the lunch bell rang, specifically to avoid Nash and Sabine. We'd texted Em to meet us at the restaurant. I was now considering eating out every day, just to avoid another confrontation. With either one of them.

I shook salt over the popcorn, avoiding his gaze. "She told me she was going to sleep with you. Not a huge surprise—I know what she wants—but it was the way she said it. She's so sure I have nothing to offer you, and she has everything you can't resist."

"And you believe her?"

I closed my laptop and finally looked at him. "I don't know

what to believe. You told her things about me. You had no right to talk about me when I wasn't there."

"I wasn't telling her about you. I was telling her about *me*. You just happen to be a big part of my life. And, unfortunately, a big part of everything I've screwed up lately. Kaylee, what I want from her and what I want from you are two completely different things."

"Could you be more vague?" I crunched into the first bite of popcorn, but found it tasteless.

"I want you the same way I've always wanted you."

"The way you used to want her?" He'd love Sabine once— for real—but claimed to have gotten over her. If he was lying, wouldn't he eventually realize he wanted her back? And if he was telling the truth, did that mean he could get over me just as easily as he'd gotten over her?

"Yeah," he said, and I had a moment of panic until I realized he was answering the question I'd actually voiced, not the ones playing over and over in my head. "But now she's just a friend."

"Have you told her that?"

"I tell her all the time."

I pushed the bowl away, my appetite suddenly gone. "She seems to be selectively deaf."

"Well, she's stubborn, and she definitely knows what she wants." He paused, and I looked up to find him watching me. "I wish I could say the same about you."

I closed my eyes, trying to draw my thoughts and a tangle of emotions I couldn't even describe into some kind of coherent stream. I knew what I wanted. But Sabine was right—I was scared to be with Nash while he was still fighting cravings, because if he gave in, even just once, the Netherworld would have him again. And if it had Nash, it would also have a piece of me. But I couldn't tell him to his face that I didn't have absolute faith in his recovery.

So I said nothing, and there was only silence. Painful, tense silence, like a wire wound so tight it would soon snap and lash us both. And finally Nash spoke, staring at the hands he clasped loosely between his wide-spread knees.

"Kaylee, do you even want me back? Because if you don't, and I make her go, I've lost both my girlfriend and my best friend."

"She's your best friend now?" How was that even possible? She'd only been here for three days! That was an insanely short period of time for everything that had changed!

"She's my best friend *again*. In case you haven't noticed, the other candidates have vacated the position," he snapped, and for just a moment, I saw a glimpse of the bitter, brittle pain he'd kept bottled up since Doug's death and Scott's descent into madness, buried beneath his own dark cravings and wavering willpower. "And as you pointed out, Tod's barely speaking to me."

"Well, then, you need to find a better friend." I stood and stomped into the kitchen with my bowl of popcorn. "Someone who won't try to carve me out of your life or feed from your friends' fear."

Nash followed me. "You didn't answer the question."

"You're not asking the right one." I set the bowl next to the sink and turned to face him. "Do I want you back? Yes. Desperately. Even though part of me thinks I shouldn't. But wanting you isn't enough anymore. I need to know that it's not going to happen again. Any of it."

"You don't trust me." He crossed his arms over his chest, the line of his jaw tight.

"And she says I never will, right?" I demanded, and Nash nodded. "Do you even realize what she's doing? She's telling you I'll never be able to trust you, while she's tempting you to betray my trust. She's engineering her own predictions."

"Is she right?"

"I don't know!" I crossed the kitchen to throw away my popcorn bag, determined to keep space between us, because when I got close to him, it was hard to remember what I was thinking, even without his Influence. When he was close, all I wanted to do was hold him and remember how that used to feel. How it could still feel, if I could at least forgive, even if I never truly forgot. "You have to earn trust, and you don't do that by hanging out with your ex-girlfriend until all hours of the night."

Nash leaned against the tiled peninsula, watching me. "I wish you would stop thinking of her as my ex and start thinking of her as my friend."

"I wish she would do the same!" I whirled on him and threw my hands in the air, exasperation practically leaking from my pores. He looked miserable, and I was pretty sure I looked crazy, so I took a deep breath and forced my voice back into the realm of reasonable.

"Okay, look." I took a deep breath, bracing myself for what I had to say next. I didn't want to do it this way—I'd wanted to wait until I had some kind of evidence—but waiting no longer seemed to make sense. "This entire conversation is probably pointless, anyway."

He frowned, hazel eyes narrowed. "Why?"

"I think she killed them, Nash. Mr. Wesner and Mrs. Bennigan, and Mr. Wells. Your 'best friend' is a murderer."

"No." Nash shook his head without hesitation, and I almost felt sorry for him. It must be hard to surface from such a sea of denial and finally breathe the bitter truth.

"What, she didn't tell you that, either? Maybe she's the one who can't be trusted."

He crossed the kitchen toward the breakfast table in one corner and pulled out a chair with his brows raised, asking me to sit with him. I nodded reluctantly and sank onto the seat he'd offered. He took the one on my left. "Kaylee, Sabine didn't kill them. I know it's weird, three teachers dying so close together, and it's definitely suspicious. But she had nothing to do with it. Why would you even think that?"

"Because *maras* suck the life force out of people while they dream." I was frustrated and half-embarrassed by my lack of proof, but thoroughly convinced I was right. "Sabine shows up at Eastlake, and suddenly three teachers are dead. And they all died in their sleep. It's not a huge leap in logic."

"Okay, but it's not a slam dunk, either. Sabine doesn't kill people. Why would she, when she can get plenty of energy from a single nightmare? She doesn't even have to feed every night."

"Well, she has been. She's fed from me two nights in a row, and she gave Chris Metzer a nightmare during third period today. That's what started our whole confrontation."

Nash nodded too many times, like his brain was only a word or two ahead of his mouth. "Okay, yeah, she told me about Metzer."

She had? Why would she admit that?

"But that doesn't mean she killed anybody. She didn't do it, Kaylee. I…" He rubbed his forehead, and I was pretty sure I'd given him a headache. "I wish you knew her like I know her. You'd understand then. She likes people to think she's tough— and maybe she is. But she's not a murderer. She's not even really a fighter. The fights she's been in were all self-defense."

All? How many had there been?

"Nash, my dad knows about the teachers." About Mr. Wesner and Mrs. Bennigan, anyway. "And he's looking into their deaths. Something's obviously wrong—I had to tell him. And I'm gonna have to tell him about Sabine, too."

"Wait." Swirls of color exploded in Nash's irises and he grabbed my hand, squeezing it on the tabletop. "Don't tell him about her. Please, Kaylee. If you think she did it, he will, too, but I swear on my soul that she didn't do this." He looked so desperate, so heartbroken, and my chest ached at the reminder of how much he cared about her. "Just give me a couple of days, and I'll prove it."

"How are you gonna do that?" I pulled my hand gently from his grasp, and he suddenly looked lost, clearly grasping at mental straws.

"Hospital records," he said finally. "I'll make Tod get them for me. That'll prove they all died of natural causes."

"Really?" I lifted one brow and crossed my arms over my chest. "So…what would the autopsy report say about someone who was drained by a *mara?*"

Nash frowned as my point sank in. "Probably heart failure." Which was ultimately the cause of any death. "Fine. But I'll find a way to prove it. Just don't tell him about her yet. If he thinks she's dangerous and that I'm hanging out with her, he'll never let me see you again. Give me a couple of days. Please, Kaylee. I don't want to lose you."

"You don't want to lose *her.*"

He took my hand again, and I let him, against my better judgment. "I don't want to lose either of you."

"What about your mom?" I asked. "My dad will ask my uncle and your mom for help looking into this, and your mom knows Sabine's back, right?"

"Yeah, but she *knows* Sabine—she'd never bring her up as a suspect. But if you do, your dad will believe you."

I thought about it and finally nodded. Why not? When he couldn't find any proof that Sabine hadn't murdered Wells,

Bennigan, and Wesner, he'd have to finally face the truth.
And surely he couldn't possibly still want her once she'd been
outed as a murderer.

Right?

"So, how'd it go?" I asked, as Alec closed and locked the
front door.

"Oh, you know. Popcorn, soda, candy, scalding-hot
butter-flavored oil."

"Not that." I smiled from the couch. It felt good to be talking about something normal. Something other than addict
ex-boyfriends, Nightmare ex-girlfriends, and dead teachers.
"The interview."

"Oh!" Alec's eyes gleamed like onyx, and I was amazed
how different his eyes could look from Sabine's, considering
they were nearly the same color. "I got it! I start third shift
next week. I gave my notice at Cinemark tonight."

"Awesome! Third shift, though? That's gonna suck."

He shrugged on his way into the kitchen. "I'm not sleeping at night, anyway. How much worse can sleeping in the
day be?"

"Yeah, I guess. We'll miss you at the theater, though."

Alec grabbed a Coke from the fridge while I gathered up
my homework, preparing to vacate his makeshift bed. He
looked tired. "You'll get over it. You don't wanna work with
an old man like me, anyway, right?" He grinned, but I couldn't
help wondering how much of that was for show.

"Oh, stop it. You may be forty-five on the inside, but outside you're a very young, very hot nineteen, and you have
nothing but good things to look forward to."

"Especially with the new job," my dad added, and I whirled
to see him standing in the living room doorway, holding a
half-eaten apple.

"Hey, why didn't you tell me he got the job?" My dad had been home for hours and had sat through an entire half a pizza and my recap of the vice principal's death without leaking a word of their good news.

"That's Alec's announcement. And don't call him hot."

I rolled my eyes, but smiled, shoving my folded chemistry homework into the textbook. "I'll leave you two coworkers to celebrate. I'm going to bed."

"So early?" My dad ducked his head to glance at the clock over the stove in the kitchen. It was just past ten-thirty.

"I'm a growing girl. I need my sleep." Actually, I was going to get in bed with my laptop and try again to dig up some dirt on Sabine.

"Common sense looks good on you," my dad declared, as I brushed past him and into the hall.

"Well, apple doesn't look good on you," I said, glancing at the tiny clump of white stuck on his stubble. "Use a napkin." I smiled, then went into my room and closed the door. Twenty minutes later, I was sitting under the covers with my computer on my lap when Tod appeared in the middle of my floor.

"Crap!" I jumped, startled, and nearly dropped the laptop.

"Sorry." Tod reached out to steady it with one hand, then sat on the edge of my bed.

"What are you doing here?" I closed my laptop and set it on the bedside table. "My dad will kill you if…"

He laughed. "The longer I'm dead, the less threat that carries."

"What's going on, Tod?"

He exhaled and reluctantly met my gaze. "I wasn't spying on them. I swear. Not this time, anyway. I went over there looking for my mom. I thought she had tonight off."

"I'm guessing you were wrong?" I was also guessing we

were talking about Nash and his ex, and my stomach twisted at the thought.

"Yeah. My mom was leaving just as Sabine pulled up."

"What does this have to do with me?" I already knew they were hanging out, and hopefully Nash was making good on his promise to make her back off.

"I think you should see this."

"Why?" My heart thumped in my throat, and I had to swallow it to speak. "Are they…?" 'Cause I didn't want to see that. Ever.

"It's not what you think. They're just talking. But I think you need to see them together to understand their relationship. To understand why he won't let her go. Because if you take Nash back, I don't think you'll be getting just him."

"Tod, I don't wanna…"

"Trust me, Kay."

12

THE NIGHT WAS COLD, and I hadn't brought a jacket. I hadn't thought much beyond making the reaper turn around while I changed out of my pajamas. "So, how do we...?"

"Get in without being seen?" Tod finished for me, and I nodded. I'd sworn Alec to secrecy as I snuck out the kitchen door, then had to walk all the way so my dad wouldn't hear me start my car. And finally Tod and I stood in front of Nash's house, staring at it in the dark. "That's the fun part. I hope."

"Huh?" I glanced at the reaper and he gave a little shrug, but the uncertain gesture made me nervous. "What am I missing?"

"I've only done this a couple of times. I don't exactly have anyone to practice on—"

"Practice on?" I interrupted, but he spoke over me.

"—but you only have to remember a couple of things."

"What things?" I frowned up at him and found his grin highlighted by the streetlight across the road. "What are you talking about?"

"I'm going to blink into Nash's room. With you."

"Is that even possible?" And if so, why hadn't he ever told us? We could have saved so much time and gas money!

"Yeah. But I'm not exactly an expert yet. I can only take one person, and I can't go very far."

"Which is why we had to travel the pedestrian route?"

"Yeah." His grin widened. "Also, I don't have enough strength—or maybe not enough experience—to keep you invisible and inaudible at the same time. So…breathe very softly and don't talk."

"Tod! I can't go in there and spy on Nash! He'll hear us, then it'll get messy, and he'll never trust either of us again!"

His brows rose, and the streetlight glittered off his blue eyes. "You're worried about *him* trusting *us?*"

Okay, obviously that would be the kettle shouting at a couple of black pots, but there was enough distrust in our fractured relationship already.

The real problem wasn't the possibility that Nash might discover us, but the fact that I'd let Tod talk me into spying on him in the first place. However, since we were already playing fast and loose with moral constraints, I saw no reason to make things worse by getting caught.

"What do I have to do?"

"Just take my hand and be quiet. And don't let go, or you'll suddenly appear in the middle of his room, and then there will be drama. And I hate drama."

"Noted."

"You ready?"

"No." I shook my head for emphasis, shivering from the cold. "But let's go before my teeth start chattering." There was no way I could keep them from hearing that.

He took my hand, and for a moment I could only watch him, getting used to the unfamiliar feel of his warm, dry palm against mine. His fingers wrapped around mine loosely, then squeezed, and I thought I saw the slightest swirling of color in his eyes.

My pulse leaped and I blinked, breaking eye contact, then blinked again, confused by what I'd almost seen.

Tod stared at me for just a second longer, then shook his head, and his ironic grin was back. "Okay, wish me luck!"

"Wish *you* luck!" I gaped at him.

"Just kidding." He put one finger against his lips in the universal signal for "shhhh!" In the next instant, my stomach seemed to drop right out of my body, like it used to on the swings, when I was a kid.

I closed my eyes. An instant later, when my stomach settled, I opened my eyes to see Nash's room coming into focus around us. My mouth fell open, and I would have gasped at the eerie *settling* feeling throughout my body, but Tod squeezed my hand again, a silent reminder to be quiet.

And that's when my ears popped, and suddenly the world had sound again.

"...that time it started pouring, two blocks from your house?" Sabine asked, and Nash laughed. They lay side by side on his bed, on their stomachs, propped up on their elbows with their sock feet resting on his pillows. A photo album lay open in front of them at the foot of the bed, and Nash turned a clear plastic page as he answered.

"Too bad you don't have pictures of that! We were so soaked my shoes squished for a day."

"Remember how we got warm?" Sabine asked, her voice softer than I'd ever heard it. Nash turned to look at her, and their mouths were inches apart.

I held my breath, and Tod's hand tightened around mine again, another silent warning. But as my teeth ground together, I knew that if he kissed her, I wouldn't be able to quiet my anger and betrayal. Not that it would matter, if that happened. Me and Tod suddenly appearing in Nash's bedroom while he made out with his ex would be the least of Nash's problems.

But he didn't kiss her. Nash only grinned, then stared down at the photo album, the slight ruddiness in his cheeks the only sign that the memory still affected him.

I should have been happy. I should have been giddy with relief to see him actually pass up an opportunity most guys would have pounced on. But instead of relief, I swallowed a bitter, acrid taste on the back of my tongue. The memory—whatever they'd done that day, when they were soaked, cold, and in love—still affected him. Because he hadn't sold it to Avari for another dose of poisoned air. He'd kept the emotional impact of his memories of Sabine intact, and gutted his memories of me instead.

"Like I could forget," Nash said, oblivious to both my presence and my pain. He flipped another page and she watched him, rather than the pictures.

"Would you, if you could? Forget?" she added, when he looked confused. "Would you forget about me?"

His eyes widened, and I could see the slow churning in them, even from across the room. "No. I wouldn't forget you, or a single moment we spent together, Sabine. You were my first everything, and that still means something, even now that everything's changed. It always will."

Her smile looked painful, like she didn't know whether to laugh or cry. "Did you try to find me, Nash?" she asked at last, after he'd flipped several more pages in silence, and I realized with surprise bordering on amazement that she sounded… bruised. Lost. "Did you even look for me, after you left?"

Nash closed the album and sat up, while she rolled onto her back, staring up at him. "Yeah. I tried to call you at Holser

House, to tell you we were moving, but they wouldn't let me through. They wouldn't even take a message."

She nodded, and her hair fell to hang down the side of his bed. "You weren't on my approved-calls list, and I lost all my privileges when they found the cell you gave me."

"I tried calling the Harpers after that, but they didn't know anything about your new foster home. The school said you'd transferred, but wouldn't tell me where. And the internet didn't seem to know you even existed."

"Yeah, it took me a while to find you, too." She closed her eyes and let her head roll to one side. "I was stupid to think you'd wait for me."

"Bina…" Nash looked like she'd just ripped out his heart and shown it to him, still beating, and as badly as I wanted to hate her, I found anger harder to cling to in that moment than ever before. She really was his first everything—including his first broken heart.

"Do you ever wonder what would have happened?" she asked, rolling onto her side to face him again. "If you'd never left? If I hadn't gotten arrested again?"

"I…" Nash exhaled heavily, and I hated the confliction I read in the slow twist of green in his irises. "Yeah, I do. But what-ifs are pointless, Bina. It can't be like it was then. Not anymore."

"It *could* be." She reached up to brush a chunk of thick brown hair from his forehead, and I bit my lip to keep from protesting. I didn't want her to touch him. Ever.

"No." He took her wrist before she could touch his hair again. "It's different now."

"Because of her," Sabine said, staring straight into his eyes. Nash nodded and let go of her. "She thinks I killed those teachers."

"I know."

"Do you believe her?"

"I know you better than that. But you haven't exactly given her a reason to trust you."

Sabine frowned and sat up facing him. "I've never lied to her. And I don't care if she trusts me."

Nash set the album on his pillow. "Yes, you do. I'm not going to be enough, Sabine. You need more than one friend."

She shook her head, and dark hair fell over her cheek. "You're all I need."

I'd never seen her look so vulnerable. In fact, I'd never seen her look anything short of antagonistic, but she was obviously a completely different person with Nash. I didn't know whether to be relieved that she had a more human side, or pissed off that that side only emerged when she was alone with my boyfriend.

"No," he said. "I was all you had back then. You never had a real shot at any other relationship because you couldn't control yourself. But you can now."

"Shut up. You're making me sound needy just to piss me off."

"I'm telling the truth." He grinned. "Pissing you off is a bonus."

"Oh, you wanna see me mad?" Sabine returned his smile and shoved him back onto the mattress, then threw one leg over him, straddling him. My heart beat so hard it bruised my chest. I tried to pull away from Tod, but he held my hand tight and shook his head, like the ghost of relationships past, demanding I only watch.

Next, would we float through the open window?

Sabine stared down at him, her long hair half hiding them both. "You forget what happens when I lose my temper?" But from the way she was watching him, all flashing eyes and sly smile, I got the feeling she had a rather unconventional, hands-on approach to anger management.

"I haven't forgotten anything, Bina." Nash wrapped his hands around her wrists and gently pushed her back onto her side of the bed. "Including Kaylee. This isn't gonna work if you can't rein it in."

"This is *only* gonna work if I don't rein it in."

"I'm serious." Nash rolled onto his side, propped up on one elbow. "You should give Kaylee a chance. She knows what you are. She could be a good friend, if you'd let her. If you'd stop trying to scare the shit out of her every time you see her."

Um...no, I could *not* be a good friend to a vengeful Nightmare. Had he lost his mind?

Sabine snorted. She actually snorted and somehow made it look endearing. "I don't have to *try* to scare her. All I have to do is let go. The hard part is not scaring the shit out of everyone else. That took a lot of practice."

I shot Tod a questioning glance. *How much more of this do I need to see?*

He just tossed his head toward the bed, where Sabine watched Nash like he was the only flicker of light in a very dark place.

Nash looked at Sabine like she was some complicated puzzle he was trying to solve, and I knew that look. He'd looked at me that way the first time he saw me sing for someone's soul, before I knew I was a *bean sidhe*. He'd looked at me like that when I was the damsel he felt honor-bound to save from distress, whether I needed saving or not. I used to love that look.

Now I hated it.

"Sabine," he said finally, when she showed no sign of breaking what was obviously a very comfortable silence. "Read me."

"What?" She frowned, looking genuinely uncomfortable for the first time since Tod and I had entered the room. "No."

"I want you to read my fear. For real. Go deep and take a look at what I'm really afraid of."

Her brows furrowed over dark eyes. "Why?" Suspicion was thick in her voice now.

"I think it'll help you understand."

"What if I don't want to understand?"

He leaned closer, looking right into her eyes. "Then you're a coward, and I'm ashamed of you."

Anger, ripe and bitter, passed over Sabine's fine features and her frown deepened. "Now you're trying to piss me off."

"I'm throwing down a challenge. You used to love a challenge. Has that changed?"

A new smile crawled over her lips, slow and dark, like the gleam in her eyes. "Nothing's changed. That's what I keep trying to tell you."

"Then read me."

Sabine sat up, and Nash pushed himself upright to face her. "You want me to make it fun? Like we used to?"

I glanced at Tod again. How could having his worst fear read possibly be fun? But the reaper didn't even look at me.

"Sabine…" Nash said, a very familiar warning in his voice.

She grinned, trying to make light of it, but mostly failing. "You can't blame a girl for trying."

But something told me I would be happy to blame her—if I had any clue what she was talking about.

"Fine. Give me your hand."

Nash held out his hand like he'd shake hers, but instead of a formal hold, Sabine threaded her fingers between his and held their merged grip between them, knuckles pointed toward the ceiling.

I thought they'd close their eyes, but instead, Sabine leaned closer to him, like she was trying to see through his pupils and out the back of his head. For several seconds, they stayed just like that. Nash blinked several times, but the *mara*'s gaze was unwavering.

However, her hand was not. By the time she finally blinked and he closed his eyes, her hand was shaking against his. She pulled her fingers from his and wiped her palm on her pants, like their shared sweat was contaminated by the fear of whatever she'd read inside him.

"What did you see?" he asked, and this time he was the steady one.

"Kaylee…" she whispered, and I nearly pulled my hand from Tod's in surprise.

Nash was afraid of me?

"You're scared of losing her." Sabine dropped her gaze, like it hurt too much to look at him. "You're terrified of it. You dream about it, because that's what he told you would happen. That demon. He said you'd lose her. That you weren't good enough for her now. That you don't deserve her. And you believe it. Your worst fear is that you're not good enough for Kaylee. And that she knows it."

My lips opened, and the breath I hadn't known I was holding slipped silently into the room.

I glanced at Tod, and he nodded. That's what he'd wanted me to see. Or at least something like that. Yet he didn't look happy.

"That doesn't make it any easier, you know," Sabine said. She scooted away from him, but seemed unwilling to get off the bed. "Knowing that."

"No. I'm guessing that makes it harder. But it's the truth, and the truth isn't always easy."

Sabine rolled her eyes. "What are you now, the Zen master? Did Kaylee tell you that?"

"Not in so many words. But you can usually tell what she's thinking just by watching her."

No, you can't! I frowned and felt my cheeks color, and suddenly I was extraglad they couldn't see us.

"Yeah, that whole subliminal 'go away and die' message comes through loud and clear." Sabine glanced around the room, and her gaze seemed to linger in the corner where we stood. I knew she couldn't see us, but her eyes creeped me out, anyway.

I'd seen enough. They were just talking now, and she obviously wasn't going to charm him out of his clothes. Or out of me. At least for the night.

Let's go, I mouthed silently to Tod, and that time he nodded. He closed his eyes, and I took that as my signal to do the same.

After another stomach-pitching second of existing nowhere, I felt ground beneath my feet and cold air on my cheeks. I opened my eyes to find us in front of Nash's house again, and as soon as I was sure I wasn't going to fall over from disorientation, I let go of Tod's hand. And immediately missed the warmth.

"Well, that was…interesting." I shoved my hands in my pockets, and Tod glanced at me in surprise, like I'd ripped the words off his own tongue. Then he smiled.

"Yeah, it…"

"I mean, how weird that they spent most of the time talking about me. I guess that should make me feel better, huh?"

His brow furrowed like he wasn't following my logic, and he glanced over his shoulder at the house, as if that would clear it up. "Oh. Yeah." Then he smiled and said, "I have a feeling they do that a lot. So…*does* it make you feel better?"

"Yes, and no." I started walking toward the street, and Tod matched my stride.

"Why no?"

I hesitated. "Because seeing her like that—with him—

makes it a little harder to believe she's a murderer." Not impossible. But definitely harder.

Tod shrugged. "So maybe she's not."

I frowned up at him. "She has to be. Who else could it be?" He opened his mouth, but I spoke over him. "And don't say it might not be anyone, because there's no way three of our teachers in two days just happened to die in their sleep, the same week Sabine moves to town."

"I agree. But that doesn't mean she's doing it."

"Then who is?"

"I don't know. But it could be anyone. Or any*thing*. Don't you think it's at least possible that you're fixating on Sabine because she's fixated on Nash?"

I stopped on the sidewalk, almost halfway between Nash's house and mine. He was right. I wasn't ready to dismiss Sabine as a suspect, but as long as I was playing cop, I might as well think like a cop, and a good cop would never rule out all other possibilities because of a personal vendetta against one suspect.

"Help me," I said, peering up at him against the glow of a streetlight.

"What?" Tod frowned.

"Help me. You know way more about Netherworld stuff than I do, and there's no way a human is doing this. If you really think Sabine's innocent, help me rule her out and come up with some other theories. We can't just let this go on. You said yourself that Wells, Bennigan, and Wesner weren't scheduled to die."

"Kaylee, I have to be at work in less than an hour."

I started walking again, and he had to jog to catch up. "When's your first reaping?"

Tod sighed. "Not till two. But I should really at least look like I'd like to keep my job."

"Come on, reaper! There's ice cream—we'll make a night of it."

Tod's brows rose and his eyes sparkled in the streetlight. He glanced at my hand, hanging at my side between us, then finally nodded. "You know I can't say no to ice cream."

"Or pizza, or pancakes, or Chick-fil-A…"

"Shut up before I change my mind."

13

WHEN WE GOT BACK to my house, I checked to make sure my dad was asleep, then dug a half gallon of mint chocolate chip from the freezer. Tod, Alec, and I ate straight from the container while they helped me make a list of every non-human creature who could possibly kill a person in his sleep.

They seemed to agree that the killer was most likely some kind of psychic parasite. But while Tod insisted that, technically, any parasitic species could feed from a sleeping victim— so we could be dealing with an incubus or succubus, a *scado,* which feeds from anger, or a *neid,* which feeds from jealousy— Alec insisted that a *mara* was the most likely suspect, because Nightmares could *only* feed from sleeping victims. The reaper scowled a lot at Alec's conclusion, but couldn't argue.

When Tod had to leave for work, I retreated to my room with my laptop and a slice of leftover pizza, hoping that without me there to grill him on creepy-crawly trivia, Alec might actually get some sleep.

Between bites of pizza and gulps from a cold can of soda, I searched the internet for anything to do with Sabine Campbell. But none of the Sabine Campbells I found online were anywhere near the right age. She didn't maintain a profile on any networking sites I could think of—at least, not under her real name—nor did I get any hits on her from school websites. Which meant she wasn't active in sports or clubs, nor was she on the honor roll at her last school.

No surprise there.

And evidently juvenile criminal records aren't searchable, because I couldn't find a single word about her illustrious criminal past.

Then, finally, around two-thirty in the morning, I tripped over a stroke of brilliance. I searched for Nash's old school. The one where he'd met Sabine.

Her name didn't come up in any of the hits, but when I added the word *arrested* to the search, I struck gold.

Two years ago, about three months after Nash started at Eastlake as a sophomore, a fifteen-year-old female sophomore was arrested at his old school for assaulting a teacher. Two months after that, a fifteen-year-old female sophomore was removed from school property for possession of alcohol. The news stories—both from the same online paper—didn't say whether or not the two girls were the same person, but I had no doubt that they were. However, after that, all the trouble at Nash's old school seemed to have been caused by boys.

The logical conclusion? Sabine was either expelled or she moved.

But where did she go between Nash's last school and East-lake? I knew I'd heard the name of her most recent school—Sabine had told Emma during their first conversation in junior English.

Valley something. Or something Valley. Valleyview? No. Oak Valley? No, but that was closer. It was something to do with nature.

And just like that, I remembered: Valley Cove. Sabine transferred to Eastlake from Valley Cove High School. I remembered Em saying that Sabine had joked that the town sported neither a valley nor any obvious cove.

After a little more searching, I came up with a single, year-old article in the tiny Valley Cove local newspaper—miraculously online—about a female junior who was suspended for vandalizing school property. She was caught in the act of spray painting "lewd images and crude language" on the side of the school building in the middle of the night.

Yup. Sounds like Sabine.

By the time I closed my laptop at three in the morning and snuck into the bathroom to brush my teeth, I was thoroughly convinced that Sabine was an unrepentant criminal. But I had absolutely no evidence that her crimes had ever included murder.

I SIT UP IN BED and unease crawls beneath my skin like an army of tiny spiders. I blink sleep from my eyes and my room comes into focus, dark, but for the glow from a security light outside my window. Something is wrong, but I can't tell what. Not yet. But my scalp feels prickled—my hair wanting to stand on end.

I smell it first, even before I hear it, and the spiders beneath my flesh writhe frantically. I know that smell. Once, a squirrel got trapped in the old trash can we rake leaves into, and when Dad found it, it smelled like this. Like rot. Like warm death.

My heart thumps painfully and I hold my breath. I don't want to smell that putrid stench, but I want to taste it even less, so I clamp my jaw shut.

Next comes the sound—a broken cadence of footsteps, punctuated by a horrible sliding sound. The steps are soft, but they get louder. Coming closer. My pulse races and I scoot back against the headboard, putting a few more worthless inches between me and whatever is step-sliding its way toward my room.

I should run. But I can't move. I'm frozen, morbid curiosity and paralyzing dread warring inside me while my door creaks slowly open.

My door shouldn't creak. It never has before. But it creaks now, and a gray hand pushes the doorknob.

I'm breathing too fast. I want to scream. Screaming has never failed me, but now my voice is as still as the rest of me. Waiting. Terrified.

Sweat drips down my spine. I feel it bead on my forehead and in the crooks of my arms. That gray hand leads to a wrist, which leads to an arm, which then leads to a shoulder, and before I know it, she's there. In my doorway. Staring at me through dead, milky eyes.

I can't breathe fast enough, and each breath smells like her. Like decay. Like things that should be rotting peacefully in the ground, not dripping thick, foul fluids on my carpet.

But the worst part is that though she should be blind, I know she sees me. Though her cracked, colorless lips shouldn't be able to move, they open. And though her throat has already rotted through, raw tendons peeking at me through the holes in her flesh, her voice still works, and I still recognize it.

I can never forget it, though I haven't heard it since I was three years old. Since the night she died. Since the night I died, and she took my place.

This walking, rotting, stinking corpse is my mother.

"I want it back," she says, and at first her voice is a whisper. She hasn't used it in thirteen years. "You squandered it, and I want it back."

"Mom?" I don't realize my own voice is back until I hear myself speak. Oh, how I've always wanted the chance to speak

to her, just one more time. But not like this. This is wrong, so fundamentally perverse that I can't believe this is happening. Yet I can't deny it, either. Not with her stench in the air, polluting my lungs. Not with her hands reaching, reaching…

"You've wasted it. You're not living, you're just dying very slowly." Each word is an obvious effort, but she keeps going. "Give it back to me." She step-hobbles closer, and some part of me understands that her legs don't work right anymore. But the miracle, really, is that they work at all. She should be nothing but bones after thirteen years in the grave.

My skin crawls, and fear is the battery keeping my heart beating. I want to run, and I'm sure now that I can, physically. But I can't run from her. She's dead, and smelly, and oddly squishy, but she's my mother.

"Mom?" I say it again, waiting for it to sink in. Waiting for her to remember me, like I remember her. But her cloudy eyes show no warmth. No love. They are empty, and her voice is hard.

"You whine. You don't listen. You refuse to really live. You don't take risks, you don't make gains, and you're never going to grow up."

Terror and revulsion burn within me now, roasting me alive from the inside. Her words bruise like blows. Denial is the only reason I'm still conscious. I hate what she is, because I know it should be me. But I love her, because she's my mother. She gave me life. Twice.

"Mom?" It's a question this time, because my mother never spoke to me like this. My mom was kind and gentle, encouraging. I don't remember much, but I remember that.

"That would be fine, if you had at least one redeeming quality." She takes an awkward step forward, and I cringe, tears forming in my eyes. "One extraordinary trait, to prove you were worth my sacrifice." Another step, and I blink. Tears

scald my cheeks, but still she comes. Still she speaks, shredding my soul with every hateful word. "Beauty. Brains. Talent. But you have none of that. You're mediocrity personified. You don't shine like I did."

Another step, and she's at the foot of the bed now. She leans forward, both hands on my blanket. Her fingers split like sausage casings beneath the pressure of her weight. Fluid oozes to stain the purple material, and I suck air in so fast I'm choking on it.

"I was the light in your father's life, shining to show him the way. But you don't shine. He gave you away because he couldn't stand to be with you. Because he knows what I know. What you know. That you're not worth it, Kaylee. You're not worth my life, and I want it back."

"Mom, no." Tears slide silently down my face, and I swipe at them. She crawls onto the bed. Her knees smear the stains her fingers left, and the stench is unbearable now.

Up close, I can see the details. Her skin is damp and gray and flaccid. Her eyelashes and eyebrows are long gone. Clumps of her hair are missing, but that's a mercy, because what's left is thin, brittle, and tangled, caked with dirt and stiff with dried bodily fluids.

"I just need your breath. That's all it takes...." she whispers. Her dress has holes, but I recognize it. She was buried in it. It used to be blue, the same shade as her eyes, but now it's faded, and stained, and almost as rotten as she is.

"Mom, you don't mean it." I'm scooting to the side now, finally in motion, but in my heart, I know it will do no good. If she can find me here, she can find me anywhere. I haven't lived up to her gift, and now she wants it back.

And she will get it. We both know that.

"You let my life rot, along with my body. If you ever loved me, give me back what I gave so foolishly...."

I pull my knees up to my chest and push myself away from her. The corner of my nightstand pokes into my back. She reaches for my leg. Her fingers squish against my kneecap. More skin splits. Viscous liquid runs over my leg, and the smell is overwhelming.

My stomach revolts. Vomit rises in my throat. Tears blur my vision. Terror squeezes my heart with fists of iron.

Finally I scream, but it's too late. It is much, much too late.

≪ 14 ≫

THAT TIME, I DIDN'T sit up in bed. I pulled the covers over my head like a child, half convinced I was still dreaming. That if I peeked into the room, she would be there waiting for me, that half-rotted perversion of my mother, demanding her life back before I could squander the rest of it.

I stayed like that until I got dizzy from breathing my own used oxygen, and when nothing crawled toward me, when the air never putrefied in my nostrils, I finally pushed back the covers and sat up.

My room looked normal. The door was still closed, but unlocked in spite of paranoid warnings from both Nash and Tod. My comforter was spotless, my knee still clean.

My mother had never stood in this room. She hadn't stood anywhere in more than thirteen years, and deep down I knew that even if she could come see me, she would never demand my life for the privilege.

My mother didn't want me dead. But I *was* afraid I'd wasted her gift. And Sabine obviously knew that.

With that realization came the blazing fury I needed to

thaw my icy fear. But there would be no more sleep for me that night. Sabine had done her job very, very well.

"ANOTHER BAD DREAM?" Alec asked, as I tiptoed past the couch on my way to the kitchen. "That's the second one this week."

Third, but who's counting?

"Don't you ever sleep?" I demanded, without slowing.

He tossed back the blanket and sat up. "I was gonna ask you the same thing."

"I slept," I insisted, heading straight for the coffeepot. "Now I'm done. Just getting an early start."

The couch springs creaked behind me. "It's four-thirty in the morning."

I knew that, with every exhausted bone in my body. "Thus the word *early*."

"You couldn't have slept more than two hours."

The kitchen floor was cold on my bare feet, and I wished I'd remembered my slippers. "What are you now, a math major?" Or my dad?

"You're doing one hell of a Sophie impersonation this morning." Alec had only met my cousin once, and that was more than enough. "What's wrong?"

After staring at the remnants of the previous day's coffee, I decided making a fresh pot would be too much trouble and opted for a soda from the fridge instead. I popped the tab as I sank into my dad's chair across from the couch, where Alec now sat watching me in nothing but the gym shorts he slept in.

I took a long drink, then met his fatigued, bloodshot gaze. "Sabine's at it again. Or still at it. Or whatever."

"Nash's ex?" Alec rubbed the top of his head with one broad hand. "What's she doing?"

"The usual. Bullying her way into my head and sending nightmares. This has to stop."

"What's the big deal?" Alec shrugged smooth, dark shoulders. "They're just dreams, right? So shake it off and go back to sleep."

I blinked at him, trying to decide whether or not to take him seriously. "They're not just dreams, Alec. They're renderings of my own fears, ripe with life force for her to suck. She's a *mara,* remember?"

Alec's eyes widened, and he sat straighter on the couch. "*Sabine's* the *mara?* Why didn't you tell me?"

"I *did* tell you!"

Alec shook his head firmly. "The other night, you said you dreamed she made out with your ex, then tonight you said you knew a *mara.* But you never mentioned that the *mara* and Sabine are the same damn person!"

I set my can down and frowned at him. "Okay, you seriously need to get more sleep. I told you she was a *mara* last night. In the kitchen, remember?"

Alec looked startled—truly frightened, just for an instant— then his entire expression seemed to simply shut down, like when the power fails and the whole neighborhood goes dark. "Last night?" he repeated, cradling his head in his hands. "Would this have been in the middle of the night?"

"Yeah. While you were working your way through a box of my dad's cupcakes."

He exhaled slowly, then mumbled beneath his breath, "*That's* what he meant about the cupcakes…"

"What?" I leaned forward and studied his face when he finally looked up. "Are you okay?"

"Yeah. I'm just…sleep deprived, I guess. I barely remember last night. So…Sabine's a *mara?* For real?"

"Welcome to the conversation." I turned my head slowly back and forth, stretching out the cramp in my neck. "She's been exploiting my fears to try to scare me away from Nash."

"Wow." Alec whistled and leaned back with his arms crossed over his smooth, bare chest. "That's messed up. I mean, that's bordering on Netherworld-level torture. At least, of the psychological variety."

I picked up the can and took another sip, willing the caffeine into my system. "Yeah, she's not exactly warm and fuzzy."

"So what're you gonna do? You can't just let her walk all over you." Alec looked more awake, and I started to relax a little, now that he was sounding like himself again.

"I know. I thought I had it all taken care of, after I smacked her, and Nash said—"

"Wait, *you* hit someone?"

My fingers clenched around the cold, damp can. "Why does everyone sound so surprised by that?" But Alec only raised both brows at me. "Okay, I'm not exactly a prizefighter. But she had it coming. And anyway, after that, Nash said she promised to stay out of my dreams. Obviously she was lying. Or else he was."

"Which do you think it is?"

I took a long drink to avoid answering. "I honestly don't know. The truth is that I haven't been able to catch Sabine in a lie so far—she's frighteningly blunt—but Nash has lied to me repeatedly. How sad is it that I can trust his serial-killer ex-girlfriend better than I can trust him?"

"Killer…" Alec said, like he was tasting the word. "You really think she killed those teachers?"

"I don't know. She's openly confessed to everything else she's done, so why wouldn't she admit to this, if she's guilty? It's not like the police are going to arrest her for dream-stalking, right? So maybe it's not her." I shrugged and let my head rest on the back of the recliner. "But I don't have any other suspects. And anyway, you said it yourself—a *mara's* the most likely suspect."

Alec frowned. "Yeah, but that was before I knew you were talking about someone you go to school with."

"What does that matter?"

He shrugged, obviously hesitating. "It's one thing to say that a certain species theoretically fits the bill for what you're looking for. But that doesn't mean that the one member of that species you actually know is definitely the killer. You can't go blaming someone of murdering your teachers without more proof than that, Kaylee."

I flinched. "Too late."

Alec blinked. "Please tell me you did not accuse a *mara*—to her face—of killing someone. A *mara* who's already not crazy about you."

"Um…yeah. I did."

"Damn." He leaned back and stared at the ceiling. "I can't decide whether you're brave or stupid, Kaylee. No wonder she's playing dreamweaver in your head."

My scowl deepened. "She was doing that already. Besides, this makes sense. She's the only one with motive and opportunity."

Alec leaned forward again and shook his head, eyeing me solemnly. "You watch too much TV. Nothing's ever that cut and dry in real life. Especially when your suspects aren't even human."

I scooted to the edge of my chair, irritated. Why was I the only one who could see what Sabine was really capable of? "She's trying to scare me into backing down, from both Nash and this investigation."

"She wants you to give up on a boyfriend you're not sure you want back, and an investigation that consists entirely of a list of supernatural creatures scribbled on a phone message pad? Sorry, Kay, but it doesn't sound to me like she's the one lacking logic."

Wow. When he put it like that, the whole thing sounded so…insubstantial. And really, really pathetic. Still… "If you were a cop investigating a murder, wouldn't you be most interested in the suspect with a criminal record?"

Alec perked up again. "Wait, Sabine has a record? You didn't tell me that."

"Yes I *did!*" I set my Coke on the end table and studied him more closely. "You seriously need to start paying better attention. I know you're still getting readjusted to the human world, but your memory has so many holes we could strain noodles through it." And this was more than simple forgetfulness. I could tell from the way he refused to look at me, and from the tense line of his shoulders.

A chill developed at the base of my spine and began working its way up slowly. "What's going on, Alec?"

Alec took a long, slow breath, and only after several seconds of silence did he finally meet my gaze, deep brown eyes practically swimming in fear. "Something's wrong, and I think I'm starting to understand what's going on. I need to tell you something, but I need you not to freak out on me, okay?"

Why were people always telling me that?

The chills traveled up my spine and into my arms, where chill bumps burst to life. "Telling me not to freak out pretty much guarantees that I *will* freak out.…"

"Sorry." He took a deep breath. "Here's the deal… My memory of the past few days doesn't just have holes in it. It has hollows. Big, gaping blank spots."

Uh-oh. "How big is big?"

Alec leaned back on the couch and scrubbed his face with both hands. "Scary big. I wake up and have no idea how I got wherever I am. I can't remember what I was doing. It's very…unsettling."

I would have gone with "bizarre and terrifying." But then, I hadn't spent the past quarter century surrounded by true terror.

"When did this...?" I began, then my voice faded into silence when the rest of what he'd said sank in. "Wait, you said you 'wake up' and have no idea what's going on. So...this happens when you go to sleep?"

The fear churning in my stomach put a bad taste in my mouth. Something strong and foul. Something distressingly familiar...

"Yeah. It's him, Kaylee." Alec's dark gaze held mine captive. "Avari's possessing me."

"No." I shook my head vehemently, even though denial wasn't really an option. "No, no, no. He can't." I made myself put my can down before I could crush it and drench myself in cold soda.

Alec stared back at me from the couch. He looked so vulnerable suddenly. Younger than his nineteen-year-old body, and much younger than his middle-aged mind and soul. "Nothing else makes sense."

"Neither does this," I insisted. "It can't be Avari. He doesn't have the strength. Not without you there to supply extra power."

For years, the hellion had used Alec like a walking snack, drawing energy and nutrition from him to fuel his own evil projects and ambitions. But without Alec at his disposal, Avari shouldn't have enough energy to possess someone in the human world. At least, not so often or for any serious length of time.

Alec sighed, and the weight that sound seemed to carry was unimaginable. "At this point, I'm assuming he's found a new proxy. I can't think of any other way this could be possible."

My head felt like it was about to explode. "You're saying Avari took over your body just to gossip with me and snag some snack cakes? No." He was wrong. He had to be. "Alec, you talked to me. Both of those times, you spoke, and it was your voice, not Avari's. That would have been impossible if he were possessing you."

Alec shook his head slowly. "No, that would have been impossible if he were possessing *you*. Or Emma, or Sophie, or anyone else he doesn't know very well. But I've spent the past twenty-six years with him, and he's been drawing power from me the entire time. He's intimately familiar with my physiology, and it makes sense that he'd know how to work my voice box, along with the rest of my body."

No. Damn it, no!

I was breathing too fast and had to focus to keep from hyperventilating. *This cannot be happening.* Avari could not have been so close to us—*inside* Alec—without us knowing! Not now that I knew the signs. The voice was the giveaway. He wasn't supposed to be able to use his puppet's voice!

"This doesn't make any sense, Alec. Why would he burn so much energy just to chat with me and eat some refined sugar? He didn't even tell me what he was doing, so he couldn't have been feeding off my fear and anger. Why would he go to all this trouble, then not take credit for it?"

Alec didn't answer. He propped his elbows on his knees and let his head hang below his shoulders, and all I could see of him then was the rapid rise and fall of his arched back while he breathed too fast and too hard.

"Alec? What are you not telling me?" Because it was obvious by then that there was more. Maybe much, much more.

But he didn't answer.

I left my chair and settled onto the couch next to him, laying one hand on his warm arm. "Alec?" I couldn't decide whether to be mad at him for holding back or sympathize with the obvious pain of whatever he was going through.

Finally he sucked in a shaky breath and looked up. "I think I killed your teachers, Kaylee. I think Avari *used* me to kill them. And I don't know how to make him stop."

My living room suddenly seemed a little darker. I couldn't think. I could barely even breathe. Too many thoughts were flying through my head—too many questions—and I couldn't focus on any one in particular.

"Alec..." I stared at the floor, willing both the carpet and my thoughts to come into focus. "Why... What..." I stopped, took another deep breath, then started over. "How is that even possible? They all died in their sleep, from what we can tell. Tod said there were no marks on them."

When Alec just stared at his feet, I continued, desperate for some concrete information to keep from imagining things were worse than they really were. If that was even possible. "Are you saying Avari can... I don't know. Are you saying he can use his own abilities through you, when he's in your body?"

I couldn't think of a more frightening possibility. Knowing a hellion had been in control of my body was terrifying. But if he could make me kill people, using powers I shouldn't even possess...

There were no words to describe the depth of the horror weighing me down in that moment.

"No," Alec said at last, dragging his gaze up to meet mine. But my relief was fleeting. "He can't use his abilities outside of the Netherworld, even when he possesses me. But he can sure as hell use *my* abilities."

"What?" My stomach tried to hurl itself up through my chest and out my mouth. "What abilities?"

I'd suspected Alec wasn't human when he'd first contacted me—by possessing Emma from the Netherworld—but so far, he'd shown no nonhuman traits. Nor had he mentioned any.

I stood and backed away from Alec slowly, giving in to the single most logical moment of self-preservation in my entire life. "Please tell me you're human, Alec. I need you to tell me you're human *right now*. Tell me you haven't been hiding something that big from me and my dad for two weeks."

And please make me believe it…

Alec remained seated; I think he understood that if he stood, I'd lose what little control I was still clinging to. And that I'd shout for my dad. "I couldn't tell you, Kaylee. I didn't want you to be afraid of me."

"It's a little late for that now, so why don't you just lay it out for me?" I backed around the coffee table and across the room. "What are you?"

Alec sighed and glanced at the couch pillow, like he'd like to rip it to shreds, or maybe clutch it to his chest. "It's a long story."

"It's not like I'm going back to sleep." I sat in the chair again and picked up my soda just to have something to hold.

"My mom's human," he began finally. "Avari caught her half a century ago and used her as a proxy for several years. While she was there, she fell in love. Not with him…" Alec said, anticipating my disgust before I could even ask the question now burning on the end of my tongue. "With someone else. With my father. He helped her sneak away from Avari for short periods of time, usually by distracting him with some plaything newer and shinier than my mom."

My stomach churned harder. "Your dad gave Avari other people to…eat? Or whatever?"

"Not always people. Hellions' interests are very broad and…" But he stopped when he read the horror surely clear on my face. "He did it for my mom. To spare her. To be with her."

And I realized with a start that I could understand that,

even if I couldn't excuse it. Tod had done something very similar to be with Addison, after she'd died with her soul in Avari's possession, dooming herself to eternal torment for the hellion's pleasure.

I nodded for Alec to go on.

"Anyway, when she got pregnant, they both realized that my mom had to get out of the Netherworld, and that Avari could never know about me. If he got his hands on a half-breed—a potential proxy who could feed him much more and much longer than a human ever could—he'd be too powerful to fight, and my mom would never get out. So my dad arranged for someone who owed him a favor to ferry her back to the human world. They never saw each other again, and I was raised here, like a human."

"She didn't tell you?" A pang of sympathy rang through me at that thought. I'd been raised the same way, in total ignorance of who and what I really was, and of what my differences truly meant. Of what I could really do.

"Not until I was nearly grown and my differences began to manifest. She told me then because I needed to know how to control myself. How to keep from hurting anyone accidentally. Her big mistake was contacting my father for advice. She sent him messages through the friend who'd gotten her out of the Netherworld, but that put her on Avari's radar again. He got to the messenger before my dad did that last time, and…well, I don't know if he threatened him or paid him or what. But somehow he convinced the messenger to bring my mother to him, instead of delivering her message. And once Avari had her, it didn't take him long to find out about me."

"How did he get you?" I asked, my voice so low I could barely hear it. Avari had done the same thing to Nash, and to my dad, and it terrified me to know that he had the resources to take anyone he wanted from our world into the Nether-world, any time he wanted.

In fact, I might never sleep again, knowing that.

"He told me I could trade myself for her. He swore he'd send her back here the minute I turned myself over to him."

"Did he?" My heart beat so hard I could barely hear him over it. And I was afraid I already knew the answer.

"Yeah. But what he neglected to mention was that she was already dead. He used her up in one gluttonous energy binge, and when I crossed over, he sent her body back to the human world."

Alec's jaw tensed, and I knew without asking that if he hadn't already had years to mourn his mother, he might have broken into tears right then. "I didn't get to go to her funeral. I don't know where she's buried. I don't even know who found her. All I know is that if I have any relatives left, I can't go see them, because I haven't aged since the day she died. And knowing what Avari's been doing with my body...I can't put the rest of my family—whatever's left of it—in danger. You and your dad are all I have here. And if I can't make Avari stop possessing me, I'm going to lose you, too."

I wanted to deny it. I wanted to put my arm around him and comfort him like the brother I'd never had. Or like an uncle, considering our age difference. But I couldn't do that, because he was right. If Avari had that much control over him, no one was safe. Least of all me and my father.

"How did he do it?" I asked. "How did he make you kill them? What are you, Alec?"

Alec looked up at me through shiny brown eyes. "I'm half hypnos."

"What's a hypnos?" I held my breath, waiting for his ex-planation, but couldn't slow my racing pulse.

"Hypnos are minor Netherworld creatures that feed from

the energy of sleeping humans through the barrier between worlds. Full-blood hypnos can't cross into the human world, but obviously I can. I think Avari used me to suck your teachers dry in their sleep." He closed his eyes briefly, then opened them so I could see his raging anger and guilt. "It turns out I'm even more useful to that hellion bastard here than I was in the Netherworld."

"You're a hypnos?" I rubbed my hands over the cotton of my pajama pants, needing to feel something real and familiar to assure me that I was still safe in my own living room. That I hadn't accidentally crossed into that world of nightmares—or succumbed to an *actual* nightmare.

"Half hypnos," Alec corrected, scowling at the floor again.

My mind didn't want to accept the concept, and my mouth didn't really want to ask the next question. But I did, anyway. "Minor creature from the Netherworld... Please tell me that 'minor creature' isn't a euphemism for 'monster of titanic proportions.' Your dad isn't some kind of demon, is he? A hellion cousin species?"

"My father is dead." Alec's words were clipped short, yet no hint of emotion showed on his face. "But, no, he wasn't any relation to hellions. Hellions deal in human souls—no other Netherworld creature does that. Hypnos are just another species of Netherworlder, most of which feed from humans in some way. Some absorb the energy that bleeds through from this world to theirs. Some drink human bodily fluids. Some eat flesh. For most species, human by-products are a delicacy—delicious, but unnecessary. Like your dad's cupcakes. However, hypnos are one of the few species that *need* some human energy in their diet to survive. They feed through the barrier."

"How did your dad die?" I asked, pushing aside the information I wasn't ready to deal with yet—the fact that Alec was at least half psychic carnivore.

"Avari killed him when I crossed into the Netherworld, to keep him from trying to send me home."

"I'm so sorry."

Alec only shrugged. "I've had plenty of time to deal. Besides, it's not like I ever actually met him."

Still, I knew what it felt like to lose a parent, and he'd suffered twice my loss. That realization reminded me that Alec had a human side as well as a monster side, which tempered my fear and horror with a bit of empathy.

But what if his Hyde half was stronger than Dr. Jekyll?

"So, do you have to…feed? From humans? Like your dad?" And like Sabine?

Alec shook his head. "I didn't even know I could until I was nearly grown. I inherited the ability to feed from human energy, but not the necessity."

Thank goodness. But suddenly another question was poking at my conscious mind. "Alec, did you pull me into the Netherworld in my sleep, that first time I saw you?" He'd been stomping his way through a field of razor wheat, wielding a metal trash can lid like a shield.

"Yeah. Sorry." He looked almost as ashamed about that as he was about hiding his species. "I was just trying to get in touch with you while you slept. Subconsciously. But it didn't go exactly like I'd planned."

Oddly enough, I wasn't angry over his admission. At least

now I wouldn't have to worry that I'd dream of death and wake up in the Netherworld again.

"So…how does it work—Avari using you to kill people?"

Alec shrugged miserably. "I don't know. I'm not really in here when he does it." He tapped his skull with one long index finger. "But I can tell you one thing. The energy he's taking from them—and it must be a lot, if it's killing them— must be going straight through me to him, because I'm not getting any of it. I'm almost as worn out now as I was in the Netherworld."

That was a mixed blessing, for sure. The thought of Alec— my new friend and confidant—devouring my teachers' life force made me sick to my stomach. But knowing it was strengthening Avari instead was no better.

"Why teachers?" I asked, and Alec's frown only deepened.

"I don't know. I don't know anything about this, Kaylee. I've never even been to your school—at least, not while I'm in control of my own body."

I frowned at a vague glimmer of light on the dark horizon. "So then…are you sure this is what's happening? 'Cause I'd be perfectly happy to continue pinning this on Sabine." And I was only partly joking.

"I know you want her to be guilty, and I'm not exactly eager to take the blame for something I had no control over. But for the past two nights in a row, I've gone to sleep on the couch, then woken up standing in the middle of the kitchen, fully clothed, with no idea how I got there. Avari's using me to kill people, and I have to make it stop."

"You will. *We* will. I'll help you." But I wasn't sure how to even begin, other than making sure no one fell asleep at school. Ever.

I stood to take my empty can into the kitchen, and his voice followed me. "Thanks, but I don't think there's anything you can do. I'm not sure there's much *either* of us can do."

"Yeah, well, that's what Avari thought last time, and look how that turned out." I tossed the can into the recycle bin and pulled a fresh one from the fridge. "We got you, Nash, and my dad out of the Netherworld and kept Avari from forcibly emigrating the entire population of Eastlake High."

Alec huffed, a harsh sound of skepticism. "Unfortunately, that silver lining is overshadowed by one hell of a gray cloud. You and Nash took a wrong turn on the road to happily ever after, and Avari's practically got on-demand access to my body and my feeding abilities."

"Avari doesn't get credit for driving a wedge between me and Nash," I insisted. "Nash did that himself, and he's only letting Sabine drive that wedge deeper." I popped the tab on my soda as I crossed the living room again, then sank into my dad's recliner. "And as for you… At least now that we know what he's doing, we have a shot at stopping him."

But the truth was that our shot was a long shot at best. The only thing keeping Avari in check before was the fact that he couldn't cross into the human world. And now that he'd found a way—not to mention a very powerful weapon to wield—he was virtually unstoppable. The hellion was playing by new rules, and we'd have to adapt to them quickly to have any hope of stopping him.

"Kaylee…?" Alec's voice was oddly soft and tentative, drawing me from grim thoughts.

"Yeah?"

"What are you gonna do? I mean… Are you going to tell… people?"

He meant my dad. My father had bent over backward to help Alec, out of gratitude. But if he found out that Alec was being used as Avari's murder weapon—and that he'd kept his species and abilities a secret—my dad would kick him out without a second thought. At the very least. He wouldn't let anyone or anything risk my safety, even if that meant turning his back on a friend.

"I don't have anywhere else to go, Kay." Alec met my gaze frankly. "I spent the past quarter of a century groveling for whatever crumbs of mercy fell from Avari's table, and the pickings were very, very slim. When I got back to the human world, I swore things would be different. Here, I have freedom and self-respect. And friends. But one word from you could take all that away. So I'm begging you, Kaylee."

Alec's eyes watered, and I could see how much it cost him to beg for mercy, when he should have been way past such bruising necessities.

"And I swear, it'll never happen again. I won't let it. I spent two and a half decades trying to get free from Avari, and I am *not* going to let him use me here like he used me there. But I need your help. I need you to keep this quiet while I figure out how to keep him out of my body. And I swear on my life that I'll never let him use me to kill again."

I wanted so badly to believe him. He looked sincere, and he sounded sincere, and both my heart and my gut believed the agony and determination clear on his face. But what if I was wrong, and he was lying? What if he'd known all along what Avari was doing, and they were working together?

Or what if, in spite of his best efforts, he couldn't stop Avari from using him? What if he knew this was the only thing keeping Avari from calling in every favor owed to him to get his former proxy back? What if Alec was willing to pay this price—to let innocent people die—for his freedom from the Netherworld, and now he was playing me for a fool to keep me quiet?

The soul-searing truth was that I no longer knew who I could trust—my own track record made that painfully clear.

I'd trusted Nash, and he'd lied to me. I'd trusted Tod, and he'd withheld the truth about what could happen to me in the Netherworld. I'd trusted my family, and they had all lied to me about who and what I am, for almost my entire life.

The only person in the whole world—*either* world—that I was sure had never lied to me was Emma, and unfortunately, the reverse could not be said. I'd lied to her countless times, trying to keep her safe from Netherworld elements.

My life was a tower of lies, and I could feel that tower leaning. One day it would fall and crush me, and everyone around me. But until then, all I could do was slap on some more mortar and cling to the framework of trust in humanity that held me upright. Even if I was contributing to my own eventual downfall.

Alec shifted on the couch, waiting in tense silence for my answer.

"No, I'm not going to tell my dad. Yet," I said, and his relief was so palpable I almost hated to ruin it. But the rest had to be said, too. His life was worth no more than the ones I'd be putting at risk by keeping his secret. "But I have to tell Nash." Otherwise, he'd keep trying to prove Sabine innocent. "And if you let anyone else die, I swear I'll drop you off on Avari's doorstep personally."

He shook his head firmly. "It won't come to that. I swear."

Please, please, please let me be right about Alec.

"Good. And I think we should sleep in shifts from now on. You know, to watch each other. You can wake me up if I look like I'm having another nightmare, and if Avari possesses you again, I'll expel him through whatever means necessary."

"What means would those be?" Alec asked, his eyes narrowed.

I shrugged. "A good whack on the head seems to do the job. You'll wake up with a headache, but that's better than having more blood on your hands, right?"

Alec nodded. "But how will you know it's him, if he sounds like me?"

I wanted to tell him I'd know. That I'd somehow be able to look into his eyes and know I was staring at a demon, rather than at my friend, but the truth was that I couldn't be sure. Nash hadn't known the difference between me and Avari once, and I'd already made the same mistake with Alec twice.

"We need a secret code word, or a security question, or something."

"A code word?" Alec chuckled, a release of the tension he'd been buried in, and I frowned at him over my can as I took another drink. "Isn't that a little juvenile?"

I raised both brows in challenge. "You got a better idea?"

After a moment, Alec shook his head.

"Then we go with the security question. It has to be something Avari wouldn't know the answer to. Something like your favorite color, or your mother's maiden name."

"My mom never married. And I don't think there's anything about me that he doesn't know. The question should be about you."

Fine. What would Avari not know about me…? The list had to be endless, but I was coming up with exactly nothing.

"What color was your first bike?" Alec asked

"White, with red ribbons."

He smiled. "That'll be the security question and answer."

"Okay." Makes sense… Assuming I wasn't talking to Avari right now. But that was impossible, right? Avari wasn't *that* good an actor. Still…

"Did he kill anyone tonight? Do you have any new holes in your memory?"

Alec shook his head. "I haven't even been to sleep yet." He glanced over my shoulder at the front window, and I twisted to see faint early-morning sunlight leaking in between the slats in the miniblinds. "And it's looking like the time for that has passed."

Except that he'd gotten Mrs. Bennigan in the middle of the day, when she'd passed out at her desk. Mrs. Bennigan had just gotten back from maternity leave, so no doubt the new baby was contributing to her exhaustion, but she couldn't be the only teacher who ever fell asleep in the middle of the day. And the less sleep Alec got at night, the more likely he'd be to pass out during the day, leaving himself—and any simultaneously napping teachers—at risk.

"You don't have to be at work till eleven, right? Why don't you sleep for a couple of hours while I'm here to watch you?"

He frowned. "You sure?"

"Yeah." I stood and headed for the kitchen. "I'm just going to make some coffee and do some homework." There hadn't exactly been time for it the night before, between spying on Nash and trying to pin the murders on Sabine.

"Thanks, Kay. I really owe you."

I pasted on an uneasy smile. "I'll put it on your tab."

TWO AND A HALF HOURS later, I sat in my car in the school parking lot, waiting for Sabine. Again. And for once, I actually hoped she'd have Nash with her. That way he'd be there to hear that she'd broken a promise to him by invading my dreams. Again.

I'd only been waiting a few minutes when she pulled into the lot and parked one row down, four spots over. I grabbed my backpack and locked the car, wishing that I'd remembered my jacket. But with nightmares, murder, and hostile invasion by a hellion on my mind, the January cold hadn't even ranked among my worries that morning.

"Sabine!" I yelled as I jogged toward her car, and several people turned to look. My resolve wavered for an instant when I realized we'd have an audience, but one glance at the smug look on her face as she stepped onto the pavement was enough to bring my determination back in full force.

"Kaylee?" Nash stood on the other side of her car with one hand on the roof. "What's wrong?"

I stopped closer to Sabine than I really wanted to be, to keep anyone else from overhearing. "Your delinquent Nightmare of a girlfriend was in my head again," I snapped through gritted teeth.

"Did you say head?" Sabine asked, drawing both my anger and my attention from Nash. "'Cause it sounded like you said bed, and I don't think anyone's *ever* been in your bed."

White-hot sparks of anger floated in front of my eyes. "Am I supposed to be embarrassed because I'm not handing it out like Halloween candy?"

"I think you *are* embarrassed, 'cause you're afraid to let anyone have even a little taste of your…candy."

My hand clenched around the strap of my backpack. "You sound like a slut."

"You dress like a prude."

"Whoa, wait a minute." Nash rounded the car in a few steps and grabbed Sabine's arm, pulling her away from me, and I had to wonder which of us he was trying to protect. People were watching us outright now, and Nash turned to yell at them, standing firm between me and Sabine. "Go on in! You're not missing anything." I felt the warm brush of his Influence—not directed at me, fortunately—and probably would have been mad at him for Influencing our classmates, if I weren't so busy being furious with Sabine. But his Influence worked—it always did—and this time no one got hurt. They all just turned and headed for the building, like a herd of human cattle.

When we were no longer the center of attention, Nash turned to Sabine. "You were in her dreams again?"

"Oh, come on. She's such a tease." Sabine shook her head, like I should be ashamed of myself. "Those mommy issues were just crying out for attention."

"Stay out of my head," I demanded, just as Nash said, "Sabine, you promised!"

She turned to him, eyes flashing in anger. "I promised I wouldn't try to scare her away from you, and I didn't. It had nothing to do with you this time. She stuck her nose into my private life, so I responded in kind."

Nash turned to me, rubbing his forehead like it hurt. "What the hell is she talking about?"

"Yeah, Kaylee, what could I possibly be talking about?" Sabine's eyes widened in fake wonder for a second before her gaze hardened into true anger. "Why don't you tell Nash where you were last night?"

My cheeks glowed like sunset on the horizon of my vision. "Kaylee?" Nash asked, but I couldn't say it.

"Even when I can't see you, I can taste your emotions like a shark tastes blood in the water," Sabine whispered, leaning around Nash to make sure I heard her. "You can't sneak up on me. You can't spy on me. I will always know you're there, Kaylee."

My face *burned* now, and I had nothing to put out the flames.

"Someone tell me what the hell you two're talking about!" Nash snapped through clenched teeth, as more students paused to eye us before heading into the building.

Sabine crossed her arms over her chest, smug and satisfied.

"Kaylee pulled the Invisible Man routine in your room last night."

Nash turned to me, suspicion and disbelief swirling slowly in his eyes. "Kaylee?"

Crap.

"I'm sorry. I just…" I wanted to explain, but I wasn't gonna blame it on Tod. Even if it was his fault. "I don't get what you see in her, and I wanted to see you both together. I needed to understand. To be sure."

"To be sure of what?" Nash demanded, his voice as low and hard as I'd ever heard it. "You spied on me to make sure I'm not sleeping with her?"

"She doesn't trust you," Sabine said, like a snake hissing in his ear. "And she never will. I can't believe you can't see that."

Nash whirled on her. "Shut up!" His irises churned with anger, roiling like storm clouds, but it wasn't all directed at her; a good bit of that anger was for me. "It's my fault she doesn't trust me." He turned back to me. "I know it's my fault, but that doesn't excuse this."

He closed his eyes and took a deep breath, obviously trying to keep a handle on his temper. "I can't believe you spied on me." His eyes flew open and his gaze settled on me with a bitter weight. "Did it make you feel better? I hope whatever you saw justifies you violating Sabine's privacy. And mine."

And just like that, my guilt was overcome by a spark of my own latent rage. "Oh, right. Like you can claim the moral high ground here, after everything you did."

"I'm not claiming anything," Nash insisted. "I just thought you were better than that. Better than *me.* Where were you hiding, anyway? In the closet?"

"I told you, she was invisible," Sabine insisted.

Nash shook his head. "Kaylee can't…" He stopped, and his

scowl deepened with understanding. "Tod. Damn it. I take it he's been practicing?"

I could only shrug.

"It's bad enough that he goes around spying on people, but dragging you into it is way over the line."

"Don't blame him," I insisted. "I could have said no."

"I hear you're good at that." Sabine grinned fiercely, bending to pick up her book bag.

"I hear you can't even spell it," I snapped, infuriated by how vulnerable I felt, knowing she knew intimate details of my personal life. Maybe by eavesdropping, I'd evened the score a little bit in that respect.

"Okay, that's enough!" Nash growled. "I've had it with both of you." He pulled his own bag higher on one shoulder and turned to me. "You let me know when you decide what the hell you want from me. I love you, and I miss you, and I'll be waiting, whenever you're ready. But don't spy on me again. Ever."

I nodded miserably as he twisted to face Sabine. "And you… You come find me when you're ready to be my friend, because that's all I have to offer right now. But as badly as I need someone to talk to, I don't need another complication in my life. And as for the two of you…" He stepped away from us, already walking backward toward the school entrance. "Work it out. Or don't work it out. But leave me the hell out of it."

Then, for the first time since our first kiss, he turned around and walked away from me without a single glance back.

"This is all your fault," Sabine snapped, as soon as Nash was out of hearing range.

I rolled my eyes. "We were fine until you showed up."

"Yeah. About as fine as a train wreck."

"We were working things out," I insisted.

"You were pouting and licking your wounds." Sabine pulled

open her car door and locked it, then slammed it shut. "You stay out of my way and I'll stay out of yours. Deal?"

"Does that mean you're giving up on him?"

"Hell, no." Sabine's eyes darkened, even as they narrowed at me. "It means I'm giving up on you."

The familiar tap of hard-soled, clunky shoes echoed behind me, and Emma came to a stop at my side. "Hey, what's going on?"

Sabine's predatory gaze snapped from me to Emma, and Em actually sucked in a startled breath. Then the *mara* turned sharply and marched into the building alone.

"I'm starting to see the creepy," Emma whispered, as we watched her go. And I hoped she'd never have any reason to see the real Sabine—or to feel her fury.

16

THE REST OF THURSDAY morning was blessedly uneventful. No more teachers turned up dead—Avari hadn't had a chance to possess Alec the night before—and that was a mercy, considering the almost universally shell-shocked faces of both the students and staff members. Avari's latest evil scheme had proved successful enough to become obvious to—though still misunderstood by—the local human populace, and the fact that he didn't care about the unwanted attention made me very, very nervous.

The only bright spot—though it was more like a dimly lit spot—in the day was the fact that I got to do my unfinished homework during algebra, which was still being treated like study hall by the long-term sub.

I went out during my free period again and bought lunch for me and Emma, and when I got back, I found Sabine sitting at one of the tables in the quad, talking to my cousin, Sophie, and a couple of her dance team friends like they were long-lost sisters.

That might have been believable—if she hadn't just brushed

her arm against Sophie's hand when she reached for a packet of mustard. Sabine wasn't just spreading her social wings—she was reading their fears.

My mood instantly soured as I crossed the quad toward them, fast-food bag in hand. "What's going on?" I asked, glaring at Sabine from behind Laura Bell, the reigning Snow Queen and Sophie's best friend. Sabine was up to no good, as usual.

I could tell because she was breathing.

"This is a private conversation," Sophie snapped. "Go peddle weird somewhere else."

"Sabine?" I said through clenched teeth, and she looked up at me with those weird, dark eyes, sporting a faux friendly smile the three blind mice would have seen through. "Can I talk to you for a minute?"

"I'm kind of busy now, Kay," she said, raising one brow at me in challenge. "Sophie and Laura were just telling me all about the dance team. Seems they're short one team member."

As if Sabine would ever even consider trying to replace the dancer whose life I'd failed to save from a rogue reaper a few months earlier.

I fought to keep from grinding my teeth. "I brought you a hamburger."

Sabine cocked her head in interest. "I never could say no to a good piece of meat."

She stood, and Sophie put a hand on the *mara*'s arm, as if to stop her—whether she wanted Sabine there or not, she'd do anything to keep me from getting what I wanted. But then Sabine looked down at her and Sophie froze when their gazes locked. When the *mara* looked away a second later, my cousin silently withdrew her hand and turned back to her teammates, obviously upset by whatever she'd seen in her new "friend's" eyes.

At least I wasn't the only one. Sabine seemed to be letting her creepiness leak out for everyone to see lately, and I credited myself with shaking her off her foundation.

"I thought we were going to stay out of each other's way," I whispered angrily to Sabine as we wound our way through the quad to our usual table.

"You're the one dragging me away from the only healthy relationship I've attempted in years," Sabine snapped. "I'd say that's you getting in my way."

"Sophie's my cousin," I said, but the satisfaction on Sabine's face said she already knew that.

"So?"

"So…leave her alone. She may be a pain, but she's not food," I insisted, pulling the first burger from my bag. "Got it?"

"She hates you," Sabine said. "For real. Her fears are a bit bland, except for a vague, inexplicable fear of you, which is interesting all on its own. But she has plenty of energy to spare, and it all tastes like spite and insecurity. Why do you care if I take a little sip? I'd really be doing you a favor."

"Just because I don't like her doesn't mean I want you feeding from her."

Sabine frowned as I handed her the burger I'd bought for myself. "I don't get you, Kaylee."

"That's painfully obvious." I took a fry from the carton, glad I hadn't included those in my bribe. "Just stay away from my family and my friends."

"Oh, real food!" Emma said, jogging the last few steps toward our table. She pointed to the *mara* and gave me a questioning look, but I couldn't explain, because she didn't know what Sabine was. "This is why I love you, Kaylee!"

I pushed the greasy bag toward Em when she sat.

"This is why we all love her." Sabine shot an ironic, predatory smile at me. "Because she feeds us."

I glared at Sabine, hoping she'd wander off, now that she had my lunch, but she seemed content to stay just to bug me, even though Nash obviously wouldn't be joining us. And since I had nothing civil to say to the *mara,* lunch would have been either really quiet or really ugly, if not for my best friend. Fortunately, Emma was a never-ending fount of pointless gossip.

"Did you hear that Chelsea Simms ratted out Mona Barker for smoking pot behind the gym during second period?" Emma said, a ketchup-dipped fry halfway to her mouth.

"Why would she do that?" I asked, cracking the lid on my bottle of Coke. "They've been best friends since, what? Preschool?"

"Mmm-hmm." Emma nodded. "And Mona always shared."

"Chelsea Simms?" Sabine looked unconvinced. "The newspaper chick? I can't picture her smoking anything. She looks too…uptight." She shot a pointed glance my way, but I just glared and ate another fry.

"Yeah, she thinks it gives her some kind of hippie, free-speech, peace-rally quality."

"Turning in her best friend doesn't sound much like peace to me," I said, and Em waved her burger for emphasis while she spoke.

"I heard Chelsea flipped out because she got demoted from editor of the school paper, for running that conspiracy theory story connecting Bennigan's death with Wells's and Wesner's. She found out first period that her best friend got the job. By second period, Mona was starin' out the back window of a cop car."

"Da-yum." Sabine whistled, looking decidedly impressed. I kind of wanted to slap her again.

I finished my fries while they discussed Mona's chances of surviving jail for even one night—Sabine provided the insider's perspective—then her chances of surviving her parents the following night, and I'd just stood to throw my trash away when the cafeteria door flew open and Principal Goody stomped outside, her flat-soled shoes clacking on the concrete steps.

Both campus security guards came right behind her.

Emma's last sentence faded into nothing and I sat back down on the bench as a hush settled over the quad. All gazes tracked Goody and the school cops, who headed straight for the last table on the left, two spots down from us. It was the football table, where Brant Williams sat with several teammates and their girlfriends—all friends of Nash's who didn't quite know how to be around him without Scott and Doug at his side.

"Zachary Green?" Principal Goody said, her drill sergeant voice almost comical, coming from such a small, prim woman. "Come with us, please."

"Come with you where?" Zach demanded, and I couldn't help but notice that he hadn't asked what he'd done wrong.

"To my office, then home with your parents. They've already been called."

"What for?"

Oh, now *he asks, when his ignorance is too late to be believable.*

"For vandalism of school property."

Instead of demanding specifics, Zach stood and let the old guard tug him toward the cafeteria, and he only dragged his feet long enough to throw a satisfied look over his shoulder at one of the other players still staring after him in surprise.

As the guard hauled Zach up the first step, the cafeteria door flew open again, and Leah-the-pom-girl nearly collided with the entire principal parade. She bounced down the stairs to make room for them to pass, and as soon as the door swung shut, she raced across the half-dead grass toward the seat Zach had just vacated.

"Did you guys see?" she demanded, sliding onto the bench

seat next to Laura Bell. "He did it in neon pink. It looks like a flamingo bled all over the lockers."

"What lockers?" Brant asked, and Leah's gaze narrowed on the player Zach had glanced back at.

"Yours." She nodded to Tanner Abbot. "And Peyton's." Her focus skipped to his girlfriend—who also happened to be Zach's ex-girlfriend, after a very messy breakup right before the winter break.

"Ouch. I thought Zach was over that," Emma whispered, as talk among the players built to a startling crescendo.

"Jealousy festers..." Sabine said, and I nearly choked on the last gulp of Coke from my bottle when she stood, facing the other table. "What'd he write on them?" she called across the quad, and every voice went silent as all heads turned our way.

I wanted to melt into the ground just to escape all the stares, but Sabine stood tall, silently demanding an answer.

Leah hesitated, glancing at Peyton—her friend—in sympathy. But in the end, the spotlight called to her; she could not disappoint her audience. "He wrote, 'skanky nympho whore' on hers, and 'limp-dick traitor' on Tanner's."

For one more, long moment, silence reigned. Then the entire quad broke into laughter and loud, eager commentary, while Peyton and Tanner huddled together in humiliation.

"Never a dull day around here, is there?" Sabine asked, sinking onto the bench again with a huge smile on her face.

She was right about that—nothing had been the same since she'd come to Eastlake.

AFTER SCHOOL, I rode to work with Emma and Alec, glad she had offered to drive, because I wasn't sure I could have stayed awake behind the wheel.

Alec looked just as tired, and when I asked, he admitted he hadn't let himself sleep at all that day, for fear of waking up somewhere other than on my couch, with mud on his shoes and a new hole in his memory.

The Thursday night crowd was enough to keep me awake and on my feet for the first half of the evening at the Cinemark, but during my break, I went to check on Alec and discovered that he'd already gone on his. I started my search in the parking lot, where he usually napped in the car on his breaks.

Unfortunately, Emma's car was empty.

When I didn't find him anywhere else in the lot, I headed back inside and glanced into the break room, then called his name outside of all the men's rooms. But Alec was gone, and he wouldn't have wandered off without telling me. Not after what we'd figured out the night before.

Think, Kaylee! I demanded, leaning against the closed door of theater two. My heart was beating too hard, and I was starting to sweat, in spite of the enthusiastic air-conditioning. *If Avari really has him, he'll be looking for someone sleeping.* But why would anyone pay to sleep in a movie theater, when you could sleep at home for free?

Maybe he'd left. Maybe Avari knew we were on to him, so he'd hijacked Alec's body the first chance he got, then simply ditched the theater? Surely a hellion wouldn't care whether or not his host got fired....

I'd taken two steps—on my way to tell my boss I had to leave—when the door to theater two opened so suddenly it slammed into my shoulder. The two college-age men who emerged didn't even notice me in the shadows.

"I swear, I'm gonna fall asleep in there if I don't get some more caffeine and sugar," the shorter, rounder of the pair said, running one hand through pale hair. "This better pay off."

"It will," the taller man said, as they headed toward the lobby and the concession stand. "Dana always leaves these tearjerkers all mushy and willing, 'cause she's grateful her life doesn't suck like the chick in the movie. Don't fall asleep, though. That'll piss them both off, then we'll have sat through an hour and a half of women bonding on screen for nothing."

And as they walked off toward the land of caffeine and sugar, what they were saying truly sank into my exhausted, frustrated brain. If a chick flick could bore them to sleep, it could bore some other poor jerk to sleep. Which made theater two my best bet for finding Alec, assuming Avari had actually caught him asleep at the wheel. Literally.

I pulled open the doors and rushed up the steeply inclined walkway toward the front of the theater, then had to pause to let my eyes adjust to the darkness. Fortunately, theater two was one of the smaller spaces, so it didn't take me long to find a familiar, close-cropped head of curls about two-thirds of the way up, several seats from the right-hand aisle.

I made my way up the steps slowly, but he saw me before I got there. Unfortunately, in the dark, I couldn't see his expression, so I had no clue whether I was looking at Avari or Alec. Or whether lights would have made any difference.

"Hey," Alec's voice said, as I sank into the chair next to him, and I took a deep, silent breath. My heart raced. It was Avari. It had to be. Why else would Alec waste his dinner break watching a six-week-old movie about middle-aged women rediscovering their lost youth?

I was even more convinced when I noticed that the man in front of him was snoring softly, while his wife munched on popcorn, oblivious.

But I had to be sure.

"What color was my first bike?" I whispered.

Alec's head turned toward me slowly, and my pulse tripped faster. "I'm sorry?"

My heart leaped into my throat, and I had to swallow it to speak. "I know it's you. Let Alec go. Now."

Alec only blinked, and my hands clenched around the armrests. Then, finally, he nodded, and the voice that replied was all hellion, oddly muted but rendered no less terrifying by the whispered volume.

"Ms. Cavanaugh, how delightful to see you again, without all the pretense."

Hearing his voice left no room for doubt—it was really Avari. I'd known that, deep down. But knowing it and experiencing it were two completely different things, which I didn't discover until I found myself staring into the unfamiliar depths of a familiar pair of deep brown eyes, lit only by the flicker of the big screen.

"Get out," I repeated, whispering through clenched teeth.

"Oh, I don't think so." Avari leaned Alec's head so close his lips brushed my ear, and my skin crawled. But I didn't dare pull away, for fear that he'd only come closer. "Alec has been very difficult to get ahold of lately, and I'm disinclined to let him go, now that I finally have him."

"You can't stay in there forever," I insisted softly, resisting the urge to rub the chill bumps popping up on my arms.

His hand settled over my wrist, as if he knew what I was thinking. "No, not forever. But I have quite a bit of energy stored up at the moment—thanks to our friend Alec—so I can hang on more than long enough to replace the meal you've interrupted." He waved one dark hand toward the man sleeping in front of him in an eerily graceful motion, which looked very wrong on Alec's strong young body.

I jerked my hand from beneath his in horror. He'd already been feeding. But with any luck, my interruption had saved the poor idiot's life, if nothing else.

"Get out!" I demanded, forgetting to whisper, and the lady in front of me turned to glare.

"Or you'll what?" Avari leaned close again. "Dump popcorn all over this badly tailored, ill-fitting uniform?"

And that's when I realized I had no idea what to do next.

My plan only went far enough to expose the hellion's presence. How the hell was I supposed to get rid of Avari? I didn't have anything to hit him with, and I couldn't afford to make a scene in the theater, anyway.

Or could I?

"Is this really what my proxy has been reduced to?" he asked. "Serving greasy concessions to the masses in ugly shirts and pleated pants. I think he was better off in the Nether. With me."

"Well, I don't think so, and neither does he."

The hellion chuckled, and the smooth, dark sound wound its way up my spine, promising me pain and pleasure so hopelessly intertwined that I knew if I gave into it, at least I'd die smiling. "Is that what he told you? That he's the victim here, rather than a full partner? He didn't happen to mention the fee he gets for renting out his body?"

"Fee?" He was lying. He had to be. Alec didn't have to tell me anything about Avari's new hobby, but he'd volunteered the information. He wouldn't have done that if he were a willing participant, right?

"He didn't tell you he gets a portion of the energy from each one?"

In fact, he'd claimed the exact opposite. "You're lying."

Another laugh, and this time his breath stirred my hair, warm and damp on my earlobe. "Ms. Cavanaugh, you are charming, even in your ignorance. I have many, many talents. Some that defy description in any human vocabulary, and more's the pity. But lying is not among them. Hellions cannot lie."

But if that were a lie itself, wouldn't that mean that everything else he'd said was, too?

I shook my head, confused. So I clung to what I knew without a doubt. I wasn't sure I could trust Alec, but I was sure I *couldn't* trust Avari.

"Get out right now, or I'll scream for security," I hissed, leaning into him this time, in spite of the discomfort crawling up my spine. "I'll tell them you assaulted me, and you can spend the rest of your time here in jail, getting to know an entirely different portion of the 'masses.'"

I had Sabine and her criminal history to thank for that little stroke of genius.

Alec's thick, dark brows arched dramatically in the flickering light from the screen. "I don't believe you'd do that to your friend."

"Believe it. Alec would rather wake up in jail when you've exhausted your resources than be an unwilling participant in another of your murders."

Plus, I could always recant my accusation later, without hurting anything but my own credibility.

"So what'll it be? Home sweet Netherworld, or the inside of the Tarrant County jail?"

"People have to sleep in jail, right?" Avari smiled, and I decided to call his bluff.

"Maybe. But I hear most people are bailed out pretty quickly, so you'd probably be the only overnight guest." No need to mention that my knowledge of the inner workings of the adult justice system came entirely from television. "And considering that you haven't had a good meal recently, I'm guessing you won't be able to hold out that long. Am I right?"

Avari's borrowed smile faded slowly. "You know I will be back."

I shrugged, trying to look like I wasn't scared out of my mind and sweating beneath my "ill-fitting" uniform. "Not if I can help it."

"But you cannot help—not Alec, and not yourself. You're in over your head, little *bean sidhe,* and if you are not careful, I'd venture that someone will be happy to relieve you of that pretty little head entirely. In just…one…bite."

I clutched the seat between us to keep my hand from shaking as his eyes flashed with malice and the promise of pain, in the sudden bright glow from the movie screen.

"Until next time, Ms. Cavanaugh…"

Then Alec's eyes closed. His hands relaxed and his head fell onto the cushioned back of his chair. He snored lightly.

I sucked in a deep breath, then let it out slowly, trying to purge my fear with the used air. Then I shook him awake.

Alec sat upright in a single, startled movement. His eyes widened, and he glanced around the darkened theater in wild panic, gripping the armrests almost hard enough to crack the cup holders.

"It's okay," I whispered, and he whirled in his chair to face me, shocked eyes still round, pupils drastically dilated.

"Kaylee?" He swallowed, and his Adam's apple bobbed. "It happened again?"

I nodded. "First, what color was my first bike?"

Alec blinked. "White, with red ribbons."

My whole body relaxed with my next exhale, though I knew I'd already used up my entire break, plus some. "Thank goodness. Yeah, it happened again. Let's get out of here." I stood and pulled him down the steps by one hand, moving so fast I almost tripped us both. In the wide hallway between theaters, I tugged him into a corner of the unused secondary concession stand.

"I'm late, so here's the short version—you must have fallen asleep on your break, and Avari got in. He found some guy sleeping during the chick flick in theater two and was chowing down on some human life force when I found you. Er… *him*. I threatened to have him arrested if he didn't vacate your personal premises immediately."

"And that worked?"

I shrugged. "I may have exaggerated how long he'd be in jail, and how alone he'd be, with no one to feed on."

Alec frowned. "What were you going to have him arrested for?"

I glanced at the sticky ground beneath my feet, avoiding his eyes. "Inappropriate, unwelcome contact with a minor."

"Sexual assault?" Alec hissed. "You were going to get me arrested for groping a sixteen-year-old girl in the back of a theater? Are you *insane?*"

I bristled over his use of my least favorite nonmedical descriptor, but I had to admit that hearing it aloud made it sound pretty bad. "It was just a bluff," I insisted, staring up into his horrified eyes. "And anyway, I would have recanted."

"Kaylee…"

"What else was I supposed to do?" I demanded. "I didn't have anything to hit you with, and I couldn't just let him use you to kill that poor man."

"Fine." But he didn't look like it was fine, and the longer he stared at me in horror, the guiltier I felt. "Just promise me you'll come up with some better threats. Preferably nothing that'll get me arrested."

"I swear. And you have to promise not to fall asleep by yourself."

"That's a lot harder than it sounds, you know."

"I remember. I spent days trying to stay awake, to keep you from dragging me into the Netherworld in my dreams."

"I *said* I was sorry about that." Alec groaned.

"And I'm sorry about this. But I gotta go. I spent my whole break talking to a hellion in the back of the theater."

Alec flinched. "I'll make it up to you."

But I didn't see how that was even possible. I started walking back toward the concession stand, where my shift was tragically Emma-less—she'd gotten stuck in one of the ticket booths—then stopped when something else occurred to me.

"Alec?"

"Yeah?" He turned, halfway to the break room, and followed when I gestured toward the shadowed alcove housing a supply closet.

"Avari said you're in on this. That you're his partner, and that you're getting a portion of the energy from each of his kills."

Alec frowned. "Kay, would I be this exhausted if I were getting any of that energy?"

Oh, yeah. Still, exhaustion could be faked… "He also said hellions can't lie. That's total BS, right?" I asked, trying in vain to think of a time Avari had lied to me. But I came up blank.

Alec's frown deepened. "Actually, that part's true."

"Then how could he say…?"

"That I was his partner in this new serial slaying?" Alec finished for me, and I nodded. "He probably didn't. Hellions can't tell an outright lie, but they're very, very good at implying things and letting people draw their own conclusions. Did he actually *say* I was in on it? Or did he just ask leading questions, then fail to correct your assumption?"

I thought hard, but I couldn't remember. The whole encounter was indistinct now, but for the memory of his hand over my arm, the sickening warmth of his breath on my ear, and the skin-crawling revulsion I'd felt over both.

What kind of world was I living in, where the only people who never lied to me were the ones out to steal either my soul or my boyfriend?

17

THAT NIGHT, AFTER my father went to sleep, Alec came into my room and we took turns sleeping in two-hour shifts. True to her word, Sabine stayed out of my head, but because Avari had made no such deal with Alec, and especially since I'd evicted him from his earlier occupation, I shook him awake every time he so much as grunted in his sleep, and every single time, I made him tell me what color my first bicycle was.

He passed the test each time. We'd dodged a bullet, but I was far from sure we'd be able to do the same thing night after night. Especially considering how exhausted I was the next morning, after nearly a week without a decent night's sleep.

Friday was a blur of desks, textbooks, and piercing school bells, made even more miserable because Nash ignored both me and Sabine again. All day long. And I have to admit that once I was sure no more teachers had died, I kind of mentally checked out of the school day. I was just too tired to concentrate.

Until some sophomore, bitter over not making the basket-ball season cheerleading squad, was caught dumping bleach from the custodian's closet all over the cheerleader uniforms hanging at the back of the team sponsor's classroom during lunch. That woke the whole school up.

As Principal Goody escorted a gaggle of pissed-off cheerleaders to the office to call their parents, she stopped in the hall and I heard her tell the team coach she'd be glad when this week was over.

I knew exactly how she felt.

That night, I had to work, with neither Emma nor Alec to keep me company. After my shift, I checked my phone for missed calls and found a voice mail from Nash. I listened to it in my car, in the dark, with nothing to distract me from the intimate sound of his voice in my ear.

"Hey, it's me," he said, and just hearing from Nash made my chest ache, after two days of near-silence from him. "I'm sorry about the other day. Are you working? You wanna come over tonight? Just to talk? We could order a pizza, and Mom made some of those fudge cookies before she left for work."

He paused, and my sigh was the most pathetic sound I'd ever heard.

"Anyway, I figured if I invited you, you wouldn't feel like you had to sneak in under the cover of…Tod. Give me a call?"

Then the phone went silent in my hand.

I dropped my cell onto the passenger seat and started the engine. Then I turned the car off and stared out the windshield.

Nothing had changed. Nash was still recovering from a serious frost addiction, I was still trying to forgive him for what he'd done, and his ex was still marching toward a very messy boyfriend coup.

But then again, maybe nothing *would* change until I gave him a real chance to make things better. Maybe I never would be able to move on until I either forgave him or let him go.

And I desperately didn't want to let him go.

I'll just stay for a few minutes. I'll have one slice of pizza. And maybe a cookie. A cookie never hurt anyone, right?

Besides, I hadn't had a chance yet to tell him what was going on with Alec, because he'd been avoiding both me and Sabine at school. So I'd stay for a few minutes. An hour, tops.

I'd definitely be home before curfew....

Twenty-five minutes later, I knocked on Nash's door, suddenly wishing I'd changed out of my uniform shirt. I'd considered it during the drive, but in the end I dismissed the thought—dressing up might send the wrong message.

If I came in my uniform, he'd know I was just there to talk. That I wasn't trying to look good or to take things beyond that first crucial private conversation. I'd made the right choice.

But I still wished I'd changed.

Nash opened the door in nothing but a pair of jeans, and suddenly I wished *he'd* changed. He was really hard to talk to when he wasn't fully clothed.

A relieved smile lit up his face when he saw me, and I couldn't resist a small grin of my own. "I didn't think you were coming." He stepped back to let me in. "I called three hours ago."

"I was at work. They make us leave our phones in our lockers." But even after my shift, I hadn't called to let him know I was coming because I wasn't sure I'd actually go through with it until I rang the doorbell. Being alone with Nash was hard. Even without his Influence working in his favor—which he'd sworn would never happen again—he was temptation on two feet. When I was with him, I wanted to touch him, and when I touched him, I wanted to touch him some more, but that would lead to all things sweaty and illogical, and logic was the only weapon I could deploy against the lure that was Nash, and the traitor that was my own heart.

He closed the door at my back, then leaned against it, and my pulse rushed in my ears as I pulled off my jacket and dropped it on the back of a chair. "Did you eat?" he asked, while I stood there like an idiot in the middle of his living room.

"Just some popcorn on my break."

"I'll call for pizza."

While he dialed, I sat on the couch and tried to get comfortable. We'd never really hung out in his living room, but I wanted to make it clear that I had no business in his bedroom. Not tonight. Not while we were still feeling things out. Figuratively.

When he hung up, Nash sat next to me, and I twisted to face him, leaning against the arm of the couch with my back to the end table lamp. Light from over my shoulder lit his face enough for me to see the browns and greens in his eyes, alternately twisting contentedly and churning with nerves.

I was relieved to realize he was nervous, too. He understood that he was getting a second chance, and he obviously didn't want to mess it up.

"Hey, I thought you should know you were right about Sabine."

He shook his head slowly. "I don't want to talk about Sabine."

"I'm just saying, she didn't kill them."

"I know. I still don't want to talk about her."

I smiled. "Looks like we still have things in common."

"I sure hope so." He reached out for my hand and curled his fingers around mine, and my pulse leaped just like it had the first time we'd touched. How could it possibly feel just like that still?

I hesitated, tempted to drop the subject and continue exploring a potential reunion. But Nash deserved to know the truth, and frankly, I didn't like the pressure or responsibility that came with being the only one who knew Alec's secret. "Wait, there's more," I insisted.

"I like more…" His eyes flashed, and my heart beat harder.

"It's Alec," I said, and Nash froze.

"What's Alec?" He pulled his fingers from my light grip and scowled. "You and Alec…?"

"No!" I rolled my eyes and crossed my arms over my chest. "Why does everyone keep saying that? He's *old,* no matter how young he looks!" And he had much more important things on his mind than dating. I took a deep breath. "Alec killed them. The teachers." I frowned. "Well, not him, exactly. It was actually Avari, but he was using Alec's body. It's kind of a long story."

"Then you should probably talk fast." Nash's irises churned too fast for me to isolate individual emotions, but his lips were pressed thin, his hand clenched around the back of the couch.

"Okay. It turns out that Alec's only half human. His other half is hypnos, and Avari somehow scraped together enough power to possess Alec and feed through him. Which only gives him more power. And evidently kills people."

Guess that wasn't such a long story, after all.

Nash's frown could have blotted out the sun. "And he's sleeping on your couch?"

Actually, now he was sleeping half the night in my bedroom, where I could watch him for signs of possession. But all I said was, "He's not really sleeping much at all, since we figured out what was going on."

"Kaylee, you have to tell your dad."

I shook my head. "He'll kick him out."

"That's kind of the point."

"No, Nash. If my dad kicks Alec out, who's going to make sure he doesn't get possessed and kill someone else?"

"Let your dad worry about that." I started to shake my head again, but Nash cut me off. "If you don't tell him, I will. This is too dangerous, Kay. Swear you'll tell him. Tonight."

And finally I nodded, feeling almost as relieved to be free from the responsibility as I felt guilty over having to break a promise to Alec. "Fine. I swear."

Nash's hand relaxed on the back of the couch and he slouched a little, obviously more at ease now that he had my promise.

"So…how are you?" I asked, ready for a subject change. I didn't want to bring up the issue that had separated us in the first place, but I felt like I should know how he was doing. For real. I *wanted* to know.

"I'm better now." Now that I was here. He didn't say it, but we both heard it. Then the heat in his gaze gave way to a different kind of intensity. "Kaylee, I'm so sorry for everything that happened. I wish I could take it all back. I wish I could do so many things differently…."

I squeezed his hand. "Nash, you can stop apologizing."

"But you haven't forgiven me."

"Not for lack of apologies." I glanced at our intertwined fingers, enjoying the familiar warmth and the way our palms seemed to fit together. "It's just a lot to deal with. Doug died because we did too little, and we did it too late. And Scott probably wishes he were dead."

Surely lifeless oblivion would be better than living with Avari's voice constantly in your head, telling you things you don't want to know, demanding you do things no sane person would do….

His hand tightened around mine, and his gaze seemed to burn a hole right through me. "What else can I do?"

"I don't think there's anything else you *can* do," I whispered. "It'll just take time. And for now, this is nice." I tried on a small smile and held up our linked hands, but Nash only frowned.

"Nice is good, but it's not enough. I want you back for real. I want to talk to you at lunch, instead of staring at you while you eat. I want to see the smile on your face and know I put it there. I want to hear your dad's voice get all low and pissed off, like it only does when I've stayed over too late."

I grinned. No one could piss off my dad like Nash.

Except for Tod.

"You know why he sounds like that, don't you?" Nash asked. "It's because he knows how I feel about you, and it scares him. He knows that he's missed most of your life, and you're not a little girl anymore, and I'm proof of that. He knows what I know, and what you'll let yourself know some day—that you love me. And it scares the shit out of him."

I couldn't breathe around the fist-size lump in my throat. That lump was all the words I was dying to say but shouldn't, all rolled up into one word clog, refusing to move. I couldn't let them out—couldn't expose so much of what I really felt while I still wasn't sure I could completely trust him—but I couldn't swallow them, either. Not anymore. Because whether I wanted to say them or not, whether they would actually change anything or not, they were true.

"Kaylee?" Nash's focus shifted between my eyes, searching for something inside me. "You can't tell me there's nothing left for me in there. I know there is. I can see it in your eyes."

"No fair peeking," I mumbled, and he chuckled.

"Nothing about this is fair." He hesitated, swallowing thickly, like he needed something to drink all of a sudden. "I know I don't deserve a second chance, but I'm asking for one. Let me prove how serious I am. Just one more chance."

I stared at him, studying his eyes. And all I found in them was sincerity and heart-bruising need. He meant it.

So instead of answering, instead of *thinking,* I leaned forward and kissed him. For once in my life, I let my heart lead the way, while the rest of me held on tight, helpless and scared, along for the ride.

Nash kissed me back, and it was like we'd never broken up. And for the first time, it seemed possible that we could just pick up where we'd left off and forget all about that messy little pit stop on the path to forever.

But that wasn't right, was it? Was forgetting even possible?

In that moment, I just didn't care about roadblocks thrown up by my brain—my heart and my body were committed to crashing through them. So I set the hard questions aside and focused on Nash. On the way he tasted, and the way he felt. Of the warmth of his fingers wrapped around mine and his free hand sliding up my arm and over my shoulder to cup the back of my head.

My mouth opened against his, and I welcomed him back, while my body welcomed back the heat he awoke in me, which had lain largely dormant over the past three weeks. But Nash was very careful, his eagerness very controlled. He was hyperaware of my boundaries, and reluctant to even approach them after what had happened the last time.

His caution was both blessing and curse. It was like trying to scratch an itch with gloves on—his passive caresses only made me want more. And maybe that was the point. Maybe he was leaving it all up to me, how far we went and when. Which would have been awesome, if I weren't trying to quench a thirst for him which had been building for the past twenty-one days.

"Nash..." I groaned, when his mouth finally left mine to travel down my neck.

"Too fast?" He started to pull back, but I wouldn't let him.

"No. I just wanted to say your name without being mad."

He grinned and leaned with his forehead against mine. "That's my favorite way to hear it. But this *is* too fast. We have to slow down, or we're going to wind up in the same position again—without the frost. Or the Influence," he added, when I frowned.

"But you're not…"

"Kaylee, *I* need to slow down."

"Oh." I tried to banish disappointment from my voice, but he heard it, anyway, and I think that made it worse for him—knowing that I wanted more. But he was doing the right thing, and so should I. "Um…okay. I'm gonna get a Coke. You want one?" I stood, straightening my shirt.

"Yeah. There's some in the fridge."

I'd made it halfway across the room when a car rumbled to a stop outside, and a wash of bright light traveled across the living room through the front window. "Must be the pizza." Nash stood, already digging his wallet from his back pocket, and I shoved open the swinging door into the kitchen, pleasantly surprised by the quick delivery.

But when I pulled open the fridge, a familiar, disembodied voice spoke to me from the other side of the door. "It's not the pizza," Tod said, and I slammed the door shut without grabbing the cans. But the kitchen was completely empty.

"Where are you?" I demanded in a whisper, as the front door creaked open from the living room. "And how do you know it's not the delivery guy?"

Tod suddenly appeared between me and his mom's small kitchen table, wearing a royal blue polo with a stylized pizza—missing one slice—embroidered on the left side of his chest. "Because I have your pizza right here, and I didn't drive."

I laughed. I couldn't help it. An undead reaper was one thing. But an undead pizza delivery driver? The jokes wouldn't stop coming.

"It's not funny!" Tod snapped. "This was your idea."

"I was joking!" I hissed, opening the fridge again.

"Well, I wasn't. Being dead doesn't have to mean mooching off all my friends, right?" he said, and I shrugged, pulling two cold cans from the top shelf. "Plus, you were right about the free pizza."

I couldn't resist another grin. "So…is there a family discount?"

"Hell, no. Nash is paying full price. Plus tip."

Before I could reply, hushed voices from the living room caught my attention. "Who's that?" I demanded, setting the sodas on the table. I headed for the swinging door, but Tod grabbed my arm before I'd made it two steps.

"It's her, isn't it? That's Sabine's car? You saw her?"

He nodded reluctantly, brushing a curl from his forehead. I started forward again, and again he pulled me back. "Let go. What, you're on her side now?"

"I'm just trying to keep this from going bad, fast."

"Shh…" I said, when I realized I could make out words from the other room.

"Kaylee's here?" Sabine said, obviously refusing to be shushed by Nash. And it's not like she didn't know I was there—my car was in the driveway! "I thought it was just going to be us."

"I didn't think she'd come. Bina, *please* go before she hears you."

I couldn't hear what came next, so I snuck closer to the door. Tod clenched his jaw, but let me go.

"Sabine, no! I'll make it up to you, but you have to go n—"

Then there was no more talking from either of them, and my blood boiled.

I shoved open the swinging kitchen door and froze with my foot holding it open, unable to truly process what I saw. Sabine Campbell had her shirt off, and she'd latched onto Nash like the parasite she really was. She had him pressed against his own front door, her tongue surely halfway down his throat. But the worst part…

He held her shirt, dangling from one fist—and he was kissing her back.

I couldn't speak. I couldn't even form a coherent thought until Tod cleared his throat at my back, and Sabine reluctantly peeled herself off my boyfriend.

Nash's face flamed, but Sabine only grinned. "Hey, Kay. Sorry I'm late to the party, but the more the merrier, right?"

"You two look merry enough without me," I snapped through clenched teeth. Then I stepped forward and let the kitchen door swing through Tod, who barely seemed to notice.

"Kaylee, wait…" Nash pushed Sabine away from him. "I didn't… She…"

"I know. She was all over you like a tick on blood." But I also knew that he hadn't pushed her away. He may not have started it, but he'd let it happen, and I couldn't help wondering, if I hadn't been there, how much farther he would have let it go.

I glanced pointedly at the shirt he still held in one hand, and his cheeks flushed nearly scarlet.

Nash whirled on Sabine and shoved the shirt at her and she took it, reluctantly covering herself. Then he pulled open the front door, grabbed her arm, and shoved her onto the porch, still clutching the material to her chest. "Don't come back," he growled, an instant before slamming the door in her face.

"Kaylee…" He turned to face me, leaning against the door.

"You didn't stop her."

"I was about to…"

"Yeah. You can tell from how far down her throat your

tongue was…" Tod said, sarcasm threaded boldly through each word.

Nash turned on him. "This is none of your business. What are you even doing here?"

"You owe me $15.99. Plus tip."

Nash looked confused until he noticed Tod's uniform. "I'll owe you," he finally snapped. "Get out."

"I'm going, too." I headed for the door as Sabine's car started in the driveway.

"Kaylee, wait."

"Where's her bra?" I asked, my hand already on the door-knob.

Nash closed his eyes and exhaled slowly, miserably. "She wasn't wearing one."

18

"KAYLEE!"

Someone grabbed my shoulder and my head flopped forward as he shook me.

My eyes flew open. Alec stood over me, his hair rendered even darker by the halo of light shining around his skull from the fixture overhead. His brown eyes were wide and worried, his generous lips thinned into a tight frown.

"What?" I wasn't even dreaming, much less having a nightmare. In fact, he'd interrupted the first almost-peaceful sleep I could remember getting in the past few days.

And even as that thought faded, I realized the problem—I was supposed to be watching him, not dozing. I'd insisted that he take the first shift sleeping under the assumption that my dad would get back from my uncle's house—where they were conferring about the sudden spike in the teacher mortality rate at Eastlake—while Alec was still asleep. That way I could explain about Avari's murder-by-proxy without having to break my promise to Alec to his face.

Obviously I'd underestimated my own exhaustion.

"Sorry." I sat up and wiped an embarrassing dribble from the corner of my mouth. "Is my dad home yet?"

"No," Alec said, and I glanced at my alarm clock in surprise. It was just after midnight. "Kaylee, this isn't going to work." He sank onto the edge of my rumpled bedspread, broad shoulders sagging in frustration and obvious fatigue. "How are we supposed to watch each other if neither of us can stay awake?"

"I'm fine," I insisted, standing to stretch. "I just need some coffee."

"If you guzzle caffeine, you won't be able to sleep when it's your turn, either, and that'll just make everything worse." Alec hesitated, and I read dread clearly in his expression. "You're gonna have to tie me up."

"What? No." I sat on the edge of my desk and pushed tangled hair back from my face, hoping I'd heard him wrong. "I'm not going to tie you up, or down, or any other direction!"

"Kay, I don't think we have any choice. Avari's just waiting for a chance to get back into my head, and how happy do you think Sabine's going to be with you, after her little stunt tonight failed?"

I'd given him the short version of my visit with Nash, skipping my promise to fill my dad in on everything.

"If either of us falls asleep at the wrong time, things are going to get a whole lot worse."

My tired brain whirred, trying to come up with a viable alternative, but in the end, I was too worn out to think clearly, much less argue. Survival and a good night's sleep trumped my deep-seated aversion to restraints—born of my week-long stay in the mental health ward—so I finally relented and trudged into the garage for the coil of nylon rope looped over a long nail on the wall.

In my room again, I turned my stereo on and cranked the volume, hoping the noise would keep me awake. Then Alec helped me cut the rope into workable sections and showed me how to tie a proper knot. Evidently he'd had practice restraining...things...for Avari in the Netherworld.

I bet the hellion never thought that particular skill could be used against him, and that thought made me smile, in spite of encroaching exhaustion, and the disturbing reality of what I was about to do.

The plan was for me to tie Alec to the chair in one corner of my room—the one I'd woken up in—but the back was one solid, padded, curved piece of wood, with nothing to tie his hands to. The desk chair was no better, and since I wasn't willing to tie him up in the living room, where my dad would see him before I'd had a chance to explain, our only other option was my bed.

I cannot begin to describe my mortification—or the flames burning beneath every square inch of my skin—when I knelt at the head of my bed to secure Alec's right arm to my headboard. "It's okay, Kaylee," he insisted, head craned so he could watch me while he voluntarily submitted to something that would have sent me into a blind panic. "This'll keep us both safe."

"I know." But I didn't like it, and my revulsion didn't fade when I tied his other hand, or bound his first foot to the metal frame beneath the end of my mattress. I had trouble with the final knot, but had almost secured his right ankle when a sudden hair-prickling feeling and a subtle shift in the light told me that someone was behind me.

"What in the hell are you doing?" my father demanded, his voice low and dark.

I whirled around so fast I fell onto one knee, and the end of the rope trailed through my fingers to hang slack. My dad stood in my doorway, his irises swirling furiously in some perilous combination of anger and bewilderment.

The music had covered his footsteps, and evidently the sound of his car.

"Maybe this wasn't such a good idea," Alec mumbled at my back, and my father's harsh laugh sounded more like an angry bark.

"Considering your current predicament, I'm betting that's the first smart thing you've said all night!"

"This isn't what it looks like." I frowned and shoved myself to my feet, then glanced back at Alec, who could only stare at me in humiliation. "Actually, I'm not sure what it looks like," I admitted, turning back to my father. "It's to keep us both safe…" I ended lamely, wishing I could just melt into my bedroom carpet and disappear.

"Safe from what?" my father demanded softly.

"From…" I closed my eyes and took a deep breath, then met his stare again and started over. "I was gonna tell you everything when you got home. Nash made me promise."

Behind me, Alec shifted on the bed—as best he could, with three limbs bound to it—and I could practically taste his anxiety.

"What does Nash have to do with you tying Alec to your bed?" But honestly, he looked like he didn't really want to know the answer to that.

I perched on the corner of my desk and turned off my stereo. "I'm assuming you want the short version…."

"That would be good."

So I sucked in another deep breath, then spat the whole thing out. "Avari's been possessing Alec and killing my teachers—we have no idea why he picked teachers—so we've been sleeping in shifts for the past couple of nights, to stop it from happening again. But now I'm so tired that I can't stay awake—" no need to tell him about Sabine just yet, since she wasn't immediately relevant to the hellion or the dead teachers "—so Alec thought I should tie him up, in case I fall asleep and Avari gets back into his body. You know, to keep everybody safe." I shrugged miserably, then watched my father, waiting for the fireworks.

"I don't even know where to start," he said. But he got over that pretty quickly. "Avari's the one killing teachers?" he said, and I nodded. "And he's using Alec to do it?" Another nod from me. "And you've known this for two days without telling me?"

"I was afraid you'd kick him out. And even if it were okay to do that to a friend—and it's not—if you kick him out, there won't be anyone around to make sure Avari can't use him as a murder weapon again," I finished, proud of my own coherence, considering how incredibly tired I was.

For several moments, my father stood mute, obviously thinking. Then his focus shifted from me to Alec. "Those teachers died without a mark on them," he said, and I could see in the angry, frustrated line of his jaw that he'd come to the right conclusion, with far fewer clues than I'd needed. "What are you?"

"I'm half hypnos." Alec met my father's gaze unflinchingly— his species wasn't his fault, after all—but looked genuinely sorry for the danger he'd involuntarily exposed us all to.

"Please tell me your other half is human," my father said, and Alec and I both nodded.

My dad sighed and pulled a folding knife from his back pocket. "Well, Kaylee, you're right about one thing—we can't leave him on his own. Not unless we want the next blood spilled to fall on our hands."

My relief was almost as strong as my confusion when he strode forward purposefully and cut Alec's left ankle free.

"Mr. Cavanaugh, it's not safe to let me sleep free," Alec insisted, as my father rounded toward the head of the bed.

"Which is precisely why you won't be sleeping in my daughter's room." He slashed the rope around Alec's left arm, then leaned over him to repeat the process with the remaining knot. "Ever."

A few minutes later, we all stood in the living room, my father unwinding a new rope he'd produced from a pile of not-yet-unpacked cardboard boxes in the garage. Alec sank into my dad's recliner and positioned a pillow beneath his head, then my father tied his feet to the metal frame of the foldout ottoman. While I spread a blanket over our poor houseguest, my dad pulled Alec's arms toward the back of the recliner, where he tied his wrists to each other, linked by a taut length of nylon spanning the back of the chair.

But even with this new precaution and my dad's much sturdier knot work, he wasn't willing to let Alec sleep alone, just in case. So when I finally headed to bed at almost one in the morning, my father was settling onto the couch with his pillow and a throw blanket, determined to protect us all from the most recent Netherworld threat. Even in his sleep.

"He kicked her out topless?" Emma shoved her spoon into the pint of Phish Food and dug out a chocolate fish, her brown eyes shining in the light pouring in through the kitchen window. After a long, mostly sleepless night, Saturday morning had dawned bright and clear, in blatant disrespect of my foul mood.

Fortunately, Emma had come bearing ice cream. Two reserve pints sat in the freezer.

I nodded, letting my bite melt in my mouth. Chocolate may not cure everything, but it goes down a lot better than any other medicine I've ever tasted.

The front door opened before I could respond, and Alec walked in, carrying a newspaper under one arm, nose dripping from the cold. He closed the door, then noticed us in the kitchen.

Before he could speak, I pointed the business end of my spoon at him and said, "Where were you? You weren't on the schedule today." He'd been gone when I woke up, both the ropes and bedding stowed somewhere out of sight.

Alec dropped the newspaper on the kitchen counter. "Apartment shopping."

My eyes narrowed. "I thought you didn't have the money yet."

"I don't. But I will soon, thanks to the new job." And I had a feeling that after the big revelation, my father had suggested Alec move forward with his plans for financial and residential independence.

Still... I wasn't taking any chances after meeting Avari at the theater. "Just humor me. What color was my first bicycle?"

"White, with red ribbons," he replied, without hesitation.

"What's with the twenty questions?" Em asked, scraping the inside edge of the carton with her spoon.

I shoved another bite in my mouth, buying time to think. But Alec was faster. "It's this stupid trivia game." He winked at me. "I'm winning."

"Oh, I wanna play!" Em said, sitting straighter. "What was the name of my first bra?"

I nearly choked on my bite. "You named your first bra?"

She frowned. "You didn't?" When I could only laugh, she turned to Alec. "You gonna guess?"

He hesitated, pretending to think. "I gotta go with Helga."

She threw the ice cream lid at him. Alec laughed, then dropped it into the trash. "One carton of Ben & Jerry's, two girls, two spoons. I'm guessing this is about Nash?"

Emma nodded, watching as Alec took off his jacket and draped it over the half wall between the kitchen and the entry.

She'd made no secret of the fact that she thought he was hot, and I couldn't exactly tell her he was nearly three times her age.

Alec raised one brow and grinned. "Isn't the ice cream therapy thing kinda cliché?"

I shook my head. "It's a classic for a reason."

"And that reason is 'cause we're underage," Em insisted. "If I could've gotten my hands on anything stronger last night, we'd be recovering from strawberry daiquiri therapy this very moment."

He laughed, heading for the silverware drawer. "So, is this girl-only ice cream, or can a sympathetic guy get a bite?"

Emma leaned over the table much farther than she had to for her next bite, to be sure he could see down her shirt. "What's mine is yours."

I kicked her under the table, as Alec dug in the fridge for a soda. He was older than her mother! And he was currently being used as the murder weapon for a Netherworld demon. Not that she knew any of that.

One more point in favor of full disclosure. I was probably going to have to tell Emma soon....

"What?" Em pouted, then licked ice cream from her spoon with it inverted over her tongue.

"That's *all* you're gonna share with him," I whispered

She stuck her tongue out at me, then took another bite.

"What were you doing at Nash's, anyway?" Alec asked, taking the chair on my other side. I think Emma scared him. Thank goodness.

"Makin' up."

Em grinned. "More like makin' out."

"Not that it matters now."

"Why?" Alec dug in, his small spoon dwarfed by both of

ours. Obviously an ice cream drama rookie. "If *she* kissed *him,* what's the problem?"

I stared at him like he'd just volunteered for a lobotomy. "He kissed her back. I saw it. He didn't push her away. He let her take her shirt off and stick her tongue down his throat."

Alec licked his spoon, then set it on the table and popped his drink open. "Okay, I may be breaking some kind of girl-bonding rule or something, but can I offer you a guy's perspective on this?"

I frowned, my spoon halfway to my mouth. "Is this gonna make me want to hit you?"

He shrugged. "Maybe. But it's the truth. Here goes: kissing back is instinct. Unless the girl smells like a sewer or has tentacles feeling you up independently, a guy's first instinct is to kiss back. That's how it works. What's important is how long that kissing back lasted. So…how long?"

"You can't be serious." I could feel my temper building like the first spark in what could soon be a roaring blaze. "You think it's *okay* for him to kiss her back just because she isn't hideous? Aesthetically speaking." I was no suffragette, but I was pretty sure the he-can't-control-himself defense was a big, stinky load of horseshit.

"No." Alec held up one hand defensively. "But I also don't think it's okay for you to condemn him, if he was the innocent kissee, rather than the instigator of said kiss."

I rolled my eyes. "Fine. He wasn't the instigator."

Alec nodded, obviously pleased with the progress. "Did she know you were there?"

"She parked right behind my car."

"And he kicked her out, right?" Emma added, catching on.

"Yeah. And he told her not to come back."

Alec turned to Emma, and she couldn't resist another grin. "Are you hearing what I'm hearing?"

"Yup." Alec met my gaze. "This was for your benefit, not his. She set you both up, and did everything she could to make you think he wanted it. And *you…*"

My frown deepened. "You think I'm overreacting?"

Alec shrugged again and dug in for another bite. "I wasn't there. But it sounds to me like you at least owe him a chance to explain."

I hesitated. Long enough for two more bites. "Maybe." But I just wasn't sure I had any more chances for Nash left in me.

I'M AT MY DESK with my laptop open, scouring the internet for a good price on a spray can of mara repellent, when the room suddenly feels wrong at my back. I don't turn. I don't even look up, because I know neither one will help. For several long seconds, we both pretend I don't know he's there. That the back of my neck isn't prickling with fear.

Finally he says my name and I can't ignore him. I slowly close my laptop and swivel in my rolling desk chair to confront the impossible.

"You can't be here." Yet me knowing that hasn't prevented it from happening.

"Surprise," Avari says, and he sounds truly thrilled. Somehow he's managed to cross into the human world in his own body, and as far as I'm concerned, he brought hell with him.

The hellion looks different than I remember him, but that's no surprise. Hellions can look like whatever they want, with one exception: they cannot replicate the exact form of any other living or deceased being. There will always be some small difference—finding that difference is the key.

At least, that used to be the rule. But if he can cross over now, do any of the other rules still apply?

Avari is now shorter than I remember him, with lighter hair. But he hasn't bothered to change his voice, and his eyes are still the featureless ebony orbs I can't forget—spheres of chaos and infinity. Madness at a glance.

"Get out." It's all my overwhelmed brain can come up with while the rest of me fights the waves of fear and despair emanating from him like radiation from ground zero.

"Not until I have what I want."

I don't ask, because I know what he wants: me. But I don't know why, and he's never felt inclined to explain. Hellions can be bargained with—I've seen that firsthand—but they never give information for free, and I'm not willing to pay.

"So how does this work?"

He takes a step toward me, and I stand, my heart beating frantically. I want to retreat, but there's nowhere to go. My desk is already cutting into my spine. "I grab you, then I drag you kicking and screaming into the Nether, where I'll take good care of you—until the next new toy comes along."

"And how are you planning to keep me there?" I'm impressed by my own nerve. I was stalling—for what? The cavalry? A brilliant idea?—but also digging for important information.

"Oh, after a couple of hours with me, you won't have the strength to cross over. You won't sleep and you won't eat until I've broken your mind as well as your body, and after that... Well, it simply won't matter what happens to you after that. You'll never know the difference."

"You won't break me." I sound much more sure than I really am. I have this strange calm now. It almost feels like acceptance. I can't fight him, and I won't scream for help and doom my would-be hero. And that means he's won, before the fight even begins. So what's the point in fighting?

Then he's in front of me, and his hands have become wicked claws. He grabs my arm and his claws sink through my wrist, and suddenly I remember the point in fighting.

Pain, the moment he touches me, and not just where he rips through my flesh. I double over, struggling to breathe through an agony like electricity being run through me. He is the lightning and I am the rod, and the strike never ends.

Pain everywhere. I smell my skin cooking, hear my hair crackle as the follicles pop from the heat. In the mirror, I see no change, but I feel every single bit of it, like life is fire and I am the fuel, forever burning but never quite consumed. He can make me hurt in every cell of my body with a single touch. He will do this for eternity, if I go with him.

And he hasn't even started on my mind yet.

NO! I'm screaming now, the magic word. They teach us in preschool. If something bad happens, shout NO! and parents will come running. If a stranger touches you, shout NO! and the police will take him away. You can always shout NO! and there will always be someone there to protect you.

But that's a lie. No one comes. NO! is a lie, and safety is a lie, and the only truths are pain and forever, and pain is everywhere, and forever has already begun.

He pulls my arm, and the pain doubles, though that shouldn't be possible, because how can you double infinity? I fall to the ground, because I can no longer stand. I can no longer think. I can only feel, and hurt, and scream, and know that it will never end. And that my grand delusions of resistance are like wielding a breath of air against a brick wall. There is nothing I can do. Giving in will not stop the pain. Begging will not stop the pain. In the end, even dying will not stop the pain.

And as my world fades beneath a swirl of gray fog, I know that I am lost, and that I will never, ever be found....

IT WAS STILL dark when I opened my eyes, and the only sound I could hear was my own breathing, too hard and too fast.

Still panicked from the nightmare. I stared up at the ceiling without seeing it, more afraid of the understanding now burrowing its way into my head than the dream I'd just escaped.

It wasn't Sabine. My nightmare about Avari didn't feel like her work—which I was definitely starting to recognize. It wasn't personal enough. There was no angst and no self-doubt, the primary colors of her dream palette.

This dream felt like...Avari. Like the hellion was playing with my mind, messing with my very psyche. But that was impossible, right? Hellions couldn't give people nightmares. Could they?

In the dark, as my breathing gradually slowed and my pulse calmed, I became aware of another sound, soft and even. Someone else was breathing. In my room.

I turned my head slowly, my heart thumping painfully, and could barely make out a familiar silhouette outlined by the creepy red glow from my alarm clock.

Alec sat in the corner chair. Silent. Watching me, like he'd *been* watching me for quite a while.

Why was he watching me? Why wasn't he tied to the recliner in the living room, which is how he'd started the second night in a row? Where was my dad?

Uh-oh.

"Alec?" But I knew before he answered. I knew from the creepy smile Alec would never wear, and the way his eyes seemed to focus on something *inside* me.

"Bad dream?" he asked, leaning forward to study me closer in the dim light, and I froze at the sound of his voice. Because it wasn't his voice. It was Avari's.

No pretense this time; the hellion was all business. Just like in my dream.

"How did you...?" I started, clenching the top of my comforter.

"How did I get Alec free from those sad little ropes?" Avari finished, and I nodded. I didn't bother ordering him to leave, because I didn't have anything to threaten him with this time without involving—and endangering—my dad. Who'd probably already been both involved and endangered, considering that Avari had somehow gotten past both him and the restraints.

"Waking up bound was a bit of a surprise, I must concede," the hellion said, leaning forward to peer at me through my friend's eyes. "Regrettably, this body does not come with extraordinary strength. Fortunately, your father—or rather, his unconscious form—proved quite useful."

"You possessed my dad?" My hands were damp, and I resisted the urge to wipe cold sweat on my covers. My father was eligible for hellion possession by virtue of having spent time in the Netherworld when Avari had him kidnapped the month before.

"Only long enough to free our dear Alec in his sleep. Your father is now unconscious, and both bound and gagged with his own restraints for my convenience. But he is otherwise unharmed, and I suggest you give me no reason to change that."

My chest ached, and each breath felt like a knife to my heart. There was no one left to help me, and very few ways for me to help myself, without making things worse for both my dad and Alec. Even if I'd been willing to leave my dad, I couldn't run, because if the hellion knew Alec's physiology well enough to make his voice work, he could certainly catch me in the older, stronger body.

Why had he stayed to watch me sleep instead of going out for his usual murder-by-proxy? He couldn't really drag me back to the Netherworld. Not using Alec's body, anyway.

"You did that? My dream?" I asked, stalling for time to come up with a plan as my heart thudded in my ears. My only real hope was to knock Alec unconscious, which would expel the hellion from his body. But I'd never hit anyone that hard in my entire life. At least, not without a weapon to wield…

The hellion nodded magnanimously, an artist reluctantly taking credit for his masterpiece. "What did you think? Dreams are a new medium for me, and I may have used just a bit too much terror, when a little suspense would have sufficed."

Fear and fury coiled within me, a startled snake about to strike, but I'd have to time my move perfectly to disable him with one unpracticed blow. "How?"

Avari shrugged nonchalantly, and it was almost as disturbing to see him in Alec as it had been to see him in Emma less than a month before. "There is a bit of a learning curve, but I'm sure I will get the recipe right next time."

"How did you get into my head?" I snapped. "And there won't be a next time." There wasn't supposed to be a *this* time. Depriving Avari of his proxy was supposed to keep him too weak to possess anyone. But not only did he clearly have the strength, he'd somehow picked up a new skill set!

"I've discovered several new talents since your last visit to the Nether, Ms. Cavanaugh. And there certainly *will* be a next time. Talents unpracticed are talents wasted, you know."

"What do you want?" I asked, fully aware that this confrontation was now mirroring my bad dream. But that was the best I could do with the memory of the nightmare-hellion's hands on me, his claws digging through my flesh, his power singeing my every nerve ending.

Avari cocked Alec's head to one side, lending him a look of vacant curiosity. "You know, I've never had trouble answering that question in the past. And now it seems I want so many things that I can't decide what to take first."

I nodded, going for bravado. "Makes sense, considering you're a demon of greed."

"Lately, that's not as much fun as it sounds like. What I really want to do is shove my hand down your throat and rip your heart out the long way. But I'm not sure if this body can accomplish such a physically demanding feat. And even if it can, if I give in to such immediate gratification, I'll lose your precious, innocent little soul. And I think I might want that even more than I want your deliciously painful death."

Don't show him fear. Don't shake and don't sweat. Hold on to your anger, Kaylee. But that was all much easier said than done. "Lucky me."

"Not in the slightest. Once I have your soul, I'll be able to kill you over, and over, and over. It's immensely entertaining— for me. Just ask Ms. Page."

Addison. My chest ached just thinking about her and the very real torture she endured daily at Avari's hands, er…claws. Because she'd sold him her soul, and we hadn't been able to get it back for her.

"So, while I'm not quite ready to kill *you* yet, and I rather like having Alec on this side of the barrier now that I've had time to consider the benefits, I have no reason at all to leave your father breathing, if I cannot bring him into the Nether."

No! A jolt of adrenaline shot through my chest. I lurched toward the door, all thoughts of patience and timing forgotten. But I didn't even make it to the end of the bed before Alec's hand closed around my arm. He jerked me backward with more strength than a human should have had, and I had half a moment to disagree with the hellion's assessment of Alec's power before Avari threw me back onto the mattress. My head slammed into the headboard, and he was on me in an instant.

He pinned me with his weight, propped on his elbows with my wrists trapped in his fists.

"Get off me!" I fought the suffocating panic building inside me as I struggled to free my arms. Flashes of four-point restraints and men in hospital scrubs played in my memory, with an all new fear born of the sheer delight in not-Alec's eyes.

"Shhhh..." Avari whispered, as Alec's cheek brushed mine. "Your father is fine, for the moment. I simply haven't yet decided what to do with him."

And that had to be true, because a hellion couldn't lie....

I went still, my heart racing, terror lapping at my fragile control.

"Would you believe that while I'm in this body, I can feel everything it feels? And it *likes* this arrangement." He shifted over me, and I bit my lip against a scream, knowing Avari enjoyed every single moment of my fear. "Have you and my Alec done this before?"

I couldn't talk. I couldn't do anything but ride the horror in silence, desperately hoping I was still dreaming. That this was part of the nightmare.

He let go of my left wrist to brush hair from my face, then wedged one leg between my knees.

Pulse racing in panic, I acted without thinking. Without stopping to consider what would happen if my rash plan didn't work. My free arm shot out. I grabbed the first thing my hand landed on. My alarm clock.

I swung as hard as I could. The cord ripped from the wall. The clock slammed into Alec's head. Avari blinked, stunned. So I did it again, grunting with the effort.

His eyes fluttered shut and he collapsed on top of me.

Tears of relief and belated terror blurred my view of the ceiling. I shoved him off of me and scuttled off the bed into one corner of my room. Alec rolled over the edge of the mattress and thumped to the floor on the other side.

For several long moments, I could only breathe, fighting not to hyperventilate. My legs shook when I stood, and my hand trembled as I wiped my eyes, determined not to give in to sobs. I crossed my room slowly, watching Alec, half convinced Avari was playing possum just so he could catch me again, and start the whole sadistic game all over. But he didn't move, other than the steady, slow rise and fall of his chest.

Once I'd crossed the threshold of my room, I raced down the hall and into the living room, where I dropped onto the floor next to my dad. He lay on the carpet on his left side, with his back to the couch, his ankles tied together, wrists bound at his back. There was a piece of duct tape over his mouth, and when I ripped it off—hoping in vain that the pain would wake him up—I found an entire ratty dish rag stuffed into his mouth.

I couldn't find my dad's pocket knife—there was no telling what the hellion had done with it—so I got a steak knife from the kitchen and carefully cut the ropes, but my father's eyes wouldn't open. And I had no idea what to do.

I should do something. I should call someone, but an ambulance seemed risky. What would I tell the police? Technically, Alec had attacked us both, but even if I denied that, the evidence wouldn't support whatever desperate lie I made up.

But I didn't want to be alone in the house with two unconscious men, both of whom had been possessed by a vengeful hellion in the past hour. So I fumbled for the phone on the nearest end table and speed-dialed the second number on the list.

I hadn't forgiven Nash, and I did *not* want to go groveling back to him when I needed help. But I did want to hear his voice. And welcome a touch that could replace the feel of Avari's unwelcome, surrogate hands on me.

The phone rang and rang, and when Nash finally answered,

I sank onto the floor in relief. "Hello?" He was still half-asleep, and I wished I could join him. Just curl up next to him and forget about the constant terror my own nights had become.

"I need help." I was proud of how steady my voice sounded, but he knew me too well.

"What happened?" Bedsprings creaked and a light switch clicked softly. "Are you okay?"

"Yeah. Just a little freaked out, and I don't really want to be alone. Could you... Would you come over?"

"Give me five minutes." The phone clicked in my ear, then buzzed with a dial tone. He didn't even know what had happened, and it didn't matter. If I needed him, he would come. No matter what.

I sat there for a moment, still reeling from the trauma of the past few minutes. Then I stood and did the only thing I could think of to protect myself while I waited: I grabbed the duct tape lying on the floor near my father's head, then headed into my room, where I rolled Alec onto his side and taped his hands together behind his back and his feet together at the ankles. It wasn't a perfect solution, but it was all I had. Duct tape, and the desperate hope that Avari wouldn't have the strength or the opportunity to possess either Alec or my dad again before the end of the longest night in history.

Then I unlocked the front door and sat on the floor next to my father's head. And waited.

A minute and a half later, my front door flew open. Nash stood on the porch, panting, wearing only jeans, a short-sleeve tee, and sockless sneakers. He stepped inside and shoved the door closed, and I stood. "You ran the whole way?"

"Mom has the car." He folded his arms around me, and I let him, even though his chilled limbs stole my warmth and made me shiver.

I was warm on the inside.

"What the hell happened?" he asked finally, pulling away to kneel beside my dad, two fingers pressed against the pulse in his neck.

"Avari. Dad's been making Alec sleep tied to the recliner, so tonight Avari used my dad to cut Alec free, then he possessed Alec and…"

"And what?" Evidently satisfied by my dad's pulse, Nash stood, his irises churning with green twists of fear and amber swirls of protective anger.

"Nothing." I shrugged miserably. "Nothing happened. I hit him with my alarm clock, and now I might need a new alarm clock, but I think Alec's okay."

"I don't give a shit about Alec." More fierce colors flashed in his eyes. "What about you? Are you okay?"

"Yeah. Just a couple of bruises." I held up my arms so he could see the faint handprints around my wrists, and Nash clenched his teeth so hard I was afraid he'd crack them. "I taped him up, so I think we're pretty safe. I just… I didn't want to be alone."

Nash wrapped one arm around me, and his hands felt warm now, through the tee I slept in. "Where is he?"

I pointed toward my room, and Nash stomped off down the hall. A second later, he reappeared, dragging a still-bound and unconscious Alec behind him. He dropped Alec on the floor and stared at him, and I understood that he was fighting a violent impulse I could only vaguely understand. He wanted to kick Alec while he was down—I could see it in his eyes.

"Nash, none of this is his fault. He hates Avari as much as we do. Maybe more."

"No. More isn't possible. Not after that," Nash insisted, gesturing toward my bruised arms. He helped me lay my father on the couch, then we curled up together in the recliner and watched them both, waiting for morning.

NASH STAYED UNTIL my father finally woke up around dawn and thanked him, then sent him home. Over coffee, I explained what had happened—my dad didn't remember anything—then I tried to pretend I couldn't see the slow swirl of fear in his eyes. If Avari had the power to possess him—a one-hundred-thirty-year-old *bean sidhe*—then his limits were few. And that was enough to scare anyone.

Alec woke up half an hour later, while my dad was in the shower.

"Kaylee?"

I rubbed sleep from my eyes, but stayed in my chair, across the room from where he still lay on the floor. "Are you...you?"

"Yeah. Shit. My arm's asleep." He tried to move, but could only shrug awkwardly with his hands bound, his forehead wrinkled in confusion. "What happened?"

I brushed hair back from my face, but stayed in my corner. "What color was my first bike?"

Guilt flooded his features when he saw my face and recognized the remnants of my recent trauma. "Kaylee, what happened?"

"Just answer the question. What color?"

"Red. No!" He shook his head when my eyes widened in panic. "White, with red ribbons. Sorry."

My gaze narrowed on him. I wanted to trust him, but I couldn't. I couldn't fully trust anyone who was in a position to actually help me. I'd never felt more alone in my life.

"Give me a break, Kaylee, please. My head feels like it's the size of a pumpkin and I'm tied up on the floor and I don't know how I got here. I'm not exactly thinking straight."

I exhaled slowly, fighting for calm. Avari had fooled me too many times. "What did you guess Emma named her first bra?"

A flicker of amusement lit his features for just an instant.

"Helga," he said, and I finally stood. "What the hell happened?"

I crossed the room carrying the steak knife, but hesitated to cut him free. I was sure it was Alec now, but when I looked at him, I saw Avari staring down at me through Alec's eyes, pinning me. And every time I thought about that, fear gave way to a miniburst of panic, deep in my chest.

"Kay?"

"You…" I stopped and started over, squatting to cut the tape so I wouldn't have to look at him. It wasn't Alec's fault. "*He…* He tied up my dad, then came into my room and…" I couldn't finish, so I finally just showed him one bruised arm.

"Oh, damn, Kaylee, I'm so sorry." Alec looked like someone had just punched him in the face. Then followed up with a kick to the groin. "You know I'd never…"

"I know." I sank onto the floor and leaned against the couch with my knees pulled up to my chest. "I don't know what to do. He'll come back. I don't think we can stop him."

"Yes, we can." Alec sat up and used the knife to free his feet. "We'll find a way." He peeled off the last piece of tape, then his hand rose to the back of his head and came away smeared with blood. Alec winced. "I guess your dad's pissed?"

I forced an uneasy grin at that. "Yeah, but I did that. Also, I'd steer clear of Nash for a while. And you should probably stay away from Tod, for good measure." Because one way or another, the reaper would hear about what happened.

And that's when I noticed the dark red stain on the carpet. I could have killed Alec. And none of this was his fault.

"This has to stop."

"I know. We'll find a way. I swear, Kaylee, this will never happen again."

But it was hard to take heart in his words, because they sounded more and more hollow every time I heard them.

≪ 19 ≫

SABINE WAS SITTING in the passenger seat of my car when I tried to leave for work at nine-thirty Sunday morning. I saw her the moment I stepped onto the front porch, and for a second, I considered simply marching back into the kitchen, where my father was cleaning Alec's head wound, trying to figure out how to keep Avari out of our lives for good. To my surprise, he was more sympathetic to Alec's dilemma this morning, rather than less, since he'd now personally fallen victim to possession.

But ignoring her would only be prolonging the inevitable. And Sabine's presence *was* starting to feel inevitable, though I'd only known her a week. The *mara* was a force of nature— a tidal wave of fear, and pain, and need—and the only way I knew to survive her was to grab the nearest tree and ride out the surge.

She didn't look up as I jogged down the porch steps; she just stared out the window, long dark hair covering the only visible side of her face. A glance up and down the street showed no sign of her car, and I decided right then not to even ask how she'd gotten to my house.

I exhaled slowly as I walked down the driveway, struggling to contain the sudden white-hot flare of my temper, determined to face my latest problem head-on.

Despite her obvious B and E, the driver's side door was locked, and Sabine didn't turn to face me when I tried the handle. Nor did she unlock the door and let me into my own car, though she'd clearly gone through some effort to let *herself* in. If I couldn't see the back of her rib cage expanding with each breath, I might have thought she was dead.

That'd be just like Sabine, to die in my car—one last trauma for me before she'd probably haunt me for the rest of my life.

Gritting my teeth, I unlocked the door myself and slid into the driver's seat. "What are you doing in my car?" I demanded, still clutching my keys for fear that if I put them in the ignition, she'd grab them and run, as the next part of whatever stunt she obviously had planned.

"Waiting," she said, and her voice was oddly nasal.

My spine tingled. Had Avari somehow gotten ahold of her, too? Had he found another body to wear while he tortured me?

But then she turned, and I understood. She wasn't possessed—she'd been crying.

Great. A bawling Nightmare. *What's next? A schizophrenic Minotaur?*

"How did you get in here?" I asked, not sure I really wanted the answer. I should have just kicked her out and headed to work—I'd probably be late as it was. But I so rarely had the upper hand with Sabine that I couldn't resist the opportunity to find out what could possibly make the big bad *mara* cry.

Sabine reached between her seat and the passenger's side

door and held up a long, thin strip of metal with a hook on one end. A slim jim.

My fist clenched around my keys. "I don't even want to know how you learned to use that." My curiosity—not to mention my patience—was fading by the second. "If you expect me to feel sorry for you, you're out of luck," I said, trying not to stare at her swollen eyes, flushed face, and tear-streaked cheeks.

"I don't want your sympathy." She sniffled, then grabbed a tissue from the minipack in my center console and wiped her face. It didn't help. "I want you to fix this."

"Fix what?"

"This!" She spread her arms, as if to encompass her entire screwed-up life. "Nash won't talk to me. I went back last night, and he just kicked me out again. He won't even listen."

I have to admit, I took a little joy in her pain; she'd certainly dished out enough for me. "I'm surprised he let you in in the first place."

Sabine frowned like I wasn't making sense. "I went in through a window."

"You broke into his house!" But then, why not? She'd broken into both my dreams and my car....

She shrugged. "Harmony always forgets to check the windows."

"That's not the point." Though I made a note to mention that little security lapse to Nash. "You can't just break into his house and expect him to be happy to see you!"

Her frown deepened. "He always was before. We never could stay mad at each other, and after we had a fight, one of us would sneak into the other's room, and instead of apologizing, we'd—"

"Stop!" I shouted, louder than I'd intended to in the confines of my car. For a couple of endless moments, I could only blink at her, trying to process what she'd almost said, while subconsciously denying that we were even having this conversation. "I get the picture, and I *don't* need to hear about it." Or think about it, or ever, *ever* get stuck with a visual. "And anyway, that's not normal, Sabine. In fact, it's messed up. Sounds like you two had nothing in common but sex."

Hurt flickered across her tear-streaked expression, and again, my heart beat a little faster in satisfaction. But she recovered quickly. "I don't think you *know* what's normal, Kay. Sometimes messed up is just the way things are. And even if we weren't a normal couple, so what? *Screw* normal. Normal is dull, and Nash and I were lightning in a bottle. We burned hard and fast, but never burned up."

I started to argue, but she spoke over me. "And it's none of anyone else's business what our relationship is built on, but just so you understand, I know Nash better than you ever will. You can't truly know someone until you've seen what he's afraid of, and even if he tells you all his deep dark secrets, you can never understand them like I do. You can never understand *him* like I do."

"Get out." I'd heard enough.

"No." She locked the passenger's side door with her elbow and crossed both arms over her chest. "Not until you fix this."

"Why should I? You haven't even apologized."

She frowned, looking genuinely confused. "I can't apologize."

My hands clenched around the wheel. "Why not?"

"Because I'm not sorry!" She sat straighter, eyes wide and earnest. "I did what I had to do. It didn't work, and now I wish I'd done something else, but I had to try, and I'm not sorry for that. I'll do whatever it takes to get him back. I thought you'd understand that."

"I do." I exhaled heavily and stared at the dashboard, then

made myself meet her pained gaze. "That's exactly why I'm not going to help you. Now get out of my car. I have to go to work."

Her gaze went dark, her full lips pressed into a thin, angry line. "Damn it, Kaylee, you're going to fix this, or I swear I'll be in your head all night long, every night for the rest of your life."

My jaw clenched so hard lights started flashing in front of my eyes. I shoved the key into the ignition and turned it, and when the engine rumbled to life, I twisted in my seat to check out the rear windshield as I backed down the drive. "Fine. If you won't get out, consider yourself along for the ride. And don't ask me how you're getting home, 'cause this is a one-way argument."

"I can do it, you know," she insisted a couple of minutes later, like I hadn't spoken at all. Like I wasn't halfway to the highway in my stupid Cinemark polo and pants. "Those other nightmares only ended because I let them. I can ride your dreams all night long—as long as I want—and you won't be able to wake up until I decide you've had enough. And that won't be until you make things right between me and Nash."

I swallowed thickly as I swerved onto the on-ramp, trying to pretend her threat hadn't scared the crap out of me. But it had. Aside from the terror she could inspire, my very worst fear was of not being in control of myself. I couldn't stand the thought of being at someone else's mercy. And she knew that. But I wouldn't bend to her threats—not even the big one.

"Threatening me isn't going to make me help you, you know," I said, wishing I could watch for her reaction, instead of staring at the road. Because frankly, I wasn't sure which was more dangerous, the highway traffic, or the *mara* in my passenger seat.

"Then what will?" She sniffled again, and wiped her face with both hands this time.

"Nothing! I don't owe you anything, and I'm glad Nash isn't talking to you! You half stripped and jumped my boy-friend, right in front of me, and you wanted to get caught. The whole thing was just another part of your mind game!"

"Well, *yeah*," Sabine said, and I glanced away from the road to see her frowning, apparently surprised by my statement of the obvious. "You knew I was coming after him—I told you that up front. It's nothing personal. But you're wrong about that last part. This isn't a game. This is my *life*, and he's the only good thing in it. He's all I've thought about in the two years I spent trying to get back to him, and I'm not going to lose him now. You have to help me, Kaylee. *Please*."

Her voice cracked on the last word, and I glanced at her again in surprise. She obviously hated asking for my help, but she'd do anything to get Nash back, and I knew how she felt.

Nash and I had made up, but not because I'd forgiven him. I missed him so much that we'd made up *in spite* of me not forgiving him. Which meant that Sabine was totally barking up the wrong ex-girlfriend.

"No, I *don't* have to help you," I said at last, and the words sounded so foreign coming from my own mouth that I actually had to repeat them in my head, to reinforce the certainty.

"You are such a selfish *bitch!* You have everything!" she shouted, and I nearly swerved into the next lane. "You could find someone else to love you—hell, all you'd have to do is open your eyes—but I can't. Nash is all I have. He's all I'll *ever* have, and I put everything I am into finding him again." She stopped yelling and swallowed thickly, staring out the windshield for a long moment while we both tried to catch our breath.

Then she turned to me again, calmer now, but no less intense. "Kaylee, I'm not asking you to shove him at me. I'm not even asking you to step aside. I just need you to stop pulling him away from me."

I flicked my right blinker on and veered smoothly off the highway at my exit, and when I didn't answer, Sabine tried again.

"What do you want?" she demanded. "You want me to beg?"

The theater was up ahead, and I picked a spot near the back of the lot. "I want you to get out of my car! I couldn't help you even if I wanted to. Nash made up his own mind."

"I know, and he's mad now, but he'll get over it. I'm pretty sure it'll take longer without makeup sex, but he *will* get over it. But he won't tell either of us that unless you get over it, too. If you forgive me, he'll forgive me, and we can go back to the way things were."

"I don't *like* the way things were!" I shut off the engine and pulled the key from the ignition. "And he doesn't, either."

"Ask him." She grabbed my arm when I tried to get out of the car. "Ask him if he really wants to be rid of me, Kaylee. He'll tell you the truth. And if he says he doesn't want to lose me—at least as a friend—and you still won't help me, then you're intentionally trying to make him unhappy. Why would you do that if you really love him?"

"That doesn't even make any sense! I…" But I didn't have anything logical to follow that up with, so I could only groan and let my head fall back against the headrest. "You are the most infuriating person I've ever met."

She lifted one brow, half-amused, even with tears still standing in her eyes. "I'm going to take that as a compliment."

"It's really not."

"Yet you haven't kicked me out of your car."

"Not for lack of *trying!*" I sighed again, but recognized

the sound of futility in that breath. It was so much harder to hate her when she wasn't kissing my boyfriend or stalking my dreams. "Sabine, I have to be on the clock in five minutes. And this isn't going to happen. You can't seriously expect me to forgive you for a topless make-out session with Nash. Much less sanction your friendship."

"Why are you always telling me what I can't do? There's *nothing* I can't do, and the same goes for you, whether you know it or not. And if you weren't so threatened by me, you'd have no problem with this."

"That's it. I'm done." I shoved open my door and got out. "Lock the doors when you go. And stay out of my car." *And out of my life.*

My SHIFT ENDED at two, and I was relieved to find my car empty. And not so relieved to find all four doors unlocked—a metaphorical middle finger from Sabine. Fortunately, I didn't keep anything in my car, so there was nothing to be stolen except the car itself, which probably would have happened if I'd been working a night shift.

When I walked through my front door half an hour later, I found a note from my father in the empty candy dish on an end table, where I usually dropped my keys. The note repeated what his voice mail had already told me: he'd driven Alec to the factory for a preliminary drug test and training video, and he'd be back by six with dinner.

What the note didn't say, but I'd heard in my father's voice, was that he was unwilling to leave Alec alone if at all possible, after last night's demon-roping marathon.

So for the first time in weeks, I found myself alone in my house. I would have loved a nap, or even just a couple of hours spent staring at the TV, with no one else around to fight me for the remote. Unfortunately, I couldn't really relax until I knew how to keep Avari out of my dreams, and out of Alec's body.

By my best guess, the only reason he hadn't tried to steal *my* body was that I couldn't feed him like Alec could. But it was only a matter of time before I made him mad enough that he'd take me over just to hurt or humiliate me. Or worse. Because if he had the power to possess a half hypnos, he had the power to possess me, and it wouldn't take him long to figure out how to use my own abilities to cross me into the Netherworld. And I couldn't just sit around with that thought eating at me like acid.

Unfortunately, I had no idea where to start looking for solutions. My dad and uncle—and probably Harmony Hudson—were already burning their respective candles at both ends, so far without a thing to show for their efforts.

My only idea—some of that weird Netherworld dreamless-sleeping herb Harmony had given Nash while he was sick—was shot down before I'd even fully expressed it. Nash said that the herb would keep Sabine from giving me nightmares—she can't mess with dreams that aren't there—but wouldn't even slow Avari down. He didn't need us to dream; he only needed us to sleep.

And I already knew from experience that the internet had nothing about hellions. At least, not about real hellions. There was plenty of info on comic book and video game hellions. But nothing of use, unless I had an enchanted sword hanging from my belt or a gang of mismatched but powerful superheroes at my back.

And even then, there were no guarantees.

I was staring at my Betty Boop phone message pad—still blank—when the doorbell rang. Surprised, I dropped my pen and pad on the coffee table and crossed the room to glance out the front window, where I found Tod standing on the porch, his hands behind his back.

Huh. Weird.

I pulled open the door and looked up at him. "What's with the doorbell?"

He grinned, and a blond curl fell over his forehead. "Just tryin' on some manners."

"Why? Who died?" I meant it as a joke, but when his smile faded, I frowned. "Please tell me no one died...."

"Well, I'm sure someone, *somewhere,* died. But no one I know." He hesitated, and I stared at him, still trying to figure out what the reaper was doing on my porch. "Can I come in?"

I shrugged and stepped back to clear the way. "You don't usually ask permission. Or use the door. So...what are you delivering today—pizza or death?"

"Both, actually." He pulled his arms out from behind his back as he stepped over the threshold, and his right hand held a grease-stained medium pizza box. "Pepperoni for you now, and a fatal aneurism to the woman in room 408, in about ten hours."

"Thanks." I took the box and closed the door behind him, a little disturbed that I was only a little disturbed by the mention of his night job. "What's the occasion?"

"No occasion. I need to talk to you, and I was hungry."

Okaaay... "What do we need to talk about?" I set the pizza box on the coffee table and flipped open the lid to find the pie still steaming and gooey with cheese.

But instead of flopping into my dad's favorite chair, Tod stood in the middle of my living room, watching me like he wasn't sure what to do next. "Are you alone?"

"Not as alone as I was a minute ago," I said, and at that, he cracked a smile—but a small one. "What's up, Tod? Is something wrong?"

"We need to talk about Nash. And Sabine."

I dropped onto the couch and grabbed a slice of pizza, then gestured for him to help himself. "Pizza isn't enough to get me to talk about Sabine. You should have brought chocolate." I chewed my first bite as he sank onto the opposite end of the couch, but made no move on the pizza. "She broke into my car this morning and wouldn't get out, so I had to take her to work with me. Then she left my car unlocked, like a tribute to suburban crime statistics."

Tod's mouth quirked in a half smile. "You're lucky she didn't take a bat to it."

"So I hear. That girl is seriously damaged."

"I know. She came to see me after she left the theater."

"At work?"

"Yeah. She's hurting, Kaylee."

"I know. Now explain the part where that's my fault."

"It's not. But she's not the only one. I talked to Nash after that."

I frowned and swallowed another bite. "You have too much free time. Two jobs, yet you're never at either of them. I'm in the wrong line of work."

He shrugged and glanced at the pizza, but didn't take a slice. "I have a lot of 'driving' time to kill, so I stopped by home—" by which he meant *Nash's* home "—on the way to a delivery address."

"Convenient."

"Yeah." He frowned. "It almost makes up for the whole walking corpse thing, huh?"

"Anyway…"

"Anyway, Nash is in bad shape, Kaylee. On Friday, he had been reunited with a good friend and was a couple of steps from getting back together with his girlfriend. Today he has neither one of those."

"He has me," I insisted. "We kinda made up. He even came over last night." *Or early this morning…*

"Yeah. You 'kinda' made up. In the sense that he'll drop everything to come running when you call, but you still haven't forgiven him enough to deal with his problems. Which means that he's still alone in every way that counts. And being alone is really hard on his willpower."

I made myself swallow another bite. "By willpower, are we talking about resisting certain Netherworld addictive substances, or certain willing ex-girlfriends?"

"I'm talking about frost, Kaylee. Demon's Breath. He can't do this on his own, and Mom and I can't be there all the time. Especially now that I have two jobs."

"When were you ever there?"

"I was around. He just didn't know it. But I'm not gonna let my brother start using again." He looked right into my eyes then, and I saw a hint of true turmoil flicker in the cerulean depths of his eyes. Turmoil and…something else. Something even more aching and suppressed. "Being alone and in pain makes everything harder to resist, and right now Nash is hurting because he knows you can't forgive him. And he's resisting something that already has a hold on him. He's fighting the undertow, Kaylee, and he needs your help."

Nash hadn't said anything to me about that. He didn't talk to me about his cravings or the lingering effects of withdrawal, because he knew I wanted nothing to do with that part of his life.

"You think I should forgive him?" Like it was just that easy.

Tod blinked and met my gaze. "I think you should give him up. You need to let Sabine have him."

20

"I NEED TO WHAT?" Tod was kidding. He had to be.

The reaper held two hands up in a defensive gesture. "Okay, just hear me out before you start yelling, okay?"

I nodded, because the truth was that I could barely speak, much less yell. My vocal cords were paralyzed by shock. Which almost never happens to a *bean sidhe*.

"Kay, you and Nash are no good for each other," Tod said. I tried to interrupt, but he spoke over my inarticulate mumble. "You know it, even if you won't admit it. He needs you, but you don't need him."

"That's not true." I shook my head, emphasizing my denial. "I do need him. I needed him last night."

"No, you didn't. He said that by the time he got there, you'd already expelled the hellion, tied up the host, and cut your dad loose, all by yourself. You're so strong, and smart, and you never hesitate when something needs to be done, and that's all…amazing." Tod's irises sparked with a sharp twist of bright blue before going suddenly still. "But Nash needs to be needed. You both *want* each other—even a dead man could see that—but you've changed, and he has nothing to offer you anymore, and eventually you're going to realize that on your own. But probably not before you've wasted years of your life—and his—with the wrong guy."

My chest throbbed like one big bruise, like my heart was trying to pound its way out through my ribs. But above that steady beat of pain, my indignation roared, drowning out everything else, demanding to be heard.

"What gives you the right to tell me who I shouldn't be with? What, you think being a few years older than me means you know everything?"

Tod's irises pulsed with a quick beat of anger, then went still when he got control of them. "No. But I think being dead for a couple of those years gives me a perspective most people don't have. I know how short life really is, and I can see things you and Nash don't understand yet. Like, maybe there's someone better out there for him. And maybe there's someone better for you."

I dropped my half-eaten slice of pizza into the box and stared at him in disbelief. "Being dead doesn't qualify you to play matchmaker between my boyfriend and his *ex*-girlfriend. Maybe she's an ex for a very good reason."

"Or maybe she's an ex because my death got in the way of their relationship. Maybe they never should have been separated. And then you two never would have met, and this whole thing would have played out differently."

Shocked silent, I could only blink for several seconds, as what he was really saying sank in. "Then he wouldn't be an addict, right? Because if he'd never met me, he would never have been exposed." I could barely breathe through the sting in his words.

"No." Tod reached for me, looking both stunned and confused, but I pulled away from him. "Kaylee, I swear that's not what I meant. I'm not even sure how you got that out of what I was trying to say…"

"Then what did you mean?"

"I just meant that if you and Nash had never met…" He stopped and closed his eyes, like he was trying to gather his thoughts. "If you hadn't met, you wouldn't have to deal with letting each other go now."

"I'm not letting him go."

"If you give a damn about him, you will. As bad as it probably hurts to think about this right now, Nash and Sabine are right for each other. Maybe more so now than they ever were before, because now they need each other. They're both messed up pretty bad, but together, their two halves make a whole, while the most you and Nash are ever gonna add up to is one and a half."

"One and a half?" I repeated, like a brain-damaged parrot. I heard what he was saying, but I just couldn't believe that some manipulative, antagonistic, dream-pirate could possibly be better for Nash than I was.

Tod nodded solemnly. "It's an improper fraction. Sad, but true."

"Actually, it's a mixed number," I said, slowly going numb as his words continued to sink in. "Fourth-grade math."

"Whatever." He glanced down, then met my gaze again and let me see a sad little swirl of color in his eyes. "My point stands, and I have to side with Sabine on this one. If you really care about him, you have to let her have him. That's the only way either of them are ever going to be whole. If you try to keep Nash for yourself, you'll only ever really have half of him."

"But he loves me." I felt like I'd just turned in a hundred circles and the room wouldn't stop spinning.

Then Tod put his hand on my arm, and the world went still.

"Yeah. He does. And it'll hurt like hell for him to get over you. But he *will* get over you. And she'll help make that happen."

"What if I don't want him to get over me?"

"Then you're being selfish." Tod leaned back and ran his hand through his hair again. "Kaylee, you're never going to be able to truly forgive him for what he did, and honestly, I don't know that you should. But my point is that if you can't forgive him, he won't be able to forgive himself. Which means that as long as the two of you are together, he's going to be living with this, trying to make up for it and failing over and over again, because he has nothing left to offer you. Do you really want to watch him suffer like that?"

I shook my head, not in answer, but in denial and confusion. "Being with Sabine won't fix that. She can't undo it, and she can't make me get over it."

"No, but she can help him forgive himself. Your relationship with Nash was all shiny and clean, but it's tainted now. It's like a stain you can never wash out. A constant reminder. But their relationship...well, it was messed up from day one, so that's kind of their status quo. It'll work between them, Kaylee. If you let it."

I could only stare at him in mounting shock and pain. And when my anger reached its crest, my temper exploded. "What is *wrong* with you?" I demanded. "How can you stand there and tell me that two people who love each other shouldn't be together? That I should just shove him into the arms of his slut of an ex-girlfriend and call it a day?"

"This is the truth, Kaylee." Tod put his hands up, palms out, in another defensive gesture. "You can't get mad at me for telling the truth."

"Oh, yes, I can." I stood and flipped the pizza box closed,

then slammed my hand down on it for good measure. "Get out." I picked up the smooshed box and shoved it at him.

"Kaylee…"

"Just go away, Tod. I have enough to worry about without adding 'taking stupid advice from a dead guy' to the list."

Tod blinked at me, and the smallest cobalt tremor of emotion rippled through his irises before he regained control. Before I could interpret what I'd seen. Then he sighed and blinked out of the room, pizza box and all.

Alone in my house again, I sank onto the couch and buried my head in my hands, my fingers pressed into my eyes so hard that red spots formed behind my eyelids. I refused to let the tears fall. Tod was wrong. So what if I didn't need Nash anymore? Wanting him was enough.

But as I lay awake that night, listening to Alec snore in the recliner he was now handcuffed to, doubt ate at me, one vicious bite at a time.

What if Tod was right? What if wanting Nash wasn't enough?

By Monday morning, exhaustion had become my state of normalcy. Even with Alec well secured, none of us had gotten much sleep for fear that Avari would possess my dad and tear up the house looking for keys to the cuffs Tod had commandeered from the local police station's supply room. For our safety, neither Alec nor I knew where my dad had hidden the keys.

But beyond all that, I was afraid that if I let myself sleep deeply enough to actually get any rest, Avari would find me again in my dreams. And lying awake only gave me more time to obsess over dead teachers, vengeful hellions, and a boyfriend who may or may not be better off with a walking Nightmare than with me.

Thanks to another largely sleepless night, I pulled into the school parking lot just five minutes before the final bell and had to park near the back, both my scattered thoughts and flagging energy focused on finding Emma, so I could ask for advice about Nash. I was halfway to the building when a scream ripped through the parking lot, and all random snatches of conversation ended in startled silence. Heads turned toward the human but obviously agonized wail, now accompanied by other enraged shouts, and the sickening thunk of some blunt instrument into solid flesh.

I shouldn't have gone; I didn't really want to know. But horror and curiosity are overpowering lures on their own, and together, they're virtually irresistible. So I found myself in the thin flow of bodies streaming toward sounds of anger and pain, fully aware that there was probably nothing I could do to stop whatever was happening.

When the crowd stopped moving, I elbowed my way to the front, then sucked in a sharp breath when what I saw sank in.

In the main aisle, Trace Dennison, one of the basketball team starters, clutched a golf club in both hands, huge feet spread for balance, cheeks flushed in obvious outrage. He pulled the club up over his head, and the crowd around me gasped.

"No, man, wait!" Derek Rogers, the captain of the basketball team, leaned against a dusty blue four-door car, clutching his left arm to the big *E* on the front of his green-and-white letter jacket. His face was ashen beneath a smooth, dark complexion, his jaw clenched in pain, and he held his right arm over his head in defense against the golf club ready to swing at him again.

"Whoa, Trace!" Two of the other team members stepped out of the crowd, palms up in identical defensive gestures, intense, cautious gazes trained on Trace. "What are you doing?

Put the club down!" the first player said, nervously running one hand through a head full of soft brown waves.

Trace didn't even seem to hear him.

The second player—Michael something?—moved in boldly, while around me, the entire crowd seemed to stop breathing. "Dennison, do *not* make me kick your ass. Put that thing down before I shove it someplace graphic."

Trace never even turned. Instead, he gripped the golf club— a putter?—like a baseball bat, and as we watched, frozen in horror and anticipation, he swung overhead again, grunting with effort and with what sounded like primal rage.

Michael lunged for the club and missed. Derek shouted. Onlookers sucked in sharp breaths. And over all that, I heard the muted thud of impact and the crunch of breaking bone.

Derek's shouts became high-pitched screams, and his right arm fell to his side, useless.

Tears blurred my vision, but shock held me in place. I didn't know what to do. *No one* seemed to know what to do, except Michael, who looked determined to put this insanity to an end, despite the obvious danger to himself.

"You're crazy!" Derek shouted between pain-filled gasps, edging down the length of the car and away from the club as Trace lifted it again.

"Trace…" Michael said, hands outstretched now, and Trace whirled on him, club held high. The crowd shuffled backward as one, but Michael didn't seem to notice. "What's the problem, man? What's this about?"

"He's my problem," Trace said through clenched teeth, glancing over at Derek, who'd clenched his jaw shut—probably to keep from screaming—clutching both ruined arms to his chest. "Seventeen point average and an MVP nomination doesn't mean you walk on water. If he wasn't such a ball hog, maybe people'd realize there's more than one man on the court!"

A ripple was working its way through the rapidly growing crowd—a single capped head sticking up above most of the others. Coach Rundell and both security guards stepped into the clearing as Trace started to turn back to Derek, already pulling the club high again, ready for another swing. Michael must have seen them, because he moved closer to Derek, dragging Trace's gaze with him, distracting him from the newly arrived authorities.

Coach Rundell wrapped one meaty hand around the neck of the club and neatly plucked it from Trace's grip, jerking him backward in the process.

When Trace turned, his face scarlet with rage, the security guards each grabbed one of his arms.

"Call an ambulance," Rundell growled, after one look at Derek's misshapen right arm, obvious even beneath his thick jacket sleeve. The younger of the two guards pulled a portable radio from his belt and spoke into it, passing along the coach's orders to the attendance secretary as they hauled a belligerent Trace Dennison toward the building. But by then, at least a dozen students were already dialing 9-1-1 directly.

Rundell helped Derek out of his jacket carefully, but the senior screamed as the sleeves slid over his arms. "Oh, shit," Rundell said. Derek's arms were both obviously broken, but his right sleeve was torn and oozing blood, the white end of a bone sticking up through both flesh and stained material.

"Okay, let's get you inside." Coach waved Michael forward to help him get Derek to the school building, both basketball players towering over the shorter, thicker football coach as several other teachers arrived and began to disburse the onlookers.

"Hey, Coach!" another voice called from the crowd, and I turned to find a freckled sophomore member of the golf team holding up the club Rundell had dropped, a long black golf bag hanging from his opposite shoulder. "Can I have this back now?"

Rundell stopped and turned toward the kid, and Derek groaned. "What was Trace doing with it?"

The kid shrugged. "He grabbed it right out of my bag and just started swinging."

"Well, I think it's evidence now. Have your dad call me." Rundell held out his hand, and the kid jogged forward to hand him the club, then the coach marched toward the building with one hand on Derek's shoulder.

"What happened?" Emma asked from behind me, and I turned to see her rounding the car on my right.

"Trace Dennison went homicidal, and now the basketball team's down two starters. He broke both of Derek Rogers's arms."

"Damn." Emma whistled as we headed toward the building.

"Yeah. It was pretty brutal." I was oddly relieved to realize that even after everything I'd seen in the Netherworld, human-on-human violence still truly bothered me.

We followed the crowd toward the side entrance, and gossip buzzed all around us, people rehashing Trace's psychotic breakdown, Mona's arrest for possession with intent, and Tanner's locker vandalism, which had been largely outshined by the rest of the chaos. Then the shrill ring of the final bell cut through the animated chatter, and the foot traffic sped up.

Great. Another tardy. Maybe Mr. Wesner's sub wouldn't notice.

As we jogged toward the building, a car pulled into the parking lot, and distantly, I noticed that it was Jeff Ryan's rebuilt '72 Chevelle. Nash had helped him work on it a couple of times, and Jeff had let him borrow it once, as a thank-you.

I waved to Jeff as I crossed the aisle, practically dragging

Em along with me. We were only feet from the school door when an engine growled behind us. Tires squealed, and I turned toward the sound to see a sleek, low-slung black car racing down the center aisle. I sucked in a breath to shout a warning, but I was too late.

The black car slammed into the passenger side of Jeff's Chevelle with the horrible *squealcrunchpop* of bending metal. I flinched and grabbed Emma's arm. And for a second or two, a thick, shocked silence reigned complete in the parking lot.

Then Jeff's door creaked open and he crawled out of his car, the passenger side of which was now wrapped around the crunched front of the other vehicle.

People raced toward the wreck. The other driver got out and started yelling at Jeff, but I couldn't understand much of what he said. Jeff was wobbly and too stunned to reply, but after one good look at his ruined masterpiece, he blinked and shook his head, then jumped into the shouting match full-strength.

Teachers came running. Some gestured for onlookers to get to class while others tried to break up the fight that had erupted between Jeff and the other driver, who were still shouting between blows.

"Holy shit, what's that all about?" Emma asked, walking backward as slowly as possible, reluctant to tear her gaze from the latest violent outburst .

"That's Robbie Scates," someone said from my left, and I glanced over to see a guy I didn't know staring longingly at Emma. "He and Jeff entered some kind of hot-rod show in Dallas on Saturday, and Jeff placed higher. His picture was in the Sunday paper. Guess Robbie's a sore loser."

"A stupid one, too," I mumbled. At least fifty people had seen him T-bone Jeff's car.

"Damn…" Emma breathed. "An arrest on Friday, and now two fights and a wreck today, before school even started!"

"Technically, school's started," I noted, dragging her by one arm toward the entrance. "We just missed the first few minutes."

"I don't think we're the ones missing anything," Em said, turning reluctantly to follow me to algebra, where our dead teacher's desk was now occupied by a clueless long-term sub.

IN SPITE OF the busy work the sub handed out—along with our tardy slips—Emma managed to fill the rest of the class in on the parking lot chaos, through a combination of whispered sentences and passed notes, until the sub finally gave up and pretended not to notice the crowd gathered around our desks.

"It's the pressure," Brant Williams opined, dark brows drawn low. "Trace needed that scholarship, otherwise he'll end up at TCJC. But he fumbled twice in the first quarter, and the recruiter never even looked at him after that."

"Well, they're sure not gonna recruit him now," Leah-the-pom-squad-girl added. "Unless maybe the golf team's really hard up."

But whether it was senior year pressure or something dumped into the school's water supply, the truth was that half the student body seemed to have gone insane over the weekend.

During second period, the fire alarm went off right about the time we started smelling smoke, and when we filed into the parking lot, the most prevalent rumor was that Camilla Edwards's science fair project—brought to school so the year-book staff could get pictures of the first state finalist in nearly a decade—had been doused with something flammable and lit on fire in one of the chemistry labs. Now those pictures were all that remained of a project she'd started more than eight months earlier.

"This is insane," Emma said, when I snuck away from my class huddle to meet her by her car. The red and blue lights from the fire trucks and police cars flashed over her face, giving her expression a look of urgency, on top of the standard bewilderment. "Why would anyone trash Cammie's project? Just to get out of second period?"

But I had no answer. All I knew for sure was that Eastlake High had lost its collective mind, and the timing was too precise to be a coincidence. I was already dealing with a new Nightmare of a student, dead teachers, and a hellion with more strength and abilities than he should have. And now some kind of violent mental defect was sweeping the student body.

It was all related. I could feel the connection in my gut, even if I couldn't make sense of it. There was something I wasn't seeing. Some piece of the puzzle I hadn't yet found. And the only thing I knew for sure was that until I put the whole thing together, no one at Eastlake High School would be safe.

21

WHEN I WOKE UP at 2:24 a.m. on Tuesday, something lay on my pillow, two inches from my face. I sat up, fumbling for my bedside lamp, instantly alert. It was a purple sticky note, taken from my own desk.

Ice surged through my veins as I reached for it, raising chill bumps all over my body, and those chill bumps blossomed into chill *mountains* when I read the note.

Three words. Infinite possibilities.

And sleeping, wake.

There was no signature, and the handwriting was unfamiliar, with an old-fashioned, curly look to it.

Avari was back. And he wanted to play.

And that's when I realized the house around me was silent. No snoring. No groaning couch springs or squealing metal recliner frame as someone shifted in sleep.

Swimming in panic, I pulled on the jeans I'd worn the day before and raced into the living room—then froze when I squinted into the dark and made out the empty recliner and the pillow lying next to it on the floor. Alec was gone.

I whirled toward the couch, but it was empty, too, except for my dad's bedding, and for one long, horrible moment, I thought he was gone, too. Then something shifted in the shadows between the couch and coffee table, and I realized it was the rise and fall of my father's chest.

Shoving the coffee table out of my way, I clicked on the end table lamp and dropped to my knees next to my dad. His hands were cuffed at his back and blood had pooled beneath his head, and when I brushed back his hair, I found a sticky lump above his left temple.

Avari had found the keys. He'd possessed my dad in his sleep, found the handcuff keys, then released Alec and restrained my father. My dad had obviously woken up at some point after Avari had taken Alec's body—otherwise, why hit him? But I'd slept through the whole thing.

And now someone innocent would die, because I couldn't master the art of defensive insomnia.

Well, that, and because Avari was a vindictive, soul-sucking demon with an appetite for chaos and a yen for my complete destruction. But I couldn't help blaming myself, at least in part, because I'd failed to stop him. Again.

But maybe I could catch him. The others had all died at the school.

Since my father was safe for the moment, I pulled on my jacket, grabbed my car keys, then headed for the front door, where I froze with my hand on the knob. Stuck to the wood, half covering the peephole, was a second purple sticky note, displaying that same antiquated writing.

A walk I take.

If it was a riddle, it was a very bad one. I already knew he'd gone somewhere. Probably to kill someone. So why start a new game now?

He wouldn't, unless he was planning to feed from my pain,

as well as from whatever energy he funneled through Alec. Which meant he was going after someone connected to me. And that narrowed things down. As did the fact that he was on foot.

But even knowing that, I could think of at least half a dozen people he might target, and I didn't have time to check on them all individually.

As I stepped into my shoes, panic-fueled, anger-driven plans of action tumbled through my brain, their unfinished edges making mincemeat of my upper level logic. In the driveway, I slid into my driver's seat and shoved the key into the ignition, and when the interior lights flared to life, I found myself staring at another sticky note in the middle of my steering wheel. My heart thumped painfully. Four words this time, in that antiquated scrolling print.

Fair maid to break.

It was more poem than riddle, but hardly brilliant, either way.

And sleeping, wake
A walk I take
Fair maid to break
Emma.

No, wait. What if he meant Sophie? My cousin and best friend were the only two human girls I knew for a fact that he knew how to find. My hands clenched around the steering wheel in frustration. Emma was my refuge from all things twisted and non-human. Sophie was my own flesh and blood. I couldn't lose either of them. But I couldn't save them both; they each lived about a mile from me, but in opposite directions.

I slammed the gearshift into Reverse, anger at Avari burning bright beneath aching fear for my cousin and my best friend. I backed down the driveway and onto the road, then shifted into Drive and took off, dialing as I drove.

Nash answered on the third ring.

"Mmm... Hello?" He sounded groggy, and bedsprings creaked as he rolled over.

"Wake up, Nash. I need help." I ran the first stop sign, confident by the lack of headlights that no one else was on the road in my neighborhood at two-thirty in the morning.

"Kaylee? Are you in the car?"

"Yeah. I need you to call Sophie and make sure she's okay." She wouldn't answer the phone if she saw my number on the display, especially in the middle of the night.

"Avari?"

"He found the handcuff key, knocked my dad out, and left me this stupid, cryptic riddle about breaking a 'fair maid.' I'm on my way to Emma's to check on her. So can you please call Sophie?"

"Yeah. I'll call you right back."

I got to Emma's two minutes later, driving way over the suburban speed limit. There were two cars in the driveway and another parked at the curb, and I recognized them all. One was Emma's, one her mother's, and the third belonged to one of Em's two older sisters. I saw no sign of Alec, or Avari, or evil of any kind.

I closed my car door softly and studied Emma's house. The front rooms were dark, except for the lamp they always left on, and since I didn't have a key, I wouldn't be able to get in without waking someone up. But then, neither would Avari, unless Alec had some kind of walk-through-walls power I didn't know about.

I practically tiptoed across the lawn and onto the front porch, where my hand hovered over the doorknob. An unlocked door would mean that Avari had beat me there. But a locked door didn't eliminate that possibility—he could have gone in through the backdoor or a window.

Holding my breath, I twisted the knob. It turned, and the door creaked open.

Uh-oh.

I stepped inside, and my blood rushed so fast the dimly lit living room seemed to swim around me. A few steps later, I could see down the hall, where a thin line of yellow light shone beneath the second door on the right. Emma's room.

My sneakers made no sound on the carpet as I crept toward her door, and when I was close enough to touch it, I heard voices whispering from inside, one deep and soft, the other higher in pitch.

Wrapping determination around myself like a security blanket, I turned the knob and pushed the door all the way open. Then blinked in surprise.

Emma sat on her bed in a tank top and Tweety print pajama bottoms, her straight blond hair secured with an old scrunchy. Alec sat in her desk chair, pulled close to her nightstand. Neither of them looked surprised to see me.

"'Bout time!" Emma said, waving me inside. "Shut the door so we don't wake my mom up."

Bewildered, and more than a little suspicious, I closed the door, but hovered near it, unwilling to move too far from the exit until I was sure it was safe. I studied Alec, looking for any sign that he wasn't...himself. "What color was my first bike?" I asked, and Emma laughed.

"You guys are obsessed with this game!"

But Alec knew it was no game. "White, with red ribbons," he said, right on cue, and only then could I relax. Kind of.

"What's going on?" My eyes narrowed as I ventured a little farther into the room. Even if he was Alec now, he'd been Avari when he planted those notes and left my house.

Something felt wrong. How on earth had he explained this to Emma?

But before either of them could answer, my phone rang. I pulled it from my pocket and flipped it open when I saw Nash's number. "Your cousin's not a morning person," he said, before I had a chance to say hi. "But she's fine."

"Thanks. I found Alec, and he and Em both seem okay. Do you think you could run over to my house and…look for that key?" Without it, I wasn't sure how we'd ever get my father out of the cuffs. "If my dad wakes up, tell him I'll be back in a few minutes, and I'm fine."

"Yeah. See you in a few."

I flipped my phone closed and slid it into my pocket, then looked up to find Emma watching me.

"Alec came to check on me," she said, in answer to my question. "He said you'd be right behind him, and here you are. *He* brought ice cream, though." She gestured to two spoons and a pint of Ben & Jerry's on the nightstand. One of the very pints she'd left in my freezer, no doubt. "Just FYI, Kay, if you're going to wake me up in the middle of the night for my own protection, then refuse to explain exactly what I'm in danger from, bringing ice cream is a good way to soothe my sleep-fuddled anger."

"Huh?" Considering the time, my lack of sleep, and the fear-laced adrenaline still half buzzing in my system, that was as articulate a response as I could manage.

Alec leaned back in his chair. "Emma, would you mind bringing another spoon?"

Em frowned, then glanced from me to Alec. "You know, if there's something you don't want me to hear, you can just say, 'Em, there's something we don't want you to hear.'"

He smiled, and I could practically see my best friend melt

beneath the full power of his attention. "Em, there are things we don't want you to hear. Also, we need another spoon."

Emma sighed, but stood. "Whisper fast," she said, then headed into the hall.

"There are notes all over my house and car from Avari," I whispered as softly as I could, the minute her footsteps faded. "What the hell happened?"

"It sounds like he found the key." Alec sat up straight, facing me as I sank onto Emma's bed. "I was here, alone, not ten minutes ago. Then she came in with two spoons. Evidently he brought her ice cream, but I'm not fool enough to believe that's the only reason for this little excursion."

"You told her I'd be coming, too?"

Alec shrugged. "He must have said that...before."

"So...he left notes for me and brought ice cream for Emma." I closed my eyes, trying to think through exhaustion, anger, and an encroaching headache. "How did you get rid of him?"

Alec shrugged. "I didn't."

"He vacated on his own..." I mumbled, as Em's muted, bare footsteps echoed toward us. "He never planned to kill her. He's just playing some kind of twisted game." But why?

Emma came back into the room before he could answer, but even if she hadn't, I doubt he'd have had anything to say. Though he'd lived with the hellion for a quarter of a century, he seemed no more privy to Avari's thought process than I was.

"So...what's up?" Emma asked, handing me the spoon. She sank onto the bed and pulled the lid from the carton of ice cream. "What's the latest cloud on the horizon of my pathetic existence?"

"Dramatic, Em?" But I had to grin. Nothing ever seemed to get Emma down. Even being told she was in danger from some mysterious force she probably would never understand.

"It's poetic. I like it," Alec said, and I swear I saw Emma

flush, which hadn't happened much since the night she'd snuck into my room at one in the morning to tell me all about losing her virginity.

"You're not pathetic, and you're not in danger." *Anymore...* "We had a scare, but it seems to be over."

"A scare of the Netherworld variety?" Emma's smile faltered. She knew just enough about the non-human side of my life to be scared senseless every time it was mentioned. And I intended to keep it that way. If she was scared, she was much less likely to dig for information. Her fear was keeping her safe. Or at least safer than she'd have been otherwise.

"Yeah, but it's fine now." I stood, eyeing Alec. "You ready?"

"Wait!" Em waved the spoons at him slowly, like she could hypnotize him with the lure of shiny metal. "Stay and have some ice cream."

"Em, it's almost three in the morning." And I had to get back to my dad.

"Hey, you two woke me up from some very pleasant dreams. The least you can do is mollify me with ice cream."

One look at Em—who only had eyes for Alec—and I knew I was fighting a losing battle. So I stayed for just a few bites, if only to keep her from making any beyond-friendship overtures toward a man three times her age.

Then Alec and I headed home, where I cleaned my father's head wound while Nash called his mom at the hospital and asked her to send Tod to the police station for another handcuff key.

We never found the one Avari had taken.

<< 22 >>

AFTER ANOTHER MOSTLY sleepless night and an early breakfast spent watching Harmony stitch the gash on my dad's head, I held my breath as I walked into the school on Tuesday morning, half-afraid of what I'd find. I knew better than to believe that yesterday's campus chaos had faded into the ether.

I was right.

I'd made it halfway to my locker when the door to the girls' bathroom flew open and slammed against the wall right in front of me. I lurched out of the way as two bodies stumbled into the hall and collided with a stretch of lockers, ringing the metal doors like a gong. Hair flew, too wild and fast for me to identify either of the fighters as I scrambled out of the immediate impact zone.

A crowd formed quickly—a living boxing ring—as each girl tore at the other's hair and clothes, clawing at exposed skin. They screeched and grunted, a primal racket of pain and rage, punctuated with just enough profanity-riddled half sentences for me to understand the cause.

They were fighting over a guy. Someone's boyfriend, or ex-boyfriend, or stupid, unwitting crush.

A couple of teachers came running to break up the fight, already haggard before eight in the morning, and as I bypassed the action, I noticed two of the school's larger coaches hauling a boy apiece down the hall in my direction. The student on the left had a split lip and a black eye. The one on the right was bleeding from a head wound and a totally *crunched* nose.

In spite of their injuries, it was everything the coaches could do to keep them apart.

"Did you hear?" Emma asked, when I finally slid into the seat next to her in algebra.

"About the fights in the hall? Caught the live show and nearly got flattened. It's like going to school in a war zone."

"Not that." Emma looked just as put together as always, in spite of her interrupted sleep. Obviously middle-of-the-night ice cream was the cure for dark under-eye circles. "They took Coach Peterson away in handcuffs this morning. The custodian caught him trashing Rundell's office, shouting that he would have been the head football coach if Rundell hadn't married the superintendent's daughter." Emma leaned closer to me, not that it mattered. Everyone else was busy passing the same news. "I swear, Kaylee, the entire school's gone insane!"

Yeah. Including the teachers, which was a new development.

By third period, there had been four more fights and another teacher removed from school grounds, for undisclosed reasons. Whatever she'd done, she'd done in the teachers' lounge, and the rest of the staff wasn't talking. Which left us to interpret her crimes as we saw fit. And there was no shortage of rumors.

After third period—my free hour—I headed across the

deserted gym toward the cafeteria, but stopped short when I heard a screech from the girls' locker room. "Sophie, no!"

I dropped my books on the polished wood floor and raced for the locker room, then threw open the door and froze in surprise at what I saw.

In one hand, Sophie held a huge pair of metal scissors with jagged blades. The ones she'd been using for her Life Skills project—pinking shears, Aunt Val had called them. In the other hand, my cousin held a thick chunk of Laura Bell's long, shiny brown hair.

Laura was bawling hysterically, her face already red from the effort, one hand clutching the back of her scalp.

"I'm…I'm so sorry!" Sophie screeched, her hand shaking violently, and a second later, she burst into tears, too.

"Give me that!" I jerked the scissors from her grasp by the closed blades, then spun Laura around to assess the damage. The center section of her hair had been clipped so close to her head I could see scalp showing through.

Great. A half-bald beauty queen. Laura was going to need therapy—I could already tell.

"Go to the office and have them call your mom," I said, unsure if Laura could even hear me over her own snot-strangled tears. "I'm sure they can get you some kind of emergency salon appointment. Or something."

Not that there was anything they'd be able to do for her, short of shearing the rest of it to match.

Laura wiped tears from her face with one sleeve, then wandered out of the bathroom in a traumatized daze, rendered virtually useless by a bad haircut. Not that I couldn't sympathize.

"Sophie, what the hell?" I demanded, as soon as the door closed, but my cousin just stood there, clutching a handful of her best friend's hair.

"I don't know!" she screeched, her words so painfully high-pitched I wanted to slap both hands over my ears. Maybe she was part *bean sidhe,* after all… "She was working on her hair, going on and on about being Snow Queen, and I just kept thinking that she never should have won. Then I just… snapped, and the next thing I know, I'm holding half her hair, and she's screaming, and all I can think is that it should have been me. It *would* have been me, if you hadn't trashed my dress. I didn't even get to compete after that!"

Her eyes widened, then narrowed in sudden understanding. And fury.

"This is *your* fault. I would have been Snow Queen if you hadn't ruined everything, like you always do! Luck of the Irish, my ass. You're like an agent of darkness. I swear, you have horns growing under all that stringy hair."

"Sounds like you found the family resemblance." I scowled and stepped closer to her, and Sophie backed up until her hip hit the sink. "I ought to cut your hair to match hers, and if you open your mouth one more time, that's exactly what I'll do." With that, I dropped her shears into the big covered trash can and stomped out of the locker room, leaving Sophie to her guilt and tears.

I was almost out of the gym—Sophie had yet to emerge— when a familiar voice shredded my remaining self-control like wood through a chipper.

"So you actually died, and she just…let it happen?"

Sabine. My pulse spiked with irritation. What the hell was she doing?

"Well, I don't think she could have stopped it…" another, softer voice said, and my anger was a white-hot ball of fury flaming in my gut. *Emma.* Sabine had Emma, and they were talking about…things they shouldn't be talking about.

"But you don't know for sure, right? I mean, you don't actually know what she's capable of, do you? All you really know is that she's not human and she screeches louder than a police siren. Right?"

I spun silently, trying to pinpoint the voices, but the gym looked empty.

"Yeah, I guess..." Em finally answered, and confusion slowed her words, like the first drink of the night.

"Don't you ever worry about the next time? I mean, being best friends with a *bean sidhe* should come with hazard pay, right? You're always in the line of fire, thanks to her."

"Actually...yeah. Something went down last night, and she and Alec wouldn't tell me what. Again." She paused as I crossed one corner of the basketball court quietly. "But everything turned out fine."

"But what if it hadn't? What if you'd become collateral damage again? Do you ever worry that she might..."

"Just let me die?" Emma asked, and I could hear the fear in her voice. My blood boiled. Sabine was goading her, reading and manipulating her fears with every word, but the actual fears were all Em's. Things she'd never told me about.

"Yeah," Emma continued. "Kaylee and Nash can't save someone without letting someone else die. One of these days, it'll be my time to go, and I'm afraid that Kaylee will just... let it happen. Or that they'll save someone else and end up killing me by accident."

"It could definitely happen," Sabine said, as I rounded the edge of the bleachers to see her smiling at me over Emma's shoulder. She'd known I was there the whole time. My hands curled into fists and my jaw clenched so hard my whole face ached.

"Sabine, what the hell are you doing?" My voice sounded lower and darker than I'd ever heard it.

"Just getting to know Em a little better."

Emma was watching me now, a familiar edge of irritation

in her narrowed eyes. "Why didn't you tell me Sabine isn't human? And don't tell me this is more *bean sidhe* business—she's not a *bean sidhe*. And why do you and Alec have Netherworld secrets now? Are you just using any excuse to lock me out of your life?"

I raised a brow at Sabine. Clearly I was late to the conversation—Em had obviously confided *several* fears.

Sabine only shrugged and grinned, so I turned back to Emma, my arms crossed over my chest.

"Did she tell you what she is?"

"More than *you* told me. She's a *mara*."

I nodded. "And did she tell you what that means?"

Emma frowned. *That's what I thought.* "She's a Nightmare, Em. Literally. She reads people's fears and exploits them for her own entertainment." Or nutrition. I was still a bit fuzzy on that detail. "And that's what she's doing to you right now. Exploiting your fears."

And that's when it hit me. The school chaos. The fights and jealousy. They had nothing to do with Avari—what did he care if a few kids got arrested or expelled?

It was Sabine. All of it. I'd heard her talking to Sophie and Laura about the Snow Queen title last week. She'd chatted with the basketball team at lunch. And now she was moving in on Emma. She was feeding from their fears and insecurities. And it had to stop.

I took a deep breath, then faced my best friend, without letting Sabine out of my sight. "Em, I swear I'm not going to let you die. No matter what. Your life is definitely a priority, so you can stop worrying about that." I closed my eyes, weighing pros and cons in my head, then met Emma's suspicious gaze again. "And I'm going to tell you everything. I promise." It wasn't fair for me to keep her in the dark—I, of all people, should have known that. "But right now, I have to deal with the mess Sabine's gotten us all into. I'll meet you in the cafeteria, okay?"

Without waiting for her answer, I grabbed Sabine by the arm and hauled her across the gym. She just laughed and let me pull her. "Where are we going?"

"To find Nash." If anyone could reason with an out of control *mara,* it would be our mutual ex. Her one true love, according to Tod.

My anger burned even brighter at that thought.

"Oh, good!" she said, as I hesitated in the middle of the basketball court, debating the shortcut to the quad through the cafeteria. But pulling Sabine through a crowd of students she'd already worked into some kind of fear-fed frenzy would be a very bad idea. So I turned right and headed for the gym exit. "But you should probably know he's not speaking to me."

"Fortunately, he is speaking to me."

"So, what, you're gonna tattle on me for telling Emma I'm not human? That wasn't your secret to keep, Kaylee. Totally my call. And if blowing my own cover happens to poke holes in your credibility…well, we'll call that a big fat bonus!"

"You are *such* a bitch." I shoved open the heavy exterior door and pulled Sabine into the parking lot, then took an immediate left, circling the building toward the quad.

"That's hardly breaking news."

"Yet the headlines just keep coming." I tightened my grip on her arm. The quad was in sight by then, but I saw no sign of Nash. In fact, all the tables were empty, which was weird, considering we were ten minutes into lunch.

"Okay, this has been real fun," Sabine said, as I stopped next to the first empty table. She jerked her arm from my grasp and faced me, her goading grin gone, true anger flashing in her eyes. "But if it isn't gonna get Nash to talk to me, I'm done with this."

She started to stomp off toward the cafeteria, but I grabbed her wrist. "Get back here." Nash would have been *so* much better at talking some sense into her, but since he wasn't there, it was up to me.

Sabine jerked her arm away again. "The novelty of your badass act is wearing off quickly."

And suddenly I realized that the lack of a crowd was as much disadvantage as advantage—she probably wouldn't hesitate to punch me if there was no one around to see it. "How could you pull Emma into this? She has nothing to do with your sad little obsession with Nash."

Sabine rolled her eyes. "I didn't hurt her. I barely even got a taste of her fear. And as for my disclosure, you of all people should know how scary it is when you don't understand the world around you. I would have thought you'd want to spare your own best friend from such painful ignorance."

I couldn't fault her logic and I'd already decided to tell Emma everything. But even if Sabine's argument was sound, her intentions were not. She'd been using an innocent bystander to piss me off, and it worked. "Just leave Emma alone."

"I don't answer to you about anything, Kaylee. Including my dinner plans."

Fresh flames of rage licked at my skin; I felt like I was standing too close to a bonfire, and if I didn't back up, I was going to get roasted. And I was fine with that—so long as Sabine got singed, too.

"You can*not* just go around feeding from people! You've turned this school into a war zone, and people are getting hurt."

Sabine rolled her eyes and crossed her arms over her chest. "I told you I didn't kill those teachers. And I'm not responsible for how a bunch of human sheep deal with the loss of a couple of shepherds."

"They're people, not sheep!" Even if they did tend to follow the herd and stand around bleating uselessly at times... "And no matter what you call them, you don't have the right to turn them against one another and get people thrown in jail, or sent to the hospital!"

Sabine frowned. "Okay, you can't even *see* sanity from where you're standing. I had nothing to do with any of that."

"Right." I stepped closer, shoving my fear of a broken jaw—or worse—to the back of my mind. "I heard you talking to Sophie and Laura the other day, and today Laura's missing a chunk of hair from the back of her head."

"Sophie sheared her BFF?" Sabine looked genuinely surprised—like she didn't already know. "Wow. Good one..."

"Shut up. Laura's bad hair day is the least of what you've done. Jeff's car. Derek's broken arms. Coach Rundell's trashed office. Cammie's torched mold spores... This school is the only safe, normal thing in my life, and Eastlake does *not* deserve to go down like this!"

"I know. That's why I'm not doing it." Sabine shrugged. "I could if I wanted to, but I kinda like it here. The food sucks, but I'm passing with minimal effort and I have friends..." She gestured to me, and my mouth actually dropped open.

"I am not your friend."

She gave me an infuriatingly good-natured roll of her dark eyes. "I think the definition of 'friendship' is open to a little interpretation from the fringe groups, Kaylee."

I crossed my arms. "It's really not."

"Whatever. My point is that none of that stuff is my fault."

I shook my head, thoroughly disgusted. "I *saw* you talking with half the people who've gone psycho!" And there was no telling how many private conversations I'd missed.

"Yeah. I was reading their fears. For later." The *mara* uncrossed her arms and shrugged. "A girl's gotta eat." She sat on the edge of the nearest table, leaning forward with her palms against the wood. "I've been in your head. I've been *all over* your boyfriend. And I was messing with your best friend in the gym. But I didn't hurt anybody. And I didn't do any of that crazy shit you're talking about."

"And I should believe you because you're just such a joy to be around?"

"Think about it, Kaylee. This isn't fear-based. From what I can tell, all these newly converted psychos are running on pure jealousy, and that's just not palatable for a *mara,* no matter how hungry I get."

Crap. I hadn't thought of that. But then, she couldn't directly benefit from making Em distrust me, either, and that hadn't stopped her.

"Fine. So you're doing it for fun."

Sabine's grin was back, and I wanted to slap it off her face. But I wasn't stupid enough to indulge that impulse. Again. "Well, there's definitely a slapstick sort of lowbrow entertainment value involved in watching your school fall apart at the seams. But a few laughs aren't worth the effort it would take to orchestrate something like this myself. And anyway, my nightmares aren't just food—they're art. I take pride in that. But this isn't art, Kaylee." She spread her arms to take in the school around us. "This is nothing but…chaos. And as much as I enjoy upsetting the balance of your sad little existence, believe it or not, I don't thrive on chaos."

Chaos…

She was right. *Maras* don't thrive on chaos—but hellions do.

Yet the violent frenzy all around us didn't feel like Avari's work—jealousy wasn't his medium—and the only suspect that left was Sabine, no matter how artfully she wielded logic against me.

"So, what, you expect your pristine record to speak for itself? You've been arrested at least twice, expelled from two different schools, and were handed off from one foster family to the next for years. I think that says pretty clearly what you're capable of."

Sabine's eyes narrowed and darkened. She stood and stepped closer, putting her face inches from mine, and for the first time, I noticed that she was at least a couple of inches taller than I was. And now thoroughly pissed. "You Googled me?"

I shrugged. "I thought I should know what I was dealing with."

"Then you should have asked me," she growled through clenched teeth. "I got expelled the first time for punching a teacher who called me stupid in front of the whole class. He had it coming, and everyone knew it. Which is why he got fired and never pressed charges. I got expelled the second time for breaking into some stuck-up bitch's locker to take back the cell phone she stole from my jacket pocket and used to send dirty emails to the entire school from my account."

"You really expect me to believe that?" Her story actually made sense, and I might really have believed it—if she hadn't spent every moment since we'd met trying to make my life miserable. Logic said that I probably wasn't her first victim.

"I don't care what you believe. But just in case you still have a brain cell functioning behind that inch-thick skull, listen up. I've never lied to you, Kaylee. Not once. I may not always say what you want to hear, but it's always the truth."

With her last word, the first wave of fear slammed into me, so cold and strong I had to fight to suck in a breath. She'd opened her mental gates, and now the full force of the terror *maras* emanated naturally was washing over me in wave after bitter wave.

"It's *your* version of the truth," I insisted, taking an involuntary step back when the black weight of my own fear threatened to drive me to my knees. "And that's about as reliable as a politician's promise."

"Well, how 'bout a few truths you can trust?" She stepped forward again, and again I stepped back, watching shadows twist in her eyes, the silent reflection of every fear I'd ever felt. "Nash belongs with me, whether he knows it or not. You were nothing but a fleeting curiosity, and he's already started getting over you."

"Pathetic…" I spat, gasping for breath as the dark oblivion in her eyes swelled, threatening to swallow me whole. "You're in denial, and it's pathetic. And so are you. What, can't you handle one little *bean sidhe* without channeling Freddy Krueger?"

Sabine's brows arched high over black irises swimming around bottomless pupils. "You think I can't rein it in?" Without waiting for me to answer, she closed her eyes, and a second later the dark cloud of fear lifted. I could breathe again, and even the sun looked a little brighter.

"Better?" she snapped, malice sharp in her voice and in her gaze. She'd pulled it in, but that only meant that the concentration of anger inside her had doubled. Sabine was an angry dog on a leash—if I kept goading her, she'd pull free, and next time she might not be able to control it. "I can play nice if that's all you can handle, but that won't change the facts." She took another step, and this time when I backed up, my spine hit the corner of another picnic table. "If I'm in denial, why are *you* the one he gave up, memory by memory?"

"He had no other choice…" I made myself stand straighter and maintain eye contact.

"There are always choices. The truth is that you're what he was willing to give up."

"No." I shook my head. I couldn't believe that. I just… couldn't.

"Oh, yeah? Then why is it he can't remember what it felt like to kiss you for the first time, but he can relive every single time he touched me, whenever he wants? I'm still up there." She touched her temple, eyes narrowed in fury, hand steady with conviction. "And I'm still in here." She laid that hand over her own heart, and I felt mine crack a little. "And I've been other places you were too scared to go when you had the chance. And now it's too late."

I couldn't breathe, and this time that had nothing to do with any fear leaking from her abusive, rotting soul. I couldn't breathe because she was right. He'd given me up, but he'd kept her. All of her.

Why would he do that?

Sabine's brows arched again, and she leaned down to peer into my eyes. "You get it now, don't you? He can still feel that initial thrill from the very first time we touched."

She ran her hand slowly down from my shoulder, and my chest felt like it was caving in. I jerked back, but she only laughed. "It was innocent, at first. Fresh and new. Exciting, like if my heart beat any faster, it'd explode. And he still feels that, every time he thinks about it."

I shook my head and backed around the corner of the table.

"What does he feel when he thinks about you, Kay? You should ask him. Or I could just tell you. He feels nothing. You're a big numb spot on his heart, and all he feels now when you're around is guilt and pain. You're killing him, and for what? So you can cling to something he didn't care enough about to preserve? You should let him go so he can find peace."

And with that, my anger flared to life again, incinerating doubt and self-pity. "I don't know how to be any clearer about this. *Nash doesn't want you*. Not like you want him. And getting me out of your way isn't going to change that, because

I'm not the obstacle in your path, Sabine. You're standing in your own way."

That one great truth strengthened me, and I stood taller, itching to show her what she refused to see. "You're obsessed with him. And not even with the real Nash. You're in love with the memory of someone you knew two and a half years ago, but you're both different people now, and here's the thing that's killing you: he's moved on. You want to believe that he never really got over you. That if you could just push me out of the way, he'd remember what the two of you had together. But you said it yourself, Sabine—he never forgot. He remembers exactly what it was like to touch you, and love you, and know you loved him back. And he still picked me."

Sabine flushed bright red. Shadows swam over her eyes, and my skin prickled with the cold concentration of terror accumulating inside her, like a balloon, about to explode. Her right hand curled into a fist, and I braced myself for the blow. But before she could swing, the lunch room door burst open and students flooded the quad, carrying trays and drinks, and talking about whatever cafeteria disaster had cut our lunch time in half.

I wasn't sure the sudden crowd would actually stop either her physical or psychological blows, but Sabine dropped her fist and glared at me like she could see right past my heart and into my soul. "You're right," she whispered, anger shining along with something deeper and more haunted in her eyes. "We're not friends." Then she spun around and stomped toward the building.

And the really weird thing was that as the rest of the lunch crowd spread out around me, I could only watch Sabine go, fighting a deep bruising ache in my chest, just like the one I felt every time I lied to my dad.

"HEY," NASH SAID, pulling even with me in the hall on the way to my fifth period French class. "We need to—"

"I don't want to talk about it."

He frowned and reached for me, but I pulled away. "Talk about what? Did something happen?"

I clutched my books and kept walking. "Doesn't something always happen?" After four months of hellion-induced pandemonium, I could hardly remember what my life had been like before I'd known about the Netherworld.

"Specifically…?"

I sighed and stopped to lean against the nearest locker. I was exhausted, physically and emotionally, and I was too worried about Alec's serial body snatcher and the unchecked series of school disasters to concentrate on class work. Or to dwell on Sabine, and whether or not I'd falsely accused her of trying to bring the school to its knees.

"I had a fight with Sabine."

"Again?" Nash forced a grin, but I wasn't buying it. "It

couldn't have been too bad—your face is intact. What happened?"

But if the past week had taught me anything, it was that if I accused her of something, he would automatically come to her defense—another point in favor of Tod's "they're meant for each other" conviction. So I tried a different tactic. "Don't you think this is weird? I mean, the school's in total chaos. Everyone's gone crazy." I hesitated, giving him time to infer my point. But he only frowned harder. "Something's wrong, Nash, and I don't think it's human in origin."

And the truth was that I had no idea how to even trace the source of the problem on my own. Of my two prime suspects, one was physically inaccessible by virtue of a hellish alternate reality, and the other was socially inaccessible, due to the fact that she now wanted to knock my head clean off my body.

"Agreed," he said at last, and I actually sighed with relief.

"Okay, I'm not saying Sabine's behind all of it, necessarily." Though that's what I'd believed an hour earlier. "But she's definitely involved somehow."

"Kaylee…"

"Just listen. I *saw* her talking to several of the kids who've gone off the deep end, and she's not exactly a social butterfly." Sabine was more like a social cockroach, skittering around in the dark, making trouble. "She has Coach Peterson for geography." I'd verified that during English, with one of her classmates. "Also, I swear I saw her in Mrs. Cook's class the other day, on my way to the bathroom."

Mrs. Cook was the teacher who'd lost it in the teachers' lounge.

"Kaylee, there could be a hundred people who have both Cook and Coach Peterson. That doesn't prove anything."

"No, but this didn't start until she came to Eastlake," I insisted.

Nash put a hand on my arm and stared straight down into my eyes. "Your turn to listen. This has nothing to do with Sabine." He glanced around the hall, then pulled me into the alcove near the restroom entrances. "This is a blitz. It has to be. I've never personally seen one, but my mom says they're not that uncommon. The news usually reports them as mass suicides—like that Jonestown thing back in the seventies?—or mass hysteria, or mob mentality. There've been witch hunts and lynchings and riots. And if this one goes unchecked, eventually Eastlake will devour itself whole and the building will crumble into a pile of smoldering bricks. Or something less dramatic, but equally bad."

"Wait." I blinked, struggling to absorb so much information so fast. "You told your mom about this?"

"No, I didn't figure it out until lunch. She told me all about blitzes when we studied herd behavior in psychology."

"So…what exactly is a blitz?"

"It's a full-scale assault on a specific population by some force in the Netherworld. In this case, that specific population is our school, obviously. But it has to be driven by a *big* force, because… Well, you know how hellions and some of the minor Netherworld creatures feed on the bleed-through of human energy?"

"Yeah." Unfortunately, I was intimately familiar with that process.

"Well, to support a blitz, this Netherworld force has to be able to do the opposite. He has to push enough energy into our world to affect human behavior. Or at least our state of mind."

Which sounded exactly like what was happening here.

"So…who could have that kind of power? A hellion?" Avari was the obvious suspect.

"Not on his own. But with help, yeah. I think it's possible." Nash sighed and glanced at his feet before looking up to meet my gaze. "Avari's the dominant hellion in our area—well, the Netherworld version of our area—and his entire existence is powered by greed. There's no way he'd let something like this go down without at least getting in on the profit. Which means he's involved, but not acting alone."

"What kind of profit are we talking about?" I asked, as pieces of the puzzle floated around in my head, looking for some place to fit.

"Energy, probably. There'd be lots of it to go around, with this large an operation. And with energy comes power."

"Would this blitz be enough to…boost his abilities?" I asked, thinking of his recent cameo in my nightmare.

"Yeah, I guess. Why?" When I didn't answer, Nash stepped closer, glancing around to make sure no one was near. The bell would ring any second, but another tardy seemed pretty petty compared to an entire school under attack by at least one hellion.

"I think Avari's had an upgrade. He was in my nightmare. And I don't mean that I had a dream about him. He was *there*. Controlling it. Hurting me. And I think he was feeding from my fear."

"Kaylee, that's impossible. Hellions can't mess with your dreams, and that's not how they feed."

I shrugged. "The only other person who can do that is Sabine. But this nightmare didn't feel like her and she hasn't claimed credit, which seems to be a point of pride with her. So who else could it be?"

Nash scowled as he thought, and I saw the exact moment understanding washed over him. "Shit. It was Sabine. Well, it was Avari *using* Sabine. If he can possess a hypnos, he can possess a *mara,* and he'd have access to anything she can do while he occupies her body. The tricky part would be catching her while she sleeps."

"Uh-oh." Avari was getting too strong, too fast, and we had no clue how to stop him. "Why didn't she say anything?"

"I don't think she knows. If she did, she'd tell me," Nash insisted. "She'd be beyond pissed, and out for blood."

I couldn't blame her there. Avari was using Sabine, just like he'd used me. As badly as I hated to absolve her of any guilt, she was a victim in this—a selfish, deluded, boyfriend-stealing victim, but a victim nonetheless.

"What I can't figure out is how he even knew she was there to use…" Nash wondered aloud.

Crap. "Um…that part's my fault." I shrugged miserably at the realization that I'd accidentally dragged the *mara* into this, then blamed the whole thing on her. "He masqueraded as Alec a couple of times before we figured it out, and one of those times, he heard me and Emma…complaining about Sabine."

Nash's eyebrows rose, like he might ask for details, then he apparently thought better of it. "Okay, I guess that's understandable."

"So, if he can possess her and feed through nightmares, or possess Alec and feed through any kind of sleep…would that give him enough energy to power this blitz?"

"I doubt it. He'd probably recoup the energy possession requires by feeding while he's in the host body, but that's not going to be enough for something this big." Nash's widespread arms took in the whole school.

"So, how is he running this thing?"

"Well, once he got it started, it would be self-sustaining. The chaos he causes would bleed through even stronger than regular human energy, and he could easily feed from it. But as for how he got it going in the first place…" Nash could only shrug. "I don't know. But we have to make it stop."

I KNEW FIFTH period was going to suck the moment Mrs. Brown turned off the lights. Because of the chaos—which everyone had noticed, but no one could explain—she'd decided to ditch her lesson plan in favor of something requiring a little less concentration from her half-traumatized students. The class let loose a universal groan when she pulled out an old documentary on the history of French architecture.

It was all I could do to keep my eyes open when the monotonous narration began.

THE NARRATOR DRONES ON about art nouveau, complete with pictures and clips of buildings I've never even heard of. I don't care about art nouveau. I don't care about art old-school, either. I care about staying awake and surviving another school day, so I can find and eliminate the source of the pandemonium.

And suddenly, my exhausted mind finds that word hilarious. Pandemonium *roughly translates to "all demons," and that seems weirdly fitting, considering Avari's relentless intrusion into my life, and into my body, and now into my school.*

All demons, all the time. That's what my headstone will read, if Avari ever gets his way.

Mrs. Brown stands at the front of the room, and for a second, I'm convinced she's read my mind. Or noticed that I'm not paying attention. But instead of yelling at me in French, she stares at the back of the room, her eyes oddly unfocused.

And that's when the scream explodes from my mouth. It's too hard and too fast to stop this time, and I am strangling on the vicious sound. Choking on it, as it scrapes my throat raw.

I taste blood on the back of my tongue and everyone stares at me. I can't hear the film anymore. Can't hear whatever they're shouting as some gather around me and others back away. I can only hear my own screech.

No one notices Mrs. Brown. No one else is watching when she collapses, and finally I understand. She's dead, and her soul cries out to me, clinging to the life she no longer has, begging to be held in place.

I want to help her, but I can't. Not without damning someone else. So I try to close my mouth, but the scream is too strong, and my jaw too weak. I claw at my throat in desperation. My fingers come away bloody, and there is a new layer of pain. But still I scream, and now I can see Mrs. Brown's soul, hovering over her body, a slowly swirling grayish form—just a representation of her actual soul, Harmony explained to me once. You can't see a real soul, and you probably wouldn't want to, she'd insisted.

But then the fog rolls in, and the real terror begins. Gray mist rises all around me. My heart trips over some beats, skipping others entirely. The fog obscures dingy floor tiles and scratched desk legs. I slap one hand over my mouth, but the sound leaks out, anyway. Thirty sets of shoes disappear into the gray. I try to back away from it, but there's nowhere to go. It's everywhere.

NO! I won't cross over. I won't!

But the scream has a mind of its own. The scream wants me to go and the fog is too thick to fight, so I close my eyes and pretend it's not real. And only once my voice fades to an ineffective croak do I open my eyes again.

This time when I scream, nothing comes out.

I KEPT MY eyes squeezed shut, afraid to look. The desktop was cold beneath my folded arms, and I could feel the crack in the seat of my chair that pinched my leg when I wore shorts. Both of those facts should have meant everything was fine. That I was still in my darkened classroom, with twenty-nine other students feigning interest in the history of French architecture.

But silence doesn't lie.

There was no tapping of Courtney Webber's feet as she listened to her iPod instead of watching the film. No scratching of Gary Yates's pencil against paper as he scrambled to finish his history essay before last period. And certainly no criminally dull narrator droning on about angles and perspective and rebellion against classical architecture.

My heart thudded against my sternum. I sat up, gripping the sides of my desk with my eyes still squeezed shut. I didn't want to look. But not looking would be stupid. Not looking could get me killed. So I opened my eyes and took in the differences—the things that hadn't bled through the barrier into this warped, twisted version of my own world.

An empty classroom. The thirty-two empty desks, devoid of scratches and names scribbled in permanent marker, gave the room an abandoned feel—the high school version of a ghost town. A barren metal teacher's desk sat up front, by the door. There was no whiteboard. No posters of le Louvre, la tour Eiffel, or le Centre Pompidou. There was no ancient television on a cart, playing an outdated, staticky video cassette.

The Netherworld. If I'd had any doubt, it disappeared with my first glance at the educational void surrounding me. I'd crossed over. In my sleep.

No! It takes intent to cross into the Netherworld, and I had no intent. I had the *opposite* of intent. Yet there I was, of someone else's volition.

Sabine.

She was mad at me. She was *pissed,* and I couldn't blame her. And she alone had the ability to mess with my dreams. Well, she and Avari, but this felt like Sabine. It was cruel on a personal level—making me dream that my wail wanted me to cross over—and she knew my fears. She knew there was little in either world that scared me more than winding up in the Netherworld.

Focus, Kaylee. I had to get back to my own world, but I

couldn't just cross over again in the middle of class. It was entirely possible that no one had seen me disappear from French, thanks to the darkened classroom and bored or sleeping students. Assuming I hadn't actually screamed my head off, in life as in my dream. But the chances of thirty people also missing my reentry were slim to none, and I wasn't exactly swimming in good luck.

I'd have to find someplace unpopulated in both worlds before I could cross over. And I'd have to find that place without being eaten, captured, or ritualistically dismembered by any of the Netherworld natives.

No problem. The last time I'd been in the Netherworld version of my high school—less than a month before—it had been completely unpopulated. Surely I could just jog down the hall and around the corner, into the nearest supply closet, then scream my way back into my own world, completely unnoticed by the Nether-freaks.

Taking deep, slow breaths to control my racing pulse, I stood and walked silently to the classroom door, only feet from Mrs. Brown's unoccupied desk. Fingers crossed against surprises, I twisted the knob, pulled open the door—wincing at the creak—then stepped into the doorway.

And froze in terror.

The walls were red. And they were moving.

It took one long, terrifying moment for me to understand what I was seeing, but understanding only made it worse. The walls themselves weren't red. I couldn't tell what color they were because they were covered—completely *obscured*—with thick red vines, pulsing, coiling, constantly twisting in one huge tangle.

My hands clenched around the door frame and three of my fingernails snapped off at the quick. Panic tightened my chest, constricting my lungs. I couldn't breathe. I couldn't move. I could only stare in horror so profound it swallowed the rest of me whole.

Some sections of the vine were as thin as a pencil, others as thick as my bicep. The larger sections were striated with every possible shade from dried-blood red to a softer, watercolor cherry, like thinned paint. The ends of the vines, very fine and limber, sported needle-thin thorns and sharply variegated leaves, greenish in the center, bleeding to maroon on the edges.

I gasped, then clasped one hand over my mouth. I knew those leaves.

Crimson Creeper.

The entire hallway was *crawling* with it. A few months before, I'd been pricked by several thorns from an infant vine growing through cracked concrete, and that had been enough to nearly kill me. What clung to walls and lockers now was probably enough to take out half of Dallas.

As I stood frozen, staring, trying to overcome fear too thick to breathe through, something brushed my right index finger. I jerked my hand away from the door frame and turned to see a thin cord of vine slowly slithering down the metal jamb, leaves the size of half-dollars reaching for me like petals toward the sun.

I swallowed a startled shout and stumbled away from the door—and into the hall. Too late, I realized my mistake, but when I turned back toward the classroom, I found that one curious vine stretching across the opening at waist height, blocking my entrance. Deliberately.

Sparing one moment for a string of silent curses—most aimed at Sabine—I stepped carefully into the center of the hallway. There was no turning back now.

I walked slowly, eyes peeled for reaching vines, while soft, dry slithering sounds accompanied my whispered footsteps.

A thicker vine slid toward my right foot. Skin crawling, I backed out of the way—only to step on a small tangle of leaves and thorns.

Several steps later, I noticed a break in the ever-shifting plant life—an open classroom door. A metallic scraping sound screeched from the opening, and I jumped, my heart pounding fiercely. I swallowed the new lump of panic and went still, willing myself to go unseen, hoping that whatever was in that room hadn't heard me. Eyes closed, I sucked in a deep breath through my nose—and nearly gagged on it.

And that's when I realized something warm and wet was soaking into the back of my shirt.

Barely suppressing a squeal of disgust, I darted forward and glanced up to find something foul and goopy and vaguely orange in color, dripping from the ceiling. From a large, tightly wrapped coil of vines, almost directly overhead. The creeper had caught something, and it was being slowly digested by tiny pores in the plant—but for the bit of Nether-slime that had leaked down my shirt.

Revulsion shuddered through me and it took every bit of self-control I had not to pull my shirt over my head and drop it where I stood, as fears of Netherworld poison and weird biological contamination threw my logic circuits into overload.

Another harsh, heavy scraping sound echoed from the classroom ahead, and I edged forward a little more. Then stopped again when a deep, rough voice slid over me, like sandpaper against bare skin.

The words sounded familiar, but the speech pattern was so foreign I couldn't decipher any meaning from sounds and syllables I felt like I should know. When no one came thundering into the hall to grab me, I silently released the breath I'd been holding and crept forward again until I stood inches from the open door.

A second voice spoke, higher in pitch, but his meaning was no easier to grasp. I could hear them moving around inside the room—a second-floor math class, in the human world—and my muscles were so tense I was starting to ache all over.

If I ever made it back to the human world, I was going to *kill* Sabine.

After a pause in the bizarre conversation, the scraping sounds resumed, and I gathered my battered courage around me like the remains of badly beaten armor. Then, using the scrapes to disguise the sound of my movement, I lurched across the open doorway and deeper into the vine-tangled hall, my heart racing erratically.

As I passed, I got a fleeting look at the backs of two tall, hairless creatures with skin so wrinkled and voluminous they looked like overgrown shar-peis. They had smooth, shiny skulls—the only unwrinkled parts of their bodies—and long, black claws tipping too many fingers to count. But even weirder than the creatures themselves was the huge stack of school desks they were both studying, puzzled, like chess players searching for their next moves.

From there, I walked on softly, concentrating on silence and speed, trying to ignore the cooling patch of fetid wetness on my back as I dodged grasping creeper vines. The next few doors I passed were closed, the classrooms quiet and presumably empty.

I was about fifteen feet from the T-shaped hallway junction when a mad scrabbling sound sent chills skittering up my spine. It sounded like a hundred cat claws scrambling for purchase on a slick floor, the whole thing accompanied by a high-pitched, foreign-sounding voice.

My arms prickled with chills, I tiptoed toward the door, which stood open about four inches. The closer I got, the louder the sounds became, and when I was less than a foot away, a chorus of younger, sharper voices joined the first in a frenzy of eager inhuman cries.

Sweat broke out over my forehead. I took a deep, silent breath and peeked around the vine-choked doorjamb and into the classroom. My throat tightened around a gasp as waves of terror and revulsion washed over me, freezing me in place for several eternal moments.

At first, I couldn't understand what I saw. There were too many limbs, gray like death, but short and dimpled like toddlers. Too many round, smooth heads, covered in soft, translucent peach-fuzz hair. Too many tiny violet eyes. Too many gaping mouths full of needle-teeth, snapping and whining eagerly.

And in the midst of what could only be a nest of pint-size Netherworld monster children stood a single adult, darker and smoother in color, but no less terrifying. As I watched, my pulse rushing in my ears, she held up an ordinary cardboard box, extended over the crowd around her. The children stilled, staring at the box in reverent silence.

The adult paused, and her smile chilled the blood in my veins. Then she overturned the box, and half a dozen round, fleshy things fell from it.

The children pounced. The air crackled with their hisses and snarls, and with the scratching of their clawed feet on tile. They fought for the bloodied treats, snatching quick, gory bites before another set of clawed hands ripped the prize away. Crimson sprays arced through the air. Teeth gleamed red beneath black gums.

It was a preschool free-for-all—a child-size slaughter—and the one adult watched, a proud, gruesome smile warping the bottom half of her round face.

Shuddering, I stepped past the door and only released the

breath I'd been holding when nothing burst from the room to devour me.

Breathing hard now, I took a second to get myself back together, then I started walking again. The storage closet was right around the corner from the bathroom. Surely I could make it that far.

But I'd only taken a couple of steps when a commanding, glacier-cold voice sent chills the length of my body. I froze.

Avari. He was right around the corner.

Damndamndamn! What were they all doing here? The school had been empty just weeks before! Sabine's life expectancy had just shrunk to a matter of minutes from the time I got back to the human world. Assuming that actually happened.

Riding a fresh wave of fear, I raced down the hall—*toward* the sound of his voice—and ducked into a bathroom niche, thick with shadows. The walls were blessedly free of vines, but covered with a thick, smelly, slowly oozing fluid.

I pressed as close to the wall as I could get without actually touching it, and stared out at the empty hall from the shadows hopefully hiding me.

"…very close now…" Avari said from around the corner, as I sucked in a silent breath tasting of fear and smelling of my own sweat. "When you have yours, and I have mine, this affiliation is over. You will slink back to your own corner of oblivion, and we shall see each other no more. Agreed?"

"Agreed," said a second voice, smooth and seductive, like the first sweet taste of a chocolate-dipped pepper, before the fire inside it roasts you alive. "I shall have the lovely Nightmare child, and you shall have your little *bean sidhe,* and we shall feast on their souls for all of eternity.…"

⟨ 24 ⟩

As they rounded the corner, I breathed shallowly through my mouth to keep from smelling whatever oozed down the wall behind me. Wishing with every single cell in my body that I was anywhere in the world but where I stood in that moment.

Avari stepped into sight, and I willed my heart to stop beating for a few seconds, afraid that even that small noise—plus the stench of my terror—would give me away. But he never even glanced at the restroom alcove. Evidently the flood of human emotion from the blitz in progress disguised my individual fear. And he was obviously too irritated at the creature who walked on his other side to bother checking the shadows for humans accidentally stranded in the Nether.

Lucky me.

The woman with him was shorter than Avari, and very thin, her hands a tangle of swollen joints and skeletal fingers beneath the tattered sleeves of a black velvet dress. Her cheeks were sharply pronounced, the hollows beneath them dark and deep. Her black orb eyes reflected a faint green glow in the little available light, and since she had no obvious pupils or irises, I couldn't tell whether or not she was even looking in my direction.

But her most prominent feature by far was her hair—an ever-dripping flow of noxious liquid, streaming over her head and down her back in distinct currents and waves. The flow was thick and black, except where the light overhead gave it a dark green tint. As I watched, she brushed a streaming strand back from her hawkish face and several drops splattered on the floor at her back, sizzling in green-tinted fizz on the grimy tiles.

I'd never seen anything like her river of hair, and I had no doubt that if it splashed me, the drops would eat the flesh right off my bones.

I shivered in my shadows, fighting to keep my teeth from chattering, but the two hellions just walked on slowly, talking, and I strained to hear every word.

"My beautiful Nightmare is ripe for the plucking—so full of luscious envy," the woman said, her words sliding over me like the seductive warmth of a fireplace. Suddenly I wanted her voice for myself, to replace the screeching abomination my own throat spewed into the world. Why should a monster like that get such a beautiful voice, when I got a shriek that could drive grown men home to their mommies? "And I would pluck her *now*," she continued, oblivious to how badly I wanted to rip her voice box from her emaciated throat and stomp it into the ground, to deny her what I couldn't have for myself.

The thought that I might be capable of such a violent act should have shocked and scared me, but it didn't. It felt…justified. Why should someone else—*anyone* else—have something I couldn't have?

"Your impatience is tiresome, Invidia," Avari said, drawing

my thoughts from the wrong I ached to right. "I've readied both hosts, but pushing them into slumber in the same moment is rather an exact science, and one rash act could bring this whole tower tumbling down on top of us."

"Nonsense." Invidia tossed her hair again as she passed out of my sight, and several vines shrank away from the drops sizzling on the tiles. "You exhausted them for just this purpose, and this flow of youthful energy will not last forever. We should strike now, while the iron is hot, lest our hosts have time to cool their heels."

"Soon, Invidia. I give my word, it will be soon...."

I didn't release my breath until I was sure they'd turned the next corner and passed out of both sight and hearing range. Their conversation played over in my head as I tried to make sense of antiquated phrasing, using what little I knew of the Netherworld and the continuing catastrophe my school had become.

The "flow of youthful energy" seemed the most obvious: the increased bleed-through of human life force the blitz provided. But as for the rest...I needed a second, more enlightened opinion. All I knew for sure was that Avari and this Invidia—clearly a fellow hellion—were planning to somehow claim me and Sabine, body and soul, with the help of a couple of preselected "hosts." And we didn't have much time to defend against whatever they were about to throw at us.

Considering the seemingly steady flow of traffic in the Netherworld version of my school hall, I decided to risk crossing over in the bathroom instead of pressing on to the storage closet, which may or may not be locked from the outside in the human world.

I eased the door open slowly, and when I saw no sign of any Netherworldly occupants, I slipped inside and let the door close behind me. The row of sinks looked just like the sinks in my world, except that the one in the middle was steadily dripping a viscous-looking yellow fluid in place of water.

Swallowing my disgust, I knelt to peek beneath the doors of the two closed stalls, glad most of them stood open. On the human side of the crossing, the second to last stall was out of order. The toilet had been broken since we got back from the winter break, and a sign hung on the outside of the locked door.

That stall held my best chance of crossing over without being seen.

The door on this side of the barrier was open, so I went in and closed it, then stepped up onto the slimy-looking toilet seat to keep a set of feet from suddenly appearing in the human world version of the stall when I crossed over. I braced my hands on either side of the stall, careful not to slip. I did *not* want to land in the goopy yellow liquid putrefying in the bowl beneath me.

Then I took a deep breath and closed my eyes, concentrating on the memory of death to summon my *bean sidhe* wail and my intent to cross back over.

I thought about Doug dropping the clip from Nash's bright red balloon, the night of his own party. He'd inhaled as I raced toward him, but I was too late; that one hit was all it took. Doug's eyes had rolled back into his head and he'd collapsed to the ground. The balloon had fallen with him, and I'd nearly choked on the scream trying to rip free from my body.

And with that memory, the wail came again, as real and as painful as it had been the first time. My throat burned like I'd swallowed fire. The scream bounced around in my skull and in my heart, demanding to be set free. Pain echoed everywhere the trapped wail slammed into me, but I clenched my jaw shut, letting only the thinnest thread of sound out, desperately hoping it would be enough.

I closed my eyes and clung to the sides of the stall when the fog began to roll in, roiling around the base of the filthy toilet and over my ankles, though I couldn't feel it. I ignored the intense need to open my mouth, to scream for that re-membered soul—one I hadn't been able to help, in real life.

And now, in memory, Doug and his soul would help me. They would send me back so I could save myself and Sabine from eternal torture, and the rest of the school from the en-ergy blitz that would soon be its ruin.

When I heard water running—the first sound not pro-duced by my tortured throat—I glanced down to find the toilet beneath me clean and white, the water in its bowl clear and odorless. Only then did I let that thread of sound recede within me, like winding up an unrolled ball of twine. A very thorny, scalding ball of twine.

"What was that?" a girl's voice asked from outside the stall, and I nearly groaned out loud. The broken stall was empty, which I'd been counting on, but the bathroom itself was not. Either someone was skipping class, or I'd crossed over be-tween bells.

"What was what?" another voice asked.

I considered hiding out until they left, but I had to find Sa-bine and Nash before they made it to sixth period, or I might not get another chance until it was too late.

Bracing myself for embarrassment, I hopped down from the toilet and unlocked the stall. When I stepped out, all four girls in front of the mirror turned to stare at me.

"Can't you read the sign?"

"Gross. That one's *out of order.*"

"That's Sophie Cavanaugh's sister."

"Cousin," I corrected on my way into the hall, and before the door closed behind me, the fourth girl made a disgusted sound in the back of her throat. "Ew! She didn't even wash her hands!"

"Or flush!"

I speed-walked through the hall, sidestepping students and teachers alike, scanning dozens of familiar faces for the two I needed. I couldn't stop Avari and Invidia on my own. I needed Nash and Sabine.

But what I found was Tod. Where I least expected him.

After glancing into Sabine's sixth period classroom with no luck, I ducked into the first-floor girls' restroom in search of her. I'd checked three of the four stalls and found them all empty when Tod suddenly appeared in front of the door to the fourth.

I shrieked a shrill profanity and jumped back so hard my elbow slammed into the third stall. "You can't be in here!"

Tod stuck his head through the last stall door, then backed up and shrugged. "It's all clear."

"Well, it might not be for long. What are you doing here?"

"Nash called me."

He had? Emma must have told him I'd disappeared from fifth period.

"Oh. Well, thanks, but I'm more than capable of sneaking around the Netherworld on my own for a few minutes." Even if I almost got devoured by man-eating plants and carnivorous kindergarteners… "So you can go polish your shining armor for someone else to admire."

I *might* have been a little irritated at him for telling me to give up Nash.

Tod frowned and brushed a curl from his forehead. "You went to the Netherworld? Why the hell would you do that?"

"I didn't do it on purpose!" I propped my hands on my hips, impatient to continue my search, but I wasn't going to be seen talking to an invisible friend in the hall. Not so soon after the recent bathroom weirdness. "Sabine took her anger issues out on me when I fell asleep in French."

"Hell hath no fury like a *mara* falsely accused."

"Nash told you? What'd he do, call you at work?"

Todd shook his head and pulled a small, slim phone from his back pocket. "Mom put me on her cell plan, now that I can pay for the additional line. Got it a couple of days ago."

"And you didn't give me the number?" I swallowed a bitter, unexpected wash of disappointment.

The reaper grinned and leaned with one hip on the nearest sink. "I was waiting for you to ask."

A flash of irritation burned in my cheeks. "That might have actually happened, if I'd known you had a phone."

His brows arched in surprise. "I figured Nash would tell you."

"Well, he didn't," I snapped.

Tod slid the phone back into his pocket. "So…you're still mad about the other day?"

"Wouldn't you be mad if I told you to give up on someone you care about? Just…hand her over to someone who doesn't even deserve her?"

Tod gave me a strange, sad look I couldn't interpret, and the blues in his irises shifted subtly for a moment before he got control of them. "Yeah. I guess I would."

And obviously that was as much of an apology as I was going to get.

"Anyway, if you didn't come to rescue me from the Netherworld, what are you doing here?"

Tod blinked, and I could almost see him refocusing on the crisis at hand. "Nash just called to tell me that Sabine sensed someone sleeping in the hall—you know *maras* can feel slumber, like we'd feel heat from a fire, right?"

I nodded, creeped out by the comparison. "So what?"

"So there was no one sleeping in the hall. Everyone was up and moving, on the way to class."

"So maybe her spidey senses are all messed up." I shrugged. "Karmic payback for sending me to the Netherworld in my sleep."

"I doubt it's that simple. Or that satisfying," he said. So did I. "The only way I know of for a sleeping person to function like he's awake is if he's…"

"Possessed," I finished for him, as the implication began to sink in and dread settled through me like lead, pinning me in place. Avari had taken control of his "host." Or maybe Invidia had taken control of hers. "Did Sabine mention the lucky victim's name?"

Tod shrugged. "She said the hall was too crowded and no one was snoring."

"Great. She's always *so* much help." I closed my eyes, trying to gather my thoughts, then looked up at him. But before I could tell him what I'd overheard in the Netherworld, the sixth period bell rang, and I nearly jumped out of my shoes.

"You gonna be in trouble?" Tod asked, glancing at the ceiling like he could actually see the bell.

I reached for the door and gripped the handle. "Nowhere near as much trouble as we'll all be in if Avari gets his way. He's playing with a friend this time, and they're up to something big."

"You mean the blitz?"

"The blitz is just a means to an end. He and his partner are trying to drag me and Sabine into the Netherworld, and they've each picked out a body here in the human world to give them hands-on involvement in the process. We have to find out who they've possessed before they can make their move."

There weren't many possibilities to choose from. A person had to have some connection to the Netherworld to even qualify for hellion possession, and I couldn't think of a single eligible party, other than me, Nash, and Emma.

And Sophie…

Shit!

Tod's blue eyes went hard and angry on my behalf—and probably on Sabine's. "What can I do?" He followed me into the hall, where I lowered my voice to avoid notice by the stragglers still making their way to class.

"Find Sophie and make her talk. If she doesn't sound like herself, knock her out. Then meet me in the quad."

Tod's lips turned up in a grim smile. "You know I never pass up an opportunity to smack your cousin."

25

TOD DISAPPEARED, and I headed straight for the gym, where Nash hung out during last period, now that football season was over.

I scanned the bleachers, glancing over several groups of students talking and watching the basketball team practice, but Nash found me before I spotted him. "Hey," he called, and I turned to see him walking toward me from the boys' locker room. "What happened?" he asked, falling into step with me when I gestured for him to follow me toward the gym doors, where we wouldn't be overheard. "Emma said you disappeared during French. Like, literally disappeared."

"Unscheduled trip to the Netherworld, courtesy of everyone's least favorite *mara*."

"Damn it, Kaylee, I'm so sorry." He ran one hand through his hair in frustration. "Are you okay?"

I shrugged, trying not to show how pissed off I was, or how scared I'd been. Like it was no big deal that his ex had nearly gotten me killed. A lot.

"A little sticky…" I plucked at the drying gunk stuck to the back of my shirt. "But still in one piece. And I *did* accuse her of trying to incite a school-wide riot. Though for the record, I think the interdimensional field trip constitutes gross overkill."

"I'll talk to her..." he said, shrugging his backpack higher on his shoulders, and suddenly it felt weird for me to be whispering to Nash in the middle of class, carrying nothing but the weight of my own guilt and fear. I'd left my stuff in French class, after my involuntary departure from the human world.

"Don't bother. We have bigger hellions to fry, before one of them drops me into the hot oil. Or Sabine."

"What?"

"I'll explain when we find Sabine," I said, leaning back against the side of the bleachers. "For now, please tell me you found the sleepwalker."

"Not even close."

"Great." I shoved a flyaway strand of hair back from my face. "Well, now we're looking for two puppets. One will sound like Avari, the other like this demon chick named Invidia. I heard them plotting when I crossed over. I'm guessing she's a hellion of envy."

Nash's brows arched halfway up his forehead. "Based on...?"

"Based on the fact that she's obsessed with Sabine, because of the amount of jealousy she's evidently festering with."

"Envy. Shit," Nash said, leaning against the wall by the first set of doors, and I could practically read his thoughts on his face as he put the puzzle together for himself. "So...this Invidia helped power the blitz?"

"Yeah." I shrugged and glanced through the glass door into the hall, itching to get moving. But discussing Netherworld business in the empty school halls in the middle of last period would not only get us in trouble, it might just get us committed. The noisy gym was a much better place to go unnoticed.

"My guess is that the power she shoved into our world to get the ball rolling came through as violent jealous impulses."

"Thus, all the fights and property damage."

"Exactly. And I'm pretty sure they *wanted* me to blame the whole thing on Sabine."

"Because you're jealous of her?" Nash said, nodding like he understood, and I bristled.

"I'm not jealous of her! I just don't think she belongs on your bed at two o'clock in the morning." Okay, maybe I was a *little* jealous of that part. "What I mean is that they framed her. I'm guessing Sabine's envy drew this new hellion into the area, and Avari saw his chance. He probably knew your ex was here before we did. He killed the teachers in their sleep to make me think she was doing it, and Invidia overloaded the kids I saw Sabine reading fears from, so I'd think she was doing that, too."

"Why?" Nash frowned. "Why do they care who you blame this on?"

"I haven't figured that part out yet. Maybe to divert attention from Alec?" I glanced at the huge clock over the far set of bleachers, and my heart thudded harder. A quarter of last period was gone. We were running out of time. "I need you to get Sabine and meet me and Tod in the quad. We need to figure out who the hellions are possessing, and evict them."

"No problem. We'll be right there."

Nash and I parted ways in the hall, where he headed right, toward Sabine's sixth period class, and I went to the left, headed toward the French class I'd missed half of, where Mrs. Brown handed me my books, along with a pink detention slip.

Funny how "teenage hero" translates to "teenage delinquent" on my permanent record.

Next I headed toward my history class, approaching from the right, so I could check on Emma without being seen by

Coach Rundell, who rarely left his desk during class. Like several of the other teachers, Rundell was showing a video instead of actually teaching, but I could hardly blame him, considering that his office had been trashed that morning and the inexplicable chaos had only gotten worse.

Emma was in her usual seat with her arms crossed over her chest, staring blankly at a television I couldn't see. The entire classroom flickered with a familiar bluish light, and half the students had fallen asleep sitting up.

Satisfied that Emma was safe, I dropped my books off in my locker, then slipped outside through the parking lot exit and made my way around the building from the outside. The quad looked empty when I got there, but before I could take a seat at the nearest table, Tod appeared several feet away.

"It's not Sophie," he said, by way of a greeting. "She's in the office, cryin' like a baby, trying to explain why she cut some chick's hair off."

"Good." At least that would keep her out of Avari's grip for the time being.

More footsteps crunched on the grass behind me, and I turned to find Nash headed across the quad toward us. Alone.

"Where's Sabine?" I asked, sliding onto the nearest bench seat.

Nash frowned, but sat down across from me. "Sabine's a no-show."

"From geography?"

"From school, as far as I can tell." He stared at his hands, clasped together on the table, his jaw clenched in frustration, eyes swirling in true fear. For her. "I looked everywhere I could think of, and she's just gone. Her books are in her locker—not that that's any indication of…anything—and her car's in the lot. And she definitely wouldn't leave campus without her car."

"You have her locker combination?" I asked, and they both just stared at me until I rolled my eyes. "It was a valid question!"

"You think she crossed over?" Tod asked, sitting on the end of the table next to ours, his legs hanging.

"I seriously doubt it," Nash said. "She *can* cross, of course, being a *mara*. But she'd be just as vulnerable there as we are. And no matter what else you think about her, she's not stupid."

"No argument there," I said reluctantly. If she were stupid, she'd be *so* much easier to deal with. "But if she didn't cross…" My words faded into uneasy silence as a horrifying possibility occurred to me. "Avari can possess her," I said, glancing from brother to brother.

"We've established this," Nash said. "He used her to give you that nightmare about him pulling you into the Netherworld."

Which was now starting to sound prophetic.

"That's my point." I stood, my thoughts racing too fast for me to process without freedom of movement. "When he possessed her, he had control of her abilities. So…does that mean he could possess her again and make her cross over?"

That thought was scary enough to make the fine hairs on my arms stand up. But even worse was the knowledge that if he could make Sabine cross over that way, he could make me do the same thing.

So why hadn't he? Why would he need human hosts, if he could just make us cross over on our own?

"I don't think that would work," Tod said, and my relief came almost before I'd heard his rationale. "You have to have intent to cross over, and even when he's in control of your body, he's not in control of your willpower. He can't make you want to cross over."

"Sabine did," I pointed out, frowning over the inconsistency—yet grateful for it.

"Sabine made you dream that you wanted to cross, right?" Nash asked, and I nodded. "She's had a lot of practice weaving nightmares. Avari hasn't. For the moment, I think you're safe from that. But we have to find a way to keep him from possessing us, or this is going to keep happening."

Tod shrugged. "Being dead seems to do the trick."

I glanced at him, arms crossed over my chest. "I think we're looking for something a little less drastic."

Nash cleared his throat, bringing us back on target. "Okay, we have to find Sabine. And whoever else they're planning to grab."

"Any idea who that could be?" Tod asked.

I shook my head. "All I know is that Avari claims to have prepared both the hosts. Which I'm guessing means that he wore them out somehow, so they'd be tired enough to fall asleep at school today."

"Well, then, the joke's on him," Nash said. "Everyone I know could fall asleep at school *every* day."

"That doesn't exactly narrow it down," I snapped, as the pressure to *do something* started to overwhelm me. "And the fact that it has to be someone with a connection to the Netherworld narrows it down too much. I can't think of anyone else who qualifies."

"I could tell you…" a nauseatingly familiar, glacier-cold voice said from my left, and I turned slowly to find Alec watching us from the entrance to the quad. "But that would ruin the surprise."

I stood so fast I nearly tripped over my own feet. "Let him go," I demanded, wishing my own voice held half the authority the hellion's did.

Avari sauntered toward us in Alec's tall, lanky body, moving much too smoothly for a human. Or even a half human. "I've been in here for almost twelve hours now—thanks to the energy produced by the cesspool of envy that is your school—and I've grown much too comfortable to give him up now."

"Twelve hours…?" But twelve hours ago, Alec was…

Dark rage washed over me, igniting tiny fires in my veins. "It was you the whole time, in Emma's room. With the ice cream."

Tod and Nash glanced at me nervously, eyes narrowed in identical questioning expressions, but I ignored them.

"You only pretended you'd let him go."

Avari shrugged. "You've made it difficult to gain access to this body lately, so why give it up once I had it?"

"But the password… How did you know about my bike?" I asked, and both Hudson brothers frowned in confusion.

"Ahh, Ms. Marshall is a veritable fount of information."

He'd tricked Emma into playing what she thought was a trivia game, then had manually hacked our password. Damn it! That never would have happened if I'd told her what was going on.

But… "I saw you." I stepped closer, and Nash and Tod moved up to stand at my sides. "An hour ago, in the Netherworld. Talking to Invidia. You didn't have Alec then."

Avari smiled with Alec's full lips, and the effect was too creepy to bear. "I had him in…what would you call it today? Limbo?"

"Paused? You had him *paused?*" Somehow, that sounded almost worse than being actively possessed. Where had Alec been, when neither he nor Avari were using his body? Some sort of mindless, metaphysical holding cell?

"Precisely. And that would never have been possible, if this generous educational institution hadn't provided me with the power to control both his body and my own simultaneously."

"Let him go." Nash stepped forward when my horror proved too much to fight through for the moment. But Avari had come to make a deal, and he wouldn't leave until he'd gotten what he wanted.

Or been physically evicted from his host.

"What do you want?" I demanded, trying to gather my thoughts and come up with a plan.

"I want you." The brown eyes that stared at me were Alec's but their expression was all hellion. "You come with me now, of your own free will, and I give you my word that I'll never possess any of your friends again."

"Stall him," Tod said, and that's when I realized Avari could neither see nor hear the reaper. And Tod had a plan. "Keep him talking. Blink if you understand," he said, and I blinked, careful not to look at him and give away his presence.

"I'll be right back," he said. I blinked again, and Tod disappeared.

"No way," I said to the hellion, hating every second that I was forced to address him in my friend's body. "You're gonna have to do better than that if you expect me to just hand myself over to you."

Alec's head cocked to the side, like he was studying a particularly interesting insect. "This isn't a negotiation, Ms. Cavanaugh. If you don't cooperate, you'll be to blame every time I feed through this body, or try on Ms. Marshall's form and find out exactly what she has to offer."

I swallowed, fighting through horror and revulsion just to be able to speak. "You're psychotic."

"We don't utilize that term in the Nether. The very concept is considered both obvious and redundant. Now, if you don't cross over this instant, I swear I will take the reins of your boyfriend's subconscious the next time he succumbs to slumber, and we'll see how well you like him when *I'm* in control."

"Don't listen to him, Kaylee," Nash insisted. "I'll never let that happen."

Avari laughed, and the cold, sterile joy sounded foreign and harsh coming from Alec's throat. "We all know you can't stop me."

"But *I* can."

I heard Tod before he appeared, and he appeared just a fraction of a second before he swung a big aluminum toaster in a two-handed grip—at the back of Alec's head.

Alec's eyes fluttered, then closed, and he collapsed to the ground, unconscious but still breathing, and at least temporarily free from the Netherworld body snatcher.

"One down," Tod said, grinning over the still form on the grass. "Let's go evict the other one."

26

TOD STARED AT ME over Alec's unmoving form on the grass, still holding the toaster, the flat left side of which was now massively dented. "Kaylee? You okay?"

"Not even kind of." I shoved hair back from my face and glanced from Tod to Nash, then back. "But having known you both for several months now, I'm starting to see 'okay' as a relative term."

Nash gave me a grim, confident smile, and Tod actually chuckled without letting go of the toaster.

"Okay. I need you to check Sabine's house, and if you find her, call us," I said, and Tod nodded. I didn't think she'd left campus, since her car was still in the lot, but with Sabine, I'd learned to expect the unexpected. And the impulsive. And the vindictive. And the just plain crazy.

"If she's not at her house, try mine," Nash added, just before his brother blinked out of sight. "I've already checked everywhere she hangs out when she skips class," he said, as we headed toward the cafeteria entrance.

I shrugged. "So we'll check again. And if we don't find her here, we're gonna have to cross over."

Nash nodded reluctantly, obviously much more willing to put us both in danger to save Sabine than he'd been for Addison.

He pulled open the door and held it for me, and I stepped past him into the lunchroom—where I could only stare. The cafeteria was *trashed*.

"What happened?" My gaze wandered the food-smeared walls, then snagged on a huge plastic jug of nacho cheese that lay busted open on the floor, oozing smooth orange processed cheese product a couple of feet from my shoes.

"Giant food fight. I'm not sure who started it, but a couple dozen people trashed the place before Goody could get it under control. She suspended thirty-eight kids. The cafeteria staff got pissed when she told them to clean it up, so they walked out, and now all those suspended kids have to spend tomorrow scrubbing the walls. Which is why they sold pizza for lunch in the hall. You didn't see any of that?"

I shook my head, still stunned. "I was busy falsely accusing Sabine during lunch." Then I'd sat in my car to cool off until the bell rang for fourth period. Somehow I'd missed the entire spectacular disaster.

Normally, I would have assumed that food fights were a little juvenile for high school, but based on the number of dented pots and busted food containers, I'd say this one was really more of a riot than anything. "This isn't going to smell any better tomorrow..." I said, stepping over the busted cheese container, on my way to the main entrance. "Let's go."

But I'd only taken a few steps when Nash's hand landed on my arm. "Wait. Did you hear that?"

I'd only heard the sticky squeak of my shoes on the filthy

floor, so I stopped and listened. And I heard it, too. A voice, soft and smooth, and feminine, in spite of the low pitch.

My chest seemed to constrict around my heart. I knew that voice, though I'd only heard it once. "Invidia," I whispered. "She's already here." And Sabine would be with her.

Suddenly I wished I hadn't divided our resources by sending Tod to look for her.

Nash held one finger to his lips and I nodded as I followed him toward the kitchen, carefully sidestepping most of the mess. We followed the empty serving lane past the glass-topped ice cream freezer and into the heart of the Eastlake cafeteria, a maze of commercial-size stoves, dishwashers, and deep stainless-steel sinks. And there at the back, between one of the sinks and a tall metal shelf filled with commercial-size cans, stood Sabine.

And Emma.

"Em?" I asked

She smiled at me slowly with a foreign tilt of her head, and that's when I understood. Emma had fallen asleep in history during the video, and Invidia had made her move. My best friend was the second host.

Emma's body stood half-behind Sabine, pressed against the *mara*'s right side, her mouth inches from Sabine's ear. She watched me closely, a predatory gleam in her normally bright brown eyes, lips half-parted, like I'd interrupted her in mid-sentence.

"Is this the sweet little *bean sidhe?*" Invidia's voice asked, while Emma's hand stroked Sabine's bare arm. "See how she taunts you? How she flaunts the boy in front of you? She knows how you feel. She knows how *he* feels, and she doesn't need him, yet she clings to him, just to keep him from you."

"Sabine, that's not true..." I moved closer slowly, scanning my peripheral vision for anything I could use against Invidia without permanently injuring Emma.

"Hellions can't lie," Sabine said, and her gaze blazed with hatred. With envy so bitter I could practically taste it on the air between us. How could she suddenly hate me, when she'd called me a friend a few hours ago? Was this because of my false accusation—which I'd actually believed at the time? Or was some of it because of Invidia, and the storm of envy she'd unleashed in our school?

Surely the lure of it was even thicker, so close to the hellion who controlled it.

"Hellions can't *intentionally* lie," Nash corrected, stepping up on my right. "But they're free to guess and make assumptions, just like anyone else."

"Look how they work together to subvert you…" Emma's long blond hair fell over Sabine's shoulder, standing out against the dark strands as the hellion's voice slid over me, sweet and smooth as honey on my tongue. If *I* could hardly resist her pull, how was Sabine supposed to, considering how badly she actually wanted what I had?

"She's changed him. Lessened him," Invidia continued, and I could see that Sabine was listening. That the hellions words were hitting their target—not Sabine's ears, but her heart. "But with her gone, you could fix him. You could have him back, and it would be like it was before. Without the meddlesome little female *bean sidhe* to get in your way…"

"Sabine, don't do this," I begged, taking a single step toward them. "Make her leave Emma alone. Em has nothing to do with this."

"This Emma-body?" Invidia looked surprised, then she exhaled a languid, seductive laugh from my best friend's throat. "Emma Marshall has everything to do with this," the hellion insisted, leaning closer to whisper directly into Sabine's ear, though we could all hear her. "She is part of the problem. Part of the effortless existence simply handed to this little *bean sidhe,* while life has given you only battles to be fought."

"Bina, please…" Nash begged, and Sabine's conflicted gaze flicked his way. But that made things worse, because she couldn't see him without seeing me, and seeing us together only reinforced the poison the hellion dripped straight into her ear.

"He's part of it, too. Part of her gilded privilege." Emma's hand reached Sabine's fingers, then trailed slowly upward again, and the *mara*'s arm twitched. "The loving boyfriend, the loyal friends, the protective father. She has everything, and you have only hunger. Insatiable, unbearable hunger, clawing, devouring you from the inside, night and day."

I edged forward again, and Nash came with me. "Sabine, you can have all that, too!" I insisted. Well, maybe not the father, but that wasn't my fault. "And you don't need to bargain with a hellion to make it happen!"

"She lies," Invidia purred, and Sabine shuddered when Emma's lips brushed her ear. "People are drawn to the sweet little *bean sidhe,* to bathe in her bright innocence. When you enter a room, they tremble and shrink back. You must work to hide the horrors they see in your eyes, and she has only to smile. You cannot have what she has—not *any* of it—on your own. But *I* can give it to you. I can give you love, and acceptance, and a smile brighter than the sun. I can give you people, and attention, and a steady stream of sleeping mortals, just waiting to scream in their slumber for you."

"She can't do it, Sabine," I insisted, stepping past a stainless-steel counter, now less than ten feet from them. "Even if she thinks she can, it won't really be what you want. She can't change your species, and she can't give you real friends. No matter what she promises."

"What does she know of your pain? Of your isolation?" Invidia hissed, and a deep chill traveled through me at the sibilance in her voice. "She knows nothing of your darkness, yet she would extinguish the one flame glowing on your horizon." Em's gaze flicked to Nash at my side, and Sabine's followed.

"You need only cross into the Nether…" The hellion slid Emma's arm around Sabine's waist in a possessive gesture. "Deliver me this young, ripe Emma-body and sign away your soul. Such a small price, for a lifetime of peace and pleasure."

"Sabine, no!" Nash cried, and when I glanced at him, I saw his irises *churning* with fear and rage. "If you cross over, you'll never make it back. She won't let you."

"Smart *bean sidhe* boy…" Invidia purred. "He still wants to protect you. If not for *her,* he would be yours. Cross over now, and I give you my word you will return, the moment you sign. You will live out your full lifeline here, with everything she has, but you truly deserve."

My thoughts raced so fast the room was starting to spin. Invidia might be able to give things to Sabine, but she couldn't take them from me. Could she?

I saw the decision in Sabine's eyes a moment before she disappeared. She loved Nash too much—and evidently envied me too much—to resist the offer. "No!" I lunged for Emma, desperate to pull her away from Sabine before the *mara* crossed over. But I was too late. My fingers barely brushed the fine hairs on Emma's arm, then they were both gone.

"No!" Nash took me by both arms and made me look at him, forcing me to see through my own encroaching shock.

Emma was in the Netherworld. And I had let it happen. Humans couldn't survive in the Netherworld, and even if Em proved to be the exception, she'd never be the same. How could she be, if she saw even a fraction of the grotesque, hor-

rifying creatures who lived there, every last one of them waiting to devour her in one way or another?

"Kaylee, we have to get them back. You have to cross us
over. Now!"

And that's when I understood the depth of Invidia's plan.
She couldn't take what I had from me and give it to Sabine.
Surely that was beyond her power. But if I went to the Nether-
world, she—or Avari—could enslave me for the rest of my life.
Or they could just kill me and take my soul, which was what
they probably had in mind for Emma. Eventually, anyway.

We'd been set up. Invidia had meant for us to hear her talking to Sabine, and she meant for us to see them cross over.
And she wanted us to follow.

But even knowing that, knowing both hellions would be
there waiting for us, we had to cross. I couldn't leave Emma—
or even the terminally conflicted *mara*—to the hellions' mercy.
Not and live with myself afterward.

"I know," I whispered, my voice having succumbed to terror and shock. *Get it together, Kaylee.* "Okay, let's think about
this."

"No, let's go get them back. I can't cross over without you,
Kaylee. Come on..."

"Wait a second." I pulled Nash to the opposite side of the
room, careful not to get too close to the walls in case the
Crimson Creeper invasion had spread to the kitchen. "We'd be
stupid to cross over in the same spot they last saw us. They'll
be right there waiting to grab us."

A current of surprise and relief twisted through the fear
churning in his irises. "Good thinking."

"Thanks."

Nash was usually the calm, cool one, but he wasn't thinking clearly at all this time. *It's Sabine.* He wanted her back as
badly as I wanted Emma back, and I couldn't help wondering

if Tod was right. Were Nash and Sabine meant to be together? Was I the only thing standing in their way.

No time for that now… "Give me your hand."

His fingers tightened around mine and a lump formed in my throat. I'd held his hand so many times before, but it had never felt this…bittersweet. Sabine needed him, and he needed to go save her. And he needed me to get him there. But what did I need from him?

"Kay?" Nash's forehead furrowed in fear and concern. "You ready?"

I exhaled heavily. "Nope. Let's go."

Calling forth my wail was much too simple that time, because of how easy it was to picture Emma dying—again. I'd promised her I wouldn't let that happen, no matter what. And I was *not* going to break my promise.

When the wail faded from my ears and the pain in my throat subsided, my eyes flew open and I scanned the Netherworld-version kitchen around us. Thin tendrils of creeper vine had snaked in from the cafeteria but, though they reached for us, slowly slithering along the walls and floor, they hadn't grown enough to completely overwhelm the room yet.

The sink faucets dripped typically rank, gloppy substances, but few of the other appliances had bled through the barrier.

Emma and Sabine stood in the middle of the kitchen, exactly where they'd crossed over, only now my best friend was back in her own body—and obviously in shock. Sabine held Em's forearm, and I couldn't tell whether the *mara* was trying to protect her or control her.

Avari and Invidia faced them from separate sides of the room, so that Sabine couldn't keep an eye on both hellions at once.

"Kaylee…?" Emma's brown eyes were wide, but not truly focused when her gaze slid to me from Invidia, whose long, sizzling hair flowed rapidly now with excitement. Drops of it rolled down her clothes without damaging the material, then fell to bubble and burn little holes in the linoleum tile. Emma winced at the sizzle. "Where are we? This is hell, right? I'm in hell?"

"It's the Netherworld, Em." My version of hell. "It's gonna be fine. I'm going to get you out of here."

"Am I dead, Kay?" Her words were slurred with shock, and my heart broke. She'd fallen asleep in history class and woken up in hell, and she thought I'd let it happen. That I'd let her die when I could have saved her.

"Soon, my dear..." Invidia crooned. "Very, very soon."

"Don't listen to her, Emma. Don't even look at her," I insisted, and for the first time, I wondered why neither hellion had simply charged them both. Or us.

"Sabine, cross back," Nash said. "Take Emma back to the human world, and we can all work this out there. You don't have to sell your soul to get your life back together."

"He's wrong," Invidia insisted, her green-tinted eyes flashing, while Avari stood silently by, apparently content to wait and see how things played out, at least for now. "You've tried it on your own, and how well did that go?"

"It went fine!" Nash shouted, irises churning furiously as he stepped forward. I followed him, reluctant to let him out of arm's reach in case I had to cross over quickly. He turned back to Sabine. "You can do this on your own, and I'll help. I've *been* helping."

"You threw me out." Her hand tightened around Emma's arm, and Em flinched, but didn't try to pull away. "You kicked me out of your house and told me not to come back."

Nash hesitated, and I read confliction on his face. He couldn't deny what we all knew had happened, but passing the blame on to Sabine, where it rightfully belonged, would only push her further toward making a proverbial—and almost literal—deal with the devil. "I take it back," he finally said. "I was frustrated and angry, and I acted on impulse, when there was probably a better way to handle the situation," he said, and I wondered if that was a direct quote from his mother.

"He'll do it again." Invidia swept a rivulet of hair over her shoulder, and drops of it splattered the floor behind her. "As long as *she's* in the way, he'll abandon you again and again. Sign over your soul, and I'll make all that go away. I'll make *her* go away."

And suddenly I was out of patience.

"Okay, look," I started, and when all heads turned my way, I had to swallow the lump in my throat before continuing. "Your soul is your business, Sabine."

"Kaylee…" Nash started, warning me with his tone.

"She's a big girl, Nash," I insisted. "She can handle the truth." I turned back to Sabine, uncomfortably aware that I also had the full attention of two hellions. "What you do with your soul is up to you. I personally think you'd be an idiot to sign it over to someone who plans to torture you for all of eternity, and that *is* what she's planning. Ask her, if you don't believe me. But I won't let you drag Emma down with you."

I propped my hands on my hips and shot Sabine a challenging glance. "You let her go right now, and then if you still want to sell your soul I'll prick your finger myself, so you can sign in blood. How's that?"

"Kaylee!" Nash snapped, but I could only shrug, hoping my attempt at reverse psychology didn't backfire. Sabine typically did exactly what I wanted her not to, so maybe if she thought I wanted her to sell her soul—or at least that it wouldn't bother me—she'd run in the opposite direction.

"Let her speak," Avari said, hands in the pockets of his suit jacket. "I find her honesty…blissfully chaotic." He was dressed like any human corporate monkey, which should have made him look harmless and…normal. But his eyes…

I couldn't stand to look at those solid black orbs; they seemed to suck the light out of the room, rather than reflect it. His eyes were windows not into his soul—he didn't have one—but into a void so deep and dark it was the very definition of despair.

"Good. Here, let's get this over with." I marched toward Sabine, hoping a show of aggression on my part would push her into action.

Sabine took a step back, pulling Emma with her. Nash called my name, but I didn't stop. And when I was halfway between him and Sabine, a sudden wink of motion drew my attention to my right. My head swiveled, eyes searching for the anomaly.

Avari was gone.

Nash yelped behind me. I spun to find Avari holding him by one arm, and suddenly I understood why neither hellion had made a move until that moment—I'd gotten pretty damn good at crossing over in a hurry, and based on what I'd seen minutes earlier, Sabine could do it nearly instantly. Neither hellion was willing to risk us crossing over and depriving them of four victims.

But once Nash was out of my reach, he was fair game.

I froze, stuck between my maybe-boyfriend and my definitely best friend, unsure what to do.

"One move, and I'll kill him," Avari said, and since hellions can't lie, I was pretty sure he wasn't bluffing.

"Kaylee, go!" Nash shouted, face already twisted with pain, and I understood that he was feeling exactly what I'd felt in the nightmare Avari had given me. "Take them and go!"

But I'd no more leave him than I'd leave Emma, and the hellion obviously knew that.

Avari glanced past me at Sabine. "Let's make a deal, Ms. Campbell."

"No!" Invidia screeched, and Emma gave a startled yip. I followed her gaze to see that the hellion of envy now sported several rows of razor-sharp, needle-thin teeth, the yellowish white of aged bone. "No deals. The *mara* is mine, and so is the lovely Emma-body. *Mine!*"

"Kaylee...!" Em moaned, and now she was clinging to Sabine.

"Sabine, get her out of here!" I snapped, splitting my attention between Invidia, Sabine and Em, and Avari and Nash.

"If you go, you'll never see him again," Avari said, and Sabine's eyes widened in panic. She wouldn't let Nash die, and as grateful as I was for that impulse, I was terrified to even think what she'd do to save him.

"What's your offer?" Sabine asked, and a horrible screech of fury erupted from Invidia's inhuman throat.

"No! Mine! I found her. I fed her. I cultivated her envy into a fragrant bouquet of desire and bitterness and rage, and she is perfectly ripe right now, and *I will pluck her!*"

Avari's gaze never wavered from Sabine. "A trade. Mine—" he shoved Nash forward, without letting go of him, and Nash moaned "—for yours." And that's when I understood that Avari was feeding from him. Draining his energy, like he'd done for more than a day, the last time Nash was in the Netherworld.

"No, Sabine," Nash gasped, as his face drained of all color. "Kaylee, don't let her do it."

I didn't know what to say. I couldn't choose between Nash and Emma. I *couldn't!*

"You'd give up a *bean sidhe* for a human?" Sabine aimed a suspicious look at Avari. "Why?"

"All you need to know is that if I get the girl, you may take your lover and cross back over."

But I understood what he wasn't saying. He wasn't giving up Nash for Emma. He was giving up Nash for me. Because if he got Emma, he could force me to trade my freedom for hers.

"Kaylee...?" Em was shaking with full-body tremors, her eyes glazing over with shock.

"No!" Invidia was wild with fury now. Her hair flowed so fast a sizzling puddle was forming on the ground at her feet. Her eyes glowed bright green, and her hands had become claws, sharp and hooked on the ends.

Sabine glanced from Invidia, to me, to Avari, then back to me, and I could see the confliction written all over her face. She didn't want to damn Emma. But she didn't want to lose Nash, either, and Avari's deal was obviously much more beneficial than the one Invidia had offered.

Then she looked at Nash and saw pain shifting the colors in his eyes, and I knew what she'd say before she could even form the words.

"Fine. Here." Sabine pushed Emma to her right. Avari let go of Nash and shoved him in the opposite direction. I raced toward Emma. She stumbled and fell to her knees. Across the room, Nash half collapsed from pain. Sabine ran toward him, arms outstretched.

And before either of us reached our goal, a dark blur flew across the edge of my vision. Invidia screeched. I turned to see her racing toward me—I was closest to her—claws bared, needle teeth snapping together, so long and curved she couldn't even close her mouth.

I dodged to the left, and she mirrored my movement from ten feet away, hissing in fury, hair sizzling in a trail behind her.

Avari let loose an inhuman roar, enraged to see another hellion so close to his prize. He stopped—just feet from Emma—

and planted his right foot firmly on the ground, like a giant determined to shake the earth. Tendrils of frost shot across the tile from his ordinary black dress shoe, racing toward Invidia, growing thicker and stronger with every inch of ground they covered. They reached her as she lunged for me. I scrambled backward in terror, and she froze. For real.

A blue sheen covered her skin. Her hair stopped dripping, instantly frozen into overlapping, green-tinted icicles. Her claws still reached for me, a foot from my face, frozen in time.

"Kaylee!" Tod shouted, and I looked up to see him standing across the room, surprised by what he'd found, but ready for action.

"Get Em!" I yelled. He nodded, then disappeared. Avari reached for Emma again, and she stumbled away from him. Tod reappeared at her side and she clutched at him. Another instant later, they were both gone.

Avari roared again, and his gaze narrowed on me from my left. On my right, something crackled sharply—Invidia was fighting the ice. Avari stalked toward me. I closed my eyes to summon my wail. But before I could produce any sound, Nash shouted from across the room.

"Come get us!"

I opened my eyes to see him holding Sabine at arm's length, refusing to let her cross them over until he knew I was safe.

Avari stood and straightened his jacket. He glanced at me on his right, then at Nash and Sabine, on his left, and I recognized the look on his face.

Greed. Pure, concentrated avarice. He wanted us all. But even a hellion couldn't be two places at once. He'd have to choose.

But then more ice crackled on my other side, and I knew he wouldn't get the chance.

Invidia's left claw shot toward me. The ice glaze over her

arm cracked and shattered on the floor. I kicked out on instinct. My foot slammed into her stomach, and she fell to her knees, still half-frozen. I kicked her again, and she fell onto her side. When her face hit the ground, three long, sharp teeth broke off of her lower jaw and clattered on the ground, as long as my little finger. Several frozen hair-cicles snapped off of her head and skittered across the floor toward Nash and Sabine.

"Sabine, cross!" I shouted. She glanced at Avari, then knelt and plucked one of the poison-cicles from the ground, holding it between her thumb and forefinger. Then she nodded at me and grabbed Nash's arm.

"No!" Nash shouted, as she crossed over with him in her grip.

I tried to summon my wail. Avari ran for me. Invidia's thawed claw wrapped around my ankle, ripping through my jeans. I jerked my foot, but she wouldn't let go. So I grabbed one of her broken teeth, my pulse racing in my ears. Avari roared in fury, feet away. Invidia's grip on my ankle tightened.

I shoved the tooth through her left eye.

Invidia screamed and let go of my foot, slapping both claws over her injury. I scrambled backward, trying desperately to call up my wail. But it wouldn't come. I was too scared to think of any death but my own.

Then strong, warm arms wrapped around me from behind. "I've got you," Tod whispered in my ear, as Avari charged us.

An instant later, we stood in the Eastlake kitchen, Tod still holding me from behind. My right foot stood in white glop from a busted bottle of mayonnaise. Emma stared at me from three feet away, eyes wide with shock.

Across the room, Nash was hunched over in pain and exhaustion, wrapped in Sabine's arms. On the floor at her feet stood a clear plastic cup with the melting poison hair-cicle inside. I didn't even want to know why she'd taken it.

Tod squeezed me, then let me go, and I whirled around to face him. "Thanks. I totally owe you."

"No. You don't," he said, and the blues in his eyes shifted slowly.

Then Emma was there, wrapping me in a hug.

"Are you okay?" I asked her, pulling my foot from the mayo.

"I think so." She let go of me and pushed strands of blond hair from her face. Her eyes were still wide and her skin was pale, but being back in familiar surroundings went a long way toward calming her down. "That was the Netherworld?"

"In all its many-splendored horror." I grabbed an apron hanging from a hook on the wall and wiped as much of the gunk off my shoe as I could.

"What the hell happened? I was in history one minute, and the next thing I know, I'm staring at some man in a suit and some…thing with rancid water for hair, who looked like she wanted to eat me whole."

"It's a long story, Em. I promise I'll tell you the whole thing. But I need just a second to…breathe."

Emma nodded, and I sat down on a stool, blessedly free of splattered condiments. And for a moment, the five of us just stared at one another.

Shocked. Relieved. And very much alive.

27

"So, the one with the hair?" Emma said, pulling the pan from the oven.

"The poison hair, dripping and fizzing everywhere?" I asked, laying a hand towel across the counter.

Em nodded and set the pan on the towel, then inhaled deeply through her nose. To try to make up for her trauma the day before, I'd promised to answer every Netherworld question she could throw at me over homemade brownies, chosen for the inherent comfort-power of chocolate.

"That was Invidia. She's a hellion of envy."

She dropped the pot holders on the counter. "The one who put the whammy on you and Sabine?"

"And half the school." I shoved the pot holders into the drawer to the left of the stove. "It was part of the blitz, remember?" Emma nodded, but didn't look very sure, so I elaborated. "Okay, think of it like a waterwheel. Once it gets going, it produces lots of power, right? But you have to put in an initial effort to get it set up. The setup in this case was one big burst of energy shoved into our school by Avari, a hellion of greed, and Invidia, a hellion of envy. That one burst irritated already existing frictions between people, and since it was powered by greed and envy, it paid off in greed and envy."

"So…Sophie cut off Laura's hair because she was jealous of that stupid Snow Queen crown."

"Exactly." I reached into the fridge and pulled out a gallon of milk, while Em got down two short glasses.

"And it made Sabine crazy jealous of you, and it made you determined to blame everything that went wrong on her."

I huffed and handed her the first glass. "Sort of. But Avari and Invidia went through some special effort to play the two of us against each other, because we were the payoff."

"That's creepy, Kay."

"At the very least." I sipped from my glass, watching her closely.

For the most part, Emma had dealt pretty well with what she'd seen, and subsequently been told. Her reaction to finding out she'd been possessed—"Did my head spin around?"— was her typical humor defense, but I saw the fear beneath. I knew what she was feeling—out of control and terrified and *used*—because I'd been there.

And I would be there to help her deal. And to fight back. We all would.

When the doorbell rang, I answered it while Em cut the brownies. Nash stood in the circle of light on my front porch, and the moment our gazes met, the colors in his irises started swirling and my heart beat a little harder.

"Hey."

"Hey," I said, then I let him fold me into a warm hug, punctuated by a kiss. I ached for more, but it wasn't the time. I couldn't help wondering if that time would ever come, because…

"So, are you gonna make us stand out here all night?" Sabine asked, stepping onto the porch behind him. "I'm freezing my ass off, and I need to talk to Emma."

I stepped aside to let them in, then closed the door and took Nash's hand when he offered it. He'd asked me out for Friday night—a real date, guaranteed free from all Netherworld interruptions and *mara* scheming—and I'd accepted. Though I had no idea how I'd talk my dad into letting me go. Nash was willing to earn back my trust, and I was willing to let him try, so long as he stayed clean. But my dad was staunchly con, regarding the possibility of a Kaylee/Nash reunion.

It might actually be easier to make Sabine give up on Nash than to make my dad accept him.

Sabine stomped past us into the kitchen, where Emma had yet to look up from her brownies. The *mara* had already apologized for sending me to the Netherworld, then almost selling me to Avari. I accepted her apology because I knew she meant it—she wouldn't have said it otherwise. And I'd apologized for blaming the murder of our teachers and near-destruction of our school on her. So in her warped world view, we were even, and the status quo was secure. She would keep trying to claw her way into Nash's heart—unsatisfied with the role of good friend—and I would continue to push her back every time she went too far.

But because Em refused to accept her apology and didn't owe Sabine one, the *mara* had become obsessed with making Emma forgive her.

It was not going well.

"Em?" Sabine launched into another round of apologies, while Nash and I sat on the couch.

"Feeling okay?" I asked, staring into his eyes to see the truth. It had been more than a day, but he was just now regaining color after being drained by Avari. Again. Of course, it helped that he no longer had to worry about me and Sabine being actively pitted against each other by a pair of evil Netherworld hellions. We weren't best friends—I'd probably never actually *like* the *mara*—but we could be in the same room without needing a referee now.

Most of the time.

"I'm better." After a lengthy pause, during which Emma tried to get rid of Sabine by offering her chocolate, Nash said, "Mom should be here any minute."

"She's on her way," Tod confirmed, and I looked up to see him sitting in my dad's favorite chair. Watching us.

"Shouldn't you be delivering pizza?" Nash asked.

The reaper shrugged. "Like I'm gonna miss this."

I frowned. "You've already seen it?"

"Um…yeah. And heard it, and smelled it, and…"

"What is it?" Nash asked, but his brother only grinned.

Harmony had been looking for a way to keep us from getting possessed ever since she found out what had happened to me a month ago, and we'd gotten a call that morning saying she'd finally come up with something. Which was the only reason Sabine and Emma had wound up in the same room so soon after Em's first trip to the Netherworld.

"Where's your dad?" Tod glanced down the hall, like my father might materialize any moment.

"Helping Alec get settled." Alec and my father had struck up an odd sort of friendship, thanks to their mutual lack of humanity and abject hatred of the hellion who'd possessed them both multiple times. My dad had even cleaned out our meager savings to lend Alec his first month's rent and security deposit.

"Knock, knock!" Harmony called from the front porch, then came in without waiting for me to open the door, carrying a large cardboard box. "Tod, give me a hand, please."

The reaper stood reluctantly and took the box from his mother. As soon as he touched it, the box started to shake and erupted into a chorus of squeals and odd, high-pitched growls.

"What's that?" I asked, standing as Tod set the box on my coffee table. Em and Sabine wandered in from the kitchen to stare suspiciously at the weird, yipping box.

"That…" Harmony began, "is part of what's going to keep you from playing host to a hellion ever again. But first…" She stuck one hand into her coat pocket and pulled out a plastic sandwich bag filled with odd, blue, stiff-looking strands of… something. "Emma, give me your wrist."

Em stuck her arm out hesitantly, while Harmony pulled out one of the cords, which turned out to be braided lengths of something fibrous.

"This is silk from a Netherworld plant called *dissimulatus*. It's very rare, which is why it took me so long to find it, but it's also very sturdy." She tied braided silk into a loop around Emma's wrist, then double and triple knotted it. The bracelet was too small to slip off, but too loose to cut off her circulation. "It won't shrink, stain, or tear, so you can wear it all the time. Even in the shower."

"Dissimulatus?" Em asked, twisting the loop around her wrist while Harmony dug in her bag for another one.

"It means 'disguise.' As long as you wear them, the silk will disguise your energy signature, both here and in the Netherworld."

"What does that mean?" Emma asked. And if she hadn't, I would have.

"Think of yourself as a cell phone," Harmony began, tying the second bracelet on Sabine's left wrist. "Constantly broadcasting a signal—your energy signature. That signal identifies you as a human female, about sixteen years old. Specifically, it identifies you as Emma Dawn Marshall. This bracelet—" she held up another one and waved me forward, as Sabine frowned at her new accessory "—is like a jammer. It's going to jam your signal. And for the rest of you—" Harmony glanced at me, Nash, and Sabine in turn as she wrapped the stiff length of cord around my arm "—it will disguise your species, as well."

"So…no one will know I'm a *bean sidhe?*" I asked, as she tied the first knot.

"Not just from tasting your energy signature."

"And that'll keep Avari from possessing us?" Nash said, holding his arm out for his bracelet.

"It'll keep him from identifying you. And if he can't find you, he can't possess you. Right?"

"But he knows where we live," Sabine pointed out, frowning skeptically. "It's not gonna be hard to find us, if he's looking in the right place."

Harmony nodded solemnly. "And that's where these come in." Without further explanation, she opened the box on the coffee table, reached inside, and pulled out a small, quaking ball of fur.

I frowned at the creature, and at the faint gamey smell emanating from it. And when Harmony shoved it toward me, I took a step back.

"He won't hurt you," she insisted, and pushed it toward me again. This time I held out both hands, and she deposited the furball in them. "This is your new best friend." She brushed blond curls back from her face, then reached into the box again and pulled out another ball of fur, and handed this one to Nash. "They don't have a name that I can actually pronounce, so you may as well just think of them as puppies. Very special puppies."

"They're dogs?" Emma asked, and Harmony smiled.

"Not fully. They're a mix of a Pomeranian and a small Netherworld critter. They're very expensive and difficult to breed. So don't take this responsibility lightly."

"Responsibility?" Sabine said, holding her "dog" at arm's length.

"Yes. It's very important that you bond with them over the next couple of weeks."

"So, what?" Emma said. "Hellions are allergic to fur?"

Harmony laughed and stroked the small creature in my hands, which had begun to sniff my fingers with a tiny, wet nose. "No. These little guys are Netherworld guard dogs. If they sense a hellion anywhere near you, on the other side of the world barrier, of course, they'll start yipping up a storm. So...if you sleep with him in your room, he'll wake you up before you can possibly be possessed."

"So...the cure for hellion possession is a pet?" I asked, running one finger down the creature's thin, trembling spine.

"Well, it's more preventative than actual cure, but it's the best I could come up with."

"My mom won't let me have a dog," Emma said, looking worried as she cradled hers to her chest.

Harmony was unconcerned. "Tod can talk her into it, can't you, Tod?" The reaper nodded. "And, Sabine, I'm sure Nash can talk to your foster mother for you." Their Influence should pave the way toward pet ownership before the poor mothers even knew what hit them.

"But I don't want a dog," Sabine said, still staring at hers like it might bite her. Or vice versa. "I didn't even want a bracelet."

Harmony frowned. "Do you want Avari in your body?"

"No."

"Then you want this bracelet, and you definitely want this

dog. Name him. Feed him. Bond with him. He's the only thing standing between you and serial possession. Got it?"

Sabine nodded hesitantly, and I laughed out loud. I couldn't help it. She couldn't have looked less comfortable if Harmony had demanded she cha-cha in a pair of three-inch heels.

"What about Alec?" I asked, pushing my new bracelet up my arm, to keep the pup from chewing on it.

"I dropped his off at his new place. Sophie's getting one, too, though I don't know how her dad's going to explain it."

"So…this is it?" Nash asked. "We're using jewelry and puppies to ward off evil?"

Harmony nodded. "Right now, guys, these puppies and bracelets are all you have standing between you and the Netherworld. Well, these little guys, and one another. For whatever reason, the dominant hellion of this area has literally moved into your high school, just across the world barrier from where you spend most of your waking hours. And he's not alone. Such a concentration of power is like a lighthouse in the dark. It's going to attract others, and your school is going to be at the heart of whatever trouble moves into the neighborhood.

"If you're going to take on the entire Netherworld population, as some of you seem determined to do, you need to at least know what you have going for you. So take a look around this room. This is it. These are the people in your corner. So I suggest you all find a way to get along. I have a feeling someday your lives are going to depend on it."

I glanced around my living room, one face at a time, thinking of everything we'd been through together. Everything we'd fought and survived. Hellions. Possession. Toxic vines. Demon's Breath. Walking nightmares. Was Harmony saying it would get worse from there?

A chill shot through me at the very thought.

But as I watched Sabine watching Nash watch me, I realized something I should have understood much sooner—as horrifying a threat as the Netherworld represented, learning to trust again in my own world might just be the scariest thing I'd ever had to do.

★ ★ ★ ★ ★

ACKNOWLEDGMENTS

THANKS FIRST OF ALL TO MY EDITOR, Mary-Theresa Hussey, who knew just what this book needed. Her suggestions challenged me to find better solutions, and the book is *so* much better for it.

Thanks to Natashya Wilson, for so much enthusiasm and support.

Rinda Elliot, for the lightning-fast critique, and for being the first to love Sabine.

Thanks to #1, who made fajitas and helped me figure out how to hurt a hellion.

Thanks to Ally, Jen, Melissa, Kelley, and everyone else in the YA community for advice, camaraderie, and for making me feel so welcome.

And most of all, thank you to the readers who have given Kaylee and her friends a place in this world. Without you, none of the rest of it would matter.

• REAPER •

To all the readers who've asked for more of Tod,
I couldn't be happier to oblige!

STARING DOWN AT the man on the bed, I couldn't help but suspect the coincidence. What were the chances he'd be brought in on my first day at the hospital? Levi was a shrewd little bastard, and the man on the bed—practically gift-wrapped for me in a hospital gown, terror dancing in his eyes—was proof of that. I was no angel in life. Why should that be any different in death?

"OKAY, I'M HEADING out..." Mom slid her purse over one shoulder on her way through the living room. "There's leftover lasagna in the fridge. And there's some bagged salad."

I nodded absently and flipped the channel to VH1 concert footage from one of the kids' networks—where I was *not* trying to catch a glimpse of my ex-girlfriend Addison, who'd dumped me for a chance at stardom when she was cast in a pilot.

"Tod." Mom sat on the coffee table, right in front of the television. "Did you hear me?"

"Yeah." I leaned to the left and she mimicked my movement. "Lasagna. Salad. Got it."

"I'm serious. Eat something green, okay?" She snatched the remote and aimed it over her shoulder, and a second later the screen went dark. I started to complain, but then I noticed how tired she looked—the beginnings of lines on a face that would look thirty years old for the next half a century—and came up with a grin instead.

"Do Skittles count?"

Mom rolled her eyes. She never could resist my smile. "Only if you save me the purple ones." She handed me the remote, but wouldn't let go when I tried to take it. "You're staying home tonight, right?"

"What am I, a leper? It's Friday night. I have plans."

She sighed. "Change them. Please."

"Mom…"

"I need you to keep an eye on Nash."

"Am I my brother's keeper?" I tried another grin, but this time she wasn't buying it.

"Tonight, you're his warden. It doesn't do me any good to ground him if I can't keep him at home."

"Then why bother grounding him?"

She leaned closer and lowered her voice, bright blue irises swirling slowly in dread and frustration, and the fact that she let me read her eyes was my first clue how serious she was. Humans wouldn't have been able to see it—only a fellow *bean sidhe*—banshee, to the uninformed—would be able to read her emotions in her eyes, but she usually hid them from us too.

"Because he snuck out in the middle of the night and drove to Holser House on a license still warm from the lamination! And an ineffective consequence is better than no consequence at all. At least, that's what I'm telling myself." She raked one hand through her hair, then met my gaze with a worried one of her own. "He's not like you, Tod. Aside from a couple of notable exceptions, you tend to think things through, but Nash is ruled by his heart—"

I nearly choked on laughter. "I think the organ he's ruled by is a little farther south, Mom."

She frowned. "My point is that he's not taking this separation from Sabine very well. I thought some time apart would help...cool things down between them. But it seems to be doing the opposite." She let go of the remote and gave me a wistful smile. "You and your brother could not be more different."

"Because he thinks he's in love, and I don't believe in faerie tales?"

"Love isn't a faerie tale, Tod. But it isn't child's play either, and it makes me nervous how intense they are together."

"You just don't want to be a grandmother," I teased, trying to lighten the mood.

"That's definitely part of it," she admitted. "My future grandchildren deserve better than teenage parents could give them. But beyond that, it isn't healthy how wrapped up they are in each other. Relationships like that burn bright, but when they burn out, they leave everyone blistered. Do you understand what I'm saying?"

"You're condoning my playboy lifestyle, right? Because I'm your favorite."

Mom laughed out loud. "At least Nash doesn't get bored a month into a relationship. You, my hedonistic firstborn, are an entirely different kind of problem."

"Hedonistic is another word for favorite, right? So that's a compliment?"

She stood, still smiling. "Eat something green. And read something without pictures. Those are not suggestions."

I turned the TV back on as she headed for the door. "I'll take them both under advisement."

"Nash!" Mom called, one hand already on the front doorknob. "I'm leaving!"

A door squealed open down the hall, and a minute later my little brother stood in the doorway, dark hair standing up all over like he'd just woken up. "And this is noteworthy because...?"

"Because this is your official reminder that your grounding does not expire with daylight. Do not leave this house while I'm at work."

Nash gave her a crooked grin—possibly the only feature my brother and I had in common. "What if the house catches fire?"

"Roast marshmallows. And if it floods, you'll go down with the ship. If there's a tornado, I'll meet both you and this house in Oz, after my shift. Got it?"

I chuckled and Nash glared at me before turning back to our mother. "Total house arrest. I got it."

"Good. I'll see you both in the morning. Don't stay up too late." Then the door closed behind her. A moment later an engine started and her car backed down the driveway.

"Mom told me to watch you. She thinks you're up to something," I said, when Nash just stared at me, leaning against the doorway into the hall.

"She's right." He crossed the room and sat on the coffee table, where she'd sat minutes earlier. "I need a favor."

"Move." I shoved him out of the way and started flipping through the channels again. "What kind of favor?"

"The kind that only you and I can do," Nash said, and his hazel irises twisted in an intense storm of greens and browns. I turned the TV off and dropped the remote on the center couch cushion. "I'm going to pick up Sabine, and I need help convincing them to let her go."

Shit. "I'm confiscating your hair dryer—you've fried your brain. You can't just 'pick up Sabine' without a court order—she's in a halfway house!"

Nash nodded, like he didn't see the problem. "That's where the 'convincing' comes in."

And by convincing, he meant Influencing. The female of our species was better known, historically and mythologically, by her iconic wail for the dying. What most of the human race didn't know was that where they heard a head-splitting scream, male *bean sidhes*—like me and Nash—heard an eerie, compelling song calling out to disembodied souls, keeping them from moving on.

Male *bean sidhes'* most prominent ability—Influence—was also vocal in nature, and much more subtle than the female's wail. But no less powerful. With nothing but a few words and some serious intent, we could make people do things. Make them *want* to do things. Like release Sabine from her court-mandated halfway house into the custody of her sixteen-year-old boyfriend.

"You really think I'm going to drive all the way to Holser House on a Friday night just to help you score a conjugal town pass for your delinquent girlfriend?"

"Not a town pass, Tod. I'm not taking her for a walk—I'm breaking her out. *We're* breaking her out. You talk to whoever's on duty while I get Sabine. Then we leave. Simple." He shrugged, like things were really that easy in NashWorld.

"*You're* simple." I leaned back on the couch and crossed my arms over my chest, trying to figure out how to explain the problem so that even an impulsive, lovesick idiot twenty-two months my junior could understand. "Okay, look...everything you've said so far will probably work." I'd certainly talked us both into and out of tougher situations before. "But what happens after?"

"After what?"

"After we leave and the night staff realizes they've just lost a girl put in their custody by the state of Texas? You think they're just going to shrug and move on? Hell no, they're going to report her missing. And at the very least, they're going to have the description of the two guys she left with." Because my Influence wouldn't last much longer than it would take for the sound of my voice to fade into silence, and no matter how powerful I got with age and experience, I'd never be able to make someone forget what they saw or did. It just didn't work like that. And Nash damn well knew it.

He shrugged, and I wanted to smack him over the head. "So we come up with another plan. It won't be the first time you snuck a girl out of her house in the middle of the night."

"Nuh uh." I sat straighter, shaking my head at him. "Don't pretend this is the same as sneaking out for a beer at the watershed. You're talking about helping a convicted criminal escape from corrective custody!"

"She doesn't belong there."

"Okay, then, genius, what are you gonna do with her once you have her? Put her in a box and poke some holes?"

"She can take care of herself. And I can help."

I searched his face for some sign that he was joking, but found nothing. "She's *fifteen!*"

Nash shrugged. "That's just a number. It doesn't say anything about her."

"It says something pretty damn funny about your IQ!" I said, and he opened his mouth to retort, but I spoke over him. "Fifteen is too young to drive, too young to get a legal job, too young to sign a lease and obviously too young to pick a boyfriend with half a brain."

Nash's confidence crumbled and fell apart, exposing blind desperation and pain so intense I could hardly wrap my mind around them. And while I wanted to believe this was all drama and hormones, *he* obviously believed it was more than that. "They won't even let me talk to her, Tod. I think they found the phone I gave her, 'cause she hasn't answered it in three days."

Finally I leaned forward, right in his face, determined to give him the wake-up call he desperately needed. "What did you expect? You date a criminal, and you're eventually going to have to share her with the state. Hell, she's probably got a girlfriend on the inside by now."

"You're an asshole."

"And you're living in a fantasy world. There are other girls out there, Nash. Maybe even a few who've never seen the inside of the police station."

He glared at me, waiting for me to cave, but that wasn't gonna happen. Not this time. Mom was right—he'd lost it. Over a *girl*. "Fine. I'll do it myself. Gimme the keys."

"No way. I'm meeting Genna in an hour."

"I thought you were supposed to stay here and babysit."

"I thought *you* were supposed to be the smart one. So why are you acting like such an idiot?"

"Just give me the keys!" Nash glanced around the living room, then lunged for the end table when he spotted the keys to the car I'd been forced to share with him since his birthday. I rammed his shoulder, knocking him to the carpet halfway across the room.

"Sorry." I grabbed the keys and shoved them into my front pocket. "But Mom says you're grounded." I stuck my hand out to help him up, but he smacked it away, glaring up at me with his jaw clenched.

Nash shoved himself to his feet and stepped forward like he'd take a swing. But he wouldn't. I could see hints of our father's build in the width of his shoulders, but I still had two inches and twenty pounds on him, and he knew better than to start a fight he couldn't win.

"I'd do this for you," he spat instead. "Because you're my brother. But obviously that concept is wasted on you." Then he stomped off to his room and slammed the door.

"You'll thank me for this later!" I shouted, trying to deny the fact that his parting shot stung almost like a physical blow.

A COUPLE OF hours later, the credits scrolled down the darkened TV screen, and Genna sighed. She sat up, and I missed the warmth of her back against my chest. I wrapped one arm around her waist and leaned forward. "Hey, I liked you there."

She twisted in my grip to straddle me, delicious pressure in exactly the right place. Her brows arched and she gave me a slow smile as she bent toward my ear. "I thought you might like me here better," she whispered, her breath an intimate warmth against my ear.

She was right.

She laid her hands flat against my chest, warm, thin fingers splayed over my shirt. My pulse spiked and I pulled her down for a kiss. My mouth left hers to trail over her chin and down her neck, tasting her bit by bit. She sat taller and threw her head back to give me better reach, shifting closer on my lap, and—

My cell phone buzzed on the end table.

I groaned, and Genna leaned back to brush hair from her face. "Aren't you going to get that?"

"Nothing on *earth* could make me take that call right now."
I tried to pull her closer, but she leaned over the arm of the
couch instead, peering at the display on my phone.

"It's your brother."

Damn it. I shifted her to one side and looked around her
shoulder at the dark hallway. "Nash, come out and get it yourself!" Then I recentered Genna on my lap. "Sometimes he
texts mom with snack requests, but I'm not gonna wait on
the lazy little punk."

Genna laughed, staring down at me. "He's been in his room
this whole time?"

"Yeah. Sulking."

"He's probably afraid of what he'll see if he comes out."

"Oh yeah?" I slid my hands slowly up her sides. "What's
he gonna see?"

"A little more of this…" She kissed me again, and Nash's
call was delivered to voice mail.

Two minutes later, the phone rang again, and I wanted to
throw it through the front window. Genna handed me the
phone. "He's not gonna quit until you answer."

I groaned and flipped the phone open, one hand on her hip,
and loud, bass-heavy music blasted from Nash's end of the line.

Oh shit. There was no music coming from the hall. When
had he snuck out?

"Where the hell are you?" I snapped into the receiver.

"I need a ride," Nash slurred into my ear, and I rolled my
eyes. He'd found a party.

"Where *are* you?" I repeated. "And how did you get there?"

"Arlington," Nash said, his words slushy but coherent. "I
walked to Brent's and he drove us out here, but now he's shit-
faced."

The tip of Genna's tongue trailed up my neck, hot and

damp, and full of promise. "We leave for Florida tomorrow morning," she whispered into one ear, while Nash barked threats into the other. "I won't see you again until school starts. But I don't have to be home for another hour…"

"You've already failed as a brother once today," Nash snapped. "Put your ass in the car and come get me."

"I'll be there in an hour," I said, only half focused on him while Genna leaned back and started unbuttoning her shirt. My pulse raced, anticipation sparking in my veins. "Just hang out until then…" I finished, vaguely aware that my voice was little more than a suggestion of sound by that point.

"Come get me, or I'm calling Mom," Nash threatened. "And *you* can tell her I'm at some stoner party in Arlington because you were too busy making out with your girlfriend to notice me leaving."

Shit.

"You're a complete pain in the ass, Nash."

"If you're not here in twenty minutes, I'm calling the hospital." Where our mom was pulling a twelve-hour shift. Nash spat out the address, then hung up before I could argue.

"Damn it." I flipped my phone closed, then lifted Genna from my lap and set her on the middle couch cushion.

"What's wrong?" she asked, frowning as I shoved my phone into my pocket and grabbed my keys.

"I have to go get Nash. But then we can take this to my room and pick up right where we left off." After a moment's hesitation—and one more long look—I pulled her up from the couch. "You'll never even know he's here." Because I'd bind and gag him if I had to, to keep him quiet.

"Where is he?" Genna buttoned her shirt, then ran her fingers through pale brown hair.

"Arlington. Let's go."

"Wait, Tod, I can't go to Arlington." Her frown deepened, and I could feel my plans for the evening being downgraded from X to PG13. "We'll barely make it back here before my curfew, and I'll be late by the time I get home."

"You want me to take you back now?" I asked, while on the inside I chanted, *please say no, please say no, pleasesayno* over and over.

"No," she said, pressing herself against me. "I want you to let your brother wait a few minutes." She tugged on the button at the waist of my jeans.

I put one hand over hers to stop her, cursing myself silently. "I can't. When left to his own devices, Nash finds trouble." And sometimes tries to break it out of jail. "You sure you can't miss curfew? I'll make it worth your while...."

"I'm sure you would." Her smile practically sizzled, and the flashes of memory that surfaced scalded me from the inside out. "But if I'm late, my mom will jump to all the right conclusions, and then my dad will *kill* you. Seriously. And what am I gonna do with a dead boyfriend?"

"Nothing that doesn't defy the norms of polite society..." I mumbled, disappointed when she stepped back and turned toward the door.

If Nash isn't dead of alcohol poisoning by the time I get there, I'll kill him myself...

Five minutes later, we pulled up in front of Genna's house, and as she'd predicted, the living room windows were still blazing with light. "Sure you don't want to reconsider?" I spread my arms and grinned. "All of this could be yours...."

"I'm reconsidering as we speak." She leaned toward me, and I met her halfway. "But we've already been spotted," she said, lips moving softly against my jaw on the way to my mouth. I glanced up to see that she was right; a tall, shadowed form stood in the front window, staring right at my car. "I gotta go." Genna pushed the door open and stepped out, small pink purse in hand. "Say hi to Nash for me." Then the car door closed, and she was halfway up the walk before I'd even shifted into Drive.

Her front door opened and her dad stepped out to put one arm around her shoulders, and as they stepped inside, she turned back to smile at me once.

And that was the last time I ever saw Genna Hansen.

"WHAT TOOK YOU so long?" Nash asked, as he slid into the passenger seat and pulled the door closed.

"I stopped to donate all your underwear to the homeless. You're gonna wanna take care of those tighty whities—they're all you've got left."

He leaned against the door, either too tired or too drunk to sit up. "And to think, most people don't understand your sense of humor."

"Fools, all of them." I flicked on my turn signal and merged with the highway traffic, typically heavy for a Friday night. "What are you doing out here, anyway?"

"Drinking alone, while my best friend and my brother feel up their respective girlfriends, with no thought for the less fortunate." His eyelids looked heavy, and I wondered how much he'd had. "Unfortunately, the juvenile justice system doesn't consider Sabine's separation from me cause for concern."

"Bastards." I swerved around an SUV, then back into the right lane. "Clearly the system is flawed."

Nash shrugged and slouched lower. "At least you got laid."

I glared at him before turning back to the traffic. "No, I got a brother who redefines the concept of '*coitus interruptus.*'"

"Sorry." Nash frowned, his unfocused stare aimed out the

windshield as I eased the car off the highway and onto the first street in a tangle of suburban neighborhoods. "But hey, since you're not busy anymore and we're out anyway…we could head over to Holser House." I started to shake my head, but he kept talking. "Please, Tod. That place is going to kill her."

Irritated, I clenched the wheel and stared at the road. "You're drunk, Nash."

"Then *you* can do the talking!" he snapped, sitting straighter now. "I'll stay in the car."

"You should have stayed in the *house!*"

"You didn't!"

My hands clenched around the wheel. "I came back with Genna instead of going out, so I could keep an eye on *you!*"

"Great job."

I shook my head, fighting the urge to punch the steering wheel. "No way. *You* snuck out and got drunk. You're not blaming this on me."

"But Mom will," he said, and it only took me a second to realize he was right. "She doesn't have to know." He twisted in his seat to face me, rather than the windshield. "Let's go get Sabine. I'll be sober by the time we get home, and we'll tell Mom she ran away on her own. Sabine will back us up, and Mom never has to know either of us left the house."

"No." *Hell* no. Mom would see through that in a second, and I'd get into worse trouble than Nash for letting him go through with such an idiotic, *illegal* stunt.

"Come on, Tod, I never ask you for anything!"

"Bullshit!" I glanced at him, furious to realize he actually believed his own load of crap! "You ask me for gas money, and condoms, and alibis, and favors and advice you never follow. And now you're asking me to drive your underage, drunk ass to break your jailbird, jailbait girlfriend out of corrective custody. And *I'm* the one who'll get in trouble when that brilliant piece of on-the-fly planning goes south."

"If something goes wrong, I'll take the blame," Nash insisted.

"No, you won't, because no one will point the blame at you. Sabine will lie to protect you on her end, and Mom will let you slide because she thinks you're some 'sensitive soul.' It's always, 'Poor Nash, he wears his heart on his sleeve, then wonders why it's always bruised.' Or, 'He's only so reckless because he lives in the moment and he *feels* things so deeply.'"

"She doesn't say that."

"The hell she doesn't. But your problem isn't the heart on your sleeve, it's the head on your shoulders. You don't *think* about things, you just *do* them, and it never even occurs to you that you could be screwing someone else over."

"You mean you?"

"Yeah, *me!* I can't turn around without tripping over whatever trouble you're in. I spend half my life cleaning up your messes, and all you do is take up space and get in my way!"

I couldn't see Nash. The suburban street was unlit, and I was staring at the road. But I could tell I'd gone too far because he went completely still and quiet. For nearly a minute. Then he grabbed the door handle, like he'd pull it open with the car still moving. "Let me out."

"What?"

"I'd hate to take up any more space in your life," he spat. "Stop the car."

I rolled my eyes, but slowed down, in case he tried to jump. "Are moronic overreactions a side effect of dating a delinquent, or is this the alcohol talking?"

"You don't know anything about me," Nash snapped, tightening an already white-knuckled grip on the door handle.

"And you don't know a damn thing about Sabine. Stop the car, or I'm gonna jump and roll."

"No, you're gonna go home and sleep it off in your own bed," I insisted, as we rolled past the last house on the block, the rest of which was taken up by a large community park.

"Stop the damn car!" I felt his Influence almost before he spoke, and his words washed over me in a rush of anger, chased by a backwash of resentment. The urge to pull onto the side of the road was overwhelming.

I slammed on the brake and we screeched to a halt at the corner in front of the park, not because he wanted me to stop, but because I was too pissed to drive. "Don't even *try* to Influence me, you little—"

Nash's eyes widened, staring straight ahead. I glanced up just in time to see a car gliding toward us on the wrong side of the road, sleek and black against the night, no headlights to announce its approach.

Adrenaline surging through me, I shifted into Reverse and cut the wheel to the right, but it was way too late. The car slammed into us head-on. There was a loud *pop* of impact and the squeal-crunch of bending metal.

The world spun around me.

Nash flew forward and his head smacked the windshield. My seat belt punched the air from my lungs as the entire dashboard lurched toward me. The steering wheel stopped two inches from my chest.

Then everything went still.

The only sound was the soft hiss of something ruptured. Every breath hurt, and my neck was so stiff I could hardly turn my head. I exhaled slowly and closed my eyes, stealing a moment in the near-silence to appreciate my pounding heart, and the fact that it continued to beat.

Then I twisted in the dark to face my brother.

"Nash?" He was slumped in his seat half facing me. His eyes were closed, his head steadily dripping blood from an injury I couldn't see in the dark. My relief bled into dread as I pushed my door open and the interior lights came on. "Nash?" I said again, but he didn't answer. He was barely breathing, and I was afraid to make things worse by shaking him awake. "Shit!"

I unbuckled my seat belt and had to slide out the door sideways, because of the crunched dashboard and the steering wheel that had nearly crushed my rib cage. The street was lit only by the red glow of my taillights—the wreck had obliterated the headlights—and I spared a moment to glance at the bastard crumpled over the deployed airbag in the other car. Where the hell were *our* airbags?

My car didn't have them. It was too old.

I raced around the rear of the car and pulled Nash's door open with one hand, while the other dug in my pocket for my phone. I flipped it open and knelt by my brother.

He wasn't breathing.

Shit!

Heart racing in panic, I felt for his pulse with my free hand, but couldn't find it in his neck. I tried his wrist—my mom had taught me years ago—but couldn't find it there, either. His heart wasn't beating.

"No!" I shouted, out loud this time. I dropped his arm and pressed the 9 on my phone, my hands shaking, my pulse a roar in my ears. "No, no, no..." I chanted, shock and guilt warring inside me as I pressed the 1. "Not like this. Not after I..."

Not after what I'd said to him. These couldn't be his last moments—drunk on the side of the road, alone except for the asshole brother who'd put him there in the first place.

If Mom were here...

If my mother was there, we could fix him. A male and female *bean sidhe,* together we could reinstate his soul and save his life. Nash would live, and I wouldn't be a killer.

There'd be a price—*someone* had to die—but it'd be worth it. Let the reaper take someone else—some old man sleeping down the street. Someone who'd already lived a full life. Someone whose brother hadn't just told him he was taking up space and getting in the way.

But my mother wasn't there, and she'd never make it in time, even if I called her. Neither would the ambulance. There was no one close enough to help Nash except me and…

The reaper.

Because no one dies without a reaper there to take his soul.

I blinked as the thought played out in my head, and with it came a chilling spark of possibility.

I flipped my phone closed and shoved it into my pocket. My head throbbed and my chest ached, and my stomach pitched at the very thought of what I was about to do—of who I was about to appeal to—but nothing compared to the nameless, formless agony rising through me with the knowledge that I'd gotten my own brother killed.

Standing, I squinted into the dark, looking for someone I probably wouldn't—and *shouldn't*—be able to see. I swallowed, my hands shaking from either fear or shock. "I know you're here, reaper," I whispered, suddenly glad no one had emerged from the nearest houses, now more than a block away. "I know you're here somewhere, but there's been some kind of mistake. It's not his time. He's too young."

"There's no such thing as too young to die," a soft, oddly high-pitched voice said behind me, and I whirled around to find a small boy watching me, freckled face crowned in hair cast red by my taillights. "Trust me."

Momentary confusion gave way to both horror and hope. "*You're* the reaper?" I stared down at him, heart pounding, and he nodded slowly.

"One of them, anyway."

Because the concept of reapers isn't creepy enough without adding dead kids to the mix.

My pulse raced with a dizzying combination of fear and anger. No good could come of arguing with a grim reaper. But I had nothing left to lose.

"Sorry about your premature death." I paused to clear my throat, then continued, trying to project confidence I didn't feel. "Missing out on puberty must suck. But this can't be right." I gestured toward Nash without taking my focus from the reaper. "Can't you double check your list or something?"

The dead child shook his head slowly, and his dark gaze never strayed from my eyes. "I died right on time. As did he." He nodded toward my brother, still slouched in the passenger's seat. "See for yourself." He pulled a folded piece of paper from his pocket and held it out to me. My hands trembled so badly I almost tore the paper when I opened it.

It was a printout of an official looking form, with a seal I didn't recognize. I read by the crimson glow of my own tail-lights. *Nash Eric Hudson. 23:48 Corner of 3rd and Elm.*

"No. Not like this." Determination burned within me, feeding flames of anger. I tore the paper in half, then ripped it again and dropped the scraps on the ground. "It can't go down like this."

"You know that doesn't change anything, right?" The dead kid put his hands in his pockets and watched the scraps of paper blow away, then looked up at me, frowning. "You're a *bean sidhe,* right? So you know how this works?"

"Yeah." My mom had always been straight with us about

death. Even when my dad died, when we were just kids. "But I also know you can change it, right? There are ways to change this…?"

The reaper raised one brow and suddenly looked much older. The difference was in his eyes—in the sudden interest I saw there.

"Please. It can't happen like this," I insisted, talking to us both now. "I wasn't paying attention, at home or on the road. This is my fault. You have to help me fix it."

"He would have died anyway," the reaper said, shrugging again. "If you'd kept him home, he would have choked on his dinner. If you'd left him at the party, he would have made his friend drive, and they'd have wound up exactly like this."

"How did you know…?" I demanded, confusion trailing into the night with my aborted question.

"I watched. But my point is that you aren't the cause of Nash's death. You're merely the instrument." He glanced at the driver of the other car, unconscious, but obviously breathing. "One of the instruments, anyway."

"I *can't* be the instrument of my brother's death!" I snapped. "That's *beyond* screwed up."

The reaper eyed me closely, like he could see beyond my words and into the thoughts I didn't voice. "Which is it you object to? His death, or your part in it?"

I hesitated, for just an instant, but he saw my indecision. He heard that moment of silence. "Both!" I shouted, running my hands through my hair, resisting the urge to simply close my eyes until the entire nightmare blew over. Because it wouldn't. "It can't happen like this. Can't you…give him more time? Please? I'll do whatever you want. Just give him a few more years."

The kid shook his head, and I realized that his hair really

was red—it wasn't just reflecting the taillights. "There are no extensions." He squatted to catch my gaze when I sank onto my knees, as my anger began to fade into a welcome numbness. "There are only exchanges. One life—" he gestured toward Nash, palm up "—for another…" He held his other empty hand toward me, miming the act of balancing a set of scales. "How badly do you want him to live?"

The question seemed to echo all around me, and it took me a moment to realize I was hearing it in my own head.

I looked up slowly to find him watching me, his intense eyes an indeterminate color in the dark. "You mean I can…?"

"I have to leave here with a soul, but it could as easily be yours as his. It's your choice."

I glanced up at Nash, unmoving, his arm hanging limp against the side of the bucket seat. The reaper was right; Nash would have died no matter what I did or said to him. But I couldn't deal, knowing that I'd ignored him in favor of a girl, told him he had no place in my life, then driven him into the path of the car that killed him.

I couldn't live my life, knowing the part I played in ending his.

My next breath was long and deep—I'd decided it would be one of my last.

"Yes. I'll do it. But I have one condition."

The child's brows rose again, this time in dark amusement. "Death makes no promises."

"He can't know." I stood, staring down at my brother. What good would it do to give him life, if he'd spend it feeling guilty for my death? I turned to the reaper. "I'll do it, if you swear he'll never know it was supposed to be him."

The child smiled slowly, and his satisfied expression raised chill bumps on my arms in spite of the warm June night. "That, I can do."

And suddenly the enormity of what I'd just agreed to hit me with the unyielding weight of eternity. Isn't your life supposed to flash before your eyes when you die? Then how come all I saw was regret?

The reaper glanced at Nash, then back at me, and the hint of a grin told me the little bastard enjoyed this part of his job. "Any last words?"

Pushing everything else aside to clear my head, I knelt next to Nash, wishing with all of my last few seconds of life that he could actually hear me. "Can't clean up after you anymore, baby brother, so don't punk out. Make it count."

I stood and started to turn toward the reaper. But then something hard slammed into my chest, and my legs folded beneath me. I blinked, and the car went fuzzy. Nash's face slid out of focus. He took a breath. Then he coughed, his eyes still closed.

The child knelt over me, red curls backlit by the moon, finally emerging from thick cloud cover. The last thing I saw was the creepy little bastard's smile....

BRIGHT LIGHT SHINED, red and veiny through my closed eyelids. I blinked, and suddenly the world was white instead. But not Heaven-white, with clouds, and robes, and chicks with wings. Hospital-white. White walls. White ceiling. White sheets and pillows, on the bed beneath me.

I sat up with a sudden flash of memory and brought my hand to my chest. But there was no pain. I took a deep breath, and everything felt fine. Which was weird.

"Welcome back."

Startled, I twisted on the bed to find the child reaper in a waiting room style armchair by a darkened window, his short hair bright red in the glaring fluorescent light. His feet didn't reach the floor and his smile didn't reach his eyes.

"Shouldn't you be getting back to Snow White?" I snapped, rubbing my chest again, still surprised when it didn't hurt. "No one ever mentioned that death would come in the form of a sucker-punching little dwarf."

The reaper raised one rust-colored eyebrow. "You may be the first person to ever use that particular description of me."

"Would I also be the first person you hit with a…what *did* you hit me with?"

"The post from the traffic sign your car knocked over." He shrugged. "And no, you're not the first. I could have killed you without touching you, but it's easier for both your family and the coroner if I give them an obvious cause of death. At a glance, impact with a blunt object should look like your chest was crushed by the top half of your own steering wheel—you really should have been buckled." The child shook his index finger at me in mock disappointment. "But the hard part was getting you back in the car."

"For a kid, you pack a lot of power."

The reaper scowled. "If you really think I'm a child, maybe I should have left you in that coffin."

I blinked, briefly surprised by the mention of my own death. "Speaking of which, what's with the encore performance?" I'd traded my life for Nash's—I'd *tried* to, anyway—but if I was still alive, did that mean he was still dead?

Pissed now, I stood and realized I didn't recognize the stiff white dress shirt I wore. "What the hell did you do?" I demanded. "We made a deal. My life for his." My hands curled into fists, but before I could do anything stupid, I realized I didn't really have any recourse. What was I gonna do, punch a kid? A dead reaper kid, at that? "I wanna see your supervisor."

The kid laughed, and my urge to punch him became an imperative. "*I* don't even want to see my supervisor." His smile looked a little more genuine, but that only made it harder to buy. "Before we go any further, my name is Levi."

"I don't care what your name is." But at least now I'd know who to blame when I got in touch with his boss.

"Relax. Your brother's alive—he was released from the hospital three days ago—and you're as dead as disco." The reaper shifted in his seat, but made no move to stand. "That's what you were buried in." His careless gesture took in my stiff shirt and the pressed black pants I'd never seen in my life.

I looked like a waiter.

"If I'm dead, why am I in the hospital?"

"This is a nursing home." He pushed himself forward, then kind of hopped onto the floor, standing no more than four feet tall. "Specifically, Colonial Manor, room 118. You're here on a temporary visitor's pass, of sorts. No one alive can see or hear you."

"I'm visiting a nursing home in the clothes I was buried in, but no one can see or hear me. Which part of that is supposed to make sense?"

"Have a seat, and I'll explain." He gestured toward the bed, and I sat reluctantly, tugging at the sleeves of the shirt I already hated.

"You're visiting *life,* not a nursing home—we're only here because this is one of the places I'm working at the moment. And you're here—in the grander sense of the word—so I can recruit you."

"Recruit me?"

"Yes." His widespread arms indicated the entire facility.

"There are nine elderly care facilities in this district and we're down one man—specifically, we've lost the man who covered the night rotation, circulating between them as needed. The sooner I fill the spot, the sooner I can get back to the managerial position I've damn well earned."

"You brought me back…" A surreal thought on its own. "…to work in a nursing home? Like, changing bedpans?" Was I dead or *damned?* "I think I finally understand the phrase 'hell on earth…'"

Levi frowned. "You're being recruited as a reaper. I thought that part was obvious."

"If by obvious, you mean cryptic and baffling." And suddenly I was glad I was sitting. "You're gonna have to give me a minute here. This may take a while to sink in."

Levi shrugged narrow, thin shoulders. "Actually, you're handling it better than anyone else I've ever recruited. I'm attributing that to the fact that you already knew about a good bit of this, by virtue of being a *bean sidhe.* Which is why I want you for the position. With any luck, your orientation and training will take about half as long as it takes most people. And the less time it takes to train you…"

"…the sooner you can get back to the managerial position you've damn well earned. I caught that the first time." *If the afterlife has managers, does that mean there's also a customer service department?*

His smile was real that time, and all the creepier because of it. "I knew you'd pick it up quick."

My thoughts chased each other fast enough to make me dizzy. "All I've picked up so far is that you brought me back from the dead to make me a reaper."

"*I* didn't bring you back. The reanimation department did that. And because you're a *bean sidhe,* they tried to keep you for themselves. But I insisted that the reapers had a prior claim to you."

"Yeah, that's not creepy or anything," I mumbled. "So, do I have any say in this?"

"Of course. It's your choice. But consider carefully before you decide, because this 'visitor's pass' is only valid for twenty-four hours, and reanimation only works once. If you take too long to decide, you're dead for good. If you turn the job down, you're dead for good. If you take the job, then give management any reason to fire you, you're dead for good. Understand?"

I nodded slowly. "Mess up and I'm dead for real. That may be the only part I *do* understand."

"Questions?"

"You bet your scythe."

Levi chuckled and stood, straightening a blue polo shirt with a Gymboree label embroidered on the pocket. "We don't actually carry scythes."

"Damn." I snapped my fingers in mock disappointment. "I gotta be honest—that was the real selling point. There's a black hood, though, right?"

His brows rose again. "A reaper with a sense of humor. This should be interesting." Levi started across the room. "Let's walk and talk. You had questions?"

I followed him into the hall, and with my first steps, it became obvious that he was right—no one could see either of us. Our shoes didn't squeak on the faded linoleum. We cast no shadows. I felt like a ghost. Displaced, like I was out of sync with the rest of the world.

Like I wasn't really there at all.

"How long has it been? Since I died."

"Ten days."

"Ten days?" I was dead for more than a week?

Levi nodded. "The reanimation process takes some time."

An aide headed down the hall toward us, pushing a bald man in a wheelchair. It was surreal, walking unseen among so many people who—even if they died that very night—had already outlived me. "And Nash just got out of the hospital?"

"He had a cracked rib and a skull fracture. They ran several tests. But he's young and resilient. He'll be fine."

"What, were you spying on him?"

Levi dropped into an empty chair in the hall, feet swinging inches above the floor, and the incongruity between his child's body and the dark knowledge in his eyes left me a little dizzy. "Experience has shown me that new recruits have trouble concentrating on the job until they know those they left behind have actually survived them. So I checked in on your brother."

"Can I see them? Nash and my mom?"

Levi frowned and crossed his arms over his chest. "Usually, that's forbidden. Watching your family makes it hard to resist contacting them, and contact with anyone who knew you before you died is a firing-level offense. Which is why we typically place new reapers far from where they lived. However, you're being recruited for a specific position and your family actually lives in this district." He shrugged. "Considering the circumstances, I don't think anyone would object to you checking in on them occasionally, so long as they never see you. But you won't find them where you lived. They moved yesterday."

Two days after Nash got out of the hospital. My mother did the same thing after my father died—moved us to a new house, in a new town. She seemed to think it'd be easier to live without him if our house held no memories of him.

Had she already given away my clothes? Boxed up my stuff? If my family lived in a house I'd never set foot in, did that make me dead *and* homeless?

I slid down the pale green wall until I sat on the floor with Levi looking down at me. Where would I go now—if I took the job—when I wasn't killing people and harvesting their souls?

Nursing shoes squeaked down the hall, drawing me from my self-pity. "Why can't they see us?" I asked, staring as a wrinkled old woman with bright red, thinning hair hobbled past us, leaning on a walker. She seemed to avoid us instinctively, even though she couldn't see us, and that made me feel a little better. If she was scared of us—even subconsciously—then we had to be real. Right?

Levi slid out of his chair and I stood to follow him. "They can't see *you* because you're just visiting." We stepped past a room full of square tables, where senior citizens sat playing cards and dominoes. "They can't see *me* because I don't want them to see me, and that's a reaper's prerogative. Selective corporeality, visibility, etc..." He glanced up at me, one brow arched. "Usually *that's* a selling point."

I felt a grin tug at one side of my mouth. There *were* obvious perks with that particular fringe benefit. "So, 'reaper' is really just a nice word for 'covert pervert?' Is that what you're saying?"

"Not if you want to keep your job for long. But the officials tend to overlook innocent observation in the rookies, because after a few years, most of them outgrow the phase."

I stopped in the middle of the hall, frowning down at him. "Okay, first of all, how open to interpretation is the phrase 'innocent observation?' And second, why would anyone *ever* outgrow that phase?"

"They outgrow it along with their humanity, Tod. The longer we're dead, the less we have in common with the living, and you don't lust for what no longer interests you."

Great. "So you're saying the afterlife is hard on the libido? FYI, that's probably not a good bullet point for your recruiting brochure."

"Yet it rarely scares away potential recruits. Any idea why?" Levi blinked up at me, studying my eyes like he could see the gears turning behind them, a hint of grim amusement in the curve of his little-boy mouth. And suddenly I understood.

"Yeah." I started walking again, staring ahead to avoid his gaze. "Because we all think we'll be the exception." Myself included. Surely if I could still be near my family—even in an altered state of existence—I wouldn't lose my humanity. How could I, if I surrounded myself with it?

When I looked up, he was still watching me, but the smile was gone. "It won't work," he said, his child's voice soft but confident. "They won't be enough."

I frowned, but held eye contact. "Reapers can read minds?"

"No, but I was always pretty good at connecting the dots." Levi shrugged, hands in his pockets. "It may work for a little while. But the more time you spend with them, the harder it'll be for them to accept your death. Even if they never see you. And beyond that, they *will* grow old, and when they die, there will be nothing left of your humanity. Death will have you eventually, Tod, and the longer you cling to what you had, the harder it'll be to let go in the end."

"So, you reap souls *and* crush hopes? Is that part of the job, or just a service you offer for free?" My chest ached, like my heart had bruised it from the inside—the first physical discomfort I'd felt since waking up dead—and I couldn't decide if that was a good sign or a bad one.

"I thought you'd want the unvarnished truth, rather than the glossy veneer. Was I wrong?"

I closed my eyes, then opened them to meet his gaze. "Bring on the truth." Even if it made me want to end my own life. Again.

Though his expression never changed, I could have sworn Levi looked...satisfied.

"So, even taking into account this unvarnished loss of humanity, does anyone ever turn you down? I mean, the choices are reap or die, right? So does anyone actually ask to be nailed back into the coffin?"

Levi nodded slowly, and I squinted at the red-tinted haze cast by the light shining through his copper curls. It was like a crimson anti-halo, gruesomely appropriate for a child of death, and a reminder that Levi wasn't there to help me. He was there to fill a vacancy.

"It happens. But more often than that, they accept, then change their minds."

"Why?"

"Some people can't handle not being a part of the living world. Others don't have the stomach for the job."

"What exactly *is* the job? Do you actually...kill people?" Because, having even indirectly contributed to my brother's death, I knew for a fact that I didn't have whatever it took to play executioner.

Levi shrugged. "It's not murder, by any means, but yes, we extinguish life when the time comes. Then we collect the soul and take it to be recycled."

"So...you killed Nash?" Part of me was horrified by the thought, but the other half was relieved that someone else was willing to take the blame.

"And you saved him."

But that wasn't right. I hadn't so much saved him as given back what I'd played a part in taking. That didn't make me a hero. It just made me dead.

And that's when a new fear broke the surface of confusion that defined my afterlife so far. "Hey, you're not gonna go back and kill him if I turn this down, are you?" Because I was far from sure I wanted to spend my afterlife extinguishing human existence, one poor soul at a time.

Levi shook his head firmly, and for once the wide-eyed, innocent kid look worked in his favor. "We made a deal, and that deal stands no matter what you decide. Nash will live until the day you were scheduled to die," he insisted.

"And when was I supposed to die?" Knowing my luck, my noble sacrifice had only bought him a couple of extra weeks, half of which he'd spent in the hospital.

"I have no way of knowing that until your exchanged death date appears on the schedule. Which hasn't happened yet." He glanced up at me. "Anything else?"

"Yeah. Why me?" What had I done to deserve an afterlife, when everyone else evidently got recycled back into the general population? "How was I chosen?"

"Very carefully," Levi hedged.

I rolled my eyes. "I'm gonna need more detail than that. If I hadn't taken Nash's place, would you have recruited him? Is that why you were watching him?"

He motioned for me to follow him again, so I fell into step beside him, ambling slowly down the bright hallway. "I was watching both of you." Levi paused to watch a nurse's aide walk past us in snug-fitting scrub pants, and I realized that he'd obviously avoided the loss of humanity—and human urges he'd never grown into in life. "But no, I wouldn't have recruited Nash. I *couldn't* have. He was scheduled to die, but I was there for you."

"What the hell does that mean?" I snapped, frustrated by his suddenly cryptic explanation. "Why couldn't you recruit Nash?"

Levi sighed. "A person has to meet very specific criteria to even be considered for this job, much less actively recruited. Reapers literally hold the power of life and death in our hands." He cupped his creepy little child-palms to illustrate. "The list tells us who to take, and when. But the decision to actually follow the list—the responsibility—ultimately rests with each of us individually.

"Imagine what would happen if the wrong person was given such a power. If a reaper had a God complex, or a personal vendetta? What if a reaper was susceptible to bribes or threats? Or even just lacked a respect for the position? We screen our candidates very carefully to make sure nothing like that ever happens. We evaluate their personal relationships and the decisions they make when something real is on the line. And then we test them."

"And you chose *me?*" I huffed. "I hate to question your dedication to the recruiting process, but it sounds more like you ran up against a deadline and grabbed the first sucker with the balls to call you out."

At the end of the hall, Levi stepped through a glass door and into a dark, mostly empty parking lot. "We've been watching you for almost two months, Tod," he said from the other side of the pane.

"Then you know my brother snuck out when I was supposed to be watching him." After a moment of hesitation, I followed him, and was surprised when I felt nothing. Not the glass I stepped through, not the asphalt beneath my shoes, and not the night breeze obviously blowing through the branches of the trees on the edge of the lot.

"Yes. But you picked him up when he called."

"Under protest. And that ride home ultimately got him killed." I shook my head, confused on several points, but absolutely certain about one thing. "You've got the wrong guy." I turned to give him a clear view of my back in the parking lot lights. "Notice the conspicuous absence of wings and a halo."

Levi actually laughed, the first look of genuine amusement I'd seen from him so far. "What I notice is that the undertaker left your pants intact when he split the back of your shirt."

"What...?" I couldn't see my own back, but a quick check with both hands verified that my shirt had been cut open along my spine and was evidently pinned together at the collar. Since it was tucked into my pants and the earthly breeze never touched me, I hadn't noticed the gaping hole in my wardrobe.

"Funeral directors sometimes do that to make bodies easier to dress. Doesn't usually matter—most corpses don't get up and walk around half-exposed after the funeral."

Funeral. Corpses. Undertaker.

What obviously amused the reaper left me horrified and hollow. "If I unbutton my shirt, am I going to find a roadmap of Frankenstein stitches?" I demanded, my voice trembling in spite of my best effort to remain calm.

This is real. I'm dead.

I sank to my knees in the middle of the parking lot, hunched over with my head in my shaking hands. I'd been on an autopsy table, and in a coffin, and in a hearse. My steps made no sound and my body cast no shadow.

I had *died,* and the world kept spinning, without even a wobble in its rotation to mark the occasion. I'd known life would go on without me, but seeing that was different than knowing it, and feeling it was worst of all.

If I turned down the job and died for good, no one would know I'd been granted one more day, and the chance to make something of my afterlife. No one would know, and no one would care. I could throw back my head right then and scream until my lungs burst from the pressure, and no one would hear me. Hell, I might not even *have* lungs to burst. There's no telling what they took out of me during the autopsy....

Levi's red brows arched as he stared down at me. "What, no quips about dissection or formaldehyde?"

I scrubbed my hands over my face and stood, glad that I could at least feel the texture of my own skin, even if I couldn't interact with the rest of the world. "Sorry, but the whole walking corpse epiphany kind of threw me off my game." Still, I had to know... "So, would you say I'm closer to a zombie or a vampire? I gotta know—are my parts going to rot and fall off, or am I forever frozen in youthful perfection?"

Levi gave me that satisfied look again, like refusing to be broken by the psychological shock of my own death was some kind of nifty dog trick I'd mastered. "Relax. You weren't autopsied. The cause of death was obvious, thanks to my quick thinking, and the coroner was one of our reanimators. Instead of cutting you open, he prepared you to return, completely intact and functioning. If you take the job, you'll look just like this forever." Levi waved one hand at my body, then shook his head and stared up at the sky. "You know, we never had to plant employees before the advent of chemical preservation. It was a much simpler time..."

"Were the recruits simpler then, too?" I asked, when he finally glanced away from the stars. "'Cause I still don't understand how I earned this whole 'get out of death free' card. You know, the lack of wings and all…"

"We don't want angels." Levi walked across the lot without looking back, leaving me no choice but to follow. "Or saints, or do-gooders. A saint would spare everyone scheduled to die, and that would lead to a drastic imbalance between life and death. We need someone who will do the right thing, even when that means ending a life. Which it usually does, for us."

So… I'd been recruited because I *wasn't* a humanitarian? I wasn't sure how to feel about that. "Why didn't Nash qualify?"

"Because he didn't have a chance to be tested."

"Neither did I."

Levi settled onto the bumper of the last car in the lot. "You've already been tested, and you passed."

"Because I picked Nash up instead of leaving him to die of alcohol poisoning? That doesn't make me worthy. It barely makes me human."

Levi shook his head. "You passed because you saved his life at the expense of your own."

"That was survivor's guilt! I couldn't face my mother every day, knowing I got Nash killed." And I sure as hell couldn't face myself.

"You claimed no credit for what you did, and you died without knowing that wouldn't be the end for you. That's the test." He shrugged and leaned forward, like we were getting to his favorite part. "To weed out the power-seekers and those who just want to prolong their own lives, we can't take anyone who actually volunteers for the position. The theory is that only those who don't want power are truly qualified to wield it. So a recruit has to willingly give up his or her life for someone else, with no expectation of reward."

For a moment, I could only stare at him. I was being granted an afterlife—naturally, it came with strings—because I'd volunteered to die? "Is that irony intentional, or just coincidence?"

Levi laughed. "I'm going to let you answer that for yourself, after you've been reaping for a few years."

"How did you know I'd do it?" My mind was spinning with the sudden realization. "You must have known. Why else would you have been watching me for so long?"

"I didn't know. I took a chance on you, and I'm really hoping it pays off. We had a position to fill, so I started weeding through the possibilities. None of those actually scheduled to die qualify, of course, but anyone willing to die *for* one of them might. Usually that's the parent of a small child, but there weren't any of those on the lists I had access to, so I moved on to siblings. Nash was one of three scheduled to die in my district, and he was the only one with a same-gender sibling close in age. Theoretically, the two of you were likely to share a closer bond than any of the others I looked at. And the fact that you're a *bean sidhe* meant that you knew an exchange was possible. Which, though unusual in a recruit, worked in my favor."

"But that's all just theory," I insisted. "In reality, one sibling could be such a heartless bastard that he'd make out with his girlfriend instead of looking out for his pain-in-the-ass little brother, thus dooming the poor kid to death by head-on collision."

Levi frowned. "You need to remember that Nash would have died anyway. Keeping him home wouldn't have stopped that. And since you took his place, I think your survivor's guilt can reasonably be put to rest now."

"You must have been dead a long time, if you think that's even possible."

Levi gave me a creepy half smile, but made no comment on his age.

"What about the other guy? The one who hit us?" I asked. "He survived, right? Couldn't you have traded his life for Nash's, and left both of us alive?"

The reaper's smile faded into an even creepier puzzled expression. "Yes. I could have. But he didn't volunteer. And if I'd taken the drunk driver instead of you, I'd still be looking for a new recruit, now wouldn't I?"

I could only stare at him, stunned in spite of my knowledge that for the reaper, filling his vacancy was the bottom line. "You let a drunk driver live and killed me instead, just to get yourself out of the nursing home?"

Levi shrugged. "The driver was of no use to me. You are."

"WHERE ARE WE?" I pulled my hand from Levi's even as the world solidified around me, and I was glad to be rid of the feel of dead flesh. Not that his hand felt different than any other hand, but knowing it was attached to a dead kid kind of creeped me out.

As did the sudden realization that my hand was now also attached to a dead kid.

"This is where they live now," he said stepping off the sidewalk and onto the grass, lit only by a streetlight on the corner.

I didn't recognize the house. I only knew the town because we'd lived there as kids, before my dad died. But this time, my mom had settled into the older section of a large development. She'd found a corner lot, but the house was too small to have three bedrooms.

There was no room for me.

And though I knew I wouldn't be moving back in, even if I took the job, that fact still stung much more than I'd expected.

Mom and Nash were trying to move on from my death, and my presence would only disrupt their adjustment. The last thing I wanted was to make it harder for them.

So why had Levi brought me?

"What is this, a bribe? I thought potential reapers were supposed to be above bribes."

He shrugged. "If you're going to take the job, there's something you need to understand first."

"Something beyond the fact that I'm dead and invisible, and I was evidently dressed by Edward Scissorhands?"

Levi ignored my sarcasm. "Yes. Officially, I'm supposed to explain to you that no matter how alive you might look, and feel, and even function, you're not alive. Not like your friends and family are. You died, and your soul was removed from your body, and even though you've been reanimated, you don't truly belong here. And you never will. I'm supposed to tell you that the sooner you come to terms with that fact, the sooner you can start to accept your new state of being and your job. And the sooner your family and friends can start to accept your death."

I frowned, arms crossed over my chest. "That sounds like advice from the Grim Reaper website."

"The recruiting handbook, actually, but you obviously get the idea."

"Yeah. So if I'm supposed to be letting everyone move on, why did you bring me here?"

"Because I think that steering you away from your family is just going to make you more determined to see them. You need to understand that stepping back into their lives would only be making things worse. They'll think they have you back, but when you start becoming more reaper, and less son and brother, they'll just have to let you go all over again. A clean break is easiest for all involved."

Maybe. But anyone who's ever broken a bone knows that even a clean break hurts like hell.

"Are you going in?" he asked at last, squinting up at me in the light from the streetlamp. "You can walk through doors and climb through windows, but walls and floors will be barriers. And, of course, no one can see or hear you."

I frowned. "That doesn't make any sense."

Levi shrugged. "Even visitors bow to physics, in one form or another."

Is that what I am? A visitor in my own family's home? I couldn't take my eyes off the house, a physical reminder that I didn't belong here. Not in their home, and not in their lives—which was just what he wanted me to see.

"When you're a reaper, there will be fewer physical rules to follow. But that's a perk of the job. No benefits until you sign on the dotted line."

"In blood?" I asked, only half kidding.

"Don't even joke about that," Levi said, and a chill raced the length of my spine. "Meet me at the hospital when you're done." Then he disappeared before I could ask him how I was supposed to get there, or why he'd be at the hospital.

As I walked toward the front porch, that feeling of displacement swelled within me. My shoes made no impression on the grass. I couldn't feel the breeze rustling tree leaves over my head. I was caught somewhere between dead and living, and even my mother had moved on without me.

As evidenced by the house I'd never seen.

I reached for the doorknob, and my hand went right through it. I should have seen that coming. Yet each new demonstration of my physical absence was more unsettling than the last.

I closed my eyes and stepped through the door, and when I looked again, I found myself in an unfamiliar room, surrounded by familiar furniture. And stacks of boxes. The worn couch against one wall still sported the stain where I'd spilled a can of Big Red on the center cushion. The end table was still cracked from where I'd fallen on it, goofing around with Nash.

The sound of running water drew my focus to a swinging door on the right hand wall. The kitchen. I crossed the room and stepped through the door, which refused to even swing in acknowledgement of my passing.

My mother stood at the sink, drying her hands on a faded dish towel over and over, staring out the window at an unlit backyard I'd never played in. Then she dropped the towel on the counter and leaned forward, gripping the edges of the sink, staring down at the drain. Her knuckles were white with tension, her back curved, half-hidden by a mass of long blond curls.

"Mom?"

But she couldn't hear me, and that reminder made my throat tight. Her shoulders shook, and suddenly she grabbed a glass from the counter, a quarter inch of milk still standing in the bottom. She hurled the glass at a fridge I'd never seen, spraying shards and white droplets all over the kitchen.

"Mom?" Nash called from somewhere else in the house, and my breath caught in my throat. Levi was right; he was okay. Or, at the very least, he was home. In this new house, which couldn't possibly feel like home yet.

"I'm fine!" my mother lied, sliding down the cabinet to sit on the floor, just outside the shrapnel zone. Her face was pale and streaked with silent tears, and I hated knowing I was the cause.

I sank to my knees in front of her, inches away, but worlds

apart. I watched her private pain, aching to heal the wound I'd caused, but there was nothing I could do. I'd never felt so worthless in my life.

Finally, she dried her face on the dish towel, then started picking up the glass. When the kitchen was clean again, familiar dishes stacked in unfamiliar cabinets, she pulled a paper plate from the stack on the table and piled it with cookies from a platter near the stove. Chocolate chip with walnuts—her go-to comfort food.

I followed her out of the kitchen and watched when she paused outside the closed door at the end of the hall. Nash's room was silent—no music and no video game carnage. Mom took a deep breath, then knocked on the door. When he didn't answer, she pushed the door open anyway and stepped inside.

My brother sat by the window in his desk chair, staring outside. He didn't even look up when she came in.

"I brought you some cookies," my mom said, and I almost laughed out loud—not that they'd have heard me. Cookies were her solution to everything. Baking them distracted her, and serving them fulfilled her. But sugar never solved anything in the end. "And there's the cake, of course."

Cake? A housewarming cake? Or to welcome him home from the hospital—to celebrate the life he hadn't lost.

"I'm not hungry." Nash crossed his arms over his bruised, bare chest, even thinner than I remembered. He'd lost weight in the hospital. But not as much as he'd have lost in a coffin.

"The doctor said you need to eat," Mom insisted.

"She also said to give me some space."

Mom frowned and set the cookies on his desk. "Doctors make mistakes sometimes."

Nash huffed, still staring out the window. "Then why'd you open this little heart-to-heart with a quote from one?"

I wanted to smack him. If my hand wouldn't have gone right through his head, maybe I would have. But Mom took it in stride. She sank onto the edge of his desk and pushed hair back from her face. "Nash, you can't sit in your room forever."

He shrugged. "Worked for Howard Hughes."

"That comparison doesn't really work for me."

"I'll try harder next time." Nash sighed. "I don't really want to talk right now, Mom."

She crossed her own arms over her chest, mirroring his stubborn posture. "Well, *I* want to talk."

Finally Nash turned to look at her, wincing with one hand over his ribs. "About what? Cookies? I don't want any. The move? I don't want to be here. Tod? I don't want him dead. But since this isn't the Republic of Nash, that doesn't seem to matter."

My mom sighed and picked up a cookie she probably wouldn't eat. "Nash, Tod's time was up, and there's nothing anyone could have done to prevent it. You have to stop blaming yourself."

The irony stung like fire in my chest, and I stumbled back a step.

Nash's expression went hard, but I could see the pain beneath. "Why, Mom? *You* blame me." She opened her mouth to argue, but he cut her off. "You don't blame me for his death— we both know how that works—but you blame me for *how* he died. If I hadn't gone out, that damn drunk would never have hit us. Tod might have died peacefully at home, instead of on the side of the road, crushed by his own steering wheel."

I blinked, stunned. I'd made sure Nash would never know what happened, but instead of absolving him of guilt, I'd saddled him with it. Nash thought it was his fault. And one glance at my mother told me he was right—she did, too.

But she didn't know the truth. He obviously hadn't told her that I'd had Genna over instead of watching him—which had set the whole thing in motion. And *neither* of them knew about the rest of it.

Nash stared at our mother, silently begging her to argue. To insist that she didn't blame him. But we could both see the truth, even if the colors in her eyes held steady.

"No." I said it out loud, glancing back and forth between them, but no one heard me. "This isn't what I wanted." But my brother stared right past me.

Mom answered, finally, too late to be believable. "It's not your fault," she said, staring at the hands clasped in her lap.

Nash actually rolled his eyes. "*I* went to the party. *I* got drunk. *I* made him come get me. It's my fault we were on the road. If I'd done any of that differently, he wouldn't have gone out like that."

I couldn't take anymore. *"It was my choice!"* I stood, but they still couldn't see me, and they damn well couldn't hear me.

My mother shook her head slowly, wordlessly denying his guilt, even as her eyes argued to the contrary.

"I wish you'd just say it!" Nash shouted, and I stood in front of him, trying to interrupt, trying to keep him from saying whatever would come next, because there'd be no taking it back. But he looked right through me. "I wish you'd just yell at me and get it over with. I know I screwed up. I know I can never fix it, and I wish you'd just say it, so we can…so we can at least *start* to move on. Because he's not coming back, Mom. I'm the only one left."

"Nash, *no,*" I said, but my words—like my presence—were worthless.

Mom sniffled. "Nash, I'm not going to…"

"Just say it!" he shouted, standing, and I tried to shove him back into his chair, but my hands went right through his chest.

"You knew better!" she yelled, and I spun toward my mom. She stood, and she was crying, and I couldn't stand it, but there was nothing I could do. "You were grounded, and you went out drinking anyway. Sabine *just* got arrested for the same thing and you saw her in that place, but it didn't sink in, did it? *You* went out and partied, and Tod paid for it. *You got him killed!*" Her legs folded and she dropped to her knees on the carpet.

Nash walked through me and sank to the floor with her. He wrapped his arms around her and they cried, apologizing to each other over and over, mourning me together. And I could only watch, my fists clenched in frustration, separated from them by death, and life, and the devastating knowledge that things could have been different—but that would only have made them worse.

I sank into Nash's chair, but the cushion didn't squish beneath my weight. In my current state—present, but powerless—I couldn't even affect the damn furniture, much less my family. I was no good to them like this. What was the point of making sure Nash lived, if he and my mom were both going to blame him for my death?

I had to take the job. I wasn't crazy about the idea of killing people for the remainder of my afterlife—I wasn't even sure I could actually do it—but I couldn't let them spend the rest of their lives thinking he was responsible for how I died. Not when the truth was the other way around.

I left them like that, crying and forgiving each other for shouting what they thought was the truth. Bonding over my death.

In the living room, I stopped cold in the middle of the floor when my gaze landed on what I'd missed before. The cake. On the coffee table. The candles looked burned, and I knew I would have smelled them, if I were really there.

I moved forward slowly, dreading what I'd see, even as the understanding sank in. The cake would be chocolate, with cream cheese frosting between the layers. The same every year, because it was my favorite. And there it was, printed in blue letters, in my mother's own curly cake script.

Happy Birthday Tod.

Today I would have turned eighteen.

I WAITED FOR the last bus of the evening with three other people, then stepped up through the folding doors when they closed behind the woman in front of me. The bus swayed beneath me as it rolled forward, but I wasn't jostled, like the other passengers. As if the rules of physics that bound me were a little less precise than they should have been. I was only *kind of* there, thus only *kind of* on the bus, and I couldn't quite shake the feeling that I was only one deep breath away from falling through the seat and onto the road, where the highway traffic would barrel right through me.

The bus stopped down the street from the hospital, and I didn't fully relax until my feet *kind of* hit the concrete and the bus rolled away. Two blocks later, I passed two EMTs unloading a man on a stretcher on my way into the waiting room, wishing like hell I could feel the air-conditioning or smell the antiseptic and bleach.

Levi sat facing the entrance. Waiting for me. "Well?" He stood as I approached, forced to project determination in my bearing, since he couldn't hear my bold, confident footsteps.

"I'm in." And I would talk to my mother, even if it got me fired. I hadn't expected an afterlife, so I wouldn't be losing much if I died again—for real this time. At least this way she would know the truth.

"I thought you would be." But Levi's smile was slow, his thin brows slightly furrowed, and I understood that he was connecting more dots in his head, and he didn't seem particularly bothered by the picture they formed. "Let's go make it official."

I STILL COULDN'T feel the wind.

Levi swore that when I got better at dialing up and down my corporeality, I'd be able to feel and smell things without becoming visible or audible. But that level of competence was obviously going to take more than two days' worth of practice.

For the moment, I was stuck with an all-or-nothing physicality, and since "nothing" had been deemed good enough for last night's shift on the nursing home circuit—hopefully my first of many—I figured "all" would work for what I had planned for the morning.

The house looked brighter in the daylight. A little nicer, but no bigger. There were still only two bedrooms and still only two occupants. I was still both dead and homeless, and the previous day spent wandering through town and watching Nash unpack between video games did nothing to make those facts of the afterlife more appealing. But the chance to talk to my mom and set things right made everything else worth it.

Assuming I didn't give my mother a heart attack.

In the shadow of the front porch roof, out of sight of most of the neighbors, I closed my eyes. I focused on what I should be hearing and feeling. The porch beneath me. The sweltering July heat. The buzz of bees hovering over a flowering vine climbing the porch post.

I thought about what I wanted. Day-to-day interaction in

the afterlife is all about intent, Levi had said. Once you've gained some control, if you intend to be seen or heard by someone, you will be.

And I damn well intended to be both seen and heard.

Then, suddenly, I could feel it. All of it. Even the sun baking the backs of my calves, the only part of me not shielded by the porch roof. My smile was equal parts relief and triumph as I jogged down the steps, my own footsteps echoing in my ears. I nearly laughed out loud when my finally fully corporeal body cast a long shadow on the grass.

But both my laughter and my confidence died a moment later, when I stood at the door again. No matter how I approached the issue—and I'd thought of nothing else for the past two days—I came up empty. There was just no good way for a dead son to greet his mother almost two weeks after his funeral.

However, when the moment came, my lack of a plan ceased to matter. Fools may rush in, but only cowards run away.

So I knocked. Then I waited, the nervous pounding in my chest a steady reassurance that I'd actually achieved corporeality. That she'd be able to see me. If she ever answered the door.

And finally, the doorknob turned. I swallowed as the door creaked open, and there stood my mother, a sweating glass of soda in one hand. Her hair was pulled back in a ponytail and a smear of dirt streaked her forehead. Behind her, I saw dozens of moving boxes, most open and half-unpacked.

She blinked up at me, looking just like she had the day I'd died, except for the dark circles under her eyes.

Then she blinked again, and her mouth opened for an unspoken, probably unformed question. The glass slipped from her hand and shattered on the metal threshold, splattering us both with cold soda and ice cubes I was relieved to be able to feel.

I grinned, trying to hide my nerves. "At this rate, you're not going to have any good glasses left."

Her mouth closed, then opened again. "Tod?" she whispered, her voice unsteady. She thought she was seeing things.

"Yeah, Mom, it's me," I said, ready to catch her if she collapsed. "Please don't freak out." But I should have known better—my mom wasn't the freaking-out type.

She reached for me with one trembling hand and cupped my jaw. Her eyes filled with tears. "You're really here."

"As of about five minutes ago, yeah." I shrugged and couldn't resist a real smile.

Heedless of the broken glass, she threw her arms around me and squeezed me so tight that I'd have been in trouble, if I'd actually needed to breathe. I hugged her back, reassuring her with my hard-won physicality until she finally let go and pulled me over the collateral damage and into the living room.

"I can't believe this," she said, the blues in her eyes swirling with a dizzying combination of confusion and wonder. "Is this real? Tell me this is real. Tell me you're back, somehow, and I haven't lost what's left of my mind."

"It's real, Mom." I wanted to stop there, without saying the part that would kill the new light in her eyes. "But I'm not back."

She frowned, and that light dimmed, but wasn't truly extinguished. "I don't understand. You're alive."

"Not in the traditional sense of the word." I sat on the arm of the couch, pleased when the cushion sank beneath my weight. "But I think I'm pulling off a reasonable imitation. Check it out." I spread my arms, inviting her to test my corporeality. "Pretty solid, right?"

She reached out hesitantly and laid one hand on the center of my chest. "But…your heart's beating."

"Nice trick, huh? I'm proud of that one."

She pushed the front door closed with one hand, unwilling to break eye contact, and I could see her warring with denial and confusion. If she were a human mother, clueless about the non-human and post-death elements of the world until her dead son showed up on her doorstep, she'd probably already be in a straitjacket. "What's going on, Tod? How are you here? I know of a few possibilities, but none of them are…" She dropped her gaze, and when she met mine again, the blues in her eyes had darkened with fear, or something close to that. "What happened?"

"You might want to sit down."

"No, I think I'll stand."

I almost laughed. She always was stubborn. That's where Nash got it.

"Fine." I sighed and scrubbed my hands over my face, my initial excitement wilting along with hers. "This would be so much easier if they actually issued black hoods," I mumbled, still struggling for an opening line.

My mother froze, her eyes narrowing. "Reaper. You're a *reaper?*"

I glanced at her in surprise. "Wow, first try. Remind me never to play twenty questions with you."

"This is serious, Tod," she insisted, her voice hushed even beyond the original whisper. She glanced toward the hallway, where music—something heavily melodic and moody—blared from Nash's room, then tugged me past the swinging door into the kitchen. "You have no idea what you're getting into."

"Uh, yeah, I do. The scythe was a little tricky at first,

but—much like golf—turns out it's all in the swing." I mimed swinging a golf club, but she didn't even crack a smile.

"I'm not kidding." My mother pulled a chair away from the table and sank into it, her frown deepening by the second. "If you've signed on with the reapers, then you're not really here. You're not alive. I'm not even supposed to *see* you. They have *rules* against this kind of thing."

I shrugged. "Yeah, but as you might recall, I've never been much for rules...."

"This isn't *funny!* Reapers don't really die, but they don't truly live, either. You can't possibly understand what that will do to you."

I sighed and sank into the chair next to her, folding her hand in both of mine. "Mom." I leaned forward, peering straight into her eyes. "I'm dead, not stupid. I know what I signed on for. Eternity in solitude. Gradual loss of humanity. General indifference toward the living, and a skewed perspective on both life and death."

"Yes, and—"

"And...there's the daily extermination of life. Which sucks. It *all* sucks. It's not like I'm looking forward to spending the next thousand years alone, disconnected from the rest of the Earth's population. But at least I'm here. I'm in your kitchen, solid and warm. I still have all my memories, and my own body, and..."

"It's not the same," she said. "You can't just pick up where you left off. You're here, but you can't go back to school. You can't graduate, or go to college, or get married. You can't have a career, or a family. You're just going to linger between life and death, sending other people on, but unable to fol- low them," she finished, shoulders slumped like I'd some- how added to her burden instead of lifting it. "Reapers either fade from life or start to enjoy taking it. They don't get happy endings, Tod."

"I know. I know all of that, Mom."

Her tears were back, and I couldn't understand that. Where was the joy? The relief? Could it possibly hurt her worse to think of me as alone and slightly less than human than to think of me as dead and gone? "Then why would you do this?"

"Because the alternative sucks!" I stood fast enough that my chair skidded several inches behind me. "I thought you'd be happy. I'm still here, and I'm still me. Would you rather I crawl back into my coffin? Because I can, if that's what you want."

"No…" She stood and reached for me, but I backed away, and she looked bruised. "I'm sorry. I'm grateful for the chance to see you again. To get to touch you and talk to you. But honestly, the circumstances scare me. You may still be yourself now, but death changes you, Tod. There's no escaping that. If you're lucky, you can slow the process, but you can't stop it. And I don't want to see you change."

"You won't have to," I said, crossing my arms over my chest. "As long as I have you and Nash, I'll still be me. And after you're gone, none of that will matter anyway. So why can't you just be happy for me? This was the only way I'd get a chance to…" I stopped before I could say it. This wasn't how it was supposed to go. I wanted to tell her calmly, not on the tail end of a fight about my afterlife, which oddly mirrored every fight we'd ever had about my future—back when I'd still had one.

"A chance to what?" She waited expectantly, and suddenly I wished I could just tell her that I didn't want my death to hurt her like my dad's did.

That was true. But it wasn't the reason I'd come, and I

hadn't signed up to ferry souls for all of eternity just to punk out on the most important truth I'd ever possessed.

"A chance to tell you that it's not Nash's fault. What happened…it wasn't his fault, and you both have to stop blaming him."

"I don't blame him." Guilt lined her face, though her irises held stubbornly still.

"You don't blame my actual death on him, I know. But you both blame him for the circumstances. But you don't understand what really happened. It wasn't his fault. It was mine."

"What does that mean? What happened that night, Tod?" she asked, sinking back into her chair, and I could tell from the dark thread of trepidation in her voice that she was starting to get the picture, even if it hadn't come into focus for her yet.

I sat across from her, leaning forward with my elbows on my knees, bracing myself for what had to be said, and for the possibility that she'd never look at me the same way again. "First, promise you won't tell Nash. You have to make him understand that it wasn't his fault, but you can't tell him what really happened. It wouldn't be fair to him."

Knowing that he lived because I'd died—even if it was my choice—would lead to survivor's guilt thick enough to haunt him for the rest of his life.

"Okay…" Mom said, but I knew without asking that if she thought it was in his best interest to know, she'd tell him, no matter what she'd promised me. There was nothing more she could do for me, but he was still alive, and still her responsibility. Nash had to come first now. And I understood that.

"I'm not sure how much you know about Grim Reapers. Do you know what it takes to qualify…?" I asked, and the sudden startling comprehension in her eyes was answer enough.

"Oh, Tod…"

"It's okay, Mom. It was my choice."

"It was supposed to be Nash?" She sounded stunned. Numb.

"Yeah." I frowned when I could see where her thoughts were headed. "But you're thinking about this all wrong. As much as I'd love to be remembered as a martyr—I'm sure that'd lead to some serious play in the afterlife—that's not how it happened."

"What do you mean?"

"I wasn't watching him that night. I left to pick up my girl-friend, and I didn't even check on him when I got back. Or at all. I don't even really know when he snuck out. Then, when he called, I bitched about having to pick him up. I yelled at him on the ride home, telling him what a worthless pain in the ass he was." I took a deep breath, then spit out the rest of it, to get the bitter taste off my tongue. "That's the last thing he heard before that asshole slammed into us. The truth is that if I'd been watching him, he wouldn't have been on that road in the first place."

At first, she could only stare at me, trying to process everything. "So you…?"

"So when the reaper spelled it out for me, I had to do it. I couldn't let me yelling at him be the last thing he ever heard."

"I can't believe you did that.…" She scrubbed her face with both hands, and stray curls tumbled over them, effectively blocking me out. I had no idea what she was thinking or feeling.

My heart dropped into my stomach, and the tone of my entire afterlife suddenly seemed to depend on what she said next. On the judgment I would surely see in her eyes. Her hands fell from her face slowly and my mother stared at me through layers of pain and regret I couldn't imagine. "I don't think you even understand what you gave up for him. I don't think you will, until we're both long gone."

"I don't think *you* understand." My own guilt was a strong, steady pressure on my chest, slowly compressing my lungs, sending an ache through my heart. "This wasn't some noble gesture, Mom. I wouldn't have had to save him if I hadn't put him in the path of that car in the first place. I just needed you both to know that it wasn't his fault. I made the call."

Finally she nodded, though she looked like she wanted to argue. "Thank you. For all of it."

I stood to go—I'd had all the post-death reunion I could stand for one day—and she stood with me.

"Are you going to get in trouble for this?" she asked. Translation: *Am I going to lose you again?*

"I don't think so. My supervisor's pretty cool, for a dead kid. He brought me here the other night, and I'm pretty sure he knows where I am now. If I get caught by someone else, he'll deny knowledge, but he's not gonna bust me himself."

In retrospect, I'd realized what Levi obviously understood from the start. Watching my family mourn wouldn't make me want to let them go. It would make me want to keep them close—and that was the only benefit worth accepting the job for.

"In that case, don't be a stranger." Her eyes teared up again and she sniffled, pulling me close for a hug. "It can't be like it was before, but you're welcome here any time."

Relief eased some of the sting from our bittersweet reunion. That was exactly what I'd needed to hear.

"Do you want to talk to Nash?"

I shook my head firmly. "Not now. I'll show myself eventually, but I'm not ready yet." This soon after the accident, I was afraid I wouldn't be able to keep the truth from him. He'd know something was weird—something beyond his brother's less-than-triumphant return from the grave—and I wouldn't be able to lie convincingly enough to cover it up.

"Okay." Mom squeezed me one more time, then let me go. "But don't drag it out too long. The longer you wait, the more jarring it'll be for him."

But what she didn't say—what we both knew—was that no matter how jarring my return was for my little brother, it couldn't be more jarring than waking up ten days postmortem in the clothes he was buried in. Nash would never know what that felt like.

Nor would he ever know that what was supposed to be the end of his life became the beginning of my afterlife instead.

ELEVEN MONTHS AND ten days after my first nursing home rotation, I blinked into the hospital's ER to find Levi waiting for me, slouched in one of the lobby chairs. The sense of *déjà vu* was so strong I was actually disoriented for a moment, as I flashed back to my earliest days as a reaper—a rookie so green I couldn't even pull off the disembodied voice trick without my entire body flashing in and out of sight like a not-so-special effect.

"Glad you could make it," Levi said, sliding out of the chair to stand less than shoulder high on me.

"Yeah, it was tough to make time between the compulsive thumb twiddling and the lure of bingo night at Colonial Manor, but I managed to fit you in."

His forehead furrowed. "Glad I rank as a priority."

"You rank as accessory to the crime that is my eternal hereafter. So, why am I here? This isn't my beat."

"It is now." He reached into his pocket and pulled out a folded sheet of paper, and that sense of *déjà vu* became a startling certainty. "We inherited a rookie from another district, and he'll be taking over the nursing home circuit. Which means you're getting a promotion."

I huffed in amusement. "From adult diapers to bedpans? Move over, Elvis, *I'm* the afterlife of the party!"

"If you don't think you can handle it, you can go back to rotating between rest homes…" Levi threatened, copper brows raised in challenge.

"Gimme that." I snatched the paper and unfolded it to find a list of four names, times, and room numbers. Roughly the same workload I'd had on my old circuit, but these reapings would all take place in the same building. Obviously consistency was a privilege of rank.

"Don't make me regret this," Levi warned, frowning up at me through a dead child's eyes. "Most reapers spend nearly a decade in the rest home circuit before moving up."

"If I weren't already dead, I'd be alive with joy," I said, and dimly I realized that Levi was responding. But I couldn't concentrate on what he was saying because my ears were suddenly full of something else. Music. A beautiful, eerie singing faintly echoing from beyond a closed set of doors. If I didn't know better, I'd swear…

But then it was gone, and Levi was staring up at me, his pouty child's mouth pursed in a frown I found *really* hard to take seriously.

"What'd you say?" I asked, fighting the urge to scruff his curls. He didn't like that. At *all*.

"I said, you're a smartass, Hudson."

I grinned. "I recognize no other kind of ass." I glanced at the list one more time, then started walking backward away from him. "Now if you'll excuse me, Death waits for no man. Except me." I shrugged, still grinning. "It waits for you, too, obviously, but 'Death waits for no kid' just doesn't have quite the same ring."

Levi rolled his eyes, then blinked out of the waiting room, leaving me to my first non-geriatric reaping, scheduled in a mere five minutes, in Triage E.

I walked through the double doors, unseen and unheard, and made my way past a nurse's station and the first few rooms, most of which were blocked from view by curtains on steel tracks. But the third room was open.

In it, a girl lay strapped to a stretcher, arching fiercely against the restraints, throwing long brown hair with every violent toss of her head. She moaned incoherently, but something in that sound drew me closer, until I found myself in the doorway, listening, picking out low, eerie notes in the last sounds she produced before her voice gave out. She twisted toward the door then, and her medicated gaze met mine, pain and panic swirling in sluggish shades of blue in her irises.

Holy shit. A female *bean sidhe*. I'd never even seen one, other than my mom.

She went still then, her limbs lax, and for just a second, we watched each other as she blinked slowly and I was unable to blink at all.

Then a nurse walked through me and into the room, and the spell—whatever it was—was broken. And only after I'd walked away did I realize that she shouldn't have been able to see me. *No one* could see me, unless I wanted them to....

Several steps later, I found Triage E, and with it, the man whose time on earth was over. Martin Gardner, 58, had suffered a heart attack, and the doctors had just gotten him stabilized—or so they thought.

But before I could help Mr. Gardner into the great beyond, shouting at the end of the hall drew my attention. I turned to find a man on a stretcher being wheeled toward me, his arm flapping as a nurse walked alongside him, trying to calm him down. "Drunk driver," the EMT pushing the stretcher said to a man in scrubs, madly scribbling on a clipboard. "Cops are waiting in the lobby. The bastard killed three people, but only broke his own arm. Figures, huh?"

As they wheeled the man closer, I saw his face, and rage shot through me, hotter than a bolt of lightning. I knew that face. I'd only seen it once, but I could never forget it, even if my afterlife stretched into eternity.

The bastard who killed Nash. And now he'd killed again.

I glanced at Mr. Gardner, sleeping peacefully with his daughter at his side. Then I turned and followed the other stretcher into Triage H.

Levi wouldn't know the difference, so long as I turned in a soul. At least, not until the exchanged death date showed up on another list, farther down the road. And if he fired me then, so what? It'd be worth it to know this asshole wouldn't be killing anyone else behind the wheel.

When the nurse finally left the room, I stepped in, taking on just enough corporeality for the man on the bed to see me. I watched his eyes widen in terror when I appeared out of nowhere. Then I leaned over and whispered into his ear.

"Time's up, you drunk driving piece of shit." His hands shook on the bed rails, and the scent of urine blossomed into the air. "Just FYI, in your case, I think it's okay to fear the reaper."

★ ★ ★ ★ ★

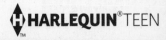

THE GODDESS TEST NOVELS

Available wherever books are sold!

A modern saga inspired by the Persephone myth. Kate Winters's life hasn't been easy. She's battling with the upcoming death of her mother, and only a mysterious stranger called Henry is giving her hope. But he must be crazy, right? Because there is no way the god of the Underworld—Hades himself—is going to choose Kate to take the seven tests that might make her an immortal...and his wife. And even if she passes the tests, is there any hope for happiness with a war brewing between the gods?

Also available:
THE GODDESS HUNT, a digital-only novella.

Be sure to look for THE GODDESS INHERITANCE coming April 2013!

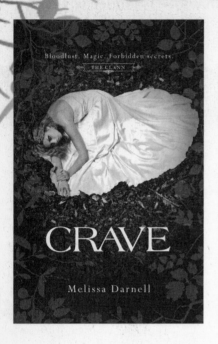